Praise for Book I of *The Banned and the Banished, Wit'ch Fire*

"*Wit'ch Fire* grabs at your heart and tears a little hole, then tears another, and another—a brutal and beautiful ride. I can't put the book down!"

—R. A. Salvatore

"I loved every page of this book. Clemens has contructed a world of magic that's never been seen before, with a cast of beings who are so engaging and entrancing that you never want the story to end. His imagery is so brilliant that every scene comes instantly to life, and while everything seems immediately familiar, the reader soon learns to expect a new surprise with every page. And just as you think he can't possible come up with anything else, a new character bursts upon the tale, bringing along a whole new level of sorcery!"

—John Saul

"Full of violence, magical pyrotechnics, and black-hearted villains."

—*Publishers Weekly*

"Classic fantasy told in a classic manner. Solid entertainment—action and adventure wrapped in riddles and mystery. Don't miss this one."

—Don McQuinn

"There are some distinguishing touches in this very Jordanian fantasy novel . . . Clemens appears to be following a cherished formula, but he does an unusually good job of dressing the routine elements with distinctive details and creating interesting characters."

—*Locus*

"Clemens demonstrates considerable skill at combining swift pacing with character development in this gracefully written beginning to a projected high fantasy quest."

—*Library Journal*

Also by James Clemens

Wit'ch Fire

WIT'CH

STORM

James Clemens

DEL REY

The Ballantine Publishing Group | New York

For my most vocal and persistent supporters,
my brothers and sisters
(and yes, I am going to list them all):
Cheryl
Doug
Laurie
Chuck
Bill
Carrie

A Del Rey® Book
Published by The Ballantine Publishing Group

www.randomhouse.com/delrey/

ISBN 0-7394-0318-4

Cover design by David Stevenson
Cover illustration by Brom

Manufactured in the United States of America

ACKNOWLEDGMENTS

To list all the folks who have contributed to the production of these novels would consume an entire book. But I would be remiss if I did not thank a few special people: my agent, Pesha Rubinstein, for getting my foot in the publishing door and pushing me further and further; my editor, Veronica Chapman, for heralding the novels in the halls of Del Rey; and both Eleanor Lang and Christine Levis, for publishing and promoting the book to the world; and a special note of appreciation for the cover artist Brom and the cover designer David Stevenson, for putting a breathtaking face on the project.

Of course I must bow a gracious thank-you to the members of my writing group, who have been invaluable in toning and honing this plot line (Chris Crowe, Dennis Grayson, Dave Meek, Stephen and Judy Prey, Caroline Williams, and a special thanks to Jane O Riva.)

And to Carolyn McCray I owe a debt of gratitude that knows no boundary for her continual support, criticisms, and friendship.

And a big hug to my special cheerleader, Maryl Olah, for her hard work and dedication in dressing up as Elena at several conventions and promoting the first novel.

NORTHERN W
GREAT WESTERN OCEAN
STEPPES
TOR AMOV
NORTH WALL
BARRIER ISLANDS
CASTLE MRYL
Windham
STONE OF TOR
PASS OF SPIRITS
WESTERN REACHES
Mirror River
Moon Lake
ISLES OF KELL
Gelph
Rumor
Boiling Seas
Ramble River
SOUTH WALL
RUINS OF TULAR

TES
N
W
E
S
SKREE
ISLES
STONE
FOREST
BLACK
HALL
GUL'GOTHA
Bay Of
T'lek
GREAT
OCEAN
Penryn
terville
STANDI
Sigiltower
rfell
PLAINS
Lands End
Shadowbrook
ARCHIPELAGO
UPPER WOODS
LANDSLIP
Port Rawl
SOUTHERN
FANG
SWAMPS
Drowned
Lake
BLASTED
SHOALS
GREAT
BOG
CRUMBLING
MOUNDS
SOUTHERN
WASTES

FOREWORD TO WIT'CH STORM

by Sala'zar Mut, novelist and playwright

(NOTE: Here follow the exact words written on the eve of Sala'zar Mut's execution for crimes against the Commonwealth)

FIRST AND FOREMOST, I AM A WRITER.

As a writer, I have come to believe that words should always be written in one's own blood. Then one would be careful what he or she chooses to write. Who would dare waste their limited quantity of vital fluid on mere flippancy and fictions? If words were pumped forth from one's heart, would they not always speak with the truth of that person's soul?

So though I write this with a cheap ink that clots upon my paper like the spittle from a dying man's throat, let me imagine it to be my life's blood that inks this parchment. And in some ways, it truly is—for from my cell, I can hear the executioner sharpening his knives upon his stone, a noise that slices as sharp as the edge he grinds. When I am done with these words, he will open up my belly so all can read what the gods have written inside me. I will become an open book. So let these words be both a foreword to this next translation of the Kelvish Scrolls and a foreword to the open volume my corpse will become when the sun next rises.

I am forced this night to write my story so that my dear wife, Delli, may die quickly under the axman's blade, rather than suffer and writhe upon the Stone of Justice. I write so she might die in peace. But as I told you before, I must be truthful with my final words. And the truth is that whether or not the quality of my wife's death hung on my actions, I would still write this foreword.

For you see, writing is not only my craft . . . but my life.

True, writing earned bread for my children and a roof over my family's heads, but it also nourished my soul. Words sustained me. Words were my heart. So how could I refuse one last time to tell a story—even if it's the story of my own damnation, a story to be used to frighten you away from the wonders inherent in the Scrolls.

I know I am to be an example to you students who hope to become Scholars of the Commonwealth. My death is to be a testimonial to the perversity and damnation that can lie within the text of the Scrolls.

So be it.

Here is my tale:

Among the dank alleys of Gelph, I chanced upon a black market dealer in items arcane who offered that which was forbidden. He stank of spiced sweetmeats and sour ale, and I was apt to shove him aside. But the scoundrel must have spied into my soul, for he whispered an offer I could not refuse: a chance to peruse words forbidden from ages past. He offered me a copy of the Scrolls, preserved on the flayed skin of a dead zealot. As a writer, I had heard rumors of such a text and suspected I would pay any price for the chance to read its words. And I was right—it cost me dearly to wrangle the copy from the foul-toothed alley man.

By candlelight, I read the entire text over the course of four sleepless days and nights. I feared someone interrupting and snatching the copy from before my eyes, so I read without stopping. My beard grew stubbled upon my cheek, but I did not cease until the last word reached my tired eyes.

The first of the Scrolls seemed so innocuous I could not understand why it was banned. I raved that such a benign work should be kept from the people, but by the end of the last Scroll, I knew . . . I knew why the Scrolls were kept locked away from the eyes of the populace. This made me more than just rave—I *raged* against the injustice! And with the words of the Scrolls giving me power, I sought to bring the story to the people.

So I devised a plan.

I thought I could convert the Scrolls into a play—change a few names and places, twist the story a bit—and still bring its hidden magick to the people. But a cast member betrayed me. On the opening night of my play, I was arrested along with my troupe and the entire audience in attendance.

Of the two hundred people hauled away that rainy night, except for my wife, I am the last still breathing . . . but their wails yet echo in my head. Over the five winters of my imprisonment, I have shed so many tears that thirst is always on my tongue. Even as I write these words, tears smear the wet ink in black trails across the tan parchment.

Yet as much sorrow as the perusal of the Scrolls has cost my family and many others, in my heart I still cannot regret reading them. The Scrolls changed me with their words. I now *know* the truth! And that knowledge can't be cut from me by the executioner's knives. I will die with the final words of the Scrolls on my lips . . . and die content.

As a writer, I always suspected that words held a certain magick. But upon reading the Scrolls, I now understand just how powerful the written word can be.

Words can be the blood of a people.

POSTSCRIPT TO THE FOREWORD

by Jir'rob Sordun, professor of University Studies (U.D.B.)

WELCOME BACK TO THE SCROLLS.

Why, you might wonder, do we waste the first few pages with the dying words of a blaspheming man? Sala'zar Mut was executed by public torture and slow decapitation at New Welk Prison in Sant Sib'aro on the morning after he wrote the preceding foreword.

His death, dear students, is the first lesson to be pondered before one should continue through the Scrolls.

Did you believe Mut's words? Did you believe that words can be the blood of a people? That words can have some arcane power? Do not be ashamed if you did, for Sala'zar Mut was a skilled writer.

But let this be a lesson to you . . . Do not *trust* words.

Mut was under a delusion, a weakness of the mind caused by the untutored reading of the Scrolls.

Let his *death* be the lesson here—not his words. Words did *not* save his life.

So, before you open the first page of this second book, you must know the following truth and harden your heart by reciting it one hundred times before the sun sets today:

"Words do *not* have power.

The Scrolls do *not* have power.

Only the Council has power."

Assignation of Responsibility for the second Scroll

This copy is being assigned to you and is your sole responsibility. Its loss, alteration, or destruction will result in severe penalties (as stated in your local ordinances). Any transmission, copying, or even oral reading in the presence of a nonclassmate is strictly forbidden. By signing below and placing your fingerprint, you accept all responsibility and release the university from any damage it may cause you (or those around you) by its perusal.

____________________ Signature

____________________ Date

Place inked print of your right index finger here: [ ]

*** **WARNING** ***

If you should perchance come upon this text outside of proper university channels, please close this book now and alert the proper authorities for safe retrieval. Failure to do so can lead to your immediate arrest and incarceration.

YOU HAVE BEEN WARNED.

WIT'CH STORM

Birthed in fire

and shadowed by the wings of dragons,

this is the way the journey began.

Outside my window, a winter's sun prepares to set into the blue of the Great Western Ocean. The sky above is not the rosy glow of spring, but a bruised jumble of purples, reds, and yellows. I sit at my desk and wait, as I have done every night since finishing the first part of her story last year. For the past hundred nights, I have watched the moon wax full and wane to a sliver several times from this very seat, a pen poised above parchment, unable to write.

Why? Why do I delay in continuing her tale? I know it is the only way to free me of the wit'ch's wicked spell. Only by writing her entire tale in truthful words can I lift her curse and finally die. So am I dragging my feet in a secret attempt to extend my interminable existence? Perhaps to live another century, or two, or maybe three?

No. Time destroys all illusions about oneself. Like water flowing through a chasm, digging an ever deeper channel, the passing of years has worn away the layers of my self-deception. This is the only reward her damnable curse has granted me: a heart that can now see clearly.

These days and nights of empty pages are *not* sprung from a desire to continue with my life, but simply from dread, a paralyzing fear for what I must write next. Some things even the tincture of time cannot soothe.

I know next I must tell the tale of her dark journey, a road blackened by the long shadow of the wit'ch. Yet I fear to put this story on paper. Not only will writing this account require unlocking and staring full in the face again the horrors that lay along the road, but also by placing ink to paper, it will make the legend more real, give substance and form to what is now only memory.

Still I must . . .

So, as the bright days and rosy sunsets of spring and summer fade behind me, I find within the icy breezes and bruised skies of winter the will once again to write. This is the season in which I can tell her tale.

It is not, however, the same season in which her story begins.

Listen . . . Can you hear the ice breaking in the mountain passes as spring finally releases winter's hold upon the peaks of the Teeth, opening the way to the valleys below? Listen as the ice moans and cracks like thunder heralding the beginning of her travels.

And like all journeys, foul or fair, it starts with a single step . . .

Book One

DARK ROADS

1

Elena stepped from the cave, pushing aside the leather hanging that kept the warmth of the mountain folk's morning fires snug within the cavern. Even though spring was already a moon old, here among the peaks the early morning hours were still laced with whispers of ice from the mountaintops. Free of the caves, the air smelled crisp, scented with pine and highland poppy, and this morning, a breath of warmth even hinted at the summer to come.

A sigh on her lips, Elena shook back the hood of her green woolen jacket and raised her eyes toward the mountains. Still tipped with heavy snow, they seemed to lean over her as if threatening to topple, and the roars from a hundred waterfalls echoed through the valley from the torrents of snowmelt. After a long winter, where both water and time itself had seemed frozen forever, the spring thaw was like a new birth.

Smiling, she took a step forward—but, as if to remind her that winter had not yet completely given up its grasp on the highlands, her heel slipped on a patch of black ice.

She cartwheeled her arms to no avail and landed on her backside upon the rocky trail.

Behind her, Elena heard the rasp of leather on stone as Er'ril pushed aside the cavern's apron to join her. "Girl, we can't have you breaking your neck before we even leave the Teeth." He reached a hand to help her up. "Are you hurt?"

"No, I'm fine." With her face burning hot enough to thaw the ice under her rump, Elena ignored his hand and struggled to her feet on her own. "I didn't see . . . I slipped . . ." She sighed and turned away from his stern expression. Under black brows, his gray eyes always seemed to be weighing her, judging her every action. And why was it that he only seemed to acknowledge her when she was burning a finger on a flame or snagging a toe on an unseen rocky outcropping? She wiped a palm over her gray trousers, searching for her dignity but finding only a sodden spot on her backside.

"The others have been waiting a long time," he said as he slid past her, leading the way up the three hundred steps toward the pass where the rest of the party had gathered. "Even the wolf should be back by now."

Fardale, in his wolf form, had left at daybreak to survey the trails that led to the distant valleys. Meanwhile, Nee'lahn and Meric had been assigned to tack the horses and ready the wagon, while Tol'chuk and Mogweed hauled and inventoried their supplies. Only Kral still remained below, saying his final farewells to his mountain clan.

"If we hope to clear the pass by nightfall," Er'ril said as he climbed, "we must be off quickly. So keep your eyes on the stairs, rather than on the clouds." As if mocking his warning, a patch of ice betrayed Er'ril's own feet. His one arm shot out, and he had to hop two steps to keep his balance. Afterward, as he glanced back at her, his face was a shade darker than before.

"I'll make sure I watch where I'm going," Elena said, her eyes bowed meekly—but she couldn't keep a grin from her lips.

Er'ril grumbled something under his breath and continued forward.

They managed the remainder of the stairs with care, each in a cocoon of silence. Elena, though, imagined both their minds dwelt on the same worry—the journey ahead, the long trek across the many lands of Alasea to the lost city of A'loa Glen. Somewhere in the sunken city lay the Blood Diary, hidden there by Er'ril centuries ago: a tome prophesied to contain the key to saving their lands from the black corruption of the Gul'gothal lord. But could they reach it, a band of travelers from different lands, each with his own reasons for pursuing this journey?

With much of the last several weeks spent plotting, planning, and outfitting the band of travelers, a mixture of relief at finally being under way and dread at leaving the security of the frozen passes swirled in each member's breast. A heavy silence, like now, hung around the shoulders of everyone, except for—

"Ho!" The call from behind them stopped both Er'ril and Elena near the head of the trail. Elena twisted around to see Kral squeeze his huge frame through what now seemed a tiny opening in the granite cliff face far below. He waved an arm the size of a tree trunk at them, his voice rolling like a boulder through the canyon. "Hold up there. I'll join you."

With his back bent under a heavy pack, he bounded up the steps, taking three stairs with every stride. Elena held her breath and winced. She was amazed that more of the mountain folk didn't break their necks upon the icy trail. But Kral seemed hardly to notice the slick stairs, his feet finding firm purchase with each step. Was it just luck or skill, she wondered, that kept the huge man from a deadly fall?

He soon drew abreast of them. "It's a good day to be off," he said, not even winded by the thin mountain air. He seemed to be the only member of the party to have no doubts about their journey. While the others had grown more silent with the approaching day of departure, Kral had swelled with nervous energy, anxious to leave. He was always rechecking their supplies, honing weapons, trimming the horses' hooves, measuring the ice melt, or satisfying some other need for their departure.

Noting Kral's wide-toothed grin as he joined them on the stair, Elena asked the question that had been nagging her. "You don't seem at all bothered to abandon your home. Aren't you a little sad to leave?"

Kral rubbed a hand through his thick black beard while his expression softened to amusement. "Spring is the usual time of our Scattering. With the winter passes now open, our people split into separate Fires and hike the trading routes. The clan will not unite again until the end of autumn. In truth, we call no place home. As long as there is rock under our boots and a heart in our chest, we are home." He nodded them forward to the head of the trail.

Er'ril refused to move, though. "Kral, you speak the truth, as all your people do, but you leave much unsaid." From his higher vantage on the hewn stairs, Er'ril stared the mountain man straight in the eyes. "I suspect I know better what spurs your hurried desire to depart."

"And what might that be, man of the plains?" Kral's eyes narrowed slightly, the amusement on his lips fading to a hard line.

"When we first met back in Winterfell's inn, you mentioned a prophecy of doom heralded by my reappearance among your tribe."

Kral's gaze darted away; he seemed to study the cracked ice on the stair.

"It's not the journey ahead that excites your heart," Er'ril continued, "but simply relief that I am leaving your people—and your clan yet survives."

"You shame me with your words," Kral mumbled to the cold stone.

"I don't mean to. That's not why I stopped you here."

"Then why?" he asked sourly.

"To thank you." Er'ril took a step closer and reached up to grasp the man's shoulder as Kral's eyes grew wide. "I've already thanked you for sheltering us and healing me of the goblin's poison, but I never thanked you for the risk your tribe took in taking me in. You knew the prophecy, yet took me into your home."

"You owe us no . . . thanks," Kral said, stumbling with his tongue. "We could do no other. We are bound to the Rock and will not shirk our duty—or its burden of prophecy."

"Still I owe you a debt, friend." Er'ril squeezed Kral's shoulder a final time, then turned around to lead the way up to the Pass of Spirits. "And we of the plains, too, know something of honor."

Elena followed Er'ril, but not before noting the shine of respect in the mountain man's eyes.

As they continued higher, toward the pass, Er'ril began to limp slightly on his right leg, the climb obviously worrying the bone struck with the goblin's knife last autumn. The dagger's poison had wasted the Standi plainsman to a hollow figure. Though he had quickly regained his muscle and form afterward, echoes of his injuries still persisted, especially with exertion. And Er'ril wasn't the only member of the party bearing scars. Each member carried wounds—not all of them visible—from their first confrontation with the Dark Lord. And who knew what other battles were yet to be fought before the party reached the lost city?

Er'ril reached the top of the trail and stopped. His eyes were toward the open pass. "I still think the plan is foolhardy," he mumbled.

Elena and Kral joined him.

The Pass of Spirits spread in meadows and gentle slopes away from them. Here spring had truly reached the highlands. Blooming crocuses spread in splashes of blues and whites, and at the edges of the pass, some flowers were even pushing right out of patches of persistent snow, as if spring itself were trying to shake its shoulders free of winter's mantle. Besides the flowers, the pass teemed with life. At the fringes of budding birch trees, the spotted red flanks of a family of deer could be seen, slowly working up the pass. Overhead a circling hawk screeched and dove into the green sea of meadow grass then sprang back out, something small and furred wriggling in its talons.

Er'ril's eyes obviously saw none of this. "Look at that wagon," he said. "It looks like a cheap tavern whore, painted and draped in bells to attract every eye and ear."

Near a small creek that murmured among mossy boulders, Elena spotted the herd of tethered horses grazing by a large covered wagon. The wagon's wooden sides were painted a burnt orange, and its canvas covering, stretched taut over a frame of bent maple saplings, had been stained dark blue with hand-stenciled white stars. Cowbells ringed its flanks, each painted a different color.

"I sort of like it," Kral said beside her.

Scowling, Er'ril marched toward the milling horses and people waiting nearby. "I should've just taken Elena by myself. Then we would not have needed this foolishness."

"It's been long decided. We all cast our stones," Kral said. "Besides the elv'in Meric—who wanted to abandon the entire journey—you were the only one who wanted to split up the group."

"We are too many. A smaller party could move more swiftly and attract fewer eyes."

"Perhaps, but if you should attract an enemy's eyes, you'll need the strengths and skills of all to keep the girl from the Black Heart's grasp. It is not just brigands and thieves we must protect her against."

"I've heard the arguments."

Elena had to half run to keep up with the bigger men. She spoke between gulps of air. "Uncle Bol warned us that we must stay together."

"I know, Elena," Er'ril said, slowing slightly to allow her to keep abreast of him. "I don't mean to disparage your uncle. He was a brave man. But the portents he attempted to decipher are tricky to interpret with accuracy. He might have been mistaken."

"He wasn't," she said firmly, and in her heart, she truly did sense the importance of keeping the group intact. Maybe in part because she had already lost her entire family: her parents burned to death by her own hand, her aunt and uncle slain by beasts of the Gul'gotha, and her brother Joach stolen from her by black magicks. So much loss would have been inconsolable without the support of those around her. After six moons together, this group had become a second family, united not by the blood of birth but the blood of battle—and she did not want to see this family sundered. "We must stay together."

"So we will," Er'ril said, but doubt rang in his voice.

"It's a sound plan," Kral argued. He pointed at the gaily painted wagon. "There stands our banner. Disguised as a small circus, one among many plying the warm roads of spring and summer, we will hide in the open. While searching eyes will seek for us along back roads, we will travel open and free, loud and noisy. Not only will this keep furtive eyes from looking too closely at us, it will also earn us coppers and gold to replenish our supplies. I say it is a sound plan."

"Yes," Er'ril said with sarcasm. "And you mountain folk only speak the truth."

Kral harrumphed and patted Er'ril good-naturedly on his shoulder. "Ahh . . . I see your time among the clans has taught you a bit of wisdom."

Close to the wagon now, Kral's loud voice drew the attention of the others away from their final preparations. Nee'lahn turned her head from where she had been cinching a saddle atop a roan stallion. She raised a hand in greeting, then froze as her eyes settled on Elena. Blinking a few times, she dropped the currybrush she had in her other hand and crossed closer to them.

As she approached, Nee'lahn wiped a smudge of mud from her cheek while speaking: "Sweet Mother, Er'ril, what have you done to the poor child? Her hair!"

Elena, suddenly self-conscious, raised a hand to her shorn hair. Where once long auburn curls had draped past her shoulders, now only a coarse crop of hair that barely covered her ears remained. And that hair was no longer auburn, but dyed as black as Er'ril's own locks.

"If we are to hide Elena within this daft circus," Er'ril said, "what better way than to mask the girl herself? So . . . meet my new son."

Er'ril watched the others gather around Elena.

Amongst the thronging party, Tol'chuk's bulk was like a boulder in a stream. Twice the weight of even the huge mountain man, the og're did not crowd too closely, seeming to sense that his massive form still unnerved the much smaller girl. Even though the creature was foul to the eye—with his leathered skin, fanged teeth, and hulking mass—Er'ril had grown to respect and admire the og're for his calmness and intelligence. It was Tol'chuk's quiet words during the oft-heated discussion of their plans that had finally persuaded Er'ril to their present course.

In contrast, dwarfed in the og're's shadow hid the quiet Mogweed. To Er'ril, the shape-shifter remained a blank slate. The skinny man with mousy hair and nervous movements hardly spoke a word, and when he did, he talked so softly he could hardly be heard. Yet, as little as the si'luran man revealed through his manner and speech, Er'ril felt something oily and slippery about him. Even now, as Mogweed studied Elena, darting quick glances from a few paces away, he struck Er'ril as being like a hungry bird studying a squirming worm. Er'ril could practically see Mogweed's mind swirling with thoughts and plans he never voiced.

Whereas Meric, dressed in his usual white linen and billowy green pants, never kept his opinions to himself. The tall, silver-haired elv'in leaned closer to Elena, reaching a narrow finger to raise her chin, but his words flew to Er'ril. "How dare you touch her? You had no right to mar the beauty of our royal line in such a manner."

"It was necessary," Er'ril answered coldly. "Her disguise might just very well keep that precious royal line of yours still breathing."

Meric released her chin and turned hard eyes on Er'ril. "And what of her mark?" He pointed to Elena's hand, where shades of ruby whorled in languid swirls. "How do you propose to hide her wit'ch's blaze?"

"My *son* will earn his keep at the circus by hauling and sweeping. And for these chores, he'll need a good pair of work gloves." Er'ril tapped his belt, from which hung a set of plain leather gloves.

"You propose to have elv'in royalty sweep and handle filth?" Meric's white skin darkened. "You've already made her a sorry enough figure with your ridiculous shearing."

Elena's face had by now flushed to match her ruby hand.

Meric knelt down by the girl. "Listen, Elena, you don't have to do this. You are the last of the elv'in king's royal line. In your veins flows the blood of lost dynasties. You must not ignore your birthright." He took her hand. "Give up this foolish quest and return with me to the wind ships and seas of your true home."

"The lands of Alasea are my home," she answered, slipping her hand free of his. "I may be descended from some lost king of yours, but I'm also the daughter of these lands, and I won't abandon them to the Gul'gothal lord. You are free to leave and return to your home, but I will stay."

Meric stood back up. "You know I can't return—not without you. And my mother, the queen, would not tolerate any harm coming to you. So if you persist in this foolish pursuit, I will be at your side to protect you."

Er'ril tired of this man. "The child is my charge," he finally said, guiding Elena away by the shoulder. "She has no need of your protections."

The wasp-thin elv'in ran a disdainful eye up and down Er'ril, then waved an arm around the pass. "Yes, I see how you protect her. Just look at the wagon in which you propose to lead her. You would have her travel like a vagabond."

Er'ril inwardly winced at the words, recognizing his own complaint from earlier. He hated to hear the same sentiment on the elv'in's lips. "It's not an unsound plan," he mumbled, knowing he was contradicting his previous words. "For centuries, I have traveled the roads myself as a juggler and showman to earn my keep. Its gaudiness will hide one plain girl."

"But just look at her hair," Meric moaned. "Was that necessary?"

Before either could speak again, Tol'chuk interrupted, his voice a rattle of rocks in his throat. "Hair grows back," the og're said simply.

Kral grunted his amusement and turned to Nee'lahn, who stood at the mountain man's side. "Well, it's settled then, lass. With Elena disguised, I guess you'll be the only woman traveling with this troupe . . . Of course, if you feel outnumbered, we could always pop a mummer's wig on the og're and call him Mogweed's sweetheart."

The petite nyphai woman swept back her long blond hair. "I don't think that'll be necessary. Now if you're all done gawking at the poor girl, maybe we can finish hitching the horses and be under way."

"Nee'lahn's right," Er'ril said, turning his back on the elv'in. "The wet passes will be ice by nightfall and—"

"Look!" Elena said, pointing past everyone's shoulders.

A huge black treewolf could be seen at the head of the pass, loping across the meadow toward them, a dark shadow in the grass.

"It's about time, Fardale," Mogweed mumbled under his breath. Er'ril heard the distaste in the man's voice and sensed there was much unspoken between these shape-shifting brothers.

The wolf swept up beside Mogweed, his tongue lolling from the side of his mouth. With his amber eyes aglow in the sunlight, Fardale fixed his brother with an intent stare. After several silent breaths, the wolf nodded his head slightly, breaking contact, then crossed to the nearby creek to slake his thirst.

"Well?" Kral asked Mogweed. "What did your dog say?"

Before Mogweed could answer, Elena scolded the mountain man in hushed tones. "He's not a dog. You shouldn't call him that."

"He's just teasing, child," Er'ril said and joined Kral at Mogweed's side. "Now what did your brother discover about the condition of the passes?"

Mogweed edged away from Er'ril, deeper into the og're's shadow. "He says many of the ways are blocked by fast and deep waters. Impassable. But the northernmost trail is clear of all but a few swollen streams."

Er'ril nodded. "Good. Then we have an opening to the valley and plains."

"Except . . ." Mogweed seemed to shrink in on himself.

"What is it, man?"

"He says that it . . . smells wrong."

Elena moved closer to them, a seed of worry growing in her eyes. "What does that mean?"

Er'ril rubbed at a throb that had developed in his temple during the hard climb here. "Yes, what does that mean?" he repeated sourly.

Mogweed studied the flowers crushed under his boots. "It's not clear. Something . . . something . . ." Mogweed shook his head.

Tol'chuk shifted his large bulk and cleared his throat. "The wolf speaks in pictures," he attempted to explain further. "The si'luran half of my blood caught some of Fardale's images, too: *A wolf with raised hackles. An empty path that smells of rotten carrion.*"

"What do you think that means?" Elena asked in a tiny voice.

"He warns that the way may be open, but something struck his wolf senses as false. So he warns caution."

In the resulting silence, Fardale trotted over from the creek to sit at Elena's side, nudging her hand with his wet nose. She absently scratched him behind his ear as he squatted on his haunches.

So much for not treating Fardale like a dog, Er'ril thought, but he kept his silence. The intimacy shared between the wolf and the girl seemed to calm the growing unease in her expression, and the youngster needed as much resolve as she could muster for the long journey ahead.

"So we go," Er'ril said. "But we keep our eyes and ears alert."

AS THE OTHERS BUSIED THEMSELVES WITH FINAL PREPARATIONS, Mogweed hung around the far side of the wagon. He had his own preparations. He spotted the bent-backed crone among the small crowd of Kral's people that had gathered to wave them all off. Nodding his head at the old woman, he slipped into the shade of the wagon. He shuffled three coppers in his palm, then returned one to his pocket. Two should be enough.

He listened as the others of his party called orders to one another. All busy. Good. Soon, he heard the wheezing breath of the ancient mountain woman as she hobbled toward the lee of the wagon. He bit at his lower lip, hating his dependence on anyone else. But the task he had requested of the old crone was one he could not accomplish alone. He juggled the coins, clinking them together. Luckily, shiny coppers bought other hands to do the work his own could not.

The old gray-haired woman, leaning on a crooked branch of polished hickory, lurched into the shade beside Mogweed. She must have once stood taller than Mogweed, but time had bent her back so cruelly that now she had to roll her eyes up to stare Mogweed full in the face. With eyes the color of black granite, she studied Mogweed silently. As sorely as the passage of countless winters had ravaged her body, he sensed a core of ice in her as hard as the eternal snow atop the windswept peaks.

Suddenly he regretted his choice of accomplices in this task.

Glancing away from her flinty eyes, he cleared his dry throat. "Were you . . . able to get what I asked of you?"

She stared, still silent for several heartbeats, then slowly nodded and reached into the folds of her battered fox-fur cloak. "We mountain folk are traders, ain't we?" she replied with a throaty cackle. She pulled out a small satchel made from cured goatskin and began to hold it out to him. But when he reached for it, the old woman pulled it back. "Whatcha want with this stuff anyways?" she asked.

He was prepared for this question. "A keepsake," he said as guilelessly as he could manage.

The crone's eyes narrowed with his words. "You're a sly one," she hissed. "Perhaps too sly for your own good."

"I don't know what you're—"

She spat at his boots. "You stink of lies."

Mogweed backed a step. Would the woman expose him? He found his left palm slipping toward the hilt of the dagger at his waist.

"But your fate is not mine to judge, and a deal is a deal," she said and tossed him the stuffed satchel. "The Rock will weigh your worth and carve your path."

Caught off guard, Mogweed struggled to catch the little bag, fumbling it in his fingers until he pinned it to his chest. Unable to find his tongue, he slipped his other hand, which still palmed two coppers, back into his pocket and retrieved the third coin. He sensed he had better be more generous with his payment to this old crone. Offering all the coppers in his open palm, he finally muttered, "For your troubles."

The old crone suddenly lashed out with her hickory staff and struck his hand, scattering the trio of coins into the mud. "Only silver will cleanse your lies from my ears."

Mogweed rubbed his injured hand, then quickly fished the rare silver from among his small cache of coins. He cautiously passed her the payment, eyeing her staff warily.

The coin disappeared among the folds of her cloak. With a grunt of effort, she turned from him, but not before sharing a final warning. "Beware what you buy with lies, sly fox. You might discover the prize is not worth the price." With that, she slipped from shadows into sunlight and vanished beyond the corner of the wagon.

Not worth the price? Mogweed fingered open the goatskin satchel and stared at its contents. A smile without humor etched his face. This prize could very well prove to be worth *any* price.

Tucked within the shadowed interior lay several of the sheared locks of Elena's auburn hair.

Proof of a wit'ch.

UNDER THE SHADOWED TANGLE OF OAK BRANCHES, A HUSH HAD fallen over the copse. Not a bird sang; not an insect whirred. Vira'ni listened for any sound. Naked, her skin the color of the softest moonlight, clothed only in the folds of her long black hair, she knelt by the rotted stump of a pine, its sides charred by old fires. She held her breath. Even a single noise could disrupt the spell.

Her children, though, had done their job well. Nothing still lived within a quarter league of the glade. From here, she could see the ground littered with the small bodies of the dead woodland creatures—tufted squirrels, birds of every feather, even a red doe lay sprawled at the edge of the copse, its neck contorted from the poisons. Satisfied, she bowed her head in preparation.

Before her, atop the worm-eaten wood of the stump, rested a palm-size bowl of carved ebon'stone. Its basin glowed blacker than the richest obsidian, while jagged veins of silver quartz etched its dark surface like forked lightning at midnight. She allowed a finger to trace its edge.

Here lay wealth—and within its basin lay power.

Using a bone dagger, she sliced her thumb and dripped the blood into the basin. Fat droplets rolled like quicksilver to the bottom of the bowl, then quickly vanished—the stone was always thirsty.

Reciting the words taught her, Vira'ni's tongue grew colder with each utterance. Without halting, for that meant death, she forced her tongue to keep moving. Thankfully it was a short litany. Tears squeezing between her clenched lids, she spat the last word through her blue, frozen lips.

Finally done, she sat back upon her heels and raised her injured thumb to her mouth, licking gently at the cut. The blood was like fire in her frozen mouth.

Now, though, came the hardest part of the spell—waiting.

As she sucked at her wounded finger, her children must have sensed her distress and approached tentatively. Vira'ni allowed them to climb up her legs and nest where they had been birthed. An especially concerned child even crawled up her belly to gently rub its furred legs against her nipple. She ignored the young one, dismissing its impetuousness.

In her mind, she went over the ritual. Had she made a mistake? Perhaps more blood—

Black flames suddenly erupted from the ebon'stone bowl, flickering like a hundred serpents' tongues above the basin.

"Darkfire," she whispered, naming the flames with lips still blue from the cold. But these flames offered no warmth. Instead the small glade grew colder for their presence. Where normal fire shed light into darkness, this flame drank the late-afternoon sunlight that dappled through the branches overhead. The wood grew gloomy as a fog of cold darkness flowed out from the flame.

The child at her breast, frightened by the darkfire's blaze, bit her teat, but Vira'ni dismissed the pain. Poison or not, the spider's bite was but a small nuisance compared to the menace that lurked within the black flame.

She bowed her head to the stump. "Master, your servant awaits."

The flames swelled. Darkness swallowed the bowl and the stump. A faint scream echoed up from the flames. Even this whisper of pain brought a shiver to her skin. Vira'ni recognized the music of Blackhall's dungeons. Her own voice had once joined the same chorus as she writhed among the tortured. And so she would have remained if the Black Heart had not found her pleasing to his eyes, choosing her as a vessel for his power and impregnating her with the Horde.

Vira'ni's hand raised to where the Dark Lord himself had touched her that final night. A single white lock now nestled within her black hair, like an albino snake among black roots. As she fingered the single snowy tress, images flashed across her eyes—yellowed fangs, ripping claws, the beat of bony wings. Her fingers fell away from her hair.

Some memories were best left untouched.

Then a voice rose from the flames, a voice that poisoned her resolve. Like a beaten dog fearing the strike of its master's hand, Vira'ni felt her bladder loosen, soiling herself as she bowed her head farther. Her bones shook with each word. "Are you prepared?" the Dark Lord asked.

"Yes, Sire." She kissed the ground fouled by her own weakness. Her children scattered from her side, the spiders skittering under leaf and carcass. Even this small remnant of the Horde knew their father's voice.

"Your region is secure?"

"Yes, Sire. My children guard the entire pass. If the wit'ch comes this way, the Horde will alert me. I will be ready."

"And you know your duty?"

She nodded, smearing her forehead in the mud. "All must die."

2

Elena closed her eyes and allowed the motion of the horse to lull her. The muscles of her legs responded to the shifts and rolls of her mount with easy familiarity, the line between beast and rider dissolving into simple rhythm.

They had been on horseback for almost a full day now, though the company had made little headway down the pass. The trundling, creaking wagon slowed them to a pace no faster than a quick walk; and to further delay matters, several swollen creeks had to be forded with care, the swift currents proving treacherous to wheel and hoof.

While the others grumbled about the meager progress of the troupe, Elena did not mind, simply happy to be once again atop her own horse. The small gray mare, Mist, was the only piece of her home to survive the ravages of last fall's horrors. Now, as she rode, it seemed as if those terrible events were mere echoes from a bad dream. If she allowed herself, she could almost imagine that she was traveling the fields and orchards of her valley home, perhaps on a jaunt to Baldy Nob Hill for a picnic. Her hand strayed to the mare's dark mane and combed the rough hair with trembling fingers. A slight smile curled the corners of her lips. For a moment, she could almost smell home in the scent of Mist's musky sweat.

"Child, you'd ride better if you kept your eyes open," Er'ril said, his road-tired voice shredding the memory of her home.

Elena straightened in her saddle and opened her eyes. Rows of alpine birch and lodgepole pine lined their path. Ahead, Elena saw the back of the wagon lurching through the rough terrain. "Mist is following the others. She won't take me astray," Elena mumbled.

Er'ril kicked his mount, one of the tall crag horses, a white stallion whose coat blended well with the ice and snow of the peaks. The Standi plainsman, dressed in knee-high black boots and a deep brown riding jacket, drew abreast of her. A band of red leather tied his black hair back from his rugged face, yet the winds of the pass caught a few locks and blew them like a banner behind him. He and his mount towered over the small gray mare and its rider.

"Have you been practicing your lessons lately?" he asked in a hard voice, his eyes glinting in the late-afternoon sunlight.

She turned away from his stare to study the pommel of her saddle. "I've practiced some." Er'ril had been tutoring her on the few basic skills that the plainsman knew about the control and simple management of magicks. Er'ril's brother, Shorkan, had been a powerful mage before sacrificing himself to the binding of the Blood Diary, and during Er'ril's decade at Shorkan's side, a small bit of the arcane skills had brushed off onto him.

The plainsman sighed and reached a hand to grab her reins lightly while controlling his own horse with subtle movements of heel and thigh. "Listen, Elena, I understand your reluctance to touch the power within you, but—"

"No. You're wrong." She slipped the glove from her right hand, revealing the bloodred stain. "I've come to accept the burden and do not fear it." Elena reached her fingers toward Er'ril's wrist, and as she knew he would, he pulled back his hand from her touch. "It's you and the others," she said, "that fear the power."

She raised her face, but Er'ril would not meet her eye. "It's not that we don't—" he began.

Elena held up her ruby hand to stop him. She needed to voice this. "I have seen how everyone tries not to stare," she continued, "how they shrink from my touch. Their fear scares me more than the magick."

"I'm sorry, Elena, but you must understand. It has been centuries since anyone has borne the mark of the Rose—and longer since a woman has done so."

"Still, can't you see the girl hidden behind the Rose?" She pulled her glove back on. "I am more than just the stain on a hand."

When she raised her eyes, she found Er'ril staring at her with a thoughtful expression, the hard lines of his face softened. "Well spoken, Elena," he said. "Perhaps I have looked too much at the wit'ch . . . and not at the woman."

She nodded her thanks. "Perhaps you should see both. Because I suspect that on this journey, both will be equally tested."

Er'ril didn't answer, but he reached a hand and squeezed her knee. "You have grown much during the six moons among Kral's people. More than I had thought."

"It must be the mountain air," she said with a whisper of a grin.

He patted her leg and offered her one of his rare smiles. Something deep inside her stirred at the sight, something touched by more than the palm on her knee. A mixture of relief and regret flooded her when he removed his hand and turned away.

Er'ril sauntered his stallion a few steps aside while Elena tapped Mist's flank to urge the horse after the retreating wagon. Elena sighed. Suddenly the journey to A'loa Glen didn't seem quite so long.

Ahead, the thunder of hooves erupted near the wagon, drawing her attention. Meric appeared, mounted atop a spirited roan filly. The elv'in lord seemed to float above his saddle as the horse galloped toward them. Meric's silver hair, tied back in its usual braid, flagged behind him, matching his mount's own tail. He and his filly flew to join them.

"What is it?" Er'ril asked.

Meric ignored him, instead bowing his head first toward Elena before answering. "Kral has called a halt ahead. He's found something odd. He asks that we all join him."

Elena gripped her reins tighter. "What did he find?"

Meric shook his head. "I don't know. He says he's never seen its like before among these peaks and passes."

Elena recalled the wolf's message: *The trail smells wrong.* She reached a hand and pulled her riding jacket tighter around her neck.

Er'ril's hand had wandered to the pommel of his sword. "Lead on," he said.

Meric swung his horse around and guided the way. As they passed the gaily painted wagon, Elena saw that Nee'lahn and Mogweed were already gone from the wagon's front. She glanced within the tented interior. It was empty. Apparently Tol'chuk, too, had proceeded ahead.

Meric led the way along the thinly marked trail. As they rounded a bend, the path beyond vanished over a steep slope. The others gathered near the crest and were studying the lower lands. Elena and her companions dismounted and joined them.

"Kral," Er'ril said as he stepped up to the mountain man, "what've you found?"

Kral just pointed his thick arm downward.

Elena stepped beside Nee'lahn. The nyphai woman wore a worried expression. Ahead, the trail dropped in steep switchbacks toward a lower rimwood forest. With the sun setting behind them, the wood below drowned in shadows. Composed predominantly of black oaks and red maples, the trees' gnarled and bent boles were a dramatic change from the straight and stately posture of the lodgepole pines and mountain birch of the higher elevations.

"That wood looks sick," Nee'lahn whispered, seeming to draw inward, as if listening with more than her ears.

"What's that stuff growing on the tree branches?" Mogweed asked.

Elena saw it, too. Strands of gossamer filaments blew and billowed from almost every branch, like ghostly mosses. Some clumped in thick patches, some in ribbons stretching longer than the trees were tall.

"What is it?" Mogweed asked, directing the question at Nee'lahn, the troupe's expert in woodlore.

But the answer came from Tol'chuk, the og're's sharp eyes glowing amber in the dying light. "Looks like webs."

Mogweed's voice rose sharply in pitch. "And how . . . What would cause those?"

Elena answered that question herself. "Spiders."

NEE'LAHN STEPPED TOWARD THE LONE OAK, SEEKING ANSWERS. THE ancient tree towered like a sentinel near the edge of the dark wood, separate from its web-shrouded brethren. Only its branches, peppered with green buds, lightly brushed the arms of its companions. *Something was dreadfully wrong here.*

"Nee'lahn!" Er'ril called. "Wait!"

She ignored him, only raising a hand to silence the plainsman and indicate she had heard his warning. The others were still trying to coax the wagon down the series of switchbacks to where the trail continued into these strange woods. She could hear their raised voices as they shouted orders to one another. Only Er'ril and Elena had followed her when she had hurried toward the forest's edge.

As one of the nyphai, steeped in the elemental magicks of root and loam, the woodlands were her charge. Nee'lahn could not remain idle while this stand of old-growth forest suffered. She would find who or what had assaulted its spirit—and make them answer for their violation!

Nee'lahn cautiously approached the ancient oak, careful not to crush the fallen acorns near the base of its knotted trunk. It wouldn't be good to offend this old man of the forest—not if she needed answers.

Bent with age, its bark burnished to a polished black by decades of winter's ice and summer's scorch, the solitary oak commanded respect. Its branches were a snarled canopy overhead—as if in form, the old man expressed his anger at what had occurred to his root brothers. But even this stout survivor had not escaped the corruption's touch. Nee'lahn spotted several melon-size horny growths sprouting like yellow boils from his trunk. They somewhat resembled the parasitic galls from nesting wasps, but she had never seen them swell so large.

Nee'lahn reached a tentative finger to touch the bark of the old man, keeping her hand well away from one of the ripe growths that protruded overhead. Closing her eyes and bowing her head, she opened herself up.

Wake and hear me, old one. I seek your counsel.

She waited for a response, searching for that stirring of spirit that meant she had been heard. Some of the older trees could become lost in dreams and were reluctant to abandon the communal song of their forest home. But such was not the case with the old man—she heard no trace of woodsong, no music of the glade in which the old man communed.

The entire forest lay silent to her calling.

A chill passed through her. Only one other forest had been so deathly still—her own woodland home, Lok'ai'hera, after the Blight had destroyed it.

"Nee'lahn," Elena said near her shoulder, but the girl's words seemed far away. "You're crying. What's wrong?"

"The forest . . . It isn't sick." Nee'lahn's voice cracked as she answered. "It's dead. Poisoned like my home."

"How could that be?" Er'ril said. "Look, the trees still bud with new growth. They seem fine."

"No. A tree's spirit will sing the moment it sprouts from seed and continue until it dies." She faced Er'ril and Elena, touching her palm reverently on the cold trunk of the old man. "I hear no woodsong here," she whispered. "All the spirits are gone."

"Yet, the trees still sprout," Er'ril continued to argue.

"It's a deception. Something has dispossessed the true spirits and taken over the trees. What lies before us is not forest . . . but something else."

Elena stepped closer to Er'ril. "Who could have done that?" she asked, her eyes wide.

"I'm not—" Nee'lahn tensed. Maybe it was just her imagination or a wishful dream, but for a breath, she'd felt a familiar touch: a tingling behind her ears, a minor chiming, like wind through crystals. She dared not hope. Then she felt him reach for her, swimming up as he drowned in poisons.

The old man yet lived! But he was in such pain.

"Nee'lahn?" Elena asked tentatively.

"Hush, he's weak." Nee'lahn turned away from the two worried faces to place both palms upon the knotted trunk of the ancient oak. *Come to me, old man,* she prayed. *Let my song give you strength.*

She hummed softly in her chest a melody taught to her as a child. The tree spirit drew closer, hesitatingly, as if wary. Nee'lahn opened farther. *See my light; fear not.* Then his song joined hers, at first just a mere whisper, but soon with a desperate fervor. It had been a long time since this tree had communed with another of the root. His song wrapped around her like the arms of a long-lost friend. Yet, Nee'lahn sensed little strength left in those once-strong arms. Though beautiful and full of the resonant depth that only the passage of many winters could cultivate, the woodsong faded with each note. The old man was using the last of his spirit to reach out to her.

Nee'lahn would not let his effort be in vain.

She sang in harmony to the old oak's chorus of pain and loss, pleading: *Tell me what has happened to those who shared your root, old one. We must know.*

The old man continued to sing, but his voice weakened rapidly. Only one word reached her clearly: *Horde.*

What did that mean?

Confused, she hummed in supplication for a clearer description—but none came. He was slipping away. She tried to sing him songs of healing and hope, but it was to no avail. The old oak's spirit died as she held his song close to her heart.

She lowered her forehead to the bole of the tree. *May the Sweet Mother make you safe,* she sent him in final prayer. Yet, just as the old man drifted into nothingness, a last clear whisper reached back to her.

Shuddering, shocked by the oak's final message, she dropped her hands from his bark. No! Not that! Tears sprang fresh to her eyes.

"What is it?" Elena asked.

Nee'lahn tried to pull her mind back to normal speech, fighting for control of her tongue. How dull simple language was when compared to the multilayered song of the root. She shook her head, still dazed by the tree's message. "We must—"

"Get back!" Er'ril grabbed Nee'lahn by the shoulder and yanked her away from the oak.

Dancing to keep her balance, she twisted around to see what had so startled the plainsman. Her hand flew to her mouth to cover her expression of disgust. With the death of the tree, the yellow galls now quaked and shook upon the dead carcass of the old oak, and a sick droning buzz reached Nee'lahn's ears.

"Back, back . . ." Er'ril urged needlessly.

They all sped in a stumbling retreat.

Suddenly, like ripe milkweed pods, the galls burst open. A flow of tiny red spiders poured forth from the ruptured sores, spilling across the trunk and branches. The stench of rotting meat flowed forth from the heart of the tree, now a nest of the blackest corruption. Within a heartbeat, thousands of spiders drifted on lines of silk, wafting in the twilight breezes.

"Mother above, what horror is this?" Er'ril cursed.

Nee'lahn knew the answer. "It's the Horde."

The spiders continued to entomb the tree in their webbing. It seemed as if the beasts were already growing, their tiny bodies swelling like blood blisters, their black legs stretching longer and thicker. So foul to the eye, there could be no doubt that poison ran strong in their bites.

"What . . . what are we to do?" Elena asked. "We can't go through that forest."

"Yes, we can," Nee'lahn said, her voice venomous enough to

match the spiders. She recalled the final chorus of the ancient oak. What he had asked of her was blasphemous to a nyphai, an entreaty that went against the grain of her own spirit—but now Nee'lahn understood the necessity.

"How?" Er'ril asked. "What do you propose?"

Nee'lahn closed her eyes, remembering the image that had bloomed in the oak's deathsong: *Flames licking at wood and leaf.* Her voice grew hard with the promise of revenge. "We burn our way through."

ELENA CHEWED AT HER LOWER LIP AND FLEXED HER RIGHT HAND, STUDYing the ruby stain in the early evening gloom. The sun had already set behind the peaks of the Teeth behind her, leaving only a shadowed twilight at the edge of the corrupt wood.

No one paid her any heed as she stood near the back of the wagon. The others were too deep in discussion on the plans for tomorrow. Only one item had already been settled—that they would not brave the forest this dark evening. Instead, they decided to camp well away from the woods with two guards posted throughout the night.

As they all argued back and forth, only Mist stood by Elena's side at the back of the wagon, the horse's nose buried in her feed bag. Elena's left hand idly ran a comb through her horse's mane, removing brambles and tangles from the long day's ride. But she did a shoddy job, her attention more on the bloodred whorls and black eddies of magick that swam across her right hand.

She concentrated on the ruby stain, remembering Er'ril's instructions. Just let the magick show; don't release it. Elena deepened her breathing and let her heartbeat slow. She needed to practice control of her magick's flow, sensing that tomorrow would test her skills. With her lids sinking partially closed, Elena willed the tips of her fingers to warm. As she watched, only half aware, the nails of her right hand began to glow a soft rose.

Now for a bit more magick.

Elena bore her will to an intensity that scared her slightly. She could feel the call of her wild magicks, a seductive chorus of power. She listened to their siren song, now well familiar with their allure after the many days of practice with Er'ril.

Elena could not deny that a part of her—the half of her spirit that was wit'ch—was attracted by the whispers of power. But rather than deny this appetite, she heeded the power's call. Er'ril had taught her that ignoring her desires would only give the wit'ch in her more strength and control over her own true will, allowing the wit'ch to overwhelm the woman.

She would not allow that!

She was *Elena Morin'stal*, and too many had already died in her name for her to give up her heritage to some siren song of power. She would not lose herself to magick's lust.

She spread her hand wide. The tips of her fingers brightened to a white heat, the color burnt clean from them. She allowed herself a smile of satisfaction. If she should prick her finger now, the wild magick would be free to flow from her, unleashed into the world. And when she finally chose to do this, it would be the woman, *not the wit'ch*, that bent the wild magick to her will.

She clenched her fist into a tight ball, feeling the energies penned up within, then opened her hand. Her magicks crackled in blazes of power across the palm and back of her hand.

Suddenly, a voice rose behind her. "What are you doing?"

Startled, Elena's magick flared brighter, like an ember fanned to flame. She fought it back down, but not before the blaze had stung her eyes, as if scolding her for not releasing its energies into the world. After it had died away to nothing, it took a moment for her stressed eyes to make out the slender figure of the shape-shifter standing behind her.

"Mogweed?" Elena slipped her hand, now dark again, back into its glove.

"Sheathing your sword, I see," Mogweed said with a fluttering smile.

"Pardon me?"

He pointed to her gloved hand. "Covering up your weapon. A sheathed sword seems innocent enough, even beautiful, until the blade is pulled free, revealing its deadly edge." Mogweed's eyes glowed amber in the weak light. "Your magick is like that sword."

"Maybe. But a sword is easier to control," she said shyly. "It doesn't try to stab people all on its own."

"Ah, child, everything takes practice. A sword is only as lethal as the skill of its wielder."

"But even a child can accidentally kill with a sword."

"True, so true." Mogweed reached to her currycomb. "Let me

help you with that." He began to work Mist's mane with more diligence than Elena's halfhearted effort.

"I can manage," she said, but Elena could not deny that Mist seemed to enjoy the shape-shifter's attention. Of course, the chunk of cured sweetroot he first offered to the horse did wonders to ingratiate the man to Mist.

"Tut, tut," he scolded her. "I enjoy it. The horses deserve a bit of kindness for their long day of labors." He glanced over to her with those strange, slitted eyes. "Now, enough about horses. I really came to see if you could use some company. You seemed so alone back here. Why aren't you with the others?"

"No one seemed interested in my ideas about tomorrow."

"Hmm . . . that sounds familiar." He offered her a smile. "I keep mostly to myself, too. I'm afraid I don't fully understand the goings-on of mankind. We si'lura are an isolated people, living deep in the Western Reaches, well away from men, except for the occasional hunter or trapper. I'm not comfortable around others—" He lowered his voice, sounding like tears might threaten. "—especially so far from home."

Elena took a brush and began wiping down Mist's flanks. "I know how you feel," she mumbled. A pang of sorrow caught her unawares. As she worked at Mist, soft music rose from the campfire as Nee'lahn began playing her lute. The lonely notes wafted outward like the gentle warmth of the campfire, spreading not only into the night but also reaching inside Elena. Er'ril had once told her that Nee'lahn's lute contained an ancient spirit of the nyphai's lost home. And listening to its mournful voice, Elena knew it was true. Its chords spoke of lost homes and vanished friends and touched Elena's heart. She had already lost so much of her own home—mother, father, aunt, uncle. Her only hope lay in the chance that her brother Joach, after being stolen off the streets of Winterfell by the darkmage, still lived somewhere amongst the lands of Alasea. Her secret dream was that along this lengthy journey she might find her brother again. "Joach," she whispered to Mist's flank, "you promised to be there for me. I am holding you to your word."

Mogweed raised his head from near Mist's tail. "Were you talking to me?"

She smiled, cheeks flushing. "No, sorry. Just remembering . . ."

He nodded knowingly. "Memories of home are always a strange mix of sorrow and joy."

"Yes . . . yes, they are." She lowered her face and hid the tears that began to well. She had always found the shape-shifter rather cold: always alone, seldom speaking, always studying everyone with narrowed, suspicious eyes. Now, maybe, for the first time she began to understand the man. Maybe the two of them weren't so different.

The two worked over Mist in silence, both turned inward. When he didn't know she was looking, Elena caught a wavery smile pass over Mogweed's face. She imagined the shape-shifter's thoughts dwelt, like hers, on bittersweet recollections of lost homes and families. After several moments of quiet brushing, Mist's coat glowed in the fading twilight.

They both stepped back to admire their handiwork.

"That's much better," Elena finally said. "Thanks."

"No, I should thank you for allowing me to help. I found it nice to talk to someone who shared my sentiments." Mogweed suddenly raised a hand and patted his leather jerkin. His fingers stopped at an inside pocket and withdrew something. "Here's a gift," he said. "Just a small token."

Elena leaned closer to see what he offered in his open palm. "It's an acorn."

"Yes, from near that big oak."

"But why did you . . . I mean of what . . . ?"

"I know it's not much of a gift. But I'm a collector. What is someone's trash is another's treasure. I heard Nee'lahn's tale. This woodland home is dead. I felt sorry—so I collected the acorn to maybe plant somewhere free of this foulness, to give the forest a chance to someday live again." Mogweed began to withdraw his hand. "I'm sorry. It was a silly offering."

"No, no." She took his hand in her own and removed the acorn. She held the oak seed in her fist and pressed it to her chest. "What a sweet and thoughtful gesture. Thank you, Mogweed. I will treasure your gift."

"I thought since we both lost our homes . . . that maybe we could at least bring someone else's back." His voice cracked with his last words. "And in that way, maybe bring back a little of our own."

Elena did not hide her face this time. A single tear rolled down her cheek. She wanted Mogweed to see how much he had touched her with his words.

He seemed at first shocked by her emotion; then he glanced at his feet, as if embarrassed or guilty. "I'm sorry . . . I didn't think . . ."

"No, Mogweed." She reached to his shoulder. For a heartbeat, it seemed he cringed from her touch, as if he suddenly did not want to be here. She squeezed his shoulder.

Before she could speak, a stern voice rose from behind her. "Elena, shouldn't you be in bed?" It was Er'ril. "We've a dangerous day tomorrow, and I want you well rested."

She removed her hand from Mogweed's shoulder and faced the plainsman. "I was just combing out Mist."

Er'ril ignored her. "Mogweed, don't you have the first watch? Shouldn't you be with Kral?"

"I was just going," he said meekly, brushing past Elena.

"And keep your eyes open," Er'ril called after him, his words more an accusation than an instruction.

When Er'ril turned back, Elena knitted her brow darkly. "You need not be so hard on him," she said. "He's not a warrior, just a wanderer—like me."

Er'ril blew out a rude noise. "I can read people. He's a shirker. Always looking for the easiest path."

Elena roughly placed her brushes and combs back into the wagon. She dumped the horse's water bucket, slightly splashing Er'ril with the contents. "Yes, you're a keen observer of people's feelings."

As she stomped off toward the spread of bedrolls, her fingers wandered to the lump in her pocket. The acorn was a reminder that looks could deceive. The acorn appeared tiny and weak, but within its shell lurked the potential for a mighty oak.

Er'ril could not see that—not in Mogweed, not in herself.

"What is the matter with that child?" she heard Er'ril grumble behind her.

Nothing, she answered silently. Nothing at all.

ER'RIL STOOD WITH HIS BACK TOWARD THE CAMP'S FIRES. IN THE DIStance, the light of the flames lapped to the fringes of the forest, but its heat barely reached his position. So far the creatures of the Horde seemed content to stay within their dead wood. Still it would be unwise for his band to let its guard down. Behind Er'ril, to protect against any marauding spiders, the group of bedrolls lay within a protective ring of small campfires. Standing just beyond their circle of warmth, Er'ril wore a deerskin jacket with a furred collar against the late evening's cold as he stood watch. Morning seemed a false promise this dark moonless night. Even the stars were just whispers poking through a thin cloudy haze that had blown in at nightfall.

Unblinking, he studied the forest, trying to pierce its mysteries. The companions had argued well into the evening on the best course through the wood. They had all quickly decided that turning back was not an option. According to the wolf, the other trails were swamped with snowmelt—and who was to say that these other paths weren't similarly blocked by corruption? No, they had to risk the wood. Yet doubt ran like ice in Er'ril's veins. The child was ultimately his responsibility.

"We must go forward," Tol'chuk suddenly said beside him, as if reading his mind. The og're had been sitting so still and quiet, like a crouching boulder, that Er'ril had almost forgotten the hulking creature was there.

"I know," Er'ril said, thankful to speak aloud what troubled him. "But are we right? We could always go back to Kral's people and wait until the other passes open."

"No, this be the correct path."

The certainty in the og're's voice drew Er'ril's eyes. "How can you be so sure?"

Tol'chuk shifted his thick body, his joints creaking like breaking saplings. In the firelight, Er'ril saw the og're pull open his thigh pouch and remove a large object. Like a fired coal, it glowed a deep red between Tol'chuk's claws. Er'ril recognized the stone: the Heart, as Tol'chuk had named the large crystal, a chunk of precious heartstone mined from deep in the og're's lands.

Er'ril had seen the crystal before, but never aglow as it was this night. His gaze was drawn to it; its gentle radiance seemed to penetrate deep within him. Er'ril found his voice strangely hushed as he tried to understand the og're's revelation. "What's the significance of . . . of the Heart?" he asked.

Tol'chuk became silent, a boulder again. Only the white flumes flaring from his nostrils into the chill air indicated he still lived. Finally, he spoke again. "I would tell you something, Er'ril. Something I have told no other."

"What is it?"

"Long ago, one of my blood ancestors, the Oathbreaker, betrayed the land most foully. And as punishment, the land cursed our people." The og're lowered his face in shame, his back bending in anguish.

Er'ril had never seen Tol'chuk so pained. Uncomfortable with the og're's display, Er'ril found his eyes drifting back to the forest's edge, but he knew he could not so easily ignore his companion's distress. He spoke into the silence. "What did this Oathbreaker of yours do?"

"No one knows." Tol'chuk held up the glowing stone. "But this be our curse. The stone holds our clan's spirits of the dead until they can travel to the next world. But the land laid a corrupt seed, a black worm called the Bane, within the heart of the stone. It now eats our spirits instead of letting them travel beyond."

Er'ril grimaced. A foul story indeed.

"I be the last descendant of this Oathbreaker, doomed by my mixed blood never to bear offspring. Prophecy says only I can lift this curse upon our people's spirits and destroy the Bane."

Er'ril glanced back to the heartstone, trying to pierce its glow and spy the black worm inside. He could not see what the og're described. "This Bane . . . How are you supposed to get rid of it?"

"I must discover what the Oathbreaker did and correct it." Tol'chuk lowered the large crystal back to his lap.

"I thought no one knows what this ancestor of yours did."

"That be true. But I was given the Heart as a beacon. It guides me where I must go."

Er'ril digested this information, beginning to understand. "The glow—?"

"It calls me forward. Leads me where I need to be. First to the shape-shifters, then to the girl. After I joined you all, the stone grew dark and quiet—so I know we all must stay together. But with the first melt of snow, it began to call again, worse as each day passed. Now it urges like hooks in my heart. We must not *delay*."

Er'ril studied the stone for several moments in silence. "I believe you," he finally said and turned back to face the corrupt forest. Though the og're's words had helped steady Er'ril's resolve on their course, they did little to ease the fear around his heart. Stone or not, prophecy did little to protect one from a spider's bite. "But, Tol'chuk, are you quite sure of your stone's pull?"

As answer, the og're lifted the heartstone toward the dark wood. The crystal flared brighter, competing now with the flames of the hearths. "We have no other path. We *must* travel through the spiders' forest."

3

Elena adjusted the damp cloth across her nose and mouth. It sat cold against her cheek. She shifted in Mist's saddle, unable to find her rhythm.

"We look like a bunch of bandits, eh?" Kral called to her as he rode beside her. Elena imagined he wore one of his broad grins under his own mask of wet cloth. The others were similarly garbed to protect them from the smoke to come. Her companions were also outfitted with hooded cloaks, to keep ash and stray spiders from hair and face.

Elena nodded at Kral. They did look somewhat like a raiding party.

Ahead, Elena could see the tall column of black smoke already marring the blue morning sky. Its source was a fierce bonfire started at daybreak by Er'ril, Nee'lahn, and Meric. It raged a stone's throw from the forest's edge, near where the trail entered the wood.

She followed the trail of smoke to the blue sky above. Why did her journeys always begin with fire, she thought, remembering the orchard blaze that had heralded the beginning of her horrors.

Elena, accompanied by the mountain man for protection, traveled slowly toward the fire and smoke. The wagon trailed behind, its bells tinkling brightly in contrast to the dire wood they skirted.

Although the morning sun had quickly burned off the dawn haze, the forest itself still clung to the night's shadows. Wisps of trailing webs, many carrying the red-blistered bodies of their makers, reached from the wood's edge toward them. They kept well away from these clinging strands, aiming for the fire.

Mogweed drove the wagon behind her, bearing Fardale and Tol'chuk. Er'ril had insisted no one should travel this trail on foot; the risk of a spider bite was too high. Even the horses' legs were wrapped in leather straps.

Elena glanced over her shoulder to where the two draft horses strained in their harnesses. Her heart went out to them. Er'ril had tried to corral Elena within the wagon with the og're and the wolf. "It's safer under the wagon's canopy," he had claimed. But she would not leave Mist tethered to the back of the wagon. Restricted by the lead, unable to maneuver, her mare would be easy prey to the crawling beasts. She could not allow that. Risk or not, she would stay with her horse.

"Yo!" Kral called to Er'ril as they neared. Elena's eyes were drawn forward. "If you stoke that fire any higher," the mountain man bellowed, "you'll be chasing us back to my clan's caves."

Er'ril raised his single hand in acknowledgement but kept his head bowed near the silver-haired elv'in. The plainsman's hand and face were smudged with char and ash.

Meric shook his head vigorously at something Er'ril said. Even from here, Elena could see the elv'in's blue eyes flash angrily.

Ignoring their argument, Nee'lahn stood between the fire and the forest, wrapped in her cloak and mask, her shoulders tight by her ears. She stared steadily toward the forest, her eyes moist with more than the sting of smoke. The nyphai raised a black hand to her cheek and brushed away a tear, leaving a smear of ash under one eye.

The jangle and clatter of the wagon as Mogweed pulled to a halt finally drew the three fire builders. Er'ril straightened and crossed toward them, trailed by Meric and Nee'lahn.

"We're ready," Er'ril said, eying Elena on top of Mist. A momentary flash of irritation mixed with worry seemed to cross through his eyes. He turned to face the others now gathered. "I've torches flaming at the fire's edge. Everyone on horseback needs to grab one. Once remounted, we'll spread out on either side of the trail opening." He pointed for where he wanted everyone positioned. "Then on my signal, we'll burn a swath through this cursed wood."

Heads nodded and everyone, except those in the wagon, approached the fire. Er'ril laid a hand on Elena's knee when she tried to dismount. "You stay by the wagon. This is not for you."

Elena deliberately removed the plainsman's hand. "No," she said with heat in her voice. She jumped from the mare's back. "This *is* for me. This *is* all for me. I understand the need to conserve my own magicks until I'm more skilled, but if we are to burn a forest, then my hand, too, will lay torch to wood. I'll not sit idle."

Er'ril's face had darkened fiercely. "Yes, this whole journey is for you, Elena. But its purpose is *not* for you to burn a forest. If we are to trust prophecy, you are our last hope against the Gul'gotha. You, child, have no right to risk—"

"First, I am tired of being called a *child*. I am well past my first bleed." She moved to swipe back her hair, realizing too late that her locks were long gone. She dropped her arm, her face reddening further. "Second, if I am to save these lands, I must learn to face adversity, not be hidden away and coddled like a babe. On this journey, I must learn to harden my heart in tempered steel. And, as you taught me, only the hottest fire can forge the strongest steel."

Er'ril just stared at her, his mouth hanging slightly open. The others had stopped to stare at them, though several eyes now darted awkwardly away.

"I will not shirk my responsibility here," Elena finished, her hands in fists. "I will face my fires."

Er'ril shook his head ever so slightly. "Fine," he said aloud, but as she tried to brush past him, he stopped her with a hand to her shoulder. "But you stick close to me," he whispered fiercely. "Lessons learned do no good to the dead."

Elena nodded and crossed toward the fire. The others had already gathered burning brands. She reached for a stump of dead wood protruding from the fire and pulled out its flaming end.

Er'ril did the same. "Mount up!" he called to everyone.

Elena and the others returned to their horses. Mist shied from the torch's flame at first, but with a few soothing words, Elena was able to calm the mare and regain her saddle. She walked Mist closer to Er'ril's white stallion. The plainsman, guiding his horse with motions of his legs, held his own torch high.

Suddenly a breeze blew up from the lower valley and scattered smoke and flaming ash from the tip of Er'ril's torch toward Elena.

Er'ril twisted in his saddle to face Meric. "Are you certain you can manage this?"

The elv'in scowled at him. "You have already asked me that a fistful of times. My answer remains the same."

Er'ril persisted. "Yes, and you have also told us a *fistful of times* that your heart is not firm on this journey. Our success here depends on your elv'in skills, Meric. If you cannot master these winds and keep the fire driving ahead of us, we will be forced to retreat."

"I know my duty. I have given my word as an elv'in lord to drive this blaze through the heart of this foul forest. My winds will not fail me."

The two men stared icily at one another for several heartbeats. Elena could tell Er'ril hated being dependent on another. She guessed that after centuries wandering the roads of Alasea alone, the plainsman had grown to distrust any arm but his own. She moved Mist between the two men. "Meric will not fail us," she said, with a nod toward the elv'in. "He knows my wishes and will not balk from his duty."

Meric bowed his head. "I see the elv'in king's wise counsel has not been diluted by generations of ordinary blood."

Kral called out from where he and Nee'lahn were guiding their horses away. He carried three brands caught up in his large fist. "If you're done warming your jaws, we've a fire to set!"

Er'ril raised his torch higher and kicked his stallion toward the forest. Elena followed, with Meric trailing. The trio aimed for the forest to the left of the trail, while Nee'lahn and Kral trotted toward the far side.

"Sick-looking beasts," Meric said as Er'ril pulled his group to a stop just beyond the eaves of the forest.

Elena found the elv'in's words to be too mild. From the forest's canopy draped a tangled curtain of webbing, snarls that hung like clotted blood from an open wound. The fat red bodies of the spiders, singly and in frenzied groups, added to the image that the trees bled.

"These are not natural beasts," Meric said. "They stink of corruption."

"Natural or not," Er'ril said, raising his torch toward a tangle of web blowing out toward them, "a hot-enough fire can burn out any corruption." He laid his torch to the mass of strands. The torch's flame jumped to the web. Sizzling and hissing, the fire ran up the strands. A handful of spiders caught in the blaze tried to scrabble away, their bodies afire. Several blazing spiders even managed to pass the fire onto neighboring webs, while others popped and burst from the poisons boiling within their bodies. Splashes of caustic poison etched the wood and bark they touched.

Er'ril raised his voice, his words echoing across the valley. "Now! Set it aflame!" He threw his torch into the forest.

Elena threw hers where Er'ril pointed. Meric moved his filly to the side a few steps, then flung his own brand deep within the wood. Deadwood that had accumulated like driftwood at the edge of a sea greedily consumed the torches' fires.

"Again!" Er'ril called out. Elena and the others returned to the fire to collect more torches. They repeated their attack upon the forest, seeding new fires and spreading the breadth of the fire's front. After four trips to the forest's edge, they were forced to stop. The blaze had grown too hot to approach closer than a stone's throw.

Er'ril called for everyone to regather. As the others joined them, Elena could not keep her eyes from the flames licking up at the sky. The fire crackled and popped like the choking laugh of a predator. What had they done?

Elena walked Mist beside Nee'lahn's horse. The small woman hung limply in her saddle. The nyphai, too, could not turn her back on the fire. Firelight reflected in her tears. "We . . . we had to do it," Nee'lahn muttered, reaching a small hand out to Elena.

Taking her hand in her own, Elena stayed silent, knowing that no words could ease this pain.

Nee'lahn continued, "I know the forest is dead . . . and I am glad to see the fire destroy the Horde that murdered this proud wood . . . But . . . but still . . ."

Elena squeezed her hand.

Tol'chuk had by now wandered over to them, his amber eyes aglow in the flames. The og're's sharp ears must have heard Nee'lahn's words. "The spirits of the trees be gone now. Free now. It be not right that these beasts feast on the carcasses. It honors the dead to send their ashes back to the sky and ground. With the way burnt clear, life can begin again."

Tol'chuk's words seemed to straighten Nee'lahn's shoulders. "Green life from red fire," she said softly.

"What was that?" Elena asked.

Nee'lahn sighed and shook her head, slipping her hand free of Elena's. "Tol'chuk is right," she said. "Even the last of our elders prophesied that my own forest home could only be rebirthed in fire. 'Green life from red fire' were the elder's dying words." Nee'lahn wiped away her tears and pointed an arm toward the fire. "Today we have not birthed a fire of destruction, but the first flame of new life."

Er'ril called to them all, drawing their attention back to the circle of companions. "The fire burns fierce enough. It's time now to give the fire its legs. Everybody load up and get ready. We must stick close to the heels of this marching flame." Er'ril swung to face Meric. "Are you ready?"

"Always." Meric reined his filly around and trotted her several paces away from the group, toward the fire's edge.

Once clear of the group, Meric settled his mount, then bowed his head with his arms tight across his chest. At first nothing happened. Elena noticed Er'ril's stallion dance on its hooves as the mount sensed its master's nervousness. What had to occur next was crucial to their plans.

They waited, everyone eying each other. Only Meric sat calmly upon his steed, his head still bowed.

Then a high whistle echoed down from the peaks, like the keening cry of a hunting hawk. Elena held her breath. At first, she felt a slight shift in the air. The smoke that had wafted toward them in waves, fouling the breezes with its stink and ash, suddenly cleared around them. Fresh air, crisp from the cold peaks, washed away the smoke.

Then it came.

In a rush that had all members of the group scrambling to keep their mounts steady, a gust of swift air swept down to engulf the group and slam into the fire's raging front. The flames swelled hugely, leaping toward the sky, as if trying to stop the wind—but the gusts grew in force.

Elena crouched lower atop Mist, offering less of a target to the gale. Behind her, the wagon's bells clanked angrily, and its canopy snapped sharply in the wind. With the gusts whistling in her ears, she barely heard Er'ril yell for everyone to make ready.

Soon the fire began to retreat from the wind, digging deeper into the forest, forging a wide path through the wood. The wind, knowing it had won the battle, calmed slightly but still blew steadily from the peaks, driving the fire onward. Their plan was to burn a swath through the forest wide enough to keep the spiders lurking to either side at bay. But they couldn't delay too long.

"Let's go!" Er'ril bellowed to them. "Stay together."

Ahead, Meric shook back his hood. His face, lit by the retreating fire, was aglow with rapture. He turned to Er'ril. "Do you still doubt my abilities?"

Er'ril led the group. "Not as long as that wind keeps blowing," he said as he passed the man.

Meric tried to scowl, but after touching the elemental power in his elv'in blood, he could not erase the wonder and awe in his eyes. For the first time, Elena could see the prince in the man.

"We must hurry," Er'ril yelled, struggling to be heard above the fire's roar.

Elena faced the burning woods. The trail, a moment ago full of flame and smoke, was now an open throat, awaiting them. Elena pulled her cloak tighter around her shoulders and kicked Mist forward.

VIRA'NI KNELT NAKED IN THE SMALL GLADE, A DELICATE FIGURE OF carved moonlight, her fingers planted to the largest knuckle in the dank dirt. She listened with her head slightly cocked. Her long hair, silky like her children's webs, draped to the leaf-strewn forest floor.

Surrounding her, the trees were now just black skeletons under shrouds of webbing. Thousands of her children scurried along the busy thoroughfares and byways of their magnificent construction, adding and building, fighting and mating. But Vira'ni ignored all this as she strained her senses. Like the trees, Vira'ni herself lay within a nest of silver web, but from her nest, eight cords of braided silk extended out to all compass points to merge with her children's handiwork. These cords vibrated and thrummed like the strings of a finely tuned lute.

In her nest, Vira'ni listened to the music of her children's instrument. Not just with her ears, but with the bones of her body. Since dawn, something had been happening. She read agitation in the faint vibrations.

One of her children scampered down a cord toward her. She pulled a hand from the dirt and reached a finger toward it. "What is it, my sweet?"

The spider crawled up onto her palm.

"You have news?"

Her child sat with its furred legs bunched under it in the center of her palm. It quivered ever so slightly.

"Don't be afraid," she cooed softly.

She raised the spider to her lips and placed the child in her mouth. Such a delicate creature. The warmth of a mother's love for a child ran through her veins. She felt its eight tiny legs dance on her tongue, and a smile turned the corner of her lips. Oh, how she loved this tiny one, but now was not the time to dally. Something was happening. The vibration in the cords increased with each breath she took.

Vira'ni moved her child with her tongue. Now tell me what you know, little one, she thought as she crunched the spider between her teeth. Its poisons swept through her instantly. The master had prepared her well.

Vira'ni swooned slightly, both hands again planted deep into the soil for support. Her vision swam in myriad hues. The trees and webs blurred. Then she saw—saw with the vision of her children—a great conflagration consuming her forest. It raged many leagues away, near the edge of her wood. She spied the fire from thousands of eyes all at once, her mind's eye fractured into a thousand pieces.

Stinging tears flowed across her cheeks as she bore witness to the holocaust: *sheets of flame consuming wood and web . . . her children fleeing . . . smoke from countless windswept fires . . . spiders aflame and dying . . .* and for a moment, *a charred wagon, its canopy smoldering, pulled by two wild-eyed horses . . .*

She spat the hollow husk of her child to the ground. "No," she moaned. "My children!" She pushed to her feet, snapping free of clinging webs.

Vira'ni looked toward the far western sky, trying to pierce the net of branches and webs. The sky above her was clear, with the sun directly overhead, but to the west, the horizon was blotted out by a huge black cloud. If not for her vision, she might have mistaken it for an approaching storm, black with angry thunderheads—but she knew better. What fed these clouds was not rain and lightning, but fire and wind.

As Vira'ni watched, she began to hear a distant roar like the call of an approaching beast, and in the skies above, tendrils and roots of smoke began to worm out of the black wall, reaching toward her.

The fire was coming this way, sweeping through the forested valley!

She shuddered as she realized its impact. It would consume all in its path! She raised a muddy fist to her mouth in horror and tore her eyes from the roiling skies. "The Horde must not die," she cried. In her breast, the numbing fear for her children was laced with the strangling terror of offending the Dark Lord if she should lose his sweet gift.

Her mind dwelt for a moment on the thought of trying to contact her lord, but by the time she could purify the ebon'stone and perform the rites, the fire would be upon her and all would be lost. That must not happen! No, she thought as she hugged herself, the call would have to wait. Once she and her children were safe, she would let the master know what had happened.

Behind her, the roar grew louder, and the day began to darken as smoke ate the sun.

She must hurry.

Scrambling free of her nest, she squatted in the damp mud, her small knees spread wide. She closed her eyes and opened that part of her, allowing the scent to flow out from her. It smelled of ripe meat and spoiled milk.

Come to me, my children.

She spread her knees wider, and they came—crawling, scrabbling, scurrying from all directions. She knew she could not save them all. Such a deed, besides being impossible, was unnecessary. She needed only to protect a fraction of the whole, only a small seed from which the Horde could grow forth again.

Come, come, she urged. *Hurry.*

Her children crowded over her knees and up her smooth legs, returning to where they had been birthed. They squirmed and wiggled their way to the angle between her legs. She smiled with motherly pride as they entered and filled her womb. As she began to hum a lullaby taught to her by her own mother, the Horde kept flowing into her, thousands of scrambling spiders, swelling her belly ever larger. Soon her stomach was as wide as a mother birthing twins. Vira'ni felt her children settling in her belly and grinned.

She carried so much more than twins.

Once her stomach was fully distended, she closed her knees. A few tardy children tried to climb up her bare legs, but she lovingly swatted them from her thighs as she stood.

Crossing to where her belongings were piled, Vira'ni quickly dressed and slipped a bag over one shoulder. The forest trail was nearby, but she would still have to hurry if she wanted to clear the wood before the fire caught her.

She set off at a fast pace, one hand holding her bag in place, the other on her belly. Though exhausted, she allowed a smile to shine on her face. She was such a good mother.

4

"Keep going!" Er'ril called, his throat burned raw with smoke and exertion. He watched the wagon's rear wheels struggle to climb over the half-burnt log that had fallen across the trail. "Mogweed, don't let those horses balk. Drive 'em hard!"

A cascade of flaming ashes swirled across the forest path, igniting tiny blazes on the wagon's canopy. It was death to stop on this trail. Though the main fire was still being deliberately driven forward by the elv'in's winds, smaller side pyres still smoldered and spat at the company as they fought their way through the ruined wood. The wagon was most at risk, a large flammable target for stray flames.

"Get those fires out!" Er'ril hollered, but his words were unnecessary. Kral and Nee'lahn, mounted on their exhausted horses, were already circling the wagon, splashing water from goatskin flasks. The tiny flames sputtered out, leaving black scars on the wagon's canopy.

"We're running out of water," Elena commented at his side. She coughed harshly and sat hunched in the saddle, wilting from the heat. The hot breath of the racing fire seemed to worsen the deeper into the wood they traveled, the heat taxing the company more than the flame and spiders. "And we still have so far to go."

Er'ril adjusted his mask higher over his nose, trying to keep his worried expression hidden. "We'll make it," he muttered.

Once she had finished dousing the wagon, Nee'lahn idled her mount beside them. "Meric nears exhaustion," she said. "He denies it, but I can see how his hands tremble on the reins. And a moment ago, he almost tumbled from his saddle."

"He'll have to manage," Er'ril said. "If the fire should expire before we breach the woods, we'll be trapped. He must keep the fire moving. We can't stop." But as if mocking at his words, the wagon's bells clanked sharply as the rear wheels failed to climb over the stubborn log and the rig settled back into the mud.

The two women's eyes stared up at him.

Kral circled around to join them. He pointed to the left of the trail. "Here they come again."

Er'ril glanced where he pointed. It seemed that the spiders somehow always sensed when the company slowed. Various troupes of the Horde had periodically threatened the company along the trail, but luckily the creatures were slow. As long as the team had kept moving, the flames and the heat had posed a bigger risk than the spiders.

Until now . . .

Across the scorched ground, masses of red-bodied spiders rolled toward the trail from the fringes of forest that lay to either side of the fire's wide swath. Scattered, smoldering embers consumed many of the attackers, their bodies hissing and curling into tight balls, but the others continued their march over their dead comrades. Even in the swirling smoke and eddying winds, tiny spiders floated upon wisps of silk, bits of poison in the wind.

Death crawled, skittered, and floated toward them.

Er'ril glanced back to the stalled wagon and kicked his stallion closer. "Lighten the load," he called to the wagon's occupants. "Toss out our supplies."

Tol'chuk's huge arm swung open the wagon's back flap. Fardale peered out as the og're began to climb from the wagon.

"No," Er'ril yelled, "get back inside. There are spiders underfoot. Just jettison our gear."

"I weigh more than all of our supplies," Tol'chuk said, ignoring Er'ril's order and continuing to haul his massive body from the wagon. The og're dropped barefoot to the trail. "We og're be thick of skin. No puny spider could pierce our hide."

Er'ril had by now pulled his mount beside Tol'chuk. "Still," he said fiercely, "I would rather lose all our supplies than you."

Tol'chuk patted Er'ril's knee. "Me, too," he said with a smile that exposed his fangs.

The og're then swung back to the wagon, bent his knees, and grabbed the rear axle in both of his huge, clawed hands. With his muscles bunching like gnarled roots, Tol'chuk hauled the back half of the wagon up, tilting the rig upon the front wheels. "Now!" he bellowed out, his voice full of the strain in his back.

The crack of a whip split the wind. The wagon lurched forward as if stung by a bee. With a groan, Tol'chuk followed, holding up the wagon, his legs driven in the loamy soil up to his ankles.

Once the rear wheels had cleared the log, Tol'chuk released the wagon. It crashed to the trail, clear of the obstruction. Seemingly satisfied, the og're rubbed his hands together to clean them of the axle grease and drew his feet from the sucking mud. "Now we can go." He stepped over the tumbled log, crossed to the wagon, and clambered back inside.

Sweat stinging his eyes, Er'ril sat stunned at the display of strength in the og're. Tol'chuk's manner, always so quiet and reserved, belied the raw force of sinew and bone in the creature. Er'ril would have to remember never to cross this particular member of the team.

"Spiders," Elena said, interrupting Er'ril's thoughts as she danced her mare beside him.

Like a wave breaking on a beach, the forefront of the spider army rolled onto the trail. At the same time, flanks of the foul troupe swarmed up the black trunks of neighboring trees and threw themselves on strings of silk toward the company. It seemed that the many beasts had one mind, one intent: to swallow Er'ril and the others in their sticky embrace.

Er'ril twisted in the saddle. "Nee'lahn, take Elena and catch up to Meric. Kral, stay here with me. We need to buy some distance from these beasts."

Ahead, Mogweed popped his head from around the front edge of the wagon. His amber eyes were huge with fear. "Sh-should I go ahead? Meric is almost out of sight!"

Waving his hand forward, Er'ril called to him. "Go! Catch up with him. And don't spare the horses!" Er'ril swung his stallion around as Elena and Nee'lahn trotted their mounts toward the wagon. He watched for a breath to make sure Elena followed his orders, then turned to Kral.

Cloaked in hood and mask, the mountain man seemed a menacing figure atop his black, fire-eyed war charger. The horse pawed its steel-shod hooves in the dirt. The spiders were now within spitting distance of the mount's legs. "What's your plan?" Kral asked calmly, showing little discomfort at the poisonous sea cresting toward him.

Er'ril hopped from his horse. "Buying us some time." He pulled free his sword and swatted his mount. The slapped horse whinnied in surprise and galloped down the trail into the mass of spiders.

Sometimes sacrifices were necessary.

The spiders swung toward the hooves that slashed into their midst. Like a single creature, they swarmed upon the horse. Its white legs and sides were soon encrusted with red-blistered bodies. The stallion reared, its neck stretched back in pain, a silent scream fixed upon its open jaws. It toppled backward to the muddy trail, writhing for several heartbeats before settling to a still form. Already loops and tangles of webbing began to enshroud the beast. Its open eye, once full of vigor and heart, was now the dull orb of a stillborn. A single red spider danced across the dead globe.

Sheathing his sword, Er'ril turned away as the sea of spiders swallowed their feast.

Kral reached a hand toward Er'ril to pull him up on his mount. "His name was Sheshone," the mountain man said, naming the crag horse.

Er'ril allowed himself to be swung behind Kral atop the huge stallion. He wished the mountain man hadn't imparted that piece of information. The nameless were easier to forget.

Kral swung his mount around and trotted him after the retreating wagon.

Er'ril did not glance back.

"What happened?" Elena asked, her face pale with concern. She watched the plainsman untether one of the two draft horses that trailed behind Meric. He stayed silent as he quickly unburdened the beast of three of the packs. He let them drop to the mud and climbed bareback atop the thick-bodied horse.

"Keep going, Meric," Er'ril ordered. "Kral, make sure these packs get tossed in the wagon when Mogweed catches up to here."

Kral grunted his acknowledgement, then reined his horse around. "I'd better get back to keep watch on our rear. That bit of horseflesh will not buy us much time." He cantered away.

Once the mountain man was gone, Elena stepped her mare beside

Er'ril. They followed Meric and Nee'lahn, who were already a fair clip down the smoky trail. "What happened to your stallion?" she asked.

Er'ril stared steadily ahead. "He's dead." The plainsman kicked his horse to a faster pace, signaling the end of this discussion.

Elena rubbed her red eyes and glanced over her shoulder as if she might spy what had truly happened on the back trail. Behind her, the wagon lurched, tilting back and forth, as Mogweed drove the rig after them. Whatever had transpired back there was hidden by the wagon and sharp twists of the path. Resigned, she settled back forward. From Er'ril's locked shoulders, she imagined the events had been hard on the plainsman—and as usual, he refused to share his burdens.

Elena found her right hand clutching the reins harder. Somehow she sensed that if she were better skilled with her magicks, perhaps she could have saved Er'ril from making the decision that hunched his shoulders now. She studied her gloved hand. Its ruby stain lay hidden from sight, yet, like a rash, its power itched across her skin, reminding her that what lay hidden could not be denied by mere deerskin.

Soon a time would come when Er'ril would not be there to bear her burdens. Then she would need to take her gloves off and make her own hard decisions. Elena contemplated the taut strain in Er'ril's back. Would she have his strength then?

Nee'lahn had slowed her steed and dropped back. "Trouble ahead. A league farther, the trail descends into a deep hollow. The flames jumped this secluded section of forest and skipped to the higher wood beyond."

"And the spiders?" Er'ril asked.

"The forest remains intact in the low wood. And so does the Horde."

Elena pushed Mist closer to the others. "Can we go around?"

Nee'lahn shook her head. "Not with the wagon—and even if we abandoned it, I doubt we could make it safely through the smoldering fires and collapsed trees."

"Let's see this wood," Er'ril said, snapping his reins to urge his mount forward.

Nee'lahn led the way. "It's just beyond the turn of the trail ahead. Meric waits."

No one spoke as they trotted toward where Meric slumped atop his roan filly. The heat seemed to worsen with each step forward, its roasting touch reaching through cloaks. Elena found herself gasping for air by the time they reached Meric.

As they approached, Elena could see the exhaustion in every muscle of the elv'in. Somehow he seemed to have shrunk in on himself—as if the draining of his elemental abilities had sapped the very substance from his being. He glanced tepidly at them, his eyes ringed in shadows, as the horses pulled to a stop beside him.

"Meric," Er'ril asked, "how are you managing?"

Meric's lips cracked as he spoke. "The fire has but a league of forest yet to consume. I will last until then." He nodded toward where a wide pocket of green forest still thrived just ahead. "But I can't help here. It takes all my concentration and skill to keep the main fire moving."

Er'ril nodded as he turned to study the obstacle, his eyes narrow with worry.

Elena inched Mist forward to better view where the trail dropped into the deep hollow. The surviving bit of forest, sheltered in the recess, lay shrouded in web and silence. No spiders could be seen moving among the strands and tangles of silver thread. In fact nothing moved. The wood lay as still as a corpse. The complete lack of any sign of life bothered Elena more than if a thousand spiders were crawling and capering among the branches.

"Maybe the fire's smoke drove them all away," Elena offered with halfhearted hope.

"I wouldn't count on that," Nee'lahn said. "The spiders have been tenacious in sticking to their nests. I wager that beyond the edge of scorched trees, the Horde still awaits us."

"Then maybe we can just torch this section of wood by hand," Er'ril mumbled.

Meric sighed and shook his head. "No time. We must stick close to the main fire as it marches, or the spiders will circle back and reclaim the wood before we can pass. Even now we delay too long. The fire escapes us as we speak."

A thunder of hooves momentarily distracted the group from the dire glade. Kral galloped his stallion up to them. The wagon was trundling not far behind.

"The Horde is on the move again. They'll soon be upon us. Why's everyone stop—?" Kral asked, but his voice died in his throat as he saw what lay ahead.

Nee'lahn explained the situation while Er'ril returned to studying the woods. Elena pulled closer to the plainsman but let him think in silence. She needed for him to realize that only one option still lay open to them, but if she voiced it, Elena knew Er'ril would stubbornly resist. No, she would not goad him and drive him away from the correct choice. Given time, he would realize the one true path ahead.

As Elena watched Er'ril, she saw the tautness in his shoulders suddenly slump and recognized the resignation in his posture. After a moment's hesitation, he twisted in his saddle, and Elena found herself staring into his hurt eyes. She knew how it pained him to ask this of her. She simply nodded at him. Both knew what must be done.

Er'ril swung his draft horse around to face the others as the wagon closed to join them. He cleared his throat to draw everyone's attention. "Spiders or not, we're going to have to force our way through this bit of forest."

Concern lit everyone's eyes, but no one voiced a protest.

Only Kral spoke, his voice edged with hard humor. "I hope we have enough horses to spare."

Elena did not understand the mountain man's words, but she did not dwell on it. Now was not the time for words or explanations. She swung Mist around to face the dark woods and took a deep breath.

With the others silent behind her, Elena slipped the glove from her right hand. Its stain was already aglow with ruby and crimson whorls. She sat straighter and willed the wit'chlight to flare brighter. An ember of brilliant light the color of a moonrose bloomed in her open palm, then spread out to her fingers.

As she concentrated, she sensed Er'ril settle his stallion beside her. "Let it build," he whispered hoarsely. "Don't let it overwhelm you. The power is yours to control."

Elena let the lids of her eyes droop lower. Her hand now blazed in the shadowed wood. Magicks crackled across her skin. The power seemed so much larger than her small frame. How could it stay contained? And once released, how could she control it?

"Careful," he warned, his voice full of worry.

A seed of Er'ril's concern found fertile ground in Elena's chest. She again pictured her parents swallowed in a wall of fire cast out from her own body. The glow in her hand faltered. She could no better control her magicks now than she had back then. "I . . . I can't . . ." she moaned.

Er'ril reached his hand to her knee. "Yes, you can, El. This magick is in your blood. It's part of you. Control yourself and you control your magick."

"But?"

He squeezed her knee. "Trust me, El. I know you can do this."

Fighting back tears, she glanced up to Er'ril. Under hair as black as shadows, his gray eyes shone with the intensity of his convictions. In the hard contours of his face, she saw the strength of the man who was her protector. She nodded and drew a small amount of Er'ril's stoniness into her. Taking a deep breath, she turned back to face the shrouded wood, clearing her mind of anything but the flows and ebbs of the magick in her blood. In a few heartbeats, the glow grew back to an intense blaze.

She *would* do this.

"Now, when you're ready, you—" Er'ril's voice was like a gnat in her ear.

"Enough!" she snarled at him, willing him silent. "You were right. I know what I must do."

Her left hand slipped to the sheathed knife at her belt and gripped its rose-handled hilt. She pulled forth her wit'ch's dagger, its silver blade shining crimson in the reflected ruby blaze.

Her magick called for blood, sang for its release.

Now Elena was ready to listen.

She drew the dagger's edge across the meat of her thumb. Their prison pierced, her magicks burst forth from the wound, a cold fire raging out into the world.

A flicker of a smile fluttered about her mouth before Elena could force her lips to a stern line—but somewhere deep inside, somewhere where Elena feared to look too closely, a part of her still crackled with laughter and wicked delight.

THE ROAR OF THE CONSUMING FLAME FOLLOWED VIRA'NI FROM THE eaves of the forest. Her brow glistened with sweat, and her breath rattled in ragged gasps as she stumbled from the wood's edge. Her hair and green jacket were coated in a fine powder of ash, and tears streaked through the soot that stained her face. With her legs wobbling under her, she kept running, trying to escape the fire's voice.

One hand still clutched her belly, reminding her why she must not let exhaustion lull her into defeat. She must protect the seed of the Horde. She must not let the Dark Lord's gift die with her. In her mind's eye, she still pictured the flaming death of her children. Whoever had burned this wood would pay—oh, yes, they would suffer for this crime! It was this rage that fueled her weak legs and tired heart.

It took her several breaths and several more steps before she even realized she had escaped the forest and had entered the meadowed plains of the lower foothills. Only when her feet splashed through a wide stream of shallow snowmelt did her eyes focus on the open fields. Around her, the last of the afternoon sunlight, smudged with blowing smoke, cast the meadow grasses in hues of rose and gold. A few scattered islands of young oaks dotted the landscape, and in vernal pools, splashes of wild daffodils heralded the spring. Among these round hills, a thousand brooks and streams coursed through the lush growth.

Free of the overhanging branches and the webs of her children, Vira'ni felt suddenly exposed and vulnerable. Her legs slowed as she continued along the trail that led down out of the highland forests toward the distant plains. She glanced behind her at the black skies, lit up from below with the scarlet glow of the flames. Like a living beast, the conflagration rolled slowly toward her, growling its anger at her escape.

She found her legs stumbling faster again. Would the fire be happy with just the forest? Though the meadow grasses were green and wet with spring growth, would that necessarily sate this hot flame and stop its progress?

She stumbled on, her hand moist on her belly. She had more to protect than just herself. She must keep going. As the sun retreated toward the horizon behind her, she struggled onward. Once she was sure she and the Horde were safe, then she could stop and let her master know what had befallen them. She kept glancing over her shoulder as she marched and splashed through the wet meadows.

With her eyes fixed upon the flames and her ears full of the fire's roar, Vira'ni failed to see the small hunters' camp sheltered beyond the rise of the next hill until she practically fell within the circle of tents. She seemed to surprise them as much as they startled her.

Vira'ni shuffled to a stop, wary of these strangers. She quickly weighed the danger. A dozen men, dressed in the green leathers and knee-high black boots of hunters, stood or sat around three fires. A handful of women, now frozen in various poses around cooking pots and spitted meats, also mingled among the men. Scattered among the larger folk, the small faces of a few children peeked from around legs and bosoms.

Everyone stood fixed for a heartbeat until a hound tethered near one of the tents let out a long, baying howl in her direction. The dog's voice set everyone in motion at once. Vira'ni backed a step away. Several of the men nudged each other and words were exchanged with appreciative glances in her direction. Spits of grilling meats began to turn again, and one broad-shouldered woman cuffed the hound and scolded it quiet.

One man separated from the group and approached her. Sandy haired with a matching broad mustache, he was a good head taller than the other hunters. His lips were set in a firm line, but his green eyes carried a trace of suspicion. "Lass, why are you out among these hills by yourself?"

Vira'ni shrunk under his gaze, letting her long black hair drape between his eyes and her face. She could not find words, still too shaken by her sudden intrusion among people.

"Where are your companions? Did—?"

The hunter's voice was cut off as a woman who stood as tall as the large man elbowed him aside. She had blond hair cropped short and wore an uncompromising set to her mouth and eyes. "Sweet Mother, Josa, can't you see she's heavy with child and practically scared out of her skin?" She nudged the hunter farther away. "Go tend to your hound before it chokes itself on its tether."

Once Josa had shuffled back to the heart of the camp, the woman placed fists on her hips and ran her eyes up and down Vira'ni. Her voice was warmer than the tone she had used with the man. "Now, child, don't fret. My name is Betta. You're safe here. Just take a few deep breaths and calm yourself."

Vira'ni straightened and moved a few strands of black hair from her face. "The fire . . ." she began, but her voice failed her.

"I guessed that from the soot and ash all over you. So you came from the wood? Were you traveling alone?"

"Yes . . . no . . . my children!" Vira'ni could not stop the flow of tears from bursting from her eyes.

Betta swallowed Vira'ni in her large arms just as her legs finally gave out. Vira'ni sank within her embrace, allowing the woman to support her for a few ragged breaths. It felt so good to unburden herself. Only another woman could truly understand the pain a mother felt at the loss of a child—to carry a life in your womb and see the world destroy it. She sobbed uncontrollably into Betta's chest as the woman stroked her hair and whispered words to soothe her.

Betta led her into the camp, sweeping her into a tent for privacy. Once the woman had settled Vira'ni into a nest of pillows and ordered a cow-eyed woman to fetch a cup of tea, Vira'ni began to regain control of her emotions. She allowed Betta to wipe her face with a cold wet rag, clearing soot and tears from her cheeks. Vira'ni tried to speak, to let her know how much she appreciated the kind attention, but Betta placed a finger across Vira'ni's lips to silence her. "Drink this; then we can talk." Betta handed her a small cup of hot mint tea. Its steam and aroma seemed to seep into her bones and give her strength.

Vira'ni savored the tea in silence, allowing it to warm her tongue and hands. Once she had finished, she felt vigorous enough to speak without crying. She handed the small cup back to Betta. "Thank you," she said shyly.

Betta settled to the pillows beside her. "Now tell me what happened. Are there others of your party that we should search for?"

Vira'ni studied her hands, willing her voice not to break with the sorrow. "No, I traveled only . . . only with my children."

"Did they not escape the fire?"

She shook her head. "It caught us by surprise. It was too fast! I couldn't . . . I couldn't save the others." Her voice began to rise until Betta placed a hand atop hers.

"Hush, now, do not blame yourself. You had to save who you could," she said, nodding toward Vira'ni's bulging belly. "Now, I want you to rest. You must be strong for the child you grow now."

Vira'ni sniffed back the tears that threatened, and nodded.

Betta pushed to her feet and began to leave.

"The fire rages fierce," Vira'ni said before the other woman left the tent. "It might yet cross to the meadows here."

"Don't you fret. We know these lands. These spring meadows run wet and will stanch the fire's path beyond the wood. And we'll have watchers out to keep an eye on the flame. If it threatens, we can break camp and be all on horseback in a blink. So you sleep. We will not let anything happen to you or your unborn child."

"You are most kind," Vira'ni said. She began to settle back into her pillows when a pain reached up from her belly to grip her heart. Her vision blacked, and a gasp escaped her throat as the fire ripped through her. For the briefest moment, she saw with the thousand eyes of her forest children: *A small woman atop a horse . . . her right hand raised, glowing like a small ruby sun . . . Death rained out from her and consumed all . . . a death more horrible than flame . . . a death born of dire magicks!*

As quickly as it came, the pain and vision vanished, leaving only a dull ache and hollowness in her chest. Betta was leaning over her, concern etched in every plane of the woman's face.

"What is it, child?"

Vira'ni stayed silent, picturing again the woman's fist aglow with wild magicks. She knew who approached, burning her way through Vira'ni's children. It was the wit'ch! The one the master craved! One trembling hand reached up to finger the lock of white hair nestled within the black. She had not forgotten her duty. The master must be served!

Her face paled as she realized how close she had come to failing her Dark Lord. The wit'ch had driven her from her post and almost slipped past her—but the wit'ch had made a mistake. The master had attuned Vira'ni to the woman's black arts. With her magick's first touch upon the Horde, Vira'ni's own body had felt its searing fire, warning her to the wit'ch's presence. Foolish child! Now alerted, Vira'ni would not fail her lord a second time—or her lost children. She would make the wit'ch suffer and writhe as all those spiders had upon their flaming webs.

But she needed help—Vira'ni raised her face to the worried eyes of Betta and recognized a potential ally, someone to help her with her duty. Especially with a little coaxing . . .

Vira'ni allowed tears to rise to her eyes. "I remember now!" she moaned loudly. "My mind tried to erase . . . to deny the horrors . . . But now it comes tumbling back in a dreadful rush! Fire and death!" She pushed up from the pillows and clutched Betta's arm. "Those who set the fires and murdered my children come this way."

Betta's eyes grew wide, then narrowed with fire. "You know who set this flame upon our wood?"

"Yes . . . yes . . ." Vira'ni stared into Betta's reddening face. "She comes with many others. I saw a wagon." Vira'ni forced her shoulders to shudder. "They murder all in their path."

"Who are they?"

Vira'ni sat straighter and cranked her voice to a fevered pitch. "Foul murderers . . . and defilers of children. Not men—but beasts!"

Betta's eyes sparked with hate; her lips bled of color. She spoke rapidly. "Our elders warned that this wood was befouled by evil, that the poisonous beasts were unnatural markers of corruption. We were sent here to watch the wood and make sure the spiders didn't spread to the meadows. And for moons now, the beasts have stayed cloaked among the trees, shunning the direct light of the sun. But now . . . Sweet Mother! Now if your words are true, the evil prepares to spread its foul reach—and fire marks their coming!" The woman broke Vira'ni's grip on her arm and stood. "I must alert the others. Those monsters will not pass here."

Vira'ni watched the woman fly from the tent, Betta's voice already raised in alarm. No, Vira'ni thought as she rubbed her full belly, the poisonous smile of a spider fixed on her lips. No, these killers of her children would not escape these hills.

5

The magick streamed in rivers of coldfire from Elena's open palm while sparks of blue flames danced like will-o'-the-wisps around her wrist. With sweat beading on her brow, she concentrated fully on her task, struggling as best she could to maintain a leash upon her magicks. Though Er'ril had instructed her in the basics of manipulation—simple lessons he had learned while serving as a liegeman of the Order—any complex orchestrations of her gifts were beyond her current abilities.

Still, what Elena lacked in skill, she made up for in raw power. Wild magick was a force few things could withstand. As her flow of coldfire washed upon the shore of the web-shrouded glade, hoarfrost and ice froze all it touched. Tree trunks burst with explosive cracks. Frozen roots snapped their hold upon the dirt, toppling ancient oaks and stately maples. Even the tenacious webs of silk were transformed to delicacies of frost that shattered with even the slightest breeze.

A cloud of frigid mist rose from the forest, driven into the smoky sky by her coldfire crackling through the glade. Her magick devoured the wood and its denizens just as thoroughly as hot flames had scoured the main forest. Two fires, twins in extremes, consumed all in their paths. As Elena watched the white mist meet the black smoke in the sky, it reminded her of the extremes of her own magicks. While studying with Er'ril, she had learned that the character of her magicks was dictated by the light that renewed her power.

Sunlight gave her power over red flame and heat, whereas moonlight aligned her to the burn of ice and frost. It was as if her magicks mirrored her own spirit, divided—two extremes again—between wit'ch and woman.

In the sky above, where icy mist met fiery smoke, spats of whirlwinds grew as the two sides fought for control. Ice-coated leaves rattled like the bones of the dead. Branches snapped and were drawn into the air. The sky itself groaned as the battle raged.

The fury of the skies spread to Elena's breast. Her magick sang in her blood, crying to join the war above. Her heart thundered to its chorus of destruction. She fought against its call as surely as the smoke fought the mist. But another part of her, the wit'ch within, sang with the harmonies of her magick, thrilled to the crackles of blue flame and screaming winds.

Elena squeezed her eyes closed against the sight of the roiling skies, pulled her attention back to herself, and centered her breathing. She concentrated on her body and searched through muscle and tendon, ligament and bone, blood and bowel. She acknowledged the soreness of her inner thighs from the long day of riding, felt the throb of a fresh bruise where her shoulder had struck a low branch, even dwelled upon the faint tenderness of her newly budding breasts. She was more than mere flows of arcane magicks. She was a woman—and that was magick enough for her.

A voice intruded. "Elena, you've destroyed the glade. Pull back." It was Er'ril. He still sat atop his draft horse at her side.

She inclined her head slightly, keeping her eyes closed. Now was not the time to be distracted by the awful beauty of her magick's crackling flows. She slowly closed her raised hand. Her fingers felt frozen to the marrow of her small bones. For a moment, she feared she would snap her digits from her palm as she willed her fist to close. Yet slowly, one by one, like a bloom closing at midnight, her fingers clenched to a fist, severing the flow of coldfire. The traces of magick still left in her screamed at the interruption. Her hand trembled with the pent-up power. *More!* sang her blood. *Taste the full rage of your wild magick!* One finger began to stretch back out.

A voice intruded again. *"No!"* But this time it was not Er'ril's clipped Standish accent. It was Elena's own voice, spoken aloud to the magick within and without. She tightened her fist, feeling her own heart beat in her clenched palm. She willed the beat to slow from its fevered pitch to a controlled throb. Without opening her eyes, she knew the brilliant radiance of her hand had faded back to its normal stain. She lowered her fist to her lap.

"Sweet Mother, child!" Kral said as he danced his war charger behind her. "Just look at that!"

Elena opened her eyes and for the first time saw the result of her magick. The wooded hollow now lay etched in silver ice, each bole, branch, and leaf entombed in crusts of hoarfrost. Thousands of spears of cloudy ice stretched out from trunks and limbs, some as long as a man was tall. But instead of draping toward the ground, these thorns of brilliance stuck straight out from their woody perches, pointing away from Elena, as if a terrible wind had been blowing out from her. Which in some ways, she realized, was true.

As Elena studied her handiwork, the smoky sky cleared for a brief instant to let the sharp rays of the late-afternoon sun pierce to the assaulted glade. Where sunlight met crystal ice, thousands of tiny rainbows burst forth. The entire glade transformed for one long hushed breath into a sweet dream—a forest of ice and rainbows.

"It's so beautiful," Nee'lahn said with wonder thick in her voice. "As if woodsong itself were given substance and form."

Elena tore her eyes from the brilliant wood. Here numbing beauty hid so sweetly the death and destruction at its heart. Hot tears flowed across her chilled cheeks. Death should never be this radiant.

"What's wrong?" Er'ril asked. "Are you injured?"

Studying her hand, Elena shook her head. Even where the dagger had sliced her thumb, no wound now seeped. It had healed without even a shade of a scar. Her right hand, though, had not escaped completely unscathed. As the magick had bled out from her wound, the stain had drained from her skin. Instead of the usual deep ruby whorls, her palm now was only slightly reddened, as if she had suffered a bad sunburn. The ruining of the wood had cost almost all her magickal reserve, leaving only a small trace of her power. She raised her hand to show Er'ril. "I'm fine. But I only have a bit of magick left."

The plainsman stared, then nodded. "No need to worry. We should be able to clear the wood from here. You can always renew once you're completely drained."

"Why must I wait until all the magick is gone before I can renew?" she asked, lowering her hand. "Wouldn't it be safer to keep my reserve full at all times?"

"Now you're thinking like a true mage," he snorted, the lines of worry momentarily easing. "My brother Shorkan used to voice the same complaint. Many mages in his time tried to discover ways to renew before their magick was fully spent. They all failed. It just doesn't work that way."

"Then maybe I should spend the last dregs of my power. Empty my reserve and renew now." It seemed the most prudent course, but the thought of again opening her magick trembled her heart.

"No. Do not even harbor that thought." Er'ril's face darkened with concern, his voice tight. "Magick is a gift not to be squandered lightly. It should only be used with true purpose. Leave it be." Er'ril kicked his horse forward and waved for the others to follow. "Now let's go."

Elena, though, urged Mist to keep abreast of the plainsman's steed. "But why? What difference does it make? Can't I use my power in whatever way I want?"

Er'ril did not look at her. "There's danger in that path, Elena. Lax and frivolous use of magicks during my time led to the corruption of many a mage's spirit."

He continued down the trail in silence, his eyes staring somewhere far from the frozen forest as they entered the dead hollow. Elena thought the conversation had ended and began to turn away, but Er'ril started speaking again, his voice thin and strained. "Soon those mages grew drunk with their powers. It twisted many of them. From this corruption, the Brotherhood of the Darkmages arose." He turned to stare at her, his gaze intense. "Be warned. More than just the danger of death is risked by the wanton use of your wild magicks—it can also blacken and pervert your spirit."

Elena sensed the truth in his words. She had felt the seductive call of her magicks and knew deep within her that a corner of her spirit already sang to the raw wildness of her power. A shiver passed through her. How long until that part of her spirit grew? With trembling fingers, Elena slipped her deerskin glove back over her right hand and resolved that she would only use her magick when no other path lay open. Even then, she would think twice.

Er'ril mumbled something under his breath.

"What was that?" she asked as she cinched her glove on tight, unsure if the plainsman had been addressing her.

After a long pause, he raised wounded eyes toward her. "You need a better teacher," he said. "I'm not learned enough to instruct you in the finer workings of your art and in the tools of safeguarding your spirit. This untutored use of your magicks risks so much."

For the first time, Elena saw the depth of pain behind his stony features and realized she was not the only one who suffered when she used her powers. "I . . . I'll manage. You've taught me well." She smiled crookedly at him. "Besides, what choice do we have? You're all I've got."

Her words softened his pained expression. "Still . . . you must proceed with caution."

"I will," Elena promised.

Meric and Nee'lahn trotted their horses up to them. Meric leaned far in his saddle, one fist gripping his saddle's horn to keep him upright. His words were coarse with fatigue. "The fire's path has almost reached the forest's edge. We've wasted too much time. We must hurry before the Horde retakes the burned corridor we've forged."

"Go on ahead then," Er'ril said. "Nee'lahn, stay close to Meric and help him." Er'ril swung around in his saddle and called to the wagon that crept slowly behind them through the iced bower. "Mogweed, lean on the whip. We must run the horses if we are to outpace the spiders."

Elena saw the shape-shifter's pale face clench with fear, but Mogweed nodded. With a crack of a whip, the wagon bucked forward. The sudden start tumbled two figures from the rear of the wagon. It was Tol'chuk and the wolf Fardale. They had jumped from the rig and now ran alongside it. Elena was amazed the huge og're could move with such speed.

Er'ril seemed more angry than impressed. "No, no, stay in the wagon," he yelled. "We can't slow to keep abreast of you on foot."

Tol'chuk answered, his voice calm and steady as he loped beside the large wheel of the wagon. "Less burdened, the horses can pull faster. And we og're be quick of foot—at least for a short way. I can race as far as the forest's edge. Fardale and I will not slow you down."

Er'ril's face shone with doubt. "The spiders . . ."

Tol'chuk pointed to the side of the trail. Entombed in ice, the blistered bodies of spiders could be seen like red blemishes in a diamond. "They be not chasing us very quickly."

Er'ril stared for a moment in indecision, then called out to Kral. "Keep to the back trail! Guard our rear!"

Kral raised an arm in salute, pulling his war charger behind the billowing canopy of the wagon.

Er'ril swung forward in his saddle and snapped his lead to urge his mount faster. "Does your mare still have enough heart in her to run the rest of the way?" he asked as Elena followed.

"Mist has a strong heart. She'll be exhausted, but I believe she can run me out of this foul wood."

"Then let's be off," he said, kicking his steed even faster. "I'm tired of trees and long to see the end of this forest."

Elena urged Mist on with soft words of encouragement. Her mare snorted briskly and tossed her head, glad to run. Elena kept close behind Er'ril's horse, following the plainsman's broad back.

By now they were almost halfway through the dead hollow, the branches a frozen roof over their heads. Down the trail, Meric and Nee'lahn were small figures. Elena could see them ride through frosted drapes of webs that blocked the trail, shattering the frozen strands into thousands of glittering fragments. As they followed, wind-borne motes of web, like a light snow flurry, still floated in the trail. Loathe to have even these pinpricks of corruption touch her skin, Elena pulled her mask, which had fallen from her face as she worked her magick, back up over her mouth and nose. Still she shivered as pieces of web settled upon her cloak and hood. Even Mist nickered warily as she galloped, needing no further encouragement to run.

Soon they were climbing back out of the hollow and entering the burned wood again. But relief at escaping the hollow was a fleeting thing. The sudden return of heat felt pleasant for several heartbeats; then the air reeked of scorched wood and smoky poisons, and the burning breath of the fire swallowed her up. Elena coughed, and Mist noticeably slowed as the heated air taxed the sweating horse.

The distance between Elena and Er'ril quickly grew. Behind her, Elena could hear the ringing bells of the wagon closing in on her. She leaned forward and rubbed a palm over Mist's wet neck. "C'mon, girl, you can do this," she urged, the heat charring her throat. "It's just a little farther."

With the smoke and ash limiting her line of sight, Elena prayed her words were not a lie. She had lost track of Meric and Nee'lahn quite some time ago as they were swallowed in the haze, and now even Er'ril had become a ghost down the trail. She thought to call out to him but realized there was no need. He could not make Mist run any faster.

She tapped Mist's flank and whispered words of encouragement, letting the mare know she needed to hurry. In answer, Mist huffed loudly, and her hooves dug harder. Her flanks heaved and rolled under Elena as the mare fought through the smoky air. Er'ril's figure grew more solid as the distance narrowed. "Good girl," she sang in the horse's ear. "I knew you could do it."

Suddenly Mist's hoof struck a stubborn root, and the mare stumbled forward. Elena fought to keep her seat, arms pinwheeling, but she lost the battle and found herself tumbling through the empty air. She braced for the impact with the hard ground—but it never came. Instead, huge arms scooped her up before she hit.

Elena glanced up into the monstrous, fanged face of Tol'chuk. As he ran, he carried her in the crook of one arm. The og're's bare skin felt like rough bark against her cheek as he held her clutched to his chest. The smell of wet goats swelled around her from his steaming body. From the corner of her eye, Elena saw the black shadow of the wolf flash past, with Mist not far behind.

"Thank you, Tol'chuk," she gasped. "I would've surely broken a bone. But I can run on my own now."

"No time," he growled, his ragged voice like grinding boulders. "Spiders be in pursuit from all sides."

Elena glanced to the side of the trail. She had been so focused on the trail ahead that she had failed to see what threatened from the corners. Thousands of faceted eyes glowed back at her from the forest's smoky edge. Rivers of spiders flowed toward them, roiling and surging like a single beast. The blistering-hot ground consumed hundreds of their brethren, but hundreds more used the bodies of the fallen as a bridge across the burning soil. It was as if the entire army had one intent, one mind. For the first time, she understood why the creatures had been named the Horde.

The og're loped in huge bounds of his muscular legs, but exhaustion bowed his back. As he ran, his free arm knuckled often to the mud for support. Half beast, half man, Tol'chuk scrabbled in a fast gait down the trail.

Suddenly a thunder of hooves swamped over them as Kral drove his huge war charger even with them. "Quick arms, og're! But I'll take the girl from you now."

Rorshaf, the mountain man's steed, seemed hardly winded, dancing on steel-shod hooves, mane flaring black as Kral kept abreast of the lumbering og're.

Tol'chuk didn't argue. No false heroics, only common sense. Elena found herself half tossed onto the horse. Kral swung Elena's small frame into the saddle in front of him, and with a coarse command in the guttural language of the crag horses, he ordered Rorshaf to race—and run the stallion did! Trees blurred to either side as they flew down the trail. In a heartbeat, she thundered past Mist and closed in on Er'ril.

"Yo!" Kral hauled his mount up to the plainsman. "The Horde closes from all sides. If we mean to escape these woods, we must do so now."

Er'ril pulled his mask from his face, his eyes wide at seeing Elena with the mountain man. He glanced behind him to see the empty saddle atop Mist as the horse closed the distance. "What happened?" he began to mumble, then shook his head. "Never mind. Kral, get her out of these woods. I'll help Tol'chuk and the wagon."

Kral nodded, and without a word, he shot forward and left Er'ril quickly behind. As Elena clutched handfuls of black mane, Rorshaf's hooves raced through mud and smoke. Elena found herself holding her breath in fear, not for herself, but for the others still behind with the spiders.

Kral leaned over Elena. "It can't be much farther," he whispered to her. Elena tried to gain hope from his words, but who could truly say how much farther the trail ran? Elena stared forward at the wall of swirling ash and smoke. Would this trail never end?

As if hearing this thought, the wall of blackness before them blew open for a heartbeat to reveal rolling meadows just an arrow's shot away. Then a gust tore the sight from her eyes, swallowing the trail back up with smoke. Had it been a mirage, a trick of a hopeful heart?

"Thank the Sweet Mother," Kral mumbled to himself. He kicked Rorshaf fiercely. "You saw it, you old bag of bones! Now get us out of this sick forest!"

The horse snorted in irritation. Then, as if to show his master the true heart of the war-charger breed, Rorshaf became the wind itself. The galloping stride of the stallion became a smooth current of muscle and motion, as if the horse's hooves failed to even touch the mud of the trail.

In half a breath, the trio of horse and riders burst forth from the forest and smoke into a world of rolling hills and meadows. With a whoop of triumph on his lips, Kral reined his horse to a slower pace as they skirted into the tall grasses. The fire had scorched the green meadow for a quarter league before the wet grasses and wide streams smothered the fire to slumbering embers. Kral trotted his stallion in a wide circle, Rorshaf's hooves splashing slightly in the flooded meadows.

Elena rejoiced in the snatches of late-afternoon sunlight that slipped through the gaps in the smoky sky. In the distance, she could see sprinkled patches of meadow flowers gracing the gentle slopes of these hills. They had made it free of the woods!

Suddenly, from behind them, Mist burst forth from the wall of smoke and raced past them into the green meadows.

"Mist!" Elena called, but the small gray was panicked and continued fleeing out among the meadowed hills. "Kral, we need to go after—"

The mountain man held up a hand, silencing her. He sat straighter in his saddle and searched the wet fields as he slowly swung his horse in tight circles. "Where's Nee'lahn and Meric?" he mumbled. "They should be—"

Suddenly an arrow shot past Elena's ear, and Kral fell backward from the saddle, almost carrying Elena with him. Alone atop Rorshaf, Elena twisted about. Behind the horse's rump, Kral lay on his back in the grass, the feathered haft of an arrow protruding from his shoulder. He fought to sit up, the wind knocked from his chest. Managing to raise himself up to one elbow, he spat something in the language of the crag horses.

Rorshaf hesitated.

"Go, you useless piece of dung!" Kral's voice thundered. *"Ror'ami destro, Rorshaf, nom!"*

The war charger suddenly snorted loudly and spun on its heels. Elena frantically grabbed fistfuls of mane as the horse shot away into the meadows. Overhead another volley of arrows rained past the racing horse.

With tears in her eyes, Elena clung to Rorshaf's back. The horse flew across the empty hills and meadows, a black zephyr across the green fields. But where would this ride end? Elena risked a glance over her shoulder and saw the edge of the forest fading behind her. Then Rorshaf passed over the crest of a hill, and the forest disappeared completely from view. And with it, all those she knew and cared for in the world.

6

Naked and alone in the tent, Vira'ni knelt upon a pillow, her swollen belly resting on her lap. The ebon'stone bowl balanced on a small oaken tray before her. The stone's surface already danced with darkfire, the black flames sapping the feeble light from the tent. She listened for the approach of any footsteps, shivering as the flames drank the warmth from her skin.

Outside, the camp was almost empty. Among these nomadic people, it was skill that judged the hunter, not whether the one who pulled the bowstring was man or woman. So most of the womenfolk had accompanied their men to hiding places among the meadows to lie in wait for those who moved through the forest. Only the children, guarded by two older women and one bent-backed man, still moved among the smoldering hearths.

Vira'ni had waited for the camp to empty before beginning the preparations for contacting her master. She had intoned the casting words and paid her debt of blood, then waited. Now all seemed quiet, a hush fallen over the encampment. It was time.

Bowing her face, she recited the final words and felt the surge as the Black Heart's essence swept within the flames of the darkfire. The shadows thickened in the tent, and the air became difficult to breathe. Vira'ni kept her head bowed. Somewhere without, a hound began baying wildly but was quickly cuffed to silence. Vira'ni felt her children surge in her womb, agitated by the closeness of their true lord. She bent down to touch her forehead to the lip of the bowl, both as honor to her master and as protection for her children.

From deep within the flame, the Black Heart spoke, his voice dripping venom more poisonous than the entire Horde. "Why do you call?"

"To let you know, Sire. She whom you await has come. I have seen her and felt the burn of her magicks."

"And she yet lives?"

"I have laid my web. She will not escape me."

"She must not!" Vira'ni felt his wrath like a snake tightening around her neck. "If the cursed child reaches the plains, she could head in any direction, losing herself among the many lands. That must not happen!"

Vira'ni's mouth dried with fear. "The . . . the Horde and I will not fail you, Sire. You can trust your servants."

Harsh laughter crackled fiercer than the black flames and held even less warmth. The darkness grew denser near the core of the ebon'stone bowl. It was not just the blackness of a moonless night, but a total lack of light and substance, as if what swelled before her was a peek into the heart of death itself. Her belly quaked with fear, and the tent grew colder than the deepest crypt. The taste of iron filled her mouth as she bit her trembling lip.

From this inky void came the voice of her lord, sounding somehow closer. "Trust? You beg for trust?"

"Y-y-yes, my sire."

The void wormed over the lip of the bowl toward her. "I will show you how much I trust you."

Vira'ni squeezed her eyes tight. Bloody saliva drooled from her lips. "Master? Please . . ." Even with her eyes closed, she could still somehow see the darkness sliding toward her. She knew wherever it touched she would be forever scarred. She crouched, frozen, like a pig to slaughter.

She felt its first touch upon her exposed knee. A gasp escaped her throat, but she knew better than to move. The master did not like it when one of his servants flinched from his touch—that she remembered well from those early lessons taught in the dungeons of Blackhall. So Vira'ni held still, pulling her mind back to that corner of her being where she knew to retreat. Three winters spent in the twisted warren of cells below the Gul'gothal halls had taught her methods of preserving her sanity. She fled to that safe space now, barely aware of the cold finger crawling up her inner thigh.

In her safe place, she hummed songs her mother had taught to her among the boats and nets of her fishing village on the storm-swept northern coast. She wrapped herself snug in choruses of lost loves and life's wonders. Here she couldn't be harmed, here nothing could touch her, here she was safe—

Suddenly pain ripped open her warm cocoon, a blazing torment worse than any she had felt during the long dungeon winters. Her eyelids snapped open, but the agony blinded her as surely as if her eyes were still closed. All she saw was blackness etched with red lightning. But as the pain ebbed slightly, her vision returned, narrow and pinched, but wide enough to raise a moan to her lips at what she saw.

A shadowy umbilicus, like the black tendril of some sea beast, now linked the ebon'stone to her womb. It pulsed and throbbed as it filled her belly with dark energies, searing her flesh with the fire of white-hot branding irons. Unable to scream as the pain trapped the breath in her throat, all she could do was writhe at the end of the burning tether. Only the magicks the Dark Lord had imbued in her veins long ago kept her heart from bursting. This protection, though, was no kind gift. Death, right now, would be a welcome guest.

But as the pain waned to a smoldering ember in her womb, death was not her companion now. The voice that filled her skull like leeches, sucking at her will, was something so much worse. "See how much I truly trust you, Vira'ni. I grant you another gift. I have taken the Horde in your belly and transformed them into something new for you to love."

"My children!" she cried, sensing her loss. "No!" This new torture was so much worse than the pain of the flesh.

"Fear not, woman. This child you will love just as well." The wicked umbilicus spasmed one final time, then detached and slid back into the ebon'stone bowl. "Enjoy my final gift."

In her belly, worms of ice roiled through the burn in her womb, eating away the pain. A sigh of pleasure whispered from her lips as the agony vanished. Her belly now felt cool and calm. Released from the storm of pain, she found herself falling limp to her pillows, curling around her swollen belly.

Deep within, she felt something stir, something strong, something ripe with her lord's black magicks. She hugged her arms around her belly, appreciating the strength in the movements of her unborn child. She closed her eyes, pulling her arms tighter, a smile on her lips.

Her master was right as always. A glowing warmth suffused her veins, and she found tears in her eyes. She did . . . Yes, she certainly did love this child. She rocked back and forth upon the pile of pillows. It wouldn't be long, she sensed.

Her child, the true seed of the Black Heart, would be born this night.

ER'RIL DANCED HIS DRAFT HORSE BEHIND THE WAGON. "IT IS ONLY A LITTLE farther, Mogweed!" he called. "We can make it!" But his words felt like a lie on his tongue. Er'ril tried to ignore the spiders closing on their flanks, but it was difficult with the constant low rustle of the Horde's march. The sound ate at the back of his skull. "Tol'chuk, they are almost upon us."

"I have large ears, plainsman. I hear them, too." The og're ran behind the wagon, pushing at its rear to ease the load of the laboring horses in front. He ran at a slow trot.

Too slow, Er'ril feared. He risked one look behind him. The trail to the rear was already awash with a sea of writhing, surging bodies. To the sides, only three horse lengths away, the Horde drove toward them. "We need more speed," he mumbled to himself.

Suddenly a loud barking erupted near the front of the wagon, startling Er'ril's mount. He had to fight to keep the horse from bolting down the trail into the spiders. Ahead of him, the wagon jerked forward out of Tol'chuk's grip, almost tripping the og're to the mud. Tol'chuk stumbled a few steps, then caught his balance and pursued the fleeing wagon. The barking continued, mixed with occasional loud growls.

Er'ril kicked his horse forward to investigate. "Tol'chuk, can you keep up?" he asked as he trotted past the loping og're.

Gasping from exertion, Tol'chuk nodded his boulder of a head. "Just get this big wagon out of my way and see how fast I run."

Er'ril snapped his reins and urged his mount to the front of the wagon. Once he slipped past the side of the rig, he saw the reason for the commotion.

It was Fardale!

The large black wolf raced behind the horses' legs, snapping at heels and dodging the occasional kick of a hoof. The wolf's eyes glowed amber in the gloom of smoke and shadow as he herded the terrified team and wagon onward.

Perhaps there was a chance . . .

Ahead, the end of the trail came into view amid the blowing black ash and soot. It was a sight to cheer the heart—except between them and freedom, Er'ril saw the path tremble and quiver with a flowing army of spiders. The Horde had outflanked them. But how?

Then Er'ril spotted the woodland stream a quarter league down the trail near the edge of the path. Its wet banks had offered the Horde an easy path through the burned wood to cut off their escape. Er'ril swung his head around. They were completely encircled by a blanket of spiders.

Mogweed seemed also to have spotted this obstacle before them and began hauling on the reins. "Fardale! Stop! Leave the horses be!" the thin shape-shifter screamed. "We must stop! Hurry!"

The wolf heeded his brother's shouted orders and raced to the front of the train of horses, now barking to help his brother slow the wagon.

Er'ril realized the folly of Mogweed's plan. If they stopped, they had no chance of escaping the bites of these spiders. They would be surely swamped as they stood frozen on the trail. Ahead, the wind blew apart the smoky drape, and Er'ril saw that escape was only a stone's toss away. So close! He clenched the reins of his mount, refusing to bow to defeat. No, if he was to die, he would end his life with a struggle!

Er'ril galloped his horse forward to keep abreast of the wagon. The team had only one defense left—speed! And Mogweed was about to destroy this single advantage. "Don't slow the horses! Keep them running! It's our only chance!"

Mogweed's eyes were wild with fear. Seemingly deaf to Er'ril's cry, Mogweed still yanked on the lead.

Er'ril realized he did not have time to argue and sway the shape-shifter. If they were to have a chance to survive, he would have to take control of the rig. Skilled from centuries of riding, Er'ril pushed to his feet atop his galloping draft horse and leapt across the open trail toward the wagon. Taking a blow to the shoulder, Er'ril crashed atop the driver's bench. Not waiting to check his bruised condition, he clambered into position beside Mogweed. The shape-shifter sat on the bench with the driver's whip frozen in his hands, his face shocked at the sudden appearance of Er'ril.

"Give me the lines," he ordered, "then crawl back and tell Tol'chuk to get in the wagon."

Stunned, Mogweed obeyed with a slight look of relief in his eyes. "What are you—?"

"I'm going to push the wagon right through them. Now go!"

Mogweed cringed and hurried toward the rear, clambering over the boxes of supplies.

Er'ril snapped the lead with a loud crack, then tucked it under his knee, snatching up the driver's whip. Now was no time to spare the horses. He gave the team a touch of the whip. "Fardale! Leave the horses and get up here!"

The treewolf was already in motion, seeming to sense the change in plans. Fardale spun on a paw, and in a blur of black fur, flew into the wagon, joining his brother under the wagon's canopy.

That left only Tol'chuk to collect. "Get that og're in—" he started to order when suddenly the rear of the wagon sank sharply. A plank cracked explosively from the back of the rig.

"He's in!" Mogweed yelled to Er'ril.

With the increased weight of the og're, the horses noticeably slowed. This was no good. "Jettison our gear!" he called back to his companions. "Everything! Toss everything!"

Behind him, Er'ril quickly heard crates crashing to the trail. But he could not dwell on their losses. He beat the horses savagely with the whip, silently apologizing for his cruelty but knowing he must not fail. Ahead, the draft horse he had been riding, now no longer burdened, flew into the sea of spiders first. The horse raced like a storm through the Horde.

If that horse can make it, then maybe . . .

A loud screech erupted from the steed, and Er'ril watched it stumble to a knee. A wave of spiders washed higher on its flanks. The horse struggled to rise, crawling in lurching motions, but then collapsed under the mass of tiny predators. The horse had not even made it a quarter of the way through the spiders.

But the poor beast's death had not been in vain. Its appearance among the Horde had diverted the spiders' attention, its blood drawing the army's bulk to the side of the trail.

Er'ril drove the wagon toward the opposite flank, where the spiders now swarmed less thickly on the trail. He cracked the whip over the sweating rumps of his team. He needed every drop of speed and heart still remaining in these horses. "C'mon," he urged through clenched teeth as the wagon entered the spiders' domain.

Among the Horde, the horses needed no further urging, seeming to sense the danger. The proud beasts dug madly at the mud of the trail, froth flying from their lips. As they raced, spiders were crushed underfoot, and a greenish smoke could be seen rising from the horses' heels as the poisons scorched their hooves. Rather than slowing them, the pain drove the horses faster. Er'ril raised his whip, then lowered it, realizing how little fear it could generate now.

He could do nothing more.

Er'ril watched spiders beginning to work their way up the leather wrappings that protected the legs of the beasts. Ahead, the trail ended within whorls of smoke and sunlight. They had made it halfway through the Horde's blockade. Er'ril clenched his fist tight on the lead. Almost there! They must make it!

But the horses were slowing, their hearts giving out after the long day of terror and racing. Smoke blew across the trailhead, erasing the promise of escape. It now seemed the entire world was just spiders and ash.

Tol'chuk's head appeared at Er'ril's shoulder. The og're stayed silent. No words could help now.

"At least the girl got out safely," Er'ril said as the horses slowed.

"All be not lost yet," the og're said. "As long as we be moving, there be hope."

With his words, the horse on the left died, crashing to the mud, its harness ripping free of the wagon. The other horse bucked, tangled in the legs of the dead horse. Then this one, too, fell to the trail—defeated. The horse never even tried to get up, simply raised its neck once, looking toward the wagon as if to apologize; then life fled from its eyes.

The wood now lay silent with death.

Escape lay only a small distance away, yet it might as well have been a thousand leagues.

Er'ril was suddenly knocked aside, his one hand grabbing for the side of the wagon to keep him on the driver's bench. From the corner of his eye, he saw Tol'chuk roll through the front opening and over the side of the wagon.

Er'ril straightened. "What are you doing?" he cried.

Tol'chuk had a knife in his clawed hands. The og're hurriedly sliced loose the tethers and harnesses to the horses and dug his nails into the backs of their spider-encrusted carcasses. With two grunts, he flipped the horses' bodies aside, as a child might a soiled rag doll, then gathered the harnesses over his own shoulder. Spiders now danced across the og're's back and legs.

"Tol'chuk . . . ?" Er'ril's voice died in his throat. What could he say? Death lay as surely within the wagon as without.

"As long as we be moving, there be hope," Tol'chuk said, repeating his earlier words. The og're leaned into the gathered harnesses, and his feet sank into the mud. He took a step, then another. Once the wagon began to roll, the og're dug harder with his legs.

Er'ril twisted in his seat, frantic for some way to help but unable to think how. He had never felt so useless. All he could do was watch as the og're bunched his muscles and dragged the wagon behind him.

Though the pace grew no faster than a crawl, at least they were moving. With blood pounding in Er'ril's ears, time slowed to match their creeping pace.

As Er'ril watched, spiders plagued Tol'chuk, but luckily the main bulk of the Horde was drawn to the carcasses of the horses, an easier meal than the thick-skinned og're. Still, enough spiders remained to thickly coat Tol'chuk's legs. And even though the og're had bragged earlier of his people's thick hides, tree bark itself was no obstacle to the corruption of the Horde. From his seat, Er'ril could see tendrils of green smoke rising from Tol'chuk's thighs as the poisons ate at his flesh, trying to weaken a spot so their bites could kill. Lines of pain marked the og're's back and neck.

Tol'chuk could not last much longer.

Suddenly a fierce gust blew down the throat of the trail and cleared the way of smoke. Sweet Mother! The meadows were only a horse length away! Er'ril jumped up. Lost among the ash and gloom, he had never suspected they were so close. "You're almost there!" Er'ril cried in encouragement to the laboring og're.

Tol'chuk raised his face, then stumbled a step at the sight. Regaining his footing, Tol'chuk leaned harder into the harnesses. The view of freedom seemed to renew the vigor in the og're's stride. His strong legs ate up the last of the distance, and the wagon was soon rolling into open meadows.

As soon as they entered the grasslands, the spiders fled from Tol'chuk's body and raced back to their shrouded trees. Seemingly the Horde feared to abandon its shadowy roost. Still, Tol'chuk continued to haul the wagon until they were clear of the trees and only green grass surrounded them.

Once safe, Tol'chuk stopped, his legs wobbling under him, and dropped the harnesses. He tried to swing around toward the wagon, but his legs gave out, and he collapsed to his knees into the wet meadow.

Er'ril leapt from the wagon and raced toward the og're. Tol'chuk's burnished skin was marred with white streaks and pocks from the assault of the spiders. When Er'ril reached him, Tol'chuk's face was still clenched with pain, and his breath rattled with wheezes and a coarse cough. The og're rolled two bloodred eyes up to Er'ril as the plainsman leaned over him.

"We did it, didn't we?" Tol'chuk gasped.

Er'ril placed a hand on the og're's shoulder. Where his fingers brushed one of the pockmarks, Er'ril's skin burned fiercely. He could only imagine the pain the og're still suffered. "You did it, my friend. It was your heart and bone that saved us."

Tol'chuk nodded. "Good. As I said, we og're be thick of skin." With those last words, Tol'chuk's eyes rolled back, and the og're slumped to the grass.

Before Er'ril could check to see if Tol'chuk still breathed, a voice cracked across the open meadow. "Back from your demon! Do not make us feather your corpse with arrows!"

Er'ril straightened and saw a band of twenty or so green-cloaked figures rise from the deep grass, each member armed with a tautly bent bow. Instinctively, Er'ril reached for his sword belt, but just as quickly, he realized this was a battle he could not win. He searched the determined faces that surrounded him.

No, now was not the time to fight.

Er'ril raised his arm and opened his palm in the common gesture of surrender.

Wrapped under a thick blanket, Vira'ni still lay nestled among the tufted pillows when she heard the hurried feet of several people running into the camp. Voices were raised in tones of jubilance, and occasional shouts of victory burst from the party. As someone ran up to her tent, Vira'ni sat up straighter, drawing an arm protectively across her belly.

The tent flap whipped open, startling her, but it was only Betta. The large woman, dressed in a stained green cloak with the hood pushed back from her cropped blond hair, pushed into the tent. Her eyes shone brightly, and she wore a wide smile. Breathless, she crossed to Vira'ni and lowered herself to one knee. "We did it!" she exclaimed, almost trembling with excitement. "We captured them all!"

Vira'ni could not have asked for better news. "All of them?"

She nodded. "You were right. They even came with a huge demon leading their wagon. Clawed and fanged, it was an awful sight. Lucky for us, it quickly collapsed."

Vira'ni did not recall any demon from her vision, but perhaps this was some other trick of the foul wit'ch. "And the girl? Did you see a small woman-child atop a horse?"

"Yes, poor thing. She seemed the prisoner of some black-bearded cutthroat. We freed her with a well-placed arrow, and she escaped from there on her own." Betta grinned proudly. "Last we saw, she was riding like the wind across the meadows."

Vira'ni's blood chilled with each word Betta spoke. No! This could not be! The wit'ch had slipped her snare. The horror of this realization must have reached her face.

"What's wrong?" Betta asked, her smile fading away with concern.

"The child—" she stammered. "The child is the demon who leads them. She wears the flesh of the innocent like a costume. She was the one who killed my children!" Her voice had now edged toward hysteria. "You must believe me."

Betta, her eyes wide in horror, raised a thumb to her forehead in a warding gesture against evil. "I don't doubt you. The other demon we saw this day proves the truth of your words." The huntress scrambled to her feet. "Stay here. I must let the others know! Hopefully, we've chased the she-beast away from our lands, but who knows the mind of a demon? Perhaps she might try to rescue her companions. We must be prepared."

Vira'ni reached a trembling hand toward Betta. "No, we must seek her out. Now!"

Betta shook her head. "Night falls. And we hunters know not to seek a wounded beast in tall grass—especially at night. No, in the morning we'll track the demon. If the beast remains in these lands, we'll drive her out . . . or see her dead. You can be assured of that!"

Vira'ni was at a loss on how to convince the woman to hunt the wit'ch this night. As she struggled for a plan, a ripping spasm jerked through her belly. A loud gasp erupted from her throat, drawing back Betta's attention. Before even the first spasm ended, a second quake of pain shook through her body, and Vira'ni fell back to the pillows, a scream on her lips.

Betta was at her side, reaching under the blanket that hid Vira'ni's nakedness. The large woman rested one of her hard hands on Vira'ni's feverish belly. At that moment, another rip of pain tore at Vira'ni's swollen gut, and with it, a wash of hot liquid flooded her legs. Instantly, the stench of corruption filled the tent.

"Your belly pushes, and your life-water flows," Betta said, her nose curling in disgust. "Signs that your child comes, but something is wrong." Betta flew to her feet and pushed to the tent's flap. "I must fetch the midwife and let Josa know about the demon child." With that, she was gone.

Alone, Vira'ni kicked back the blanket and pushed to her elbows as the agony faded for the moment. Between her legs, she saw the spread of greenish black fluid staining the pillows. The smell was thick with rot. It was not life-water that flowed from her womb, but the brackish brine of a tortured birth.

Vira'ni lay back among the pillows. She had experienced a birth like this once before. In the dungeons of Blackhall, the guards had abused her most foully; and one night, while stretched on an altar, a winged beast had come to lay his seed in her. Moons later, in the soiled hay of the dungeon's floor, she had birthed a stillborn child. Then, too, her life-water had run black, and the stink of death had lain upon her womb. In the filth, she had gathered the dead child in her arms, rocking and moaning. Not again! Long ago, she had lost a cherished baby and could not survive the death of a second infant. She cried so loudly that her master took pity upon her and took her dead child. Using his black magicks, he transformed the babe into the Horde. The one became many. Once finished, the Black Heart returned the now-living children into her belly to thrive and never leave her again. Even now tears rose to her eyes at the sweet memory.

Agony suddenly slashed at the bones of her pelvis, pulling Vira'ni back to the present. She could feel the child thrashing in her womb. Her face shining with sweat, she smiled past the pain.

This would be no stillborn birth.

Suddenly, an old woman thrust through the tent's opening, her arms laden with two pots of water, one steaming, and a load of scrap cloths. The smell of sick birthing seemed to strike the newcomer like a blow. The woman scowled dourly, and with a slight shake of her head, crossed to Vira'ni.

"Honey," she said with a voice scratchy with age, "don't you fret. I been a midwife for going on forty winters and know a thing or two about bringin' young 'uns into the world. Everything'll be fine."

Vira'ni, though, could see the lines of worry on the old woman's face and sensed the midwife had recognized the smell of death. But Vira'ni simply nodded.

The woman set her pots of water beside the pillows, then fished a few dry mint leaves from a pocket and crumbled them into the water. "My name's Greddie, but everyone calls me Auntie Dee," she said as she worked. "So just you relax and let Auntie Dee take care of you and your young 'un."

Suddenly a burst of pain tore into Vira'ni like the huge knobby roots of a tree. Her scream drew Auntie Dee to her side in a heartbeat. Lost in red pain, Vira'ni barely noticed the old woman lay a cold cloth across her hot forehead then slide around to crouch between her twitching legs. Thankfully, the agony retreated as quickly as it had come—at least for now. Gasping, Vira'ni lay limp among her pillows.

Humming softly to herself, Auntie Dee grabbed Vira'ni behind the knees and pulled her legs up and open. "Now listen, child, I want you to push when I tell ya." The old woman raised her face from between her legs. "And *not* before I tell ya, you hear?"

Vira'ni's hair clung to her wet face, and her skin ran hot and cold all over. "I'll try."

Auntie Dee frowned up at her. "No. You will not *try*, you will *do*! Are we all clear on this here?"

Vira'ni swallowed a lump in her throat. "Yes, ma'am."

"Good girl." Auntie Dee's face disappeared as the old woman leaned down to examine Vira'ni closer. "What are all these marks down here?" she asked as she probed and prodded.

Vira'ni knew they were the tattooed symbols of power the Dark Lord had marked upon the entrance to her womb. "I . . . I'm not sure . . ." Then the pain struck again, so suddenly, without warning, like lightning from a clear sky. Vira'ni's back arched off the pillows as her womb ripped open.

"Push!" she heard Auntie Dee yell, but it sounded so far away. "Push! I can just see the head! Push or you'll lose the child!"

The words sank through the agony. She *must* not lose her child! Not again! Never again! With a cry frozen on her stretched lips, Vira'ni curled her shoulders up off the pillows, bearing down on the fire in her belly. She clenched her teeth and forced every muscle into one purpose—to push this child into the world.

"Almost . . . almost . . ." Auntie Dee chanted before her. "I thought the child dead for sure. But look at that little imp squirming to get out!"

Vira'ni ignored the mutterings of the old woman. With a final sharp intake of breath, she clutched handfuls of pillows in her fists, tearing through the fabric with her nails and gouging the flesh of her palms, then with a scream that split the night, she shoved her child from her womb.

Afterward, she fell back to her pillows, like a puppet with its strings slashed. She lay there shuddering and trembling from the exertion for several breaths before concern for her child drew her up on an elbow. Auntie Dee had not said a word yet.

Vira'ni struggled up, panicked that something was wrong, then with relief saw Auntie Dee with her baby. Her child had its eight jointed legs wrapped around the old woman's face, clinging to her skull. Auntie Dee lay sprawled across the floor of the tent, her heels drumming and spasming in death throes. Vira'ni sighed as her baby's four wings beat the air, drying its wet membranes before it could fly. It mewled softly and sucked greedily at the wrinkled neck of the woman, its two sets of jaws digging and working deeper into the soft tissue. As she watched, blood ran in thick pools from the wounds. Children were always so messy with their eating.

Still Vira'ni could not help smiling warmly at her child. It was so good to see a baby suckle for the first time.

7

Elena fled from the setting sun. Shadows chased her and the horse across the meadows as she clung to Rorshaf with both fists wrapped in his black mane. Her mount thundered over green knolls and splashed through soggy fields. She had long given up trying to control the horse's flight; the reins lay just beyond her reach, and her screamed commands had been ignored by the stallion. Fleeting thoughts of leaping from the saddle had passed through her mind, but a fall from such a height at this speed would surely break a bone if not her neck. So she clung with her cheek pressed to the wet mane of the horse, praying Rorshaf had some destination in mind.

Still, as much as her fears dwelt on the mad ride, her heart lay far behind her. What had befallen the others? When last she had seen Kral, the mountain man was collapsed in the meadow, an arrow shaft protruding from his body. There had been so much blood. She squeezed her eyes closed as if she could pinch the image from her memory. And what of her other companions?

Er'ril's face floated like a ghost in her mind's eye. He was her guardian, her knight, her teacher. Even as she escaped this ambush, she knew all was lost if Er'ril did not avoid this noose, too. How was she supposed to travel the lands of Alasea by herself? How was she to avoid the Dark Lord's minions and find the lost city of A'loa Glen? No, she needed Er'ril and the others.

Pushing upright in the saddle, Elena grabbed a firmer handhold in Rorshaf's black mane and hauled savagely on it. "Stop, curse you! Stop!" Tears blew off of her cheeks as the horse raced on. Like a flea battling a dog, Elena fought the horse with her thin arms. She had to stop Rorshaf before she was carried too far away. But her will meant little to the war charger's drive. With twilight swallowing the hills in shadows, the stallion continued to thunder across the meadows.

"Please," Elena cried into the fading light. "Please stop." Despairing, she slumped and buried her face in Rorshaf's mane. "I don't want to be alone." Her last words were a moan.

Then, as if her sobs finally melted the iron heart of the horse, the cadence of the hoofbeats slowed from full gallop to canter to walk. Elena raised her face to watch the horse pull up to a wide stream blocking the way forward, its waters polished a silvery rose in the last of the evening's light. A scattering of dragonflies darted on pearlescent wings through the reeds and thrushpoles at its edge.

Near a solitary willow whose branches brushed the shallow waters, Rorshaf danced to a stop, his muscles trembling from exertion. Elena slid off the horse's back, almost falling as her own tired muscles betrayed her. She caught herself and reached for the fallen lead that dangled in front of the stallion. She had to keep the horse walking, or he would stove up. She tugged on the lead, expecting the stubborn war charger to resist, but Rorshaf followed her as she walked along the stream's edge.

A battalion of frogs plopped from the mud into the river as Elena moved ahead, angry croaks spreading a warning through the ranks. With the scent of water lilies perfuming the twilight air, meadowlarks wheeled and glided over the waters, catching flitting insects. Elena slapped at her arm as a rivermidge bit at her hot skin. Rorshaf huffed and swiped his tail at a similar plague of biting flies drawn by his sweating coat.

Elena kept the stallion walking, and after a time, Rorshaf's trembling flanks began to calm. Still, she kept him moving until a small eddy from the stream blocked the way forward, a tiny harbor of silver waters. She let him drink from the still waters, but only a little. She also knew she should rub the horse down before night truly fell, but right now exhaustion weakened her own legs. Elena knelt by the water's edge on a flat stone.

Staring into the quiet stream, she could clearly see her own reflection in the water. She removed her gloves and raised a hand to her shorn hair. Who was this woman? Her face seemed so foreign, smudged with ash and char. She leaned down, reached a hand to the stream, and splashed cool water over her brow and cheeks, trying to find the face of the girl who used to run wild through her family's orchards. With water dripping from the tip of her nose, she watched the stream's disturbed surface quickly settle back to still. She stared into her own eyes in the wavering reflection. That young girl in the orchards was long gone.

As she leaned over the waters, movement caught her eye. A small pendant had fallen from her shirt and now dangled and swung from her neck over the water. She reached a hand to cup the tiny carved vial that hung from the twisted cord. The cord was braided from the hair of her dead aunt Fila. A rush of memories assaulted her: fond memories scented with cinnamon and flour from time spent in her aunt's bakery, and foul memories full of blood and terror. Aunt Fila had died on the streets of Winterfell to buy Elena a chance to escape the claws of a skal'tum.

Tears rose to her eyes. She clutched the vial tight in her right fist, jabbing a sharp corner in her palm and drawing blood. "I need you, Aunt Fila," she called to her own reflection.

Elena expected no answer. She had tried many times while among Kral's people to contact her aunt with the magicks in the amulet. She had failed each time. Either the elemental magicks in the vial's water had seeped away, or her aunt was now beyond her reach. Still it brought her some small comfort to keep this token of her family by her heart. She squeezed the vial tighter, remembering not just her aunt but also her Uncle Bol, who had given her the amulet and instructed Elena on its use. "Seek my sister in reflections," he had urged Elena among the ruins of the old school. "If able, she will come."

Elena let her hand drift open as a pang for all she had lost reached her heart. The vial, now free of her fist, swung over the waters. A drop of blood from her pierced palm rolled from its jade surface to strike the water with a small ripple. As the ripple spread, a milky light bloomed upon the surface of the water.

Eyes wide, Elena watched the light swirl like spilt cream. "Aunt Fila?" she whispered.

The pool of light continued to spin and spread.

"Please, Aunt Fila, I need you." Elena reached to clutch the amulet again, her tears joining the waters.

Then, like a whispered memory, the glow settled into the faint image of her lost aunt, the familiar face draped in swirls of light.

Elena's throat tightened with tears and emotion. She had lost so much of her family. The sight of her aunt awakened old wounds that had only recently healed.

The image grew clearer. The stern lines of her aunt's face became distinct, her eyes sharp with fire. Words arose from the water, quick and urgent. "Child, time runs short, and the distance is too great to maintain this contact for long. But you're in great danger. You must flee!"

These were not the words of comfort Elena had expected to hear. "Flee? But . . . but where?" Elena stuttered, the dam of tears bursting.

"Hush, child. Enough of this nonsense. Wipe your face. Tears are just wasted salt."

Obeying her aunt's words without thinking, Elena wiped at her eyes. Aunt Fila, a rock-hard and industrious woman, was not accustomed to argument. Even death had not softened her iron resolve.

"Now look over your shoulder."

Elena craned her neck around. In the far distance, evening had consumed the higher meadow. But buried among the hills, a spattering of red flames glowed near the horizon.

Aunt Fila spoke behind her. "The camp of your enemies. There lie your friends. But between you and your companions stands a creature of the foulest ilk, of the blackest magicks. To free them, you must defeat it."

Elena turned back to the ghost in the water. "But how? My magick is almost spent."

Her aunt frowned at her. "I can sense that. Your magick is like a beacon to me. But it shines only feebly now, and what comes for you this night is blacker than the deepest pit. You can't defeat it. Not yet. You must run."

Elena sniffed back her tears. "But what of the others?"

"They are lost."

"But I can't just leave them."

"You are all that matters. You must survive to reach the Blood Diary. The prophecy must be fulfilled!"

Elena remained silent.

Aunt Fila's voice softened. "I know that what is asked of you is difficult. But hard choices were made by all to bring us to this point in history, to give us one chance for a new dawn in this black time. You are the land's only hope."

Elena pushed to her feet.

"Good girl." Her aunt's voice grew faint, and the light faded from the water. "I can't maintain the contact any longer. Use this night to escape from here. The plains beyond the hills are wide with hundreds of small towns and villages. There you will find refuge." The light in the stream was now only a feeble glow. No image could be seen, but faint words still rose from the water. "I love you, sweetheart."

Elena watched the glow completely vanish. "I love you, too," she whispered to the dark water.

With the light gone, true night descended around her. Elena turned to face the mountains and meadows behind her. The campfires seemed brighter in the deepening darkness. Sorrow tightened her shoulders. With her heart heavy as a stone, she twisted away from the distant flames. Her aunt's words echoed in her head: *You are the land's only hope*.

Elena placed a boot into Rorshaf's stirrup and pulled up into the war charger's saddle. This time she kept the reins firmly in hand, determined not to be dragged once again by a panicked horse. Elena sat straight in the saddle, her hands clenched into hard fists as she searched her heart. She was tired of being hauled blindly against her will, whether by a wild horse or wild forces. It was time she chose her own path.

She swung her mount around to face the distant campfires. With a silent apology to Aunt Fila, Elena kicked Rorshaf's flanks. The stallion reared, huffing loudly, then dug his steel-shod hooves into the mud and cantered off toward the clustered flames.

Prophecy be damned! Those were her friends.

ER'RIL TESTED THE BONDS THAT HELD HIM FAST TO THE WOODEN STAKE. The leather straps were solid, the knots tight. He tried pulling at the stake, but the pole was thick and had been pounded deep into the dirt. It failed to budge.

"It's no use," Kral whispered from where he stood tied at a neighboring pole. His right shoulder was wrapped in a bloodstained bandage, his face haggard.

"And use caution," Meric added in a hiss. "They'll beat you if they catch you trying to wriggle free." The elv'in, who had been captured earlier, stood staked beyond the mountain man, sporting a new bruise on his cheek as proof of his words. He nodded toward two guards who leaned on spears a few paces away. Dressed in green hunting cloaks and caps, both men were broad shouldered and hardened by years of winter camps. Songs of victory from the nearby campfires kept the guards distracted and masked the team's exchange of words.

Er'ril searched the immediate area. Mogweed was the only other of the companions staked here. The shape-shifter hung sullenly in his bonds, head down. Er'ril turned a worried face back to Kral. "Where's Elena and Nee'lahn?" he asked.

"They took Nee'lahn to question her just before you arrived." Kral lowered his voice, and a hard grin shone through his black beard. "But Elena escaped. I sent her off on my war charger. She's safe."

Er'ril allowed himself a sigh of relief. "Where did she go?"

"I gave Rorshaf orders to carry her until he reached water, then stop. If trouble arose, he was ordered to mind the girl from there."

"Your horse understood all this?" Er'ril asked doubtfully.

Kral's grin grew broader. "I raised him from a foal. He'll mind my commands and watch over the girl."

Er'ril let the mountain man's words sink into his heart, but they offered little comfort. Horse or not, the child would not last long on her own.

"Where's the og're?" Meric interrupted, his blue eyes searching the surrounding meadows. "And the wolf?"

Er'ril nodded toward the wagon. "They have Tol'chuk trussed up tighter than a pig, with ropes and iron chains. I thought him dead, but he began to moan and thrash as they dragged him through the mud behind three horses. He's groggy from the spiders' poisons, but I think he'll live . . . as long as they don't take a sword to him."

"And Fardale?" Kral asked, his grin now faded.

Mogweed answered, his head still hung in defeat. "My brother ran off, proving his coward's blood."

"He had no choice," Er'ril argued. "Hunters have no love for wolves. They would have surely peppered his body with arrows if given the chance."

"Still, he abandoned me," Mogweed added sourly.

Suddenly a scream—a woman's scream—split the night. The four men staked to poles froze. Er'ril's first thought was that they were torturing Nee'lahn. But before rage could set him to struggling with his bonds, Er'ril saw the tiny nyphai woman being shuffled around a tent, escorted by two large women. Nee'lahn's jacket was ripped, her violet eyes wide with fear. At spearpoint, she was driven back to an empty pole and lashed to it.

The stationed guards tried to get some answers from the women, but their questions were waved away. "It's women's business," one of the escorts scolded as she knotted Nee'lahn's bonds. "Some commotion over at the birthing tent. Sounds like the lass is having a difficult birth." Once the nyphai was secure, the escorts gathered their spears and left.

The guards scowled at the five prisoners, then swung away. They resumed their post, but this time took up positions a few paces farther from the stakes and closer to the circle of fires, their necks craning to get a better view of the stirred-up camp.

Er'ril bent his head to meet Nee'lahn's eyes and kept his voice quiet. "Did you learn anything? Like who these people are and why we were attacked?"

Nee'lahn, shivering slightly in her bonds, swallowed a few times before speaking. "They . . . they think we sport with demons. Someone told them we killed their children and corrupted the forest."

"What! Who?"

"They didn't say. But I overheard one of the questioners, the headwoman named Betta, mention something about a young girl from the forest who was about to give birth. She seemed very anxious, as if something was going wrong."

"You think this girl might be one of our accusers?"

She shrugged. "I'm not sure. But this Betta woman left to check on the birthing. And I think it was this headwoman that screamed. Something is dreadfully wrong."

Er'ril's brow furrowed. "If anything goes sour with that birth," he grumbled, "I can guess who'll be blamed."

Kral rumbled beside Er'ril. "I spotted hunters gathering bundles of wood—more than is needed for their campfires." He raised his brows suggestively. "If we don't want to burn, we'd better find a way to remove ourselves from here."

"I'll not argue with that. But how?"

No one answered.

Er'ril's mind slipped and slid over various plans. None seemed realistic. Even if they escaped their bonds, what of Tol'chuk? Could they just abandon the og're? And what of their gear? The wagon was easy to replace, but one of the captors had ripped the ward to A'loa Glen from Er'ril's jacket pocket, absconding with the small iron-sculpted fist. How were they to proceed without the key to unlocking the magickal barriers to the lost city? Er'ril ground his teeth with frustration.

"He's back!" Mogweed's loud squeak drew all their attentions. Even one of the guards glanced over his shoulder to scowl at them, but he turned quickly away as a second scream billowed from across the camp.

"Quiet, Mogweed!" Er'ril commanded.

The shape-shifter stood agitated in his bonds. "Over there," Mogweed said with a nod. "Behind that bush."

Er'ril glanced where Mogweed indicated. "I don't see anything." Perhaps the shape-shifter was deluded by fear. Then Er'ril saw it, too: a pair of yellow eyes glowing behind the branches.

"It's Fardale," Mogweed said with relief in his voice.

The treewolf's black form was indiscernible from the shadows of the high meadow grass and low bushes, but the intense amber eyes were unmistakable. Good. Er'ril added this new factor into the plans for escape. With the wolf's aid, perhaps there was a chance. "Can you speak with him?" Er'ril asked, hope beginning to fill his tight chest.

Mogweed's eyes were already locked upon his brother's. "Fardale says he's scouted the camp—and warns it reeks of the corrupt stench he'd scented before." Fear now shook the shape-shifter's voice as Mogweed turned to face Er'ril. "It . . . it's the scent of the spiders. But here the foulness has grown much stronger."

VIRA'NI WAS SO PROUD OF HER CHILD. HER DEAREST ONE HAD ALREADY grown so much larger as it feasted on the midwife. It sat on Auntie Dee's chest, now grown as large as a small calf. Underneath it, the old woman's wasted flesh now clung tight to skull and bone, her many wrinkles gone as her sunken skin stretched flat across the bony planes of her face. How much younger Auntie Dee now appeared! What a fine gift Vira'ni's child had granted the midwife for her work this night.

But, of course, that wasn't her child's last gift.

"Now, I know you're hungry still, but we have much work to do if we are to prepare to catch our little wit'ch."

Her baby craned its face toward her. Two sets of mandibles chewed at the air, dripping blood onto the chest of the old midwife. It mewled softly at her, its membranous wings vibrating. Six stalked eyes waved at her in supplication.

Vira'ni raised a palm to her cheek. Oh, how beautiful was her child! But this was not the time for cuddling. Maybe later. Right now preparations must be made.

"Give your auntie a kiss for helping us, honey. Be quick about it. We must hurry."

Her baby swung back to the old woman and buried its muzzle between the midwife's sagged breasts, digging through her shift and into the flesh. Vira'ni smiled as she heard the ribs break. Such an obedient child.

With legs latched tight to the old woman's torso, it worked its head into the midwife's ravaged chest to reach her heart. Vira'ni then saw the large red glands at her baby's throat convulse as her child delivered its final gift into the old midwife. Once finished with its kiss, her baby clambered off the old woman's chest, its eight jointed legs dancing backward, its four membranous wings vibrating with excitement.

Auntie Dee's body, which had long ago grown still as the child had fed, now began to twitch upon the ground. The old woman's mouth opened and closed like a fish stranded on a dry bank. Then her glazed eyes began to glow a soft red.

Suddenly the midwife bent at the waist, sitting up. Her mouth hung slack, and a blackish drool dripped from her lips. Fingers flailing, her hands scrabbled across the floor as the baby's poison spread to all corners of the dead woman.

Just then, behind Auntie Dee's shoulder, Vira'ni saw the tent flap stir. Her child scrambled to the side of the door as Betta bowed her way inside. "Is the birthing done?" Betta asked as she pushed the flap of the tent wide open. The huntress straightened once through the doorway, but her face twisted with disgust. "Sweet Mother, what's that stench?"

Vira'ni just smiled proudly. Auntie Dee tried to answer, but only a choking gurgle flowed from her damaged throat.

"Auntie Dee?" Betta approached the back of the old woman sitting among the tumbled pillows.

Drawn by the voice, the midwife slowly turned her head, her neck twisting all the way around. Her vertebrae popped and cracked like snapping branches until Auntie Dee faced Betta.

The huntress stared, her eyes huge with horror. She stood frozen, her hands fluttering around her throat like startled birds. Then Betta screamed, a beautiful screech that pierced the tent to fly through the camp.

Auntie Dee lurched to her feet, swinging around to return her head to its proper place. She stepped toward Betta on shaky legs, a gurgle still flowing from her bloody throat. With palsied motions, Auntie Dee pointed to her own chest as if to show Betta where Vira'ni's baby had kissed her. The old woman's spasming fingers dug at the raw-edged wound in her chest, ripping at it. Then with a sudden jerk, Auntie Dee tore her rib cage open.

Betta screamed a second time, but sadly it was not as piercing.

From the midwife's open chest, a spawn of black-winged scorpions burst forth. Each a thumb's length long, they swarmed over the panicked huntress, stingers jabbing. With her hands batting at the creatures, Betta fell backward out of the tent, coated with the scrabbling bodies of the poisonous beasts.

Naked, Vira'ni followed, pushing aside the teetering figure of the ravaged midwife. Hollowed out, Auntie Dee collapsed in a rattle of bone and skin upon the pillowed floor. Vira'ni ignored the old woman and crossed to the tent's opening. She threw back the flap and found Betta lying on her back just beyond the doorway. The huntress's skin had already started to blacken, and her belly had bloated like a dead cow left too long in the summer sun.

Beyond Betta, a ring of hunters stood limned in their camp's fires, faces stunned in horror.

Vira'ni ignored them and spoke to Betta's still form. "Now don't be selfish. Share the kiss, my little ones."

With her words, the swarm burst from the corpse's belly in a thick black cloud, spreading out to consume the waiting hunters. Screams rose into the night as ebony stingers spread their deadly kisses. A small child ran panicked among the fleeing legs toward Vira'ni, tears flowing across her cheeks. Vira'ni knelt to collect the frightened child in her arms. "Hush, my dear, there's nothing to fear."

Vira'ni pulled the child tight to her naked bosom. What a sweet little girl with those pretty curls! She was almost like a tiny doll. Vira'ni covered the child's ears to muffle the screams of the camp. Poor thing. Children were always frightened by loud noises. Vira'ni remained crouched by the sobbing child and waited.

It didn't take long. Around her, hunters collapsed in agonized poses to the flattened meadow grass, and their cries soon died away as the poisons took effect. Vira'ni sighed and stood up, still carrying the child in one arm. Everywhere bodies lay strewn around the camp. One sorry fellow had even fled into one of the fires to escape the kiss of the scorpions. As the flames charred his bones, thick oily smoke billowed into the night sky, the smell of burning flesh tainting the chill breezes.

Vira'ni scowled at his flaming form. Sweeping back her long black hair, she turned away from the sight and crossed toward where the prisoners were staked at the camp's periphery. The scorpions knew her will and had left the five butchers of her children alone. She would deal with the murderers personally. As Vira'ni maneuvered between the small cluster of tents, the child in her arms continued to sob. "Hush, little one," she said, then lowered the child to the ground.

Too stricken with terror, the little girl collapsed to the dirt, crying and rocking back and forth. Vira'ni stepped over her and continued toward the stakes. "Now there's no reason to carry on like that," she said as she left. "Why don't you play with my baby? You two will have fun."

Vira'ni knew her own child had been following close at her heels, its scaled legs scrabbling and scritching in the dirt. As she continued onward, Vira'ni heard the sobbing child scream once behind her; then there was only silence. Vira'ni smiled. Every child needed a playmate.

Now she came within sight of the five stakes.

Vira'ni stopped behind a low tent and studied them. Four men and one woman, she noted. Murderers all! Her warmth and goodwill after birthing such a fine child dried to a hard knot in her gut at the sight of them. She stalked into the open, unashamed by her nakedness. Why should she be the one ashamed? Her shoulders shook with suppressed rage. She stepped over the blackening bodies of the two guards and kicked aside a fallen spear.

Her baby, now done playing, scurried up next to her. Its wings beat at the air as it tried to gain flight. Already hungry again, it mewled plaintively at her. Vira'ni sighed. A mother's work was never done.

Ahead, the female prisoner gasped at the sight of Vira'ni's baby. At least this small woman had the good taste to recognize the astounding beauty of the child. A surge of pride warmed Vira'ni's heart. Perhaps Vira'ni would even let the woman feed the baby before killing her.

Then one of the men, the prisoner with only one arm, dared to speak. "Sweet Mother! It can't be!"

Vira'ni turned hard eyes toward the man.

"Is that you, Vira'ni?" he asked, his eyes wide and shocked.

Surprise froze Vira'ni where she stood. Even the hungry cries of her child seemed dull in her ears. She gazed at the bound man, seeing him clearly for the first time: black hair, ruddy complexion . . . and those eyes! Those piercing eyes the color of stormy skies. "Er'ril! I knew it! I knew you weren't dead!"

Both stared in silence at each other.

Then the huge black-bearded man cleared his throat. "Er'ril, you . . . you actually know this woman?"

Er'ril nodded. His words were like dry leaves crumbled underfoot. "Yes. Long ago. We were once lovers."

8

Elena heard the screams from the camp die quickly in the wind. What was happening? Fear and worry clenched her hands on the reins of her mount as she rode across the dark meadows. Were they the cries of her friends? She shook her head to dismiss such thoughts. Even from two leagues away, Elena could tell that many more voices were raised than were numbered in her party. Still, it was possible her companions' voices were mixed in with that dreadful night music.

But now, nothing. Even the tree frogs and crickets had been quieted by the screams, as if the entire world held its breath. This abrupt silence was worse than the cries. Elena could almost sense death in the quietness of the night.

With the fires of the camp as a beacon, she urged the war charger to faster speeds, but even Rorshaf had his limits. After almost a full day of outracing flames, spiders, and ambushers, the horse's gait could achieve only a shaky gallop. Still Rorshaf fought his fading heart to obey his rider, his chest heaving, his breath trailing in twin streams of white, like banners in the cold night air.

Suddenly, Rorshaf stumbled as a hoof struck an unseen obstruction. Elena twisted in the saddle to maintain her perch. Rorshaf, though, was a skilled crag stallion, and among the icy cliffs of Kral's home, good balance was bred into the horses' bones. Rorshaf caught himself up before he rolled, pulling back into his gallop.

With a heave, Elena hauled herself straight in the saddle. Biting her lower lip, she pulled back on the reins and slowed the horse to a walk. She was being foolish. Her urge for speed had been a blind reaction to the screams. Her heart, rather than her head, had guided her actions.

Elena glanced across the fields. The sliver of moon was too pale to shed more than wan light across the waving grass, and pools of mist collected in the folds between the round hills. Racing too quickly through the dark meadows risked another stumble, a broken leg, or worse. And what was she hurrying toward? To what end? Her aunt's words echoed in her head: *Between you and your companions stands a creature of the foulest ilk, of the blackest magicks . . . You can't defeat it.*

Elena pulled Rorshaf to a stop. In the far distance, near the horizon, a vague, reddish glow marked where thousands of embers still smoldered in the rimwood forest. Not far from the horizon, the fluttering flames of the nestled camp danced shadows across the hills. She stared, unblinking, at the fires.

What was she to do?

The thought of turning back and obeying her aunt's instructions to flee passed through her mind. It was *not* too late. She could take Rorshaf, and even in the horse's weakened state, she was sure they could reach the distant plains by morning.

No! Elena waved this thought away. She would not abandon her friends. That was not a choice.

But then again, what were her choices?

She removed the glove from her right hand. The "mark of the Rose," as Er'ril referred to her hand's ruby stain, had faded with her magick's release to a pale sunburn. Only a little of the magick's strength still coursed through her veins. For a moment, she considered again the thought of dumping the residual magick she contained and renewing now, bringing her Rose to full bloom. Even though Er'ril's warnings were fresh in her ears, fear of facing the unknown enemy with only a fraction of her power scared her more.

Elena found her other hand reaching and pulling free her sheathed dagger. The knife's bright blade caught the scant moonlight and shone like a small lamp in her hands, drawing Elena's eyes. She was sure the dagger was visible for hundreds of leagues.

The knife's brightness gave Elena reason to pause. The release of her magick would be a far greater beacon this night than a shining blade. If she were to drain her magick, all eyes would be upon her, including the evil at the camp. Elena lowered the dagger back to its sheath. She was unwilling to expose herself to whatever lay in wait among the flickering campfires.

As she pondered her choices, a plan began to grow within her. She might be low in power, but there was also a certain strength in shadows and surprise. With luck and the cover of night, there was a chance to free her friends without needing the power of a full Rose. Who was to say she even needed to confront the foul creature?

With this in mind, she climbed off the war charger. Rorshaf would be too noisy and large for her to creep unseen upon the camp with him. She must go on foot. While her mind whirled with plans, she pulled the packs and saddle off the war charger and walked him to cool his heated skin. Once satisfied the horse's heart had calmed, she hurriedly rubbed him down, then tossed his lead around the thin bole of a scraggly meadow oak.

"Stay here," she whispered at the horse.

Rorshaf pulled lightly against the tether and rolled a large eye toward her. Elena could tell he did not like the situation but would obey.

Elena ruffled through the packs, loading all she would need into one satchel. As she buckled the pack, her eyes spotted Kral's ax tied to the abandoned saddle. Its red iron surface had been honed to a dull sheen, but no amount of grinding or polishing had been able to remove the black stain that marred its surface—a foul blemish where the blood of a skal'tum had etched the metal.

Without thinking, Elena crossed to the weapon and unlashed it. Hefting the ax, she weighed it in her small hands. Though heavier than she could truly wield, its strength and sharp edge gave her comfort. Propping it over one shoulder, she faced the distant campfires. She would need to be as hard as the iron of the ax.

Clutching the hickory haft of the weapon, she set out toward the fires at a hard pace. With over a league to travel, she wanted to reach the camp while night's cloak still hid her. As she marched, her thoughts dwelt on her companions. Were they still alive? Was this dangerous journey needlessly putting herself in jeopardy? Her steps did not falter. In her heart, she somehow knew they lived. Whether this hope was wishful thinking or some invisible bond that had formed between her and her friends, she did not know. But she could not leave without the others.

As she continued, the night grew colder, her white breath marking her steps, but the exertion of slogging through the muddy meadows kept her warm. Soon the camp was only an arrow's flight away. She circled a bit to the right to place a large hill between her and the encampment. She wanted her approach to be as furtive as possible.

By now though, even without seeing the camp's interior, she knew something was amiss. No snatches of voices or clatter of cooking pans echoed from the far side of the rise. Worse yet, a foul but familiar stench marred the night's winds: burning flesh. Elena found herself cringing, unnerved. She knew that stink too well. Tortured images of her parents wrapped in cloaks of flame bloomed in her mind's eye. She fought these memories back. Now was not the time.

She slowed her pace as she neared the looming mound, searching its crest for sentries. Either they were too well hidden or no one stood guard. She crouched low in the tall grass as she continued toward the deeper blackness at the base of the bluff. From here, she must be cautious. All her plans depended on stealth.

Around her, the grasses lay silent. Not a bird whistled in warning; not an insect whirred for a mate. In the quiet, her footsteps seemed so loud, but Elena knew her own fears amplified the noise. Still she tried to move more carefully, her ears straining for any other sounds.

Her wariness allowed her to hear the whispered snap of a twig to her left. She spun around, raising the ax, just in time to see the large black shape materialize out of the grass before her, as if the shadows themselves had been given form. From the black hulk, fangs glowed in the scant moonlight, and sharp yellow eyes narrowed in warning.

A fleeting image formed in her head: *Two limping wolves meet in a wood. Back to back, they face the hunters.*

Elena dropped Kral's ax and ran to the shape-shifter. It was Fardale! Wrapping her arms around his neck, she buried her face in his thick fur. She allowed herself a moment of relief, then pulled back. If the wolf still lived . . . ? She retrieved the dropped ax. "The others?" she whispered at the shape-shifter. "Do you know where they are?"

Fardale swung around, then glanced back over his shoulder at her: *A wolf leads another past a hunter's hidden snares.*

Elena nodded. Though she bore no si'luran blood, she understood the shape-shifter's message. Over the long winter, she had heightened her ability to communicate with the wolf, her magick allowing her to forge a bond where blood did not. She waved him onward, but before Fardale obeyed, he sent one last image. Elena's eyes grew large, and her heart clenched. Before she could speak, the wolf slipped between the grasses, his form dissolving again into shadows.

Elena followed on numb legs, the image still vivid in her mind: *A naked woman of stunning beauty stood before a family of trapped wolves. From her loins, poisonous vipers flowed toward the pack.*

ER'RIL FOUND HIS TONGUE THICK IN HIS THROAT. HOW COULD THIS BE? He stared at the naked woman before him, her bare thighs fouled with black blood. Her face, achingly beautiful, was as cold as polished stone, and her ebony hair, once a solid drape of night, was now marred by a squirming streak of white. But worst of all, Er'ril saw madness dance in her eyes.

As he stood lashed to the stake, his mind fought to match the memories of a young maiden from ten winters ago with the woman who now stood before him. He remembered when they had first met. It had been along the harsh northern coast, in a town constantly shrouded in sea mists, where the air had always tasted of salt and ice. He recalled the young woman, a fisherman's daughter who had shyly caught his eye as he juggled for coppers in a seaside tavern.

Inexplicably, he had found himself drawn to seek out the company of this young maiden. Her delicate face and silken hair had seemed so out of place among the wind-hardened people of these northern lands, like a soft-petaled rose growing in rock. He could not take his eyes from her as he juggled his flaming brands.

So after his last set on the cedar-planked stage, he retrieved his collection pan and the few yellow coins inside it, then shouldered his way through the crowd of bearded men and haggard women to reach the small woman near the back of the tavern.

She kept her eyes lowered demurely as he stepped before her table. Even as he introduced himself, she barely acknowledged his presence. When she spoke for the first time, her voice was as tender and soft as her skin. "My name is Vira'ni, she had said, her long black hair spread like wings to either side of her raised face. In her moist blue eyes, he saw a sadness that spoke to the emptiness in his own chest.

Er'ril sensed at that moment that they both needed each other. He needed to step from the road for a while, and she needed a heart to call her own. And so they had talked well into the night and into morning.

Eventually he was introduced to her family and accepted like a long-lost son. He had thought to spend only a few days but discovered a certain simple pleasure in life by the sea. He helped repair the family's damaged boat, and before he knew it, days became passing moons. Vira'ni's father taught him the nets and the vagaries of the sea, while her brother showed him the mysteries and wonders of the coast and the wet forests around them. And during all this time, he and Vira'ni grew closer. Her father even seemed pleased with the choice his daughter had made. "One-armed or not, you have a strong back and a good heart," he had once told Er'ril as they shared a pipe before the fire one evening. "I would be proud to call you son."

It was this time spent along the northern coast, fishing and crabbing, that reminded him what he missed most from his distant past: the warmth and quiet peace of a family around him.

Words suddenly intruded on his memory, pulling him from the sea back to the stake in the meadow. He found himself staring into Vira'ni's wide blue eyes. "Why did you leave me?" Madness and darkness now lay behind those eyes that had once shone with love. Her voice rose toward hysteria, one hand reaching up to tug at the white streak in her hair. "You knew I was with child. *Your child!*"

Er'ril looked away from her. "I didn't mean to hurt you," he mumbled. And he hadn't. Time and the warmth of her family had eventually healed the hollowness in Er'ril's chest. Cured of his road-weary sickness, he had come to his senses and knew he had to leave. Among Vira'ni's family, he had gained the peace he needed, but at what cost? Vira'ni's pregnancy had finally forced Er'ril to recognize the selfishness of his actions. He would never age, but Vira'ni and his child would. He knew his path was not the way of home and children. That road was for men who aged, for men who grew old with their wives, not for a man who had lived hundreds of winters and who might live hundreds more. No, the empty road was his only true home.

So, knowing that to delay any further would only hurt Vira'ni worse, he staged his own death. One day, he had set out on a small boat as a storm approached and simply never returned, letting his death be blamed on the cruel mistress of the northern coast.

"I didn't understand," he said now, struggling to explain. "I thought—"

Vira'ni interrupted, her eyes far away in the past. "My father was so ashamed of me! To be with child . . . and without a husband. After you disappeared into the sea, my father dragged me off to an old crone in the hills. She gave me a potion of crushed leaves that cramped my belly." Her face winced as if recalling this pain. "The blood. So much blood! The potion stole the child from my body. My poor sweet child."

Er'ril's heart grew cold with her words.

"But I had heard rumors," she said, her eyes bright, "of a one-armed juggler far to the south. I knew it had to be you! I knew you couldn't be dead. So after a handful of days, once I stopped bleeding, I fled from the old crone's hut and went to seek for you. From village to village, I searched." Vira'ni's voice cracked with her next words, as if the memories hurt her even to speak of them again. "Then . . . one evening on the road, he found me. Black wings, teeth, the hissing of snakes. He snatched me up and took me to his dungeons." Tears rolled down her face as emotions warred within her trembling body. She turned wild eyes upon him. Hate and hurt mixed in her twisting expression. "Where were you? Why didn't you protect me? I couldn't stop him!"

Er'ril looked away from her. "I'm sorry," he whispered, but even to him the words sounded hollow.

Her face hardened. She wiped brusquely at her tears, her eyes narrowing as if seeing him for the first time. "I don't need your pity, Er'ril. The Black Heart was kinder to me than you." She laughed sharply and pointed to her feet. "In his dungeons, his winged beast came to me one night and granted me this gift—a new baby to replace yours."

About her legs capered a creature of nightmare. The size of a large dog, it was all wings, jointed legs, and gnashing jaws. From its black maw, poison dripped and flowed, hissing where it struck the mud.

Er'ril's eyes widened with horror.

"Here is a love that won't abandon me!" she said, then turned to the foul beast. "Why don't you give Er'ril a little kiss? For old times' sake."

The creature mewled, its eight legs digging at the mud. Stalked eyes swung toward him; then the beast scrambled in Er'ril's direction.

Though he recognized the horror of what approached, a larger dismay gripped his heart. He should never have just abandoned Vira'ni. He was as much to blame for the tortured woman before him as anyone. Er'ril closed his eyes and leaned his head against the pole, ignoring the creature as it reached his legs and snuffled at his boots like a hound on a scent.

And which of them, the Dark Lord or himself, had treated Vira'ni more cruelly?

In his heart, Er'ril was afraid he already knew the answer.

Elena crouched in hiding along the bank of a swollen creek, clutching the ax in her hands. The gurgling water masked any sounds around her, making her nervous and edgy, and the occasional croak of a mud frog made her jump with each eruption.

Shivering from more than just the cold, she clenched her teeth until her jaw ached. Where was Fardale? He had left her buried in a patch of scrubby hawthorn bushes beside the flowing stream as he checked the way forward. Though she knew her fears stretched her perception of time, she was sure the wolf had been gone longer than necessary. Had something happened?

She pushed higher on her knees and peered between the branches of the bushes. The flames of the campfires lit the darkness just beyond the shoulder of the hill ahead. From where she spied, it seemed as if she were alone in the meadows.

As her ears strained, she occasionally heard snatches of words barked from where the fires crackled. But maybe it was just her imagination. She sank back deeper into cover and sat with her arms wrapped around her knees. The longer she waited, the more certain she was that failure would be the only outcome of this night's venture. Who was she to think she could free the others? Her companions had far more strength and skill than she, yet they had still been captured.

Her mind fought for any plan, but none seemed sound.

As despair and worry settled around her heart, a rustling of grass sounded from behind her. She swung around and saw the familiar black shadow slink along the creek bank toward her, yellow eyes ablaze. A sigh of relief escaped her throat.

The treewolf glided toward her. Elena saw he carried something in his jaws. It glinted in the moonlight. When he reached her hiding spot, he dropped the object in the mud of the bank, then crossed to lap silently from the creek.

She studied the muddy object, a puzzled look on her face. Why had the wolf brought her this? She had to remind herself that Fardale was no simple dog; a keen mind lay behind his wolfish features. She leaned closer to the object, and then like the dawn rising after a stormy midnight, a plan grew in her mind. She stood up suddenly. Of course! She held her breath, daring herself to believe it possible. She gripped the ax firmer in hand and allowed a small hope to beat back her despair.

Fardale crossed back to her, his eyes expectant. She knelt on one knee and hugged him for the second time that night. "Thank you, Fardale," she whispered in his ear.

He licked her once on the cheek, acknowledging her gratitude, then pulled from her grip. His eyes glowed at her, and images flowed: *A wolf who lags behind the pack is attacked by the stalking bear*.

She nodded, knowing they needed to hurry.

After a final intent stare, as if weighing her resolve, Fardale swung around on his paws and led the way back up the bank.

Elena quickly collected the glinting object from the mud and followed.

NEE'LAHN WATCHED THE SPIDER BEAST SPREAD ITS FOUR WINGS, EACH over an arm's length long. In the firelight, flows of black iridescence ran like oil over their membranous surfaces. It shuffled back from Er'ril's legs, mewling in what could only be pained hunger. Nee'lahn sensed that the creature was in its infancy, a pupa with legs, that its true adult form had yet to be seen. Only by feeding could it force its body to its next stage.

Her arms struggled for some weakness in the knots that secured her, but the ropes were thick and well tied. Even Kral, his face red with effort, could not budge the stubborn restraints. The other two men, Meric and Mogweed, seemed resigned to the uselessness of fighting their bonds. Meric stood straight in his ropes, his eyes scowling, while Mogweed simply cringed.

Nee'lahn stopped battling her ropes, recognizing that muscle and bone would not win this night. Still, she was not ready to give up. Not yet. Perhaps with wits and cunning—

Then suddenly it was too late.

The creature, which had settled into a motionless crouch, legs bunched under it, burst forward in a blur of wings and scrabbling limbs. It leapt at Er'ril.

The plainsman gasped as the spider beast slammed into his chest. Eight legs latched around Er'ril's torso, clamping him even tighter to the wooden pole. The spiked ends of the beast's legs dug into the wood. Er'ril's face purpled from the constriction, and for the first time since meeting him in Winterfell, Nee'lahn saw fear in the man's eyes.

The demoness named Vira'ni cackled with glee, her lips pulled back in a feral grin. "Kiss him, my sweet!" she encouraged her creature.

Nee'lahn knew that any chance lay in immediate action. The words leapt from her lips. "Stop! Call off your beast!"

Vira'ni swung her poisonous gaze toward the nyphai.

Nee'lahn continued before she lost her resolve. "The Dark Lord would not want you to kill Er'ril."

The demoness took a step closer to Nee'lahn. "And why is that? You think you know of my master's wishes?"

From the corner of her eye, Nee'lahn saw the spider beast lowering its twin gnashing jaws toward the plainsman's throat, but she kept her gaze fixed on Vira'ni. "I know the Black Heart wants the girl child," Nee'lahn told her. "More than anything, he wants the wit'ch."

These words seemed to reach through the woman's madness. Vira'ni's sharp, mocking smile faded.

"Only Er'ril knows her whereabouts," Nee'lahn lied. "Kill him and you lose any chance of discovering where he has hidden her."

Vira'ni made a soft noise at the foul creature, and the beast froze, obedient, its jaws only a finger's breadth from the skin of Er'ril's neck. Nee'lahn could see worry and doubt weaken the gleam of vengeance in the demoness. Vira'ni seemed to shrink in on herself. She backed a step away.

"The wit'ch . . . Yes, the wit'ch." One of Vira'ni's hands wandered like a lost kitten to her hair, playing with its black strands. "We must get the wit'ch for my lord. I mustn't fail him." Her eyes wandered back to Er'ril. "We'll play afterward."

Nee'lahn allowed her clenched muscles to relax a breath. Sweet Mother, it had worked.

She watched Vira'ni step to the beast and raise a single finger to caress one of its quivering wings. "Now, now, get down from there. We mustn't hurt Er'ril . . . at least not yet."

Nee'lahn watched with relief as the creature pulled its legs from the wood one at a time and climbed off its perch. It shook its wings in frustration and screamed at the night. Its screech—the voice of the dark beyond the firelight—touched upon the ancient fears buried in the marrows of all living creatures. Nee'lahn found her knees weakening at the sound.

Thankfully, Vira'ni soothed and quieted the creature with a palm upon its back. "Hush now, no tantrums. I know you're hungry." The demoness raised her arm and pointed. "Go feed."

Nee'lahn's eyes flew wide in horror. In a flutter of wings and scratching legs, the beast sprang at her.

"Thank you for reminding me of my duty," Vira'ni said. "As reward, you may take Er'ril's place."

The back of Nee'lahn's head cracked into the pole as the spider beast crashed upon her. It latched its eight jointed legs around her, pinning and encasing her small form from ankle to chest. Tiny lights danced across Nee'lahn's vision from the blow to her skull, but the spinning sparks were too weak to block the sight of the frothing jaws diving toward her neck.

As the beast tore open Nee'lahn's throat, pain drove her quickly into oblivion. Only the tiniest moan escaped Nee'lahn's lips as she died, a soft sighing note carried away in the wind.

9

Elena crept through horror. Bodies lay like scattered firewood around the camp. Not only men and women, but also children and gray-haired elders. Their blackened bellies had bloated like ripe melons, and small creatures could be seen squirming under their stretched skins. Elena kept her eyes away, steeling her heart, lest fear chase her off. Only the animals had been spared. Around her, horses nickered nervously and dogs slinked between the tents with lowered heads, as if fearing the strike of a stern hand. The surviving beasts shied from her as the large treewolf led the way. None of the hounds contested their passage.

She continued creeping through the outskirts of the camp. Fardale seemed to be circling around the tents, aiming for the eastern edge of the camp. From there, she could now definitely hear snatches of raised voices. Some few had survived. But who?

Clutching Kral's ax in her left hand, her palm grew slick on its hickory handle. Hidden in a pocket near her heart was the muddy object Fardale had stolen from the camp. Its weight helped firm her resolve. She could do this, she kept intoning in her head. She stepped over the ravaged body of a child, keeping her eyes averted. She must stay strong, keep control. Her right hand was clenched into a fist, empty but not weaponless. Elena had bloodied her hand with the wit'ch's dagger, and soft coruscations of power lapped and danced around her wounded fist as she held her power at bay.

She was ready.

Elena stepped around a tent and found Fardale crouched just

ahead. He flashed his eyes toward her. *The forest cat prowls low in the brush to surprise the rabbit.*

Elena crouched lower, almost crawling, as Fardale padded silently away. With the heavy ax cradled on her shoulder, she tried her best to keep up with Fardale, but the wolf's paws floated across the trampled grass and mud, and a gap quickly grew between her and the wolf. Biting her lower lip, she struggled with her back bent after the fading black shadow. Ahead, Fardale vanished beyond the corner of the last tent.

She hurried after him, but when she reached this last tent, she paused. Beyond the corner lay only open meadow with nowhere to conceal oneself. Holding her breath, she peeked around the edge of the deer-hide tent. What she saw there almost caused her to lose control of her tightly held magicks.

Five poles were staked into the ground with her friends lashed to them. A creature of sick dreams climbed away from one of the posts. It was all wing, black scale, and jointed legs. And before them all, watching with intensity, stood a slender, naked woman draped in long black hair, a single lock etched a milky white. The woman seemed to sense Elena's eyes upon her and turned in her direction. The woman's face was as white as her moonlit lock and as cold as a sunless cave. Elena darted back behind the tent before the woman's eyes spotted her.

She shivered, not from the sight of the woman or the creature, but from what else she had seen for that brief moment. It could not be! Yet Elena knew it was true. Though what stood lashed to the last pole was just loose skin and brittle bone, she recognized the honey blond hair and the green shift that adorned the desiccated figure. It was Nee'lahn.

Elena could not stop the tears. She huddled behind the tent and held her bloody fist before her mouth, trying to keep her sobs from being heard. She had come too late! Nee'lahn was dead.

A cold voice rose from beyond the tent. Elena knew it came from the strange woman. "Now, Er'ril, where is the wit'ch?"

"I'll tell you nothing, Vira'ni. You can kill us all."

"Oh, Er'ril, you never did understand me. I didn't kill the little blond woman to threaten you. These others truly mean nothing to me. They're just food for my baby. My master has given me a tool to extract the information from you, with or without your consent—but the method is so messy."

"I'll not betray the child."

"But, Er'ril, you're so good at abandoning children. Even your own."

"The wit'ch is beyond your reach, Vira'ni. I hid her well. She is beyond even the reach of the Gul'gothal lord."

Elena trembled where she hid. Er'ril was lying. But why? As soon as she wondered this, the answer came to her. Er'ril must know about her flight atop Rorshaf and thought her halfway to the plains by now. With his deceptive wrangling, he hoped to extend her lead. He was willing to sacrifice himself and the others just to buy her extra time.

She could not let him make this sacrifice, especially since it was a useless gesture. She was not racing across the plains in flight. She was here. Their deaths would do no good.

The woman continued speaking. "Maybe you tell the truth, Er'ril, but I will still find where you sent her. But first, my baby is still so hungry. Isn't that so like children? They eat until they're full, and moments later they're crying for more."

Elena heard a keening mewl rise from the meadows that made her flesh crawl. It sounded like the plaintive wail of a lamb she had once found ravaged by a bandicat, a cry full of blood, pain, and the certainty of death.

"My baby must grow strong to take wing and hunt down your wit'ch."

Elena pulled to a crouch and wiped the tears for Nee'lahn from her eyes. No more would be sacrificed this night. Blood from her fingers stung her eyes as she wiped her cheeks clear—and with her blood's touch, the world changed around her. She saw with new eyes. The magick in her blood had cast some minor spell upon her vision. She could now see inside the flesh of her hand and view the blaze of azure light trapped within, opening her eyes to the flows of magick inside her.

The woman's icy voice cut through Elena's moment of wonder. "Now go feed, my sweet. Why don't you try that big man over there? He looks strong and will feed you well."

Elena lowered her blazing hand and stood. She must stop this slaughter. Now was not the time for stealth and shadows, but something bolder . . . something riskier. It was now time to make a stand.

"So, once again, where is this wit'ch of yours, Er'ril?"

"I told you—"

Hefting the ax over a shoulder, Elena stepped from behind the tent. "Here I am," she answered calmly. Her quiet words rang clear in the hushed and deadly night. "You want a wit'ch? I'm here."

ER'RIL WATCHED THE GIRL STEP FORWARD, SHOCK AND HORROR SQUEEZing the breath from his chest. Elena had Kral's ax over her left shoulder, and blue crackles of power sparked about her right fist. The child obviously did not know what she faced. Neither weapon she bore was strong enough to vanquish the twin threats here. Between Vira'ni's twisted spirit and the spider beast, Elena had no chance to win this night, and with the others bound tight, none could come to her aid.

As Elena approached, Er'ril saw that the child's cheeks were bloody, and a strange azure glow shone from her eyes. What new magick was this?

"Why, look! Er'ril, your little lost sheep has wandered home," Vira'ni commented casually. "My master taught me much about her wit'chery and magick. And I can tell you this—from the hue of her hand, she's rather weak right now. At least the deaths of my children in the forest weren't a total waste."

Er'ril could not contest Vira'ni's words. "Get back, Elena!" he called. "It's a trap!"

Kral and Meric echoed his words. Only Mogweed stayed silent, cowering and trembling.

Elena ignored them all, not even looking in their direction. She concentrated on Vira'ni. "Get your monster away from Kral," Elena said with fire in her voice.

The spider beast had frozen at the sudden appearance of the girl. An arm's length from Kral's boots, the creature crouched unmoving. The large red poison sacs on either side of its head pulsed like foul hearts.

"My baby?" Vira'ni answered. "But the sweet thing's not finished growing yet and needs more nourishment." She waved a hand, and the spider beast's legs again began to move in Kral's direction.

"Then you leave me no choice." Elena lifted the ax in both hands and threw the heavy blade with the strength of both shoulders. It arced toward the spider beast. Er'ril was amazed that the ax flew as fast and as sure as it did. He suspected some of the girl's magick must be behind the power of the throw. Still, as Er'ril had judged, neither was a match for the evil in this meadow. The spider beast darted to the side, and the ax missed, landing between Er'ril's and Kral's stakes, burying its blade deep in the mud.

Vira'ni's eyes had followed the ax's path with a momentary wince; then she laughed loudly when it landed harmlessly. She spoke to the ax. "Goodness, she is a feisty one, isn't she?"

With Vira'ni's attention diverted, Er'ril noticed Elena stare intensely at him for the first time, obviously wanting something of him. Once she had caught his eye, the girl slipped an object from her breast pocket and hurriedly rolled it toward his stake. Glinting in the moonlight, it bounced and tumbled across the grass to land near his toes. He studied the muddy object, his eyes wide. How did . . . ?

Unfortunately, Elena's secretive movements did not completely escape Vira'ni's attention. "Now what are you up to?" Keeping her eyes on Elena, she backed toward Er'ril's stake. "What's this little love note she's passing to you?"

As Vira'ni glanced closer to the object, bending slightly away from Elena, the child pointed toward the ax. Er'ril suddenly understood. But could he make it work again? From the corner of his eye, Er'ril saw Kral struggle with the spider beast as it reached his legs and climbed upon him. With what little movement Kral could manage with his ropes, the mountain man kept jabbing his knees at the creature's belly to keep it unsettled, but this battle would not last long. Er'ril concentrated on the object at his toes. He must make it work.

"How cute!" Vira'ni said, leaving the muddy object untouched. "It's a tiny iron sculpture. I thought it was a rose at first, but now I see it's just a small fist." She faced Elena again. "Not very romantic, my dear."

Elena backed a few steps away, raising her red fist high in the air. Crackles of power blazed in the night.

Vira'ni followed. "Very pretty. Now see what I can do." With a long, sharp fingernail, she sliced a deep cut in her forearm. Blood welled quickly, but Vira'ni smeared it over her chest and face before it could drip to the mud. Instead of staining her skin red, the blood seemed to draw shadows to her flesh. About Vira'ni's form, inky pieces of night coalesced around her, drawn to her naked skin and clinging to her like a lover's caress. She now wore the darkness like a shield.

"I will give you one last chance to free my friends," Elena said, seemingly unfazed by the demonstration of Vira'ni's power.

"Or what?" By now, shadows trailed and roiled around Vira'ni like serpents. As they grew in strength, the meadow dimmed, the shadows sucking hungrily at the fire and moonlight. The shadows themselves soon crackled with black flames. "You think you can douse the darkfire that the Black Heart has granted me?"

"Let's find out," Elena answered. She backed farther away, leading Vira'ni with her.

"It's too late to run, my dear."

Struggling to shut out the women's warring words, Er'ril closed his eyes. He knew the girl was just trying to buy him time, keeping Vira'ni distracted. He must not lose this chance. Elena needed his help. With his heart pounding in his throat, he recalled his battle with the rock'goblins. How had he made the ward work? He remembered the boy's name, the one whose fist lay carved in iron before him, the one he had slain long ago. *I need you,* he whispered in his mind. He formed the boy's name on his lips: *I need you, De'nal.*

With the silent utterance, his shoulder stump suddenly bloomed with a searing fire. He gasped as he hung in the ropes, his legs weak with the flare of pain. Then just as quickly the agony vanished. Yet all was not as it had been. Er'ril now sensed the presence of a phantom arm attached to his shoulder, like a distant memory of his old limb of flesh and bone. He opened his eyes and saw the iron fist floating in the air before him. It was again his own fist, attached at the end of his phantom arm. He stretched and flexed his hand and watched the sculpted ward obey, iron fingers opening and closing to his command. He clenched the hand back to a fist. He had done it!

Lowering the iron hand, he saw that Elena had managed to draw Vira'ni out of sight behind the tents. He could hear their voices raised in challenge. He must not waste the slim chance the girl had won.

A groan to his right drew Er'ril's attention. Kral was losing his battle with the spider beast. The creature now straddled the man's large chest, scrabbling to secure its position, its legs digging into Kral's flesh. With his phantom arm and iron fingers, Er'ril reached and grabbed the hickory handle of the ax. Pulling with a force stronger than his real limb, he hauled the blade up from the mud and lashed out at the beast.

He only managed to smack it with the flat of the blade, but it proved enough. Caught by surprise, the beast was knocked clear of Kral. In a flurry of wings and tangled legs, it landed on its back.

"Swing around," Er'ril hissed at Kral. "Your ropes!"

Kral twisted his body around the pole to expose the cords that bound his arms and shoulders. "Hurry!" he spat back at Er'ril. Nearby, the creature was already righting itself, shaking out its disturbed wings. From its two jaws, a scream of fury pierced the night.

Sweat beaded his brow as Er'ril swiftly swung the ax. With two swipes, Kral stood in a tangle of severed ropes.

The spider beast leapt at Kral's throat, but the mountain man drove a fist the size of a small boulder into the creature's face, knocking it away from him. "Begone, you foul-faced dunghill," he shouted. The beast rolled into the higher meadow grass.

Er'ril freed the mountain man's legs. "Take the ax," he called, giving up any pretense of subterfuge. "Get me out of these ropes."

Kral obeyed, accepting the ax from Er'ril's iron fist. The mountain man moved with grace and speed, using his huge ax like an extension of his arm.

Er'ril shook off his ropes.

"Get me out of here, too!" Mogweed whined loudly.

Er'ril pointed at the shape-shifter. "Free Mogweed and Meric—but the three of you keep that beast here! I'm going after Vira'ni and the girl."

"Wait," Kral warned. His eyes were on the edge of the grass line. "Here it comes again."

The beast leapt from the meadow's edge. Its stalked eyes were aglow with red rage; green poison dripped and sizzled from its slathering jaws. But it seemed shaky on its legs, teetering as if blown by strong winds. Its body shuddered, and its swollen belly convulsed. It screeched—not with rage but with pain.

"Something's wrong," Kral mumbled.

"Get me out of here!" Mogweed cried again, spittle shining on his lips.

Meric spoke for the first time, his words directed at Mogweed. "Fool, keep your tongue still."

The beast seemed attracted by their voices and took a scatter of steps toward them, then suddenly stopped as if unsure. Its eyestalks waved erratically, and it began to wobble on its legs. It tried to take another step but instead toppled to the ground. It scrabbled at the mud, and its wings fluttered weakly for several heartbeats. Then, after a final, violent shudder, it lay limp. The glow faded and died in its eyes.

"It's dead," Mogweed said, his words both a question and a statement of relief.

"But what killed it?" Kral asked.

Er'ril ignored the question and the mystery. Elena was more important. He waved Kral toward the two men still roped to the poles as he turned to leave. "Free them, but don't be so sure the beast is dead. Watch it closely."

Er'ril turned to leave, but before he could step away, Mogweed's voice quaked. "L-l-look!"

Er'ril glanced back. The beast lay quiet, its eyestalks limp and dead, but now its wings had begun to dry and curl like sun-seared leaves, and its eight legs withdrew into its black body. With these transformations, its belly section swelled, and something inside its poisonous heart began to thrash and squirm.

"Get me out of these ropes!" Mogweed squealed.

Kral was already there, slicing the shape-shifter's bindings. "What's happening?" Kral asked as he moved to free the elv'in from his ropes.

Er'ril stood frozen in indecision. "It's molting," he said. "Shedding into its new form." Er'ril knew he should leave this matter to Kral. But Mogweed would be of no aid to the mountain man, and Meric was still too weak from his daylong manipulation of the winds to be of any real help. Er'ril paused. He feared pursuing Elena without first seeing what manner of monster was at his back.

He did not have long to wait.

The skin and scale of the spider beast's belly split open, and from its heart, an oily green mist blew into the night, glowing like some sick fungus on moldering wood. Er'ril sensed that one whiff of that oily fog would kill instantly. All four men backed farther away from the carcass.

What squirmed free from its dead shell plopped, steaming, onto the mud of the meadow. Pale skinned, like the belly of a dead snake, it lay curled, a moist bundle on the mud. Here it was at its most vulnerable, but the fog of poisonous mist hung around it like a protective barrier.

The men could only watch as it began to uncurl, arms stretching out, knees bending free. It rolled to face them, swiftly gaining its bearing and strength. What crouched before them was no weak babe, fresh from a womb. Instead, cunning already shone in its eyes. It swung its feet under itself and stood on its two bare legs to face them.

"Sweet Mother," Kral swore near Er'ril's shoulder, amazement thick in his voice. He lowered the ax he had been about to hurl.

Before them rose a wonder. Long black hair framed a face of soft skin and full lips, breasts the size of ripe apples, and a slim waist above long, shapely legs. Her simple beauty shone forth like a beacon from all the horror of her birth. Not only did she share her mother's beauty, she was her mother's twin.

It was Vira'ni, born again.

"Sweet Mother!" Kral swore again, backing now in horror, his ax clutched tight.

From behind this beauty's shoulders, membranous wings spread forth, all bone and leather. Black blood could be seen coursing through the thick vessels in her wings. A feral smile spread the she-demon's lips to reveal rows of sharpened teeth. A red tongue, longer than an arm, slithered from between pointed fangs, curling about her face like an angry viper. She hissed at them and raised hands that sprouted razored claws, a sick green oil sheening their tips. What stood before them was a creature of pure poison.

Er'ril groaned. "I thought her mad . . . deluded . . ."

"What? What is that thing?" Kral asked as they backed another step, raising his ax protectively.

"The Dark Lord . . . He . . . he finally succeeded in mating a human with a skal'tum, mixing human blood with the lineage of the dreadlords. *This creature . . . this monster truly is Vira'ni's child.*"

The cursed beast crouched lower on its legs, arms and wings raised high.

"Watch out!" Meric called from behind their shoulders.

They all retreated in a bunch.

It called after them, its voice a hissing cackle. "Now why are you all running away?" It leapt toward them. "Come give usss a little kissss."

Elena continued to back farther into the heart of the camp. Once again she was among the litter of bloated and blackened corpses and had to be careful where she placed each foot as she retreated from the demoness. The air stank of smoke, blood, and excrement.

Had she bought the others enough time? Elena could not know for sure, so she continued her slow retreat, drawing Vira'ni with her.

She studied the woman. The demoness lay wrapped in shadows, her pale skin roiling and flowing with inky blackness while ebony flames of darkfire danced across her skin.

Yet that was not all Elena saw. With the trace of blood magick still tinting her vision, Elena could spy deeper within the demoness. Buried in the woman's chest, a tiny white flame flickered. Already this night, Elena had seen such flames near the hearts of her two friends, Meric and Kral, and recognized these tiny blooms of energy.

It was elemental magick!

Vira'ni—unknown perhaps even to herself—was an elemental! Of what forces, Elena could not fathom. But the small white flame was not alone in the woman's chest. Around this tiny flicker, a maelstrom of black magicks roiled, drawing sustenance from this sweet flame just as the flames of darkfire dancing on Vira'ni's skin drew energies from the firelight and moonshine.

This roiling force made Elena's stomach sicken and set her heart to pounding. Black energies seemed to fill Vira'ni's entire body, from the tip of each finger down to each toe. How could Elena ever think of defeating this creature? She backed another step. If only she could keep the woman distracted until Er'ril came to her rescue. Maybe the two of them together could . . .

Vira'ni spoke from within her shadows, startling Elena. "I think I'm done herding you, little lamb. I've got you where I want you."

Herding her? The words made Elena's heart grow cold. What did she mean?

Vira'ni waved her arm, and darkfire blazed forth from the woman's fingertips. Elena winced and raised her crackling fist like a shield, but the assault was not directed at her. Black flames arced forth from Vira'ni's hand to dance across the corpses around her, igniting them. The fire's touch upon their blackened flesh was like the touch of life upon a seed. The swollen bellies of the dead hunters burst wide, releasing a swarm of black scorpions into the meadow. Some scuttled in the mud toward her, while others were winged and took flight in tiny black clouds.

One scorpion, with its stinger raised, scrambled toward her toes. Elena waved a hand at it as if warding it away. A drop of blood flew from her fingertip and struck its armored back. The scorpion blew apart into gray mist and vanished. Elena stared, wide eyed, for a heartbeat. Sweet Mother, her blood could kill!

She danced back from the approaching army of scorpions.

Unfortunately this put her closer to Vira'ni. "See, the Horde doesn't want you to leave either," the woman said gleefully.

Elena ignored her, an idea forming in her head. She clamped her left hand around her right wrist and squeezed. Blood from her wounded palm bled faster, dripping down a single finger. Elena spun in a slow circle, seeding the ground with fine drops of her blood, creating a circle around her.

"What are you doing, child?" Vira'ni had stepped closer and reached a hand toward Elena. Where the woman's fingers crossed the ring of blood, her nails began to smoke. Vira'ni yanked her hand away and rubbed at her fingers. "Now that wasn't very nice."

Scorpions swarmed toward Elena from all directions, both on the ground and in the air. The night was thick with their buzzing wings and chattering claws. But whenever the poisonous beasts reached her barrier, they vanished in puffs of mist. Soon, a thickening gray fog began to build around her from the number of vanquished scorpions.

Elena cringed within her small island. How long would her power keep them at bay?

"Now where did you learn to form a mage ring?" Vira'ni asked, her voice only mildly irritated. She waved a hand and halted the assault of scorpions. The beasts stopped their approach, waving their claws and slashing their tails in agitation. A writhing sea of armored scale and stingers surrounded her, only a bootstep from her toes. "What a nuisance," Vira'ni said sourly. Scorpions clambered over the woman's bare feet, and a few winged ones landed in her hair. She kept plucking them out.

"You . . . you don't know half my power," Elena boasted. She raised her hand and pointed it at Vira'ni. It was with some small satisfaction that Elena saw Vira'ni take a step back.

Then the demoness seemed to collect herself and pushed a strand of black hair away from her face. "Perhaps you're right, but within your ring, you're trapped. If you unleash your magicks, you'll break the seal." She shrugged. "So right now, I can't get to you, and you can't get to me. But with sunrise, the spell will break, and my Horde will be waiting." She waggled a few fingers at Elena. "I guess I'll leave you to their care. Besides, I'd best check on your friends and make sure they're all comfortable. I wouldn't want to be known as a poor host."

Elena trembled where she stood. Her knees felt as if they might give out at any moment. What was she to do? She watched Vira'ni swing away from her and step casually through the sea of scorpions. Elena clenched her fists. Where was Er'ril?

ER'RIL SWUNG HIS IRON FIST, USING THE FULL STRENGTH OF HIS PHANtom arm, and smashed it into the leering she-demon's face. Her head bounced back, and the force of the blow shoved her an arm's length away.

Her wings snapped angrily at the air. "That hurt!" she said, but she seemed otherwise unharmed by the massive blow. The dark magicks of the skal'tum protected even this mixed-blood creature.

Kral stepped up next. "You think that hurt!" He swung his ax in a mighty arc toward her neck, but she was quick as a snake and darted back from his blow. Kral barely managed to catch his balance to avoid the parrying swipe of her clawed hand. He danced back from her.

They again stood staring across a narrow space at each other. Meric and Mogweed had retreated a few paces farther back, leaving the fight to Er'ril and Kral.

"Any ideas?" Kral hissed at Er'ril.

"I don't know. She's the first of her kind."

"I just need one good strike," Kral said. "My blade is still tainted with the blood of the skal'tum from last autumn. It'll penetrate her dark protections."

"Yes . . . but can you do it? She's smaller than one of her full-blooded brethren, but she's just as tough and much faster."

"If we attack together—you go in low and I'll go in high."

The creature laughed sibilantly at them. " 'You go in low and I'll go in high,' " she mimicked them. "Besidesss toughness, I also have the *hearing* of one of my 'full-blooded brethren.' " She cackled again at them and tossed back her hair.

Even this small gesture reminded Er'ril of her birthmother. How much else of Vira'ni was in this monstrous being? "You may be half skal'tum," he said, pleading to that part of her that might be Vira'ni, "but you are also half human. We don't need to fight."

"Who sssaid you had to fight? I'm not a cat. I'd prefer if I didn't have to play with my meal first. You could just stand there."

With a snap of wing, she leapt at them.

The attack was so sudden Er'ril could only manage a glancing punch to the demon's shoulder; still, it was a lucky blow. The strike sent her spinning on one clawed foot. Er'ril ducked under her wing as Kral struck out with his ax. While rolling to the side, Er'ril saw the iron blade strike home, a clean blow to the side of her head. But Kral's ax bounced harmlessly from the beast's cheek without even raising a bruise. The rebounding ax tumbled from Kral's startled hands. The mountain man tripped backward in a hurried retreat.

Fortunately, the force of the blow had knocked the she-demon to a knee, so she was unable to immediately attack. Er'ril helped Kral to his feet. The ax now lay at the demon's heels.

She rubbed her jaw and turned poisonous eyes toward them. "You were right, mountain man, that *does* hurt more."

"Why . . . How . . . ?" Kral stammered, obviously struck dumb at the lack of damage from his blow.

"Didn't you know the rulesss?" she said sadly. "I'm a newborn."

Er'ril groaned. He suddenly knew why the ax had failed to bite. They were in horrible trouble.

"What does she mean?" Kral asked.

"I didn't think . . . It's been so long."

"What?"

"Tell him," the she-demon hissed, pushing back to her feet. "He should know what he facesss."

Er'ril pulled Kral farther back. "When the skal'tum are newborns, they're gifted with a thicker layer of dark magicks. It's to better protect their young."

"Then how do we harm it?"

"We can't. Not even sunlight will weaken its protection. Only after a newborn kills its first prey, thus proving its strength, will its dark magicks become vulnerable." Er'ril nodded toward the she-demon. "She must feed before she can be harmed. And I can think of only one way to do this."

"How?"

Er'ril darted a glance over his shoulder toward Meric and Mogweed, then faced Kral with worried eyes. "One of us will have to sacrifice ourselves to her."

10

"WAIT," ELENA CALLED TO VIRA'NI'S BACK.

The naked woman stopped her casual stroll through the sea of scorpions and turned back toward Elena, grinding one of her creatures under her heel as she swung around. "What is it, child? I've work to do."

Elena's mind scrambled for some way to delay Vira'ni. Er'ril and the others could not have escaped yet, or the plainsman would be here by now. She must earn them more time. Ignoring the sea of scorpions at her toes, she studied the maelstrom of black energies seething and surging within the body of the demoness. Her own fist crackled with only the mildest tempest of blue coldfire, a mere summer squall compared to the raging storm within Vira'ni.

Elena's eyes suddenly narrowed in suspicion. How was it that Vira'ni had such power? From the way all the others had talked, Elena had thought herself the only female to wield magicks in ages. How did it come to be that a woman now stood before her whose power equaled, if not surpassed, her own?

Elena remembered a lesson from her father's teachings of swordplay to Joach: *Even the strongest opponent has a weak spot.*

But where was Vira'ni's weakness? The woman seemed steeped in powerful magicks. Yet how could that be? If Vira'ni was not also a wit'ch, what kept the magick inside her?

Elena's eyes suddenly flew wide as a thought occurred to her. Near the woman's heart, Elena still caught glimpses of the small silver flame buried within the surging storm of dark magicks. Could that be the answer? A plan formed in Elena's mind. With a tremble, she glanced to her toes and the scorpions surrounding her. If she was wrong, she would pay with her life.

"What is it?" Vira'ni repeated. She was about to leave again.

Elena spoke clearly, trying to fill her voice with confidence. She had to draw the demoness nearer. "I see a secret inside you. Deep inside you, a flame of power."

One of Vira'ni's eyes crinkled in suspicion. "Yes, it's the magicks the Black Heart bestowed upon me."

"No, that black fire is only a parasite upon your own true power, sapping that which you were born with."

"I don't know what you are talking about. This is nonsense." Yet Vira'ni had not turned away in disgust. Instead, intrigued by Elena's words, she took a step closer.

Elena continued, keeping the woman interested. "You're an elemental. Your spirit is bound to the land."

"What are you prattling about, child? I have no magickal gift."

Elena swallowed hard. So Vira'ni was unaware of her own nature. How was Elena to get her to believe? She took a different course. "What about your mother or father? Did they ever show the gift of land magicks?"

Vira'ni waved the question away and began to turn.

"No, think about it. Did either one show any signs? Any strange talents?" Elena could not keep traces of desperation from her voice.

Vira'ni hesitated, then spoke in a cold voice. "I don't know. My mother died when I was young, but my father often talked of how she could sing the crabs and lobsters into our traps . . . even the ironcrabs of the deep that could tear a man's arm off. But what does any of that matter?"

"It proves your mother had the gift, so you must have it, too. It is in your blood."

"Nonsense."

Elena had to persuade her to try to use her power, to wake her blood for a moment. "Look inside. Remember the sea . . . Remember the sound of waves on rock, the taste of salt in the air—and look!"

Vira'ni glanced suspiciously at Elena, but the small silver flame seemed to grow slightly brighter.

"At least open your heart to the possibility!"

"I . . . I . . ." Deep within the shell that was Vira'ni, the elemental fire burned fiercer as her blood sought to remember its birthright. Vira'ni took a step closer. "I think . . ."

The silvery flame flared to a sharp incandescence, momentarily beating back the black fires within the demoness.

Tears appeared in Vira'ni's eyes. She took another step closer, now only an arm's length from Elena. She seemed weak on her legs. "I sense it now. So clear! So beautiful." A profound sadness entered her voice, thick with tears. "I remember!"

For a moment, Elena saw a glimpse of the woman buried within the black magicks. But she could wait no longer. The black magicks of the Dark Lord already churned hungrily and would not be kept in check by the flare of silver flame for longer than a few heartbeats.

Opening her right fist fully for the first time, Elena struck out. She reached toward Vira'ni and felt a jolt of pain as her hand passed over the circle of blood, piercing her protective mage ring. Then her splayed fingers touched Vira'ni's naked skin. Not waiting even a breath, Elena willed her power to flow into the woman's chest.

Streams of magick wound from each fingertip into the demoness. Elena studied her magick's path, and with the aid of her enhanced vision, discovered she had better control over the flows and weaves of her power. Reaching toward the woman's heart, the edges of Elena's magick were consumed by spats of black fire. Wit'chfire died quickly when confronted by the might of the Dark Lord's dire power. Still, there was a chance. If only the path to the silver flame could stay open a moment longer . . .

She thrust deeper with her magicks.

"What are you . . . ?" Vira'ni was awakening to the assault.

The black magicks began to collapse back toward the silver flame. No, just a moment longer. Elena's trace of magick was but an ember before a raging firestorm, but there was no retreating. She forced her fingers of magick toward the fading silver flame near Vira'ni's heart. If she could join her magick to Vira'ni's, get the small elemental flame to flare bright enough, perhaps the silver fire could drive off the black. She lunged and sent her magick into the elemental flame, stoking the fire with her own.

Her power flowed, and like oil thrown on fire, the silver flame flared into a raging storm.

The black energies fled from the fierce light.

Elena allowed herself a moment of hope. It was working!

"Don't . . ." Vira'ni's voice was weak and trembling. Elena stared up at the woman's eyes. They were now so clear and lucid that they appeared almost a different color. Tears welled in those eyes. "It hurts . . . Don't make me remember who I am."

"You must," Elena said. The flame in the woman wavered with her words. Elena fed more of her wit'chfire into the blaze. "Fight it!"

Panic widened Vira'ni's eyes. "Stop! You can't defeat him this way. You don't understand what you're doing." Like an army massing, the black magicks grew thicker at the edges of the silver flame. The energies now crackled wildly within the small woman's body. "You're making him stronger in me!"

Elena hesitated. She had only the smallest bit of magick left.

"You don't understand!" The woman now howled. *"He feeds on me!"*

As Elena watched, the black energies swelled, drawing substance from the stoked flame.

Understanding suddenly dawned in Elena. Sweet Mother, it *was* feeding on Vira'ni's elemental power. Her efforts had only succeeded in strengthening the black magick, giving it fuel for its fire. The silver flame faded, its energies drawn into the darkness.

Once again, a mad gleam crept into Vira'ni's eyes. But before she was overwhelmed, the woman's hand reached up and grabbed Elena's, pressing it firmly to her cold flesh. "It's not too late!" Vira'ni moaned.

"What?" Elena cried. "I don't understand!"

Then it was too late. Elena could see the other's eyes go cold, her expression harden to granite. The grip on Elena's wrist spasmed tighter. The woman was gone—and the demoness was back.

Er'ril kept his eyes fixed upon Vira'ni's spawn, reluctant to face the others. The she-demon grinned harshly at him, wings spread wide, eyes aglow with hunger. She seemed to relish the pain of his decision.

Er'ril ground his teeth, his jaw aching.

If there was to be any hope of harming the creature, one of them must die first. Only death could wear thin her dark protections. But who would volunteer to be her first kill?

If not for the fact that he alone knew the true path to A'loa Glen,

Er'ril would not hesitate. He had lived more than his share of winters. But as guardian to the girl and the only one capable of unlocking the Blood Diary, he could not sacrifice himself. And worst of all, he had to ask someone else to take his place.

Kral spoke beside him. "Take my ax, Er'ril."

Meric had crossed to near the mountain man's shoulder and pushed the ax back toward Kral. "No, 'tis your tainted blade that can kill her. I'm too weak to fight this night, while you're still strong. The blood of my lost king must be preserved, even if it means my death."

Mogweed huddled in their shadows. "The elv'in speaks wisely," he muttered.

The she-demon cackled at them. "If you mice are done with your chattering, perhapsss I should make the choice for you."

Time had run out. Er'ril could think of no words to argue against Meric's statement. He glanced at the silver-haired elv'in. Meric's blue eyes were sharp with purpose. Er'ril regretted all the hard words the two had shared. It was clear the elv'in cared as much for Elena's safety as Er'ril did, even if it was for different reasons. Er'ril stared at the large bruise that marred Meric's left cheek, proof already of his brave heart. Now Meric stood ready to show the full depth of his resolve and spirit.

Er'ril found the elv'in's eyes staring into his own. No further words were needed. Er'ril nodded his head, the decision made.

Meric stepped forward—just as a howl shattered the night.

All eyes, including the she-demon's, swung to the left. From the wall of meadow grass, a huge wolf leapt into the clearing. It was Fardale. He crouched with a loud growl flowing from his throat, the hackles on his back raised high.

"It seemsss we have another volunteer," the she-demon said with a sharp smile.

"Get back," Mogweed screamed to his brother. "You can't harm it!"

Fardale glanced at his brother, his amber eyes glowing like twin moons in the night.

"Oh," Mogweed whispered and slunk farther into the shadows of the others.

Er'ril sensed that some silent communication had been shared between the two. "Did Fardale tell you something?" he whispered quickly.

Mogweed kept his eyes toward the she-demon and his growling brother. "He's freed the . . . There's another—"

Again the quiet night was shattered, this time by a rumbling bellow that came from the other side of the clearing. It was no wolf. It rose from the tall meadow grass and kept rising and rising. How could something so large have moved so quietly upon them, especially burdened?

It took a shocked moment for Er'ril to recognize Tol'chuk. The og're held a squirming dog over his head, its muzzle clamped shut in one of his large, clawed hands.

The she-demon snapped her wings and swung to face the new challenge. But before she could turn, Tol'chuk threw the dog at her. The squirming weapon cartwheeled across the clearing, limbs scrambling at the empty air.

Instinctively, the she-demon struck out at the flying object. Poison-tipped claws lashed out at the dog, knocking it aside. The hound crashed to the mud in a limp pile, its chest raked open, dead from the poison before it even struck the ground.

"My, my," the she-demon said, "you do seem to be running short on weapons. What next, a sheep? A goat?"

Using the distraction of the dog, Tol'chuk had by now stalked into the clearing.

Er'ril noticed that his companions had succeeded in surrounding the she-demon. But of what use was that? She still had her dark magicks. Meric glanced once at Er'ril, then swung back toward the winged beast and walked toward it.

Er'ril's heart ached, but he knew there was no other choice.

Mogweed suddenly snatched at Meric's billowing white shirt and tugged the elv'in to a stop.

"Leave him—" Er'ril began to say.

"The . . . the dog!" Mogweed stuttered in a faint whisper. "It's dead."

"So?"

Mogweed's voice snapped louder. "The monster killed it. Didn't she?"

Er'ril's eyes grew wide with understanding.

The shape-shifter's words seemed to have reached the she-demon, too. Her eyes glanced to the dead hound near her clawed feet. The fanged smile faded on her face as she realized the truth. She *had* killed. She had taken the life of her prey. Her magicks were now vulnerable.

Her eyes met Er'ril's for just a heartbeat. Er'ril grinned, but his lips were hard. "Do this for Nee'lahn," he hissed at the others. "Take her down."

Kral whopped in triumph and led the charge toward the encircled she-demon. She tried to take flight and escape, but Tol'chuk dragged her by a wing back to the mud and grass. The others swamped her, Kral's ax a blur of revenge. Er'ril turned his back on the fight. He was no longer needed here. Elena, though, had been left with Vira'ni too long.

Behind him, he heard a screech that shivered the small hairs on his arms. It was a death cry.

Without glancing back, Er'ril ran from the she-demon's dying screams. He felt no satisfaction, not while Elena was still in danger. With his iron fingers clenched into a fist, he raced over the small rise that separated him from the main encampment. He prayed he wasn't too late.

He crested the rise to peer into the circle of tents of the main camp. Among the sputtering fires, a sea of blackness surged and flowed across the trampled soil. Scorpions! Their glossy armor reflected the firelight in poisonous glints.

But this was not the horror that caught Er'ril's breath in his throat. In the center of this poisonous sea, Elena struggled. Vira'ni held the girl tight as the scorpions descended in a swarm upon the pair.

"Elena!" he called out to her.

ELENA HEARD HER NAME CALLED, BUT KNOWING HER PLAN TO DEAL WITH Vira'ni had failed, she stayed silent. She had squandered her magick in a futile attempt to defeat the demoness. At least Er'ril was free, she thought as she stared into the baleful yellow fire in Vira'ni's eyes. Hopefully, the others were safe, too. If nothing else, she could die knowing she had bought them their freedom.

Vira'ni yanked on Elena's arm and pulled her closer. "I hear a little bird calling your name."

Elena ignored her words, too. Her eyes were on the dying war of energies waging within the woman's breast. The silver flame of elemental power had waned back to a weak flicker. Black energies whirled around this small pyre, still drawing licks of substance from the flame.

It was a mesmerizing dance of power.

It's not too late! The last lucid words of the woman mocked Elena. How? How was it not too late?

The magick churned and wheeled around the tiny spark of flame.

Then Elena suddenly knew.

As scorpions skittered up her boots, she pressed her palm more firmly against Vira'ni's chest, as if trying to keep the demoness at bay. *If only . . . if only it isn't too late.*

Elena thrust once more into the woman's chest with the last dregs of her wit'chfire. Again fingers of power wound toward the tiny elemental flame, dodging spats of black energies. As she worked her magick, the final streams of her energies became an outstretched hand. Reaching, she closed her wit'chfire upon the small bit of elemental magick—and squeezed.

Like pinching out a candle's flame, her magicks snuffed the small brightness from Vira'ni's chest, extinguishing the woman's elemental fire.

In the void, the black energies collapsed around Vira'ni's heart, swallowing the last traces of Elena's magicks. With her power spent, her special vision dimmed and disappeared. She could no longer see the flows of magicks.

Elena removed her hand from Vira'ni's chest. Her fingers were so cold—and so pale. Not even a trace of the Rose remained.

Suddenly a hand grabbed her wrist.

Elena jumped and tried to pull away, but the grip was iron. She stared up at Vira'ni's wild eyes. The demoness grinned and wrenched at her arm.

Elena gasped from the pain, too stunned to fight. "Now quit squirming. You—" Vira'ni's face suddenly took on a vaguely confused expression, as if she had forgotten what she had been about to say.

The grip on Elena's wrist spasmed tighter for a heartbeat, squeezing a cry from Elena. Then the hold on her wrist relaxed, and Vira'ni's hand fell away.

Free, Elena stumbled backward. Scorpions crackled under her

heels as she crushed them. She stamped others from her boots. The scorpions seemed as stunned and confused as Vira'ni. Some were even stinging each other, while others stood as still as their mistress.

Vira'ni suddenly shuddered, as if shaking cobwebs from her naked body. As she trembled, the white streak in her hair faded and darkened to match her other black locks. For a moment, Elena thought she saw a dark mist seep from the woman's skin and fade out into the night.

A winged scorpion landed on Elena's arm, stinger raised. Elena cringed and started to swat at it when the poisonous creature collapsed and dissolved into a glistening black clump on her arm. It was clotted blood. Elena shook it off in disgust.

Around Elena's boots, the other scorpions also collapsed into bloody piles that steamed into the chill night. Like the ripples from a pebble dropped into a pond, the dissolution of the scorpion army spread outward from the two women until the poisonous creatures were gone.

The Horde lay dead.

Vira'ni moaned, drawing Elena's attention, though the girl stood unmoving, still wary of the naked woman.

Vira'ni swooned and fell to her knees in the mud and blood. Her ashen face had paled even further, as if her very substance had left her body. She raised her face toward Elena. The mad gleam was gone. "Is it . . . is it over?" she asked, tears flowing down her cheeks.

Suddenly from behind, someone grabbed Elena's shoulder and pulled her away from the kneeling woman. Her heart leapt to her throat until she realized it was only Er'ril. The plainsman stepped between Elena and Vira'ni.

"Get back!" he snapped at Elena. The iron ward floated in the air before Er'ril, its cold fingers open and reaching for Vira'ni's throat.

"No," Elena said, tugging at his real arm. "Leave her be. She's no danger now. The dark magicks have fled her."

"How?" he asked with narrowed eyes. His shoulders were still tight with fury.

"She was an elemental. The Dark Lord somehow bound his black energies to her land magick. Once that was gone, the foul energies had no hook in her and were cast out."

Er'ril stayed silent, but he lowered his iron fist.

"It's over," Elena said softly.

Er'ril realized the girl was right. "Vira'ni?" he asked tentatively, his voice softening as his anger fled him.

She raised her face toward his, and a mixture of pain and loss glowed in her eyes. Then her countenance settled into simple sorrow. As he watched, her skin paled and her flesh seemed to shrink to her bones. She was dying.

He stepped toward her. Behind him, Elena began to protest, believing he meant to attack her. He waved her back and knelt beside Vira'ni. After a moment's hesitation, he reached and took the woman in his one arm. At his touch, she collapsed like a teetering stack of blocks in his embrace, too weak to hold herself upright. He gently lowered her to his lap and fingered stray black hairs from her face; he had always hated when hair got in her eyes.

As he stared at her, his heart remembered the face he had once kissed and the woman he had once loved.

From where she lay, Vira'ni stared back at him. "I'm so . . . so sorry, Er'ril." Tears glistened in the firelight on her cheeks. "I . . . What I did . . ."

The plainsman reached out and touched a finger to her lips. "Hush . . . hush, it wasn't you."

Vira'ni trembled under his touch, too weak now even to speak. She reached for his hand, her fingers fluttering like a weak bird, but she was too feeble; her hand fell away.

Er'ril knew her death was near. He wiped the tears from her cheek and took her hand in his own, entwining their fingers. He bent down close to her. He would not abandon her again, not now.

Her eyes were barely open. He pressed his cheek against hers and whispered in her ear. "I'm the one who is sorry, Vira'ni. I should never have left you."

She struggled to speak, her breath catching in her dying throat. "I . . . I loved you."

He leaned closer and gently kissed her on the lips. He felt her relax under him. "And I loved you," he whispered as he lifted his lips from hers, but she was already gone. He held her cold hand for several long breaths, his cheeks damp, his head bowed.

Beside him, his iron fist fell to the mud, once again just a motionless sculpted fist. He ignored the loss of his phantom arm, praying Vira'ni had heard his final words.

For truly, he *had* loved her.

TWO MORNINGS LATER, ELENA STOOD BY NEE'LAHN'S GRAVE AT THE EDGE of the rimwood forest. In the shadow of the dead trees, they had buried their companion. The spiders were long gone from the wood, destroyed like the scorpions when the Dark Lord's magicks fled.

Elena knelt by the grave. The fresh-turned soil was like a blemish at the meadow's edge. The team was due to head out for the plains today, but Elena wanted to do one last thing before she left.

She stared at the small stone at the grave's head. It pained Elena to look upon it: Once again, someone's life had been spent to help her on her journey. It seemed the path she forged would always be marked with blood and tears. Sniffing back a sob, she gently scooped a small hole in the loose soil of the grave.

Kneeling back, she reached and removed a small acorn—the seed Mogweed had given her—from her breast pocket. She placed it in the shallow hole and carefully layered soil over it. "If I can't bring back your forest home, Nee'lahn," she whispered, "let me at least bring back this one tree."

Elena stood up, wiping the dirt on her gray trousers. "Let life come from death. Let this be the true marker of your final resting place."

Wiping away her tears, she turned her back on the grave and looked out past the rolling meadows toward the rising sun.

It was time.

The others were waiting for her. The wagon was already loaded and hitched. They had scavenged the hunters' horses to replace those of their own that had been killed. The only bright moment of the past two days was when Kral had gone to fetch Rorshaf and found Mist grazing in the meadow with him as if nothing had happened. Elena had been overjoyed to see the small gray mare again and had hugged Mist tightly as the horse struggled to get to the grain bucket.

Otherwise, the past two days had involved too much grave digging and hurried activity. The bodies of the hunters had to be buried, along with Vira'ni and the she-demon she had birthed. Er'ril would let no one else touch Vira'ni's body. He had nestled her gently in the grave, and then, as if tucking in a child after a nightmare, he had leaned and placed a lingering kiss on her forehead. Only Elena saw the plainsman's tears as he filled the grave with cold dirt.

Amidst all the sorrow, the team united in support of each other, forging bonds where none had existed before. Even Mogweed was well congratulated for his sharp wits in helping defeat the winged beast. He strutted around the camp, his chest swelled with pride. Meric, who especially held the shape-shifter in high regard, even offered his filly to Mogweed.

Only Er'ril seemed subdued and withdrawn from the others. He had buried Vira'ni himself and since then had had little to do with preparations for their departure, only giving a curt command now and then.

Elena sighed. The rolling meadows held too much sorrow for all of them. The sooner they left, the better.

Still, she had one last chore to do. Gazing at the meadows aglow in the rosy light of dawn, she raised her right arm high and bathed her pale hand in the morning sunlight. She filled her heart with longing and hope and willed the gift to come to her. In response, her hand vanished in a blaze of brilliance.

Taking a deep breath and girding herself, she lowered her arm. Her right hand returned again to her wrist, her skin now afire with whorls of red magicks.

Elena stepped away from Nee'lahn's grave—the first step, she sensed, on the long road ahead, a road that would eventually lead her to the Gul'gothal lord himself. She clenched her red fist into a hard knot and marched toward the dawn. She would make the Black Heart pay for all the blood, the sorrow, and the tears.

Magick crackled furiously around her fist as she crossed the rose-tinged meadows.

"I'm coming," she spoke to the rising sun and the darkness that lay beyond it. "And nothing will stop me."

Book Two

SEAS AND MISTS

11

Joach lived as a prisoner in his own head.

As his body stood in the Great Kitchen of the sprawling Edifice, awaiting his master's supper, Joach stared out of two holes in a skull that felt like a hollowed-out pumpkin. He watched his arms move and his legs shamble, while inside his head he screamed for someone to help him. But his lips remained slack with a continual rope of drool hanging to his chin. He could feel the saliva slobbering from his mouth but could not get his hands to move and wipe it away.

"Eh, you! Boy!" jeered the greasy-haired kitchen urchin, poking Joach in the shoulder with a dirty spoon. "Did your mum drop you on your head, or what? Git away from me before you slobber in the soup kettle."

Shoved by the spoon, Joach's legs stumbled back a step.

"Leave 'im be, Brunt," the cook said from a neighboring hearth. He was a wide-bellied man, like most cooks, wearing a stained apron that covered him from neck to toe, sashed at the waist. His cheeks glowed ruddy from the heat of the kitchen's many hearths. "You know he ain't right in the head, so quit pestering 'im."

"I heard he was left in the woods by his parents for the wolves to finish off." Brunt made a snapping motion toward Joach.

"M-m-master wants m-meal," Joach heard himself stutter with a slurred tongue. That was the extent of his conversation. Just enough words to let others in the Edifice know his ordered duty. The kitchen help ignored his garbled words. He might as well have been another spoon or pot.

"Naw, naw," the cook said. "He was kicked in the head by a horse and everyone thought 'im dead. Were all set to bury 'im, they were! Then that old crippled brother, he came along and plucked 'im up. Took 'im here. Rescued the drooling dolt. Now that's kindness!" The cook spat into a skillet to test its heat before continuing. "Speaking of kindness and dolts, if you want to keep working in my kitchens, you'd better get back to stirring that stew, or it'll burn!"

Brunt lowered his spoon to the fish stew with a grumble and continued to stir. "Still, that kid gives me the woollies. He just stares at you with his nose dripping. It's downright sickening."

Even if he had been able to control his lips, Joach would not have argued with the boy. Ever since he had been stolen from the cobbled streets of Winterfell by the darkmage named Greshym, Joach had been under the demon's spell, a thrall to the ancient one's commands. While he still lived in his head, aware and feeling all, he was unable to stop his body from obeying the murderer of his parents.

Unable to speak freely, he could not even warn anyone who lived within the walls of the Edifice of the snake that lived among them. Greshym posed as a white-robed brother of the Order, but in truth was a creature of the Dark Lord.

A platter of meats, cheeses, and a bowl of steaming fish stew was shoved toward his chest. Joach's arms caught the handles of the wood platter. He had been ordered to fetch supper, and as always, his body obeyed. In his head, he dreamed of poisoning the meal but knew it impossible.

"Be off with you, you slack-jawed oaf!" Brunt said with a sneer. "Get outta my kitchen!"

Joach turned to go, his body ever obedient. Behind him, he heard the cook scold his boy. "Your kitchen, Brunt? Since when is this *your* kitchen?"

Behind him, he heard a slap and a yelp from Brunt, but Joach's legs were already carrying him out of the kitchen and down the hall.

As he shambled through the twisting corridors and stairways of the Edifice, winding his way back to his master's chamber, he stared at the laden platter and put aside all thoughts of poisoning the meal. The fish broth smelled of garlic and butter, and the meats and cheeses were cut thick and generous. Even the loaf of cold bread seemed a miracle of flavor.

Pangs of hunger wailed in his belly, but unless his body was given the order to eat by the darkmage, Joach could do nothing to fill his empty stomach. Over the many moons since he was stolen from his sister's side, his body had wasted into a scarecrow. Often whole days would pass before the darkmage would remember to tell his servant to eat—and lately, those days of hunger were becoming even more frequent.

Joach was now mostly forgotten by his master and, like a neglected dog, he wasted away, awaiting his master's next word.

As he shambled past a mirror in a hall, he caught a glimpse of his reflection. His face, formerly sunburned from his work in the orchards, had paled to a slug's complexion, and his flesh had shrunken on bone. His cheekbones poked from under bruised eyes. His red hair, overgrown past his shoulders now, hung tangled and matted. And his green eyes stared back at him, dull and glazed.

He was the walking dead.

No wonder the kitchen urchin had wanted him out of his sight. Joach himself was relieved when his body moved past the mirror and the image was gone.

For the past moon, Joach had given up the fight against his spell-cast enslavement, resigned to his fate. Occasionally he would still scream in his bone prison, but no one ever heard. Now death seemed the only real possibility of escape. He pulled back deeper into his skull and curled up on himself. Starvation would eventually claim his body; then he would be free.

Despondent, he ignored his body as it struggled the platter into his master's cell. The room was barren of any significant trappings or decorations. Only two thin beds, an ancient wardrobe, and a worm-worn desk occupied the room. A threadbare rug covered the floor, but it did a poor job of keeping the cold of the stones from one's feet. Though a small hearth continually glowed with embers, its feeble heat did little to dispel the chill that always hung in the air. It was as if the room itself knew the evil it contained and kept warmth and cheer from its occupants.

In addition to the ever-present chill, the room was also always dim. Besides the single oil lamp on the desk, the only other illumination came from a small-slitted window that overlooked one of the many tiny courtyards that pocked the great structure. Somewhere beyond the walls of the Edifice sprawled the half-sunken city of A'loa Glen—and beyond that only the sea. Since arriving, Joach had seen neither sea nor city, nothing but the halls and chambers of the sprawling Edifice huddled in the center of the once-mighty city. Like a second prison, it held his body as surely as his skull held his spirit.

"Put that platter on the desk!" Greshym ordered. The darkmage was already wearing his cowled white robe. That meant the demon was going somewhere. He never wore the robes when alone. The fabric seemed to irritate the darkmage as much as its pure white color mocked his black heart. He shook the sleeve of his right arm lower to hide the stumped wrist, then pulled the hood over his bald head with his good hand. He stared at Joach with those milky globes of the near-blind.

Even though Joach had no control over his body, his flesh still crawled as those eyes settled on him. It was as if his body, too, knew the menace that lay like poison behind those milky globes.

"Come," Greshym ordered. "I've been summoned."

Joach's legs stepped aside to let the darkmage pass, and in the process, he almost dumped the fish stew on the mage's pristine robe.

"Put that cursed platter down, you fool!" Greshym snapped as he swept through the doorway. "Do I have to tell you everything?"

Inwardly, a tiny smile formed in Joach's mind. Maybe there was a little rebellion in his body yet. He set the tray down and followed the darkmage back out to the hallways once again.

Over the moons of his enslavement, Joach had learned more about his prison than any of its denizens suspected. Chambermaids, servants, and even other brothers of the Order spoke freely around Joach, thinking him a brain-addled fool who would not repeat their words. So truths were spoken in his presence that would otherwise be kept silent.

He had learned that the Brotherhood was a group of scholars and other men of skill who had banded together in secret to preserve A'loa Glen and the traces of ancient magicks still contained within the sunken city. They kept A'loa Glen cloaked and the paths to the city warded against trespassers. Besides the Brotherhood, only their servants and a handful of others roamed what was left of the ancient city. A'loa Glen was lost to the world, a city of myth, kept hidden from the eye of the Gul'gothal lord by both time and magick—*or so the Brotherhood supposed*.

Only Joach seemed to know about the darkmage who masqueraded as one of their own. But what was this murderer's purpose here in a half-deserted city?

Joach followed the bent back of the crippled old mage. After a few twists and turns, he could guess their destination—the westernmost tower, named the Praetor's Spear after its sole occupant.

During his slack-jawed eavesdropping, Joach had also learned what the others in the Edifice thought of the solitary figure who lived alone in the western tower. Though the Praetor led the Brotherhood, he was seldom seen and little was known of his past. His true name had long been wiped away, as was tradition for this post. Some said the Praetor had lived for over five hundred winters, while others said it was just different men who bore the Praetor's name, succeeding one after the other.

So who truly was the man in the tower? And what business did the darkmage have with the leader of the Brotherhood?

Greshym had visited the Praetor in his tower four times since Joach had arrived at A'loa Glen, but Joach had learned nothing of the mysterious leader. Each time, Joach had been left standing by the stairs that led up to the distant room as Greshym continued on to his rendezvous. He was never allowed to accompany the old man.

Even his body seemed to know this routine. Joach's legs began to slow when the darkmage finally wound through the dusty corridors and reached the lower stair of the Praetor's Spear. Joach was ready to stop, anticipating the signal to halt—but it never came.

Greshym started up the spiraling stair.

Without the order to stop, Joach's body had no choice but to follow. That had been his master's last command.

He climbed after the darkmage. The stairs seemed endless, curving ever upward. They passed an occasional slitted window, and Joach caught glimpses of the ruined city below. Toppled towers lay strewn in crumbled piles of stone and moss; lakes of brackish brine dotted the landscape where the sea bubbled up from below. In some of these dark green lakes, the peaks of ancient buildings protruded like steep islands. And sea mists drifted languidly through the remnants of the once-proud city, ghosts of those that once roamed its streets and hawked wares from its open doorways. While above all, gulls circled the ruins in slow spirals, like foothill vultures eying a dying calf.

Yet the view's most profound effect came from something unseen, something felt in the bones—an aching melancholy for all the beauty and wonder lost forever. Glimpses of the ancient majesty of the city could still be seen in the occasional sparks from windows of stained crystal set like jewels among the ruins or in the towering marble sculptures, now tilted or marred with damage, of honored men and women whose faces spoke of grander times and higher purposes. Though the city was dead, it still spoke tales of a glorious empire, of a peaceful era. It spoke of Alasea before the Gul'gotha raped her lands.

If Joach could cry, he would as he looked upon his land's ancient past. Here sprawled a small reflection of Alasea as a whole: a land of beauty, broken and dying.

Joach's body continued its climb after its master. They passed a few stationed guards, but their eyes seemed blind to the crippled man and the doltish boy. Joach recognized the glaze in their eyes as he passed. He had seen it in his own eyes in the hall mirror: the walking dead.

A chill crept into Joach's skull. Did Greshym's grip reach so far? Or were there other darkmages masquerading in white?

At the top of the stairs, a huge oaken door blocked the way farther. Two dull-eyed guards stood with spears to either side. Greshym ignored them and strode toward the door, his staff thumping loudly, making no attempt at stealth.

Joach followed.

The heavy door swung open on silent hinges even before Greshym reached its ornate handles. No hand opened this door. Beyond the threshold, Joach could sense a palpable evil. Like a thick fog, it flowed out from the open doorway.

Though he did not want to enter the chamber beyond, he could not balk at entering. His body continued its shambling pace after the darkmage. Joach cowered deeper into his skull, trying his best to hide.

As he entered the well-lit tower chamber, he was surprised at how warm and inviting the room appeared. Three large hearths glowed cheerily with licking flames. Fanciful tapestries hid the stone walls of the tower, reflecting bright colors in the firelight, while couches and thick-stuffed chairs of expensive red silk dotted the heavy rugs. Huge windows with insets of stained crystal showed the blue sky, and below one of these windows, sunlight shone brightly on a huge polished table that held a crystal-and-marble model of A'loa Glen as it had stood before its fall—a thousand jeweled spires, with walkways that passed from tower to tower through cloud, fountains, and parks.

Joach had to pull his attention away. It hurt too much to look at its pristine beauty. So much lost.

His gaze settled on the lone occupant of the room. He stood tall by the western window, staring out at the sunken city, his broad back to them. He wore a long white cassock, its cowl thrown back casually.

Greshym cleared his throat.

The man, who could only be the Praetor, swung to face them. Joach was surprised at how young the man was. He had expected the leader of the Brotherhood to be a gray-haired elder, not this black-haired young man. Gray eyes studied the darkmage from a hawkish ruddy face. Joach recognized the countenance of a Standi plainsman. Traders from the neighboring plains had often visited Winterfell selling bundled leaves of tobacco or wagon loads of barreled spices. It was so odd to see such a familiar reminder of home so far afield.

Those gray eyes shifted from Greshym to settle for a moment on his own. Joach tumbled backward in his skull. What he saw in those eyes was nothing of home: it was maggots and clotted blood. It was black fires that consumed the flesh of those you loved. It was evil. Here stood the source of foulness that Joach had sensed in the room. It flowed from those eyes, black wellsprings of corruption.

Thankfully, those eyes left his own after only a heartbeat.

"Why did you bring the boy?" the figure asked, his clipped Standish accent clear in his words.

Greshym glanced at Joach as if surprised to see the boy standing in his shadow. He sniffed derisively and turned back to the tall man. "I simply forgot. He's been dragging behind me for so long that I don't even see him anymore."

"It's not wise to be forgetful here. The Brotherhood grows suspicious."

Greshym waved this statement away with a twist of his staff. "The Brotherhood is made up of fools. It always has been. Let them have their rumors; they'll never suspect the truth. Now what news of our wit'ch?"

The Praetor's eyes twitched at Joach, then just as quickly away. "She moves once again," he said coldly. "She has fled the Teeth, escaped the hills, and lost herself among the peoples of the wide plains."

"How? I thought the Dark Lord had laced all the trails leaving the thawing mountains with legions of his ill'guard. What happened?"

"She slipped past one imbued with the Horde, killing her."

"Curse that damned child!"

"You know the wit'ch's resourcefulness at surviving, Greshym. Or have you forgotten Winterfell? Besides, she is guarded well by my brother."

Greshym stamped his staff on the rug with a muffled thud. "Speaking of your brother," he said, irritation thick in his voice, "how is it that Er'ril still lives? You never did explain that. He has no magick."

The Praetor's eyes grew hooded, and his face darkened. "Something the Black Heart hadn't anticipated. The Blood Diary has claimed Er'ril as its own. It protects him against the ravages of time."

Sighing loudly, Greshym continued. "And what of the Diary, Shorkan? Have you discovered a way to unlock the cursed tome?"

A slight shake of the Praetor's head answered this question. "Not without Er'ril. He is the key."

During his long imprisonment, Joach had learned to read the darkmage's moods. These last words seemed to wound Greshym. "So there's no way to get to the book," he mumbled sourly.

A trace of anger entered the Praetor's words. "What is this concern about the book? We don't need it in our hands. As long as it resides here in A'loa Glen, locked or not, it will serve its purpose in luring the wit'ch here. If she survives the traps set by our lord, she will fight and bleed her way across the lands just to put herself in our hands. Our lord's plan is wise. We simply wait."

Greshym seemed hardly to have heard the words; his voice was vague and distracted. "Still, if I could get to the book . . ."

The Praetor leaned closer to the darkmage. "What? What could you do?" Joach could almost feel the menace in the man like the sun's heat on his skin. Greshym backed a step, bumping Joach.

"Then I . . . then I could destroy it and eliminate the risk of its ever falling into the claws of the wit'ch. It's dangerous letting the wit'ch get so close to the book." Greshym cleared his throat and shook some semblance of spine back into his pose. "That's all I meant."

Joach knew these last words were a lie. And the Praetor seemed to sense it, too. He walked around the darkmage, eying him up and down suspiciously. Greshym did not flinch from his scrutiny.

Finally, the Praetor pulled his cowl back over his head dismissively and turned away. "Go now. Listen and study. We must be ready for her."

Greshym began to swing around, but the tall man spoke again. "And take better care of your servant. He reeks like rotting fish."

Joach would have flinched and blushed at these words, but instead his body continued to stand, slack and dumb, beside the darkmage.

"Why do you keep the boy anyway?" he continued. "Be rid of him."

Greshym scowled. "I think not. Like the Blood Diary, the boy is a card whose value is yet unknown in this game. I'll keep him until our hand is fully played."

The Praetor walked to the window and waved them away. "Then at least clean him up."

Greshym bowed his head slightly and turned on a heel. Leaning on his staff, the old mage limped toward the large ironbound oaken door. "Follow me," he snapped at Joach.

The boy's legs obeyed, and Joach shambled in the darkmage's wake.

In his head, though, Joach reviewed their words. He knew whom the two had been speaking about. The wit'ch had to be his sister Elena.

He sobbed quietly in his empty skull. His sister yet lived! It had been so many moons since he had heard mention of her. He had not known if she had died in Winterfell or what had become of her. Now he knew! Elena was free.

But as much as this relieved him, a greater fear gripped his heart. Elena was coming here! She would be captured or killed. He remembered his promise to his father before he and Elena had fled their burning home: to protect his younger sister. And he meant to keep that promise! But how could he? He couldn't even keep from fouling himself.

His body shambled after its master, but in his head, he railed against the chains that bound him. He must find a way out of this imprisonment and stop his sister from coming here.

Yet, regardless of his passion, his legs still kept following the darkmage's footsteps, and drool once again rolled from his cracked lips and dripped from his chin.

How? Joach cried in his head. *How am I to break free?* Where was the door out of one's own skull?

GRESHYM LIMPED BACK THROUGH THE CORRIDORS THAT LED TO HIS room. His mind seethed with black thoughts. How dare Shorkan order him about like some low servant! He had once been the man's teacher! Of course that was long ago, and they had been different men—whole men, before the forging of the Blood Diary had split their spirits.

Now Greshym hardly recognized his former student. Had he himself changed as much? He didn't think so. After imbuing half his spirit in the book's forging, he was still the same man, only now he was able to think more clearly, able to see his heart's desires more keenly. He now had no nagging doubts about facing his innermost lusts. Once, guilt and regret had tied his hands, and sorrow and pain had guided his acts. Now he walked free, unfettered by constricting emotions, able to loose his baser desires and pursue his lusts with all his energies. He now dabbled freely in the blackest arts just to see what would happen, his ears deaf to screams and pleas for mercy. The forging of the book had opened his spirit to all its secret demons, allowing him to rejoice in them without shame, to pursue them without guilt, finally to live his life true. The book had freed him.

He cursed under his breath as he struggled down the stair. So why had he lied to Shorkan about his real reason for his interest in the Diary's destruction? It was not, as he had explained, to keep the wit'ch from gaining it. No, he wanted the book destroyed for his own selfish reason.

He spat on the dusty floor. He had lied because Shorkan would never understand. The fool seemed content with his wounded spirit. And why shouldn't he be content? Shorkan had everything. Not only did he have boundless power and the freedom of an unlocked heart, but he also had something Greshym did not: *youth*.

Shorkan never aged. He appeared the same black-haired young man as when the book was forged, still vital with youthful energy. The passing of winters had left him untouched. Whereas, due to some trick in the magicks, Greshym's body had continued to age. His joints grew hoary with pain, his eyes bloomed with cataracts, and his hair fell from his wrinkling skin.

Whenever Greshym saw Shorkan standing tall and handsome in his tower room, his heart burned with the injustice. This disparity wore on him as his body declined. Like water dripping on rock, it dug a well of discontent deeper and deeper into his spirit.

He had been treated most foully and was determined to reverse this injustice. Over the centuries, he had studied the black arts in secret—reading texts bound in runes, practicing on small animals and children—until at long last he had come upon a method to regain his youth. It could work, but it *first* required freeing his spirit's other half—and to do that, the book must be destroyed!

To this end, he would let nothing stand in his way. He cared naught for his allegiances to the Dark Lord, nor for his promises to Shorkan. His unfettered heart felt no compulsion to obey these two who thought themselves his masters. The book had freed him to act on his heart's desires, and in this matter, too, he would do as his spirit willed.

Greshym continued through the halls of the sprawling Edifice, striking the oak of his staff hard on the stone.

Let all who stood in his way burn!

He stopped at the crossing of two halls and leaned heavily on his staff as he glanced down each hall. As he stood, breathing harshly through clenched teeth, his shoulder was bumped from behind, almost knocking him down. Twisting around, he swung on his assailant.

It was only the cursed boy. He snapped his staff forward and struck the boy across the ribs. "Keep back from me," he hissed.

Unfazed, the boy did not even blink, just stumbled a step away then stood staring at him with that omnipresent glaze in his eyes.

Greshym swung back to study the hallways. The boy was like a rash on his skin: always there, a constant irritation. He shook his head, dismissing the irritation, and considered the choice of halls. His hips ached, and the thought of his soft bed tempted him back to his cell, but if he was ever to regain strength and vigor in his limbs, now was not the time to listen to complaining joints.

With the wit'ch under way, he must delay no further. Who knew how long before she came knocking on the door to the Edifice? If he was to succeed, he had to begin now. Decided, he set off down the hallway to the right.

"Follow," he called to the boy, "but keep one pace away from me!"

The hall led away from his room and toward the Grand Courtyard. Greshym scowled at the thought of crossing the decaying park contained within the walls of the courtyard. While he reveled in its rotted wood and brine-choked roots, its occasional cluster of thriving green leaves or single bright blossom always reminded him of its former grandeur. These shards of past glories galled him and sickened his belly with old memories. Yet this was not the real reason he detested the Grand Courtyard. In truth, a small part of him feared the place. Traces of Chyric magick, sustained and preserved over the centuries, still lay like pools of poison among the gardens.

The Grand Courtyard, nestled in the center of the Edifice, had been the nexus of Chyric power for the entire city. It was the root from which all of A'loa Glen grew. Though the city itself was now long dead, echoes of its magicks still whispered along its garden paths.

Greshym pulled his shoulders tighter together. He hated the place. Yet, this day, he had no choice but to walk its paths. The only way to the catacombs was through the courtyard.

He continued down the long hall with the boy in tow. Footsore, his ankles throbbing, his heart beating like a scared rabbit in his chest, he finally reached the gilt-and-glass doors that led to the courtyard.

The two doors towered twice the height of a man and contained an inlay of stained glass and crystal that formed a pair of the entwining branches of a rose bush, its thorns glistening in the afternoon sunlight. The roses themselves were crafted from ruby and heartstone—the twin symbols of the Order. Whole townships could be bought for the price of one of those roses.

Flanking the doors, two guards bearing long swords stood to either side of the threshold. One stepped forward and swung open the door for the white-robed brother.

Nothing was denied a brother of the Order.

Greshym bowed his head in thanks and passed through the portal into sunlight. The boy followed in his usual shambling gait. Squinting, he looked into the Grand Courtyard and remembered another reason he hated the place. Speckled like white mold on an old corpse, others of his white-robed brethren moved through the relic of a garden. He had forgotten how crowded the courtyard could be, especially when the sea mists lifted and the sunlight shone brightly.

He suppressed a groan and stepped farther within the garden.

"Brother Greshym?" A voice rose to his left. He heard the scrape of loose rock as someone stood up near the edge of one of the graveled paths. "How delightful to see you up and about! The sun has been drawing out everyone today."

Greshym turned toward the speaker, but he kept the edge of his cowl tilted down to partially hide his face. How had the cursed fool recognized him? Then he remembered the boy. Of course, everyone knew his doltish servant. Even now he saw the man glance pitifully at the spell-cast boy.

"Why, Brother Treet," Greshym answered, attempting to squeeze the irritation out of his voice. "A truly handsome day it is. How could I resist? My old bones were craving warmth and dragged me down here."

The pudgy man, his cowl thrown open to the sunshine, smiled. Hair the color of dried mud lay sparse on his exposed pate, and his eyes were too far apart. He looked like a surprised cow, Greshym thought.

Suddenly the balding man's eyes widened. "Oh! Then you haven't heard!"

Greshym inwardly groaned. Gossip ran like wild dogs through the halls of the Edifice, thrashing all in its path. He did not have time for this nonsense and pretended not to hear the man's words. At his age it was easy feigning deafness. "I . . . I should be going before my ol' legs give out on me. This winter's damp still has a grip on my creaking knees." He leaned heavily on his staff in emphasis.

"Why then, a little walk in the gardens is just what you need," Brother Treet said consolingly. "I'll come with you."

"How kind, but there's no need. I have my boy here." He began to turn away.

"Nonsense. I must take you to see the koa'kona tree. You can't miss this."

Greshym almost cringed at his words. "I don't have time—"

"Ah, then you truly *haven't* heard, have you?" The glee of someone with a secret to reveal was rich in Brother Treet's voice. "Come. Come see. It's wondrous. An omen of good fortune."

As much as Greshym balked at stepping within a stone's throw of the monstrous dead tree in the center of the gardens, Brother Treet's excitement piqued his curiosity. What was the daft man spewing about? "What is this talk of good omens?"

"I won't ruin the surprise. You must see for yourself." Brother Treet led the way down a gravel path, his sandals crunching loudly in the quiet garden.

Greshym followed the pudgy man. Hiding his scowl, he waved the boy to stay near his heels. Of all the traces of ancient Chyric magicks, the koa'kona tree at the garden's heart was the most potent. Its limbs had once stretched far into the sky, higher than any of the city's spires. Before dying, its trunk had grown so thick that ten men with linked arms could not circle its girth. The mighty tree had once shaded the entire garden under its green-and-silver leaves, and at night, its purple blossoms would open and begin glowing like a thousand sapphire stars.

To the people of A'loa Glen, the tree had been the living heart of the city.

Yet, as majestic as the tree appeared, it was nothing compared to its roots, poking like massive gnarled knees near its base. The roots dug deep into the island and spread like a web under the city. To those in power, here lay the *true* heart of the city. The old mages of A'loa Glen would concentrate their magick into the tree's roots, creating a living nexus of energy. Then the roots' thousand branches, crisscrossing and winding under the city, would spread the magick throughout A'loa Glen, sustaining its spell-cast spires and other impossible wonders.

But that was long ago.

As he marched after his fellow brother, Greshym stared up at the long-dead tree and felt a twinge of sympathy. Time had been no kinder to the tree than to Greshym. After the fall of A'loa Glen, the tree had succumbed to the ravages of passing winters and the loss of sustaining magick. Now the tree was a skeleton of tiered branches, most of its limbs long rotted and fallen to decay. Occasionally though, like a dying man opening his eyes to peek one last time at the world, a few leaves would grow in small clumps on one branch or another. But it had been ages since even that had occurred.

The tree was now just a lifeless monument.

But dead or not, Greshym still shied from its presence. Whispers of ancient magicks seemed drawn to the tree, hanging about its branches like moss. Though these traces of ancient magicks were weak, there was still danger. It was an intricate weaving of black magicks that kept death from Greshym's heart, a fine web of power and blood, and even a passing drift of Chyric magick could unravel or weaken a part of the complex black spell that sustained him.

So Greshym had learned to walk with care among the decaying gardens of the Grand Courtyard, especially near the koa'kona tree. But this day, he did not have much choice. Though his mission to the catacombs required traveling the edges of the courtyard, it was curiosity that drew him toward its heart. He knew better than to risk such a path, but when his blood developed a desire, Greshym was not easily dissuaded. So he followed Brother Treet deeper and deeper into the gardens, passing other brethren along the way.

Greshym noted that as he neared the tree the number of white-robed brothers who gathered there grew, becoming a solemn pilgrimage to the tree. Some brothers led others, heads bowed in whispers, while others walked singly, eyes raised toward the barren branches. What was luring such numbers of his studious brethren?

With each labored step, his curiosity grew. Why hadn't he heard of any of this? Anger became mixed with curiosity. He stared at the sheer number of white robes descending on the tree. Why had he heard nothing?

As if reading his thoughts, Brother Treet answered. "It just appeared this morning. But news is traveling fast."

"What?" Greshym snapped, no longer capable of feigning an affable good nature.

Brother Treet glanced toward him at his sharp retort.

Greshym collected himself and waved the man on. "I'm sorry, Brother Treet. It's my old joints complaining and being testy. I'm afraid this trip may not have been a good idea."

His words seemed to console his guide. "No worries, Brother. We're here." Treet turned forward and gently pushed the gathered men aside. "Make room," he scolded. "Let an older brother through."

The sea of robes parted. Brother Treet stepped aside to allow Greshym to pass forward. "It's a sign, an omen," he said breathlessly as Greshym limped past. "I just know it!"

Greshym feigned a misstep, crushing Brother Treet's foot with his staff as he struggled among the gawkers. Only the sinking gravel kept the man's toes from breaking, but the pain purpled his pudgy face. Greshym continued on as if unaware of the harm he had caused. He finally reached the shadow of the tree's trunk.

Around him hushed voices whispered in prayer and astonishment. Just overhead—Greshym had to crane his neck backward—a low-hanging branch ended in a small cluster of green leaves.

Greshym scowled. It had been almost two decades since the tree had sprouted any growth. A stray breeze fluttered the patch of leaves, their silvery undersides flashing and dancing in the sun. The crowd murmured in awe at the sight.

Is this what drew them all? From within his cowl, Greshym grimaced his disdain. *A handful of leaves!*

He was about to turn away when brightness caught his eye. Buried within the cluster of leaves, a spark of color flashed—a sapphire blazing in a fluttering sea of green and silver. A purple blossom! Curled and closed in slumber, it rocked gently on its branch.

Greshym stared in shock, his bleary eyes struggling to understand. The koa'kona had not bloomed in over two hundred winters! Yet there it was! Hanging and rolling in the sea breeze, a lone jewel from the distant past.

He backed a step away. He suddenly felt it: like a chill that passes down a spine, raising the smallest hairs. He backed another step, bumping into the boy who stood ever present at his shoulder. Too stunned to scold, he just herded the boy behind him as he retreated. But the chilling sense of danger crept after him. He recognized his unease—and its source. It was Chyric power, white magick, flowing out from the single bright blossom. He had not felt its touch so strong since ages long lost.

His eyes wild, his staff knocking knees and shins, he stumbled back as the crowd surged forward, their voices suddenly rising loud with astonishment.

"Sweet Mother!" someone called at his shoulder.

"It is a miracle!" another exclaimed in wonder.

All about him, voices echoed these words. Somewhere a bell began ringing.

Greshym's heart clamored in his breast; his breath choked him. He stared in horror.

Overhead, the blossom's petals slowly opened. A gentle light glowed from their heart, brightening the petals with a soft azure luminescence.

Greshym recognized this gentle radiance.

It was the glow of Chi.

JOACH STUMBLED BACKWARD AS THE DARKMAGE HERDED HIM AWAY FROM the tree. If not for the press of the other white-robed brothers, he would have fallen over his own tripping feet. His legs felt numb and tingled with tiny pinpricks. He reached out and clutched at the sleeve of a neighboring brother to secure his stance, but even his fingers, numb and tingling, failed him, and cloth slipped from his palm.

A choking gasp escaped his throat as he realized what was happening. Thankfully, the rattling noise was lost in the commotion of raised voices around him. No eyes looked in his direction. His vision squeezed toward darkness as he moved one limb, then another. First, he took a step back, then raised his hand before his face and clenched his hand into a fist.

Free! Sweet Mother, he was free of his prison! His body was once again his own.

The tingling in his flesh quickly faded to echoes along his bones as the spell of binding unraveled. Unsure what had freed him, Joach continued to retreat through the crowd, the darkmage backing with him. So far, Greshym had failed to notice the change.

A skinny white-robed brother turned in his direction as he bumped past. Eyes wide with wonder, the man's voice was dazed, his words breathless. "It's a miracle. Can you not feel the magick?"

Joach did not know what the fool was talking about. He tried to flee, but the man had gripped his arm with excited fingers. "Look," the brother said, pointing with his other hand toward the huge tree's limbs. "Its flower blooms in daylight! It's a sign!"

In reflex, Joach's eyes drew to where the man pointed. He spied a drooping purple flower buried within a cluster of leaves. The petals appeared to glow from under the shadows of the wide leaves—probably a trick of light.

Yet, as his eyes settled upon the flower, a calm overtook his hammering heart. Like the touch of a summer sun on his cold skin after diving deep into the chilly waters of Torcrest Pond, it warmed through his body. Somehow Joach understood that here lay the key that had freed him from prison. He did not understand how or why, only that some magick in that glowing flower had broken his bonds.

With this thought, as if to confirm this supposition, the petals of the flower broke apart and drifted like purple snowflakes toward the ground, their duty done. A sigh of regret rose like a mist from the crowd around him. Clearly some momentous event had been anticipated, and with the fall of petals marking the end of the miracle, disappointment rang clear in their voices.

"It's over," said the man beside Joach. The brother's fingers fell from the boy's arm.

Greshym's voice suddenly rose from near his shoulder. "Leave my boy be," he snapped at the skinny robed brother, but the darkmage's voice lacked its usual fire, sounding more distracted, almost fearful. His eyes stared at the falling petals for several heartbeats. Finally turning, he waved the tip of his staff, and his gaze flashed over Joach, hardly seeing the boy. The edge had returned to his voice as the last of the petals settled to the dirt. "Leave the poor boy be. He doesn't understand all this."

"Well, neither do I," said the other man. "You're the oldest of the Order, Brother Greshym. What do you make of these events?"

"Just echoes of the past," he mumbled harshly. "Some memory in the dead wood, like a dream coming to the surface. Nothing to get stirred up about."

The dismissive words sagged the skinny brother's shoulders and faded the light in his eyes. "You're probably right," he said sadly. "Still, I shall see if I can collect one of its petals before the others all get to them."

Joach noticed the brothers had clustered around the bole of the huge tree and were bent reverently collecting the small fallen petals.

"Come," Greshym said to Joach as the other left their side. The darkmage turned his back and stomped his way through the garden. "Follow me," he ordered.

Joach found his feet following, not because of any spell, but simply because he did not know what else to do. It was clear that the darkmage still thought Joach was his slave, a thrall to his words and commands. The man was mostly blind to Joach's presence and did not seem to notice his new hesitations or extra movements.

As he walked, a fleeting thought to call out to the other brothers and expose the snake among them passed through his mind. But restraining thoughts kept his tongue silent. Would they believe him? The others all thought him a brain-addled fool. Who would believe that not only a revered member of their order, but also its very leader, the Praetor, were under control of the Gul'gotha? And even if he could convince them, what if there were other darkmages unknown to Joach? If the Praetor, the head of the Order, was under the Dark Lord's black dominion, surely there might be others. For his risk, would Joach only succeed in chopping off the head of the weed, leaving the foul root intact? Then would anything be truly gained if he spoke out? These worries kept his voice silent.

Nothing would be gained by speaking—at least not yet!

A different plan formed in his head as he shuffled behind the white robe. His legs had weakened from starvation, and it was easy to mimic his usual dull pace. What if . . . ? The more he pondered his plan, the firmer his resolve became. Greshym only gave Joach glancing attention, barely seeing him most of the time. And Joach, trapped in his head these many moons, had learned what was expected of him and how he should act. But could he truly pull it off? Could he masquerade as the spell-cast slave of the darkmage? And by doing so, perhaps learn more about Greshym's schemes? Joach could not answer this last question.

Even if he learned nothing, he could always explore ways to escape the island. But in his heart, Joach knew he would never use that escape route—at least not alone.

He pictured his sister Elena's face: freckles on her nose, eyes crinkled as she concentrated. He had no idea where among all the lands of Alasea his sister might be now, but he knew Elena was headed to A'loa Glen. If Joach could not find her and warn her away, he could at least learn in secret what traps were being laid here and try to thwart them.

So Joach continued after the bent back of the darkmage. He knew his best chance at helping his sister lay in deceit, in masquerading as a slave. He would fight fire with fire, deception with deception. As Greshym and the Praetor wore false faces, so would he!

Elena, he whispered in his skull, *I'll not fail you again*.

For a heartbeat, the purple flower appeared in his mind's eye, glowing much more brightly in his memory that it had in reality. Was it mere chance that had freed him? Or like the black snakes that hid among the white folds of A'loa Glen, were there perhaps allies of the light—maybe others who might help him—hidden in the black shadows?

With Greshym's back turned, Joach glanced furtively around the courtyard. Shadows and sunlight danced along the paths of the decaying garden. The bright and the dark mingled together.

If there were others out there who could aid him, how would Joach be able to recognize them in this play of sunlight and shadow?

Whom could he trust?

Somewhere beyond the high walls of the Edifice, a gull cried a lonely call across the empty sea. The cry echoed in Joach's chest.

In this matter, he knew he was alone.

12

The gull's cry swept over the waves toward where Sy-wen's small head bobbed in the gentle surf. Her eyes followed the bird's flight across the blue sky. As her webbed fingers swept back and forth in the salty water, keeping her stationary in the sea, she imagined the various landscapes the gull had flown over. She pictured towering peaks, forests of dark shadows, and empty meadows wider than the sea. Tales were spoken of such places, but she had never seen any of them.

She craned her neck back to view the spread of sky and cloud, her green hair floating like a halo of kelp around her. The gull disappeared to a dot in the sun's glare. Sighing, Sy-wen turned her attention back to the churning white surf where the sea met the shore of the nearby island in an angry rumble. White froth spewed high in the afternoon sunlight, and black rocks glistened like the backs of whales while over it all, the ocean roared as it attacked the stone island, as if angry at the interruption of its blue expanse.

Sy-wen thrilled at the war of sea and rock. It touched something deep inside of her, something she could not name. She studied the island. Her eyes filled with the views of its green-draped peaks, of its cascading falls of spring-fed water, of its arched stones of windblown rock. Beyond this one island, others could be seen like the humped backs of great sea beasts marching toward the horizon.

Archipelago.

Even the word that named the maze of islands set her heart to beating. Here was mystery and lands unknown—forbidden territory for the mer'ai. Only the banished of her people walked those broken shores and sharp rocks.

As she kicked her powerful legs to hold her head above water, she felt the familiar gentle brush of a warm nose against the back of her thigh. Sadly, she spread her legs to allow Conch, her mother's mount, to slide under her. Once she was seated on his familiar back, Conch arched up, raising Sy-wen higher. Soon only her webbed toes still touched the sea. From atop Conch's back, she could see past the churning barrier reef to the interior of the island. Above the foam and spray, she spied the towers and straight-edged buildings of the lan'dwellers, those of her folk banished from the sea so long ago.

She raised her arms wide and caught the sea breezes in her splayed hands. How would it be to swim through the air like a gull, to fly among those towers and peer in the windows at those who lived life at the sea's edge? Did they miss the oceans and cry all night for their long-lost home, as Mother said?

In front of her, Conch's head surfaced. The jade seadragon's scaled neck sparked, scintillating in the sunlight. He huffed explosively as the scaled flaps that blocked his nose opened, expelling old air. He rolled one large black eye toward his rider, blinking his translucent lid open and closed.

Sy-wen shrank under his gaze.

Though not bonded to the dragon as her mother was, Sy-wen had been raised with the giant and had learned his moods. Conch was frustrated with her. He hated it when she swam close to the stone islands that dotted the sea. Yet from the relieved tremble in his throat as he rid himself of his stale air, she also sensed the great beast's worry and concern.

She rubbed a hand along his long sleek neck, scratching the sensitive nest of scales by his ear holes. Her touch calmed his irritation. She smiled as he turned away. Conch had always been such a worrier. Even when she was a child, he had always watched over her, a constant shadow as she grew into a young woman.

Yet as much as it pained her, Conch's guardianship would soon end. Sy-wen must soon bond her own dragon and leave Conch behind. Having already begun her woman's bleed, she was no longer a child. For the past ten moons, immature seadragons had already been flocking to her, drawn by each moon's virginal bleed—a flurry of whites, a scattering of reds, even a few jades like Conch. But she had fought them all off. As an elder's daughter, she knew her duty and must soon choose, but she was not ready. Not yet.

Tears suddenly rose to her eyes. She did not want to lose Conch, not ever—not even to bond one of the rare blacks, the mightiest of the seadragons.

After her father had died, Conch had become her guardian—and her companion. She could hardly remember her true father, only a vague memory of laughing eyes and warm, strong arms. Even her mother, too involved with her duties as an elder, seldom left their clan's home inside the belly of the giant leviathan, the whalelike creature that housed her family's clan of mer'ai. Without siblings, Sy-wen learned quickly how empty the oceans could be. With only Conch at her side, she had wandered the seamounts and the elaborate coral reefs, always alone.

Lately, she had found herself lured to the islands. Whether it was some growing unease as her womanhood and its responsibilities beckoned, or simply a swelling dissatisfaction with the empty sea, Sy-wen could not say. She had no words for the continuing draw that pulled at her heart.

Maybe it was simply her stubborn nature rebelling against her mother's restrictions. After her first excursion near the islands, her mother had vehemently forbidden her to venture near the Archipelago again, warning against the fisherfolk with their spears, telling tales of how the banished, angry at the loss of their true home, would lure mer'ai to their deaths on the rocks. She had never seen her mother so disturbed: voice cracking, eyes red, almost wild. As fury and frustration had choked her mother's words, Sy-wen had only nodded in agreement, eyes lowered in obeisance, acting properly scolded and chagrined. But once her mother was gone, Sy-wen had simply dismissed her warnings.

No words, not even angered ones, could sunder the lines that had so snugly hooked Sy-wen's heart.

So, against her mother's will, she often snuck away from the leviathan and swam alone to the edge of the Archipelago. There, she would drift in the currents, studying the islands carved by wind and sea. Curious, she would watch for any signs of the banished, one time even swimming within sight of one of their fishing boats.

But always, as now, Conch would eventually follow her scent and venture forth to collect her up, carrying her back to where their leviathan home swam slowly in the Great Deep.

The seadragon, loving Sy-wen as he did, kept silent about her wanderings—not even telling her mother. Sy-wen knew how hard it was on the sweet giant to keep a secret from his bondmate. Recognizing his pain, she limited her visits to the islands to only occasional excursions. Still—she glanced behind her and stared at the island one last time as Conch began to swing around—she would be back.

Sy-wen rubbed the dragon's neck, telling him she was ready to leave.

Conch snorted the last of the dead air from his series of lungs. Under her, the seadragon's chest swelled as he drank in the fresh breezes, preparing to dive.

Before submerging, Sy-wen slipped loose the stem from one of the air pods at her waist and bit off its glued end. It tasted of salt and seaweed. She inhaled to test its ripeness. The air was still fine. Even if the pod had staled, there was no danger. Sy-wen knew Conch would let her use the siphon at the base of his neck. Though tradition allowed only a bondmate to share a dragon's air, Conch had never refused Sy-wen.

Sy-wen slipped her feet into the folds behind his front legs, and Conch tightened the footholds to secure her.

Satisfied, she tapped Conch with the heel of her hand three times, signaling she was ready to go. A rumble shook through the great beast and his form sank under the waves, taking Sy-wen with him. Just as the water swamped her face, Sy-wen's inner lids snapped up to protect her eyes from the water's salt. The translucent lids also sharpened her eyesight in the silty water.

After the rush of swirling bubbles cleared, leaving only a few stragglers chasing them into the Deep, Sy-wen stared in awe at the full sight of the creature she rode. From nose to tail, Conch stretched longer than six men. "Dragon" was the mer'ai's word for the great beasts who shared their world under the waves, and though the seadragons had their own name for themselves, Sy-wen found her people's title most fitting. Wings spread out to either side as Conch stretched his forelimbs wide. Gentle but powerful movements rippled through the wings as the dragon sailed through the sea. His snaking tail and clawed rear legs acted as skilled rudders, guiding them in a slow curve around the lee of the islands and heading toward the open waters.

Slow undulations swept through the length of Conch's body as his form glided deeper. Schools of fish darted in unison to either side of his flowing body, splashes of blues and greens. Below, rows of reefs marched under the wings of the dragon, dotted with the glowing yellow and bloodred blooms of anemones. At the fringes of the reef, tall fronds of kelp waved as they passed.

Sy-wen stared at the massed coral below her. It was like flying, she thought, soaring above distant mountain ranges. She smiled, biting on her air pod's stem. Her eyes grew hazy as she watched the seafloor flow under her. A patch of clouds far overhead blotched the landscape in patches of shadow and filtered sunlight. She dreamed of flying in the sky with Conch.

Suddenly Conch twisted sharply in the water, diving deep toward the peaks of coral. Startled, Sy-wen almost lost her lips' hold on her air spout. She quickly searched for what had startled the dragon. There was little for a seadragon to fear in the wide Deep.

Except . . .

Sy-wen craned her neck up. Far above her, the shapes that she had thought were clouds shadowing the ocean floor were actually the bloated bellies of boats. She quickly scanned the barnacled bottoms of the fisherfolk's vessels. Seven—no, eight boats! Sy-wen did not have to be told what this meant. A solitary boat usually just carried pole and net fishers: nothing to fear. This many—Sy-wen's heart climbed to her throat—this many boats meant *hunters*!

Sy-wen clung to Conch's side as he wove his wings and body so deep that his belly scratched the sharp peaks of the reef. The waters near the islands, though, were too shallow. They would be easily spotted by the ships above. Conch struggled to find deeper water. From the corner of her eye, Sy-wen spotted trails of blood flowing back along their trail from the dragon's coral-wounded belly.

Drawn by his blood, as if by magick, schools of sharks appeared from the black waters. In only a few heartbeats, monstrous rocksharks, longer than three men, glided from dark valleys in the reef.

Sy-wen realized what Conch was trying to do. He had purposely wounded himself, luring the larger predators from their hidden homes, trying to lose himself among the more common denizens of the reef.

Conch slowed his glide through the water, letting the other predators within his shadow. He pulled hard once with his wings, then folded them under his body, narrowing his silhouette as he flowed through the water. Only the slow undulations of his body now propelled them forward.

Sy-wen risked a glance upward. A huge rockshark, with a snap of its large finned tail, swept just over her head. Sy-wen leaned down closer to Conch's neck. The shark would not dare risk attacking until he knew the dragon was near death, but the hulking rockshark was not the true threat here.

Farther overhead, the last of the boats glided past. Staring over her shoulder, Sy-wen slowly expelled the air from her sore lungs as the bellies of the hunting fleet faded behind her. They had made it!

Sy-wen sat straighter on Conch's back and rubbed a hand along his neck. Tears of relief mixed their salt with the seawater's. Her silly curiosities had almost killed the gentle giant. A new resolve grew in her breast. Where words had failed, fear and danger had finally managed to dig free the stubborn hooks in her heart.

Never again. She would *never* return to these islands.

Her mother's words had been wise, and like a child, she had dismissed that good counsel! Sy-wen's hands clenched to fists. Maybe it was time to look toward her approaching womanhood with a more open heart. Maybe it was time she grew up and looked at the world with the wisdom of an adult, instead of the dreaming eyes of a child.

She glanced back as the last of the boats drifted away from them. *Never again!*

Suddenly, below them, the seafloor exploded upward, swallowing them in a storm of silt and sand. Conch's body contorted violently under her. The scaled folds that secured her feet spasmed open. Sy-wen was thrown from Conch's back. Her air siphon ripped from her teeth as she tumbled through the water.

The sea gagged her throat as she swallowed a mouthful of salty water. In the blizzard of sand, she struggled to resecure the stem of her air hose. She must not lose her air. As her body slowed its tumble, instinct drew her fumbling fingers to the pod fastened to her waist belt and felt along its surface until she discovered the base of the stem. Thank the Mother, it was still intact. She hurriedly followed its length and pulled its end to her lips.

She drank the air hungrily while using her webbed hands to hold herself in place. Able to breathe again, she could now think. What had happened?

Swirling sand obscured her vision. She swam backward against a mild current, letting the flow of the water clear the silt around her as she kicked and paddled. Where was Conch?

Suddenly, like the sun pushing through a break in the clouds, the storm of sand settled enough for Sy-wen to get a quick glimpse near the heart of the storm. Conch, his long green body coiled up on itself, struggled savagely with something, his legs slashing, his neck twisting and contorting. It looked almost as if he were fighting himself. Then Sy-wen saw Conch's adversary. It was wrapped tight around his body, and the more Conch fought, the tighter his opponent gripped him.

A net! A snare set in the sand to catch him!

As Conch struggled, a single black eye rolled in Sy-wen's direction and fixed on her. For a brief moment, he stopped his struggle, hanging still in the tangled net. *Flee,* he seemed to call at her, *I am lost*.

Then the sand swallowed her dear friend away.

No! Sy-wen swam into the sandstorm, paddling fiercely. She had a knife and a stunner at her waist. She would not abandon Conch. She dug and clawed her way through the clouds of silt. It seemed forever that she fought the murk. Then, suddenly, she was free, back in sunlit waters, the wall of swirling sand at her back. She twisted around. She had swum through the entire cloud of silt. But where was Conch?

Above, movement caught her eye. She glanced up and saw her friend bundled in a tight ball in the clinging net, being hauled and drawn toward the surface. The bellies of the boats were now clustered in a circle around the ascending dragon.

Sweet Mother, don't let this happen!

Sy-wen fought her way toward the surface, but she was too late. She had wasted too much time fighting the swirling sand. She watched, her heart thundering in her ears, as Conch was drawn to the surface.

She kicked toward the planked bottoms of the boats. She must still try. Aiming for the largest vessel, she slid under its keel, and guided by a hand slipping over its barnacled surface, she floated upward until her head bobbed in the shadowed curve of the boat's leeward side.

Voices suddenly struck her ears, strident, their thick accent making them difficult to understand. "Look at the size of that beastie!" someone called from almost directly overhead.

Sy-wen sank lower until only her eyes and ears were above water. She watched as Conch rolled in the tangled net, sluggishly writhing as he tired.

"It'll fetch a shower of silver. We'll all be rich!" another shouted gleefully.

A sterner voice rang out from the boat above, guttural and full of threat, a voice of command. "Git the beast's nose above waters, you daft fools! You want to drown it!"

"But why do we want it alive? What difference—"

The stern voice again. "Jeffers, if you poke it one more time with that spear, I'll plant it up your hairy arse!"

A voice called back. "It's still fighting, Cap'n!"

"Leave it be! Give time for the sleep potion to reach its heart!" Then the man's voice lowered so only the men near at hand could hear. "Sweet Mother above, I can't believe it. So the rumors were true about seeing a seadragon at the fringes of the Archipelago. Who would have thought?"

"Not been one seen in these parts since my grandpa was young."

"Yah, but I've heard talk of occasional sightings in the Great Deep." He made a low whistling noise. "Wonder why the beast ended up here in the shallow coastals? And why it kept coming back?"

"Probably an ol' one. Getting daft in the head."

"Well, whatever reason, it'll bring us enough silver and gold for a lifetime. Look at that beaut!"

Sy-wen could not stop the tears from flowing down her cheeks. *Conch*, she silently sent to him, *I'm so sorry*.

"Quite a catch it is, Cap'n. Makes you almost want to believe those ol' stories of mer folk."

The other laughed. "Now, Flint, don't you go daft in the head."

"Just saying it makes me wonder."

"Well, you'd best wonder about the riches we'll fetch with a living seadragon at Port Rawl. Seadragon's blood is as rare as heartstone. I heard tell that vials left over from the last dragon—the beastie caught up near Biggins Landing ten years ago—still fetches six gold coins a drop! Now wonder about that, Flint!"

Glee entered this other's voice. "I can just imagine the look on that old snake Tyrus when we haul this treasure to port."

"His men'll have to tie him to a mast to keep him from tearing that lice-ridden beard from his face in his jealous rage."

They both chuckled.

"We're both going to die rich men, Flint." Then the voice again rose gruffly and shot across the waters. "Jeffers! What did I just tell you about that spear!"

"But, Cap'n . . ."

"Each drop of blood is wasted profit! Samel, git that Jeffers belowdecks. The next one who stabs the dragon gets fed to it!" Then his voice lowered. "Fools!"

Sy-wen had already stopped listening. Her eyes were on her friend tangled in the net, a pool of blood spreading around him. Drawn by the blood, occasional fins of sharks broke the water but were chased off with spears. By now, Conch had stopped struggling, lying limp in the ropes. She could see he still breathed. But for how long?

Sy-wen's chest hurt from suppressing her sobs. What was she to do? It would take her until well past nightfall to return to the leviathan and tell the others what had happened. But even if the elders decided to risk freeing him, Conch would be long gone, lost among the hundreds of islands of the Archipelago.

She closed her eyes and made a choice. She could not abandon her friend. His life depended on her.

Opening her eyes, she slipped a hand to her waist and freed the shark-tooth knife from her belt. Repositioning her air stem, she dove under the waves and kicked and swam toward her friend.

In the distance, sharks circled warily. Sy-wen could see their black eyes watching, unblinking. The spears kept them at bay so far.

Sy-wen swam deep under Conch until the sunlight was blocked by the netted dragon. Floating up in his shadow, she reached his underside and ran a hand along the net. The oiled ropes and knots had dug deep into Conch's flesh. Blood seeped where the tight ropes had sliced his skin during his struggle. A deep gash in a tangled fold of a wing bled near her hand, and she found herself reaching for the injury as if her touch could make the wound disappear. *Oh, Conch, what have I done?*

Before her fingers touched the dragon, something suddenly slammed into her ribs—*hard*. Sy-wen gasped, losing her air stem and swallowing a mouthful of seawater. The blow pitched her out from under Conch into the sunlit waters. Gagging, Sy-wen spun around and dug for the surface. Seawater seared her lungs. Near blind with pain, Sy-wen saw her attacker swing back around toward her. It was a rockshark. With her attention so focused on her wounded friend, Sy-wen had failed to see the shark. She knew better than to let her guard down when sharks smelled blood in the water.

She kicked in retreat. Her head broke the surface of the sea at the same time the huge shark fin crested the waves. It stood taller than her whole body. Coughing and choking, she held up the tiny knife and reached for the stunner at her waist. She had fought before—she would not let a shark stand between her and Conch.

She raised the knife, but she never had to use it. A massive spear flew bright across the sparkling water and slammed into the base of the fin. A fountain of blood flew up from the buried blade, and the rockshark exploded out of the water, thrashing against its death.

Sy-wen stared, stunned by the sight of its cavernous mouth lined by hundreds of teeth. She cartwheeled her arms to clear away from its spasms. Even a dying shark could kill.

Voices rose behind her.

"Good throw, Kast!"

"What an arm!"

Sy-wen spun around. She was once again near the lee side of the main boat. She glanced up at a pair of bearded, scarred faces staring back at her, their black eyes unblinking.

She never knew sharks could leer.

Before she could react, a net flew over the rail of the boat and swept down over Sy-wen. She kicked off the boat's side, trying to escape, but her feet slipped on the algae-slicked planks. Rope and knot descended on her, wrapping around her like a living creature. Her knife was knocked from her fingers.

She fought, but like Conch, her efforts only aided in tangling her further. Seawater swamped her mouth and throat. Unable to surface or reach her air pod, she gagged and thrashed but could not beat back the dark. Like the sea itself, the swelling blackness drowned Sy-wen, sweeping her away.

KAST IGNORED THE COMMOTION ON THE DECK BEHIND HIM. He stood at the prow of the *Skipjack* and watched the rockshark die on his spearpoint. As the king of sharks, its body and blood would drive other sharks away from the wounded seadragon.

Still Kast continued his watch, his eyes drifting to where sunlight sparked off jade scale. Except for a barrel of additional spears at his side, he stood alone. None dared approach too closely unless invited. His almond-shaped eyes warned all who neared of his heritage.

Kast had been born and raised among the savage tribes south of the Blasted Shoals—the Dre'rendi, a people known for their piracy and hard living. He even sported a tattoo on his neck of a seahawk, talons bared in attack. It was the symbol of the most savage and predatory of the Dre'rendi tribes, the Bloodriders. Kast wore his black hair pulled into a long tail that draped to his waist, leaving his neck exposed for all to see the tattoo. It was not done in false pride or to brag of his heritage, but in simple warning. Sea folk were a rowdy lot, and it was best that a man know who he insulted or accosted, lest blood be drawn. So Kast kept his tattoo exposed, forewarning all to stay clear.

Alone by the bowsprit, he studied the seadragon, shading his eyes with a hand as if supposing it all a mirage of sun and water. Yet the dragon did not dissolve into mist and vanish. It was as real as his own bones and sinew. Kast studied the folds of wing tangled in the net, the hint of pearled fangs protruding from a narrow snout, the black-jeweled eyes the size of a man's fist.

Raised on the sea, he had never supposed such wonders still hid below its waves. He had seen rocksharks that could swallow a man whole, silver-bellied eels longer than the *Skipjack*, and even spiny lobsters that killed men with a touch. But he had never seen such a creature as this dragon! Such a beast spoke of another time, an age when myth was forged in blood.

As he contemplated the sight, he brushed the tattoo of the seahawk on his neck with a finger. Could it be . . . ? He remembered the madness that had shone in the blind seer's eyes as he writhed on his deathbed. He recalled the garbled words, the hand clutching his arm as the old man died. Kast shook his head, dispelling the past, and dropped his hand from his throat. Why had he followed the words of a madman?

Captain Jarplin's voice suddenly cracked across the deck behind Kast. "Git her out of the water!" he ordered."You're gonna kill her!"

It was the urgency in Jarplin's voice, more than the content of his words, that finally drew Kast from his study of the seadragon. He glanced toward the starboard rail, where already a group of deckhands had gathered.

The captain leaned over the rail and yelled again over the side. "That's it, men, haul her on up!"

Intrigued at what new treasure was being fished from the sea and satisfied that the blood of the slain rockshark would keep other predators away, Kast signaled a fellow mate to take his post and crossed to join the group of men. Hired for his skill at tracking and hunting the pathless expanses of the sea, Kast had no obligation to help with the nets and lines, yet still he often joined the deckhands in their duties, ignoring their obvious discomfort at working so closely alongside a Bloodrider. He cared not whom he made nervous. That was not his concern. Kast needed to regularly work under the sun, testing the worthiness of his arms and the strength of his back. A Bloodrider did not let his skills wane.

Kast bumped an onlooker on the shoulder, a red-haired, clean-shaven youth. His voice commanded attention. "Tok, what's been found?"

The boy glanced toward him, his eyes widening, then backed a step away. "Not . . . not sure, sir," Tok answered. "A stowaway, we thinks. Some girl that was trying to sneak off the boat."

"A stowaway?" Kast could not keep the disgust from his voice. Stowaways were gutted and tossed to the sharks among his own people.

"The Hort brothers spotted her a'sneaking into the Deep," Tok added nervously.

The captain's voice barked again. "Clear away, you lollygaggers! Haul that net up here." Jarplin bullied through the crowd of deckhands. The captain's broad shoulders told of the strength still in his old arms, and though his hair silvered toward gray, Jarplin was as hard and tough as any of his men. His green eyes let nothing escape his notice. Known for his quick anger, the captain's justice was swift and often brutal, but still he ran a tight ship, and over the three winters aboard the *Skipjack*, Kast had developed a grudging respect for the man. "What are you all doing?" Jarplin called out as he reached the bearded Hort brothers. He shoved other men away from the rail. "Clear on out!"

Kast watched as the two brothers hauled their dripping net over the rail and dropped their cargo to the deck. Seawater and oiled ropes splashed across the planks.

The men all backed a step, letting Kast now get a clear view of the catch.

"It's only a li'l girl," someone said.

Kast's brows lowered. Tangled in the net, a small figure lay sprawled across the deck. Bare chested, with only a hint of breasts, she wore a pair of tight breeches made of some slick material—sharkskin perhaps. It took him a few additional heartbeats to realize that the dark green seaweed snarled in the net along with the girl was actually her hair. How could it be? After so many ages . . .

"She does not breathe," Kast heard himself say, stepping forward.

Captain Jarplin pushed through the men that crowded around the catch. "Git that net off her!"

The boy Tok danced forward with a knife in his hand, ready to slice the girl free.

The captain spotted him. "Tok, put that knife away. I won't have a perfectly good net wasted on a stowaway."

The boy stopped, his freckled face reddening.

Kast, though, continued toward the prone girl, a knife flashing into his own palm. He bent to the net and began sawing at the ropes. "She isn't a stowaway, Captain."

"I don't care what . . ." Jarplin's voice trailed away as he saw clearly for the first time what his precious net held.

The captain's first mate, Flint, stood at Jarplin's shoulder. He was a thin man, hardened and worn by storm and sea into a figure of tanned leather and sharp bone. His voice was as coarse as the scrabble of gray beard on his chin. "You heard the captain, Kast. Git away from the net and let . . ." Then his words died, too. A long low whistle escaped his cracked lips. As his eyes settled on the cargo, Flint rubbed at a small silver star fastened to his right earlobe. "That . . . that ain't no stowaway."

The captain raised a hand, silencing his first mate.

Kast sliced through the knots with snaps of his wrist and deft knowledge of where to cut. The girl was free in only a few breaths. Kast lifted her from the tangled ropes. His eyes raised to the circle of deckhands, and they all backed from the intensity of his gaze, leaving him room to lay the slight form on the cleared-off deck. He straightened her limbs and checked for the beat of her heart.

She still lived, but her lips were blue and her skin pallid and cold. She would not live much longer. He rolled her onto her stomach and straddled her, then used both palms to squeeze the water from her lungs. More seawater than he thought could possibly be contained in her small frame sluiced across the planks. Satisfied that he had rid her of most of the water, he flipped her back around and bent her neck. He lowered his lips to hers and breathed life into her chest.

As he pinched her nose and worked the bellows of her lungs with his own air, he heard the others murmur around him.

"Look at her hair. It shines like algae floatin' on dead water."

"Did ya see her hands? Webbed like a duck, I tell ya."

"Kast is wasting his time. She is lost to the Deep."

Others grunted their assent to this last statement.

One mate, though, snickered. It was one of the Hort brothers. " 'Course Kast isn't wasting all his time. I wouldn't mind kissing the lass, too. And those little muffins on her chest look mighty tasty." He laughed coarsely.

Kast ignored them all. He focused on his duty. In and out, he worked her chest.

Finally, the captain's voice rose behind him, and he placed a hand on Kast's shoulder. "She's gone. Leave her be. The sea has claimed its own." He pulled Kast up.

Red faced, Kast sat back on his heels, studying the young girl. His efforts had returned a bit of color to her lips, but nothing more. She still lay unmoving. He let out a rattling sigh, conceding defeat. She was lost.

Then suddenly the girl coughed harshly, wracking her whole form. Her eyes fluttered open and fixed upon him. "Father?" she mumbled and reached a hand toward where Kast knelt over her. Her fingers touched his throat, resting for a heartbeat on his seahawk tattoo.

Kast jumped back from her fingers as if stung. Where she had touched, his tattoo suddenly burned like a brand on his skin. He stifled a gasp, his cheek and throat burning with an inner fire. His heart thundered in his throat.

Shocked and speechless, he watched the girl's eyes roll back and her arm swoon to the deck. She drifted away again.

Kast bent over the girl, one hand rubbing his neck. The fire was already fading. Obviously the child was delirious, but at least she now breathed. "We need to get her somewhere dry and warm," he said. The men had fallen silent around him when the child had awakened. He scooped her up in his hard arms.

"Take her to the kitchens," Jarplin said. "The heat of the hearths should warm her up. But once she's able, I have a few questions for the lass."

Kast nodded. He had questions of his own. He waited no further and whisked her across the deck.

Behind him, he heard the captain address his men, his voice gruff and irritated. "And the rest of you, get back to the rails. We have a dragon to haul to port."

Bent over, Kast crawled through the narrow companionway that led to the lower cabins. His nose was assaulted with old smells of unwashed bodies mixed with the acrid scent of salt and vinegar from the cooking stoves. After the bright sunshine, it took him a moment for his eyes to adjust to the dim passageways of the lamplit lower decks. Blinking, he hauled his cargo down the hall toward the galley near the stern.

His mind whirled on the events of the day, his skin still aching with a dull burn. First the dragon, then the girl. What did it all mean? He remembered the child's green eyes staring into his own, dazed and confused. Could it be the prophecy? For a breath, he again pictured the blind shaman of the Bloodriders dying on his fouled cot in a back room of Port Rawl. His last words echoed in Kast's head: "A Bloodrider's oath is tattooed on his flesh. Though the sworn words are forgotten, the flesh remembers." The shaman had then clutched Kast's arms with the last of his strength. "You must go north of the Shoals, Kast. The tattoo will soon blaze with its old promises. Do not forget. When the seahawk burns, the oceans will run red with blood, and the riders will be called forth to fulfill their oath—to mount again and drive the great dragons from the sea."

A shiver passed through his body as he carried the girl down the passageway. The shaman had been his teacher, his master. But was it prophecy or madness that drove the blind seer's last breaths? He had obeyed his teacher's last words and traveled north of the Blasted Shoals, leaving behind the lean, swift ships of his people for the heavy, swollen-bellied boats of the Archipelago. For over ten winters, he had exiled himself to respect his deathbed promise, growing more bitter as each winter passed without incident.

But now—could this be a sign?

Confused, Kast dismissed these thoughts as he reached the kitchens and pushed through into the heated room. He needed the girl alive. Perhaps answers would come from her lips, answers he had been seeking for a decade since the death of his teacher. He would get his answers!

As he carried the girl into the warmth of the ship's galley, Kast spotted Gimli, the cook, bent over a bubbling pot, his old cheeks ruddy from the coals, his brown hair sticking straight up from the sweat and steam. Gimli glanced at Kast as he entered, his eyebrows rising as he spied Kast's burden.

"Whatcha got there?"

Kast kicked aside two stools and laid the girl across an ironwood table. "I need dry blankets, and a cloth soaked in hot water." He checked to ensure she still breathed. Her chest rose and fell steadily. Relieved, he went and hurriedly gathered blankets from a neighboring cabin.

As he reentered the kitchen area, Gimli was pulling a scrap of cloth from a pot of boiling water. He juggled it over to where Kast was draping the child's small form in heavy, coarse blankets.

Kast took the steaming cloth. Ignoring its burning heat, he wiped down the girl's face and upper body. The girl moaned under his touch, her lips moving as if she were speaking, but nothing intelligible came out.

As the cook looked on, Kast finished his ministrations, wrapped the girl from the neck down in blankets, and gently positioned a down-filled pillow under her head.

"Who is she?" Gimli asked.

Kast had no answer and stayed silent. He pulled a stool beside the table and sat on it. He wanted to make sure he was the first to speak to her when she awoke.

The cook shrugged at Kast's silence and turned back to his duties, armed again with his ladle.

Alone, Kast's fingers wandered to the green locks of the child's hair drying on the table's planks. Gimli had failed to ask the right question. He shouldn't have asked *who* the child was—but *what*.

Kast did know that.

He whispered to the blanket-wrapped figure, naming her heritage: "mer'ai." He touched her soft cheek. Here lay myth given flesh. "Dragonriders," he said in a hushed breath.

The ancient slave masters of the Bloodriders.

13

Sy-wen swam in murky dreams.

She pictured men whose mouths were filled with row after row of shark's teeth . . . She fled from a dragon, torn and bloody . . . She dodged a seabird that clawed at her eyes. She kicked and paddled to escape these horrows. She must flee!

Then her father suddenly came and picked her up in his strong arms, pulling her from the horrors in the sea. He kissed her and carried her to safety. She smiled up at him and found she could finally rest. He would help her. Darkness then swallowed her away—not the cold blackness of death, but the warm embrace of true sleep.

She slept deeply, but over time an urgency slowly grew in her heart. She was forgetting something. No, not something—someone. She moaned as she struggled against the whispers of slumber in her ear. Who had she forgotten? Then a new voice filled her ears, drowning all else away. A harsh voice, coarse and spoken with a thick tongue.

"That girl—spread out on the table like that—looks a mite more appetizing than the cook's stew, Kast. How about letting my brother and me have a taste of her?"

As the darkness shattered into shards around her, Sy-wen's eyes opened. She found herself in a narrow room that reeked of salted fish and burning coals. Around her, empty tables were strewn with dirty bowls, cracked spoons, and half-eaten crusts of bread.

Where was she?

As jagged pieces of memory tumbled into place, Sy-wen shrank back from the three men staring down at her. She remembered Conch, captured and bleeding. She remembered the tangling net that had pulled her from the sea and recognized two of the men here as the bearded pair who had caught her. Their leering faces were hard, but not as hard as the third man's. His features made the others seem like mere babes. Yet the severity in his face was not born of harsh cruelty, like the other two, but was more like rock hardened by the beating of a winter's surf. His features shone with a proud nobility won through time and deeds rather than birth and circumstance. His black hair was swept back from his face and revealed a red-and-black tattoo of a hawk emblazoned on his cheek and throat.

She knew this man, too. Her eyes were drawn to the curve of a tattooed wing upon his throat, and the panic in her heart subsided slightly. He had saved her. He would protect her.

One of the bearded men spoke up. "Looks like the lass likes my voice. I come a'calling, and she wakes right up."

"Leave us," the tattooed man said in a low voice. He did not even turn toward them.

"The galley is a common room, Bloodrider. We have as much right to be here as you."

The tattooed man tilted his neck to face the speaker. "You've had your dinner, Hort. Clear on out."

"And I suppose you could make us both," the other answered, menace thick in his throat. His companion stood at his shoulder, supporting the man's threat.

Sy-wen ignored the growing tension. Her eyes were still fixed upon the man's tattoo. She could not look away. She stared at the crown of feathers atop the hawk's head, the sharp points of its clawed talons. With the stranger's neck bent like this, it seemed the hawk's red eyes blazed directly at her, digging deep inside her.

As she stared, she suddenly found her heart beating faster. It became difficult to breathe. Unable to stop herself, she wormed an arm free of the wrappings around her and reached out to touch the tattoo.

She had a need.

Her fingers brushed a wing that stretched across the man's throat. At her touch, the man knocked her hand away, flinching back as if struck by an eel. He reached a hand up and rubbed his tattoo as if trying to erase it from his flesh. "Don't," he said coldly, his eyes wide and wary.

She answered, her words coming from deep near her heart. "I have need of you." She reached out to him, and he backed a step away, out of her reach. "Come," she insisted.

One of the others laughed nearby. "Looks like the lass likes Blood-riders, Kast. Maybe after you're done with her, we'll show her what real men . . ."

Sy-wen did not hear them. She had a *need*, and the sight of the tattoo had cast a spell over her. It told her to demand what she wanted of this tattooed man. A part of her struggled against these strange compulsions, but it was a whisper before a roar. She could not resist.

Neither could the man. He obeyed her order to come and stepped toward her, his eyes now narrow with fury. It seemed he could not resist the compulsion any more than she could, as if they both danced to some ancient music in their blood, sung and orchestrated by her need.

He leaned toward her, exposing his neck to her.

She reached and covered the tattoo with her palm.

He spasmed under her touch, and his narrowed blue eyes flamed to red, matching the hungry, hunting eyes of the hawk.

As her blood compelled, she named her desire. "Take me from here," she said. "I must escape."

"You're already gone," he answered in a voice filled with fire. He leaned over and scooped her up.

The bearded men stared at them, jaws hanging open. One of them made the mistake of speaking. "You're not going anywhere with the girl, Kast." Then he made the fatal mistake of blocking the tattooed man's path, a knife raised in threat.

Sy-wen watched, and though her senses were dulled by whatever spell had been cast, she still knew the stranger moved far quicker than her eyes could ever follow—even when burdened with her weight.

In a blur of sharpened steel, the man named Kast twirled, a knife appearing in one of his palms. Before either bearded man could speak or raise an alarm, they were clutching throats slashed from ear to ear. Their pig eyes seemed not to know they were already dead. Blood flowed down their stained shirts. They fell in unison to their knees as if in final prayer. One raised a bloody hand in supplication toward the tattooed man, then both fell forward onto their bearded faces.

Inside she screamed at their sudden deaths. She had never seen so much blood. Yet still she did not fight the man's murderous arms. Instead she spoke to him in encouragement. "I must escape," she said, repeating her heart's desire.

He nodded, his red eyes aglow, and lifted her higher in his arms. He stepped over the corpses and carried her toward a portal.

As soon as they left the chamber, Sy-wen smelled the sea in the narrow passageway. The scent of home came from directly ahead. Hurry, she urged silently. Her guardian climbed the stairs at the end of the hall and carried her to the open deck of the boat.

Night had fallen. Below stars as bright as the full moon, the ships' full sails billowed like drifting clouds on a black sea.

A strong breeze blew through her hair as Sy-wen was carried across the decks. Around her, a scattering of men worked the riggings and sails. A few fishermen saw Kast and raised a hand in welcome. Nearby, a boy with shocking red hair sat and worked at coiling a long rope.

"Kast, whatcha doing with the girl? Is she dead?" The boy dropped his rope and stood up. His eyes were bright with curiosity. The boy now stood between Kast and the starboard rail.

As the man walked directly toward the boy, Sy-wen felt him shift her weight in his arms, freeing one of his hands. She realized what was about to happen. Oh, no! The bloody knife glinted in the starlight.

The boy crinkled his brow, and a small laugh escaped his throat as he saw the blade. "Whatcha doing, Kast?"

No, no, no, she sang to herself. Don't do this! She could not move or stop what was happening. The spell trapped them both.

Then, whether the man heard her silent wish or obeyed some inner compunction of his own, he hesitated. "Run, Tok . . . Get away," he said, his voice strained, his words garbled.

The boy had frozen in place, a confused look on his face.

Kast raised the dagger, but his arm trembled. "Go, boy," he spat between clenched teeth. "Now!"

Suddenly a new man appeared from behind Kast's shoulder. He stepped between Kast and the boy. He was an older man, all worn edges and sun-wrinkled skin. A scrabble of gray beard marked his chin, but it was the small silver star fastened in his right lobe that caught her eye. Its brightness seemed so out of place on the gray man—yet at the same time also somehow so right.

Kast spoke to him, his voice a gasp as he fought the spell that bound him to Sy-wen. "Flint . . . take the boy . . . Get away."

"Oh, enough of this nonsense," the old man grumped. He raised a fist to his lips and blew through it. A fine dust puffed into Sy-wen's face.

The powder stung her eyes and nose. She sneezed violently, almost throwing herself from her guardian's arms. She blinked a few times, then darkness pulled her down.

Kast's blood raged against the assault on the girl. He lunged with his dagger, but as soon as the girl slumped limp in his arms, it felt like a bowstring had snapped within his chest. His vision sprang clear of the red fire that had blinded his thoughts and sight.

He stared at the knife poised at his first mate's throat. What was he doing?

Flint pushed the dagger away with a single finger.

The boy Tok peeked around the old fisherman's shoulder. "What's happening?"

Flint opened his palm and raised it to the boy. "Does this smell odd?"

The boy bent and sniffed. His eyes blinked, and he sneezed a quick little burst before sliding to the planks.

"Sleep dust," Flint explained.

"What . . . what's happening?" Kast asked.

The old man wiped his hand on his breeches and shook his head. "Who would have guessed after so many centuries that the bond-oaths of the Bloodriders still tied them so tightly to the mer'ai?"

"What are you talking about?"

As answer, the old man pulled a woolen scarf from his pocket and held it out to Kast. "Cover your tattoo. We don't want that happening again."

"What? What happened? I don't understand." Shaken, he sheathed his dagger and accepted the scarf. "Flint, what's going on?"

"No time." The old man peeked at the girl in Kast's arms. "Such a pretty face for so much trouble." He sighed and glanced up and down the deck. "If you wish to escape, we must hurry. This night won't last forever. I've awoken the dragon and freed him of the ropes. But he is gravely injured, and any delay could mean his death."

Kast backed a step away. He had wrapped his neck in the woolen scarf. "I don't know what scheme you plot, Flint. But I'll have none of it."

"Quit being such a fool, Bloodrider. You just killed two shipmates. That'll get you hung before the *Skipjack* reaches port. Come or die."

Kast still stood frozen in indecision. Suddenly an explosion of voices erupted from belowdecks, angry voices. The captain's voice was among them.

Flint raised his eyebrows questioningly.

"Where do we go?" Kast asked.

"I have a skiff tied near the stern. Carry the girl." He turned and led the way toward the rear of the boat.

Kast followed. He glanced at the sleeping mer'ai girl in his arms. What was going on?

A trail of snoring men marked Flint's trail across the deck. Kast eyed his wiry back. Who was this man he had worked alongside these past three winters? He was certainly more than just a ship's first mate. Curiosity drove Kast after the old man. Flint knew more about what had happened this evening than Kast did, and he was determined to learn all the old fisherman knew of the mer'ai, their dragons, and the strange hold the girl had upon him.

Kast joined Flint by the stern rail, where a rope ladder draped over the side. A small, single-sail skiff rocked in tow behind the larger boat.

"Can you climb down with the girl?" Flint asked.

Kast nodded. The child was light as a wisp. Below, he could see the dragon's jade snout secured to the side of the skiff. Its huge wings billowed under the waves to either side.

Flint must have noted where he looked. "He's old, and his wounds are deep. It will be lucky if we can reach the healers before he dies."

"Where are you taking him?"

Flint climbed over the side of the boat. He looked Kast squarely in the face and spoke a name that revealed his madness. "To A'loa Glen."

As the old man's face vanished out of sight, Kast stared at the open sea behind the boat. Starlight reflected in the midnight waters. A'loa Glen. The mythical lost city of the Archipelagoes. Surely Flint was mad. Sailors had searched many centuries for the sunken city, and nothing had ever been found.

Still, Kast remembered his old teacher, the Bloodrider shaman, long dead from riven fever. Kast had followed a madman's fevered words before, so why not again? He hoisted the child over his shoulder and reached for the ladder.

Below, he saw the seadragon sluggishly spread its wings.

Besides, Kast thought as he climbed onto the ladder with a child of the ancient mer'ai over his shoulder, this night even myths were becoming real.

Something stung Sy-wen's nose and pulled her from sleep. She blinked away the traces of slumber and found two men staring at her. She remembered these two men, but she was still too dazed to know if she should fear them or thank them. "Where . . . ? Who . . . ?"

"Hush, child. My name is Flint," said the one with the gray beard, the silver star in his ear glinting brightly at her. "You're safe." He waved a tiny vial in front of her nose. "Sniff more of this, my dear. It'll help clear the cobwebs from that pretty little head of yours."

Sy-wen winced at the smell, but it did seem to help her eyes focus. Above her head, a sail bulged taut with the night wind. She was in a small boat. Stars lit the night sky still, but to the west, a rosy glow promised morning.

Wobbly, she struggled to sit up. To either side of the skiff loomed the shadowy silhouettes of island mountains, hulking behemoths that threatened to topple as the boat raced through the sea channel between them.

"Careful there, sweetheart." The old man helped her up and pulled a blanket around her shoulders. "I think it best if you keep yourself covered."

She lay near the skiff's prow. Pulling the blanket more firmly around her bare chest, she stared back toward the stern and recognized the other man in the boat. He sat with one hand on the rudder and would not meet her eye. Though his neck was covered with a gray scarf, she knew him to be the tattooed man, Kast, who had rescued her from the hunting fleet. He was the one who had cast some spell over her—or maybe it was the other way around. She shook her head, still confused. The events earlier seemed like a watery dream.

The old man sat back from her, pocketing his tiny vial. "I'm sorry for using the sleep potion on you, my dear. But it was the only way to break the oathbinding between you two."

She did not understand his meaning and pushed higher on the pile of blankets. If she could just find a bit more strength, she could throw herself over the boat's side, but her arms trembled with the exertion of just sitting up. She sank back to her blankets. One hand wandered to the five-legged starfish attached to her belt. It was still there! She had lost her knife, but they had foolishly left her with the stunner—a weapon. She eyed the two men and let her fingers drop from her waist. She only had the single stunner. She must bide her time.

Then an explosive snuffling near her left elbow startled her and drew her gaze toward the starboard edge of the skiff. A familiar scaled nose rose above the boat's lip. A fine mist blew out into the night from his flared nostrils. "Conch!"

She reached out a hand and brushed her fingers along the hard ridge between his nostril flaps. Responding to her touch, Conch nudged at her palm. Thank the Mother, he still lived!

Leaning closer to the boat's edge, she saw the tether that leashed the dragon to the side of the skiff. Though he still lived, he was yet a prisoner of these fisherfolk.

The man named Flint must have read her thoughts. He spoke as Conch nuzzled her hand. "We mean no harm to your bondmate, child. He is gravely injured and needs a healer's attention."

She kept her gaze away from the men. "I can take him to our own healers," she said, keeping silent about the incorrect assumption concerning Conch's bonding to her. "The mer'ai are wiser in the ways of dragons than you lan'dwellers."

"Perhaps," he answered as the tattooed man looked on, "but I'm afraid Conch took a severe stab into his chest, puncturing his hind lung. He'll not be able to submerge to a depth to reach your leviathan. His best hope to survive lies with the healers at A'loa Glen."

Sy-wen crinkled her eyes at the mention of this city, distrustful. She had heard old stories of such a place, fanciful tales full of magick-wrought wonders and creatures from all the lands. Surely it was just an imaginary town.

Kast spoke from beside the rudder, his voice filled with bitterness. "A'loa Glen is a myth, Flint. What makes you think you could find a place that sailors have searched for for centuries without discovering?"

Flint nodded toward Sy-wen. "The seas hold many mysteries, do they not, Kast? How long has it been since one of the Dre'rendi has laid eyes upon a mer'ai?"

Kast lowered his eyes. "It has been many centuries . . . before the arrival of the Gul'gotha to our shores."

"Yet, is she not flesh? Is she merely a creature of myth?"

Kast glanced at Sy-wen, then back to the old man. His eyes were hard. "But A'loa Glen has never been discovered. What makes you think you can find it?"

"Simple," Flint said with a shrug. "It's my home."

Kast's eyebrows rose in surprise, then lowered, bunching up upon his forehead like thunderclouds. "You're daft, Flint. Your home is Port Rawl. I've been to your house by the Blisterberry Cliffs."

"Ah, that's just a place to dry my bones when I'm out of the sea."

Sy-wen cleared her throat. She cared nothing about any of this talk. She had only one concern. "Can these healers of yours save Conch?"

"If we can get him to them alive, I believe they can."

Sy-wen pulled her hand away from where Conch snuffled at it. Her palm was covered in black blood that blew from his wounded chest. She held the bloody hand toward the old man. "He will not live much longer."

Flint's eyes narrowed. The genuine concern in the old man's face touched Sy-wen. He was truly worried about Conch, too. "I did not think his wounds were so deep," he muttered, obviously shaken.

His concern loosened her own resolve. Her voice cracked with emotion. "Please," she said with tears, "if you can help save him . . ."

He placed a warm palm upon her knee. "I'll do my best." He swung to face Kast. "We need to swing around the leeward side of the next island. Do you know the Arch of the Archipelago?"

Kast nodded. "I know the place."

"That's where we must go." Flint glanced toward Conch. "And we need as much speed as you can beg from the wind."

Sy-wen huddled on her blankets, a prayer on her lips. "Hurry," she whispered.

Kast must have heard her. His gaze focused on her. "I will get your dragon to port alive," he said with a rude sharpness. "The seas and winds are the heart of a Bloodrider."

She stared back into his determined eyes, silent for several breaths.

Finally, Flint drew a hand between the two of them, severing their gaze. Once Sy-wen turned aside, the old man lowered his hand, seemingly satisfied, and nodded toward Kast. "Just make sure you keep that tattoo of yours covered."

"Why?" Kast asked gruffly.

The old man turned his back on Kast and stared out over the water. "Old magicks, old oaths," he mumbled, then waved away the question. "Now concentrate on the sails and rudder."

But Kast had one more question. "If you're from A'loa Glen," he asked, changing the tack of the conversation as he worked the rudder, "why sign on as the first mate on the *Skipjack*?"

Flint still did not turn toward the other. "To keep an eye on you, Kast," he said with a shrug, then touched his silver earring. "Your people will hold the fate of A'loa Glen in the bellies of your warships."

LATE WITH GRESHYM'S EVENING MEAL, JOACH RACED DOWN THE deserted hallway, his footfalls leaving little puffs of dust as he ran. No one had been in this passage in ages. He clutched his map in one hand. Had he missed a turn? Breathless, he stopped at an intersection of halls and unfolded his scrap of parchment. With his heart beating urgently in his ears, his finger followed the charcoal lines that roughly outlined the hallways and passages of this level of the Edifice. "Curse this place," he mumbled to himself as he realized his error. He tapped the intersection where he should have turned.

Slipping a sliver of charcoal from his pocket, he extended the detail of his map to this location. Error or not, he could not waste any bit of information he gathered on this place. Once done, he folded his map and wiped his fingers on his trousers.

He swung around and followed his steps in the dust back the way he had come. He frowned at the footprints. Perhaps he should whisk away the signs of his trespassing in these halls. Then he shook his head. Time was running short, and he still needed to reach the kitchens to collect the darkmage's supper. Besides, no one had been this way in a long time, and Greshym would grow suspicious if he delayed much longer. For the past moon, Joach had been using the short space of time when he was sent for meals to do some exploring. But each time he had to hurry. He did not want the darkmage to grow wary if his meals came too late.

Joach reached the proper intersection and made the turn that headed toward the east staircase. He fled as fast as safety allowed, his ears pricked for any voices or the sounds of other steps. Too many denizens of the Edifice knew the addle-brained servant of Brother Greshym, and Joach could not risk anyone seeing him walk faster than his usual slow, dull-eyed shamble. Luckily, the halls remained empty, and he reached the stairs without encountering anyone.

He paused at the floor's landing with his head cocked, listening to the stairwell. These stairs, spiraling down the inside of the easternmost tower, a tower named the Broken Spear, were seldom used. This section of the Edifice seemed to have been abandoned. Dust and debris cluttered the passages and halls. Still, Joach knew the value of caution and kept himself vigilant—and this time, it proved wise.

Faintly, he heard muttered voices echoing from far below. Someone was on the steps. Joach backed away, then shook his head and stopped. He could not wait for them to leave the stair. He had already delayed too long. So he slumped his shoulders and let a dribble of drool froth his lips. Sighing, he walked heavy footed down the stairs, practicing a stumble now and then.

He had perfected the manners of a simpleton. No one gave him more than passing notice. So he scuffled down the spiraling steps, again assuming his role of the doltish servant boy. As he progressed, the voices grew more distinct. The conversation sounded heated, angered, but the words spoken were unclear.

Curiosity perked in Joach. The brothers in A'loa Glen were always so calm and sedate, interminably cooperative with each other. Seldom were voices raised in anger. Occasionally Joach overheard debates concerning various esoterica of magick or a difference of opinion on the translation of a certain line of prophetic writing, but again discussions were always civil and respectful.

The voices on the stair, though, were anything but courteous. Maybe it was just two servants arguing over some trivial matter. The hierarchy of the servant class in the Edifice was fickle and often led to arguments, even the occasional fight.

Joach continued down the steps. Snatches of words began to reach him. Two distinct voices, one high and sharp, the other low and dour.

"You blaspheme . . . Such is not the way!"

"I heard it . . . Ragnar'k . . . truth in tongues of fire!"

"Ragnar'k . . . moves for no man . . ."

Joach rounded a curve in the spiraling stair and had to suppress an expression of surprise when he discovered two white-robed brothers on the steps below. They had their cowls lowered as was custom when brothers conversed.

Two faces raised to stare up at him. Joach's left foot slipped, and he stumbled down a step. He caught his balance and kept his expression dull, incorporating his accidental misstep into his usual role. The two brothers were unknown to him. Joach was not sure they would recognize him, but he could not take any chances.

One of them nodded toward him as he shuffled down the remainder of steps. "It's just that odd bird's servant. You know, that old bent-backed brother."

The other eyed Joach up and down. "Brother Greshym. I heard about his addled boy."

The two brothers were a contrast in form. The taller of the two was massive shouldered and broad backed, with skin so dark he seemed a shadow in his robe. The other, skinny as a sapling, had skin so pale even his eyes and lips seemed bled of color. Both, though, had shaven heads and a single silver star adorning the lobe of an ear.

From the corner of his eye, Joach stared at the five-pointed stars. Perhaps they were the symbol of some chapter of the brotherhood. He had never seen their like before. As he continued down the stair, both men grew quiet. Their caution in speaking in front of him only heightened his curiosity.

Still, Joach did not stop when he reached the landing the two men shared. He did not have the time to dally and ponder these men. He still had to reach the kitchens. So he shambled past them without even a glance. Yet, as soon as he was a distance down the steps, out of the men's direct sight, he heard their voices again.

The dark man spoke, his voice deep and more hushed now. "Brother Flint's signal was spotted from the watchtower just after twilight. He should be arriving at the Grotto just after the sun rises tomorrow."

Joach slowed his steps, listening.

"Then we should be off, Moris. Our time to act runs short."

"Do you think the Praetor suspects?"

"If he does," the smaller brother hissed, "we're doomed, and A'loa Glen will fall."

Joach stopped in midstep. Could it be . . . ? It sounded as if these two also knew of the evil that lurked within the walls of the Edifice. But were they allies or some competing menace? Joach chewed at his lower lip. Though his suspicions ran wild, he had grown to realize over the past moon that he needed help. All the maps and drawings he could muster would not save his sister Elena. He had to take a chance. He had to trust someone.

He turned and scrambled back toward the landing above. But when he got there, the brothers were gone. Joach checked the halls that led out into this level of the Edifice. Nothing. He listened for steps, both in the hallways and on the stairs above. It was as if the brothers had simply vanished.

He stood on the empty landing, frozen in indecision. He had no clue where the two had gone, and to search for them now would only delay Joach past the point of maintaining his ruse with Greshym. Cursing silently, he continued down the stairway toward the kitchens.

He would watch for those two men again.

Once the boy was gone from the landing, Moris pulled his eye away from the peephole in the hidden door. His large dark frame filled the tiny passage. "You were right, Geral," he said to his small pale companion. "Your ears are sharper than mine."

In the dim passageway, their white robes were like the lost shades of the dead. Moris could see his fellow brother turning to lead the way through the secret halls of the Edifice.

"I was sure I'd heard the boy stop after he was out of sight," Geral said. "Who would have suspected the boy only played at being a dolt? A clever way of gleaning information. He almost exposed us. The dark forces grow more cunning here."

Moris followed. "Do you truly think he is a tool of the Gul'gotha?"

"Of course. Why else would he maintain this ruse?" Geral glanced over his shoulder at his towering companion. "However, what it does make me wonder about is the loyalty of the boy's supposed master, Brother Greshym. Has this revered brother also been lured to the dark magicks and do he and the boy work together, or has the boy been sent to spy upon our esteemed brother, to learn his secrets? It gives me much to ponder. I hate to think that someone named after one of our sect's most gifted seers has given his heart to the Gul'gotha."

"Hmm . . ." Moris considered his friend's words. He was not as certain about the boy's allegiance as Geral. He had seen the expression on the boy's face as he had searched the landing. The boy was scared. It was not the face of a cunning creature of the Dark Lord, but only of a frightened child. Still he kept these thoughts to himself. Geral did not like his views questioned, and the two of them had already been arguing all day. Moris was tired of parrying words with his fellow brother. So he kept his silence on this minor matter.

"We must avoid this boy as much as possible," Geral said.

Moris made a noncommittal grunt and fingered the silver star in his ear. In this matter, too, he disagreed. The boy deserved further attention. Moris could not so easily dismiss the fear he had seen in the lad's eyes.

Geral continued speaking as he led the way to their concealed warren of rooms. "Our sect has kept its secret ways since before the fall of Alasea. We must be extra cautious during this pivotal time. All can be so easily lost from a loosely spoken word."

"I know, Brother."

Moris followed Geral's narrow back down the winding stairs that led below the base of the abandoned tower. The stairs led deeper and deeper under the Edifice. A few flickering lamps marked their course. Soon the walls of the narrow stairway were no longer mortared blocks but simply plain rock hewn from the stone of the island itself. Eventually the stairs ended and a maze of corridors led outward.

Geral continued onward without pause. Around Moris, the corridors widened enough for his large frame to finally straighten, and the scent of mold and brine swelled in the passages. It was the scent of home.

They turned a sharp corner in the passageway, and a room larger than the Grand Ballroom of the Edifice opened before them. Even after his twenty winters as a member of this sect, Moris' blood still thrilled at the sight.

The walls of carved rock spread like wings to either side. Imbedded in the stone were thousands of crystals, some the size of a bird's eye, others as large as an og're's fist. Their facets reflected the flames of the sputtering torches to glow like a subterranean starscape.

Both brothers touched the silver stars in their ears and paused in the entryway. As impressive as the walls were, the true reverence of the room lay in the gnarled cord of root that ran from the distant roof of the chamber to the center of the floor. The knobby, crooked shank of growth, as broad as Moris' shoulders, was the taproot for the ancient koa'kona tree, the true heart of A'loa Glen. Here was stored the last vestige of its Chyric energies.

Around the chamber, a handful of other brothers of their cryptic order had their heads bowed as they communed with the tree. Some had hands raised to one of the crystal stars on the walls, delving for prophetic visions.

Their sect, older than the Brotherhood itself and formed when Chi had still blessed the mages of the world with magick, had not abandoned their duties. They continued to work at unraveling the paths of the future through the search for prophetic visions. Long ago, their words had predicted both the disappearance of Chi from these lands and the rampage of the Gul'gotha. They had tried to warn their fellow mages, but their words were judged blasphemous. The others could not fathom that the spirit Chi would ever abandon them, and so those of their sect were declared heretics and banned from the Order; they were exiled from the shores of A'loa Glen.

Hard truths are never easily accepted.

Yet, even the sect's banishment had been foreseen by some members of their group. A small cadre of seers disobeyed the Order's edict and vanished into the walls and secret corners of the Edifice. Over the hundreds of winters since, they had worked in secret. With or without the help of the Brotherhood, they prepared for the future dawn.

The sect of the Hi'fai would not abandon its duty.

Moris lowered his fingers from his silver star and stepped into the chamber. Long ago, their sect's most powerful seer, the mage named Greshym, had spoken the vision that forged the Blood Diary. He had then sacrificed his life in the binding of the book, giving his blood to prove the validity of his vision. Could Moris offer any less?

Moris crossed to near the huge root and knelt. He himself had spoken the vision of this night—when once again Ragnar'k would move, when the blood of a dragon would mark the beginning of the battle for A'loa Glen.

Book Three

SHADOWBROOK

14

Elena tried not to flinch as the daggers flew toward her. Two blades of honed steel flipped through the midday sunshine, reflecting sparks of brilliance as the twin knives tumbled over the heads of the onlookers. The knife thrower, Er'ril, stood on the far side of the town square, blindfolded. Even though Elena knew the fold of cloth binding Er'ril had been artfully slitted and impeded Er'ril's sight only a bit, she still could not keep from holding her breath and squinting nervously at the descending daggers.

She heard the voice of one of the townsfolk raise nearby. "The boy's daft! Standing there like a cow while someone throws knives at his head."

A neighbor agreed. "But who's more daft? The boy or his father? Imagine throwing knives at your own son!"

Then it was over.

Thunk . . . thunk . . .

The two daggers imbedded into the oaken door at Elena's back, one to each side of her head, missing her ears by only a breath. She let out a sigh of relief and stepped forward. As she bowed deeply to the audience, a drop of sweat that had nothing to do with the day's heat rolled off her nose to strike the stage's plank. She straightened with a wave, matching Er'ril's own wave from across the town square.

For the past three moons, the company had been traveling the countryside, performing as a small circus from village to village. This stop, though, was a large town, at least twice as big as her hometown of Winterfell. It was the first such city they had ventured into. The town of Shadowbrook, named after the river that ran through its center, was one of three shipping towns that marked the plains, one for each major river that crossed the region. River barges loaded in Shadowbrook with the wares of the plains—baled tobacco leaf, bushels of the rye grain grown only there, aromatic oils drawn from herbs unique to the region—and transported them to the coastal cities to barter for trade goods. Due to its commerce center, the riches of the plains flowed into Shadowbrook, and Er'ril hoped to earn enough here to book passage on a ship to the coast.

His decision had proven wise. Over the past four days, the performances had gone well.

A scatter of applause met the end of Elena and Er'ril's performance. Waiting by the side of the stage stood Mogweed, dressed in a red-and-green hunter's costume, with Fardale at his side. A few children were pointing at the huge treewolf, their eyes wide. Fear and awe could be heard in their whispered voices. Mogweed and his trained wolf were a popular show and earned more coppers from the crowd than the supposed "father and son" knife show.

As she hopped from the planked stage, Elena fingered her cropped hair, stained black to match her "father." A few of the young girls who had been watching Fardale cast sneaking glances at her. The shy gazes and quick smiled whispers suggested a few were enamored by this exciting new circus "boy." Elena sighed, tiring of her charade.

Still, the deception had kept them safe.

Thousands of circus troupes plied the wide plains of Standi, earning their profits while the crops were rich. Come winter, the flow of coppers would dwindle with the sun's warmth, but for now, the plains were dotted with gaily colored wagons and performers of many an ilk. It was easy to get lost and disappear among them.

Occasionally their troupe encountered small groups of armed Gul'gothal dog soldiers patrolling the plains, and all of Elena's party knew for whom they were searching. One evening, the company had even performed for a battalion of the rough men, but none of the soldiers had raised an eye at their troupe. As a matter of fact, the captain of the battalion had paid them a silver coin as a bonus. The disguise had worked well.

Over time, the horrors of the foothills faded, though the mourning and tears for Nee'lahn did not. Her lute still traveled with the company as a reminder of their fallen friend, almost like an accusation for failing to protect her. Oddly enough, it was Meric who had finally insisted on taking responsibility for the fragile instrument. "We were once enemies," he had explained. "But long ago our two peoples worked together. I would like to return this to the elv'in as symbol of the beauty and nobility of the nyphai. Perhaps in its music, the nyphai can still in some small way live." One night, Meric had played the instrument, and for a moment it seemed his words were true. In the music, Nee'lahn's spirit had seemed to sing out to them. Tears and sad smiles had reflected the campfire that night, and for the first time, it seemed they could at last put her memory to rest.

So the days had passed. At first everyone had felt relieved that no further assault descended upon the party and that no chase dogged their trail. But as time wore on and hundreds of leagues disappeared under their wagon's wheels, the companions began to glance over their shoulders again and jump a bit at sudden noises, and the nightly campfires were stoked with a few more logs to drive the darkness farther back. It was as if the entire troupe was holding its breath, awaiting the next attack.

The quiet and peace had begun to wear on them.

Sighing, still edgy from her performance, Elena pushed aside the thin curtain behind the stage and almost ran into Meric. He stood in the wings, awaiting his turn. He slipped a small sparrow into one of his billowing sleeves with an embarrassed look. His crude magick act was seldom well received. His haughty nature seemed to shine through to the audience and rub against their grain. Only during his finale, when he used his elv'in magicks to levitate, did the crowd respond enthusiastically.

Meric stepped aside with a slight bow. "Milady," he said with simple grace.

Elena frowned at him. "Careful," she warned, suddenly irritated. "Remember, I'm supposed to be Er'ril's son, not your long-lost bloodline."

He waved off her concern with a flip of his thin wrist. A few bird feathers blew out of his cuff with this motion. His pale face reddened slightly. "I should go out there," he mumbled. "Mogweed will soon be finishing."

She nodded and continued toward the wagon. The shielding curtain ran from the wagon's edge to the back of the stage, so Elena did not have to confront any more doe-eyed audience members. To her right was an empty warehouse that awaited the fall's harvest. It was the perfect site in the square to set up their circus, as there were no prying eyes to peek backstage.

After Meric disappeared behind the curtain, Elena had a moment to herself; all the others were occupied with the show. Onstage, she heard Fardale howl, his cry raising a tinkling of nervous laughter from the audience. Elena knew that on the far side of the stage stood their troupe's only other attraction—a sideshow with a single exhibit. In a curtained cage guarded by Kral crouched Tol'chuk. People were charged a copper to view the imprisoned og're. Most viewers laughed at the poor quality of the constructed "monster," who was wearing fake goat horns on his head and painted-on whiskers. None suspected that what stood before them truly was an og're—and that was the way Er'ril wanted it. For a troupe to have a "real" og're would wag too many tongues and perhaps attract undue attention, so they added fake embellishments to mask Tol'chuk's true nature. Still, with Kral standing rock faced before the cage with his huge ax, and with a sign near his feet that warned FOR THE AUDIENCE'S OWN PROTECTION, the novelty attracted hordes of gawkers.

So with everyone else occupied, Elena had a solitary moment to herself, a rare event in such close company. As the only female among this company of men, she enjoyed these moments to herself. She smiled and walked toward the back of the wagon, scratching at the band of cloth that flattened her chest and bound her breasts.

It was then that Elena was attacked—though it would take some time to recognize the chance meeting as an assault. From the corner of her eye, she saw movement and jumped back from the shadowed doorway of the warehouse.

A small, naked boy stepped out from the shelter. He could have been no older than three and stood staring at her, sucking his thumb. He was dirty as the bricks of the warehouse, with mud-colored hair and a soot-smeared face. His face, like those of all children his age, was round and full of open honesty. Oblivious of his nakedness, he smiled around his thumb and pointed at her.

Elena knelt down closer to him. "Are you lost?" she said as if coaxing a puppy to her.

He pulled his thumb from his lips with a loud slurp. "You shouldn't be here, lady."

Elena smiled. How did the little boy know she was a girl? Maybe her voice had given her away. "It's all right," she answered him. "I'm with the circus."

"Circuth?" he lisped.

She slid off the glove from her left hand and offered her bare palm to him. She knew better than to reach for him with her ruby-stained hand; the odd sight might frighten the child. "Now where's your mommy and daddy? Were they watching the show?"

He took her offered hand with a shy smile. His palm was cold, and slimy from filth. A shudder ran through her legs at his touch. It was like gripping a dead fish.

But his eyes, shining brightly up at her, disarmed her. "I don't have a mommy or daddy," he said, a slight giggle in his voice as if he were amused at such a thought.

Her heart went out to the little fellow. To be orphaned so young, he probably didn't even remember his parents. A bit of anger grew in her chest. An orphan or not, how could his caretakers leave him so poorly kept and looked after? "Then where do you live?" she asked.

"Live?" He scratched his oily hair with his dirty fingers.

"Where do you come from?" she repeated.

He brightened with her words. "Oh, I don't come from here."

She sighed. Of course the child must live in Shadowbrook. A naked three-year-old child didn't just wander into this large city on his own.

"Who are you with?" she tried again. Someone must be responsible for him.

"I'm hungry," he said, obviously tiring of the subject.

Smiling sadly, she guided him toward the back of the wagon. "I think I just might still have some sweetcakes left from this morning."

He crinkled up his nose at her suggestion.

She was surprised by his response. What child didn't like sweetcakes? "Then what are you hungry for? We have some dried beef and bread."

He suddenly stopped and, with surprising strength, drew her to a halt. His voice became suddenly lustful, nothing like a child's. "I need your magick," he said hungrily.

She gasped at his words but could not free her hand from his grip. The boy looked up at her with that same clear face of a child, but in his eyes lurked something much older.

A second, gruffer, voice arose behind her, startling a gasp from her as she swung to face this new threat.

"Good performance today." It was Er'ril. The plainsman was pushing through the curtain toward her, the fake blindfold in hand.

"Er'ril!" she cried out to him.

The terror in her voice had him immediately at her side.

"What is it?" His gray eyes were sparking with deadly intent, one of his throwing knives already in his hand. He scanned the empty space between the curtain and the warehouse.

Elena remained mute. She stared down at where the boy had stood just a moment ago. He was gone, but cold fingers still held her. They were not a child's hand. In her grip was a clinging handful of wet moss. Oily strands and coarse vines were wrapped tightly around her palm.

"What is it?" Er'ril repeated, lowering his blade slightly as his gaze settled on her.

She held out the fistful of mossy growth toward him. "I . . . I don't know."

TOL'CHUK CROUCHED WITHIN THE CAGE, HIS LEGS CRAMPING FROM THE confinement. The curtain draped around his cage blocked his view beyond, but he could hear Meric's voice onstage. The elv'in was close to the finish of his act, and soon the show would be over for the day.

Straightening the pair of goat horns on his head, he awaited the next curious townsperson to spend a copper to view the "monster." Over the past three moons, he had played along with this farce, growling and hissing at the patrons for their amusement, but his most ferocious attempts at instilling terror usually only resulted in laughter, especially when the goat horns fell off. None believed him a real og're. But then again, he actually wasn't a *real* og're, since half his blood came from a si'luran heritage. Sighing, he worked his calf muscle with the claws of one of his hands.

Kral, his supposed jailer and guard, hissed at him through the curtain. "Someone comes. Be ready." The mountain man's voice grew louder as the possible patron approached. "Come see the beast of the mountains! Dragged from his foul lair after killing forty men and feasting on their bones!"

Tol'chuk shook his head at the man's theatrics. Kral's words bordered on lies, except that Tol'chuk's people *had* actually killed over forty men and *had* feasted on their bones. It just hadn't been this particular og're who had committed these atrocities. Kral, with his mountain honor, had at first balked at hawking such an obvious exaggeration, but over time, the road had worn away his misgivings, and the mountain man had grown quite fond of his role as the troupe's barker. His deep thundering voice suited his assignment well. As Kral continued his litany of horrors, Tol'chuk groaned loudly.

"Did you hear that!" Kral said in conspiratorial tones to someone beyond the curtain. "He stirs! Beware his rage and blood lust!"

A child spoke. "Mommy, I don't want to see the scary monster."

"Oh, honey, it's just a trick." This was a woman's voice, sounding tired and exasperated. "Someone in a fancy costume. Don't you want to peek at it?"

"I don't wanna!" The child's voice edged toward a tantrum.

"Fine, then I guess we should be heading home."

"I wanna pet the big doggie!"

The voices began to fade as the pair drifted away. "That was a wolf, honey, and his master has put him to bed." The child began a whining complaint.

Kral poked his head through the curtain. He wore a huge grin. He seemed to enjoy his current occupation. "Sorry, we lost them."

"I heard," Tol'chuk grumbled sourly.

Suddenly another woman's voice rose from behind Kral, startling him. Few snuck up on a mountain man's back without his awareness.

"I'd like to see your monster," she said. Her speech was sure and swift as a mountain stream in spring.

Kral quickly recovered from his surprise and swung to face her, his staged words already on his lips as the curtain flap dropped closed. "Why, yes, come see the beast who has slew forty men and . . ." Then the mountain man's voice suddenly cracked. "And . . . he . . . umm, I mean . . . it—"

"Feasted on their bones," the woman finished for him. "Yes, I've heard it all before." The clink of a coin in the pan marked the woman's payment. "Now if you'd be so kind as to step aside, I'd like to see this og're of yours."

Kral's tongue stumbled on words he had repeated a thousand times. "Be . . . beware his . . . blood lust."

"Yes, yes, of course, I will." The woman bent her way through the curtained canopy to step before Tol'chuk's cage. Kral, his cheeks bright red, stood behind her, holding the flap up.

Tol'chuk studied the woman and understood the mountain man's sudden consternation. She was a formidable sight. The woman stood as tall as Kral and only slightly less broad of shoulder. She wore her long blond hair braided back into a tail that reached past her waist. Dressed in leathers with iron bindings, she seemed more a warrior than Kral, and the twin blades in crossed scabbards on her back added to the impression.

Yet, as gruff as her physique and dress were, her face was that of a handsome woman. She had full lips, a slender face, and eyes bluer than the skies at twilight. These finer features were obviously not all wasted on Kral. The mountain man could not seem to look away from her, his lips still parted in midspeech.

"Why did you put such ridiculous ornaments on him?" she glanced back at Kral. "What's the purpose of the great horns?"

The mountain man's features darkened further, and intelligent speech was clearly beyond him. She seemingly saw through their sham and for anyone to argue otherwise would only heighten the awkwardness of the situation.

"Well?"' she said tersely, as if well accustomed to her questions being answered without delay.

Tol'chuk answered her. "It be a disguise," he said. "True monsters be often killed in villages."

The woman did not even raise an eyebrow at his words. "Have you no dignity?" she asked. "To crouch in filth and play the buffoon?"

Taken aback by her brutal summary of his condition, it was Tol'chuk's turn to be at a loss for words.

She spun to face Kral, her motion fluid and graceful, like some fierce cat. "Free him of this cage," she ordered. "I won't stand for this."

"But—?"

Her eyes were fire. "I would have words with the both of you," she said. "But I will not speak while—" She suddenly twisted back to the cage. "What is your name, og're?"

"Tol'chuk."

"Hmm . . . *he-who-walks-like-a-man,*" she translated. "A cruel name." She returned to stare at Kral, ignoring Tol'chuk's shocked expression. How had she known the meaning of his og're name? "As I was saying, I will not speak while Tol'chuk is locked up like some mad dog. Now free him."

Kral nodded, too abashed to speak a further word, and fumbled with his keys. He unhinged the lock and removed the chains that barred the cage door.

The woman stood with her hands on her hips until her orders were obeyed. As Tol'chuk half tumbled from his cramped cage, the tall woman studied him with an odd set to her lips, as if she was about to say something but held back.

Soon Tol'chuk was stretching his crooked legs on the cobbles of the street. Working a kink from his back, Tol'chuk raised a pained face to her. "What be your name?"

She inclined her head ever so slightly. "Mycelle Yarnosh."

"How be it that you know the og're's tongue?"

She waved his question away. "We have more important matters to discuss, like what an og're is doing so far from his mountain home in the first place."

Kral finally found his ability to speak. "I . . . I see no reason why this is any concern of yours."

She rounded on him, bringing her face close to his. "Because I went through a lot of trouble to track you all down."

Her words pushed Kral's hand to the haft of his ax.

She did not even glance at his threat. "You play at games when all your lives are in jeopardy. Why do you tarry here in Shadowbrook? You know better than this, man of the mountains. When you are hunted, to stop is to die."

"What do you speak of, woman?" Kral's gruffness had returned.

"If I could find you," Mycelle stated heatedly, "so could the Gul'gotha. I've been tracking you since the foothills, and your guide has wisely kept you moving, escaping even my skill. But now this stupidity!" She threw a hand in the air. "Has it just been the luck of the lame, rather than wisdom, that has kept you from the dogs of the Dark Lord?"

Tol'chuk closed in on the woman. She seemed to know too much about them. He sniffed at her, scenting her strength but also an underlying fear, a bitter tang. Anything that could trigger such a response in her was truly something to worry about. He spoke at her shoulder. "Why have you been hunting us?"

"Is it for bounty?" Kral asked.

She sighed and shook her head with exasperation. "Have either of you been listening to me? If I was here for a fistful of silver, a legion of dog soldiers would have your innards for their victory stew. Now if we are done dithering, perhaps you could introduce me to this wit'ch of yours."

Kral's ax was now in his hand; he had armed himself so swiftly that Tol'chuk had not even seen him move. Yet the woman had. Both her blades were already poised, one at Kral's throat, one above Tol'chuk's heart. The og're looked down at the sword tip touching his chest. Not only did she know the og're's language, she also knew the one weak spot on an og're's body where a single thrust could kill. Both her weapons were held with a casual steadiness that was more threatening than the edges of her twin swords.

Tol'chuk was the first to speak. "Kral, hitch your ax. If she meant us harm, we'd be both dead."

Kral was not a dullard. He carefully returned his ax to his belt.

"And you—Mycelle—if you know of the wit'ch, then you know we will lay down our lives to keep her from harm. So sheathe your blades and let your tongue do your talking."

With a single motion, she swept both swords into the crossed scabbards on her back. She reached and pushed back a single lock of hair that had escaped her braid. "I mean your wit'ch no harm. I have dogged her trail to offer my blades and service to her." She nodded toward the town beyond the curtained alcove. "But I may have come too late. There are two ill'guard stationed here, and they can sniff magick."

"Ill'guard?"

"Spawn of the Black Heart himself, imbued with foul magickal beasts. They make plans already to close off the city. Then they will hunt the streets for your company and the wit'ch you guard."

Kral glanced at Tol'chuk, his question clear. Should they trust her?

"If you're to escape," she continued, "it must be within the day. My skills will be of great help."

"And what do you want in return?" Kral asked, still doubtful.

"That is between me and the wit'ch," she said coldly.

Kral eyed the og're again. Tol'chuk shrugged at him. It would be best to bring her to the others, he decided. Let the matter be settled then.

Tol'chuk spoke to her, letting his threat ring clear in his voice. "If you betray us, you will need more than two swords to keep me from your throat."

She smiled at him, a bit sadly, then raised a palm to touch his cheek. "Is that any way to speak to your mother, Tol'chuk?"

Kral watched the og're's face change multiple colors at the woman's statement and her touch on his cheek.

The og're backed away from her. "How could . . . Where did . . . ?" Tol'chuk then collected himself with a shake of his head and stated firmly, "You cannot be my mother."

Mycelle lowered her voice, a certain tenderness entering it for the first time. "I can see your father in you quite clearly." She pointed vaguely at his face. "The way your eyes are pushed a bit too close together. And that nose! That is your father's nose."

Tol'chuk's hands wandered to his face as if trying to feel the truth of the woman's words. Kral sensed the woman spoke with an honest heart. "She does not lie," Kral asserted.

"But how . . . Why?" Tol'chuk's thousand questions were plain on his rocky features. He seemed unable to sort them in any coherent order.

Mycelle placed a hand on the og're's arm. "I fell in love with your father. It's just that simple."

These words quieted Tol'chuk. "If what you speak is true, why did you leave us? I was told you died in the birthing caves."

She nodded and grew pensive. "In some ways, I did. You know of your si'luran heritage, do you not?"

"Tu'tura," Tol'chuk mumbled.

"Yes," she said with a bit of fire. "So the og're tribes have always named us: *Tu'tura, "baby stealers."* We were despised by the clans. Yet your father knew my secret and still had the heart to love me. But blood is blood, and with your birth, I could no longer hide the fact that I was not truly an og're. Your half-breed birth spoke my deception to the rest of the clan. I was hounded and almost killed. Your father rescued me, taking me beaten and bloody to the ancient og'res in the deep caves."

"The Triad."

"Yes. They carried me to a magickal gate in the mountain's heart and cast me out, warning that I must never return or I would be slain. They said the spirits in the gate would take me where I needed to go."

Tol'chuk nodded with her words, as if he knew what she spoke of. "The Spirit Gate," was all he whispered.

Mycelle did not seem to hear him and continued her tale. "I was cast east of the Teeth, deep into the lands of man. Wounded in body and spirit, I was barely able to transform myself, but I did—into the form of a human. Weak and dying, I was found and taken in by a kindhearted woman who cared for me. It was she who—"

Her words were interrupted by Mogweed's sudden appearance at the curtain flap. The shape-shifter still wore his stage costume, his hair disheveled. "Something's happened to Elena," he said in a rush. "She's safe, but Er'ril wants us all at the wagon." Only after speaking his words did he seem to notice the woman standing behind Kral. Mogweed's face blushed as he realized he had spoken openly in front of a stranger, breaking the company's code of silence.

Kral clapped Mogweed on the shoulder. "Don't worry. She already knows about Elena."

"Wh-who is she?" he whispered.

Kral shrugged. "She claims to be Tol'chuk's mother."

Mogweed's brow crinkled as he glanced around Kral's wide shoulders to peer at her. "But Tol'chuk's mother was si'luran," he muttered. "That woman is *not* one of my people. Her eyes . . ." Mogweed waved to his own slitted pupils. For those who knew the creatures of the Western Reaches, the strange amber eyes with catlike pupils marked a shape-shifter in any form. This woman's eyes were normal, like any other human's.

Mycelle must have heard his words. "But I am si'luran. Or more truthfully, I *was* of your people. I have since settled."

Mogweed's eyes grew wide, a mixture of shock and disgust clear in his expression. "You . . . you settled? Were you forced?"

"We don't have time for this," she said, dismissing Mogweed with disdain. "The story is long, and Elena is not as *safe* as you so blithely stated. At least not here in Shadowbrook. Take me to her."

Her words seemed to snap the others from their interlocked gazes.

"She's right," Kral said. "Let's go." He led them through a back flap of the curtained alcove and slipped behind the stage. As he walked, he pondered the day's sudden events. First the warrior woman with her wild claims, and now there was something wrong with Elena. Was there a connection? Once past the backdrop behind the stage, Kral spotted Meric and Fardale huddled with Er'ril near the rear of the wagon. In the middle of them, Elena sat on the cart's boot, showing them something clasped in her hand.

Kral cleared his throat, and all their eyes swung toward the mountain man's group as they marched along the curtain.

Er'ril's brow darkened as he saw the stranger among them, his suspicions plain in his expression.

But Elena was the first to speak as her face also responded to the newcomer. Her eyes crinkled in confusion, then widened with shocked delight. "Aunt Mycelle?" She leapt off the wagon and raced over to the woman, throwing her arms around the supposed stranger. Tears burst from the girl's eyes as she buried herself in the woman's embrace. "I can't believe you're here," she sobbed and squeezed tighter, as if needing further contact to dispel her disbelief. "You're really here!"

The woman returned her hug just as affectionately. "Child, how you've grown."

"Who is this woman?" Er'ril said darkly.

Mycelle answered with a warm smile for Elena. "I'm not really her aunt . . . but her Aunt Fila and I did share a different sort of sisterhood."

Into the stunned silence, Kral spoke. "You knew her aunt?"

"Yes. She was the woman who found me and cared for me after I passed through the Spirit Gate."

"Ah . . ." Kral said, suddenly seeing how fates were twisting together.

Er'ril's face had blackened with ire. "Could someone explain what you are all talking about?"

His question was ignored.

Mycelle pulled Elena's wrist up. "What's wrong with your hand?" The woman's eyes had narrowed with concern.

Kral leaned closer. Elena's left hand was crisscrossed with looping shreds of mossy vines. It seemed as if the tiny leaflets and corkscrewing branches grew out from the flesh of her hand.

"It won't come off," Elena said. She tugged at a fragment of the tenacious growth. "It's stuck."

Mycelle knelt on one knee and studied the girl's hand, flipping it one way then another. Her lips were tight. "Does it hurt?" she finally said.

"No, it's just sort of tight."

"Hmm . . ." She twisted a leaflet from the moss and sniffed at it.

Er'ril had by now shouldered his way beside them. His eyes were still suspicious. "Do you know anything about this?"

"This is swamp moss," Mycelle said, picking at another strand. "It isn't just clinging to her. It's growing into her."

"What!" Er'ril pulled Elena back from her, but the girl shook him off and stood on her own.

Mycelle stood up and wiped off her fingers that had touched the moss. "Elena's been bewit'ched."

15

Mycof and Ryman stared across the tai'man board, both deep in thought on their next moves. The bone and jade pieces were spread between them in an intricate parlaying for dominance on the wormwood gaming board. Both combatants sat hunched over their pieces, dressed in motleys of green silk shirts, red woolen jackets, and black tasseled slippers.

Though similarly attired, it was their matching features that drew an eye. Obviously of twinned birth, the pair's likeness to each other was disturbingly exact. Where most other twins had slight differences, minor imperfections that set them apart, these two had no such telltale signs. It was as if both had been carved by an artisan of impeccable skill from the same bone as the tai'man pieces. Their ivory faces, each slender as a woman's, with features small and pale, made each seem more a statue than a man.

The left corner of Mycof's lip twitched slightly up.

"You have made a decision, Brother?" Ryman said, noting this abrupt outburst from his twin. Mycof was always such an exuberant tai'man player.

Mycof glanced at Ryman. He saw the ridicule in his brother's eyes for his obvious lack of control. Mycof fixed his unruly lips back into a thin line. "Sorry," he said, and reached to move a piece; he mounted it atop Ryman's stallion.

"Is that the move I have been waiting all afternoon for?"

"You are mounted," Mycof answered. "Three moves and I will have your castle stormed."

Ryman stared at the board. Had his brother gone mad? Then with this thought, he saw the trap. It was his turn to let one eyelid open a bit wider in surprise.

Mycof enjoyed his normally stoic brother's enthusiastic response, and enjoyed even more Ryman reaching a finger out and toppling his own castle, admitting defeat. Still, Mycof kept his features still: Not a lip parted, not an eyelash moved. He would savor this moment and not ruin it with a ridiculous display such as a smile. Mycof caught Ryman studying him from under his white bangs. Mycof kept his face placid.

"You are in rare form, Brother," Ryman finally conceded. He used a polished nail to sweep back his stray hair from his red eyes.

"Another game?"

"Evening approaches, and the Pack will soon be ready to hunt. Perhaps it would be best if we waited until the morn."

Mycof conceded the logic of his brother's plan with a slight bowing of his head.

"Quit patronizing me!" Ryman scolded; even his cheeks showed a thin reddish hue.

Mycof had not realized how upset his brother was at the defeat. "I was only acknowledging the full value of your assessment. Evening doth approach, and the Pack grows most hungry for blood."

Ryman heard the solidness of his brother's words and used Mycof's even tones to help harden his own constitution. The flush faded from his cheeks. "Then we should retire to the cellar." He stood, keeping his gaze well away from the board. He did not want to be reminded of his defeat.

The careful shunning of the board was noted by Mycof. He stood up and followed his brother toward the door. At the threshold, the back of his hand brushed his brother's sleeve. This token of affection was not unappreciated by Ryman.

"Thank you," Ryman said, his lips barely moving. "I think this day's challenging game overheated both our bloods."

"Certainly it was a most riotous contest."

They left together, two ivory statues draped in expensive finery. Their slippered feet whispered through the scattered rushes that covered the castle's stone floor. Servants stepped aside, casting their eyes down as the two lords of the Keep passed. Few but the servants ever set eyes upon the pale brothers, and the sun never did. Mycof and Ryman were not unaware of the whispered rumors about them, but no one questioned the twins' heritage and right to the castle.

Their parents, long gone to their crypts, had been deeply loved by the people of Shadowbrook. It was the Kura'dom family who had founded the city long ago, and it had been the twins' father who had most recently overseen the flourishing of Shadowbrook through wise contracts and trade agreements, expanding the flow of riches into the city. The entire town had shared in this new wealth, and in memory of their fine parents and ancient lineage, most folk just shook their head at the eccentricities of the brothers.

So no one said a word to Mycof and Ryman as they wandered deeper into the less-traveled regions of the Kura'dom stronghold. It was their right. It was their home.

The stronghold, known in Shadowbrook simply as the Keep, was older than the town around it. It had started as a small signal tower, one of many once scattered throughout the Standi Plains. Most had fallen since to rubbled ruin, but this one, positioned strategically and profitably near the banks of the Shadowbrook River, was a seed that had grown the town itself. And as the town had spread like roots from a tree, the tower itself had grown in fits and starts: a wing extended here, a third story built there, even four stumped towers added to surround the old signal tower. And in recent times, battlements, walls, and even a thin moat had been constructed around it, though these last works were more decorative than purposeful. The moat had a park built at its edge, and stately black and white swans swam its waters in languid circles around the Keep.

Proud of the castle gardens and handsome soaring battlements, most townsfolk had forgotten the true seed that had sprouted their town. The ancient signal tower was buried deep within the fanciful facade, a crumbling structure of rough, ill-fitted stones that was the heart of the Keep. Only a handful of men still remembered its ancient name—*Rash'amon,* the Bloody Pike, named during the first of the Gul'gothal battles five centuries ago, when a thousand men had given their lives to defend the plains. Its bloodstained battlements, lit by hundreds of siege fires from the encamped d'warf armies, had glowed crimson for an entire moon. Only with the death of its last defender had the tower finally fallen to the d'warves.

Yet this ill history was not unknown to the twins.

This was their *true* heritage.

Mycof and Ryman glided in silence from their heavily curtained room in the Keep's west wing toward the narrowing passages that led to the inner tower. As they progressed, the ceilings lowered, and the walls to either side closed in until the pair were forced to walk in single file. Finally, as the roof began to brush their white hair, they reached a door of beaten and carved brass gone green with stain. Mycof slipped a silver key from his sleeve and unlocked the way into Rash'amon.

Swinging the door wide, a waft of air washed up from below. Mycof inhaled the sweet scent. It smelled of mold, damp dirt, and a hint of something richer, a musky scent that thrilled through him. Ryman also paused at the threshold, his eyelids slightly lowered as he, too, reveled in the dank reminder of what lay below.

"Come, Brother," Ryman said in a thick voice and led the way down. "It's almost twilight."

Mycof saw his brother's hand tremble slightly as he reached out to the moldy stones for support in his descent down the steep, narrow stair. Mycof also felt the rush of anticipation in his own limbs. He had to restrain himself from hurrying his brother forward.

Ryman, though, still sensed his brother's growing urgency, like a storm cloud over his shoulder. He increased his pace.

With Ryman's back turned so he could not see, Mycof allowed himself a smile. The two brothers knew each other so well. As they continued down the winding stair, the passage grew darker. No maid or servant kept the torches burning along the length of this inner staircase. Only Mycof and Ryman had keys to open the brass door that led into the bowels of Rash'amon.

Yet, faintly ahead, far down the staircase, a glow began to grow.

Now, without any urging, both brothers sped down the stair, oblivious to how their slippered feet gave them the poorest grip on the damp stone. The reddish, burning light called to them.

The pair passed other doors, but these openings had long been bricked closed and were ignored. Down and down they wound. Only the glow held Mycof's attention. He licked his lips. Hunger grew in his belly like a flame.

By the time the twins reached the bottom of the stairs, they were running, breath rasping though clenched teeth. On this lowest level of the Bloody Pike, a thin sheet of black water soaked the stone floor, oily with mold and aglow with the reflected light from the cellar room ahead.

With their feet splashing in the water, soaking their expensive silk slippers, Mycof and Ryman rushed for the deepest room of Rash'amon and the secret it held. They dashed through into the dank cellar.

Here the floors were no longer stone; like all good cellars, this one had a dirt floor—or more precisely, mud. Over the hundreds of passing winters, the tower had settled into Shadowbrook's water table, and the river now swamped the dirt floor.

Ryman reached the room first, immediately sinking to his ankles in the river-soaked muck. He had to pull each foot free to move forward from here. The filth made sharp sucking noises with each step as he moved toward his goal. He had already lost both slippers to the greedy mud, but he gave them no thought. They were easily replaced. Behind him, Ryman heard Mycof struggle along with him.

Both their eyes were on the object in the center of the room, half sunk in the muck.

Crouching naked, like a toadstool growing in a black cellar, was the object of their devotion. Its squat body was a lump of bone and muscle molded by a cruel artist into only a rough approximation of limbs and torso. Its hooked nose dropped like melted wax over its fat lips, and black eyes had sunk deep into the planes of its face. Before its belly floated a spinning sphere of black ebon'stone afire with ancient memories of blood-soaked Rash'amon. Their master's bald, craggy features were aglow in the reflected bloodfire of the globe.

It was the seeker, he who had discovered the twins five winters ago and had gifted them with the Pack, a reward for swearing their service to the Black Heart.

Mycof and Ryman fell to their knees in the thick mud, ripping the silk clothes from their bodies. Their twin faces were contorted into spasms of ecstasy and savage delight. Their normally placid features were now storms of wicked emotions.

They bowed before their god, smearing their faces in the filth, and thus displayed their allegiance to Lord Torwren, the last of the foul d'warf lords.

Er'ril picked up the final juggling dagger and set the blade to the grindstone. He positioned himself near the shadowed doorway of the warehouse where Elena huddled with Mycelle. He had been shooed away by the tall swordswoman as she examined the girl. She seemed to know more about what had happened to Elena than he did, so for now he tolerated her orders.

Around Er'ril, the other members of the troupe were involved in their own chores as they closed down the circus for the evening: boxing their props, caging and feeding Meric's sparrows, and sweeping up their corner of the town square. To the side, Kral grumbled as he wrestled the curtains back into the wagon. The twilight sky warned of rain, and the entire circus must be wrapped up. Only the wooden stage would be left on the square, since dismantling it would be too much work.

It cost an expensive tithe to keep their stage in place, but Er'ril had at least managed to barter for the fee to include the storage of their wagon and supplies in the nearby warehouse. The troupe itself was housed in a small inn on the north side of the square, the Painted Pony. It was a shabby establishment, but Er'ril knew that the more frugal their living expenses, the sooner they would earn enough for the barge passage down to the coastal city of Land's End.

As the others busied themselves, Er'ril honed his dagger with swift strokes upon his grindstone—but his attention was not on his work. His eyes were fixed on Elena and Mycelle. After declaring the child bewit'ched, the woman had refused to say anything further until she questioned Elena more about the odd boy who had confronted her.

As Er'ril studied the two of them, the evening gloom and fog began to roll in from the river. He set aside his grindstone, satisfied with the blade's edge. With the scrape of metal on stone finally ended, their voices carried over to him.

"Is this where the boy appeared from?" Mycelle said. "This doorway?"

Elena nodded. "I thought him only a lost child."

As he eavesdropped, Er'ril polished his blade with a sheen of oil and stored the knife beside the six other daggers in the wooden case. The hilts were nicked and scarred from long use, but the blades were shiny and clean, as if newly forged. He knew the value in maintaining good weapons.

Mycelle finally straightened in the doorway, drawing Er'ril's eye with her movement. "A lost boy—now that is just like her."

"Like who?" Elena asked.

Mycelle did not answer. She only looked around the square with her head slightly cocked, as if she were keying on a sound only heard by her ears.

Both intrigued and suspicious, Er'ril snapped closed his wooden case and crossed to join them. "I overheard you," he said. "Have you truly a suspicion who is behind Elena's attack?"

The tall woman only glowered at him and motioned him to silence.

Er'ril continued. "What did you mean when you said Elena's been *bewit'ched*?"

Mycelle stayed silent, still listening, then shook her head. She spoke slowly to Er'ril, as if speaking to a dolt. "Bewit'ched . . . it means a wit'ch has cast a spell on her."

The tension thickened like a rolling fog between them.

Elena spoke into the strained silence. "But I thought I was the only wit'ch?"

Mycelle smiled at her. "Now who told you that?"

Elena glanced at Er'ril.

"Men!" the woman scolded, rolling her eyes skyward. "It looks as if I came just in time." She sighed, then continued. "Elena, you're the only true *blood* wit'ch. But a few women who bear strong elemental magicks have declared themselves wit'ches of the land. Sea wit'ches, forest hags, water wit'ches. I believe it was one of these land wit'ches that has done this to you."

"Who?"

"I have a suspicion, but it'll take more investigating."

By now, Meric and Fardale had come closer. The two must have also overheard Mycelle's words. The wolf sniffed at Elena's hand.

Er'ril glanced to the streets to see who else might be listening. The square was empty of all but a few evening stragglers. Luckily, the threat of rain had kept even these last few hurrying to accomplish their final errands before the storm blew in. None glanced toward the circus troupe.

At his elbow, the elv'in asked, "Do you think the Dark Lord is involved in this?"

"No, I sense no corruption in this magick." But Mycelle still seemed distracted, her eyes narrowed in concentration.

The woman's edginess slipped into Er'ril. He glanced warily about the square. "Maybe it would be best to continue this conversation at the inn," he finally said.

Mycelle nodded. "The first wise words I've heard you speak, Er'ril."

With the circus locked down for the night, Kral and Tol'chuk hauled the wagon through the barnlike gates that led inside the rafted warehouse. Two pallets lay along one wall. Tol'chuk and Fardale had been spending their nights in the storehouse, both to guard their belongings and to keep suspicious tongues from wagging about the og're and the treewolf.

Tol'chuk at first objected about being left out of the discussions, but some silent exchange passed between him and Fardale, and he grew silent. Mycelle also laid a hand on her son's arm. "We'll talk soon," she said.

Tol'chuk did not answer. He simply turned away and went to care for their horses. The troupe's mounts were also kept at the warehouse, corralled in a small yard behind the stout structure. It was cheaper to water and care for their own mounts than to pay an additional fee to stable them at the inn. Besides, the Painted Pony's barn was riddled with rot, and rats the size of small dogs rooted through the barn's dingy hay.

Of course, their own accommodations were not much better at the inn. The rooms were small, dark, and reeked of the fish frying constantly in the inn's kitchen. Being a river city, siltcod and mudfish were the staple of the inn's dinner fare, and variety did not seem to be in the cook's vocabulary.

Once the wagon was secure, Er'ril led the others toward the inn.

As they pushed inside the cramped common room of the Painted Pony, Mycelle had her own opinion on Er'ril's choice of accommodations. "Yes," she said, eying the three ale-stained tables occupied by a handful of sullen-faced dockworkers, "I do believe it is high time you began traveling with a woman."

Two of the rough men glanced in Mycelle's direction, their eyes widening at the fine sight of the tall blond swordswoman. As a leer crept into their expressions, Mycelle stared them down, her eyes glinting with steel. The dockworkers suddenly found their mugs of ale particularly fascinating and turned away.

"Where are your rooms?" Mycelle asked.

Er'ril led the way, stopping only to order a cold supper to be prepared. "At the top of the stairs," he said. The crooked steps creaked under his weight. "I've hired two rooms."

"How generous of you," Mycelle said sarcastically as she followed with Elena.

Soon the six of them were crowded into the larger of the two rooms. Mycelle's perpetual scowl deepened when she surveyed the room, but she kept her sharp tongue still. The chamber's two beds were planked cots with the barest ticking to cushion a body. The single window looked out upon the inn's courtyard and, though open, only seemed to draw the summer heat into the room rather than cool it. To add to the stifling quality of the quarters, the low ceiling seemed to press down upon them all. Kral had to lean to keep his head from striking the rafters.

"Let's all get settled," Er'ril said. "It seems we have much to discuss tonight."

Mogweed and Meric claimed one bed, while Kral and Elena sat upon the other. Only Mycelle and Er'ril still stood. The two of them faced each other like two wolves about to fight for leadership of the pack.

Mycelle spoke first. "After examining Elena's hand, I don't believe the bewit'ching poses an immediate risk, but more dire threats hunt these streets. Shadowbrook is a danger to her."

"I can take care of Elena myself," Er'ril said. "I've got her this far. I'll get her to A'loa Glen. Why should we trust you?"

Kral began to answer this question. "She is Tol'chuk's—"

But Mycelle silenced him with a glance. "If you don't mind, I'll tell my own story."

And she did.

Er'ril listened with little patience as the swordswoman told of her journeys from the Western Reaches and of her time with the og're tribes. She stared Er'ril straight in the eye as she spoke, offering no apologies for her actions. Even Er'ril could sense the truth of her words. "After Tol'chuk's birth, I was cast out and taken in by Elena's aunt. It was Fila who taught me who I truly was, and about the special gift born in my blood. She explained why I was so unlike the other si'lura who were content in their forest home, how this gift had driven me to leave the Western Reaches for far horizons."

"And what was this gift?" Er'ril asked.

She nodded toward the beds. "Like Kral and Meric, I was also born with land magicks in my blood. Kral is rich in rock magicks, and Meric has the gift of wind and air."

Both Kral and Meric glanced at her uneasily, obviously sharing Er'ril's own concern. "How do you know about them?" Er'ril asked.

"It is my gift. I am a seeker."

"A seeker?"

"An elemental hunter. In each generation, there are a few who are born with a special empathy for elemental magicks, those who can read the land magick in others. I am one of them. The magick in others calls out to me like a silent song. It draws me like a lodestone. This is *my* elemental gift."

"And Aunt Fila discovered this in you?" Elena asked.

"She was a wise and talented woman." Mycelle bowed her head in memory. "Due to my skills, Fila invited me into the Sisterhood and taught me how to use my magick. She knew there would come a time when the elementals would play a role in either saving or damning our lands. She once told me, 'The wit'ch is the key, but the elementals will be the locket in which the key is kept safe.' Fila gave me a purpose to my life."

"But what did Aunt Fila want you to do?"

Mycelle answered, but kept her eyes focused on Er'ril. "As a seeker, I was to journey the lands of Alasea, discover those gifted with elemental powers, and warn them."

"Warn them of what?" Er'ril asked gruffly.

"To warn them that I was not the only seeker among the lands." She let those words sink into them before continuing. "The lord of the Gul'gotha has recruited his own seekers. They, too, scour the countryside, searching for young elementals. Where I only warned, they would rape. Imbued with tools of the Dark Lord, his seekers could corrupt the gift in these youngsters and forge them into a black army, the ill'guard, a foul legion of the most dire black magicks."

Er'ril's eyes widened with her story. He pictured Vira'ni's midnight hair and smooth skin. His face darkened with the memory. He saw the shock of recognition in the others' eyes, too. "I think . . ." he mumbled. "I think we've already met one of these corrupted elementals."

Now it was Mycelle's turn to show surprise. "You faced one of the ill'guard and survived?"

"Barely," Elena said softly.

"Of what use is your warning?" Er'ril said with sudden heat. "If any of these elementals are caught, they can't resist the Dark Lord."

Mycelle reached into a pocket. "No, there is a way to resist the corrupting touch of the Gul'gotha." She removed a jade pendant carved in the familiar shape of a tiny vial.

Elena sat straighter on the bed. "That's just like the one Uncle Bol gave me to talk with Aunt Fila's ghost!"

Her words crinkled Mycelle's brow. The woman obviously did not understand what Elena meant. "I did get this from your Aunt Fila," she conceded. "One of the Sisterhood was skilled at carving jade. As I journeyed, I passed these vials out to the elementals I discovered. If ever confronted, swallowing the contents of the vial will keep one from falling prey to their dire magicks."

"So there is a way to resist this corruption," Er'ril said. This revelation wounded him. If only Vira'ni had met this woman . . .

Elena's face, though, had brightened with hope. "Does the vial contain some sort of magickal elixir?"

"So I told everyone," she answered. For the first time, her gaze lowered to the floor. "But I spoke falsely. The vials only contain poison."

A shocked hush spread through the room.

Mycelle continued. "Death is the only way to keep the corruption from claiming you. The Sisterhood judged it better to die than to become a mindless creature of the Dark Lord. Once possessed, there is no way back." Mycelle paused and took a deep breath. "However, we could not risk that this selfless choice would be made by all. So I spread both the poison and the lies to ensure this would not happen."

Mycelle glanced up, then quickly away. The horror must have been plain on everyone's face.

Mogweed was the first to speak, his voice incredulous. "You helped kill people."

The swordwoman raised her head and turned to face each person in the room. Her eyes were bright with threatening tears, her voice sharp. "Do not judge me! I made my own choices—and I will *not* recant them. I have done things that have wounded my heart. I abandoned my og're lover and my son. I shed my own si'luran heritage, forever trapping myself in human form. I've given poison to children while accepting thanks from their mothers. But I will not apologize for my actions." She frowned at Er'ril. "This is the final war. If the curse is ever to be lifted from our lands, we must all bleed."

Finally, her chest heaving with emotion, she closed her eyes and lowered her voice. "This silent war between myself and the seekers of the Dark Lord has been raging since before Elena was born. Without my efforts, there would be a wall of ill'guard between you and A'loa Glen. It was my lies and poisons that cut a bloody path for the wit'ch to follow." She opened her eyes and stared at Er'ril with an intensity that iced his bones. "Are you now too timid to walk my path?"

Er'ril swallowed, unable to answer. He did not know who frightened him more—the ill'guard or this woman with a heart of ice.

Kral was the first to speak. "We've all made hard choices."

"Yes," Elena said timidly, "but we were *given* the choices. These deceived innocents, these elementals who go about with poison around their necks, have had the choices taken from them. They will end their lives by their own hand without even knowing it."

"But which is kinder?" Mogweed asked. "Knowing or not knowing?"

Glances were exchanged.

No one had an answer.

Mycelle was the first to break the silence. "You may soon discover the truth of my sentiments. Here in Shadowbrook I've already sensed two of the corrupted elementals, a pair of the ill'guard who hunt this city. While you debate my morals, they will have your hearts roasting on their darkfire spits."

Her words caught their attentions and awoke the fears that had been slumbering in all their breasts since their battle with Vira'ni.

"What should we do?" Kral asked.

"We do what we must to survive," Mycelle said, her voice thick with venom. She pocketed her vial of poison. "It's what I've done all my life."

"RISE," THE D'WARF LORD INTONED, HIS VOICE A COARSE ITCH IN MYcof's and Ryman's ears.

The twins raised their fouled faces from the mud. Mycof could taste the dank river sludge on his lips. It was the sweetest nectar, but

Mycof knew there were finer tastes still to be appreciated this night. Kneeling beside him, Ryman's eyes mirrored his own lusts.

The floating sphere of ebon'stone slowed its spin and settled into the d'warf's pale hands. Spats of crimson bloodfire still skated over its black, polished surface, and veins of silver could be seen in arcs of jagged brilliance on the surface of the ebon'stone talisman.

"Are you ready to accept the Sacrament?" the d'warf asked. His eyes searched them, his gaze squirming over them like a blind river eel. He judged their worth.

"Yes, Lord Torwren," they both recited. "Our bodies we give to you."

The d'warf rose on gnarled legs. "Then come and accept your master's reward." He held the ebon'stone toward them.

Crawling on hands and knees through the mud, they approached the talisman.

"Come," Torwren urged, his voice a raw scab. "Give up your cool flesh for the heat of the hunt. Lord Gul'gotha has need of your talents tonight. Other elementals have entered Shadowbrook. They must be found and brought to Rash'amon for the Sacrament."

Ryman felt a twinge of jealousy at the d'warf's words. He did not care to share the secret rites deep under the Keep with anyone but his own brother. Still, his eyes were full of bloodfire and ebon'stone. He could not resist obeying.

The Pack was hungry for the hunt. The hunt meant blood.

The two brothers each raised a muddy palm to the talisman. Ryman pressed his flesh against the cold stone and knew he touched the heart of his master. He felt his bowels loosen and his bladder give way. It did not matter. The heat of his spirit was drawn into the stone.

To complete the Sacrament, Mycof closed the circle. He reached with his free hand and took Ryman's fingers in his own. The two brothers were now linked, both together and to the stone. With the touch of flesh on flesh, the spell was complete, and the Pack was called again into the world.

Ryman stared at his brother as the spell took hold of their bodies. It was like looking in a mirror. How handsome he was! Ryman grinned as the pain ripped into his body. He watched Mycof's skin ripple and knew his did the same. Black boils the size of bruised thumbs arose upon their pale skin. Mycof matched his brother's white-lipped grin.

The Pack was coming!

Soon a thousand boils marked their flesh on face, arms, chest, belly, buttocks, and legs. Mycof watched one especially large growth on his brother's left cheek ripen and stretch as what lurked within the boil struggled to start the hunt. The boil burst with the tiniest spray of blood. Mycof felt a similar sharp eruption near his own right nipple. It felt like the bite of a wasp.

Soon a storm of wasps stung their flesh.

The twins moaned in the ecstasy of the Sacrament.

From the boil on Ryman's cheek, a black, segmented worm coiled forth. It stretched and waved from its burrow. Soon hundreds of others were doing the same. Mycof stared in awe at the beauty of his brother; tears rose in his eyes at the sight. His brother's naked pale flesh was festooned with hundreds of the writhing, questing tendrils of blackness. Mycof knew his own body was gifted with the same dark beauty.

Ryman's and Mycof's eyes met, and they knew it was time.

Like leaves falling in autumn, the worms dropped from their burrowed nests and fell to the watery mud with small splashes and plops. There, the sweet creatures drank the brackish waters and ate the river's mud, swelling as they consumed their meal. Soon spiky hair sprouted and grew along their squirming lengths. Small clawed limbs burst forth from the sides to lift them from the mud. Red, beaded eyes and whiskered snouts grew forth to end their blind grubbing, and pale, scaled tails whipped back and forth, anxious for the hunt.

Pocked and bleeding, the two brothers stared proudly at the army of rats that lay around their knees. The Pack was ready.

The d'warf lord spoke. "It is done. Let the hunt begin."

With his words, the two brothers fell backward into the mud as their minds entered the Pack. Mycof and Ryman were now one with their offspring, a thousand eyes, a thousand sharp teeth hungry for blood. They sent the Pack flowing up the steps of Rash'amon, spreading out through the hundreds of cracks in the ancient stones. Scurrying forth from the Bloody Pike and out through the Keep, flowing, rippling in all directions, they reached the streets of the sleeping town of Shadowbrook.

Deep under Rash'amon, though, the two brothers still lay sprawled in the mud. Their eyes were now blind to the d'warf leering over them, yet their ears could still hear him.

"Go," he whispered as he crouched over them, his thick lips brushing the edges of their ears. "Bring me the magick."

AS TOL'CHUK HAULED A BARREL OF WATER ACROSS THE WAREHOUSE, HE felt a prickling atop his foot. Glancing down, he discovered a fat river rat crawling over his clawed foot. Disgusted, and already in a foul temper at being left in the warehouse, he kicked savagely at the rat, meaning to gut it with a claw, but the sleek creature was too quick and skittered away with an annoyed squeak, as if offended that the og're should get in its way. He scowled at its retreat. He hated rats. With the river only a few blocks from the town square and with the warehouse mostly empty, the foul creatures competed for residence in the hollow, raftered building.

Fardale stood at the open doorway that led to the horse yard and swung his nose toward Tol'chuk. The treewolf was a black outline against the sea of fog that had rolled in from the nearby river. The roiling mist was like a living creature, more substantive even than the ghostly images of the neighboring buildings. As if swallowed by the great white beast, the nickering and stamping of the horses were the only signs that the yard was occupied by anything but the occasional bold rat.

In the weak light cast by the two oil lamps in the warehouse, Tol'chuk saw the treewolf's hackles raise in a ridge along its neck and back. With his eyes aglow, Fardale sent to him: *Carrion lays spoiled on the trail.*

Tol'chuk crossed to the wolf, the water barrel still clutched under one arm. He knew better than to dismiss Fardale's keen senses. Beyond the doorway was just a wall of fog. "What do you scent?"

Fardale raised his muzzle to the slight wind that blew in from the night, then glanced up to the og're.

An image of spiders appeared in Tol'chuk's head. He knew Fardale was *not* referring to the ordinary spiders nesting in the rafters feasting on flies and moths. Tol'chuk scratched one of the many scars that pocked his thick hide from the old healed bites of the Horde.

"Be there another demon?" he asked.

Fardale's eyes glowed. *A wolf sniffs many scents near a watering hole . . . a swirl of odors, too many to make clear.*

Tol'chuk tightened his grip on the water barrel. The treewolf was not confident of his abilities among the myriad smells of the bustling town. "Perhaps we should bring the horses inside. Caution would be wise this odd night."

Fardale's answer appeared in Tol'chuk's head. It was the image of Er'ril. The wolf wondered if they should raise the alarm among the others.

Tol'chuk grimaced. A moment ago, he would have welcomed any excuse to go to the inn and join the others, but was Fardale's vague sense of unease reason to abandon his post? What could he tell the others except that the wolf smelled something his nose could not identify? The same had been true for himself when he had first entered Shadowbrook. The town was a swamp of unusual odors and scents.

He pondered his choices until the horses in the yard erupted in a sudden flurry of panicked whinnies and striking hooves. Blinded by the fog, Tol'chuk and Fardale froze. The horses, lost in the fog, sensed or saw something.

As Tol'chuk and Fardale tried to pierce the veil of mists, a huge black shape swelled up directly before them. They scattered backward as a horse flew between them into the warehouse. It was Mist, the girl's mare. The horse's eyes were rolled white in panic, and the beast's lips were frothed with fear.

Tol'chuk backed from the doorway after the horse. "Fardale, go to the inn! Warn the others!"

The treewolf retreated with the og're deeper into the warehouse. His eyes glowed for a brief instant toward Tol'chuk: *Two wolves, back to back, hold off the hungry bear.*

"Yes," Tol'chuk argued, leading the way to a side door. "But eight wolves be even better, especially if they have swords." He kicked at the door, not bothering to search for the lock's key. Planks splintered, and the door crashed wide. "Get me help!"

Tol'chuk turned away. Fardale hesitated at the open doorway, but Tol'chuk refused to allow further contact.

The wolf vanished out into the fog in a whisk of shadow and fur.

Tol'chuk noticed the mare retreat to the farthest, darkest corner of the warehouse, but his attention stayed focused on the door to the rear yard. Fingers of fog probed into the warehouse, questing tendrils that slid along the floor and curled toward the roof.

Furtive movement up in the rafters caught Tol'chuk's eye. Tol'chuk ducked, then realized it was only a line of small rats whisking in a column along one of the oaken beams, scrambling away from the foggy doorway. Something had spooked even these wily creatures. He began to glance away when one of the rats tumbled from its perch to strike the dirt of the warehouse floor. Its pelvis cracked with a quick snap, but still it tried to drag its carcass away from the door, away from the fog, tiny claws digging at the dirt.

What was happening? The rats above panicked, climbing over each other, squeaking in fear. Two more rats fell from above. Their necks were mercifully broken by the fall, their struggle over.

Still the broken-backed rat fought to flee, squeaking its alarm. Tol'chuk crossed and stood over it. Its panicked squeals rasped Tol'chuk's raw nerves. It was making too much noise, masking the approach of whatever lay out in the yard. He brought his clawed foot up to squash it, but the small rat's nose swung toward the og're. Its tiny black eyes were full of pain and fright, and a keening whine flowed from its throat. Tol'chuk hesitated, his foot hovering over the beast. Finally, he gritted his teeth and lowered his foot, leaving the rat untouched.

Tol'chuk cursed himself. He had been among these humans too long. Bending over, he scooped up the injured rat. He hated rats, but he hated more to see something so small and frightened suffer. Unsure what to do with it, he finally dropped the quivering beast into his thigh pouch. As it settled inside, the rat's constant squeaking stopped. It had sought a place to hide and had now found it.

As the warehouse grew quiet again, Tol'chuk turned to the doorway. The other horses were out there. Tol'chuk crossed and retrieved one of the oil lamps. In his other arm, he still carried the water barrel. Its weight and solidity gave him some anchor against the tenuous menace within the fog.

Raising the lantern, he approached the open doorway. He finally noticed that the horses in the yard were now silent. Even the rats above had either fled the warehouse or found a place to hide. It was as if the fog had dampened all noise as well as it masked the views.

His rasping breath was the only sound in his ears as he reached the open doorway. He held the lantern out into the night, but the fog just became that much thicker, a billowing white cave around his light.

Then, as if an emissary from the fog, a single rat stepped within the sphere of Tol'chuk's lamplight. Yet the word *rat* was a poor description for the mud-slick creature before him. Whereas the creature in his pocket was brown furred and the size of an og're's fist, this beast was as black as the pools of flaming oil deep under the caves of his home and as large as his own head. Yet the most menacing of its features were its red eyes. They shone toward him, not with the reflected light of his lamp, but with an inner fire, as if blood itself were the oil of its flame.

It hissed at him, instantly raising every stubbled hair on Tol'chuk's body. The demon rat—and there could be no question that that was what stood before him—crept toward him, nose raised as if smelling not only Tol'chuk's odor, but scenting his very spirit.

Tol'chuk backed a step, then tossed the water barrel at the creature. His aim was sure, and the barrel crashed atop the rat. Water splashed, and broken slats scattered. The rat stepped out from the ruins of the barrel, unharmed and more determined. Its red eyes glowed with a deeper intensity. As their gazes met, Tol'chuk heard the whispered screams and ancient cries of the dying in his ears. He felt something of himself being drawn within those fiery eyes. Beyond the screams, he now heard wild laughter, two voices sharing a wicked delight. Tol'chuk's vision began to dim as he was drawn into a world of bloodstained towers and the wails of the lost.

Then a sudden agony gripped Tol'chuk's chest, hooks of fire tearing his heart.

Tol'chuk gasped but knew this pain—the Heart of his people called. Yet he had never felt it so strongly. His numb fingers dropped the lamp with a tinkling crash. Flaming oil splashed his thighs and the frame of the doorway. The agony tore Tol'chuk back from the sucking pit of the demon rat's eyes. He stamped and patted the flames from his skin, but his own bones still ran with an inner fire.

Struggling to breathe past the pain, Tol'chuk backed in stumbled steps. His fingers fumbled to his thigh pouch, seeking to free the Heart. His hand closed over the stone. The Heart had once protected him against an assault by the og're who had killed his father. Maybe it could help here.

He yanked the stone free, expecting its blazing red light to blind his eyes. He held the stone forth and stared with despair. The Heart was dull: no fire, no glow, not even a flicker. He sensed the horrible truth through his fingertips.

The Heart was dead, its magick gone.

By now, the rat had reached the doorway. Its sleek blackness and red eyes were lit by the spreading flame from the burning lamp. It seemed to have grown larger. Behind it, a score of other rats, twins to this one, crawled out of the fog, eyes afire. They all stared at Tol'chuk, hundreds of pinpoints of fire.

He could not resist them, not so many. Unaware, Tol'chuk fell to his knees. His vision dimmed again.

Ancient screams and savage laughter filled his ears.

16

Elena stared at Mycelle, forgetting for the moment the strands of moss that bound her left hand. She studied the planes of the woman's face and the crossed scabbards on her back. Mycelle had once been like an aunt to her, but now it was as if a stranger stood before her. She could not reconcile her childhood memory of "Aunt My" with these poisonous revelations of the role she had played as a seeker of the Sisterhood.

While growing up, Aunt My had been one of the few womenfolk who shared Elena's interest in the hidden paths and secret treasures buried among the mundane orchards of her valley home. While others tried to interest her in needlecraft and cooking, Mycelle had walked with Elena, hand in hand, through the fields. They had had long talks, and Elena had enjoyed how her aunt treated her like an adult, not holding back, honest in all regards, teaching her about her life and even bits of woodlore. She had showed Elena how to move quietly through the trees to peek at a family of deer; how to start a fire with only a stick and a bit of twine; which wild plants were safe to eat, which healed, and . . . and which would make one sick.

Elena remembered and suddenly shuddered. *Leaf of hemlock, root of nightshade*. Even then Mycelle had known so much about the natural poisons of the world.

Mycelle, always keen eyed, noticed Elena's distress. She placed a hand on Elena's shoulder, and when Elena tried to pull away, she held her tight. Her words, though, were for the others. "I want everyone out of here," she said smartly. "Plans on how to deal with the ill'guard will wait a few moments."

Er'ril, of course, objected. "If there is danger, we need to leave now."

"Rash actions will only draw eyes and risk all. Presently the ill'-guard do not seem aware of Elena, or we wouldn't be speaking now." Mycelle stared Er'ril down. "Tonight we plan; by dawn's light we move."

Er'ril seemed about to argue further.

Mycelle's razor voice softened its edge. "Up to now, you have done well in protecting Elena. I can't fault any of you on this. But not all wars are won with swords and magick. Some battles turn on the strength of a heart. And there are words I sense Elena needs to hear, woman to woman, before she continues. Give me this moment alone."

Elena finally spoke. "Please Er'ril, do as she asks."

Er'ril stood with his lips drawn thin. He did not like this. Kral stood up and laid a hand on Er'ril's arm. "We could at least pack up the other room."

Meric and Mogweed were already standing, too. "And we'll go fetch our dinners," Meric said, nodding to include Mogweed. "Planning works best on a full stomach."

Er'ril's shoulders finally relaxed, and he nodded. "Fine. You have your moment." The four men filed out of the room. Er'ril was last. He glanced back before shutting the door. "But only a *moment*."

Mycelle bowed her head slightly, both acknowledging his words and conceding her thanks.

Er'ril shut the door. "Keep it locked!" he yelled through the thin pine planks.

Mycelle shrugged off her scabbards, then sagged and collapsed beside Elena on the bed. "How have you put up with him this long?"

The way Mycelle rolled her eyes and her expression of tired amusement touched old memories within Elena. Here was the woman she knew from her past, not the iron-blooded warrior from a moment ago.

"Aunt My . . ." Elena did not know where to begin.

Mycelle turned to face Elena. For the first time, Elena saw the deep wrinkles that now marked her aunt's face and the tired, bruised eyes. Her journeys across the lands had cost her more than her brave words had revealed.

Mycelle reached with both palms to cup Elena's cheeks and sighed as she stared into Elena's eyes. Then one of her hands lifted to finger Elena's shorn and dyed locks. "Your beautiful hair," she said sadly.

"It . . . it'll grow back," Elena said, glancing down.

Mycelle sighed. "Yes, but in your eyes, I can see other parts of you have been equally marred—things that don't grow back." Pain entered her voice. "You've grown, Elena. More than I think you suspect."

Tears threatened, but Elena refused to cry.

Mycelle lowered her hands. "I was supposed to be there for you in Winterfell. Aunt Fila suspected you might be the one, but we weren't sure. The Sisterhood had been wrong in the past. When I got word of Aunt Fila's passing, I tried to make it back to the valley, but by the time I got there, you all were gone. I should have been there for you. Someone should have been."

"Joach helped me," Elena said, choking on her brother's name. "But he . . . but he—"

Mycelle patted her knee. "I know, Elena. The Sisterhood learned what had happened. I was sent to search for you."

"Why?"

"Several reasons. Not only to help protect you, but also to instruct you in the skills of war. How to handle a sword and a dagger."

"But I have my magick."

"Some problems are more easily resolved with a sharp blade than a cast spell. You were to be trained in all manner of warfare. This we could teach you. But this—" Mycelle lifted Elena's gloved hand and slipped off the deerskin that hid her ruby stain. "—this we know too little about. Over the centuries, so much has been muddled in rumor and myth. I'm afraid that with the death of your uncle, we lost much. He had been assigned to root through the ruined school for any ancient texts that taught the intricacies of magick. He was to help you. But with his death, the little he had learned was lost, and the skal'tum burned his cottage, destroying the rest."

Elena spread the fingers of her ruby hand, her heart quailing with hopelessness. "Then in the ways of magick, I'm on my own."

"Yes, but some of the Sisterhood believe this might be best," Mycelle said. She placed her own hand over Elena's ruby one. "And I share this view."

Crinkling her brow, Elena faced Mycelle. "But why?"

"Prophecy has always said it will be a wit'ch—a woman mage—who will call forth the drums of war against the Gul'gotha and bear the torch of freedom." She leaned closer to emphasize her words. "Not a man. The order of male mages could not resist the Gul'gotha before. So why seek their old knowledge or old ways? There must be a reason a woman was chosen—why you were chosen! A new path is needed—a woman's path!"

Elena shrank under her intense gaze.

Mycelle recognized Elena's fear. Her voice softened, and a hand again raised to her cheek. "I'm sorry," she said. "I didn't mean to frighten you."

"I don't want this burden," Elena said quietly. She could not stop the tears now. Hot trails flowed down her cheek.

Mycelle pulled Elena into her arms and hugged her, gently rocking the girl. "Something tells me," Mycelle whispered, squeezing her tighter, "you haven't had enough of this on your journey here."

They held each other in silence for several moments. Elena could sense the warmth and love in these arms. It was not the love for a prophesied hero, but simply the love of family.

Too soon, Mycelle finally lifted Elena's face from her bosom and wiped away her tears. "You have your mother's beautiful eyes," she said softly.

Elena swallowed hard and sniffed back her tears.

"And that's all I really wanted to tell you. I didn't mean to scare you or burden you further. I just wanted to remind you that you're not just a sword . . . or a ruby hand . . . but you're also your mother's daughter. A woman. And this may prove your most important strength against the darkness ahead."

With a small frown, Mycelle again fingered Elena's shorn hair. "Among all these men," she said, her frown becoming a gentle smile, "just don't forget you're a woman."

They shared one last quick hug. "I won't," Elena said, remembering that mountain morning so long ago when she had raised both her hands to the dawn's light—one red, one white. She had clasped her hands together, declaring herself both wit'ch and woman. Had she somehow even then known the truth of Mycelle's words? "Woman and wit'ch," Elena mumbled.

"What was that, hon?"

Before Elena could speak, a fierce pounding rattled the door to the room. Er'ril's voice spat through the pine planks. "The wolf brings word! The warehouse is under attack!"

Without a word, Mycelle flew off the bed and into her scabbards. "Hurry, Elena," she urged. Then, more to herself as she bustled to the door, "Damn my ears, I would've sworn I sensed something earlier." She threw off the latch and flung open the door.

Elena bounced off the bed to follow, her heart in her throat.

Er'ril stood, red faced, with his fist raised. He backed a step to make room for them. "We must hurry."

"What's happening?" Mycelle asked, pushing past Er'ril into the hallway. Elena followed her.

"I'm not sure," he said. Er'ril turned to lead the way, but the woman's voice stopped him.

"We're not going," she said simply, calm and sure.

Er'ril swung around. "We've no time to argue. Tol'chuk's in trouble!"

"And you would take the wit'ch into the jaws of a trap?" she answered. "Into danger?"

Er'ril paused at her words. "I . . . I . . . We can't just leave Tol'chuk. Kral and the others are already on their way over."

"Kral is a fierce warrior. I've seen him handle his ax. If what lies at the warehouse cannot be handled by an og're and a mountain man, then it is foolhardy to take Elena there."

Elena spoke up, her voice sounding meek in her ears. "But I can help."

Mycelle placed a hand on her shoulder. "I'm sure you could, honey. But using your magick here would be like setting a blazing beacon for the Dark Lord's minions to follow. You are the future, and we cannot take that risk."

"But we have to at least try . . ." Elena glanced toward Er'ril for his support.

She did not get it. His eyes blazed with frustration. "As much as I detest leaving the others," he said, "Mycelle is right. You know the contingency plan. If danger separated us, we would meet in one moon at Land's End on the coast."

"But—"

"Then it's settled," Mycelle interrupted. "I suspect the ill'guard in town are on the move. We must do the same if we are to survive."

Elena raised hurt eyes toward Mycelle. "But Tol'chuk. He's your son? Would you abandon him a second time?"

Her heartfelt words cracked Mycelle's firm resolve. The woman glanced away from her, but Elena saw her right hand clench into a fist and her shoulders tremble as she held her emotions in rein. Mycelle's words were pained. "I did it once. I can do it again."

Elena watched Mycelle's expression slowly harden back to iron. Her eyes dried of pending tears, and her lips became firm lines of determination. Elena stared at this transformation. On this journey ahead, would she herself ever grow so strong? And, worse yet, did she even want to? Elena stepped between Er'ril and Mycelle. "No," she said quietly. "I'll not leave Tol'chuk or the others."

Er'ril raised a hand to his brow and sighed. "It's a wise plan, Elena. If we let the others draw the fire here in town, we can slip away undetected. We will meet again in Land's End."

"No."

Mycelle reached for her, but Elena stepped back. "Honey," Mycelle said, "we must leave or—"

"No. You just told me that there was a reason a woman was fated to carry this magick. That it was a woman's heart that would make the difference. And, right now, my heart says we stand together."

"You must not risk it," Mycelle said. "You are the future dawn."

"Fate be cursed," she said. "If I'm to battle the Dark Lord, I'll confront him as myself, not as some creature of prophecy." Elena turned to look Mycelle in the eye. "I'm sorry, Aunt My, but I will not become you. I will not harden my spirit against the world. If I must fight, I'll do it with my whole heart."

Elena marched toward the stairs. "I will not leave Tol'chuk."

On his knees already, Tol'chuk fell to one arm on the dirt floor, his other claw still holding the Heart aloft though the stone was dull and dead. Before him, flames lapped up the blazing door frame to consume the back wall of the warehouse. Even the hungry fire failed to brighten the facets of the stone.

Without the stone's strength, what hope did he have to resist the black magick here?

Past the burning threshold, a hundred red eyes stared at him from the rear yard. His head rang with the song of the demon rats, an ancient chorus of torment and laughter. It sapped his will and his strength. He could not resist.

As he struggled, an inner fire continued to burn through his bones. He knew this familiar pain. It was the Heart of his people trying to fight off the black magick—but it was failing. He squeezed the stone in his claw with the last of his energy. Why would it not blaze?

Too weak, his arm finally dropped. He ground the precious Heart under his weight as he fell forward. Just before consciousness fled him, he saw the rats swarm toward him—and worse, he felt the magick of the Heart abandon him.

KRAL WAS THE FIRST THROUGH THE DOOR. HE SAW THE OG'RE CRASH TO the dirt floor of the warehouse. At first, he could not see any threat here except for the spreading fire. Had smoke overwhelmed Tol'chuk? Ax in hand, he scanned the warehouse. All he spotted was Elena's gray mare backed in a corner.

Fardale whisked forward past Kral's thighs.

"There!" Meric called. His thin arm pointed toward the fire.

His sharper elv'in eyes had detected furtive movement near the blazing doorway. Huge black rats, dozens of them, flowed through the burning portal.

Fardale was already beside the og're, hackles raised, a growl flowing from his throat. His head lowered as he stared down the creatures. The rats stopped their approach toward the og're, spreading in a line to face the wolf.

Kral did not need to be si'luran to understand Fardale's meaning. His stance said it all. Here was the danger the wolf had scented earlier.

But it was just rats.

Kral's ax lowered slightly.

Then the pitch of Fardale's growl changed to a high whine. The wolf trembled. His whine became a hopeless howl that echoed through the rafters. What was wrong?

As the wolf howled and began to teeter on his legs, the rats in front of Fardale suddenly swelled larger! Their bodies, huge already, bloated to the size of small dogs. Fardale fell limp beside the collapsed og're.

Meric and Kral had stopped halfway across the warehouse.

"What's happening?"

"Black magick," Meric answered. The elv'in stood beside Kral, his silver hair floating in wisps about his face, drifting contrary to the night's breezes. Meric had touched his elemental magick. "Beware them," he said. "They steal the life from you and use it for their own."

The rats again approached the og're.

Meric raised his hands in a warding gesture, and a blast of wind blew out from him. The edge of the sudden gale knocked Kral to the side. He had to stumble a few steps to keep his balance. The wind blasted through the warehouse toward the rats. Straw and dirt billowed into the air, and the flames of the fire flared brighter with the breeze.

Caught by the gale, one rat tumbled back into the fiery wall. Its body instantly blew ablaze as if coated with oil. It howled like no beast Kral had ever heard. The small hairs on Kral's arms bristled at the noise. With its eyes burnt black, it raced in blind circles for several heartbeats then lay still, a smoking pile of bone and charred fur.

The other rats ignored their companion. With claws dug deep into the packed dirt of the floor, they resisted the elv'in's storm. Though not blown away, they were at least held at bay.

It was a standoff.

The rats' noses raised in unison, as if sniffing at the elemental wind. They swung their gazes hungrily toward Kral and Meric.

"Beware!" Meric hissed. A sheen of sweat marked the elv'in's brow. How long could the elv'in keep this up? Overhead, the wind-fed flames had raced madly up the rear wall and reached the rafters. The heat now was like an open hearth before his face. And how long until the warehouse collapsed into fiery ruin?

"I'll try to drag Tol'chuk and Fardale away from them," Kral said, hitching his ax on his belt. "Hold them off!"

"Use caution, mountain man. I sense they'll not let their prey escape them so easily."

Kral crept forward, crouching low. The wind at his back threatened to tumble him forward into the line of rats. Step by step, he crossed the warehouse toward the og're and the wolf. Once close enough, he saw that his companions still breathed. A wash of relief broke Kral's concentration. His heels slipped, and the wind caught him, driving him to his knees.

Growling into his beard, he pushed up. He kept his gaze away from the rats and stared at Tol'chuk's clawed foot. Just a bit farther.

Three steps later, he was close enough. He reached an arm out. Just as his fingers touched the og're's foot, the wind died. The sudden lack of support dropped Kral on his rear. He spun around.

The elv'in stood, staring back toward the door they had entered. Mogweed had been left at the entrance to guard their retreat, but there was no sign of the shape-shifter. Instead, a flow of demon rats poured through the opening.

He and Meric were surrounded.

Meric struggled to raise his arms, but the elv'in was caught in their spell. He backed a step, then fell to his knees. "Flee!" Meric called to him as he dropped. "Beware their eyes!" The elv'in collapsed to the dirt.

Ash rained down from the burning rafters. No longer blown back by Meric's wind, smoke now choked through the warehouse. His eyes stinging, Kral shoved to his feet. He would not abandon his friends.

Nearby, a thunder of hooves startled Kral. He shied away as the girl's terrified mare bolted from the shadows and flew through the rats that stood between it and the exit. One of its iron-shod hooves crushed a rat into a foul smear on its way out the door.

The horse vanished into the foggy night.

Overhead, a beam suddenly cracked from the heat, showering ash and drawing Kral's attention. He made the mistake of looking up.

A huge rat clung to one of the intact rafters above. Its red eyes latched onto his own. Kral could not look away. The red eyes grew larger and larger in his mind until all he saw was the bloodfire that lit the core of the creature. In his ears, he heard the cries of the dying, pleading wails to end their agony. Death was the only escape. It was a song of despair, and it wound its way around Kral's heart.

No!

Kral fought against it. The granite of his mountain home flowed through his blood and hardened his heart. His magick fought the despair of the song. Yet still he weakened. Kral fell to his knees.

In his mind's eye, he saw an ancient tower besieged by d'warf armies. He saw the bloodstained stones burn red from the siege fires.

Kral clamped his hands over his ears, but he could not muffle the screaming. He saw the tower's guardians slaughtered and their blood poured over the stones.

See, the song and images urged, even the strongest stone cannot resist the darkness. Resistance only prolongs the suffering.

Unable to break his locked gaze with the demon rat, Kral was forced to listen. Yet he ground his teeth. Listening was not believing.

He was *not* a tower! He was a mountain!

Kral crawled backward across the floor as flaming ash burned his skin and singed his beard. The rat followed him atop the rafter, refusing to let Kral escape its eyes.

Victory was impossible, the ancient dying cries sang to him.

More rats joined this one. They circled Kral now.

Why flee? Just lie down. Escape was just a cruel dream.

Kral bit his tongue, using the pain to stay focused. No! The mare had escaped!

Drawing on the last of his ebbing strength, he grabbed for one final weapon. He raised up on his knees and whistled sharply with the last of his breath. Then he fell back to his hands in the dirt.

The rats closed in on him.

Was he too late?

Suddenly an explosion of cracking planks erupted behind him. Kral, locked by the black magicks, could not glance back. Sparks and embers blew in a swirl around him as a large shape dove in from the rear yard. It was Rorshaf, his war charger. Its huge black body galloped forward and shoved between Kral and the demon rat, breaking their locked gazes. The sudden collapse of the link between them sent Kral's vision spinning. All around him was a blur of flames, hooves, and shadow.

Kral fought against this confusion. He felt teeth sink into his right hand. Bone cracked, and flesh tore. The pain drew his vision to a tight focus. He saw a large rat worrying his hand. He flung it off him with a swinging whip of his arm. The rat flew off, one of Kral's fingers still in its sharp teeth.

Pain fired his hand, but he became rock and walled off the agony. Kral raised his bloody palm and grabbed Rorshaf's thick tail, tangling his fingers in the coarse black hair. *"Ror'ami nom, Rorshaf!"* he yelled in the tongue of the crag horses.

Rorshaf reared, trampling two more rats under his hooves, then leapt forward, dragging Kral along behind him.

Kral fought to keep his bloody hold on the horse's tail as he was bounced and rattled across the warehouse floor. He kept his eyes closed. He could not afford the numbing weakness that accompanied the sick gazes of the rats.

Splintered wood ripped into his side as Rorshaf dragged him through the ruined doorway. He finally opened his eyes as he felt the cobbles of the town square strike his hip and heard his ax blade clatter on the stones. He allowed himself to be dragged a bit farther, then let go, too exhausted to hold on any longer.

He tumbled to the street and rolled a few times before stopping.

"Kral!"

The mountain man opened his eyes and found Er'ril leaning over him. Elena stood beside him, holding her gray mare by a lead. Mycelle raised a sword in each fist, eyes aglow with the spreading flames of the warehouse. Other townspeople bustled behind the trio. Word of the fire had spread quickly through the foggy night. Somewhere a bell rang loudly.

"What happened?" Er'ril asked. "Mogweed came running. Something about rats—"

Kral fought to free his tongue, lifting his torn hand. "Not rats," he muttered just before his consciousness fled him. "Demons."

BENEATH THE TOWER OF RASH'AMON, LORD TORWREN CROUCHED OVER the ebon'stone sphere, his splayed nose almost touching its polished surface as it lay cradled in his wrinkled palms. The d'warf lord's eyes were wide in the dim chamber as he stared deep into the black orb. Images of fire and shadowy figures danced in the ebon'stone heart.

As he watched, one of the prey escaped the Pack. Torwren hissed his irritation. Three others still lay under the thrall of despair upon the floor of the warehouse: a wolf, a man, and—if he was not mistaken—an og're! He cared nothing for the dog, and though the og're was a novelty, the misshapen creature was of no import. It was the silver-haired man who drew the d'warf's attention.

A seeker for many centuries, Torwren recognized the white fire nestled near the heart of this thin man. Here was one of the elementals he had sensed in Shadowbrook in these last few days. The fire burned strong in this one, much stronger than in the foppish twins he used as tools in the city. This one could be forged into a potent ill'guard, perhaps one of the most powerful. Maybe even strong enough to withstand—no, he would not let that thought grow full in his mind, not while he was linked to the ebon'stone. His master listened often to these links, hanging like a spider above his web of talismans.

No, he dismissed his secret hope and concentrated on the Pack. He merged his will deeper into the stone talisman. The shadowy images became crisper as he delved for the minds of the twins.

Ryman. Mycof. Listen and obey.

Laughter answered his call. In the warehouse, the rats swept toward the fallen prey, ready to slake their blood lust.

No! The feast must wait. The town awakens. Bring me the man—unharmed!

The twins ignored his call, the scent of blood too strong in the flaming room.

Torwren frowned. As a seeker, he despised the ill'guard, even those he helped create. They were wild, twisted beasts hiding in the skin of men. He spat his orders out to them. *The master commands! Disobey and I will rip the Sacrament from your hearts.*

This gave the brothers pause. The rats stopped, tails slashing in agitation. Then slowly they backed away from their meal.

Bring the man to the tower.

He watched the rats converge around the silver-haired man. Thin of limb and features, the man's inner fire burned that much brighter, almost as if his scant flesh was but a feeble excuse to house the elemental magick. He was truly a strong one. Lord Torwren's lips spread into a hungry leer as he stared into the ebon'stone sphere.

Bring him to me!

The rats piled onto one another, becoming a squirming, hissing mound of fur and teeth. Forged of river mud and life force, the writhing bodies melded together, creating a living mass of raw flesh, the Pack in its pure form.

As the d'warf lord urged, the Pack transformed itself. Bone, fur, skin, teeth fought for form until a hulking creature arose from the fray—half rat, half man. Covered in black fur, it crouched on two thickly muscled legs and reached for the thin man with clawed arms. Its bestial head, snouted and covered in spiked whiskers, sniffed at its prey. Thick lips pulled back to reveal row after row of shredding teeth, and bloodfire raged behind its eyes.

Torwren sensed its rising lust. He drove his will into the stone. *No! Harm him and suffer my wrath!*

The beast raised its head and hissed at the flaming rafters, its claws digging at the empty air in frustration. It knew its master but fought against the restraint.

Obey!

With a final wicked swipe at the smoky air, it growled thickly and scooped up the thin man under one arm. Burdened, it loped across the burning warehouse toward the rear door.

A few of the demon rats stationed as guards had failed to merge to form the huge beast. As the creature passed, these stray rats shook, and leathery wings sprouted from their backs. They took flight after their leader, fluttering past its massive shoulders and into the foggy night. One rat, though, still dallied, working on something in its jaws.

Torwren looked closer. It was a finger. The prey who had escaped earlier had not gone uninjured. A spark of elemental fire marked the blood that seeped from the severed finger. Another elemental! The rat seemed to sense Torwren's attention. Fearing the d'warf's wrath, it dropped the finger and shook out its buried wings, ready to follow the others.

Wait, he sent to this quivering fragment of the Pack. *Bring me your meal!*

Hesitant, the demon creature retrieved its prize.

Good, good . . . Now follow the others.

With a small squeak, the rat spread its wings with renewed confidence and took to the air, carrying the prized object in its tiny jaws. A whisper of elemental fire traced its path out into the night.

Torwren watched the progression of the Pack through the back alleys and byways of Shadowbrook.

Satisfied that his orders would be obeyed, Torwren allowed his eyes to close. He settled the ebon'stone talisman into the mud of the tower cellar and removed his hands from the sphere. One finger traced an arc of silver along its smooth surface.

If only his people had never discovered the vein of ebon'stone under the mountains of their Gul'gothal homeland, then maybe . . .

Torwren shook his head. Foolish, idle thoughts. His people had made their choices—just as he had himself.

He lifted his finger from the stone and sighed. He pictured again the strength of the magick in the prisoner caught this night. And what of the one who had escaped? If he was just as strong? If Torwren could forge both to his will?

Torwren pictured two ill'guard with the brutality of potent magick.

Dare he hope?

Elena watched with a hand over her heart as Er'ril examined Kral.

Er'ril wrapped a tight bandage around the mountain man's bloody fist. "He'll live," Er'ril said, pushing to his feet. He glanced at the huge war charger standing guard over its fallen master. "We don't have time to move the man, but Rorshaf will watch over him."

Er'ril tossed a copper coin to a boy gawking at the flames of the burning warehouse. "Keep a hand on our mare," he told the child, taking Mist's lead from Elena and holding it out toward the boy, "and you'll get another copper for your trouble."

"Y-yes, sir!" The boy stared at the shiny copper in his palm as he blindly accepted the lead.

Around them, the square now bustled with men bearing buckets and women manning the two pumps in the square. A chandlery and a cobbler's shop to either side of the warehouse were being soaked to protect them from the spreading flames and embers.

A large bearded man ran up to their group. It was the man who had rented the warehouse to them. "What happened?" His eyes were fixed on the burning structure.

Er'ril straightened and drew his sword. "That's what we are about to find out." Er'ril turned his back on the man and led the way toward the warehouse.

The front of the building still resisted the fire, but from the roof, flames spat high into the night air, and smoke billowed out from the open doorway. The warehouse would not stand much longer.

"Hurry," Er'ril urged.

Mycelle followed, hovering beside Elena.

Short of breath from both smoke and fear, Elena gasped as she ran. The heat coming from the building swelled like a sudden breeze off a raging bonfire. Her cheeks grew ruddy from the heat, and her eyes watered.

Er'ril stopped a man in an apron who had been hurrying by with a bucket. "Douse us!" he ordered.

The man, sweat and soot marring his face, stared at him as if he were mad, but the sword at his belly kept his tongue silent.

"We have friends inside," Er'ril urged. "We must help them."

The man's eyes grew wide, and he waved a heavyset woman over to him. She bore a bucket in each hand. "Help us, Mab'el!" he called. "These folks are gonna try and see if anyone is alive inside."

The woman shambled to them, a frown on her lips. "Daft idea. They're just gonna git themselves killed, too."

"Hush, Mab'el!" The man took his bucket and dumped it over Er'ril's head. "What if it were me in there?" he said.

The woman soaked down Mycelle. "I'd let you burn," she said. "Be rid of your lollygagging ways, I would!" Still her eyes shone with concern for them all.

"The boy, too," Er'ril instructed, indicating Elena.

The heavyset woman glanced in surprise.

Mycelle answered her unspoken question. "He's a firebrand," she said, naming Elena as an elemental who could control flames. "If our friends yet live, we will need his skill."

Mab'el nodded knowingly and poured her second bucket over Elena's head. Elena shuddered at its frigid touch, but the well water instantly washed away the fire's heat.

Er'ril studied her for a moment, as if judging Elena's fortitude.

She stared him straight in the eye until he nodded and turned toward the warehouse.

Soaked and dripping, they ran toward the warehouse door. Smoke stung the eye and burned the nose, but the summer storm that had threatened at sunset finally arrived. A stiff breeze blew the smoke across the square, thinning it enough to breathe, and a crack of thunder split the sky.

Rain began pelting the cobbles. Behind Elena, cheers arose from the townsfolk.

With her back to the commotion, Elena slipped her glove from her right hand and exposed her ruby stain to the flames. It took her a moment to free her wit'ch's dagger from its sheath at her belt, the rose-carved pommel catching on the mossy strands that bound her left hand. Once free, she notched her thumb and used the blood to mark her eyes.

Mycelle noticed her action. "Elena, what are you doing?"

"The blood allows me to see the weaves of magick around me," she answered.

Satisfied, Mycelle nodded, as if this were a common statement for a young woman to utter.

As they arrived at the shattered doorway to the warehouse, Elena reached for the well of power in her heart. She felt the familiar surge of rich energies, her skin tingling. Ahead of her, Er'ril entered the warehouse, crouching low to avoid the worst of the smoke. Elena followed with Mycelle, who watched their rear, both swords in hand.

Coughing, Elena waved smoke from her face, the heat drying her cheeks to a burn in only a few breaths. She looked around her.

The inside of the warehouse was a smoldering battlefield. Flaming sections of roof and rafters lit the chamber, and smoke curled like a living creature through the room. A portion of the rear wall had fallen in and crushed their wagon. It was a ruin. What had not been smashed had caught flame and burned.

But the loss of their supplies was the least of their concerns.

"Over there!" Er'ril pointed to the large form collapsed on the far side of the building. "Tol'chuk," he said. "And I think that's the wolf beside him."

Elena stared, willing her magick to grow in her fist. Her right hand began to glow with a nimbus of energy. Elena's vision shifted as the magick suddenly tinged her sight. Mycelle, beside her, bloomed like a white candle in the night, her elemental flame strong and clear. The seeker's skill was strong in her.

Glancing across the chamber, Elena's spell-cast vision seemed unaffected by the smoke and sting. "It is them," she said, confirming Er'ril's statement, "but I don't see Meric." Swinging in a slow circle, she scanned the room.

Nearby, she could make out faint areas of a reddish fire—not the red of a clean flame, but something more sickly. She crossed to one spot and discovered the remains of what looked like a huge rat, a hoofprint smashed clearly into its black flesh. But this was no ordinary rat. She leaned closer. Like an ember in a dying hearth, a foul fire glowed out from it. A part of her knew its name. "Bloodfire," she whispered.

"Get back from that," Mycelle warned. She sheathed one of her swords and pulled Elena away, her nose curling in distaste. With her elemental skills, Mycelle must have also sensed the corruption here.

Elena straightened, remembering Kral's words. *Not rats. Demons.*

"They're gone," Elena said, glancing about the smoldering room as she followed Er'ril. Rain began pelting through several new holes in the roof. Where the cool rain met the flames, sizzling steam arose around them as the fires were doused. The bloodfire also began to fade from the chamber. "They've fled."

"Who?" Er'ril asked as he cautiously led them around piles of smoking debris. He had his sword raised, ready for a sudden attack.

Elena pushed past him, shrugging off even Mycelle's restraining grasp. "The creatures of the ill'guard. They've fled from here. It's clear."

"Are you certain?" Er'ril asked.

"Yes."

"I, too, sense their presence has faded," Mycelle added. "They end their hunt this night. But by tomorrow's light we must be gone."

No longer fearing demons, the trio hurried to Tol'chuk and Fardale. Their companions lay sprawled on the dirt floor, eyes open but unaware. Quick attempts to revive them failed.

Er'ril grabbed one of Tol'chuk's legs and nodded for Mycelle to grab the other. "Can you drag the wolf by yourself, Elena?"

She nodded, distracted. With her blood-tinged vision, she saw the brilliant glow shining forth from the og're's thigh pouch. Its light shone in tiny piercing rays through the stitching in the pouch's hide: the magick of Tol'chuk's heartstone talisman, she guessed.

"Elena?" Er'ril asked, noticing her pause. He and Mycelle had the og're's legs already in hand.

Elena straightened and swung in a circle. If her blood-tinged eyes could see all forms of magick—from Mycelle's elemental fire to the glow of Tol'chuk's heartstone—then why didn't she see Meric's fire? The shattering realization took hold of her. "He's gone," she said, her voice trembling and cracking.

"What are you talking about?"

"Meric. His elemental magick should be a beacon in here. I don't see it!"

"Maybe he's hidden behind one of these mounds of debris," Er'ril offered. "The smoldering fires might be masking him."

"Or he could be dead," Mycelle said, coldly practical.

Er'ril glanced sourly at her. "We'll search for the elv'in after we get these others out of here." He began to drag the og're across the dirt.

"We won't find Meric here!" Elena suddenly declared. Somehow she knew this was true. "He's been captured!"

A section of roof suddenly crashed off to the side, startling them all. Though the fire seemed to be losing its battle to the rain, the flames had weakened the supports to the warehouse. Posts groaned, and the roof bowed ominously.

"Captured or not, we need to get out of here!" Er'ril said fiercely.

Elena glanced one last time around her, grabbed Fardale's rear legs, and struggled to haul him after the others. The wolf was heavier than she had suspected. Groaning and straining, she fought his limp weight across the floor.

"Are you all right?" Er'ril called back to her.

"I'll manage!" she spat back at him. At least her burden kept her distracted from their missing companion.

By the time they neared the door, a few townsmen had braved the dwindling flames and pushed into the warehouse, led by the aproned man who had doused them with water. "Give 'em a hand, gents!"

The men helped haul Tol'chuk and Fardale out to the cobbled streets of the square. Elena slipped her ruby hand back into her glove and reined in her magick. Her vision returned to normal.

"What manner of beast is this?" one of them mumbled who handled the og're.

"Some misbirth," another hissed at him. "Poor creature's only fit to be a carnival freak."

"Maybe it were best if we'd left him to the fire."

No one spoke against these sad words.

Once out in the clear air, Er'ril directed the men in hauling their injured to the Painted Pony.

"I'll fetch a healer," one of them offered.

"No need," Er'ril said. "All they need is a day or two in a warm bed."

Er'ril then left with a few other men to search the warehouse for Meric. Elena did not follow. She knew it was useless. She and Mycelle guided the men, burdened with her fallen comrades, to their rooms.

The innkeeper of the Painted Pony watched the parade of men with wide eyes. "If they be sick, I don't want them in my inn!" he hollered at the men. "I won't have no contagion in my establishment!"

"As if you're concerned, Heran, about the health of your patrons!" scolded the aproned man, shoving crusts of bread from underfoot. Elena had learned the bold man was the town's cobbler. He owned the shop next to the warehouse.

As the innkeeper grumbled, they continued up the stairs.

Mogweed met Elena at the door to their rooms. "I finished packing both—" His eyes grew wide at the number of men and their burden. His eyes settled on the limp form of his brother in the huge arms of the town's blacksmith. The emotions that warred across the shape-shifter's face made it seem almost as if he had regained his shifting skills. He backed to let them all in.

Once settled in their rooms, Elena thanked the men and offered them a handful of coppers from the troupe's reserve.

The cobbler shook his head at her fistful of coins. "Here in Shadowbrook, kindness does not have to be bought with coppers."

The other men mumbled their agreement, then left.

Directed by Mycelle, Mogweed went to fetch hot water.

Alone now, Mycelle stepped up to Elena. "You should get out of those soaking clothes before a chill sets into you."

Nodding, Elena slipped off her jacket. Her eyes were fixed on the trio of slumbering friends. Why did they not awaken? Not even the rain seemed to stir them.

Behind her, Mycelle gasped. Elena glanced back. Mycelle had frozen midway in removing her scabbards. Her eyes were on Elena, her expression shocked.

"What is it?" Elena asked.

"Your . . . your arm!" Mycelle pointed to the girl's left side.

Elena raised her bare arm. Her own mouth gaped in horror. The mossy strands had spread from her hand, coiling and sprouting up to her shoulder. Her entire arm now ran with vines and tiny leaves. A small purplish flower even adorned her elbow. "What is happening?" she asked, her throat tightening.

Mycelle tossed aside her scabbards and crossed to Elena. She scrutinized her arm. "The boy who bewit'ched you on the street. He said he needed your magick."

Elena nodded.

"This is disastrous," Mycelle said, picking at a vine near her shoulder. Her face grew dark. "I had thought it only a minor nuisance."

"What?"

"When you loosened your magick in the warehouse, it must have given fuel for this bewit'ched growth." She looked at Elena gravely. "The swamp vines feed on your magick."

Elena pulled back from Mycelle.

"The more you use it, the thicker it will grow. Until . . . until . . ." Mycelle's lips tightened. She did not want to voice her thought.

"What? Tell me!"

Gripping Elena's shoulders, she stared her square in the eyes. "You must *not* use your magick anymore. Swear it!"

"But why?"

Mycelle released Elena and turned away. Her firm voice dissolved into tears. "If you continue to use your magick, the vines will kill you."

17

Burdened with two crates, Er'ril pushed into the room to find Elena resting on a corner of a bed beside the limp form of the wolf. She had a blanket wrapped around her shoulders, her eyes on Fardale. Nearby, Mycelle was bent over Kral, working with needle and thread on his injured hand. Her scabbards leaned against the walls.

"I found no sign of the elv'in," Er'ril said as introduction. "Were you able to revive any of the others?"

His question was answered with a sullen shake of Elena's head.

Er'ril's eyes narrowed. Something was amiss here. "What's wrong?" he asked as he dropped the two crates he had recovered from the burned wagon. The horses, shaken and sweating, had all survived and were corralled behind the inn's decrepit barn. A few more crates were stashed in the hall, carried here by a couple of helpful townspeople. All else was a ruin. "Where's Mogweed?"

"He's gone to fetch hot water," Mycelle answered from where she worked on Kral. "I've a few herbs in my supplies—raspberry leaf and dried rivenberries—stimulants that may perhaps draw them from this strange slumber." Her words were halfhearted, with none of her usual heat. "I sent a man to fetch my gelding and bags."

Mycelle worked a bandage around Kral's fist, then faced Er'ril. "But we've more to worry about. I'm afraid I poorly misjudged Elena's bewit'ching. The spell was cast with more skill then I initially suspected."

Before her words were finished, Er'ril was already at Elena's side. He knelt where she sat on her bed.

Silently, Elena showed him her moss-encrusted fingers.

"It looks the same—" he began to say. Then Elena drew the blanket up her bare arm. The vines and pea-size leaves ran a twisted course around her arm to her shoulder. He could not keep his eyes from widening in shock. "What does this mean?"

Mycelle told him her suspicions.

Er'ril sat back upon his heels. "But if she can't use her magick, how do we hope to reach A'loa Glen?"

Mycelle crossed to them. "We don't. Not unless we can lift this bewit'ching."

Elena dropped the blanket back over her arm. Er'ril patted her on a knee. "How do we rid her of the spell?"

"Only the one who cast it can undo it," Mycelle said. "We'll have to take her to the wit'ch."

Er'ril stood. He recognized the worry in her eyes. "You suspect who cast this spell."

"Yes, I do. The moss that grows on Elena's arm is a type of vine named choker's nest. It grows only in the In'nova Swamps." Mycelle looked at Er'ril intently.

"But that's almost a moon's journey from here," Er'ril argued.

Mycelle frowned at him, clearly tired of his stating the obvious.

Before further words could be spoken, Mogweed forced his way into their room, encumbered with a pail of steaming water and a set of riding packs over one shoulder. "I've your supplies and the water you wanted," he said, seemingly oblivious to the tension in the room. "Where do you want them?"

"We'll talk more of this later," Mycelle said to Er'ril. "Right now, let's see about your companions."

Before Er'ril could object, she waved Mogweed to the space between the two beds where the og're and the mountain man lay. The shape-shifter set the pail down roughly, sloshing water across the pine floor planks. Mycelle took the packs from him. "I need mugs," she said.

Mogweed stared blankly at her a moment. Then his brows lowered. "I'll get them," he said with an exasperated sigh.

As he left, Mycelle fingered through her packs. Finally, she extracted two parchment-wrapped packages. She called Elena to her side. "Crush these leaves and berries," she said, tossing her two tiny packages.

Er'ril realized he would get no further information from Mycelle, not until some attempt was made to revive their companions. "How can I help?" he said.

Mycelle tested the water in the pail with a finger. "See if you can raise Tol'chuk a bit. When I dose him, I don't want the elixir to drown him."

Er'ril nodded and slid to the far side of Tol'chuk's bed. He pulled the blanket lower so he could get to one of the og're's arms. He freed the thick limb from the blanket. As Er'ril gripped Tol'chuk's wrist, he noticed two things: Tol'chuk's flesh was as cold as a day-old corpse, and the claws of the og're's hand clutched a large object in their sharp grip.

Er'ril immediately recognized the glinting object still stubbornly clasped in the sleeping giant's fist. It was the Heart of his people. Though unconscious and half dragged here, the og're had never let it drop.

Curious, Er'ril attempted to pry open Tol'chuk's massive fist; perhaps here lay some clue to what had occurred in the warehouse. It took the strength of all his fingers to drag open a single claw.

"What are you doing?" Mycelle asked sharply.

Er'ril continued to fight the og're's grip. "Trying to free Tol'chuk's heartstone."

"Why?"

Er'ril glared up at her, swiping away a fall of his black hair from his face. "The stone might give us some clue to the threat we face." Er'ril went back to freeing the stone. Finally, with sweat on his brow, he pried open the last of the claws. Fully exposed in the og're's palm, the facets of the heartstone seemed oddly subdued in the lamplight. Er'ril reached for it.

"Don't!" Elena suddenly cried. She had stopped crumbling the dried herb and stared at Tol'chuk with a studied expression.

Er'ril's hand froze. His fingers hovered over the stone.

"What is it, honey?" Mycelle asked, drawing nearer.

"The Heart usually glows with at least a trace of og're magicks," she said, waving at the stone. "In the warehouse, as he lay sprawled, I saw his pouch ablaze with magicks. I guessed it was just the stone! But if he held the Heart in his fist, then it must . . . must be something else." She pointed to his blanket-covered waist. "Something in his pouch."

Er'ril pulled his hand back from the stone and grabbed the blanket's edge. He swept down the woolen covering. The goatskin pouch was still tied around the og're's broad thigh. The pouch bulged with something other than its usual sacred object.

Glancing briefly to the others, Er'ril reached for the leather draws. He tugged them open just as something in the pouch suddenly thrashed. Startled, Er'ril yanked away his fingers, accidentally striking the heartstone with the edge of his hand.

As the stone knocked free of the og're's palm, the opening of the thigh pouch suddenly burst forth with a sharp brilliance. Blinded for a heartbeat, Er'ril backed a step. He blinked away the dazzle. The flare of radiance soon died down to a smoldering red glow. Yet the light was not quiet. The intensity of the glow rose and fell rhythmically like that of a beating heart.

"Stand back," Mycelle warned, her voice suspicious.

Elena took a step closer. "Something's coming."

The contents of the pouch wormed toward the opening. As they watched, the strange object in the pouch suddenly poked free of its glowing cave. Its whiskered snout tested the air. Then its body slid from the pouch's interior.

"It's a rat," Er'ril said.

"Kral had mentioned rats," Mycelle said, placing a hand on Elena's shoulder. "Spawn of the ill'guard."

Elena shook her head. "This is not one of them. It's injured." She pointed to the twist in the rat's spine as it struggled free. The rat seemed unhampered by its injury. Its slow crawl from the pouch was more caution than disability. Its eyes seemed to watch everything at once.

"The glow . . ." Elena began to say.

Er'ril noted it, too. The radiance followed the rat from the pouch. No, that was not exactly right. As its tiny clawed legs drew the last of its body free, the source of the rich light became clear.

"The rat's glowing," Mycelle said, wonder etching her hard voice.

The rat was the usual mud brown of the common river rats. But from its lice-ridden fur, a rosy glow ebbed and flowed, a nimbus of light that gave the drab creature a certain beauty, as if the radiance highlighted all that was good and noble in the beast.

"What does it mean?" Elena asked.

Both Er'ril and Mycelle just stared.

Suddenly the door banged open behind them. All of them jumped, even the rat.

"That stingy innkeep would only give me one mug!" Mogweed said sourly as he entered the room.

"Quiet!" All three of them scolded him, freezing him in place.

The rat, startled by the sudden intrusion, fled up from Tol'chuk's waist and scrabbled across the og're's barreled chest to hide under his craggy chin. It cowered there, its light flaring brighter with its fright.

The glow bathed Tol'chuk's face, casting each rough plane and deep wrinkle of the og're in sharp relief. As the radiance had improved the aspect of the common river rat, the glow seemed to highlight the character and strength hidden within Tol'chuk's coarse features.

"He is so much like his father," Mycelle murmured, her voice so soft, so unlike her, that Er'ril did not know for a moment who had spoken. He glanced up to see a single tear shine in the swordswoman's eye.

As they watched, Tol'chuk's wide-splayed nose twitched. The glow, like pipe smoke, was drawn inside the slumbering og're as he breathed in deeply. His lips began to move silently, as if he were speaking in some deep dream. His open eyes, which had been staring blindly at the thin rafters above, slid closed.

"What's happening?" Mogweed asked.

Mycelle shushed him. She reached a hand to Tol'chuk's shoulder. "I think he now slips into normal sleep. The spell is lifting." She leaned closer to the og're. "Tol'chuk, can you hear me?"

Tol'chuk snored thinly for a few heartbeats, then spoke in a throaty whisper. "Mother? Mother, where be you?"

Mycelle patted his shoulder. "I'm here, Son. It's time to wake."

"But . . . but Father wanted me to tell you something."

Glancing at the others, Mycelle's expression was clearly worried.

Tol'chuk continued to mumble. "Father says to tell you that he be sorry he made you go away. His heart still hears your voice, and his bones still remember your heat. He misses you."

Mycelle's voice cracked. She did not hide her tears. "I miss him, too." She gripped Tol'chuk's shoulder tighter. "But, Tol'chuk, it is time to come back here. There is still much to do."

"I remember . . . I remember," he said with rising heat. "The *Bane*!" Tol'chuk's eyes jerked open, a stifled cry escaped his lips, and his body spasmed as he came fully awake. He glanced around him. "What happened? Where be I?"

He tried to rise, but Mycelle placed a hand on his chest, over his heart. "You're safe."

The rat, though, seemed to realize that it was not safe and hobbled down one of the og're's arms. Tol'chuk glanced at it, his fanged lips curling in disgust. He tried to fling it away, but Elena grabbed the rat with both hands and snatched it up.

"Tol'chuk, this little one just saved your life," she said, cradling it to her chest. Its scaled tail wrapped around her wrist. It no longer glowed and seemed a normal rat again. It chewed absently at the tiny vinelets wrapping her fingers, then spat them out.

The og're's eyes grew clearer. "I know that rat," he said. "That crooked tail. I put it in my pouch."

"Why?" Mycelle asked intensely, as if her question were of utmost impact. "Why did you do that?"

Tol'chuk pushed to a seated position. He shivered, finally feeling his chilled skin. "I don't know. He was injured." Tol'chuk shrugged.

"Hmm . . ." was Mycelle's only comment.

"What?" Er'ril asked.

Mycelle nodded toward the floor. "Give him back his heartstone."

Er'ril bent and retrieved the priceless gem from where it had been knocked to the floor. It was heavy. Er'ril could barely fit his fingers around it to grip it one-handed. He lifted it.

"The Heart . . ." Tol'chuk said. His expression was worried. He held out his palm.

Er'ril placed the stone in the og're's hand. As soon as it touched Tol'chuk's flesh, the facets of the stone blew to fire. The light sparked and shone throughout the room.

"It's come back to life!" Tol'chuk exclaimed. "I thought it dead. I felt it abandon me."

Mycelle nodded. "It did."

All but Tol'chuk turned to stare at her.

"What do you recall of the attack of the ill'guard?" she asked.

Tol'chuk's eyes rose to meet hers. "The who?"

Mycelle explained about what had happened to him and the others. Tol'chuk's eyes seemed finally to focus on his two companions, slumbering and pale, on the neighboring cots. "Meric is gone?" he asked, his voice wounded.

"What do you remember about the attack?" Mycelle repeated.

Tol'chuk swallowed some hard lump in his throat. "They came in the form of demon rats. Their eyes shone with some sick inner fire."

"Bloodfire," Elena said and ignored the others' stares. She nodded for Tol'chuk to continue as her fingers soothed the small rat.

"Their eyes drew me into them . . . into a world of pain and despair. I could not resist. I became lost and could not find my way back. I weakened with their song of screams and hopelessness. I tried to resist with the Heart, but it was dead, just a lump of stone in my fist."

"No," Mycelle said. "The magick was protecting itself. What you describe I have heard before. There is a form of ill'guard black magick that feeds on one's life force. In this case, the demon rats sapped your spirit with their despairs—a most potent magick. And with the Heart storing the spirits of your dead, the ill'guard could have drawn off even these last stray bits of life force . . . stealing your ancestors away forever."

Tol'chuk's eyes widened with her words.

"So to protect itself, the spirits and their power fled into another vessel, something blocked from the spell-cast eyes of the ill'guard." Mycelle nodded toward the rat in Elena's arms. "It stayed there until it could return to you and share its energies to revive you."

No one said anything for several heartbeats.

Finally, Er'ril broke the silence. "But what of Kral and Fardale?" he asked. "Could the stone cure them, too?"

Mycelle stepped back and waved Tol'chuk toward the other two beds. "Let's find out."

LORD TORWREN CROUCHED LOWER IN THE MUD, LISTENING. HE HEARD the scrape of stone from one of the many tunnels that burrowed out from the cellar region of the tower. The Pack had returned. He reached and grasped the ebon'stone sphere. Pushing a fragment of his spirit into the stone, he ignited the well of bloodfire within. Tiny flames began to skate over its surface, and the room brightened with its sick fire.

Near his feet, the pale forms of Mycof and Ryman lay sprawled in the mud. Their naked skin ran bloody with the light of the flames. They were twin shells, empty now, that awaited the return of their creations.

A scrape again sounded from a nearby tunnel.

The d'warf lord raised his eyes.

Through the dark eye of a tunnel opening, the beast shambled into thc cellar. Red eyes shone with baleful flames, while oiled black fur reflected the bloodfire of the talisman. A scattering of heavy bats flew in behind the creature to settle into the mud. Wings retracted, and the bats became rats again. One scurried over to offer its prize to its master. Torwren ignored the severed finger dropped at his lap. His eyes were fixed on the burden carried under a thick arm of the monstrous beast.

The captive was a wraith of a man, all limb and neck. Silver hair, tied in a braid, dragged in the mud as the demon beast lumbered into the room. The magick in the prisoner struck his senses like a wash of icy water. Over the many centuries he had served as a seeker for the Dark Lord, he had never come upon one so rich in elemental fire.

Torwren sniffed at the dank air. He smelled ocean breezes and the scent of winter storms. An elemental of wind and air! He had never chanced upon one skilled in this element. He wondered how the black magick of the ebon'stone would twist this unique power. What manner of ill'guard would arise from this man?

His heart beat faster than it had in ages. This one was strong! "Shackle him," the d'warf lord ordered, pointing to the iron manacles bolted to one wall of the cellar.

The beast swung its whiskered snout toward Torwren and hissed, its blood lust bright in its eyes. But the Pack, even here in its strongest form, seemed weak and small compared to the power he had just scented.

"Do as I command!" Torwren raised the ebon'stone sphere, and bloodfire spat higher. Wicked flames reached for the creature.

It cowered away, subdued by his show of power. With its shoulders hunched against the brightness of the talisman, it stepped over the pale forms of Mycof and Ryman. Crossing to the far wall, it roughly yanked and twisted the thin man's limp form until his two wrists were clamped in iron bands. The beast stepped back.

The prisoner now hung from his wrists, his toes unable to reach the mud floor.

Satisfied his captive was secure, Torwren faced the black beast. "The hunt is done this night," he hissed at it. "Return to your slumber!"

Resistance was plain in its hungry eyes. It took a step toward him, claws rising.

Torwren shook his head at its display. Such a poor tool for his use! He lowered the ebon'stone talisman, touching first Mycof, then Ryman. With the caress of the stone, their limp bodies spasmed tight as drawn bowstrings. Their backs arched from the mud, necks stretched back, jaws opened in silent screams.

The beast froze in its approach. Rows of yellow fangs glinted as it hissed its frustration.

"Begone!" the d'warf lord ordered. He ran a wrinkled palm across the polished surface of the stone. As his hand quelled the fire, the beast simply collapsed into a mound of squirming black worms. "Return to your hosts!"

The worms twisted and roiled in a mass toward Mycof and Ryman. They rolled over the taut bodies of the twins then burrowed home, squirming into their mouths, up their noses, and into every opening in the pair's bodies. The pale forms gagged and choked on the worms as the Pack returned to roost. Their bellies swelled with the worms until the two brothers appeared as bloated corpses.

Then their bellies subsided as the magick given substance returned to its original energies. The power ran again through the blood and bones of the twins. Mycof was the first to rise from the mud; again his features were those of a statue, all emotion drained away by the hunt. The young man's colorless thin lips sighed. Ryman arose next, his red eyes glancing briefly at his brother, then at Torwren.

"Return to your rooms," Torwren said.

"The hunt . . . ?" Mycof dared.

Torwren pointed to the wall where the prisoner hung. "You have done well. The master is pleased."

His words raised a shadow of a smile from each. Torwren knew this was an ecstatic response from the brothers after the Pack had drained them. "Go to your beds and rest." Torwren retrieved the bloody finger from the mud near his knees. "We will hunt again on the morrow's twilight."

These words raised even a greater smile, a hint of teeth showing. Their blood lust had been denied this night, but the thought of another hunt promised another chance to slake their hunger.

The two brothers slowly climbed from the mud, helping each other up. With a barest bow of heads, they turned and retreated to the door that led to the tower stair.

Once gone, the d'warf lord raised the torn finger to his nose and sniffed at it. He scented caves of stone and the muskiness of mined ore. Rock magick! Even this small token promised another elemental of savage fire. He brought the finger to his lips and tasted the blood and tore into its flesh. Its taste and trace of magick would help guide him this night. Tonight's hunt must not fail.

Not if he was to allow himself a hope.

Two ill'guard to be bent to his will. Two of such strength! His eyes closed as he imagined the power at his command. Power enough to defy the Black Heart and seek the Try'sil.

He put aside these dreams and raised his gaze to the captive hung in iron on the wall. First, he had a spirit to break and cast upon the bloodfire of his ebon'stone pyre. Like his d'warf ancestors, skilled masters of the forge, he would hammer and fold this one into a blade of the keenest edge and fiercest steel.

He raised the ebon'stone sphere whose hollow heart had been filled with the blood of the last defender of Rash'amon. Torwren still remembered the screams of the soldier as he had cut his beating heart from his chest and used the hot blood to fuel the ebon'stone sphere.

The d'warf lord reached for the power of the stone, sensing the soldier's living spirit trapped in the stone along with his blood. Over the ages, the man's bright spirit had been twisted and demented by the horrors in which Torwren had employed the fire of the soldier's dying heart. Unable to resist, the stone blew ablaze with the fire and despair of this long-dead soldier. His screams sounded in Torwren's ears as the d'warf lord climbed from the mud and approached his new prisoner.

What he had done to this soldier would be a kindness compared to his plans for the captive hung on the wall. Yet Torwren did not falter. He knew the lessons of his ancestors.

The hardest steel had to be forged in the hottest flame.

PULLED FROM A FIERY NIGHTMARE, KRAL OPENED HIS EYES TO A RED flame. Panicked, his heart thundering, he beat frantically at the threat, but his arms tangled in some clinging netting.

"Lie still, Kral!"

The mountain man recognized Er'ril's voice, and the world snapped to focus. He lay on a cot in one of their rooms, snared in a woolen blanket. His side ached, and his hip throbbed. He groaned as he remembered his wild ride through the burning warehouse.

Tol'chuk lowered his glowing heartstone from Kral's face. "He awakens."

Kral stared up into the og're's worried face. The last time he had seen Tol'chuk, the og're had been sprawled out on the warehouse floor. He glanced to the neighboring bed. Fardale sat atop the next cot, leaning into Elena's fingers as she scratched the wolf behind one ear. With relief, Kral realized they had escaped, too.

The mountain man found his tongue still thick in his throat. "What happened?"

"You were attacked by the ill'guard," Er'ril said. "They drained your strength with a spell of despair, but the magick in Tol'chuk's heartstone broke its hold on you." The plainsman's words were spoken without joy.

Recalling Meric's collapse in the warehouse, Kral glanced around the room, expecting to see the elv'in. "Meric?"

"He's vanished," Er'ril said with heat. "We were hoping you had some clue as to what might have happened."

His thoughts still confused, Kral freed an arm from his blankets and discovered his right hand wrapped in a bloody bandage. It throbbed and ached. He remembered the rat gnawing away his finger. A shudder traveled through his limbs. He had never felt so cold, not even among the snows of his mountain home.

Mycelle stepped forward with a steaming mug. She frowned at Er'ril as she passed Kral the cup. She scolded the plainsman. "He's still weak. Give Kral a moment to clear the dregs of the ill'guard's spell before you interrogate him."

Shivering, Kral accepted the hot mug with his good hand, his fingers wrapping tightly around the cup to absorb its heat.

"Drink it all," Mycelle ordered, straightening. "The tea will give you strength."

Kral did not argue. At first, he just sipped the sweet tea, but as its warmth traveled from his belly out to his fingers and toes, he found himself gulping it greedily. He drained the cup and leaned back in his bed, closing his eyes. He held out the mug. "More?"

Mycelle took the mug from him with a grin. "There was enough rivenberry in that cup for a brace of stallions. Just give it a few moments to work through you."

Her words soon proved true. After a few breaths, a soothing warmth spread through Kral, and the blanket began to stifle him. He tossed it back. Even his aching side protested less sharply. He pulled himself up higher in the bed.

Er'ril weighed Kral with his eyes before speaking. "Now what do you recall about the warehouse?"

Kral cleared his throat and started his story. As he related his tale, the expressions of the others grew grimmer. ". . . Then the demons surrounded us. Already tired from using his magick, Meric dropped quickly. Then the rats were upon me. It was only Rorshaf's strong legs that saved me from further damage at the beasts' teeth." He held up his bandaged hand.

Mycelle pushed down Kral's arm. "I've knit your torn skin with needled sheep's gut and applied a balm of bittersroot to help it heal clean, but you must rest it."

"Wounds heal," he said, dismissing her warning. He knew from past injuries that his magicks would speed his healing. He was rock.

Er'ril spoke next. "So after you fell, the rats attacked you."

Kral nodded. "I sensed a bloody hunger in their eyes," he said, his brows growing dark. "If Meric is gone, I fear the worst."

Mycelle sniffed dismissively. "Put aside those fears," she said as she hauled a pail from beside the bed. "Meric lives."

"How can you be so sure?" Er'ril asked.

"They left Tol'chuk and the wolf. If they were simply after meat, they wouldn't have left behind such a rich supply."

Elena shifted on the neighboring cot. "So why take Meric and leave the others?" the girl mumbled.

Mycelle answered. "Because he's rich in elemental magicks—excellent fodder for the Dark Lord's ill'guard army." Her voice grew grave. "But his abduction raises a larger fear."

"What is that?" Er'ril asked.

"With their purposeful choice of targets, I now suspect that I'm not the only seeker here in Shadowbrook. Someone else hunts the city." She glanced at Kral and nodded at his hand. "They've had a taste of you and will come after you again. Once the Dark Lord's seeker has caught your scent, he will not give up the chase. You're too strong an elemental, a prize trophy for any seeker."

Her words silenced the others.

Mogweed was the first to speak. "What of Elena? Can this seeker sniff her out, too?"

Mycelle placed a hand on the shape-shifter's shoulder. "Mogweed, you're the only one who's thinking straight. It's tragic that Meric is lost, but Elena should be our priority. I don't believe this seeker is aware of her. Elena's magick is not elemental. It's blood magick. She is invisible to my seeking, and I suspect to all others, too. But Kral will draw the hounds of the Black Heart like the blood of a wounded fox. That we must consider."

"What are you suggesting?" Er'ril asked.

Kral found the woman's hard eyes settle on him. "Kral must not come with us."

Stunned expressions spread through the room. Kral's face, though, stayed rock. "She is right. I will only draw attention to Elena."

Elena stood up from her bed, her face red, near tears. "No, we all must stand together. We can't leave Kral behind." The blanket fell from her shoulders.

Kral stared wide eyed at the spread of vines and leaves up her arm. He interrupted the girl's declaration. "What happened to Elena?"

The girl glanced to her enshrouded limb, and the fire seemed to leave her body. She sank back to the bed as Er'ril explained about the bewit'ched link between the vines and her magick. "She must not touch her magick," he finished, "or the growth could overwhelm and kill her."

"Then that's even more of a reason for me to leave," Kral said firmly. "She can't afford a confrontation with the minions of the Dark Lord. The best way I could help is to lead them astray, distract the hunt from her."

"No!" Elena said, but her voice was now less sure.

Kral sat up straighter and threw his legs to the floor. He stared at the young lass. "Elena, I would die before I let my blood draw attention to your trail. You have no say in this matter. I will travel no farther with you."

"But—?"

He placed his good hand on her knee. "No."

Elena stared around at the others for help. None would meet her eye. Her shoulders slumped. "Then what is our plan?"

Mycelle answered, speaking a breath before Er'ril. "Daybreak nears. We must leave soon thereafter. To leave before dawn would draw too many suspicious eyes. We will leave while the town awakens and the river barges set sail."

Elena turned teary eyes toward Kral. "And what will you do after we leave?"

"I will stay. Meric is somewhere here in Shadowbrook. I mean to find him and free him."

"But we could help you."

"No. Without your magick, you are useless." Kral saw how his words pained her, but as a mountain man, he had learned that true words were often hard to hear. "You'd just be in my way, someone I would have to guard."

Tol'chuk spoke into the pained tension. "You would not have to guard me, man of the mountains. I will stay with you."

"What?" Kral swung on the og're.

Tol'chuk held his chunk of heartstone. "The Heart can fight the spell-cast sleep of the ill'guard. If you find Meric, you may need my help."

"No, Tol'chuk," Er'ril said, mirroring Kral's own thoughts. "Your words are noble, but your strong arms and your magick are best used to guard Elena."

Kral nodded.

Mycelle stepped into the argument. "Elena is the important—"

"Enough!" Tol'chuk's shout shook the thin, planked walls. He shoved the heartstone before him. He pointed it first at Elena, and the stone grew dark, its bright facets dimming. Then he swung his fist toward Kral—and the stone blew to a blinding radiance!

The mountain man leaned away from its brilliance.

Tol'chuk's arm trembled with his fervor. "As it has always done, the Heart commands me where I must go. I must stay with Kral." His eyes defied anyone to question him further.

The display silenced everyone.

"Then it's decided," Mycelle said, staring at her son with cold eyes. "Kral and Tol'chuk stay and draw off our enemies. Perhaps they may succeed in freeing Meric, but if not, their deaths won't be in vain." Mycelle turned to face the others. "But before we firm plans, is there anyone else who would like to stay?"

Kral saw one arm rise, and his mouth dropped in surprise.

Mogweed stood behind Elena with his hand in the air.

ELENA SHUT HER EARS FROM THE RAISED VOICES AROUND HER. THE SMALL crook-tailed rat nuzzled deeper into the warmth of her embrace. She, too, wished to burrow somewhere away from all this commotion. She stared at the wrap of foliage on her left arm. Tugging at a coil of vine, she followed to where it burrowed into her flesh. Because of this mossy growth, the team was falling apart. As Kral had said, without access to her magicks, she was just useless baggage, a burden to those around her.

She wiped back a tear.

In just a night, all she had practiced, learned, and accomplished was now nothing. The wit'ch was gone. She was again only a child to be watched over and protected. She had thought the long journey here had forged her spirit into something more, honed her sharper than the scared girl who had fled through the burning orchards of Winterfell, but now that her powers had been stripped from her, what she discovered was that all her maturing had been only as a wit'ch. The woman was still the same scared girl.

Kral's gruff voice drew her eyes. "Mogweed, there is no need for you to stay. Of what use are you?"

The shape-shifter stood straight before the others' stares. "Exactly! Of what use am I? Am I of any more use in accompanying Elena? I am not a warrior who can protect her. But I do have eyes and ears. And here in Shadowbrook I can be of use. I can search for signs of Meric just as well as either of you— Even better than Tol'chuk! Are you going to let this monstrous og're wander through town making inquiries and searching for clues to Meric's whereabouts by himself? I don't think that's a wise course. If Meric is to be found quickly, which he must if the elv'in is to have any chance of avoiding the corruption of the seeker's touch, then as many eyes and ears as possible will be needed on these streets. You will need me. Elena will not."

Mogweed trembled slightly, whether from the intensity of his conviction or simple nervousness, Elena was not sure. Elena sniffed back her tears. Though she may not have grown on this journey, the shape-shifter had. The cowering, mousy man had developed a certain pride and willfulness, even a nobility.

"Why?" Tol'chuk asked him. "Why risk yourself?"

Mogweed's tight shoulders sagged slightly. His voice lost some of its firm resolve. "I claim no great brazenness of spirit. In fact if fighting is needed, I will most likely run. I am no warrior. It was my weakness and fears that drove me from my guard of the warehouse when the demon rats came. In some small way, it was my cowardice that allowed Meric to be captured. I would at least like a chance to correct my mistake. Meric is more than just a companion to me. Since saving his life, he and Elena are the only two who have shown me true friendship." He smiled thinly at Elena. "And right now, I am of no use to the wit'ch. I never was."

Elena opened her mouth to protest. The shape-shifter had offered her many a kind word, boosting her spirit when it was low.

Mogweed held a hand toward her and continued speaking. "But here in Shadowbrook, I can perhaps offer what is needed to save Meric—an extra pair of eyes and ears."

Er'ril stared at Mogweed with a measure of respect. "You argue your point well," he said. "Maybe it is best for you to stay, Mogweed."

The shape-shifter bowed his head slightly in Er'ril's direction.

Elena saw Fardale's amber eyes flash at Mogweed. She caught a part of the wolf's sending: *The runt of a litter faces the snake without trembling.* Fardale was proud of his brother.

Mogweed's cheeks flushed. He turned away from the wolf, apparently embarrassed by the praise.

Mycelle finally spoke, ending the long discussion. "It is late. Dawn nears, and we could all use some rest before the day's trials tomorrow."

For once this night, no one argued.

Lost in their own private thoughts, everyone began drifting to their own beds. Elena stood up, heading for her cot in the next room, but Mycelle's voice stopped her. Elena glanced back at her.

Mycelle stood before Kral, her riding packs over one shoulder. "Take this. You may need it."

Kral stared sourly at what her palm held. He glanced up into her eyes. "Then I'll need two," he said. "In case I do find Meric."

Nodding, Mycelle reached into a pocket of her riding pack.

Elena turned away, her heart shuddering. She recognized the pair of objects Aunt My was giving Kral: two jade pendants carved in the shape of tiny vials.

LATER THAT NIGHT, AS THE OTHER MEMBERS WERE SETTLED INTO THEIR beds, Mogweed still fiddled with his bags atop his cot, checking to be sure he had what he would need for the days ahead. As he fished through the contents, he pushed aside a dog's muzzle made of iron. Long ago, he had collected it from the remains of the sniffer that had attacked Fardale in the og're's mountain domain. The chains clinked as Mogweed moved it aside. He glanced up. No eyes turned in his direction.

As he continued his search, his fingers brushed against the black stone of a shallow bowl buried deep in his personal pack. Mogweed had discovered the artifact among Vira'ni's belongings in the foothill camp and had stolen it. At his touch, the bowl grew colder, almost icy. There was something strangely thrilling about its stone surface.

Still, he pushed the bowl aside. He did not know if the iron muzzle or the bowl would ever prove useful, but he was a pack rat and collected what interested him. He continued his search.

His fingers wormed through the other contents: a moldy acorn from the dead rimwood forest; a broken string from Nee'lahn's lute; a sliver of windstone from Meric, given as a thank-you for saving his life. Finally, he discovered what he wanted—a small hide satchel hidden in the deepest corner of his pack.

His fingers wrapped around the bulging pouch.

He had not lost it!

He clasped his prize a moment, not even daring to remove the satchel to confirm its contents. He could not risk someone seeing him. He allowed himself a small smile in the darkness. His interminable wait was finally over. The time to act had finally come.

Though he didn't know how his other collectibles would ever prove useful, here was something that would prove *invaluable*. With a seeker here in Shadowbrook, someone close to the lord of this land, Mogweed sensed a rare opportunity. If he could guide this seeker to Elena, give the wit'ch over to the Dark Lord while her magicks were choked by the vines, then perhaps as a boon, this king of black magicks might break the curse on Mogweed's body, freeing his trapped spirit to shift again, to embrace his si'luran heritage—and finally be free of his twin brother!

For a moment, he thought of Fardale. He remembered his brother's praise for his decision to stay. A flash of shame passed through his heart, but he hardened his will. Fardale was a fool. Time was running short. If they didn't find a way to rid their bodies of the curse, then in less than four moons their forms would settle forever into their current shapes.

Mogweed stared down at his wan figure. That must not happen!

He let the satchel drop back into his pack. He must be brave these next few days. He must find this seeker hidden behind these demon rats and offer what he held in his pack: the shorn hair of Elena, proof of a wit'ch.

18

From the end of the longest pier, Elena stared at the river. The dawn was too bright and cheery for such a somber departing, mocking the heavy hearts gathered at Shadowbrook's docks.

The night's storms had washed away the early-morning fog, and sunlight sparkled on the wide expanse of the river, a green snake that twisted toward where the sun rose. Across the river, a pair of alabaster cranes took flight, the tips of their wide wings tapping the water as they flew low across the sluggish current. Tall, bobbing reeds waved in the calm delta breezes that traveled up from the distant coast. Elena caught even a scent of sea salt in the crisp morning. She drew her cloak tighter around her. The morning still had an edge of the night's chill, but from the clear skies, the summer sun would soon bake away the slight nip in the air.

Behind her, the town was already awake, intruding on the peace of the river morning. The gruff shouts of barge captains cracked across the waters as bales and crates were loaded. Snatches of work songs rose like vapors from the river as dock men hauled cargo and sailors secured the barges that were due to set sail today. The excited voices of passengers and families were like so many chirping birds around Elena.

Yet one voice broke through the cacophony. Kral was speaking to Er'ril. "So you'll take the river to the coast? To the city of Land's End?"

Mycelle answered him, interrupting any response from the plainsman. "Our specific plans are best left to our own. If you're captured . . . well . . ." She did not have to finish her statement. If captured, their plans could be tortured or magicked from Kral.

At these words, a sudden worry arose in Elena. She turned her back on the bright river and faced the others clustered on the dock. "If they don't know where we're going," she said, drawing their attention, "how will we ever meet up again?"

"I've been thinking on that," Er'ril said. "If we—"

"We must travel separate paths," Mycelle said dismissively. "It's too risky. If we meet by luck, then we meet. If not . . ." Mycelle shrugged.

Elena stared at Kral, Tol'chuk, and Mogweed. Tears choked her words. "But—?"

Er'ril placed a hand on Elena's arm. "Hear me out first." He stared at Mycelle, then fished a folded map from a pocket and knelt on the ironwood dock. Spreading the map, he pinned it to the wood with one of his throwing daggers. The delta breeze tugged at the parchment's edges. "Gather around me."

"Careful what you say, plainsman," Mycelle warned as she came closer.

Er'ril scowled at her. He used a second dagger to gesture vaguely to his map. "I have a friend who lives on a lonely stretch of the coast; I won't say precisely where. That is where I plan to take Elena. We will rest, then hire a boat to travel to the Archipelago." He raised his eyes to the trio who would remain behind to search for Meric. With his dagger, he pointed to a small town on the coast, its name scrawled in tiny letters.

Elena leaned down closer to read the name: Port Rawl.

"If we make it to safety," Er'ril continued, "this is our rendezvous. In exactly one moon's time, I will send Mycelle to look for you in Port Rawl."

"I know that place," Kral said with a scowl. "Swamptown. Not an easy place to meet."

"I've been there before," Mycelle said. A hard glint entered her eyes, confirming the mountain man's words.

Elena studied the map, understanding now how the town had earned its nickname. The city was nestled in the center of the Drowned Lands, a pie-shaped wedge of coastline that lay lower than the surrounding countryside. Fed by rivers flowing down into it from the higher lands, it looked to be a desolate, inhospitable region of bogs, fens, and swamps, bordered to the east by brackish coastal marshes and locked from the higher lands of Alasea by a ring of towering cliffs called the Landslip. From anything she had ever heard, only the foolhardy traveled those poisonous, snake-infested lands.

The only town that laid claim to this territory was Port Rawl. Even Elena had heard tales of Swamptown. With its natural isolation and easy access to the maze of the Archipelago islands, it had become a haven for thieves, cutthroats, and those simply wishing to disappear from the world. It was less a town than a shabby gathering place for pirates and other hard men. Murderous tales of the warring castes that ruled the town and its ill-gotten bounties had thrilled many a cold winter's night for Elena and her brother.

"Why meet there?" Kral asked sourly. He cradled his bandaged hand.

"No one asks questions in Port Rawl," Er'ril answered. "Curiosity gets one killed in Swamptown."

It was an old adage. Those words ended many tragic tales about the town.

"And where should we meet?" Tol'chuk asked. "Do you know an inn?"

"None I would dare recommend," Er'ril said. "Just find a spot and wait. Mycelle will search you out with her seeker's instinct." He glanced up at the woman to confirm his statement.

Mycelle nodded. "I'll also be able to tell if any of you've been corrupted here in Shadowbrook. The stench of black magicks is easy to sniff on one who has been turned."

Elena straightened from her crouch over the map. "Then you'll do it, Aunt My?"

"If I must. Er'ril's plan is sound enough. If these others become tainted, I will know it from a distance and avoid contact. Even if they catch me in some trap—" She fingered the pendant through her thin shirt. "—they will learn nothing from me."

Her words both chilled and comforted Elena. Since she and Joach had been chased from their home in Winterfell, this motley band had become her family. She did not want to see them cast to the winds, separated forever. Still, as much as the thought of reuniting with the others bolstered her spirit, the way Mycelle clutched the poison pendant spoke of the danger that lay ahead for all of them.

Er'ril yanked free his dagger and refolded his map. "We should be loading on the barge now," he said, staring meaningfully at the others.

Kral nodded and stepped away. Even the name of their barge had been kept a secret from the others. Tol'chuk and Mogweed began to follow Kral.

"Wait!" Elena ran up to Kral and wrapped her arms around his waist, hugging him tight. The mountain man was so wide that her arms could not reach completely around him. She leaned her cheek into his belly. "Come back to me," she whispered to his belt.

Kral's voice thickened. "No tears, Elena." He patted her head with his good hand, then broke her embrace and knelt before her. "My people are nomads. When we break our winter's camp, we don't say teary good-byes to each other. We say *'To'bak nori sull corum.'* "

Elena wiped at the tears in her eyes. "What does that mean?"

Kral placed a finger on Elena's chest. " 'You are in my heart until the roads wind us back home.' "

Sniffing, Elena could not trust her voice. She just nodded and hugged him again. Then she went to the others.

Tol'chuk whispered in her ear as she hugged him, his breath tickling her neck. "I'll watch over them. They will come to no harm." Elena smiled gratefully at him. She left him so he could say his good-byes to Mycelle. Mother and son had spoken alone for a good part of the night, and Mycelle's eyes now shone brightly with threatened tears as they hugged.

Elena approached Mogweed. The shape-shifter was his usual awkward self, plainly uncomfortable with her attention. He squeezed her once and stepped back. He nodded to his brother, touching Fardale briefly on his head before retreating. Mogweed's eyes met Elena's for a brief moment. "We will meet again," he said.

Though his words were meant to reassure, Elena had a sudden foreboding. Here on this dock was the end of something. From here, different fires would forge each of them. When next they met, none would be the same.

Fardale nudged at her hand, and she absently scratched him

behind an ear. The wolf sensed her pain and wished to share it. Beside her, Er'ril and Mycelle stared as the others left the docks and headed into the streets of Shadowbrook.

"To'bak nori sull corum," Elena whispered as she lost sight of her friends.

ER'RIL SUPERVISED THE LOADING OF THEIR HORSES ONTO THE BARGE; once they reached the coast, they would need their mounts again. The barge was a wide, low-slung ship with a makeshift corral for the animals built in the center. At first, the captain was reluctant to allow the beasts on his ship, but the quantity and quality of Mycelle's coin quickly changed his mind.

From the rail of the barge, Elena and the swordswoman watched as Er'ril and the dockworkers worried the horses up the planking onto the ship. Elena's mare, Mist, went first with little trouble, easily led by a proffered apple in the palm of one of the workers. Mycelle's golden-skinned gelding put up more of a fight until a stern word yelled from the rail by Mycelle quickly doused the fire in the horse. The beast was then led by halter up the planking to the corral.

Er'ril's stallion, though, proved most stubborn. Collected from the hunters murdered by Vira'ni in the foothill camp, it had still not bonded well to Er'ril, even after the long journey across the plains of Standi. He had selected the mount for himself because he knew good horseflesh. With its wide withers and thick neck, the bloodlines of this beast could be clearly traced to the great wild horses of the Northern Steppes, a most hardy and fierce breed. Its color also spoke its heritage: a dappling of golds, blacks, and silvers on a field of white, an inbred camouflage to blend with the snowy fields and rocks of the steppes.

While two dockhands hauled on a lead from the front, Er'ril took the risky position near the horse's rear. He had his hand wrapped around the base of its tail and was twisting the tail up, trying to drive the horse forward. Each step was hard-won, and when a step was lost as the horse retreated, the dockworkers swore their frustration.

"Use a whip on it!" the captain yelled from the bow of the ship. He was a squat man with short, muscular limbs who always seemed to be tossing his arms in the air at the antics of his crew. He was doing so now. "We lose the light with this fool's pursuit!"

A crewman ran up with a switch in his fist.

"Strike my horse," Er'ril said coldly, "and I'll plant that whip so far up your arse you'll be tasting that switch for years."

The deckhand hesitated. When the man saw the serious glint in Er'ril's gray eyes, he backed away.

Turning his attention back to his mount, Er'ril found the stallion staring back at him. It studied Er'ril for a moment, then snorted and tossed its head; with no further coaxing, the great beast clambered the planking onto the barge.

Er'ril led the horse to the corral and made sure that all the water buckets were full, that the hay was fresh, and that their grain buckets were not overflowing. It wouldn't do to have the horses get colic while on board. Satisfied, he patted his mount on the nose and crossed to join the others.

"We're all set," he said as he approached the group by the rail. While Er'ril had bedded down the horses, the barge captain had joined Mycelle and Elena. Elena had one hand on Fardale's neck, absently running her gloved fingers through his ruff.

"Then we can be off!" the captain said. His face was flushed as he stalked away. Obviously whatever discussion he had been sharing with Mycelle had upset him, but Er'ril imagined the woman had that effect on most people.

Er'ril nodded to where the captain was blustering for his deckhands to cast off from the pier, his arms already shaking at the skies. "What were you talking about?"

Mycelle waved the question away. "He wanted full payment for the trip to Land's End in advance." She shook her head and turned to study the scurrying workers on the docks. "How dare he think me such a fool?"

"When you flash so much silver," Er'ril said, "you're bound to entice their greed."

Mycelle turned around to face Er'ril. She leaned against the rail as the crew began to use long poles to push away from the docks. "You think me such a fool, too," she said, her gaze sharp. "It was with forethought that I was so generous with my purse. Here among the poorly paid workers, talk of a rich couple and their son—" She laid a hand on Elena's shoulder. "—voyaging to Land's End will have spread along the docks. It is a good disguise in which to hide Elena. Like your circus, it is sometimes best to hide in the open."

Er'ril could not fault her logic, but tried anyway. "Then to maintain this ruse, shouldn't we just pay this captain our passage in full?"

Mycelle frowned at him. "And pay him for a voyage we are not taking?" She snorted. "Now who's the fool?"

Er'ril lowered his voice. "So then you're still considering my plan, the one that we discussed last night: to swap barges along the way." He repeated his arguments from the night before. "It's over an eight-day journey to the coast, and though changing barges may slow us down, it will help shake any dogs from our trail."

Mycelle just stared at him. "That's a daft plan," she finally said, ignoring Er'ril's darkening expression. "I have no intention of ever taking Elena to Land's End."

"Then what—?" His voice was sharp enough to draw the attention of a nearby deckhand.

"Watch your tongue, plainsman," Mycelle warned.

Er'ril bit his lip to keep from another outburst.

Once the deckhand had wandered away and their corner of the ship was empty, Mycelle continued. Wisely, she still kept her voice low. "In two days' time, we will off-load from the barge and head south to the Landslip."

"The Landslip? But to follow the cliffs to the coast will take almost an entire moon."

"We're not going to follow the cliffs. We're going to descend them."

Er'ril's hand clenched into a fist. Surely, this woman was mad! "You mean to take Elena into the Drowned Lands? Nothing lives among those treacherous swamps and bogs but creatures of poison. Not even trappers or hunters venture far into there."

"You are wrong," Mycelle said. "One person lives within the deep swamps: an elemental of strong magicks. I have sensed her in the past as I ventured along the Landslip. With the help of a swamp guide, I once tried to reach her, but she is sly and her lands confounding. After seven days, with my guide near death from an adder's poison, I was forced to flee the swamps. I figured if I couldn't reach her, then neither could the seekers of the Dark Lord. So I left her on her own, believing I would never need to search for her again."

Mycelle paused as a pair of deckhands passed, hauling and rolling lines of rope.

As they waited, Er'ril considered her words. He was no fool. He knew what Mycelle was thinking. Once their corner of the rail was empty again, Er'ril spoke. "This elemental hidden in the swamp—you suspect this is the one who's bewit'ched Elena."

Mycelle nodded. "And the only one who can lift the spell and free Elena's magick." She picked at the girl's loose sleeve that hid the spread of vines on her left arm. "This is her message to us. Bring Elena to her or she will kill the child."

"So we have no choice?" Er'ril asked.

Mycelle remained silent.

Elena, however, answered, speaking for the first time, her voice sullen and resigned to her fate. "I hate snakes."

From the shadows of the dock, Mogweed watched the barge leave with his brother and the wit'ch. Oars rose and fell as the boat drove for the deeper channel of the river. He noted the name carved and painted on the stern of the ship: *Shadowchaser*.

Satisfied that no last-minute switch would occur, Mogweed slipped behind the edge of a blacksmith's shack. The hammering from inside the establishment echoed in his head as he wandered back toward their inn. He rubbed at his temples as he walked, trying to erase the seed of a headache that threatened. Still, he allowed himself the smallest smile as he reached the town square.

Er'ril thought himself so sly with all his secret maneuverings, yet Mogweed had found it simple to discover both the name of the barge and its destination. Almost all the dockworkers knew of the haughty woman with her one-armed husband. Her generosity with silver had attracted many ears and eyes. A few whispered questions and an exchange of coppers had bought Mogweed all the information he needed. Among the backstreets of Shadowbrook, gossip was a commodity traded as surely as baled tobacco leaf or casks of herb oil. Knowledge was a vital trade good, and Mogweed now possessed the most valuable tidbit of information in Shadowbrook.

He knew where the wit'ch was headed: to Land's End.

With this knowledge and the satchel of shorn hair, Mogweed would buy himself a boon from the king of this land. He strode with a certain authority in his step across the threshold of the Painted Pony.

The innkeeper stopped him as he approached the back stairs.

"Them large friends of yours be gone already," the pudgy man hollered to him. "They told me to tell you they would meet you for supper."

Mogweed nodded and felt generous. He fished a copper from his pocket and tossed it toward the innkeep. The man snatched the coin from the air and made it vanish. Mogweed turned to leave.

"Hold on there!" the innkeep added. "Some messenger boy came runnin' in just after the others left and gave me this note for you folks that burned the warehouse." He held out a folded scrap of parchment with a wax seal in place.

"Who's it from?" Mogweed asked as he accepted the note.

"It bears the seal of the lords of the Keep." The innkeeper's eyes shone with curiosity.

"Who?"

"Lord Mycof and Lord Ryman. Them's as live in the town's castle. Odd birds, but their family's been lords of the Keep since my great granddad was suckin' his mammy's tit." The innkeeper leaned closer to Mogweed. "Now what would the likes of them want with circus folk, hmm?"

Mogweed hesitated, a spike of fear rising as he touched the seal. Would they have to pay for the warehouse? Should he wait until the others returned before reading the note? The hungry gleam in the innkeeper's eye, though, reminded him of the important lesson he had learned in Shadowbrook this morning. Knowledge was a vital commodity.

He thumbed open the note and unfolded it. It took just a moment to read it.

"What's it say?" the innkeeper asked, all but drooling on the scarred counter.

Mogweed folded the note. "They . . . they want us to perform at the Keep tonight, just at twilight."

"A private performance! By gods, you must have caught them lords' attentions. I've never heard of those birds asking for such a thing before. Quite an opportunity!" The news initially delighted the innkeeper; then the man's piggy eyes narrowed. "If you think of moving to a richer inn after this, remember you booked your rooms for a whole quarter moon. You'll still have to pay."

Nodding, Mogweed retreated on numb legs. He stumbled up the steps. Behind him, he heard the innkeep already spreading the news.

Mogweed keyed open the door to his room and slipped inside. He leaned back on the door as it latched closed. He took his first deep breath since reading the note. He had expected to have a few days to plot and plan. He thought it would take some time to discover the whereabouts of the ill'guard and their seeker.

He opened the note again and looked at it—not at the words of invitation, but at the seal fixed in bloodred ink on the bottom of the paper. Mogweed had been in such a hurry to open the note that he had not paid heed to the same imprint in the wax. But he could not ignore the seal's clear impression on the parchment.

The crest of the lords of the Keep was two creatures, back to back, scaled tails wrapped around each other, raised on hind limbs, teeth bared in menace.

Mogweed touched the crest with a trembling finger. "Rats," he mumbled to the empty room.

He suddenly knew the identity of the two ill'guard in Shadowbrook.

He held their invitation in his hands.

As he leaned on the door, he took several deep breaths. A plot began forming in his head. He slipped a dagger from his waist sheath and carefully trimmed the parchment to remove the inked seal. He crossed to the lamp of the room and held the seal up to the flame. Its ink glowed bright red in the flame, as bright as the locks of Elena's shorn hair.

He studied the seal. His fingers no longer trembled.

Though their circus troupe was divided, he must convince Kral and Tol'chuk to attend this command performance. Mogweed laid out his arguments in his mind. *The lords of Shadowbrook would be powerful allies in their search for Meric. How could they possibly pass up this rare chance to gain access to the many resources available at the Keep? It could make the difference between saving and losing Meric.*

Mogweed grinned sharply at the scrap of parchment.

How could Kral or Tol'chuk refuse?

He held the paper closer to the lamp's flame until it caught fire. Then he dropped the burning scrap to the floor and ground its black embers into the planks.

Only he would know the real invitation behind the words written on the note—an invitation to death.

Mogweed rubbed the ash from his fingers.

Knowledge truly was power!

"Do you think they will come, Brother?" Mycof asked as he lounged back on his reclining sofa, a pillow cushioning his head.

"How could they not? Even if they suspect us, they will still come nosing for their friend. Either that, or they'll simply flee from the city and solve our problem anyway." Ryman lay on a matching sofa of the softest silks and down of goose. His brother's constant questions began to grate on him. "But I still believe they will come," he added. "They fought hard and will not flee."

Mycof knew he irritated his twin, but he could not silence his concerns. "Do you think the . . . the d'warf suspects?"

"He is surely too busy with the new plaything we fetched him last night." Ryman's voice edged with exasperation. "He will think us too exhausted by last night's hunt to plot against his goals."

"Are you sure?"

"Our inquiries were discreet. Only we know the prisoner was the magician from the circus that rented the warehouse. Surely this other elemental whom the d'warf seeks is also among this troupe." Ryman sat up straighter on his sofa and looked Mycof in the face. His brother's smooth brow contained a single wrinkle of worry. Ryman's heart went out to his younger brother. He had not suspected how deeply this scheme had unsettled his twin. He reached a hand to the neighboring sofa and touched Mycof's silk sleeve. "This is just like a game of tai'man," he consoled. "Moving pieces hither and yon to our best advantage. Because of our skilled hunting last night, we must now contend with another who will share our private Sacrament." Ryman could not keep the disgust from his voice.

"That is," Mycof offered, refusing to consider this horrible prospect, "if the thin man survives the ebon'stone."

Ryman patted his brother's sleeve. "Yes, that would be nice if he died, but if we mean to keep yet another from intruding on our nightly hunts, then we must take matters into our own hands." Ryman leaned back into his couch. "Before the hunt is called tonight, all in the circus must be dead and disposed of. The d'warf will think his prey have been spooked and run off, and we will again have the hunt to ourselves."

"As long as the prisoner from last night dies."

Sighing, Ryman closed his eyes. "Even that is being taken care of. Remember how skilled I am at tai'man."

Mycof remained silent. He did not voice his private concern. Just yesterday, he himself had beat Ryman at tai'man.

So might not another?

Sweat ran in rivers and streams across Lord Torwren's naked flesh, a brackish swamp that stung his eyes and collected in the folds of his skin. In chest and belly, his two hearts hammered in discord as the ebon'stone sphere hovered in the air, spinning with furious fires. He wiped brusquely at his eyes and swore under his breath.

A seeker's work required both strength of will and stubbornness of bone. To forge an ill'guard warrior out of a pure elemental was difficult work. Torwren, however, knew better than to complain. Being a seeker was far better than being an ill'guard. He, at least, had a measure of free will—unlike those bent to the stone.

Torwren studied his victim.

His prisoner hung in manacles upon the wall. The man's shredded clothes lay in the mud under his hanging toes. With the first searing touch of the ebon'stone's flames, the spell of sleep had been burned from the man's eyes. In the prisoner's gaze now, the d'warf lord sensed that the man knew what was happening. The prisoner's silver hair had been singed from his scalp, and his lips had blistered from the heat. Even now his muscles spasmed and quaked from the d'warf's last assault upon his inner barriers, yet he still stared with a cool indifference at Lord Torwren. He did not scream; he did not plead for mercy.

Scratching at his belly, the d'warf planned his next attack.

The thin limbs and sallow skin of the prisoner were deceptive. Where he should be weak, the d'warf lord found only strength. The man had a font of inner fortitude that had nothing to do with the richness of his elemental abilities. As Torwren worked on him, the flavor and depth of this man's elemental fire was like a tantalizing prize dangling just out of his reach, but before he could possess this gift, he must dig free the prisoner's spirit and give it to the stone where the dark magicks would twist it to his will. Then the magick would be his to possess, his to forge into the mightiest of ill'guard.

Torwren frowned at his prisoner. The man confounded him. His stubborn spirit still refused to burn with the bloodfire. Still, Lord Torwren knew the value of patience and persistence. A slow drip of water eventually wore through rock, and the power at his fingertips was much stronger than mere water.

Yet, to be so close to his centuries-long dream . . .

He pictured the Try'sil and let his thoughts wander to what he could do once he retrieved the lost treasure of his ancestors. He shook his head. He must cast aside these stray thoughts, especially as he worked so intimately with the ebon'stone talisman. He must not raise the attention of the Dark Lord.

He firmed his thoughts as he reached once again for the stone.

"Wh-who are you?" the prisoner mumbled, his cracked and blistered tongue forming words with difficulty.

The voice stopped Torwren's fingers. Few of his subjects were ever capable of speech after the initial testing. Intrigued, he lowered his palms away from the sphere. Perhaps a bit of conversation might reveal a weakness in this prisoner. Besides, he had the time, and seldom did he come upon the pleasure of a true adversary.

He bowed his head slightly in greeting toward the shackled man. "I am Lord Torwren," he said with a wave of a wrinkled hand. "And I don't believe I've had the pleasure of your introduction."

Even though his scalp still curled with tendrils of smoke, the man's eyes were cool. "Lord Meric," he said, his voice stronger, proud. "Of the House of the Morning Star."

"Hmm . . . of noble birth," Torwren grinned, his thick lips revealing the wide teeth of his people.

"I know you," Meric said. "You are a d'warf lord."

Torwren bowed again. "You are keen. Few of my people still live, and I am the last of the lords. How do you know my people so well?"

The prisoner's head began to sag with exhaustion. The pain had finally weakened him. "We were once allies," he said with a trace of sorrow. "We once called your people friends."

His words crinkled Torwren's brow. A knit of worry began to rise in his chest. "Who are you?"

The prisoner's sky blue eyes rose to stare at Torwren. "Have you forgotten your honor? Your allies? I am of the elv'in people."

"A stormrider!" Torwren could not keep the name from his lips. Surely this man was mad. D'warves were long-lived, known to reach an age numbered in centuries, yet none of his ancestors spoke of the elv'in as anything but fanciful tales, creatures of myth. And the most crucial story surrounding the stormriders concerned the gift that the elv'in had bestowed upon his people. Stunned, Torwren dared to speak its name aloud for the first time in centuries. "The Try'sil."

"The Hammer of Thunder," the prisoner mumbled, his head again falling. "Its iron forged by lightning borne in our magick-wrought thunderheads."

Torwren backed from the prisoner. The man knew the secrets of his d'warf heritage! Could what he claimed be true? Could he truly be one of the ancient elv'in?

The d'warf lord studied the scorched and blistered figure: the thin limbs, the delicate features. His twin hearts rallied as he began to believe. Hope surged through his bones.

The prisoner had to be a sign. It could not be mere chance. Surely this elv'in, so rich in raw elementals, had been delivered into his hands by destiny, crude material for him to forge into a baleful weapon.

In his ears, old memories of his home in Gul'gotha echoed up from the past: the strike of hammer on iron anvils, the sighing song of the bellows, the roar of a thousand forges. Since the rise of the Black Heart among his people, the forges of the d'warves had gone cold, the smithies now empty and silent. At the bidding of the Dark Lord, his people had cast their lives upon these foreign shores until only a scattered few still lived.

Now, as the last of the lords, it was up to him to reclaim his heritage—and to accomplish that he must first possess the Try'sil.

With the fervor of one who knew his task was righteous, Lord Torwren reached for the ebon'stone sphere.

As his fingers touched the talisman, he merged his mind into the stone. His will became bloodfire, and wild flames swept out from the stone's polished surface toward the elv'in. Black magicks crackled in the flames. Torwren saw the flames reflected in the prisoner's blue eyes.

It was destiny!

"No!" the prisoner screamed, seeming finally to recognize his fate.

Torwren ignored his plea and swept his flaming will at the prisoner, forcing his way into the elv'in's wracked body, working into his mouth, up his nose. The man spasmed with the touch of fire. With its burn, the prisoner's heels beat at the stone wall of Rash'amon. The flames flowed into the man's body, burning their way inside of him, violating him, carrying Torwren into the heart of the elv'in.

Once inside, the d'warf lord began his forging. Flame and hammer were the tools of the ancient blademasters, and they would be his, too. With centuries of skill, he burned at the stubborn spiritual attachments of the elv'in and hammered away at his barriers and resistance. Somewhere far off, he heard the prisoner howling at the assault.

A tight smile stretched the d'warf's lips.

Long ago, elv'in nobles had granted his ancestors the power of the Try'sil. And once again, it would be the hands of an elv'in that would return the sacred Hammer of Thunder to its rightful heritage.

Such a balance of fate could not fail!

Torwren renewed his attack, like a mad dog upon the flesh of a newborn. Somewhere deeper in the ebon'stone, something scented the d'warf's new fervor. Something ancient and corrupt of spirit twisted in Torwren's direction, drawn by the sudden blood lust. Blind to his task and wrapped in the surety of his action, the d'warf ignored the red eyes that cracked open to stare out from the stone's blasted heart.

Buried in the volcanic crèches under Blackhall, the Dark Lord stirred.

19

As the sun touched the western horizon, Kral led the others toward the massive gates of the Keep. Tol'chuk followed, cloaked to hide his og're form and burdened with their half-singed gear. Mogweed hung behind.

With their approach, Kral's eyes appraised the fortifications: The moat was too shallow with too many trees growing nearby. Archers could easily harry the battlements. The mortar that set the stones had too much sand and would poorly resist a good battering by catapults. The iron portcullis that protected the gate of the Keep was more decorative than substantial. He scowled at the construction. It would not stand against a determined assault.

Still, his party had not come to lay siege to the battlements. They had come under the ruse of entertainment to try to win a favor from the lords of this town. Surely these leaders would understand the danger that lurked and hunted their streets, and they would want to protect their people. Kral again eyed the fortifications of the Keep. Then again, perhaps not.

But what choice did they have?

Kral, accompanied by a cloaked-and-hooded Tol'chuk, had wandered the dockside bars and inns, seeking information about the demon rats. Met with laughter and ridicule, all they had learned was that the town of Shadowbrook, like most river cities, had always been plagued by rats. Yet, after a few coppers had exchanged hands, darker stories arose. Over the past seasons, bodies had been turning up half chewed by the vermin. Unusual activity, the townsfolk claimed, but the past winter had been both harsh and long. What hungry creature would not seek imaginative means of filling its empty stomach?

Kral had clutched his wounded hand under the table. He knew it was more than mere hunger that drove these ravenous beasts. With heavy hearts, Kral and Tol'chuk had returned to the Painted Pony. At the inn, their arrival had been met with strange well-wishes and pats on the shoulders. When Kral had asked about the source of the commotion, the innkeeper had given him a knowing wink and told him to speak to their mate upstairs.

Mogweed had been waiting with the news: Their troupe had been graced with an invitation to perform at the Keep tonight. Kral's first response was to dismiss it. They had no time to waste clowning for some pair of lordlings. But Mogweed's arguments proved wise. Another day spent in fruitless questioning would get them no closer to Meric. But here was a chance to gain strong allies in their search for the ill'guard. Perhaps the lords would even offer a battalion of armed guards to accompany them.

The shape-shifter's reasoning had won him over, but now Kral questioned his decision. He shook his head as his boots stomped across the drawbridge over the moat. The two guards stationed to either side of the Keep's entrance looked as decorative as the fortifications. He could only hope that the lords employed more hardy stock inside the Keep than these two fanciful, thin-limbed guardsmen.

Dressed in dark blue, with flourishes of tufted lamb's wool and even a spray of crane feathers, the pair of guards began a synchronized dance that involved much clicking of boot heels and slapping of sword sheaths. They ended this play with their swords crossed before the entrance to the Keep, as if this would truly stop Kral or Tol'chuk from entering the castle. Kral suspected even Mogweed could give this dandified pair a good fight.

Kral cleared his throat and spoke to the guards. "We come at the request of the lords of the Keep," he said as introduction.

The two guards repeated the dance in reverse until the way ahead lay unbarred. "You are expected," one of the guards intoned with exaggerated grandness.

The other guard continued the memorized litany. "One of the castle's housemen awaits you beyond the gate to take you to the Musician's Hall."

Kral nodded and led the way through the massive wooden gates of the battlements. Tol'chuk and Mogweed followed.

"They be like puppets playing at warriors," Tol'chuk grumbled, waving back toward the twin guards. "Only puppets be more real."

Kral grunted his agreement as they passed under the battlements to reach the Keep's yard. Paved in cobbles, the courtyard was at least neat and tidy. An orderly stable lay to one side, and a low-roofed stone barracks was on the other. Directly across the yard were steps that led up to the castle proper.

Like the battlements, the castle was clearly built for the comfort rather than the protection of its lords. The balconies and balustrades that adorned the front of the castle would all but invite the hooks and ladders of a marauding force, and the windows were wide and many, making for easy access into the heart of the castle.

Kral shook his head. This was no keep as much as it was a pretty plaything, a bauble to please the eye. Kral began to doubt the wisdom of this night's plan. Surely there was no real support to be garnered from the lords of such a place.

Scowling, he met the tall, scrawny houseman who stood fixed in a half bow in the center of the yard. At Kral's approach, the man straightened. Dressed in silks and slippers, the man's perfume struck Kral's nose before he was within three steps of the fellow.

Mogweed sneezed like a cannon.

The sudden noised seemed to awaken this lanky marionette. "Ah, you've come," the man said graciously, one hand raised in solicitous greeting. His eyes ran over the three men. "We were perhaps expecting more performers?"

Kral kept his voice even. "I'm afraid a few are sick in bed. But we will manage."

The man's brows rose a bit, eying Kral's bandaged right hand doubtfully. "Ah, good. Yes, yes, resourcefulness is a virtue." He spun on a heel. "My name is Rothskilder. I will be your liaison with Lord Mycof and Lord Ryman. If you will follow me, I will take you to the hall where you may set up—" He glanced over his shoulder. "—and clean up before the lords' attendance this evening."

Mogweed had sidled forward. "You are most generous."

Kral could not tell if the shape-shifter was honest or sarcastic. Mogweed's tongue could be as slippery as the belly of an eel.

They followed Rothskilder to a small alley that lay between the barracks and the castle. Apparently circus folk did not use the main stair. They passed a wide side door propped open to the night. The familiar squabble and clink of a kitchen greeted them.

"Come, come," their guide insisted, leading them into the commotion of this night's dinner preparation.

Glancing around him, Kral wondered for a moment if dinner was included with their performance. The savory aroma of roasting beef and boiling potatoes almost made him forget about the true goal of this night. Even if they could not convince the lords to help, maybe they could at least get a meal of something other than their usual staple of salted fish.

Tol'chuk, too, seemed to drag as he passed through the kitchen. Kral caught the og're staring at a rack of lamb spitted above glowing embers. Their eyes met, sharing their appreciation of the cooks' skill. Too soon, they were led to a wide hall and away from the scents of the kitchen's hearths.

With thoughts on his belly, Kral followed the slender figure of Rothskilder through the back halls of the Keep, the paths and byways of the servants who kept the castle running. The halls narrowed, and the ceilings lowered. Kral glanced to the poor construction of these dim halls. Apparently little was spent on the servant wings.

The man hummed and whistled as he led them deeper into the Keep.

"How much farther?" Mogweed asked, his breath sounding winded from the single crate he carried.

"Just a bit. I'm afraid only noble guests and their manservants are allowed in the main halls, so I must take you on a circuitous route to the Musician's Hall. I apologize for the inconvenience."

As they rounded a bend in the halls, the walls on the left side abruptly changed to rough blocks of stone. These were not mortared together but hewn and stacked.

The houseman must have noticed Kral pause by the wall. "Yes," Rothskilder said, slowing his step and frowning at the stones. "This is the most ancient section of the Keep. Such crude construction." He waved dismissively at the wall. "I don't know why the craftsmen didn't just tear it down when the castle was built."

Kral, though, could not keep his eyes from the stones. Even as their guide continued forward, Kral lagged behind. Tol'chuk and Mogweed were soon a few steps ahead of him.

Kral raised a hand to the stone. His fingers trembled. His blood responded to the stones. He sensed the force throbbing forth from them. As a single finger touched the stone, his mind exploded with the ancient voices of dying men.

Man the fires, you good men! . . . The d'warves have breached the south wall! . . . Beware their lords! They come with black magicks! . . . Archers to the west! . . . The bloodstone! The bloodstone!

Kral weaved on his feet. He reached to the wall with his injured hand to support himself. It was a mistake. With its touch, his mind was taken from him.

The castle hall vanished, and Kral found himself alone atop a high tower. A sickle moon looked down upon him, offering little light. But a reddish glow lit the horizon on all sides as Kral spun around. He ran to the tower's edge and leaned over the parapet. Below, a river glowed red with a thousand siege fires. Cries of the tortured climbed with the smoke from the fires. Kral lifted his hands from the stone of the parapet. They were wet with blood. The whole tower was drenched in the blood of the slain.

A noise, a scrape of heel on stone, sounded behind him.

Dreading to look, but unable to resist, Kral turned.

In the center of the tower crouched a naked figure. It stood no taller than Kral's belt buckle but was as heavy as the large mountain man. Kral knew this creature. Here squatted a monster from the past. He remembered the oft-repeated tales of the bloody D'warf Wars, like the story of Mulf, the ax master who had held the Pass of Tears for an entire day and night against the d'warf armies. It was said these sickly creatures had driven his ancestors from their homes in the far north, destroying and forever fouling their ancient mountain homeland, casting them forever as nomads among the lands of man. Legend around the clan fires was that only after the last d'warf was dead could Kral's people ever return home.

Kral reached for his ax. He knew that these fires and screams were from centuries past, that this was all an ancient nightmare trapped in the blood-soaked stones and that only the magick in his blood allowed him access to this ancient tragedy. Still, dream or not, he would kill this d'warf.

On the tower, the d'warf leered at him. "Now who are you?" it spat out with a sneer. A black stone sphere spun in the air over the d'warf's shoulders. Bloody fire crackled along its surface. In brighter spats of the stone's flames, a different scene, ghostly and vague, cracked through the dream. A man hung in chains in some dungeon, his skin blistered, his body wracked with burns.

Somehow Kral knew this scene was not a part of the ancient nightmare. It was happening now! This d'warf was not a figment of the past, but as real as the mountain man himself—and Kral suddenly knew the man who hung in those chains.

"Meric!" he gasped, raising his ax.

Kral's outburst startled the d'warf. A moment of uncertainty crept into his sunken eyes. "Where are—?"

Suddenly the scene was wrenched away. Kral found himself back in the castle's hallway. Tol'chuk leaned over him and lifted Kral to his feet. Mogweed stood nearby, a hand raised nervously to his throat.

Rothskilder, their guide, hovered a step away. "Is he sick, too? Like those others in your troupe?" The fear of contagion was trembling in his voice.

Kral cleared his throat and pushed free of the og're's arms. He raised a hand to his feverish brow. "No," Kral said. "I simply tripped and struck my head."

Suspicion bright in his eyes, Rothskilder nodded and turned. "It is not far to the hall."

After a narrow-eyed glance at Kral, Mogweed followed their guide. Tol'chuk kept even with Kral, obviously concerned he might collapse again. "What happened?" he whispered as low as an og're could manage.

Kral studied the rough-hewn stone wall. They passed a door of beaten brass that stood in the center of this ancient section of the tower. Kral nodded to it and walked past it without another glance. "Meric is beyond that door."

Tol'chuk stumbled a step at his declaration but caught up to Kral. "What are we to do?"

"When the time is right, we'll tear this place down to its roots," he growled.

"What's down there?" Tol'chuk asked cautiously. He seemed to sense the seething fury in the mountain man.

Kral pictured the squat toad of a creature. "Something blacker than the hearts of demons."

A gentle tapping at their door drew the twins' eyes. A raised voice spoke with measured respect from beyond the threshold. Their manservant Rothskilder knew better than to expect them to answer, but he was forbidden from entering uninvited. "As you requested, my lords, I have made your guests comfortable in the Musician's Hall."

Mycof glanced at his brother. "As usual, dear brother, you were right. They have not fled the city." Mycof straightened the lay of his green silk robes. "Pity that we must foul our own fingers with such unpleasantness."

Ryman snugged the sash of office over one shoulder, positioning the crest of their house over his heart. One finger traced the two snarling animals. "It is our duty. House Kura'dom has always had to dirty their hands to keep Shadowbrook in the family. Once again, we protect what is rightfully ours."

"And protect the purity of the hunt," Mycof said, a trace of lust in his voice. Twilight was near, and the nightly ritual already called to his blood.

"Yes," Ryman said proudly, throwing his shoulders back, "it must stay in the family."

Mycof loved it when his brother waxed noble. He touched his crest with two fingers. "To House Kura'dom."

"To the blood of our people," Ryman finished, mirroring his brother's stance. It was an ancient family slogan.

Mycof's mouth grew dry, and the slightest tremble shook his shoulders. The blood of Shadowbrook was their heritage! How dare the d'warf ask them to share the hunt with strangers! "To the blood of our people," Mycof repeated. A bright bead of perspiration stood on his brow.

"Calm yourself, Brother. You mustn't let fury rule you. The best plans are carried out with a cold heart."

Mycof sighed, releasing his anger. Ryman, as usual, was wise. He forced a relaxed pose. "All is prepared then?"

"Of course." Ryman led the way toward the door.

Mycof followed behind his older brother. As they proceeded across their room, he studied the fall of the robe and cloak about

Ryman's shoulders. His brother's white hair was striking against the dark green of the cloak, perfect in form and movement.

Ryman opened the room's door to find Rothskilder bowed before the threshold.

"My lords," their manservant intoned, awaiting their order.

"Lead the way," Ryman instructed, his lips barely moving.

Mycof knew his brother, like himself, found it distasteful to speak to another. Their voices were meant only for each other's ears. When they must speak, they whispered, sharing as little of their voices as possible with their servants.

Rothskilder knew their manners and engaged them in no conversation as he led the way toward the Musician's Hall. Still, nervousness kept their guide's tongue wagging. "I have the guards posted, and the exits secured as you ordered."

As the twins walked shoulder to shoulder, Ryman glanced to his brother as if to say I told you so. Everything was in order.

In acknowledgment, Mycof bowed his chin ever so slightly. Still, Mycof asked their manservant, "We will not be disturbed?"

His whispered voice, unexpected, startled Rothskilder. The man almost glanced toward Mycof, then caught himself and continued down the hall. "Just as you requested, this is a private audience," he said humbly. "You will not be disturbed."

Behind Rothskilder, the twins glided like two silk ghosts, their slippered feet moving in step together, their green cloaks swishing in unison as they proceeded.

Neither twin spoke, but each knew the other's thoughts. Mycof's and Ryman's eyes met briefly as they turned the last corner. Both brothers already had their fingers touching the hilts of the poisoned daggers hidden in sheaths strapped to their wrists.

The House of Kura'dom knew how to protect what was theirs.

LORD TORWREN CROUCHED IN THE MUD OF THE CELLAR. NEAR HIS TOES, the ebon'stone talisman lay half sunk in the muck. Its polished surface no longer ran with flames. After the axman's blunt intrusion into the sphere's dreamscape, Torwren had been unable to maintain the concentration necessary to keep the fires lit. Who was this strange hulking man? The d'warf had recognized him as the elemental who had escaped last night's trap, but by the dancing gods, how had he entered the stone? The talisman was bound only to Torwren. No one but he should be able to enter it freely.

Nearby, the elv'in prisoner groaned in his shackles.

"Yes, yes," he waved in distraction at the wracked man, "I'll get back to you in a moment." He had only begun to forge the elv'in's spirit. There was still much left to do, but the oddity of the intruder kept Torwren distracted.

"You . . . you will never have me," the prisoner gasped weakly.

Torwren glanced in his direction. A seed of an idea began to form. "Meric, wasn't it?" he said, stepping toward the prisoner.

The elv'in's face darkened. His eyes grew colder, and blood dripped from his cracked lips.

"It seems that a friend of yours is prying where he shouldn't," he said.

Sullenly, Meric lowered his head. "I don't know what you're talking about."

"The other elemental, the bearded giant." Torwren saw the glint of recognition in his prisoner's eye. "Tell me about him."

"I'll tell you nothing." Meric spat in his direction.

"The stone can make you talk," Torwren bluffed. "But the fire's touch won't be as pleasant as it has been thus far." Once the elv'in was converted to the ill'guard, he would be unable to keep any secret from the d'warf, but the process took too long; Torwren wanted to discover this other elemental's secrets now. He smiled warmly at Meric, satisfied that his statement had paled the elv'in's features. The threat of pain was often worse than the experience itself. He remained silent and let the elv'in dwell on his words.

Finally, in a trembling voice that lacked the fire of a moment ago, the prisoner gasped, "Take that cursed stone of yours and—"

"Now, now, is that any way to speak to your host?" Torwren ran a finger along the elv'in's exposed ribs.

The prisoner's skin shuddered at his touch. The elv'in could not keep a small moan from slipping past his lips. The display of weakness unmanned the prisoner; Torwren saw despair in the hang of his head.

He stepped back and went to reach for the stone half sunk in the mud: Just a push and the man would be singing like a split-tongued raven. But as soon as his fingers touched the sphere, Torwren knew something was wrong. He gasped and snatched his hands away. The stone's surface, usually warm with its inner fires, was as cold as the dirt of a winter's grave. It felt as if he had touched his own frozen and dead heart. The d'warf shuddered and backed from the stone.

As he stared, the dank mud around the sphere began to freeze, ice and frost sheening in the torchlight. The mud cracked as it froze. Then the ice spread from the stone in ripples.

What was happening? Torwren retreated from the ice, his wide feet sinking into muck. Soon his back was against the wall.

The prisoner, hanging on the stones beside him, raised his head, his eyes suspicious and wary.

Torwren met his gaze. Was this some elv'in magick? Had he misjudged the extent of this elemental's skill? Or did it have something to do with the bearded stranger's intrusion within the stone? He glared back at his prisoner. "What do you know of this?"

Behind the glaze of pain, confusion was evident in the elv'in's expression. "What . . . ?"

Torwren turned away, realizing the elv'in was unaware of what was happening. The ebon'stone still lay in the center of the room, a pool of ice flowing out from it. As the ice finally reached the d'warf's feet, the mud froze around his sunken ankles, locking him in its frigid embrace, the cold so intense that it felt more like fire.

The shock of its touch drew a moan from the d'warf lord.

He suddenly understood what was happening. Oh dancing gods of the Forge! He crashed to his knees in the mud. His left ankle, trapped deeper in the mud, cracked. Terror gripped his heart so fiercely that Torwren did not even feel the pain of his wailing ankle.

With his lips pulled back in a rictus of fear, Torwren watched the ebon'stone rise from its nest in the cracked and frozen mud. It floated in the air and began to spin. This time, Torwren had nothing to do with the magicks that drove the stone's flight.

"No," he moaned. Not when he was so close! His hands scrabbled at his ears, as if trying to block his realization. Not after so long! Tears rose from eyes that had not cried in centuries. He knew his mistake, felt it in the ice that clutched his ankles. After discovering the elv'in heritage of his prisoner, he had engaged the stone without his usual caution. He had been so certain that the elv'in's appearance was a sign of his destiny, a divine portent that the Try'sil would soon be his, that he had let his guard drop.

He ground his fists at his throat and groaned. After so long a vigil, all had been lost in a single moment of hope. Despair ran like the mud's ice through his veins.

The ebon'stone sphere slowly flew toward him.

Its black surface no longer ran with bloodfire. Instead its surface grew blacker; the faint lines of silver impurities disappeared until the stone sphere was a hole in the world. It sucked the warmth and feeble torchlight from the room.

Torwren knew it was no longer a sphere of stone, but the pupil of the blackest eye, a pool through which a monster stared out from his volcanic lair.

It was now the eye of the Dark Lord.

Awakened to Torwren's traitorous heart, the Black Heart had come to exact vengeance. The Try'sil, the Hammer of Thunder, was the only tool that could break the bond that held his people thrall to the Dark Lord. Torwren had been his people's last hope. His elemental skill at seeking had kept him from the tight leash that bound the other d'warves to the Black Heart's will. With only a narrow room in which to maneuver, he had plotted and waited centuries for his chance to reclaim his heritage.

He cried his despair to the stone roof of the cellar. As with the original defenders of Rash'amon, no one answered. But this time, the roles were reversed. He was not the one wielding the black magicks and smiling at his suffering victims. No, this time, he was the one crying to the blind heavens.

He stared at the black eye and despaired.

With his death, all hope was lost.

Resigned to his fate, he spread his arms as the ebon'stone approached. Death would at least end his pain. Once within arm's reach, the stone stopped its flight and hovered before him. Torwren closed his eyes—and waited.

For several heartbeats, nothing happened. Torwren's breath grew ragged, and his knees began to quake. He remembered how he had toyed with the prisoner: Agony threatened was often a worse torture than the actual pain.

Frightened, Torwren opened his eyes.

The ebon'stone sphere still spun in the air before his chest, but now its surface was again afire—not with the red flames of bloodfire, but with the midnight flames of darkfire.

Before he could wonder at this, the fire burst forth to envelop him.

At its touch, every bone in his wrinkled body blew to flame. Torwren fell backward, welcoming his death at long last.

Yet, as the pain grew more intense, his hearts still continued to beat. He willed them to stop, knowing that the coolness of death lay just a thin curtain away. He let himself go, releasing his spirit to the grave. Just as his last, weak grip on his essence loosened, he realized his error.

No!

His eyes whipped open. Blind to all but the darkfire that lapped and crested over his body, he still saw clearly what was happening. It was not death that welcomed his spirit, but the twisting magick of the ebon'stone.

He writhed and screamed, but it was too late.

The Black Heart was not destroying him. He was *forging* him, perverting his spirit as Torwren himself had done to so many others, changing him into one of the Dark Lord's creatures—into one of the foul ill'guard.

AS TOL'CHUK AND MOGWEED UNPACKED THEIR MEAGER SUPPLIES, KRAL glanced around the Musician's Hall. A small raised dais decorated in gilded roses occupied the far wall. Two tall-backed chairs of oiled ramswood and silk pillows stood atop the dais, the two cushioned thrones of the lords of the Keep. The rest of the chamber was empty, just polished marble floors reflecting the many bright lamps along the walls. Overhead, a crystal-and-silver chandelier lit with a hundred candles draped across the arched ceiling like an intricate spider's web sparkling with drops of morning dew.

Kral could imagine the lavish minstrels and parading guests who usually occupied this room. It was a chamber that called for extravagance and fanciful productions.

With a growing frown, Kral judged his own troupe. Dressed in road-worn clothes and gear singed black at the edges, the three circus performers seemed lost in the large hall. Something was wrong here. Kral sensed it in the same way he knew when the ice of a frozen lake would crack under him.

Tol'chuk came up to him. "We be about ready. Mogweed will start with a few of Meric's tricks just to set the lords at ease."

Kral nodded. They had no intention—or even the ability—to

perform a complete show. The crates of gear were just decoration, a thin guise in which to gain access to these two lordlings.

"Tol'chuk," Kral said, "be wary this evening. Something rings false here."

The og're nodded. "I now wonder, too, why we truly be called here. Did you see the guards at the doors?"

Kral nodded.

Nearby, Mogweed was fishing through a crate. Kral saw him slip a small goatskin satchel in a pocket. Then he pulled forth a small bowl of the blackest stone and set it upon another crate. Kral's brow crinkled. He did not remember ever seeing such an item among Meric's magickal paraphernalia. Just the sight of the stone made his skin crawl. Kral rubbed his arms to collect himself. He was too edgy. It was just a bowl.

Suddenly, the large wooden doors near the main entrance were swept open by two stately armsmen. Standing in the threshold was Rothskilder, the man who had led them here. Behind their thin-limbed guide stood two men of shocking visages.

Like a trick of mirrors, the two men were identical reflections of each other. Draped in matching green cloaks and silks, the pair moved in synchronous step as they entered the Musician's Hall. Their faces were disturbingly foreign, and Kral could not help but stare. Hair whiter than virgin snow and eyes a reddish pink, like those of cave newts, told Kral the birthright of this pair. Among his people, an occasional babe was born with such features. It was considered a bad omen. In the past, such babes had been considered to be touched by ice demons and were often abandoned on the snowy mountaintops to die. Such ingrained superstitions were slow to fade; even now Kral could not help but shudder slightly at the sight of the twin lords. He stared at their skin, pale as bleached bones. It was bad enough to birth one such cursed child, but to birth an identical pair of them struck Kral as a bad omen for the lineage of the Keep.

Tol'chuk grumbled beside him, keeping his voice low. "I do not like the scent of these two."

The og're's nose was keener than his. Kral did not argue.

Rothskilder bowed. "The Lords Mycof and Ryman," he announced in a formal nasal cadence, "viceroys of Shadowbrook and princes of the great Keep, inheritors of the House of Kura'dom."

Without a word, the two lords crossed to their pillowed chairs.

The guards stood straight backed, with swords in hand. Rothskilder stood just inside the doorway.

The pair ascended the dais. As they sat, one of the two raised a single finger from where it had settled on the throne's carved wooden arm. With this signal, Rothskilder backed out of the room in an extended bow. The guards followed, sweeping the doors closed behind them, and soon the two lords were alone with Kral's group.

From across the hall, the eyes of each group studied the other.

Around them, the sounds of bars dropping into place sounded from behind all the doors. They were being locked in with the two lords.

Finally, one of the two pale figures spoke, his words quiet but reaching Kral quite clearly. His words were soft and did not attempt any false pretenses. "Thank you for coming. Now which of you circus performers is the elemental who escaped our hunt last night?"

MOGWEED HEARD THE SHARP INTAKE OF BREATH FROM KRAL. THE shape-shifter had sensed Kral's edginess after his strange faint in the back halls. Since then, the mountain man's suspicions had been high. Mogweed had feared for a while that he might call off this evening's meeting. Luckily, the man had a fool's courage and had continued forward.

"Now come," the lord continued from the dais, "if you step forward, we'll let the others live."

While Kral and Tol'chuk recovered from the shock of the lords' casual revelation of their ill'guard status, Mogweed thought quickly. He had a dozen plans worked out in his head. None of them supposed the lords would speak so boldly and openly. He had expected artifice and trickery. Still, Mogweed twisted a way to use this to his own advantage. He cleared his throat. He would have to be just as bold. He stepped forward. "I am the one you seek," he stated simply. "If you know of our troupe, then you must know of my talents in controlling our wolf. It is my magick. I can beast-speak." He placed his fists on his hips. "Now let the others go free."

The twins glanced to one another briefly, the smallest smile thinning their lips.

Kral hissed beside him, "Don't do this, Mogweed. Their tongues lie. They mean to kill us all."

Mogweed, with his back to Kral, rolled his eyes. The fool thought he meant to sacrifice himself. Such honorable men as Kral were quite blind to any subterfuge under their noses. He ignored the mountain man's further protests. "Let the others free," he said, "and I will give myself to you freely, without a fight."

Tol'chuk snatched at his sleeve, but Mogweed shook loose and took another step toward the dais. He needed to convince these two minions to take him to their master. Once there, he could reveal the whereabouts of the wit'ch and gain not only his freedom but the gratitude of the king of this land.

Mogweed saw the amusement in the twins' eyes at his veiled threat. This pair would need more convincing. As he stepped forward, he snatched up the black stone bowl from where it rested on a nearby crate. "Do not be deceived. I escaped you before when you had the advantage of surprise. Don't think that I can't harm you now." Shuddering at the touch of the foul stone, he held up the bowl like a trophy. "This I took from one of your ill'guard brethren—after I destroyed her and ground her bones to dust. Be warned!" He thrust the bowl toward the pair.

With satisfaction, he saw fear dampen their frozen smiles. "Ebon'stone," one of them mumbled to the other in recognition.

Mogweed pushed his slim advantage. He needed to get this pair of lords alone. When he spoke his betrayal, he wanted it to be a private conversation. He did not know where this evening would end and wanted to maintain the ruse of his loyalty to Elena for as long as possible. "Let the others go, and you will have what you want without bloodshed. This I swear."

Kral had crept up behind him. "Don't do this," he whispered. "We will fight our way from here together."

Mogweed watched the lords lean toward each other. Their lips moved but no words reached him. Mogweed had a few moments. Just as it was necessary to trick the lords into freeing the others, he had to convince Kral and Tol'chuk to leave. If they tried to fight these demons, there was a likelihood Mogweed could get killed in the melee. He swung toward Kral. "If these twins are the ill'guard," he whispered to Kral, "then I'm sure Meric must be held somewhere here in the Keep."

Kral nodded. "I know where he is."

This revelation shocked Mogweed. He blinked a few times and

almost lost the weave of his lies. "You . . . How? . . ." He clenched his teeth and collected himself. "Then all the better. I will distract them as long as possible. You two go for Meric."

"What about you?"

Mogweed allowed himself a small smile. He knew better than to lie to Kral. "I will manage. I have a plan."

Kral studied him a moment, his voice full of respect. "You surprise me, shape-shifter."

Mogweed's cheeks blushed. "Free Meric," he urged, then faced the lords.

As he turned, the lords rose from their private counsel. One of the lords used a polished fingernail to brush back a strand of white hair. "We accept your generous offer," he said.

The other slipped a small silver bell from a hidden compartment of his chair and rang it twice. Before the echo of the ringing chime faded, the main door was unbarred and swung open.

Rothskilder stood in the threshold, head bowed. "You called, Sires?"

"The two larger performers have fallen ill," the lord with the bell stated softly. "Guide them from the Keep and back to their inn, please."

"Of course, my lords. Right away." Rothskilder waved two guards from deeper in the hall forward. "Do as our lords command," he instructed with a snap of his fingers, then quickly faced the chamber again. "And the third performer?"

"Once the others are gone, we will be enjoying his company in private." Mogweed caught the twitch of a leer on the other lord's face. Then his features settled back to calm.

Mogweed's knees trembled. For several heartbeats, he had to restrain himself from calling the others back to him. Tol'chuk must have sensed his discomfort and glanced toward him. The shapeshifter offered the og're a weak smile. Tol'chuk touched a claw to his heart and then to his lips. Mogweed knew the sign. It was an og're's good-bye to a friend.

Mogweed found his own fingers repeating the sign.

As much as it suited his schemes to free the others from this trap, somewhere deep in his heart, Mogweed felt a twinge of relief that Tol'chuk would live.

Mogweed pushed aside these feelings. He must be strong. Now he would need all the skill and cunning he had learned along the difficult road to this room. In his mind's eye, he pictured a mustached man dressed in a red-and-black uniform. Silently, he mouthed the name of his initial teacher in the ways of trickery: *Rockingham*. But even such a skilled practitioner as Rockingham was finally destroyed by the black magicks of the Dark Lord. If Mogweed was to survive, he would have to surpass his teacher.

As the doors to the hall swung slowly closed, Mogweed set the stone bowl on a nearby crate. Alone with the two ill'guard demons, he reached to his tunic's pocket for the pouch hidden inside. No coins lay within the goatskin satchel, but he prayed its contents would buy him his heart's desire.

Swallowing hard, he pulled free the pouch.

"What do you have there?" one of the lords asked.

"What the Black Heart hunts," he said calmly. He had somehow thought his betrayal of Elena would be more difficult, but he discovered no remorse in his heart. He smiled at the lords of the Keep. He had their full attention now. Their pale faces had blanched further at the mention of the Dark Lord.

Opening his satchel, he drew forth several strands of red hair. "I can lead you to the wit'ch."

Kral stood up from where he crouched over the two collapsed guards. "They'll live," he said, hitching his ax to his belt. He had used the haft to club the men unconscious. He flexed his bandaged hand. It ached, but he had still managed the ax well. "Now let's go."

He led the way along the hallways at a half run. They passed the occasional startled servant. One young girl burdened with an armload of folded linen screamed, threw her work in the air, and ran. Kral could only imagine the picture the two of them made: a bearded mountain man barreling through the halls with an ax in hand followed by a loping og're, fangs bared and claws scraping at the scatter of rushes on the floor.

Kral had no time for niceties or subtleties. He had to reach the brass door that led into the old tower before—

Suddenly a loud ringing echoed through the halls. Though unacquainted with the ways of the Keep, Kral knew an alarm when he heard one.

"They know we be loose," Tol'chuk grumbled behind him.

"It's just a bit farther," Kral answered. "Hurry!" By now, the halls had narrowed, and the ceilings were lower. They were close. Half crouched, they sped down the passages.

Crossing a side hallway, a voice yelled from down the intersecting corridor as they passed. "This way, men! They flee toward the old tower! Cut them off!" The sound of booted feet thundered toward them.

Kral swore under his breath. It was not far, but they needed time to get past the brass door. He prayed it was unlocked but knew better than to put much hope in this, especially since he knew who and what lay below. It was doubtful a prisoner would be kept behind an unlocked door.

Tol'chuk called to him just as they rounded a corner and found themselves racing along the crumbling stone of the ancient tower. "They come from both directions!"

As if the og're's words had cleared his ears, Kral suddenly heard the clatter of boots and yelled orders arising from both behind and in front. Troops were working to pin them in the passage.

Kral shifted his ax in his bandaged palm. "There!" he yelled as he spotted the glint of brass. They rushed to the door as the calls of the men grew clearer around them. Kral tried the latch. Locked.

He backed and raised his ax.

"No," Tol'chuk said. "Let me."

The og're took a few steps back. Then, with an earshattering roar, he flew at the door. His legs, thick as tree trunks, shot his rocky shoulder like a battering ram at the door. The collision sounded like thunder in the narrow hallway.

Kral gasped a bit. He had not thought an og're could move so fast.

Tol'chuk bounced off the door. Dented, the brass door had bent but still held fast, crooked on its hinges. The og're pushed back to his feet, rubbing his shoulder. "Stubborn door," he muttered as he stood. The hallways now lay silent around them. Both the inhuman roar of the og're and the loud crash had given their pursuers pause. But for how long?

Throwing back his shoulders and shaking the kinks from his neck, Tol'chuk crouched for another run at the door.

"Hold on there," Kral said. He grabbed the iron handle with both hands, and rather than pushing, he yanked on the handle. The door had dented inward enough that the locking bar was bent and loosened from the frame. Kral struggled with it, iron scraping stone. "Lend me your back," he groaned as he pulled. Kral's boots began to slip on the stone.

Tol'chuk wrapped his claws around the top of the handle beside Kral's fingers. Together, they hauled on the door, arms trembling, backs arched as they fought the stone's hold on the door.

Finally, with a loud screech of metal, the door popped open, throwing both of them to the floor. Just as they fell, an arrow shot over the tops of their heads, almost grazing Kral's scalp. It struck the wall and clattered to the floor. Kral and Tol'chuk glanced at each other, then rolled through the open portal to the tower stairs beyond.

The armsmen were wary, but the arrow was a sign that their fears were fading. They would soon be upon the intruders.

"I'll guard the door," Tol'chuk said as he reached and yanked the bent door back in place. Iron again scraped stone. "It be their strength of arm against mine to open it." Tol'chuk took a wide-legged stance, the handle gripped in both his claws.

Kral clapped the og're on the shoulder. Knowing his back was well protected, he raised his ax and started down the stair.

Tol'chuk called to him. "Be wary. This tower stinks of blood and fear."

"I've my ax and my arm," Kral mumbled. "They'll cut me a swath to Meric." His stride ate up three stairs with each step as he rushed toward the root of the tower. As he ran, the stones called to him with ancient cries and the clash of swords. He ignored their song, refusing to be overwhelmed again. Only despair lay behind the tower's music.

He reached the bottom of the stairs, his boots splashing in water, and ran toward the flickering light from a chamber ahead. Only when he was a few steps away did he slow and ready himself. He ran the haft of his ax up and down his palm, heating his grip and his blood. He remembered his ancient teacher Mulf and the stories the old man would tell when well into his tales of his own battle with the d'warf armies. Amid drunken flourishes, Mulf had instructed the young Kral in the ways of battling d'warves. He could still hear the old man's slurred words. "They have two hearts. Belly and chest. Difficult to kill with a sword's thrust. But an ax, my boy—ah!—now that is a weapon to fight a d'warf." The old man had then lifted his long white beard and made a slicing motion across his exposed throat.

"Cut his head from his body, then two hearts make no difference." His ancient master's laughter carried him forward into the cellar chamber.

Kral burst into the room, boots sinking quickly in the icy mud. The roar on his lips died to a squeak as he saw what lay within the cellar chamber.

Meric, burned and bloody, hung from shackles on the wall. The elv'in's eyes did not even turn in Kral's direction; they were fixed on the play of forces in the center of the chamber. And Kral quickly found his attention drawn there as well.

Half sunk in the mud stood the d'warf from his dreams, a wrinkled pale slug of a creature. Ice hung from the folds of his flesh, and his feet were trapped in frozen mud. His arms were raised in supplication above his head—not to the gods in heaven but to an inky stone sphere that hovered above his raised fingers. Flames of darkness crackled over the sphere's surface.

Kral stared, frozen, unable to move, as if he too were trapped in ice. Just the sight of such mindless evil numbed his body. If he could have moved his limbs, he would have fled; but unable even to breathe, he just stood with his ax half raised.

It was as if a black sun had risen from some netherworld.

As he watched, the sun began to set, lowering toward the raised hands of the d'warf. Black flames blew lower, lapping along the d'warf's skin. Kral saw his nemesis' face contort with fear and agony. Then the sphere swelled with darkness and descended upon the d'warf, swallowing up the pale creature.

Kral knew it was not just magick that lay within the darkness, tormenting the d'warf, but something so foul that the mountain man's spirit quailed against its mere shadow. If he could have closed his eyes, he would have.

As he stared, the darkness swirled and tightened around the d'warf, seeming to sink into his wrinkled flesh. In only a few heartbeats, the blackness had drawn fully into the toadish figure, leaving only a few wisps of darkfire dancing along his foul skin. The sphere was gone, and in its place stood the same squat d'warf, no longer pale of flesh, but black as the darkest midnight, a shadowy statue carved by a depraved hand.

Somehow Kral knew that the d'warf was no longer flesh, but some type of foul stone—the same ore as composed the bowl Mogweed had stolen from Vira'ni. He remembered the twin lords' name for it.

Kral's lips formed the word: *ebon'stone.*

As if his silent word was heard, the d'warf's eyes snapped open. The eyes raged red with an inner fire. Lips of stone parted to reveal yellow teeth. "How nice of you to join us," a voice whispered up from the statue's throat. Stone flowed again, and a beckoning arm raised. "Come join your friend."

Kral recalled the few words he had shared with the d'warf lord atop the dream tower. He knew the creature that spoke through that stone throat was not the same d'warf. Something else had merged with the creature as surely as the stone had merged with the d'warf's flesh.

Raising his ax, Kral heard his own voice tremble. "Who . . . who are you?"

Meric seemed finally to notice the mountain man's appearance. "Flee, Kral! You cannot fight this . . . this creature!"

The elv'in's voice, though, freed something within Kral. His heart, weak with fear, suddenly hardened to rock. His fists clenched the haft of the ax, his knuckles whitening. A d'warf, black or not, was still a d'warf—and could surely die like one!

Giving no warning, Kral rushed the foul creature. His ax swung in a deadly arc. The d'warf could not even raise a stone arm in time to block his blow. Mulf had taught him well, and Kral knew where to strike.

With all the strength of his shoulder and back, Kral swung his ax into the neck of the d'warf. The shock of the impact jolted up his arm, numbing his limb and raising a gasp of surprise from the mountain man. Kral rolled to the side and twisted his ax for a second strike.

The d'warf still stood where he had been. In streams of darkness, stone flowed, and the creature raised an arm to rub at its neck. "Thank you. That felt good. My stone skin is still hardening, and a few more strikes like that will temper my ebon'stone flesh quite well."

Kral raised his ax, determined to hammer his way through the magick stone, but as the numbness in his arm finally faded, he noticed the change in balance of his weapon. He glanced at his ax. The blade was gone. He held only an empty haft. Near the feet of the d'warf, he spotted where his ax head lay shattered in fragments upon the thawing mud. Its hard-forged iron and finely honed edge were now just shards.

The d'warf lord smiled at Kral's shocked face. "It seems your usefulness in this matter has ended. Oh, well, we will have to make do with what we have." The creature's arm began to rise.

Meric called weakly to him. "Kral, run!"

It was too late.

The d'warf pointed his arm at Kral, and darkfire burst forth like a black fountain from his hand. As if the flames themselves were fingers, the fire clutched Kral's neck and lifted him off his feet. He was thrown to the wall and pinned with his toes dangling above the mud. The fingers of flame dug into his flesh, reaching for his bones.

"No!" Meric yelled.

"Enough of your noise!" the d'warf scolded.

As Kral's vision dimmed, he saw the stone d'warf raise his other arm and point it at the elv'in. Darkfire burst forth to grip Meric's neck just as tightly as Kral's.

"Now let's finish what I began earlier," the d'warf said, his eyes flaming with burning blood. "The Black Heart has shown me the foolishness of hope, burning away my ridiculous notions of resistance. I shall teach you each the same. You both shall serve the Dark Lord faithfully as his newest ill'guard soldiers."

His rasping laughter chased Kral into oblivion.

20

"Do you believe him?" Mycof asked, unable to restrain a tremble from his whispered voice. Even the mere uttering of the Black Heart's name struck a chord of terror that shook his placid demeanor.

Ryman glanced to his brother, his neck slightly bent in Mycof's direction. "Surely he lies to save his skin," he answered, but Mycof heard the hesitation in his twin's voice and saw Ryman's left eye twitch.

This nervous display further set Mycof's teeth on edge. "Still, it is one thing to slink behind the d'warf's back, but to betray the . . . the . . ." Mycof could not even speak his name. "What if the man does not lie? Do we kill him and risk it?"

Ryman's hand fingered the hidden dagger in its wrist sheath. How he itched to plunge it into this sallow-faced elemental's heart. He stared at the little man holding a goatskin satchel in one hand and a few strands of red hair in the other. How dare this rabble ruin his finely crafted plot to eliminate any rivals to the hunt! Whether this man could lead them to the wit'ch or not, he refused to share the Sacrament with such filthy vermin. The man's clothes were drab and worn, to say nothing of his tangled hair, crooked teeth, and cracked, yellowed fingernails. Ryman suppressed a shudder. To share the intimacies of the hunt with one such as this! Ryman pulled free his dagger. Never!

Mycof placed a finger on Ryman's arm, fearing any rash action from his brother. "Remember your words earlier. The best plans are carried out with a cold heart."

Ryman remained silent for several heartbeats, then lowered his dagger. "Yes, you are correct. My words were most wise." Still, Ryman did not sheathe his dagger. Shifting his position on the pillows, he leaned toward the man standing before the dais. "Now how are we to know these old hairs are from the wit'ch, as you claim?"

His question had been meant to upset their adversary's tight resolve. It failed. The man just maintained his half smile. "Take me to your master here in the Keep," he answered. "He will judge the truth of my words. He is a seeker, is he not, one skilled at sensing the magick in others?"

The dagger in Ryman's hand trembled. How he wanted to carve that grin from that foul face. Yet he forced his wrist to steady. This one may be a skilled tai'man player, but Ryman was a master of the board. "Give us a few strands, and we will take it to the seeker."

"I would prefer to show him the proof myself. Only I know where the wit'ch hides."

"And what do you wish in exchange for this knowledge?"

"Only my life and a boon from the Black Heart: a small reward of magick as payment for my work, a small pittance of the vast magick he wields." The man then lowered his voice. "And it is a mighty magick, too. I have seen those who have gone against the wishes of the Dark Lord . . . even in minor matters." The man shook his head sadly. "I can only imagine how he would treat a greater betrayal."

Mycof again touched his brother's arm. "Perhaps it's best if we take him to the d'warf," he whispered.

Ryman's fingers clenched on his dagger. "If we take him to the d'warf, then Torwren will know we were planning to thwart him. Either way, we put ourselves at risk of punishment." Ryman sensed that the trap he had so artfully set was now closing in on him.

"I would rather suffer the wrath of the d'warf," Mycof countered, his shoulders shuddering, "than face the ire of the Black Heart."

Ryman sat undecided on his pillows. Was there another way out of this tangle? In the past, he had been in worse situations upon the tai'man board and, through sly plotting, had eventually achieved a victory. Of course, then he only risked his pieces. Here, he played with his life. Now he would need all his skill.

Ryman's eyes searched the room for some answer. They settled on the ebon'stone perched on a crate. His left eye twitched. He sensed an answer might lie within that bowl. If they could bypass the d'warf and take this matter directly to the Black Heart himself, then by the time the d'warf learned of the twins' betrayal, they would have the Dark Lord's sanction as a barrier between them and Torwren's wrath. Ryman's lips thinned. "I have a new plan," he said, his usual humor returning. "We have no need to disturb our master here in the Keep." He nodded toward the bowl. "With that, we can take the matter directly to the Black Heart."

The slightest gasp escaped Mycof's lips. Ryman allowed his grin to grow a bit wider. He always enjoyed it when an unexpected move on the tai'man board shocked his younger brother. But even more, Ryman relished the surprised look on his adversary's face. The fool did not know with whom he matched wits.

"H-how?" the man stammered. "How do we use the bowl to speak to him?"

"Blood," Ryman answered, again delighted by his opponent's look of horror.

"Whose?"

"Any elemental's blood will suffice." He raised the dagger. "Yours will do nicely. Since, as you so boldly announced, you *are* an elemental."

The profoundly sick look on the man's face actually raised a chuckle from Ryman. How he loved a good game of tai'man—especially when he won.

No further yells rose up from the depths of the tower. Tol'chuk was certain he had heard Meric's voice a moment before. Grinding his teeth in frustration, he stood by the brass door. Should he go investigate the fate of his companions or maintain his post?

The Keep's troops had long given up attempting to draw the door open. After only a few failed tries at yanking the door loose, they had pulled back, swearing and yelling that the door was soundly locked and would not budge. Someone had called for a battering ram. Someone else had called for them to wait the thieves out since the tower had no other exit. "Starvation will drive their sorry arses out of there or kill 'em for us," someone had finally declared—and so the matter had been decided. It seemed none of the troops were all that anxious to chase the armed men into the crumbling tower anyway.

As Tol'chuk had waited, his keen ears had occasionally heard some murmuring or spats of raucous laughter from beyond the brass door, but no further assault was made.

He slowly unwrapped his claws from the iron latch. He saw no good reason to maintain his post, and the silence from below wore on him like the gnawing beak of a mountain vulture. Tol'chuk started down the curving stairs. He had promised Elena to watch after her companions. He would not fail her.

He sped silently down the steps, fearing to alert whatever lay below. As he reached the last step, his wide-splayed feet splashed in the water covering the floor. He paused, his ears cocked for any evidence he had been heard. Faintly, a moaning arose from the chamber ahead. Steeling himself against what he might find, he continued forward. The air had grown colder, more than the darkness and the sunless halls warranted.

He edged toward the opening and peeked inside. It was best to know what he faced before he burst into the room. His eyes grew wide at the sight.

A squat figure painted in black oil stood in the center of the chamber with its arms raised. Twin fountains of dark flames flowed from the creature's hands to pin his two companions to the wall. Meric and Kral writhed under the grip of the black magick's touch. Horrified, Tol'chuk pulled back around the corner. He had to stop this somehow. This he knew! At the sight of his companions so foully trapped, he needed no tugging from the Heart of his people to call him forward—yet the fiery hooks had again blown to flame in his chest.

One claw clutched his thigh pouch. The Heart seemed to burn through the hide. What was he to do? Would the magick of the heartstone vanish as it had before?

Suddenly, as if to chide him for his doubts, a rat ran across his foot, half swimming in the brackish waters covering the floors. Out of instinct, he began to kick it away when he noticed its crooked tail. As it swam away toward the cellar door, Tol'chuk saw it was the same rat that had carried the Heart's magick for a brief time. Frowning at it, he wondered if it had somehow followed him.

Seeming to sense the og're's scrutiny, the rat glanced back at him. Its eyes glowed in the dark hall, the ruby red of the heartstone. With a shock, Tol'chuk realized the rat still harbored a trace of the Heart's magick. The animal chittered at him, scolding him, then swung around and crawled into the cellar chamber.

Tol'chuk waited a heartbeat. He did not know the meaning of the rat's appearance, but he would not let the little beast contest his own bravery. He swung into the opening. The rat, even injured, was quick on its tiny feet. It flew across the mud, already half the distance toward the black demon.

As Tol'chuk stepped into the room, the toadish creature swung its gaze toward the og're. Eyes of flame stared at him briefly, then turned away as if Tol'chuk were no threat. "Another guest," the demon said in a voice that seemed to echo out of stone. "Come join us. I'm just about finished with these two."

"Leave them be!" Tol'chuk bellowed. He stepped farther into the light so the creature could see him fully: few were undaunted by an og're. Tol'chuk bared his fangs, exposing their full lengths.

Yet it was not his fangs that drew the black figure's eyes. The tiny crooked-tailed rat, now almost near the legs of the demon, suddenly screeched wildly. Glancing at the small attacker as it reared on its hind legs, the demon's expression was at first mildly amused; then its eyes suddenly flared with fire. It pulled back from the rat, and the twin fountains of darkfire collapsed back to their foul source.

Freed of the flame's grip, Kral crashed to the mud, and Meric slumped on the wall, hanging from iron shackles. Neither companion moved.

Tol'chuk did not have time to go to their aid. The demon pulled its thick legs from the mud and retreated from the rat. Tol'chuk knew that there was no way this tiny creature had panicked the demon. It had to be the trace of magick in its beady eyes. The black demon must fear his Heart's magick!

Reaching to his pouch, Tol'chuk freed the chunk of heartstone and pulled the blazing Heart forth. Even Tol'chuk was blinded for a moment by the radiance. Its bright light burst through the room. The flickering torches on the walls seemed like the mere glow of fireflies before the brilliance of the heartstone.

The demon raised its black arms before its face and fled the light. Tol'chuk followed it farther into the room. He sidled toward Kral to see if he still lived. The demon made no approach to stop him. It matched Tol'chuk's pace as he crossed the chamber, keeping its distance.

"Stay back, or I will destroy you!" Tol'chuk growled with as much threat as he could manage. He had no idea why the Heart intimidated the demon or how to use it, but the demon was unaware of his ignorance, and Tol'chuk meant to keep it that way. "Back!" he said, thrusting the stone forward.

He did not need to maintain the ruse for long. Once the doorway was clear, the demon bolted for the exit. It had to pass closer to Tol'chuk, but the og're made no move to stop it. Let it flee. He had his injured companions to worry about.

The demon paused at the doorway, glaring back at Tol'chuk. Its black lips pulled back in hatred. "We are not finished," it said.

Tol'chuk lowered the stone, knowing the demon had no intention of attacking. It meant simply to flee.

"I will not forget this—or you!" The demon's raging eyes stared Tol'chuk full in the face as if memorizing his features. Then the hatred in its black face shifted like molten stone. Its eyes grew wider, and it stared with a mixture of horror and awe at Tol'chuk. It stopped and took a step toward the og're. "You! It cannot be. How . . . ?"

Unnerved by the demon's strange attitude, Tol'chuk raised the stone. "Begone!" he thundered.

Still the demon hesitated.

Suddenly the small rat was again at the demon's toes, harrying him with squeaks and squeals. The fierce intrusion of the little beast broke the demon's gaze on Tol'chuk. It glared at the rat, then in a fury of motion, it vanished out into the hall. Tol'chuk listened to the splashes of its footsteps as it ran off, then waited to be sure the demon had truly fled. After a few breaths, a flurry of screams suddenly rattled down from above. The guards stationed by the door were obviously quite surprised at what lurked at the root of their tower stronghold.

Seemingly satisfied, the rat groomed its muddy paws.

Satisfied too, Tol'chuk lowered his heartstone and returned it to its pouch. He bent to Kral. At his touch, the mountain man groaned, and his eyes opened. "What happened?"

"The demon has fled. If you be living, I must check on Meric."

"I be living," Kral said sourly, sitting up with a coarse groan. "But I'm not sure that's a good thing."

Tol'chuk nodded and crossed to Meric. He yanked free the shackles and settled the elv'in's limp body in the mud. The reek of burned hair and flesh clung to his wracked form.

"How is he?" Kral called to him, climbing to his wobbly feet.

"He be weak and sorely injured. But he breathes!"

His voice must have reached Meric. The elv'in's eyes fluttered open. "I more than breathe, og're. It would take m-more than a few burns to kill elv'in royalty." Even these few words split Meric's burnt lips, and blood welled at the corners of his mouth. Pride or not, it would take a long time for the elv'in to heal.

"Rest, Meric," Tol'chuk warned. "I will carry you from here."

Meric protested at first, but even his attempt to sit up on his own failed. The elv'in's face darkened with embarrassment.

Tol'chuk scooped him up. "It be no weakness to ask a friend for help."

Meric reached and squeezed the og're's wrist, silent thanks clear in his touch.

Standing up with the elv'in in his arm, Tol'chuk faced Kral. "Can you manage on your own?"

Kral was retrieving fragments of iron from the mud. "Just point me toward that d'warf and see how fast I move."

Tol'chuk nodded, relieved at the strength in the other's voice. "For now, let the demon flee. We have one more friend still to rescue."

Kral straightened. "Mogweed. I almost forgot."

Suddenly, the tower walls groaned, and dust billowed down around them in choking clouds. The walls themselves began to quake.

"What's happening?" Meric muttered.

"The d'warf," Kral said, waving them toward the exit. The mountain man explained as he led them in a rush up the steps. "I saw it in a dream. He led the savage troops that besieged this tower long ago and slaughtered its defenders. He used the men's dying blood to bathe the stones and perform arcane acts. I wager the blood magick of the ebon'stone was the only mortar that kept the tower standing all these years. When the d'warf lord fled, he took his magick with him. At long last, the tower will fall, and its defenders can finally rest."

The rat, now finished with its grooming, noted the tremoring of the tower and dashed away through a crack in the wall.

Tol'chuk appreciated its wisdom. "If we don't hurry," he said, "we be resting forever with those long-dead defenders."

Kral grunted acknowledgment and hurried up the steps. Stones began to crash behind them, and the stairs shook, trying to betray their feet.

They fled faster. Behind them, amid crumbling stones and clouds of dust, the ancient battle for Rash'amon finally ended.

MOGWEED FELT THE FIRST TREMBLE OF THE CRUMBLING TOWER AND thought it was his own fear wobbling his feet. Certain his death was near at hand, he watched Lord Ryman rise from his chair, dagger in hand. In the candlelight from the chandelier, the blade's surface glinted an oily green. Mogweed could almost smell the poison on the dagger.

Lord Mycof whispered from where he sat. "Brother, did you feel—?"

Then the hall rocked with a grating groan. Mogweed had to wave his arms to keep upright. "What's happening?" he cried out, giving up any pretense of hiding his fear.

But Ryman's eyes were also wide with fright. He turned to his brother as if an answer could be found in his twin's pale features. "Check with the guards," he ordered.

Mycof fished out the silver bell. He rang it and waited. Nothing happened. He looked to his brother with a confused expression. Apparently a summons had never been ignored before. Mycof picked the bell up again and shook it violently. "Ryman?" he called over the ringing chime.

Ryman strode on his thin legs to the main door and pounded a fist upon it. "Guards! Attend your lords!"

A small voice answered him. "My lords, the guards have fled!" Mogweed recognized the voice of their foppish manservant. "I can't lift the bar on my own!"

"Then go to one of the smaller side doors, Rothskilder, where the bars are lighter."

"Yes, Sire. Right away!"

"Wait!" The floor again shook. Overhead, the chandelier danced, raining hot wax from the drip pans of the many candles. "What is happening out there?" Ryman yelled.

Mogweed yelped as a large drop of wax struck his cheek. He dashed from under the chandelier, placing himself closer to the dais.

"Rothskilder!"

No answer was forthcoming from beyond the door. The manservant had already run to obey his lord's order.

Ryman swung to face Mogweed as Mycof cowered in his chair, the silver bell gripped like a weapon in his small hand. "What do you know of this commotion?" Ryman asked, his face a mask of anger.

Mogweed took a step away. "Me?"

The lord threw back his cloak and raised his dagger. "This talk of wit'ches was all a ruse. What have you done?"

Mogweed thought quickly. This fellow was beyond reason. Madness lurked behind those wild eyes. Mogweed retreated from the dagger. He found himself back among the crates of gear. "I did not lie. I came here to alert you of the wit'ch."

"Liar!"

Mycof had risen from his chair, his lips trembling. Suddenly a violent shake cracked one of the gilded rafters near the rear of the hall. It smashed to the marble floor with a terrible boom. "Ryman! Make it stop!"

"I will, dear brother." The murderous glint in his eyes left no doubt as to his intention as he stalked toward Mogweed. "By killing this traitor."

"Hurry! We must find the d'warf. He'll know what to do. He'll give us the Sacrament and free the Pack. We'll be able to escape."

Mogweed's mind worked on Mycof's words. These two seemed dependent on their seeker to free the beasts within them. This gave him a bit of courage. If their demons were trapped, maybe he could fight these pampered lordlings. Or better yet . . . "Wait," he called to Ryman. "I can help you free your demon rats. You don't need your d'warf master."

Ryman's eye twitched, but he kept his dagger high. Mogweed could see the lust in this one's eyes, a frothing desire to fight the iron bit that controlled him. Ryman had been yoked to this d'warf; now he strained to be released, to act on his own. Neither of these silk-draped lords were accustomed to taking orders. "What do you speak of?" Ryman spat at him.

"The ebon'stone bowl was not the only item I stole from the female ill'guard. She bore talismans that granted her the Sacrament any time she wished." Mogweed backed into one of the open crates. "Let me show you."

Mycof climbed from his dais. "Is what he says possible, Brother?"

"I have heard the like. Not all ill'guard are slaves to their seekers." Ryman turned narrow eyes toward Mogweed. "Show us this magick."

"Yes, yes, of course." Mogweed dug through the packed supplies, keeping one eye on Ryman's dagger. Mycof had crossed to stand beside his brother. He prayed the objects he sought were somewhere in here. He moved a fold of magician's cape and spotted the familiar gleam. "Luckily, I have a pair."

Mogweed turned, holding a glittering prize in each hand. He held them out, but when Ryman reached for one, he snatched them back. "You must swear to let me go free."

Mycof answered, a thin trail of saliva on his lip. The muscles of his face spasmed as he stared at the magickal items. "I . . . we swear."

"How do we know this will work?" Ryman hissed. "That this is not some trick?"

"I have the ebon'stone bowl, do I not? Who but the ill'guard have such items?" Mogweed hoped this last statement was correct.

Ryman considered this. "Perhaps you speak the truth, but before we let you go, we will sample your supposed magick. If it works, you are free to leave. If not, you die."

Mogweed nodded sagely. He knew Ryman was lying; the bastard had no intention of letting him leave either way. Still, Mogweed pretended to ponder this offer. He held up his bribe, then snatched it back again, delaying the exchange. "Wait. I want one more concession."

"What is it?" Ryman clenched his fist in impatience.

"Afterward, I want to be taken to your master. I must let him know of the wit'ch."

"Fine. Once we're free, you can tell the d'warf whatever you like."

Mogweed nodded. In both the lordlings' eyes now, desire had become a raving lust. Mogweed had held out long enough to draw their hopes to a fevered pitch. He stared at the pair of hungry eyes for several silent heartbeats, then tossed one gift to each lord.

"Careful!" Ryman scolded. "I almost dropped mine."

"Sorry." Mogweed bowed his head. "You must care for them as your most prized treasure. It is your freedom."

"How do they work?" Mycof held the pendant up by its twisted thread. The jade vial dangled and sparkled in the hall's light.

"You drink the contents. Refill the vial with plain water by dawn's light, and by nightfall the magick in the jade stone will have changed the water again to the Sacramental elixir."

Ryman glanced suspiciously at Mogweed. "You'd better pray it works."

"Oh, I am," he mumbled. "Trust me, I am. Please try it."

As if on cue, the hall shook again. The chandelier's crystals tinkled overhead.

Mycof unstoppered his vial. "Hurry, Ryman!"

Ryman did the same, then took his brother's hand in his own. He raised the vial in a toast to his twin. "To freedom," he said soberly.

"To freedom," Mycof echoed.

In unison, the two brothers raised the jade vials to their pale lips and swallowed deeply. Once done, they both wore thin grins.

"Keep the vials around your necks," Mogweed encouraged. He mimicked placing an invisible pendant over his own head.

Ryman nodded, and both brothers hooked the pendants around their necks.

"Good, good," Mogweed continued. "Now wait for it."

Mycof was the first to blink a few times. A hand raised to his throat. "I . . . I feel something! It's . . . it's happening!"

Ryman was swallowing hard and suddenly coughed. He raised panicked eyes to Mogweed as he fell to his knees. Mycof toppled straight backward, his head striking the marble hard. Blood welled in a small pool on the polished floor.

Panic faded from Ryman's eyes as he died. He fell back to join his twin brother, two toppled statues.

Mogweed sighed loudly. "To freedom," he mumbled to the twins.

Suddenly a loud commotion erupted near one of the side doors. Mogweed turned, expecting to see Rothskilder unbar the exit. Instead the thick oaken door blew into the hall. Mogweed's eyes grew wide as the door crashed and splintered on the marble tiles.

He had not expected such an explosion, but he was correct about Rothskilder being at the door. The limp and bloody body of the manservant was clutched by his thin neck in the monstrous grip of a thick squat creature carved of black stone.

It stalked into the hall, its eyes ablaze with inner fury. Its sick gaze settled upon Mogweed, then on the dead twins. "What have you done with my servants?" it asked, throwing aside the lifeless corpse of Rothskilder.

Mogweed stepped back.

Here was the dire master of the Keep, the seeker who had controlled the ill'guard. Mogweed knew better than to try lies here. "They were in my way," he said, fighting to keep his voice even. "I came here to see you, but they had other ideas."

The black d'warf strode toward him. It crossed to within an arm's length of the shape-shifter. Mogweed held his position. Now was not the time to show weakness. The d'warf's voice was molten lava. "What news was so dire that you had to slay my creations?"

Mogweed reached to his belt and slipped the goatskin satchel free. He fingered out a pinch of Elena's hair. "I know . . ." He had to swallow a hard lump in his throat and start again. "I know the Black Heart seeks the wit'ch. I can lead you to her." He raised the strands of hair. "Here is proof."

The d'warf's gaze narrowed, intrigued. As the floor quaked under him, he held out his palm, ignoring the rumbling stones.

Mogweed reached the strands toward the open palm. As his fingers neared the black flesh of the d'warf, Mogweed felt the same queasiness as when he handled the ebon'stone bowl. He dropped the hair into the black hand, then snatched his own hand back.

"Hmm . . ." The d'warf raised the hair to his wide nose. He sniffed at it suspiciously, like a dog on a rotted salmon. One eye grew wider. He lifted his face to Mogweed. "You do not lie!"

Suddenly relieved, Mogweed grinned foolishly. "I can lead you to where she goes. I spied on her . . . She went by boat . . . You see, it heads . . . um . . ." Mogweed could not seem to stop blathering.

"Enough," the d'warf said. He sniffed again at the piled strands, drawing the thin hairs into his thick nostrils. The d'warf closed his eyes and leaned his head back. A moan somewhere between pleasure and pain groaned from his lips. His skin began to flow like thawing ice, swirling in patterns of black stone and veins of silver. Flames of darkfire flared in spurts along his skin, growing larger until they cracked like raging torrents over rock. Soon flames of the deepest red mixed with these black flames. The d'warf became a pillar of warring fires.

Suddenly the eyes of the d'warf snapped open.

Mogweed gasped. He knew it was not the d'warf who now stared out at him, but something far fouler. He had no resistance against the evil that pulsed from those black orbs. It washed over him like the oily hands of some intimate lover.

As Mogweed tried to pull away, words, low and hissing, flowed out from its flaming throat, words that ate at Mogweed's brain like hungry eels. "What do you seek?"

Terrified and unable to answer, Mogweed fell to his knees. Bile filled his throat. What had he invoked with the wit'ch's hair? As he shuffled back, flames suddenly lanced forth from the d'warf's mouth, curling and twisting like some fiery tongue. Mogweed screamed, but once the flames brushed his chest, his breath froze in his lungs. His fingers rose to rip at his stricken throat.

Then the flames were gone, and he could breathe again. Gasping and choking, he fell to his hands on the marble tiles.

The d'warf leaned closer to Mogweed. The black lips parted to smile without warmth. Flames blazed like breath as it spoke. "I know your craven heart, shape-shifter."

Mogweed cringed. He knew nothing could be hidden from this black spirit. Games of sly tongues and misdirection would be laid bare by searing flames. Mogweed bowed his head to the tiles, showing his fealty to one so dark.

"Through your deceit, you have delivered to me the scent of my most prized prey. For that we will let you live. But the boon you came begging after—the return of your si'luran heritage—that we deny you."

Tears of despair ran down the shape-shifter's face.

"Only the wit'ch at my feet will free you," the Black Heart grated.

Mogweed dared to raise his face. "But I can lead you—"

The flaming eyes settled on Mogweed, sickening the shape-shifter's stomach and numbing his tongue. "We've forged this vessel of ours, this d'warf, into a blood hunter. It has no need for your guidance, shape-shifter. Once the hunter scents a magick, he can follow its trail anywhere."

Mogweed bowed his head, despairing. "Then what do you ask of me? You will have your wit'ch without me."

Flames tickled his neck, freezing his flesh, as the d'warf leaned closer. "Trails sometimes grow cold. So for now, stay with those who aid the wit'ch. A time may come when I will ask more of you."

Suddenly a thunderous boom echoed from somewhere deeper in the Keep. Dust and smoke washed through the open door into the hall. The floor shook, knocking Mogweed flat. He covered his head with his arms as debris rattled down from the ceiling. Deeper in the hall, a bronze sconce clattered to the floor. When the rumbling subsided, Mogweed pushed up.

Nearby, the d'warf still stood as if nothing had happened. The flames had faded from his skin, and Mogweed sensed the d'warf was once again in possession of his black body. The black figure simply squinted at the clouds of debris. "You'd best leave the Keep," the d'warf rumbled. "What is built on a poor foundation seldom stands for long."

"What?"

The d'warf ignored him and strode for the main doors of the hall. As it neared the barred doorway, an arm raised and black flames leapt out to strike the thick planks. The fanciful doors exploded outward in a storm of splinters and smoke. Without a glance back, the d'warf vanished out of the hall.

Mogweed pushed to his feet just as a new eruption arose from the back of the Musician's Hall. He swung around in time to see Kral burst into the chamber with Tol'chuk at his heels, Meric in Tol'chuk's arms.

"You found him!" Mogweed enthused, trying his best to fake his relief past the icy numbness from the touch of the Dark Lord.

Kral glanced to the bodies of Ryman and Mycof. "How did you manage this feat?"

Mogweed used his toe to shift the amulet resting on Ryman's chest. "Remind me to thank your mother, Tol'chuk. Her gift of poisons proved of substantial merit."

Kral clapped Mogweed on the shoulder, almost knocking him to his knees. "You continue to surprise me, shape-shifter."

As Kral grabbed a box under each arm, Mogweed stared dully at his back. "If you only knew . . ." he mumbled.

THE BLOOD HUNTER HAD BEEN ON THE TRAIL NOW FOR TWO DAYS, TIRELESS, needing no sleep. Only the occasional stray trapper or farmer alone near the river sustained him: The meat of a fresh heart kept his inner fires burning for a day and a night. So he ran, keeping near the river's edge, slogging through the mud and reeds of the south bank. The scent of his prey was strongest in the delta breezes of the river, so he kept close to its source. He must not lose her scent.

Torwren forged across a small tributary that left the Shadowbrook River to wind its way south. Once free of the small stream, he hastened along the Shadowbrook. Nothing would block his chase. Running along the bank, trampling through a nest of crane eggs, he had traveled another half a league before he realized the scent was gone from the river winds. He stopped and raised his nose to the breeze. Clean.

He stared back up the river. Why had she left the river? It was the fastest means to reach the coast. Suddenly questioning his new ability, Torwren again lifted his nose. Still nothing. He backtracked up the bank until again he stood in the nest of the crane, amid broken shells. He tested the air. Still nothing.

Panic began to fuel his foul heart. Where had she gone?

He continued up the river until he reached the shallow tributary and splashed his way across again. The sun was almost gone; the shadows from the forest south of the river crept from the woods.

If the Dark Lord should learn of his error . . .

Then he sensed it, a scent like lightning from a summer storm. It was her! He swung around. Where had she gone?

Then he spotted it. The mud by the bank of the stream showed a single hoofprint. The blood hunter knelt by the print and sniffed. A grin split his black lips.

He stared south along the narrow tributary. "I smell you," he mumbled as darkness descended. "You cannot escape me. I will chase you to the coast if I must."

He stood up and began to lope along the stream into the forest.

"Even if you reach the coast," he said with glee, "I have a surprise waiting for you." Torwren pictured the two elementals pinned by his black magicks to the wall of the tower cellar. He had been interrupted in the forging of them into ill'guard soldiers—but he had not totally failed.

While one had escaped unscathed, his other elemental captive had not.

A most potent and black ill'guard had been forged in the cellar that night. None would suspect the evil now cloaked behind the face of one of the wit'ch's trusted guardsmen.

Upon stone lips, Torwren tested this traitor's new name, his ill'-guard name.

Legion.

Book Four

DRAGON'S ROAR

21

THE MORNING AFTER ENCOUNTERING THE PAIR OF STRANGE BROTHERS on the tower stair, Joach lay awake on his thin pallet, staring up at the wood rafters. The sun was near rising, and he had not slept the entire night. The words of the two men still whispered in his ears, especially one word: *Ragnar'k*. Why did the word hold such an odd fascination to him? Was it a name? A place? He could not seem to loosen the word from his mind. He glanced across the room, searching for any distraction.

On the far side of the cell, Greshym lay on his back atop the blankets, hands folded across his chest like a corpse laid out for viewing. Unlike Joach, the darkmage slept soundly, a coarse snore marking each breath; but like Joach, his eyes were open, too. His milky globes glowed red throughout the night, and not just from the reflection of the embers of the hearth. Somehow Joach sensed the mage's eyes watched throughout the night while his body rested.

Yet as strange as this was, Joach had grown accustomed to it. He had learned Greshym's habits and patterns. The darkmage would continue to sleep until the sun's light reached the slitted window of their room. Then, like the dead rising, he would awaken and order Joach to fetch him his morning meal.

This day Joach did not have the patience to wait for the sun. He was anxious to return to the staircase in the east tower, to search for clues of the two men. Yet, he knew he could not move from the bed until ordered. The darkmage's eyes would see him.

Trapped, he stared back up at the ceiling. Silently, his lips formed the word that nagged his slumber.

Rag . . . nar'k.

When he shaped the last syllable, Greshym snapped upright on his bed, as if somehow the silent word had stabbed through his slumber. To reinforce this impression, his ancient face twisted toward Joach. For the first time, he saw confusion and fear in the wrinkled features.

Joach continued his blank-eyed stare, praying for the mage's gaze to leave him. He needed something to convince the mage of his continued enslavement, something to distract those prying eyes. A burning in Joach's belly reminded him of one way to perhaps accomplish this, a way to debase himself in such a way that the darkmage would not question his lack of will. As he lay on his pallet, Joach loosened his bladder, soaking his clothes and bed. An acrid smell swelled in the tiny cell from the soiled bedsheets. Joach continued to lie still, unmoving in the spreading wetness.

The odor must have reached the darkmage. "Curse you, boy!" Greshym swore. "You grow more like a babe each day! Now get out of bed and clean yourself up."

Joach did as he was ordered. He slid from his pallet and slipped out of his dripping underclothes. Slack jawed and naked, he dragged his feet in a slow shuffle to the washing basin. Using a rag soaked in the cold water, he wiped himself clean.

"Get dressed and fetch my morning supper," Greshym ordered as he stared up at the still-dark window. He grumbled sourly under his breath and lay back down. "Wake me when you return."

Still damp, Joach had to keep from hurrying when he donned a dry set of underclothes and pulled into his breeches and brown shirt. It was early, and the halls would be nearly deserted: a perfect chance to explore. As his heart raced, he kept his movements dull and fumbling. With his shirt buttoned wrong and only half tucked in his breeches, he shambled toward the door.

As his hand reached for the latch, Greshym mumbled something to himself. "Frozen in stone and thrice cursed . . . Ragnar'k will not . . . cannot move . . . Just dead prophecies."

Joach's hand froze on the iron latch at the mention of Ragnar'k. Had the mage somehow sensed his thoughts? His ears strained for meaning in the darkmage's rumblings. What did it mean and—

Greshym suddenly barked, obviously noticing his pause. "Get going, boy! Before you foul yourself again!"

Joach jerked and almost gasped at the sudden eruption. He fought to maintain his dull attitude, but Greshym had already dismissed him and stared again at the rafters. Joach yanked on the latch and hauled himself from the room on legs that trembled for real. He closed the door and leaned upon it, sighing softly in relief.

It took him a few deep breaths to calm his laboring heart. Stretching a kink from his neck, he followed a familiar path among the twisting halls of the Edifice. Few others were awake this early, so he kept his pace mostly hurried, only stopping briefly to collect the scrap of parchment and sliver of charcoal from a cubby hidden in a crumbing section of wall. His mapping tools vanished quickly into his pockets, and he continued toward his destination, the tower named the Broken Spear.

The mystery of Ragnar'k nagged at him, and though he knew not why, he somehow sensed that great importance lay in solving this riddle.

Without any significant delays, he reached the stairs that wound up the easternmost tower. He listened for voices or footsteps. Nothing. Satisfied that he was alone, he clambered up the stairs, taking two steps with each stride, and climbed to the landing where the two mysterious brothers had spoken the night before.

Joach again glanced into the halls that led out onto this level. Had the men gone this way? In the early-morning gloom, the halls were murky and the dust thick on the floor. Dust! Joach bent closer to the floor. If the men had gone this way, there should be tracks on the stone. He cocked his head and squinted. The dust lay undisturbed for as far as he could see. The two brothers had not left the staircase. He straightened, scratching his head. He knew they hadn't come down, so that left only up.

Joach stared at the winding staircase and fingered the map in his pocket. There was only one level above this one. It was the floor he had explored and mapped yesterday. That level, like this whole wing of the Edifice, was just crumbling stones and lonely spiders. What manner of business did these two have above?

There was only one way to find out. Joach climbed the remainder of the stairs to the last level. He started out into the halls but stopped as his eyes scanned the floor. He saw one set of footprints leading out and one set heading in. Joach placed his shoe onto one of these tracks. They were his own prints from yesterday. No other steps marred the pristine layer of dust.

"They didn't come this way," he murmured to himself, his brow furrowed.

Stepping back into the stairwell, he frowned. Where had they gone? He crept down the stairs more slowly, his mind grinding on the riddle: not up, not down, not into the halls. So where? His mind came up with only one answer. They went *in between*.

Reaching a finger to the outer wall of the stairwell, he pondered the possibilities. Among the servants, he had heard rumors about secret passages and chambers long bricked closed. He had overheard maids whispering about hearing voices in the walls. Ghosts, the women had feared. But were there perhaps other secrets buried deep within the stones of the Edifice?

He continued down the steps, dragging a finger along the wall. The bricks seemed to be fitted snugly together. He reached the landing again and laid both palms upon the wall of the staircase. He felt only smooth stone. Studying the floor of the landing, he knelt closer but saw nothing. Even rubbing his palms and fingers along the floor, he almost missed it. If not for his dogged search and his certainty that the men had left the stairwell via a hidden door, Joach would never have discovered the fine scratch in the stone's surface. He traced his finger along the arc of etched rock as it led to the wall again.

If a door swung open and rubbed slightly against its stone porch, it might leave just such a mark. He stood up and again studied the section of wall. Now he at least knew where the hidden door lay, but how did it open?

Suddenly, from the lower stairway, he heard the slight rub of heel on stone. Joach swung around. Two figures stepped around the stairway's curve. He froze, sure it was the two brothers come to capture him. But as the shadowy figures approached closer, their faces were revealed in the feeble light of the landing's single lantern. It was *not* the brothers, but two others whose hard faces and cruel smiles nevertheless meant trouble.

"See, I told you I saw that drooling idiot come this way." It was Brunt, the mean-spirited urchin who had tormented Joach's trips to the kitchens over the past seven moons. At his shoulder loomed a more muscular brute of a boy at least four winters older than Joach. This other boy was unknown to Joach, but the cruel set to his thick lips and the mischief that shone in his piggy eyes were a twin to Brunt's expression. These two were looking for trouble, and unfortunately, they had found Joach, an easy target for their cruelties.

They crept toward him like dogs upon a wounded fox.

Joach kept his posture slack and his face expressionless. If he fought or tried to run, they would know his secret, and with Brunt's tongue, it would only be a short time until word of his subterfuge reached Greshym.

Joach stood on the landing. He would have to accept whatever torment was inflicted upon him. He had no other choice. In the kitchens, Joach had learned to keep a watchful eye on Brunt, suffering the occasional burn or knuckled punch from the boy. So far, vigilance had kept him from serious injury, but in his excitement this day, he had slipped; now he would have to pay the price.

Brunt stepped up onto the landing beside Joach. "Look at this, Snell. He can't even button his shirt." The boy's fingers lashed out and ripped a button from Joach's shirt.

The boy named Snell snickered. "Can't he talk?" the other asked.

Brunt leaned closer to Joach's face. His breath stank, and Joach had to struggle not to cringe back. "He kin talk, but only like a dumb parrot. He keeps repeating the same words over and over." He then stuttered in imitation of Joach. "M-m-master wants m-meal."

This earned more snickers from Snell.

Brunt's chest puffed out with his audience's approval. "I always wondered if I could git him to say something else, even if it is only to git him to cry out." Brunt slipped a small carving knife, obviously stolen from the kitchen, from a pocket. "Maybe I'll slice him up like a haunch of beef."

"Give him a poke, Brunt," the other boy encouraged, a gleeful lust in his voice. "Go ahead and make him bleed a bit."

"Or maybe more than a bit," Brunt added.

Joach's mind spun. He would be of no use to Elena dead, and from the feral gleam in Brunt's eyes, Joach did not doubt the boy would go so far. Brunt liked causing pain, and in this abandoned section of the Edifice, the boy might try to see how far he could carry out his cruelties.

Brunt raised the knife to Joach's cheek and dug its tip into his skin with a twist of the blade. Joach held still, though his right fist clenched tight behind his back. Brunt pulled the knife away and studied its bloody tip with obvious fascination.

"Let me try," Snell said, reaching for the knife.

Brunt yanked the blade away. "No, that was only a nick. I want to wet the entire knife with his blood."

"Then I'm next, right?" Snell asked huskily, his hands opening and closing with blood lust.

Brunt's voice had become throaty and low. "Oh, don't worry. We'll each take several turns."

Joach now knew that the two had no intention of ever allowing him to leave these stairs. Here in the sprawling Edifice, there were plenty of places to dispose of a body.

Joach had no choice. He had to survive.

Brunt came at Joach again with the blade.

Joach straightened from his slouch and slammed his clenched fist into Brunt's face. Bone crushed under his knuckles.

Brunt squealed, dropping the knife and clasping his hands around his bloody nose. Snell, who had already fled two steps away, was stopped in a crouch, waiting to see if he should run or attack.

Joach snatched up the knife and spoke clearly. "Brunt, if you ever touch me again, I'll cut your manhood from you and feed it to Snell."

Joach's sudden words seemed to shock Brunt even more than the pain from the broken nose. The realization that he had been duped bloomed in Brunt's expression, and the boy's eyes grew red with rage. "Let's see you try, fool," he spat. "C'mon, Snell, it looks like the game's getting a bit more interesting."

Without a word, Snell ran down the stairs, abandoning Brunt. The boy's hurried footfalls faded to silence as the two remaining combatants stared each other down.

The betrayal of his companion did not seem to faze Brunt. He just shook his head and faced Joach. A hand reached into a second pocket and removed another knife. "I don't know what game you're playing, but I'm gonna end it."

Joach backed a few steps up from the landing.

Brunt followed. "I'll make you scream before I'm done with you."

Joach continued to retreat as his mind fought for ways to deal with this situation. If Brunt vanished, Snell would likely stay silent, fearful of being tied in any way to the disappearance. Joach fingered his knife. With Brunt gone, Joach could again resume his role as the dullard without worry of exposure.

With a sudden growl on his lips, Brunt rushed up the steps toward Joach, his jagged-edged knife raised. Taught the ways of sword and knife fighting by his father, Joach recognized that Brunt held his weapon too high, leaving his belly exposed. Brunt had more fury than skill.

Crouching swiftly, Joach jabbed at Brunt's soft midriff with his own knife. But at the last moment, Joach turned his wrist, driving his fist rather than the blade into the boy's belly.

Stunned, with the breath knocked from him, Brunt made a half-hearted slash at Joach, but Joach easily caught his wrist with his other hand and bent it savagely back. Pain numbed the boy's fingers, and his weapon clattered to the stone steps.

Joach twisted Brunt around until he held the boy tight, the blade pressed to his scrawny throat. With Brunt silenced, Joach's masquerade could continue. His hand trembled as he held the knife.

"Do it, coward," Brunt choked out. Tears ran from his eyes.

It was instinct that had caused Joach to turn the knife from Brunt's belly a moment ago. He was not a killer. But now he had time to ponder his leniency. Brunt would surely expose his charade if he were left alive, so any hope of helping his sister lay in this boy's death.

Joach closed his eyes.

He had no choice. He shoved Brunt away from him.

He was not a cold-blooded killer—not even for his sister. "I'm sorry, Elena," he whispered to himself.

The boy stumbled down the steps to the landing below, falling hard on his knees. Brunt twisted to face Joach. "I'll tell everyone!" he screamed up at him. "They'll all know you're a fake!"

Joach did not answer.

"You've ruined yourself!" Brunt yelled as he pushed to his feet. "I'll tell!"

Then, behind Brunt, a section of the landing's wall swung open. The brush of air must have alerted the boy, drawing his attention to the huge white-robed brother who filled the doorway.

The dark-skinned man threw gray dust into Brunt's red face. "You'll tell no one," the large man said softly. "Now sleep."

Brunt waved the cloud of dust from his face, then slumped to the floor limply. With a thud, his head struck the stone.

The brother ignored the unconscious boy and stepped over him. He stared up at Joach, his silver earring flickering in the lantern light. "Come down here, young man. It's time we talked."

AS DAWN NEARED, KAST LEANED HARD INTO THE RUDDER. SALTY SPRAY bathed his face as he brooded in silence, his lips narrow and bloodless. Flint still refused to explain the meaning of his earlier words from the prior night. How could the fate of the mythic city of A'loa Glen lie with the Bloodriders? He had never set eyes on the island and doubted it even existed.

Kast shook his head and swung the sails to help turn the boat. Responding to his skilled touch, the skiff curved into the narrow channel between the twin islands of Tristan and Lystra. The islands' two volcanic peaks towered to either side, the rock of their mountaintops aglow with the sun's first rays.

A gasp of wonder arose from the mer'ai girl as she stared forward.

Kast knew what triggered her response. Directly ahead, a towering span of weathered stone bridged the narrow channel between the islands, a sweeping arch of volcanic rock carved by wind and rain.

"It is called the Arch of the Archipelago," Flint said to the girl, sliding closer to her by the prow. "Have you heard any of the songs about it? Songs of the doomed lovers Tristan and Lystra?"

The girl shook her head and turned toward the old man.

Kast could tell from Flint's worried glances toward the seadragon that he was trying to keep the child distracted from the failing health of her beast. The dragon could barely raise its snout above the waves; its eyes had dulled and its wings fluttered weakly as it struggled to keep even with the boat.

"At one time," Flint continued, "the two islands were joined as one. Only a small river valley divided the two mountains." He pointed to the northern island. "The young man, Tristan, lived among the clans that claimed the slopes of that peak, while Lystra was the daughter of the clan leader who declared the southern peak as his property. Their two peoples were often at war." Flint shook his head sadly.

"What happened?" Sy-wen encouraged him.

"One day, while out hunting, Tristan found Lystra bathing in the river between the two peaks. She sang so sweetly as she swam that in a single breath, he fell in love with her. Hiding in the tree line, he added his voice to hers, singing his love to her. Enchanted with his music, Lystra's heart was swayed, and she called Tristan to her. Within the river, the two lovers embraced, lingering in each other's arms until the men of each clan dragged them apart." Flint leaned close to the girl and lowered his voice. "But their love could not be denied. In midnight trysts, they would meet by the river, their love growing ever deeper."

By now the girl's eyes had grown large.

"Then their forbidden love was discovered, and they were once again torn apart. Lystra's father cast a spell that called the sea to swell up and separate their two peaks and keep his daughter forever from the son of his enemies. Unknown to her father, the night the spell was cast, Lystra and Tristan had met for one last kiss by the river. As the spell took hold, the young lovers refused to break their embrace as the sea rose between them. While the swelling waters tugged them apart, they still tried to hold tight. With arms reaching for each other, they sang of their unending love. Their music and pain flowed up to the gods themselves, who took pity on the young lovers and changed them to stone so Tristan and Lystra could be forever united, forever embracing across the channel between the islands."

Sy-wen sighed and glanced toward the span of stone.

"To this day, the Arch is a special spot," Flint finished. "In boats adorned with flowers, lovers come to recite their vows of love and be united under the Arch. In the hearts of these fresh lovers, the ancient song of Tristan and Lystra can still be heard."

"How beautiful," Sy-wen mumbled.

Kast had heard enough of this nonsense and cleared his throat. "It's just stone," he said sourly. "Just rock carved by wind and rain."

Flint groaned. "Does a Bloodrider's heart have no room for romance?"

Kast ignored the question and nodded ahead. "We've reached the Arch, as you instructed. What next?"

But Flint would not let his words pass so easily. "You think the Arch is mere stone, nothing more?"

Kast just stared straight into the old man's eyes.

Flint waved toward the Arch. "Then sail on through it."

Kast adjusted the spread of the sail and straightened the rudder. He aimed for the channel that passed under the Arch. He had traveled this path a few times with boats of the fishing fleet. The Arch marked the end of the chain of islands and the beginning of the Great Ocean itself. It was the gateway to the open sea.

Sy-wen made room as Flint slid toward the prow of the skiff. From inside his sealskin jacket, he removed what looked like an ivory knife. As he held it up toward the cresting sun, Kast saw that it was not a blade but the tooth of some large beast. It was a handspan long, slightly curved, with a chipped, serrated edge. Kast could not imagine what manner of beast the tooth came from.

"What're you doing, Flint?" Kast called to the man.

"Just trying to remove the scales from your eyes," he said.

Kast now had the boat squarely pointed toward the center of the Arch. The edge of the sun lay directly ahead, just peeking up from the curved blue horizon.

"Look!" Sy-wen suddenly called out, pointing ahead.

Kast had already seen them. In the open waters beyond the Arch, a group of familiar boats rounded the cliff head of the Isle of Tristan and bore full sails toward them. It was Jarplin's hunting fleet. Kast had thought he had lost the boats by skimming through a network of channels too shallow and too narrow for the larger ships. Whether through dumb luck or skill, the fleet had found them again.

"They must've been circling the deeper channels around the Archipelago hunting for us," Flint commented.

Kast bore down on the rudder, trying to make a sharp turn before reaching the Arch. Maybe they had not been seen yet.

But Kast's hope was short-lived. Across the far waters, raised voices echoed to them. They had been spotted.

At the prow, Flint swore. Kast thought he was mad that the fleet had cut them off, but his next words made the focus of his anger clear. "Damn it, Kast!" he yelled over his shoulder. "Straighten this boat around. We must cross the Arch."

"We'll end up smack in the middle of the fleet," he argued. "Is that what you want? Stealing Jarplin's dragon will not make us welcome guests aboard his ships."

"Just do as I say, Bloodrider!" Flint glanced at him, his eyes hard. "If you've ever trusted a man, trust me now!"

For a flash, Kast pictured his teacher, the blind seer of the

Dre'rendi. Then it was his turn to swear loudly, his voice pained as he made his choice. Why was he always a fool for a madman's words? He hauled on the rudder and yanked the sail, and again the skiff sped straight toward the span of volcanic stone.

Kast stared ahead as spray spat at him from the waves, mocking him with salty stings. Past the Arch, the seas filled with the billowing sails and sharp prows of the fleet. As he aimed the skiff toward them, Kast wondered who was the real madman on this boat.

"Hurry!" Flint called out. "We must reach the Arch before they do!"

Kast swung the sail, seeking stronger breezes, tacking with the skill of his people. But the bigger boats had the better winds and swifter speed. The fleet bore toward the Arch like a surging storm of sail and rigging. Kast struggled with the skiff, but they would never win this race. And he knew why. "The dragon slows us too much," he mumbled to himself.

He had meant his words only for himself, but the girl heard him.

She turned hard eyes toward him for a heartbeat, then swung to the starboard rail. Lowering a hand to the water, she sang out across the black waters. Within a moment, a nose reached toward her from the water.

She leaned over the rail. "Conch, we must be swift to escape these sharks." She nodded toward the rolling fleet.

Though unfamiliar with seadragons, Kast recognized the pain in the creature's black eyes. The Bloodrider also saw the understanding.

Conch puffed explosively and nudged Sy-wen's hand aside. His body heaved in a huge swell beside the skiff and dove forward. In humps of undulating muscle, he swam to the front of the boat, now dragging the skiff behind him.

Kast fell backward as the skiff jumped forward.

Flint, at the prow, finally realized what was happening. "No!" he yelled. "The exertion will kill him. That must not happen!"

Sy-wen answered him. "He will die anyway if captured again. This is his only chance, and he knows it. Conch would rather die in the sea than in the nets of the hunters."

Flint's lips were tight as he considered her words. He turned forward.

Silence descended upon the skiff. The seas ahead were a wall of gnashing prows. Kast used all his hard-earned skill to tack with the wind, trying his best to ease the dragon's burden. Yet his efforts seemed minuscule compared to the power of the seadragon. Kast's long braid of black hair now waved behind him as the skiff sped across the waters.

Sy-wen cowered near Flint, her eyes fixed on the other ships cutting through the waves to intercept them.

"Almost . . . almost . . ." Flint intoned at the prow.

The sea channel beyond the Arch was now so crammed with boats, Kast did not know if even the small skiff could maneuver between them.

Ahead, as the dragon crossed the Arch, Flint leaned over the front of the boat, one hand holding him from toppling into the sea, the other extending the long white tooth forward like some miniature battering ram before the prow. "Godspeed!" he yelled.

The man was surely mad.

Then the skiff, dragged by the dragon, reached the Arch—and time slowed to a thick syrup. Kast saw the tip of Flint's tooth pierce the space under the span of rock. And where the tooth touched, the view through the Arch changed! Like a drop of dye dripped into water, this new image spread out from the tip of the tooth. It grew large enough to swallow the skiff as it sped through the Arch.

Once they passed under the stone vault, Kast released the guide rope, and the sail fluttered slack to the single mast. The skiff slowed its glide across the waves. Kast stood up near the boat's bow. *This cannot be!*

He searched around him, his eyes wide, his lips parted. Mindless of the boat's balance, he swung in a circle. The Arch was gone! Jarplin's fleet was nowhere in sight. Around him, very distantly, he could make out other islands of the Archipelago. He would swear to the south of them stood the Isle of Maunsk, but that island lay a thousand leagues away from their last position.

Kast swung around to stare astern. The sun now rose *behind* the boat, not in front of it. His legs began to tremble.

"Sit down, Kast," Flint said. "You'll capsize us."

His legs, weak already, obeyed. Kast sat down and found Flint's eyes upon him.

Sy-wen sat straight backed in her corner of the skiff, her green eyes large and moist as she too searched the waters around her. The blanket over her shoulders had fallen away, exposing her bare chest.

Kast glanced quickly away. "Wh-where are we?" he asked.

Flint pointed to a large island directly ahead of the skiff's prow. Kast had been through these waters before and did not remember this island. Squinting, he peered at it.

It was shaped like a large horseshoe, its curving shore open like inviting arms. Three mountains marked its silhouette, one at each end of the island and the largest in the center. Yet as unique as this island appeared, it was what sprouted up from the centermost peak and spread outward toward the other mountains that captured Kast's gaze. Hundreds—no, *thousands*—of towers and domed buildings sprouted and dotted the island. Near the shore, the broken tips of some spires rose from the sea itself, like some man-made reef.

"Is it . . . Is it . . . ?" Kast could not find his words.

"It is," Flint said with a nod. "There stands A'loa Glen."

Sy-wen tested the name on her own lips. She was obviously stunned, too. "A'loa Glen . . . ?"

Kast's mouth was too dry, his tongue stuck in his throat. "How did we . . . ?" His next words had an edge of anger in them. "I've been through these very waters!"

"Yes, of course you have," Flint said. "But the island is cloaked in sorceries. Its shores can only be seen or approached via three paths, and even those secret ways require certain keys." Flint held up the curved tooth.

Kast could not tear his eyes from the sight of the mythic city. "The . . . the Arch . . . ?"

"And you thought it was mere stone," Flint said with a tired smile. "Now if you two are done gawking, maybe we can sail to port and get some help for this child's wounded dragon."

Sy-wen jumped slightly and leaned over the boat's edge. She blushed, obviously embarrassed at having forgotten her friend in the excitement. "Conch?" she called in a worried voice, a hand reaching toward the waves.

With a huff of expelled air, Conch's flared nostrils rose from the water, but he was too weak to reach her palm, exhausted by his run for the Arch. "He's in poor shape," Sy-wen said, stating the obvious.

"We're almost to safety," Flint consoled, but his worried brow weakened the reassurance in his words.

Kast took a deep breath, then reached for the sail's rope. The simple routines of sailing always calmed his heart. As he worked the ropes and rudder, the sail caught the wind again and swelled out.

With the skiff under way, he found his tongue again. "Flint, you said the Bloodriders would judge the fate of the city. What did you mean by that?"

Flint turned toward the sunken towers of the city. "You'll find all your answers at A'loa Glen," he said, then lowered his voice to a cryptic mumble. "But I hope you know the right questions, Kast."

JOACH SUPPRESSED A SHUDDER AS THE STONE DOOR SWUNG SHUT BEHIND him. He was now trapped within the narrow, dimly lit passage with the large, white-robed brother. The dark-skinned man had introduced himself as Brother Moris and, after hauling the snoring Brunt under one muscled arm, he had waved for Joach to accompany him inside the secret passage.

For a moment, Joach regretted accepting the brother's invitation. He pushed one hand against the door behind him. It was snugly locked. The tunnel ahead of him was blocked by the large man, now burdened with Brunt.

"What . . . what are you planning to do with the kitchen boy?" he asked, shying around the bigger questions for the moment.

"He has a sick spirit and could grow to be a threat to the island. After using a potion to cleanse his memory, we will dump him at the orphanage in Port Rawl. He'll be no further threat to you."

Though Joach shared no love for the cruel boy, he was taken aback by the casual manner in which the brother planned to orphan the boy. "His parents . . . ?"

Moris glanced over his shoulder at Joach. The brother had his cowl thrown back in the tunnel, and his bald head shone in the flickering lamplight. His low voice reverberated in the hallway. "Don't worry, Son. The boy has no parents. All the servants here have been scavenged from orphanages across the lands or were folks rejected by the world at large." The brother continued down the hall. "We only choose those without a past to join us here."

Joach followed the brother's wide back to a tight staircase that wound down toward the bowels of the Edifice. "And what of me?"

"That waits to be seen." Moris spoke as he marched ahead. "Why did you return here this morning?"

Joach swallowed hard. "I heard you yesterday on the stair—"

"You were eavesdropping."

"Y-yes, but I had to. I don't know who to trust here."

"So while acting a lie, you sought the truth?"

Joach heard the doubt in the other's voice. "I guess—"

"Who sent you here?"

"Sent?"

"Yes, who sent you to spy upon our Brother Greshym?"

Joach stumbled a step and stopped. Did these cloaked brothers not know about the darkmage, or worse yet, were they in league with him? If the last was true, he was doomed.

Moris heard him stop and swung around, his eyes narrowed in suspicion. "Do you serve the Dark Lord?" he said harshly. "Did you come at the bidding of that nesting serpent in the tower—the Praetor?"

Joach's eyes grew wide. So these brothers knew of the evil that masqueraded as their leader! Joach found his tongue twisted as he tried to speak. Here truly were allies! "No . . . no, not at all. Just the opposite. I know he is evil. I was stolen from my home by the one you name Greshym. But like the Praetor, he is a creature of evil, a darkmage. They are in league together." Joach stood on the steps in the secret staircase and spilled forth his story. Like a river bursting its dam, words tumbled from his lips. He told of his abduction, his enslavement by Greshym, the cruelties he had endured, and his eventual release in the Grand Courtyard. Tears now flowed down his cheeks.

Moris listened to his tale in silence, seeming to know that any interruption of the story would lead to Joach collapsing in blubbering tears. It was a tale that needed telling, and Brother Moris simply let it flow from the boy.

". . . I didn't know who else worked in league with the Gul'gotha, so I continued acting like the dumb servant while I explored for a way to escape. I didn't know who to trust." Joach's words finally ran dry in his throat.

Moris reached his free hand to Joach's shoulder. "You can trust me."

Joach's legs trembled with the brother's touch. It had been so long since any kindness had been shown to him.

Moris leaned closer to his face. "Can you make it down the stairs? I think this is a tale that needs sharing with my brothers."

He nodded.

"You are one tough boy, Joach," Moris said, clasping his shoulder tighter. "Braver men would have folded under the assault you endured. You should be proud."

Joach sniffed back his tears and straightened his shoulders. "I did it for my sister."

"Ah," Brother Moris said with a slight smile on his lips. "And where is she now? Is she still back home in Wintertown?"

"Winterfell," Joach corrected. He had only glancingly mentioned Elena in his story. Feeling protective of her, he was hesitant at revealing the true role she had played, so he had skipped over parts of the story that dealt with wit'ches and blood magicks. But was his decision wise? Here was someone who could be trusted, and if Elena was headed to A'loa Glen she would need allies, too.

"If able, we'll get you back to your sister," Moris said as he turned away and started down the stair.

Joach did not follow. "Wait," he called. "My sister is not in Winterfell anymore."

Moris stopped, swinging back around once again. A trace of impatience twitched his cheek. "Where is she then?"

Joach lowered his face, ashamed at having to reveal the part of the story he had left out. "She is coming—"

Suddenly a deep resonant intoning throbbed from far below. It reached up through the stones and rattled his bones. He found further speech impossible. Each tooth in his skull ached with every rumble. He covered his ears, but it did not help. It was not a noise heard with the ears as much as it was an assault on the whole body.

From Moris' narrowed eyebrows and cocked head, the brother heard the rumble, too.

What was happening? Joach wondered. Fear finally freed his tongue. "What is that noise?" he muttered, his voice sounding meek and dull compared to the bottomless tones reaching up from below.

His voice broke the spell that had swept over Moris. The brother shifted his burden higher under his arm and glanced with suspicious eyes in his direction. "You hear something?"

A fleeting thought that the man was perhaps mad passed through Joach's mind. How could he not hear it? His entire frame vibrated like some plucked bowstring with each note. "How could I not? It's . . . it's *huge*." He knew it sounded stupid to use that word, but it best described how it affected him.

Moris climbed a step closer to him. "You truly hear!" he said with wonder. Then, in a more contemplative tone, "What are the odds of that?"

"What is it?"

Moris did not seem to hear his question. "We must hurry. It is the summons."

"I don't understand," Joach said as Moris swung around.

"Only a handful of people born can hear this music," he explained as he led the way down the stairs again. He kept the pace brisk. "It is the single trait that separates a Hi'fai from the others of the Brotherhood."

"You mean no one else can hear this?" Joach asked, having a hard time keeping the doubt from his voice. "The whole Edifice must be shaking with this noise."

"No, only those born with a certain elemental ability in their blood, a magick born of the land."

Joach pictured his sister's blazing red hand. "But I hear it . . . It almost tears at me."

"Yes, the magick must be strong in you. I would love to explore your genealogy sometime, but right now we must answer the call." He increased his pace. "We must hurry."

"Still you haven't answered my question," Joach persisted as he followed, almost trotting to keep up. "What is that noise? Where does it come from?"

Moris glanced one last time in his direction and silenced Joach with his answer. "It is the song of the stone dragon, the voice of Ragnar'k."

22

THE SUMMONS!

Greshym awoke with his heart thundering for the second time this morning. He sat straight up on his bed. Earlier he had thought he heard the name *Ragnar'k* whispered in his ear, pulling him from sleep. But only the spell-cast boy shared his cell. Dismissing it as just an echo of some deeply buried memory, he had settled back to his bed. But once reminded, the old memories could not be so easily hidden away.

None but the Hi'fai knew the ancient name of the stone dragon, and that sect had been disbanded ages ago, drummed from the Brotherhood, its members long dead. Greshym would have been among them, too, had his cowardice not saved him. Deep under the Edifice, he had dabbled in divining the future, but his visions had frightened him. Ripping the star from his ear, he had fled, afraid to face his own auguries. It had proven to be a timely act of cowardice. A moon later, the elders ordered the exile of the Hi'fai from A'loa Glen. Greshym had then watched from the docks as his fellow brothers were led off in shackles.

He never saw any of them again.

No, none but he still lived who knew the name of Ragnar'k.

Finally content that the whispered name was nothing but a fragmented dream, sleep had found him again. He had rested deeply until, rippling up from the bowels of the Edifice, the summons had torn into him.

He had flung himself upright, expecting the ancient feeling to disappear like the ghostly name of Ragnar'k, but it had not! The raking call followed him from his nightmares into the waking world.

It was the call of the stone dragon!

The shuddering wail did not fade as he slid his feet to the threadbare rug covering the cold stones.

Something was amiss. With the sinking of A'loa Glen, the lower regions of the Edifice had flooded. When he had first arrived with Shorkan ages ago, curiosity had driven him to seek out the passages that led to his old warren of cells below the castle. What he had found were just halls drowned in brackish waters and doorways bricked closed. There was no way to reach the chambers below the Edifice. Greshym had assumed that the mysteries of the nether regions were secrets lost in the past.

That was, until now.

But what did it mean?

He stood up. His legs trembled slightly. Grabbing his poi'wood staff, he sensed the black energies that wormed within the wood of his crutch. It stoked his confidence. He knew not what trick was being played here, but he must let Shorkan know.

As he swept into his white robe, a passing concern that his boy had not yet returned skated across his mind, but he let it glide away. It was still early, and the kitchens were probably just completing their morning cooking. The kitchens had been running slow for the past few weeks. He pictured Joach standing dull eyed by the hearths, awaiting the preparation of his master's meal. If Joach returned before him, the boy would simply wait in the cell for his master's next order.

Greshym crossed to the door and left his room. Following the twisting corridors and dusty halls, he reached the Praetor's Spear and climbed to the roost of his fellow darkmage. The guards as usual ignored him as he worked his way up the tower stairs. Even as his heart pounded with each rumble from Ragnar'k, he had to rest frequently on his climb; his old body tired so easily. Finally, he reached the huge ironbound oak doors and rapped his knuckles hard.

Shorkan was not expecting him, and it took two more series of knocks before the door finally swung open before him. Greshym bustled into the room, appreciating its warmth and thick carpets after the drafty chill of the halls.

But his reception by Shorkan was anything but inviting. "Why do you disturb my slumber?" he asked coldly. The Praetor stood in a heavy red robe, sashed at the waist. He had obviously been asleep. His black hair was in unusual disarray, and his gray eyes still gleamed red with exhaustion. Through the windows of the tower room, Greshym could see the sun was well up.

He bowed his head slightly, already irked at the youthfulness that mocked him from the other's face. "Something is wrong," Greshym said. "Can't you hear the wailing?"

"What are you blathering about?" Shorkan said with irritation. "I heard nothing except for someone knocking too early upon my door."

With the summons still quaking the marrow of his bones, Greshym was slightly shocked that this other, so much stronger in the black arts, felt not even a twinge of the stone dragon's call. But then again, Shorkan was not Hi'fai and had *never* sensed the voice of Ragnar'k. He did not have the elemental magick and was ignorant of the sect's many secrets.

For a breath, he thought of keeping what he knew from Shorkan, but if something were truly amiss, he might need the other's strength. "Shorkan," he began, "though you are the Praetor, there is still much you don't know of this castle."

Black fire flared in the other's eyes. The stubborn pride of youth still ran hot in Shorkan's blood. The pet of the Dark Lord did not like someone questioning his knowledge. His words were laced with threat. "I know more than you suppose, Brother Greshym."

"Then perhaps you can tell me all about why this island, of all the others of the Archipelago, was chosen as the site of A'loa Glen."

A wisp of confusion crinkled the edges of Shorkan's eyes.

"You don't know, do you?" Greshym did not wait for an answer. "There is also much you don't know about me. You know I was once a Hi'fai. It was my prophetic writings that gave you the recipe for binding the Blood Diary."

"I don't need a history lesson, Greshym."

"Ah, but you do. For though you used my visions, you never bothered to wonder about the Hi'fai themselves. By that time, they had been banished, and being the good little mage that you were, you half accepted the elders' edict that they were heretics, practitioners of sorceries that were not pure gifts from Chi. Had you not wondered exactly what my old sect was doing?"

"I knew enough. Your kind sought divinations of the future."

"Yes, but how, Shorkan? How?"

The other shrugged. "What difference does it make? The Hi'fai are long gone."

"Not completely," Greshym added, enjoying the other's consternation. "Though I turned my back on my brothers, I am still Hi'fai. It is in one's blood."

"What are you saying?"

"I am *saying* that at least one member of the ancient order still walks the halls of the Edifice."

"You?"

"Yes, me! One did not simply join the Hi'fai—you had to be born to it. To become a Hi'fai, you had to be gifted with a form of elemental magick, a magick that linked you to the dreaming."

Shorkan's brows knit together. "Weavers! Are you telling me that the Hi'fai were both mages and dreamweavers?"

"Yes. We used our elemental gifts to enter the dreaming and see glimpses of the future."

Shorkan turned and began to pace as he spoke. A bit of excitement had entered his voice as he thought he understood. "Of course, the elemental energies alone would not let you pierce time's veil. So you used your Chyric powers to bolster your inherent elemental ability. This is amazing."

"No." Greshym let the word sink in and smiled inwardly as the other stopped his pacing. He loved the confusion on Shorkan's face. The damned fool always thought he knew everything. "No, we never used our Chyric powers. It had nothing to do with Chi. Some members of the Hi'fai were not even mages, just weavers."

"Impossible."

Greshym shrugged and just allowed the other to stew.

"But how?" Shorkan finally asked.

"We had help."

"Whose?"

"The one who calls to me as we speak."

"I don't hear anything."

"Only weavers can hear the summons. Ragnar'k calls out for a gathering."

"Who . . . who is this Ragnar'k? I never heard of such a one."

"He is the reason this island became the birthplace of A'loa Glen.

Of all the islands, this is his home. He was here before the first tower was built."

"Who is this person?"

"Not a person. He is a creature of pure elemental power, a nexus of weaving energy buried in the heart of the island. Like a lodestone, his power attracted the mages who went on to build on this island. None knew of his existence until he called out to the mages gifted with elemental magicks and gathered them to him. Deep under the rock of the island, the sect of the Hi'fai was forged by his summons."

"And what matter of creature is this Ragnar'k?"

"I'm not entirely sure. Half buried in the volcanic rock of the island's core is a crudely carved statue of a dragon. Posed as if curled in slumber, it is more just a rough outline than a true rendering. Some say Ragnar'k is a spirit trapped in this statue; others say he truly is a sleeping dragon, lost in slumber for so many ages that he has forgotten his own shape, letting it fade into this crude form. Continually asleep, his spirit lives in the dreaming, outside time itself, no longer fixed in the present but flowing throughout time. When we communed with him, we could see glimpses of the future and the ancient past."

Shorkan's eyes had grown huge. "And you told me none of this before?"

"We were sworn to secrecy. After the fall of A'loa Glen, I thought Ragnar'k long dead, drowned in his subterranean lair. What do ancient histories matter today?"

"So why tell me this now?"

"Ragnar'k is *not* dead. He has begun to call again. His voice speaks to the magick in my blood."

Shorkan began to turn away. "Then let us seek out this Ragnar'k. He could prove a useful tool in the hands of the Gul'gotha."

Greshym snatched at the cuff of the Praetor's robe, surprised at how sick such a thought made him. His emotions confused him. What did he care if Ragnar'k was consumed by the Dark Lord? Still he did not let go of Shorkan's sleeve. "We . . . we can't do that. The paths below are all flooded or blocked off. There is no way to reach him."

"I will find a way. With you guiding me, I'm sure we can forge a new path." Black energies began to crackle along the edges of the

Praetor's red robe. "The master has granted me gifts to keep nothing from my reach."

Greshym let go of the robe and wiped his hand on his white cloak, as if removing a sticky foulness. As the call of the stone dragon echoed in his head, he regretted his decision in coming here. For some reason, he did not want Shorkan near Ragnar'k. His hesitation kept his tongue silent on one last matter concerning the dreaming dragon, one other prophecy concerning Ragnar'k.

Actually it was more a promise than a vision: When he was most needed, it was said that Ragnar'k would wake from his eternal slumber, shake off the rock of the island, and move again. His awakening would mark the beginning of the Great War, heralding its first conflict: the battle for A'loa Glen.

Greshym shuddered. No, he did not want Shorkan near Ragnar'k, fearing he might disturb the giant's sleep. But was the dragon truly slumbering? Why, after so long a time, had Ragnar'k begun to call again?

And why, behind the song of the stone dragon, could Greshym hear the horns of battle and the clash of steel?

Greshym followed Shorkan's broad shoulders as he headed for the oaken door, but his knees shook. Somewhere far below the roots of the tower lay a beast Greshym had fled long ago.

And centuries later, he was in no hurry to return.

Some beasts were best left sleeping.

A forest of stone towers glided past either side of the skiff. Here stood the mythic city of A'loa Glen. Sy-wen had to lean far back to see the tops of the shattered structures. Craning her neck, she stared up at the ancient monuments of the drowned city. Algae and moss choked the bricks of the lower levels, while nesting terns and gulls argued for territory among the crannies of the higher levels. Windows long open to the wind and rain stared back at her, almost accusingly. How dare she disturb the graves of the dead?

Sy-wen found herself cringing slightly from the sight.

"Swing a bit starboard!" Flint called from the tip of the prow. The older man leaned over the edge of the boat and studied the waters ahead for obstacles. He had an oar across his knees that he had been using to slowly paddle them through the ancient byways of the sunken city. They had cut the sail as soon as the boat entered the watery graveyard of leaning towers, cracked domes, and crumbling walls. It was too dangerous to allow the wind alone to guide them through the treacherous maze.

Near the bow, Kast swung his own oar to the opposite side of the skiff and gently prodded at the algae-slick brick of a nearby pillar. Crabs clinging to the ancient stones skittered away from the tip of his oar. The boat spun a bit to the right, and Kast began to paddle again.

Conch surfaced with a weak huff of expelled air near Sy-wen's elbow. She reached for his nose, but he sank again, too tired to keep his head above water for longer than a breath. He weakened rapidly as he swam through the choking kelp beds and reefs of brick and stone to keep up with the slow skiff. Emotions warred within Sy-wen. She knew they needed to hurry if Conch was to reach the healers while he still breathed. But at the same time, she wanted to slow and allow the exhausted Conch to rest. Even this dragging pace severely taxed her dear friend's heart.

Sy-wen rubbed at the tender webs between her fingers, nervous and fearful for her mother's bondmate. If Conch should die . . .

"Almost there!" Flint called with a renewed vigor in his voice.

The boat rounded the bole of an immense tower to get a clear view of the coastline ahead. The city climbed out of the sea in a series of terraces that led up the slopes of the centermost peak of the island. Now closer to the shore, Sy-wen saw that what had seemed the crown of the mountain was actually a huge castle built on the peak's summit. Sprouting from the top of the massive, towered structure were the skeletal branches of a monstrous tree, leafless and long dead like the city itself.

A stray sea breeze chilled her skin. She shivered as the boat glided closer to the shoreline. To either side of the city rose high, sheer cliffs that seemed to reach out toward the tiny boat. Her eyes wide, she studied the world of the lan'dwellers. Except for the rare times she would sun herself on an isolated sandbar, she had never walked on land. Though her heart began to beat fiercely in her throat, a part of her thrilled at the chance to explore the paths walked by the banished. She continued to stare at the countless windows that opened onto abandoned homes. "I never imagined there were so many," she mumbled.

"What was that?" Flint asked from nearby.

Sy-wen shrank shyly from his gaze, but his concerned eyes loosened her tongue. It helped to talk. "I was just surprised that there were so many of our people banished from the sea."

"Banished?"

Sy-wen waved her arm to encompass the city ahead and behind them. "All those homes. I never knew so many of the mer'ai had been forced from the sea onto the land."

The old man's eyes crinkled in confusion for a heartbeat, then relaxed into amusement. He chuckled under his breath. "Oh, my dear child, who ever gave you the idea that the shores were only populated by exiled mer'ai?"

Her cheeks reddened with his laughter. She was half angry, half embarrassed.

He reached a hand and patted her knee. "Sy-wen, not a single mer'ai has walked the shores of the Archipelago for over five centuries."

The shock must have been obvious on her face. "But . . . ?"

"Before the fall of Alasea, the mer'ai and the fishermen of the shorelines lived alongside each other, working the seas together in harmony and cooperation. It was a time of peace and shared prosperity. But then the Gul'gotha came, and darkness claimed the land. To escape the reach of the Dark Lord, your people fled to the deep oceans, exiling themselves forever from the corruption of the land. For the five centuries of the Dark Lord's reign, no mer'ai has since returned to the shores of Alasea."

Sy-wen sat back upon her pile of blankets, stunned by his words and story. "Five centuries? But the banished of my people, where did they go if not to the land?"

Flint shrugged, but Sy-wen caught a quick glance toward Kast before the old man turned away. "I don't know, but your people were always harsh in their punishments, unforgiving as the sea itself."

Wrapping the blanket tightly over her shoulders, Sy-wen sank deeper into her own thoughts. So then where *did* the banished go if not expelled to the world of stone and rock? She remembered how a dragon bonded to one of the banished mer'ai would pine for many moons, the seas echoing with its lost, forlorn cries. The great-hearted beasts only did this one other time—when their bondmate died.

Sy-wen's heart grew cold. A stony realization began to settle in her chest. Tears came to her eyes.

If what Flint said was true . . .

She choked back a sob, her heart unable to deny his words. If the old man spoke the truth, then those who broke mer'ai law weren't banished—they were *killed*.

Remembering the pining wail of the dragons, she stared up at the cliffs ahead. Tears blurred her sight, and her stomach began to sicken. She was suddenly less concerned about leaving the sea.

Behind her, Kast spoke up into the silence. "Where to now, Flint?" he asked. "I see no port, no dock."

"The city's piers are over yonder," Flint answered, waving toward the opposite side of the city. "But we aren't going to the main port. Too many eyes, too many questions."

Kast lifted his oar from the water. "Then where?"

Flint pointed toward one of the sheer cliff walls to the left of the city. "Guide us over there, Kast."

Sy-wen kept her arms wrapped around her belly as the boat slid toward the towering wall of rock. She listened to the little paddled splashes as the skiff was propelled.

"Head toward that fall of rock just ahead!" Flint's words drew Sy-wen's eyes. His arm pointed to where a section of the cliff wall had cracked and tumbled into the sea. "We need to get to the far side of the rubble and out of sight of the main city."

Kast grunted his acknowledgment and adjusted his paddling to round the boat toward the rockfall. He used the paddle as a rudder to turn them into a tiny bay formed by the boulders and cliff walls.

Sy-wen glanced behind them. With the view blocked, she no longer saw the towers of the terraced city. She twisted around. Even the sunken section of the city was out of the direct view of the tiny bay. It was as if the city had vanished in a blink.

"Now what?" Kast asked gruffly.

Sy-wen studied the cliff face. Were they to dock here and climb the jagged, damp rock?

"This is the entrance to the Grotto," Flint explained. He raised a hand to his lips and made a sharp, warbling whistle.

"Not more magick," Kast grumbled sourly. He gripped his paddle on his lap with white knuckles.

Sy-wen shrank down, not knowing what to expect. She prepared for another jump in location like at the Arch. Still, what actually occurred startled her.

A section of the cliff face suddenly shimmered and parted into huge folds, revealing the mouth of a sea tunnel behind it. She cringed back from the miracle. Then she spotted the two robed men on either side of the entrance with long hooked poles in their arms. She blinked a few times as the men used the poles to draw wider the entrance to the tunnel. It took her a few moments to recognize what was happening.

Kast put into words her own surprised realization. "It's not magick, just a camouflaged leather drape."

"Sealskin actually," Flint corrected. "It takes the dyes better when painted to match the rock of the cliff, and weathers well, too."

Kast swore under his breath as he turned the prow of the boat to point at the opening.

"Not everything requires magick," Flint continued. "It is a precious commodity and not to be wasted when a simple trick works better."

"Wh-where does it lead?" Sy-wen asked as the boat swung toward the tunnel.

Flint squeezed her hand reassuringly. "It is only a little ways."

Flint's words proved to be somewhat false. The sea tunnel led deep into the island, twisting this way and that. It took a moment of coaxing to encourage Conch to follow. But Sy-wen's touch and soft words finally convinced the weakening dragon. She saw the shocked look, mixed with awe, on the faces of the silent entrance guards as they glided into the tunnel.

As they traveled, Sy-wen studied the walls, which were aglow with occasional torches. To either side of the channel was a stone walkway used by the entrance guards. Behind the boat, Sy-wen could see Conch's nose occasionally surface. The passage was too narrow for the dragon to swim beside them. Even this bit of separation made her edgy. She kept glancing back to her friend to ensure he still followed.

Finally, after a time that seemed like forever, the tunnel emptied into a fair-size subterranean lake. The crystal-calm waters were wide enough to accommodate even one of the larger fishing boats that hunted the sea.

"There is a dock directly ahead," Flint said, pointing.

Sy-wen sat up straighter. The far side of the lake ended at a small rock beach. She spotted a wooden jetty protruding like a tongue at them.

Kast guided the boat toward it. "Where are we?"

Flint had his ear cocked as if listening to something other than the tattooed man's question. He held up a hand for silence, then turned to them, his face much more dour. "We must hurry. Time runs short. The summons is already well under way."

"What are you talking about?" Kast asked.

"The dragon awakens," Flint said, a trace of fear in his voice.

Sy-wen stared behind her at Conch. What did he mean? Of course the seadragon was awake.

"Paddle toward the pier," Flint insisted.

A group of white-robed men appeared from a nearby tunnel and rushed down the wooden dock. Their clopping steps echoed across the still water. Even from across the lake, Sy-wen could see that their arms were burdened with red, steaming pots.

"The healers," Flint said with a nod toward the gathered men. He dug his paddle deep into the water to encourage the skiff to a faster speed. "They've been waiting since dawn."

Kast also lent his strong arms and back to propel the boat toward the dock. Within a few anxious moments, hands were reaching out for flung mooring lines, and the skiff was secured to the pier's end.

A relieved sigh flowed from Sy-wen's chest. They had made it! She allowed herself to be hoisted from the boat, keeping the single woolen blanket wrapped over her bare chest.

Flint spoke at her side, his voice hurried. "We have no time to lose. You must get your bondmate to beach himself up on the shore here so the healers can work on him."

Sy-wen nodded. Throwing the blanket from her shoulders, she dove cleanly into the shallow water. Ignoring the frigid snap of the sunless pool, she swam to where Conch rolled listlessly beside the skiff.

He swung a large black eye toward her as she touched his neck. His scales were so cold. Her fingers found the rope tether tied around his withers. He needed to be cut free. Her fingers reflexively sought her knife sheath. Empty. She had forgotten it was lost when she had been captured.

She kicked to the surface and found the eight healers staring back at her. Flint stood among them, while Kast was finishing securing the skiff.

"Cut his tether!" she called. "He can't reach the shore while tied to the boat."

"Kast!" Flint called out, but the tattooed man had already heard. A flash of silver, and the knot that held the dragon to the boat was severed.

Conch's snout surfaced beside Sy-wen. He snorted and shook his head slightly, as if sensing his freedom.

"Come with me," Sy-wen urged her friend.

Reaching a hand to his chin, she encouraged him to keep his nose above water and follow her as she swam toward the pebbled shore. "There are healers here who will help you mend."

Conch snuffled and bumped at her hand. He would do as she asked.

As she guided her friend, Sy-wen soon felt the shore rise under her feet until she could stand in the shallows. Wobbling a bit, she backed until only her ankles were still in the water. Free of the sea, her body seemed weighted with anchors. Both the slippery rocks and her own inexperience with walking on land kept her balance shaky.

Conch followed her, heaving himself in short bursts of energy until he finally lay exhausted at the shore's edge. He tried to raise his head for one final push, stretching his neck toward Sy-wen. But it was too much for his weakened body, and his head sank back down to the smooth pebbles.

"That is far enough," Flint said at Sy-wen's shoulder. "My healers can work on him from here."

Already the white-robed men were splashing through the shallows, the edges of their robes tied high around their thighs. Stone pots of steaming liquid lined the shores. The smell from them reminded Sy-wen of stewing seaweed, but an acrid sharpness underlay the herbal scent.

Flint must have seen her gaze and curled nose. "Balm of willowbark and bittersroot. It will give Conch's wounds strength against festering and will ease his pain."

Sy-wen nodded, barely hearing his words. The gaping gash on Conch's chest from a spear thrust held her attention. The scaled edges had curled back from the wide wound, exposing the muscles and bone underneath. Sy-wen knew the dangers of even minor injuries in the sea. Parasites and contagion soon took root in open wounds, leading to pestilence and the rot of flesh. As she stared, seawater drained out from the ragged-edged hole in splashing gouts with each shuddering breath of the dragon.

Witnessing the extent of his injuries, Sy-wen's heart sank. To confirm her fear, she caught one of the healers glance to another and shake his head mournfully. They, too, knew death when faced with it.

Oh, Conch! Tears flowed down her cheeks, and her knees began to give way. Flint caught her before she fell. He waved Kast to his side. "Help me. She does not need to see this."

"No, I want to stay and—" But her words died into sobs.

She felt Kast scoop her in his arms again.

"I know somewhere warm," Flint said. "She can rest while the healers work their medicines."

"Lead on, then," Kast said in his coarse, thick voice.

Flint nodded. As he turned away, he mumbled something under his breath. Though the words were unclear, from his strained and sullen tone, the regret he felt was quite evident. He cleared his throat and nodded forward. "It's just a little ways."

The passage from the lake chamber reeked of the healer's willowbark potion. Its scent was a constant reminder of Conch's dire health. No one spoke as Flint led them through the twisting corridor. Sy-wen lay still in Kast's arms, too tired and scared for her dear Conch to protest being treated like a child.

They crossed other side passages as they journeyed on through the maze of tunnels. Sy-wen tried to pay attention to the path they followed but soon lost count of the twists and turns. Even the reek of the healer's medicinals finally faded.

Kast glanced frequently behind him and crinkled his brow in concentration. He hitched Sy-wen higher in his arms. "I thought you said it was only a little ways," he said after a while.

Flint's only answer was an arm pointed forward. He seemed preoccupied, listening, his head cocked to whispers only he could hear.

Kast followed with a grumble in his chest. Sy-wen suspected the big-boned man was just as lost and confused by the passages as she. But with no other choice, he followed Flint.

After a time that seemed endless in the narrow passageways, the old sailor finally stopped by a torch sizzling in an iron sconce. The tunnel exit was just ahead. From the echo of their footsteps, the chamber beyond sounded large.

Flint turned to them, his words and manner odd. "Here is where we need to be," he said. The boldness in the old man had faded to a sullen attitude. He would not even meet either of their eyes. "Come. It is time to see how this endgame plays."

"What are you saying, Flint?" Kast's voice had an edge of menace.

"Come." He led them into the neighboring chamber.

Kast followed, though his eyes searched ahead warily.

Sy-wen shrank farther into Kast's arms as they entered the large cavern. It was roughly circular in shape, the walls imbedded with glowing crystals of varying sizes. The source of the glow was the reflected light from a twisted column of woody growth, its cracked and gnarled surface dancing with flows of light. It reminded Sy-wen of the glowing algae beds that lit the deep reefs of the ocean trenches. The light had a quality that seemed unnatural for this land—for this world, even.

"Wh-where are we?" she asked.

The room was also occupied by other people in white robes—close to fifty, Sy-wen estimated. They were all positioned at various stations along the walls, hands raised to the glowing crystals. Were they other healers?

Sy-wen wiggled free of Kast's arms. It took her a few moments for her legs to support her. She leaned on Kast. The robed men—and Sy-wen spotted a few women's faces among the cowls—glanced toward them as they stepped within the chamber.

"I must show you something." Flint led the way across the room.

Kast and Sy-wen followed. Sy-wen kept one hand on the large man's arm to keep her feet steady, but she soon found her land legs. She took a few steps on her own but stayed near Kast's side just in case. Around her, the eyes of the robed ones followed their course. Whispers passed among these others; not all of them sounded friendly.

Flint paused near the glowing trunk that pierced the center of the chamber. He touched his thumb to his lips in respect. "The ancient root of the koa'kona," Flint explained, then continued to the far side of the room.

Rounding the thick root, Sy-wen kept a wary watch on its glowing surface. But once she was past it, her eyes saw the far wall of the room. A gasp escaped her throat.

Etched upon the wall was a monstrous relief of a seadragon curled up on itself as if asleep, its wings folded back in slumber. The carved sculpture encompassed the entire back wall of the cavern. The dragon depicted, carved of a stone blacker than the surrounding rock, was gigantic, three times the size of any dragon that ever had swum the oceans. But even this estimate was questionable since it lay curled up on itself, its body wound round in a snaking spiral until the tip of its tail touched its snout. Its huge head, with its eyes closed, lay buried in the center of the coil. Even if she jumped, she did not believe she could touch that stone head.

"Ragnar'k," Flint whispered, awe evident in his tone.

The single spoken word drew the attention of a small, robed man nearby. He removed his fingers from a crystal the size of a whale's eye and pushed closer to them. His eyes ran like cool water over Kast and Sy-wen, then settled on Flint. He pushed back his cowl from his bald head. He, too, wore a silver star earring. "Brother Flint, you should not have brought them." The man's voice was chilly. "They are not of the Hi'fai. They have not been summoned."

"Brother Geral," Flint said, matching the ice in the other's voice, "I truly wish this burden was not mine, yet it is not Ragnar'k that has called them here—but prophecy."

"You and Brother Moris are fools," the other hissed, glancing nervously at the dragon sculpture. "I've already communed with Ragnar'k, and his dreams this morning are confused, agitated. Something has disturbed the dragon's rest." He glanced significantly at Sy-wen and Kast. "Nothing will be prophesied this day. If Moris ever answers today's summons, he will find no support for his claim."

"Just because you don't share Moris' vision does not make it false," Flint answered.

"But he was never a strong weaver. To put so much credence on his visions is . . . is *foolish*." The man now almost trembled with anger.

Flint placed a hand on the other's sleeve. "I know his words frighten, Geral, but they can't be ignored. Other weavers have had similar visions throughout the ages. Ragnar'k will awaken. I can tell from your face that you know it to be true. The dragon's dreams are confused because already he no longer slumbers as deep. Like a sea-dragon rising to the surface, his spirit wakes."

Geral tore his robe free of Flint's fingers. "You and the others should have been cast out from the sect."

Flint shook his head sadly. "Do we repeat history, Brother? The Hi'fai were once cast out of A'loa Glen because of words of doom. Do we now do the same?"

Flint's words seemed to shake the man, whose voice receded from his rage. "But Moris speaks of our own doom, the death of our sect." The other obviously sought some consolation from Flint.

He did not get it, "We *are* doomed," Flint said. "The Hi'fai have protected Ragnar'k for countless centuries. After today, we will no longer be needed. It is the time for someone new to take on our burden." Flint reached a hand and gently touched Sy-wen's arm.

The other's shoulders slumped, resigned. "Is she mer'ai?" he asked in a tired voice, finally recognizing her presence. His eyes, cold before, had softened into sympathy as they settled on her.

Flint raised Sy-wen's hand. Confused by their words, she did not object as Flint parted her fingers to reveal her webbing.

"You were always a good fisherman, Flint," the other conceded with a quiet snort. "I heard you netted her dragon, too."

"In the Grotto, injured but alive. The healers work to save her bondmate."

Sy-wen tired of this misinterpretation and cleared her throat to draw their attentions. "Conch is not my bondmate," she said meekly.

Flint patted her shoulder. "Just because you haven't actually conceived a child does not preclude him from being your bondmate. It is your moon's blood that bonds you."

"I . . . I know." She blushed a bit with the intimacy of the conversation. "Conch is my friend, but we are *not* blood-bonded. He is my mother's dragon."

Flint's expression grew wide with shock. "But the prophecy was clear . . . the spell of release . . ." He sank to the stone beside her and gripped her shoulders. "Conch *must* be your bondmate!"

She shook her head while the small man pulled up his cowl. "I told you Moris was wrong," Geral said. Relief had raised the pitch of his voice.

A deeper voice boomed behind them. "I am not wrong."

All turned to stare at the huge, dark-skinned man who had come up behind them. He threw back his cowl, his bald pate reflecting the glow of the root. "Ragnar'k wakes. This is certain. I can hear it in his voice. But the prophecy was precise. When the stone dragon moves, the mer'ai and her bonded must be present for the spell to work . . . or A'loa Glen is doomed."

A red-haired boy suddenly bumped his way beside the hulking, dark-skinned man. His hands covered his ears. "It's so loud," the boy cried, his voice raised as if trying to call above the sounds of a storm. He winced in pain.

Sy-wen studied the boy. He seemed to be her own age, and his green eyes contained as much confusion as her own.

"It's the boy from the stairs!" Geral said with sudden heat. "Moris, how dare you bring him here? He's a creature of the Dark Lord!"

"No, he is a strong weaver," the dark-skinned man said. "Ragnar'k calls him, too."

Geral backed from all of them. "You break our laws, Moris! Flint! You expose our most sacred secrets to foreigners. And for what? Some diddled vision! The prophecy is not coming true." He pointed a finger so angrily toward Sy-wen that Kast stepped in front of her protectively. "She arrives without a bonded dragon. The prophecy is proven false!"

As the man retreated farther, others gathered around Geral. His rage seemed to be igniting those near him. Mumbled words of agreement began to spread. "They must be cast out!" Geral finally declared in a booming voice, bolstered by the others and his own fear.

Even more robed men came to support him.

Flint tried to argue with them, but the dark-skinned man placed a hand on the old man's shoulder. "We have failed," Moris said calmly to Flint. "The vision was precise. Without the bonded dragon, Ragnar'k will die as he wakes. He will drown in the very rock that has held him safe for these many centuries. He cannot be pulled free of the stone without the strength of a mer'ai and her bondmate."

"I'm sorry," Flint said. "I just assumed . . . She was a mer'ai, and she protected the wounded dragon."

Suddenly a loud crack exploded across the room. All eyes—even Geral's—turned to the carved dragon.

Sy-wen knew, regardless of the arguments otherwise, that all here expected the stone dragon to move. But it was the boy who pointed out the true source of the noise. "Over there!" His sharp voice drew all their attentions.

To the left of the dragon, the stone of the wall churned as if made of molten rock. As it eddied and swirled in slow, heavy circles, it grew blacker, a bruise upon the wall. Soon, where once rock stood, an oily shadow now stained the stone. As they all watched, a fist suddenly burst from the shadowy, churning blackness—a fist that gripped a long staff with black energies crackling down its shaft. The staff seemed to draw the light and the warmth from the cavern.

Sy-wen sickened at the sight of the malevolent force that danced along the shaft. Her belly began to churn to match the swirling shadows. She backed away, bumping into Kast. The strange boy now stood near her shoulder. Only she heard his whispered words. "He's found me. I've led him here." Terror laced his words.

From the wall stepped a robed man cloaked in inky shadows. He was hunched and bent over his staff. His face was wrinkled and blotched, his eyes milky with age. Behind him followed a second, taller man, a contrast in form to the first. Straight backed with smooth features, he surveyed the chamber. His face might be considered handsome, but it was the beauty of a carved stone: cold, hard, and cruel.

Sy-wen shuddered at the sight of them. Her insides quaked.

"It is the Praetor!" Geral called from behind Sy-wen. "We've been betrayed!"

Flint spoke without hope. "Our doom is upon us."

His words reached inside Sy-wen to her shuddering, queasy belly and lit her innards on fire. Gasping, Sy-wen suddenly clutched her stomach and fell to her knees, her eyes blind with the rising pain. She rocked back and forth, her arms tight. It had never been this bad.

The boy was the only one to bend to her aid. "We must run," he said, trying to get her to stand.

Answering him was beyond her; even standing was impossible as the searing pain lanced through her lower belly.

Mother below, please not now!

Her prayer was not answered. A final spasm gripped her belly.

Blood spilled from between her legs, soaking through her skintight leggings, more blood than she had ever shed on any of her moon's cycles.

"You're bleeding," the boy said, letting go of her shoulder. "Hey, you, she's bleeding! We need to get her out of here."

Kast bent over her, pulled down by the boy's tugging arm. His eyes grew wide at the sight. He hurriedly took the scarf from around his neck and reached to stanch her bleeding.

Sy-wen shoved his arm away, but her eyes fell upon the tattoo of a diving seahawk. Free of the scarf, it once again lay exposed on Kast's neck. She froze, her breath held in her throat, her eyes fixed by the red-and-black tattoo. Her gaze met the hungry stare of the hunting hawk. She could not stop herself, not with her heart thundering so loudly. Unbidden, her hand rose toward Kast.

Flint suddenly yelled from nearby, but he sounded far away. "No! You must not!"

He was too late.

Her fingertips touched the seahawk.

23

As Joach stooped at the foot of the carved dragon, chaos swirled through the cavern. He seemed tossed upon a sea of white robes. Some fled past him, trying to escape the two darkmages, while others surged toward the foul men, knives appearing from folds in their robes. It seemed not all were so willing to forsake their cavern sanctuary to the Dark Lord.

From the far side of the cavern, black flames snapped and spit among the white robes. In all the fury, Joach had lost sight of Greshym and the Praetor. Screams and rallying yells echoed across the cavern, but more chilling than the crackle of black fire was the occasional icy laugh that rose from the battle. It was the mirth of a black-hearted conqueror amused by the slaughter and the blood on his hands.

Unsure in which direction to flee, Joach simply remained crouched beside the young girl. His mind spun, and his heart wailed with guilt. How had Greshym followed him? The darkmage must have known Joach's act was a ruse all along, and he had used Joach as a cat to flush out the rats in the Edifice.

As he crouched, the song of the dragon continued, throbbing and racing through the marrow of his bones. It sang to his own heart; it sang of release, of escape. Joach wished he could answer it.

Beside him, Joach saw the bleeding young girl reach a hand toward her large, black-haired protector. She touched the man's tattooed neck, almost like a lover. "Kast," she mumbled softly, "I need you." But the man suddenly spasmed as if her fingertips were hot coals. A mixture of a gasp and a sigh escaped his throat.

Joach reached toward the man to see if he needed aid, but as his own fingers touched Kast's sleeve, his mind suddenly swelled with dragon song. The room vanished around him, and Joach found himself floating high above a midnight sea. Below him, he saw waters dotted with sleek, red-keeled ships, their prows depicting fierce dragons. Thousands of lanterns swung from the ships' riggings, lighting the boats and the seas around them. Yet this was not the sight that caused his blood to thrill. Among the boats, riding the waves like horses in a prairie, were countless seadragons, smaller twins to the one named Ragnar'k, and atop their backs were sleek, barechested riders. Joach knew the old fables and put a name to these dragonriders.

The mer.

Suddenly the view swung closer, as if he were a falcon diving toward the scene. He landed upon the deck of the largest of the ships. Weatherworn and sea-hardened men surrounded him. But he focused instead on a tall man standing on the foredeck. With dark hair peppered in gray, he could have been an older brother of the one named Kast. Yet somehow Joach sensed this was no brother but an ancestor. He knew that what he viewed now had occurred in the distant past. The players were long dead, the boat long rotted and sunk.

A smaller, thin-limbed woman stood before this hard man. Her silver-green hair matched that of the girl in the cavern. As the woman raised a tiny hand toward the other's neck and touched the tattoo, Joach noticed two things: Her hands were webbed, and the tattoo—some type of hawk—matched the one on Kast's neck. The man, who Joach somehow knew was the leader of these ship-bred men, arched back from the small mer woman's touch, his mouth open in ecstasy.

Then the woman spoke. "Mark all your male children as they come of age with the poison dyes from the blowfish and reef octopi as we have taught you. There will come a day when we will call you again to our sides, again to be our sharks above the water. Do you make this oath willingly and bind your people to us?"

"I do," the man gasped. "Our blood is yours to cast upon the seas."

She removed her fingers from his neck. "Then be free until we call you again to claim your dragon heritage."

Suddenly the vision snapped away, and Joach was once again in the cavern. Someone had grabbed his shoulders and was yanking him away from Kast and the girl. Disoriented, Joach could not find his footing and fell hard to the stone floor. He glanced up, rolling away a bit, expecting to see Greshym's hoary face. But it was Moris who grabbed at his arm.

"Keep back from them," the dark-skinned brother warned.

"What's happening?" Flint asked.

Moris' eyes shone brightly, almost as if tears threatened. "Don't you see? I *was* wrong. Ragnar'k warned that a mer'ai and her bonded must be present for him to survive his waking. Since Ragnar'k is a dragon himself, we both just naturally thought this meant one of their bonded dragons. But can't you see how we were wrong?" He pointed at Kast.

The Bloodrider picked up the girl.

Joach regained his feet and watched the eyes of the girl's protector glaze over. Joach recognized his dull, slack expression. It was a form of the spell that had enslaved him to the darkmage.

Joach could not keep silent. "He's bonded to her," he said. "Just like in the past. The ancient oath."

Both brothers glanced briefly at him.

Moris spoke first. "I told you the boy was a strong weaver."

Kast carried the girl away from the conflict still raging on the other side of the chamber. He hurried toward the exit.

"We should follow them," Joach said nervously. He saw how few of the white-robed people still resisted the darkmages. The smell of charred flesh filled the cavern. Bodies lay scattered across the stone floor, their white robes singed by darkfire. Joach spotted Shorkan and Greshym, two black islands in a sea of white. Black flames danced out from them to lap at those who threatened. So far the darkmages had ignored Joach's group. They seemed more interested in the huge glowing root in the center of the chamber.

"What should we do?" Flint asked as he watched Kast stride away. "Go to the aid of our besieged brothers? Flee?"

Joach liked this last choice, but kept silent by Moris' side.

"No, Flint," Moris answered; his voice had a tone of exultation. "The winds of prophecy blow through this cavern. Nothing we do from here will change the outcome." He waved his arm to encompass the entire cavern. "All this is just so much sound and fury. The purpose of the Hi'fai is ended. It is the time for new warriors to carry on the battle for the Light. We are finished."

"But we must . . . Shouldn't we . . . ?" Flint's hands were clenched into fists. Joach could tell Flint resisted Moris' words. He was not a man used to inaction.

"Watch," Moris said simply. He pointed toward the wall behind them all.

The sculpted dragon was the same as ever. Joach did not know what to expect. The dragon still called, but since the strange dream of the ships, the song no longer seemed directed at him.

Suddenly a small, white-robed man darted in front of the carving. Joach was startled to recognize him as the one who had been speaking with Moris on the stair, Geral.

"You have destroyed us all!" Geral screamed, his red eyes drilling at Joach. "You led the demons to us!"

Moris placed a large hand on Joach's shoulder and faced the raging brother. "Geral, it was over ages ago. This morning was foretold before A'loa Glen had a name. Be at peace."

A dagger slid into Geral's hand from a hidden wrist sheath. "Not until I cut this pestilence from our home." Geral leapt at Joach.

Stunned, Joach found his legs frozen. He raised his arms and winced down, expecting the man's weight to slam atop him. But it never happened. After a long heartbeat, Joach looked up. A gasp choked out of him, and he scrambled backward.

Geral was stopped in midleap, held above the stone floor by a smoky claw. Geral struggled within its grip until he was tossed aside. His head struck a wall, and he collapsed in a tangle of limbs.

"Stand back," Moris warned, pulling Joach with him. "Ragnar'k comes."

Free of its burden, the claw reached farther out from the wall. It was a sculpture of the blackest smoke. It stretched toward the floor of the cavern and touched a small wet stain on the rock near the carving's base.

"Of course," Moris whispered with sudden insight. "Her blood calls the dragon forth. The mer'ai girl has not bonded. As with all dragons, her scent lures Ragnar'k. He cannot resist her call. It is the ancient instinct of his bloodline."

As they watched, a dragon's head carved of smoke rose from its slumber to extend toward the blood. Its snaking neck unwound from its coil. Vague in form, it silently edged toward the blood, wisps of smoke trailing up from it as if from a spent fire. It seemed to have no real substance, but Geral's unmoving body warned otherwise. The dragon hunched over the small pool of blood, drawing forth the rest of its body from the rock. Forelimbs bent tight to the rock, and it snuffled at the scent. Then it raised its huge head and seemed to spot the girl retreating in Kast's arms.

The pair had reached the large root and were skirting its edge. On the far side of the root, Joach saw Greshym raise a hand and point. Even with his weak eyes, the old mage had spotted the awakening dragon. Shorkan turned to study the smoky beast. Joach enjoyed the look of surprise on the Praetor's usual placid features.

"We are powerless to interfere from here," Moris said behind him. "What will happen now is beyond our ability to change."

As he spoke, the beast continued to pull free of the rock. Wings of smoke spread from its hunched back to reach for the roof of the cavern. As more of the dragon escaped its rocky prison, it bunched up on itself, its tail snaking free of the stone to whip back and forth like an angry cat. It was a monstrous, hulking shadow crouched over the blood of the girl. Its nose followed the path of Kast across the chamber.

Then it opened its cavernous jaws and screamed its lust. Joach fell to his knees, his hands over his ears. The pain ripped through his head. He noticed others fall to the stone, too, some rolling with the agony of the screech. Joach saw even Greshym collapse, his poi'wood staff rolling from his stunned fingers.

"He's killing us!" Flint exclaimed, bent over in agony.

"No," Moris said. He had somehow kept his feet, though his face was a mask of pain. "He bellows his challenge."

Joach noticed that three people seemed unaware of the ripping scream. The Praetor was unaffected by or simply deaf to the dragon's roar, as were two others: Kast stepped over the white-robed brothers as he headed for the exit. The girl lay curled in his arms, her gaze fastened to the tunnel opening.

The Praetor's attention focused on the pair as they crossed the cavern. Shorkan strode forth to intercept them, drawn to these two, obviously suspicious of the strength that kept them untouched by the mysterious assault. He raised his arms. Black fire coursed the length of his sleeves.

Joach's vision began to blur from tears of pain. The cavern became blotches of light—some dark, some bright. Then as suddenly as it had struck, the roar ended, leaving a quaking hollowness in his assaulted skull. He wiped at his tears just in time to see the monstrous, shadowy beast surge across the cavern. One moment it was a hulking, seething wall of shadows; then in a blink it was gone.

It flew in a streak of smoke, a maelstrom of tendrils and clouds as it bore down upon the unsuspecting pair. It banked around the gnarled root in a swirling eddy of smoke. Joach winced, knowing that blood would be shed here.

The Praetor also spotted its flight and backed suspiciously from it. Behind him, Greshym struggled to rise, using his staff as a crutch. Without turning, Shorkan reached a hand back, and Greshym's staff flew from the old one's weak fingers to the Praetor's fist. Greshym, suddenly unsupported, fell to his arms and knees. Shorkan raised the staff before him. His black magicks, drawn like lightning to an iron rod, flowed out from the Praetor's body to encase the staff in flame.

Shorkan held the blazing weapon before him defiantly, ready for battle.

But his challenge was ignored. The shadow dragon sped without hesitation past the darkmage to descend upon its true quarry. Just before it struck, Kast must have sensed the approaching menace and swung around, the girl under one arm, a knife appearing in his fist as if from the air. It was a poor match for what he faced, but Kast did not falter. He crouched in readiness as it struck.

Kast and the girl vanished into the heart of the smoky cloud. Whether consumed by the dragon or crushed, Joach cringed against what would be revealed. As he pushed finally to his feet, assisted by Moris, he watched the outcome with wide eyes.

The cloud roiled about the pair, occasional glimpses of the dragon—a snaking tail, an unfurled wing, a claw that grasped toward the roof—sprouting like sudden blooms. But nothing was revealed of the two buried at its heart.

Near the struggle, Greshym had pushed to his feet, still bent with his one hand resting on a knee. He hissed at Shorkan, his words loud enough to reach Joach's ears. "Kill them all before it's too late!"

The Praetor stood his ground with his staff of darkfire raised before him, but he made no move to obey the other.

"Now is the only time you can stop Ragnar'k," Greshym implored. "If he takes root, he will become flesh!"

At that moment, the smoke dragon drew tighter around the pair; its tendrils coalesced, and its pall darkened. The swirling smoke became an eddying black pool around them.

"Strike now!" Greshym screamed. "Destroy it!"

"No!" Shorkan said. "I will have it for my master. The Black Heart will find a use for this magickal beast."

"You fool!" Greshym stumbled forward and tried to grab his staff from the other.

Shorkan elbowed him away. "Stand back!"

As they argued, the smoky fog suddenly surged up to form the figure of a dragon, its head raised toward the ceiling, its wings spread wide. It screamed once again, a piping roar of triumph.

The noise blasted through Joach, closing off all his senses. Blinded, he did not even feel himself fall to the stone floor. One moment he was standing, staring in awe at the dragon triumphant, and the next he was pushing himself off the floor, his teeth aching. He rubbed at a tickle on his neck. His ear bled.

This time, even Moris had not been able to keep his footing. The hulking brother shoved to his knees with a groan. Blood welled from his ears, too.

Joach raised his head, his temples throbbing with even the slightest motion. Across the chamber, Greshym fared no better. He lay sprawled upon the floor, unmoving. Hopefully dead, Joach prayed.

But as before, the Praetor stood untouched. He searched around himself, mystified, still unsure what assault kept knocking the room to its knees. He then studied the only other pair untouched by the onslaught. Nearby, Kast crouched, the girl still in his arms. But—

"Sweet Mother, the dragon is gone!" Joach blurted.

Flint rolled to his knees. "Where did it go?"

The Praetor was the first to respond in a coherent fashion. He still held Greshym's staff, which was afire with black magicks. "I don't understand what quality of magick you two possess," he said coldly, obviously believing the two to be the source of the smoke trickery, "but my master will find you both fascinating."

Kast spoke up. "Who are you?"

"Ah, you speak."

"The bond between Kast and Sy-wen has been sundered," Flint mumbled beside Joach.

The girl spotted the darkmage and struggled to free herself of Kast's arms, but he held her secure. Though no longer obligated by magick, he still protected her. "You'd best let us pass," Kast said with menace. He still had his knife in his hand.

Greshym groaned and crawled toward the Praetor. "You . . . you cannot defeat Ragnar'k," he warned. "We must flee."

Shorkan kicked aside his groping hand. "Flee? They have revealed their magick; now it is time to demonstrate mine."

With these words, Shorkan pointed his staff—not at the pair but at the glowing root. Fire lanced out and struck the thick stalk. At first, the root's glow seemed to hold the darkfire at bay, but then fingers of flame spread open like some loathsome black claw and grabbed the root's trunk. The chamber jolted violently with its contact.

Moris and Flint both gasped.

From its foul grip on the trunk, a river of darkfire now linked root to staff. The staff then began to suck the energy of the root to itself, bleeding the tree of the last of its ancient magick. Under the assault, the taproot began to crumble to dust, its very substance dependent on the magick at its heart.

Overhead the roof groaned as its single support faded. Boulders crashed to the floor.

As the last of the root's magick was consumed, the well of darkfire could no longer be contained to the staff's length. Black flames cascaded down in fiery torrents and bathed the darkmage in a robe of fire. His entire body now flowed with power. The air grew frigid as the darkfire drank the heat from the cavern. Black ice rippled across the floor from the mage's toes. Where it touched the collapsed forms of any of the white-robed Hi'fai, their flesh cracked and shattered.

Who could hope to withstand such a creature?

Kast stood his ground. "Stand back," he warned again and raised his small dagger higher. Its blade reflected the sick light of the black flames.

From inside the tower of black flame, mad laughter echoed forth, the sound drawing the last of the warmth from the room.

The Praetor stepped toward them.

Sy-wen watched the creature sculpted of fire stalk toward them. She shook her head to clear the spell-cast glaze from her eyes. How many other nightmares hunted this cursed cavern? She vaguely remembered that some smoky demon had threatened them, but where had it vanished? And now this fire demon laughed at them and blocked any chance of escape.

Kast held his dagger higher and backed away, but she knew what approached could not be defeated by a quick wrist and a sharp blade. She had only to look to the cavern floor littered with singed bodies to know the true danger they faced. She wriggled in Kast's arms. "Put me down," she scolded. "Let me at least fight before it kills us."

Kast hesitated a heartbeat, then lowered her to the stone floor. Sy-wen's legs betrayed her—her weight out of water tricking her limbs—and she fell hard on her backside.

"That's helpful," Kast grumbled under his breath. Even when faced with his own death, he had time to insult her. A second dagger had appeared in his other hand.

Red faced, Sy-wen scrambled to her feet, scuttling backward while doing so. "I . . . I can fight."

She straightened and reached to her belt. No dagger lay sheathed there, but she was not weaponless. Her fingers found the star-shaped crustacean attached to her belt. The stunner's poisonous sting could stop a full-grown rockshark, and Sy-wen was a skilled wielder of the weapon. She narrowed her eyes and pulled the stunner free, using a finger to flip off the protective shell that housed its stinger.

Cradling it in the webs of her hand, she pulled her arm back and stepped in front of Kast.

"Fie, girl! Stand aside!"

She ignored him and studied the figure for a weak spot. It was best to strike a rockshark's eye.

"So the little one thinks she has claws," the demon hissed.

Sy-wen ignored his words, too. Studying the creature, she noticed the only part of the demon free of flame was its face. Just as well! She swung her arm, and with an experienced flip of her wrist, the stunner shot from her webbed fingers. It spun and flew true.

Sy-wen had only the feeblest hope the weapon would immobilize the demon, but perhaps it could at least delay the creature enough for Kast and her to escape. Her strange attack caught the demon off guard. He tried to block the stunner with the staff, but he was too slow, and the arc of the spinning sea star curved deceptively. It struck him just below the eye, fastening immediately to the demon's flesh.

"What is this th—?" Then the demon crashed to his knees. He dropped his staff and dug at his face with both hands.

Sy-wen's blood quickened. She had done it! Glancing back at Kast, a look of pride shone on her face.

"Get back, girl!" he yelled.

Sy-wen's breath caught in her throat as she swung around. The demon had managed to rip the stunner from his face. But that was impossible! A stunner always buried its five legs deep into the tissue, too deep to remove without a blade. Then she saw her answer. Where the stunner had struck, black flames shot out of the demon's face. His magicks had driven the tiny beast from his flesh.

The demon rose to his feet, but did not stop there. He kept rising on a pillar of black fire. His face was sculpted rage, his eyes pools of black energies. He spread his arms, and fire lanced forth to shake the roof. Loose rock rained down and rattled like hail upon the floor.

"I would kill you now," he boomed, his voice as black as his flames. "But placing you at my master's feet will be a greater punishment!"

Kast leaned over to protect her from the falling rock. "I'm sorry," he whispered. "I should've kept you on Jarplin's ships."

Sy-wen leaned closer to him and did not object to his sheltering embrace. They were doomed, but before they were destroyed she would seek the small comfort of his arms. She raised her face to his. "No apologies, Kast. If I couldn't have gained my freedom," she said, "I would rather have died anyway."

She saw the tears that marked his eyes, like rain on rock. His voice was a strained, choked whisper. "Yes, but did I have to deliver you to it?"

She reached a hand to his cheek. This time it was no spell that drew her fingers. She wanted to wipe away his tears. No man should die with such guilt in his heart. As her hand touched his face, her eyes grew wide. She finally saw what lay *new* upon the man's skin. Her fingers brushed across it.

The tattoo of the hunting seahawk was gone, and in its place was the finest rendering of a fierce dragon, black wings raised for battle, red eyes ablaze with the hunger for blood.

She stared into the dragon's gaze and recognized him, knew him as her mother knew Conch. Her heart leapt toward the dragon as her hand stretched toward him. The tattoo was her bonded, and like all mer'ai, she knew her bondmate's name.

Ragnar'k.

With her finger's touch, the world blew out from under her.

JOACH JUMPED BACK, SLAMMING INTO MORIS BEHIND HIM. SWEET Mother! His eyes could not make sense of what was happening. He had thought the dark-haired man and the girl doomed. Shorkan rode waves of flame and crested above them like a striking snake. But now . . .

He had seen the girl reach to touch the man's cheek and neck, perhaps in a tender good-bye or something deeper. But at her touch, the man's flesh blew out from him in sheets and tangles of black scale. His clothes ripped so savagely that a torn shoe landed near Joach's toe. The frenzied motion was a blur of wing and claw.

Shorkan shied away from the maelstrom of scale and bone, skirting backward atop his column of flames. Greshym rolled away, almost caught in a splash of the Praetor's fire. "I warned you," the old mage hissed at the leader of the Brotherhood.

A roar raked the cavern walls and washed away any further words from Greshym. All eyes turned to where Kast and the girl had once stood. A second roar split the cavern stillness.

The girl was still the same, though wearing a dazed expression. She rode atop the back of a monstrous dragon. Thick black legs ground silver claws into the stone itself. Scaled wings, scintillating with sparks of rich colors, swept upward like huge ribbed sails, reaching for the roof. Yet all this was nothing compared to its huge head: eyes aglow with a red fire; jaws open, revealing curved fangs longer than a man's forearm. It stretched its neck again and roared at the two darkmages.

This was no smoke dragon, no magickal wail. It was flesh and fury.

With the force of its roar, the black flames of foul magicks were blown back like a candle's flame before a gale. As Shorkan cringed away, the flames were snuffed and stripped from the Praetor's robe, swept away to dash harmlessly against the far wall. The cavern shook with the dragon's thunder and the play of wild forces.

Greshym crawled to his knees and grabbed at Shorkan's doused sleeve. "He's too strong. You can't defeat Ragnar'k without a heartstone. We must retreat to your tower."

Shorkan's hands clenched into fists; his shoulders shook. His black eyes bore murderous hatred at the great beast.

Greshym pulled harder on the Praetor's sleeve. "You once taught me to know my battles, to know when it was best to fight. Heed your own words, Shorkan!"

Shorkan unclenched his fists and backed beside Greshym. The younger mage kept his eyes on the dragon, but the hulking beast kept its place, claws dug deep in the rock. Right now, it simply guarded the girl. As long as the darkmages did not threaten, it only watched them warily, muscles tensed and ready, head low with menace. Shorkan seemed finally to recognize the danger here and pulled Greshym to his feet. "You have much to explain," was all he said to his fellow mage, but his voice was iced venom. He waved a hand to the floor, and a well of swirling blackness opened at their feet.

"Wait!" Greshym yelled.

But it was too late. The two darkmages fell like heavy boulders into the darkness, vanishing and taking the cursed doorway with them. The floor was once again ordinary stone.

The cavern suddenly shuddered violently. Rock dust and fair-sized pieces of the roof crashed to the floor. What was left of the mighty root cracked and crumbled. The walls groaned.

Moris gripped Joach's shoulder. "We must get out of these lower levels. Come." He led Joach and Flint across the chamber, aiming directly for the dragon. The handful of surviving Hi'fai in their stained white robes were already hurrying toward the single exit.

The dragon seemed to sense the trio's approach. It swung its head menacingly at them. Its wings, which had relaxed slightly once the darkmages had vanished, twitched farther up. Eyes glowed red with warning. Words, unspoken by any tongue, bloomed in Joach's head: *Come no farther.*

Joach stopped, as did the others. Moris and Flint exchanged glances. They had heard the silent words, too.

The girl spoke from atop the dragon. Her voice shook. "He says to come no farther," she warned.

Flint answered her. "We heard, Sy-wen. It's dreamspeak, the tongue of Ragnar'k. We've listened to his dreams and muttered words for ages. But I'm surprised you can hear him, too. You've no weaver's blood in you."

"We have bonded," she said simply, quietly.

Bonded, the dragon echoed.

Moris stepped forward and spoke to Ragnar'k. "We do not mean you or your . . . bonded . . . any harm."

The girl named Sy-wen swallowed hard. "What is happening? Who were those demons? What happened to Kast?"

"I'm not sure, my dear," Flint answered.

"I want to get off this dragon," she said, a trace of worry in her voice.

"Fear not; I don't think he would ever harm you."

Never harm you, the dragon again echoed.

The room shook again, and a large boulder crashed only a few spans away.

"We need to leave here," Moris said. "It's about to collapse."

Joach eyed the exit longingly, then looked back at the dragon. "I don't think Ragnar'k will fit through those passages."

"We can't leave him," Flint said.

"But the boy is right," Moris argued. "He'll never fit."

"I'm getting down," Sy-wen said, reaching and beginning to slide around the dragon's neck. She shook all over.

The dragon snuffled at her but did not try to stop her. *Bonded,* he repeated and nudged her chest. His nose flaps parted to take in her scent. *Smell good.*

Whether from the tickle of its nose flaps or his dreamspoken words, Joach saw a ghost of a smile play about her lips. Then her feet touched the stone, and she almost fell, catching her weight just in time by grabbing an edge of wing. "I must get used to this," she said, straightening.

As she pulled her hand from the dragon's flesh, Ragnar'k blew inward with a folding of scales and flesh. Neck and tail coiled in on themselves. Wings snapped down and melded into a spinning cocoon of rippling textures.

Sy-wen yipped in fright and stumbled back into Flint's arms.

"Steady, my dear," he consoled.

In a handful of heartbeats, the flurry of bone and flesh settled into a familiar form. Kast again stood before them, naked as a newborn. All eyes were wide in surprise, but Kast's were narrowed in suspicion.

He ignored his own nakedness. "What happened?" He searched around the cavern. "Where's the fire demon?"

"So many questions," Flint said with a wry twist to his lips, "but before we search for answers, you'd best cover yourself, Kast. There are ladies present."

The large man seemed finally to recognize his nakedness and the red-faced girl who was trying her best to avert her eyes. He grumbled and accepted a cloak Moris retrieved from one of the dead brothers.

"What now?" Kast asked, cinching the cloak. It was miserably too small for him, barely reaching his knees.

"Much strangeness has happened this day," Moris said as the cavern shuddered again. "But this place is no longer safe, and I don't mean just this cavern, but all of A'loa Glen. We need space to piece this all together, to figure out what truly happened here, and more importantly, to plan. A dark time lies ahead. The Praetor knows he is exposed and will lock down the city with his black magicks. I, for one, don't want to be here when he calls the beasts of the Gul'gotha to the island—not until we're prepared."

"I think we all agree with that," Flint said.

All heads nodded.

"Then let's be off," Kast said, heading for the tunnel.

"Wait," Joach said, his eye falling on an object he did not want to leave here. He ran quickly across the floor and reached for Greshym's discarded staff. It still lay on the stone where Shorkan had dropped it. Joach remembered Greshym's agonized cry just before he was whisked away. The darkmage's eyes had been on his abandoned staff.

"Perhaps it's best if you leave the foul thing," Flint said.

"No. It's his focus of power. He covets it," Joach said as he carefully picked it up. It felt like ordinary wood, if not a bit oilier than most. Tears rose to his eyes, and his words began to choke. "He stole my home, my parents. So I'll take this from him now, and one day I'll return and make him truly pay." Joach's voice hardened. "But first I must find my sister before they do."

"What do they want with your sister?" Flint asked.

Joach strode past him. He was tired of secrets. "She's a wit'ch."

24

Kast followed last behind the others. None spoke. All of them were lost in their own reveries. Kast still could not fathom what had happened to him. He remembered the demon in the flaming cloak descending upon them; he recalled Sy-wen reaching for his cheek . . . then nothing. The next he knew he was standing naked before the others, staring dumfounded around him.

As he strode behind Sy-wen down the passages, he rubbed at his neck and cheek. It still itched with a mild burn, as if his tattoo had been freshly needled into his skin. What did this girl have to do with all this? On Jarplin's ship, they had shared some strange spell-cast union. He remembered the events in great detail: the death of the Hort brothers, the bloody dagger in his hand, Sy-wen's cool bare skin against his arms as he carried her from the ship's kitchen. All this he remembered with a fresh clarity, but this time, he recalled nothing. There was a gaping hole in his memory.

And he hated it.

What had truly transpired? Why did the mer'ai girl now glance back at him with a trace of fear in her eyes?

The passageway gave a sudden, violent shudder. Kast barely kept his footing. Ahead, Sy-wen fell to her knees. A cracking roar echoed to him from behind, followed by a roiling wall of rock dust that flew up from the deeper corridors to swallow the company. Choking, Kast pulled Sy-wen to her feet as the dust cleared. He meant to keep a supporting hand on her. But she pulled from his grip, shying away from him.

"Thank you," she mumbled, stumbling forward, not meeting his eye.

Flint called back. "The dragon's chamber must have finally given way! We'd best hurry. This whole level may go!"

The pace increased. The group bunched together in their haste, almost running down the winding passageway.

Urgency washed away Kast's noisome ponderings. The Bloodriders knew when to focus on a task, and right now, freeing themselves of this subterranean maze was critical. Answers to the mysteries of today's events would have to wait.

The passages were still hazy with floating dust. Kast could barely see the large dark-skinned man who led them, but his words traveled back clearly. "The Grotto is our only hope," Moris said, breathless from the run. "Pray the sea channel is still open."

Flint answered him. "We may have to swim. There's only the one skiff."

"What about Conch?" This from Sy-wen.

"We'll just have to wait and see, my dear. After all that has occurred, I don't know if the healers . . . if they had enough time to mend your mother's dragon."

Kast understood the meaning behind the hesitation in Flint's voice. The seaman feared the healers may have abandoned the dragon, fleeing for their own lives.

The redheaded boy named Joach spoke into the long silence that followed Flint's statement. "So there's another dragon?"

Kast's brow crinkled with the boy's words. What did he mean by *another*?

No one answered the boy's question. The party became silent except for their raspy, dust-choked breaths as they ran.

Just when Kast was beginning to wonder if Moris had gotten them lost, they rounded a bend in the corridor, and the acrid tang of medicinals struck his nostrils. But under its bitter odor was the scent of home: the smell of the sea.

They had reached the Grotto.

The company poured out of the tunnel onto the pebbled shore of the underground lake.

Red-glazed pots lay tipped or broken on the shore, obviously hastily abandoned. Only one of the eight healers still stood in the ankle-deep water beside the huge jade-scaled dragon. Bald like the others, but with skin as red as a peeled plum, he raised scared eyes toward them; then his expression settled into relief when he recognized Flint.

"Where are the others, Brother Ewan?" Flint asked.

"Gone back into the tunnels," the healer said, wiping a damp palm over the crown of his head. "Some ran to aid the others. Some simply ran. One tried to make off with your skiff, but my knife's edge changed his compulsion toward thievery."

"And the dragon?" Flint asked, his eyes on the girl, who had already waded into the water to lay a hand on the beast's nose. The dragon was too weak even to raise its head, though it did acknowledge her presence with a weak nudge at her fingers. Joach had wandered near but kept his distance from the pair.

"He still breathes," the healer declared, then added in a lower voice, "but barely. The balm of bittersroot has eased his pain, and he rests; but I fear he will not survive."

Moris approached Flint. "We must be off now. If the dragon is too sick, it would be best to leave him. To survive this day, we must move quickly. An ailing dragon will slow us."

The healer, Ewan, supported his words. "If he moves, he'll die. I doubt he could make it out the sea tunnel before he expires."

Flint took their dire news with a darkening frown. "I told her I would save her dragon," he mumbled.

Moris laid a hand on Flint's shoulder but remained quiet.

Kast knew there were no words that would help. Sometimes life offered only cruel choices. Bloodriders knew this all too well. Still Kast could not ignore the tears on Sy-wen's face as she knelt beside Conch, pressing her cheek to her friend.

"Then there's no hope?" Flint asked.

Silence was his answer.

"I will tell her," Kast heard himself say before he knew his tongue had moved.

Flint glanced at him with a slightly surprised expression. Then his eyes grew serious, and he nodded.

Kast walked toward the girl, his legs suddenly heavy.

Behind him, Ewan mumbled to the others. "It's a shame that the healing properties of seadragon's blood can't heal a dragon's own wounds."

His ruminations were ignored until Flint suddenly blurted out, "Can the blood of another dragon help Conch?"

Kast slowed his pace toward the girl. Did Flint have a plan?

The healer's voice was hopeless. "Certainly, but it would take quite a bit. The seadragon's injuries are severe, and we've only a few drops in the Edifice's apothecary . . . not nearly enough to help this one."

Kast sighed. The dragon would die. He continued walking, his boots splashing at the water's edge.

"Wait, Kast," Flint called to him.

He stopped and glanced back.

Flint hurried toward him, his eyes bright. Moris followed. "Sy-wen," Flint urged, "come over here."

She raised her head from her friend's side at Flint's words but did not stand. "He's dying," she said with such despair in her voice that Kast took a step toward her.

"I know, I know, but this is no time for crying. Your tears will not help him, but something else may."

She sniffed and wiped at her nose. "What?"

"Just come here. If you want to save Conch, you're going to have to help."

Sy-wen looked at him doubtfully, then pushed to her feet. Joach helped her over the slippery stones to join them. "What do you want me to do?"

"I need you to call forth the dragon again."

Kast saw the frank terror in her eyes. What was Flint blathering about?

Sy-wen's voice shook. "I couldn't . . . I don't know how."

Flint persisted. "What did you do to call Ragnar'k last time?"

Sy-wen glanced at Kast. He frowned back at her. Did she expect him to have an answer? Then he felt her gaze shift from his face to his neck. She raised a finger and pointed to his tattoo.

All eyes swung toward him. Involuntarily, he took a step back. "What?" he muttered. "What are you all gawking at?"

Flint's eyes had grown wide; then he snorted a laugh. "So that's where the little snake ran off to?"

"What?" Kast repeated.

Flint reached for Kast's sleeve. "Come," he said and tugged him to the water's edge. He pointed to Kast's reflection in the still water. "Look at your tattoo."

Kast scowled. What did this fool—? Then it was his turn for his eyes to widen. His hand reached up to touch the tattoo etched into his skin during his manhood ceremony. The seahawk was gone. A dragon blazed upon his skin now. He glanced at Flint. "What's going on?"

Flint pulled him back to the girl's side and explained what they had all witnessed in the cavern.

As he listened, Kast found it harder and harder to breathe in the moist cavern air. "Are you saying I changed into this dragon . . . this Ragnar'k?" Disbelief was thick in his throat.

Flint ignored him. "Child, how did you trigger the transformation?"

She refused to look Kast in the face. "I touched him—" She waved her fingers, almost apologetically. "—on his tattoo."

Moris spoke next. "It makes an odd bit of sense. They were oath-bonded when Ragnar'k merged with them. His essence must have been caught up in the spell."

"Touch!" Flint added, his expression wide with sudden understanding. "Ragnar'k vanished back into the tattoo once the girl dismounted from his shoulders. Just as touching is necessary to maintain the original oath-bond, it must be necessary to keep the dragon in the flesh." Flint turned to Sy-wen. "Can you call him forth again?"

Sy-wen took a step away.

Kast was too stunned to move. He did not know how to wrap his mind around the idea that some dragon lay inside him.

The boy Joach, fingering the mage's staff in his hands, asked a question that must have been in all their minds. "Why do you want the dragon back?"

"I want his blood," Flint said simply, as if it were obvious. "I believe Ragnar'k's blood might cure Conch."

Sy-wen's nervous fear faded. "Do you think . . . Conch might live?"

"The mer'ai use dragon's blood to heal wounds, do they not?" Flint kept his voice calm and quiet.

Sy-wen nodded, then shot a quick glance at Kast. "But I can't ask him . . . ask him to become that dragon again. What if he gets stuck that way?"

The same thought had been rolling in Kast's own head. He balked at letting the beast take him over again. What if it refused to return to the tattoo?

Then Sy-wen's eyes found his own. He watched hope and fear mix in her eyes. She refused to ask this of him, but her silence was stronger than a thousand pleaded words.

Kast reached out to her and grabbed her hand. His haste made his fingers rough. He did not want to retreat from his decision. "Do it," he said, and pulled her fingers toward his neck.

She resisted at first, struggling to free her wrist.

He stared her in the eye, and suddenly old words, buried deeper than flesh, appeared in his mind: *There will come a day when we will call you again to our sides, again to be our sharks above the water. Do you make this oath willingly and bind your people to us?*

He answered aloud in the old tongue of his people. "My blood is yours to cast upon the seas."

She started at his words. He could see something stir in her, her expression glazing over. Their two peoples were forever linked by blood oaths, promised words, and ancient magicks. He saw an ancient midnight sea appear in her eyes. "Thank you," she whispered, no longer resisting him.

He let her wrist free, and she reached to touch him.

Sighing, he closed his eyes.

Her fingers touched his skin—and he was gone.

Sy-wen sat atop the dragon again, its flesh hot through her thin leggings. The others had scattered to all sides as, at her touch, Ragnar'k had unfolded and spread around and under her, lifting her atop his scaled back. She looked down upon the others and could not clearly explain the tears that trailed down her cheeks.

Sy-wen, the dragon whispered to her, almost a purr, as if tasting her name on his tongue. *Bonded.*

She found one of her hands reaching to rub his neck, finding the spot Conch liked scratched.

Good. Fingers good. The dragon stirred under her, then . . . *Others are here.* The dreamspeak held a note of menace.

"They're friends."

He seemed to accept her statement, changing his attention quickly. *Hungry. Blood scent strong.* Sniffing, the dragon's snout lowered and swung toward the lake. His voice boomed in her head. *Little dragon will taste good.*

Sy-wen noted with alarm that it was referring to Conch. Cannibalism among seadragons was not unknown. "No, the little dragon is a friend, too."

Flint approached closer to them, Moris at his side. "Sy-wen, can you explain to Ragnar'k what we want?" Flint asked. "I think you'll have to convince him."

Sy-wen swallowed hard. "Ragnar'k, the little dragon is hurt and needs help."

His fierceness and hot hunger touched her. *Pain strong. I will eat the little dragon, and it will not hurt anymore.*

Sy-wen tightened her voice. "No. I wish him healed. Your blood will help the little dragon."

An intense feeling of irritation and exasperation entered her from the dragon, but she also sensed resignation and acceptance. *Bonded,* he said simply, acknowledging her wish.

She waved Flint over. "He'll do it."

Flint drew a blade, but Ewan was at his side and pushed the old man's hand down. "I have a bleeding lance," he said, his eyes huge as he stared at the great beast. "It will leave less of a wound."

Nodding, Flint waved the healer forward.

"Grab two of those pots," Ewan ordered. "That should be enough to help the seadragon."

Sy-wen watched the healer cautiously approach the thick neck of the beast. He mumbled something under his breath about drawings in old texts. He slipped a long, slender glass tube wrapped in cotton from a pouch at his waist. One of its tapered ends came to a sharp point.

He raised an eye questioningly toward Sy-wen. "Tell him this will hurt a bit."

Pain?

"He can hear you."

Ewan laid a hand on the great beast's neck. The dragon flinched under the girl. She soothed him, both with her hands and with messages of calm.

Searching landmarks on Ragnar'k's neck, the healer finally positioned his glass lance. "Are you ready?"

Sy-wen probed the dragon and nodded.

He struck fast and sure, deep under a thumb-size scale.

Sy-wen gasped and swatted at her own neck. It felt like the sting of a sea nettle. The dragon did not flinch, though his eyes closed a bit, indicating he felt the prick. Sy-wen rubbed at her neck. So she shared more than just his thoughts.

She watched the bright red blood flow down the glass funnel into the awaiting bowl that Flint held. In a short span, both bowls were brimming full. "That's enough," Ewan finally said, withdrawing the glass lance. He pressed his fist against the wound.

Moris and Flint each held a pot of dragon's blood. "What do we do with this? Smear it on Conch's wounds?"

"No," the healer said. He removed his fist from the dragon's neck, then leaned closer to inspect his handiwork. He nodded in satisfaction and with a final pat on the dragon's neck turned to face the others. He sighed loudly. "According to old texts on the mer'ai, the other seadragon must drink the blood."

"Great," Flint said with a frown.

With a shrug, Moris led the way into the shallows. The boy went with them.

It all went smoothly. Just the scent of blood revived the dying dragon. Conch raised his head as the men approached with the two pots. He slurped hungrily at the thickening blood as the pots were dumped between his sharp fangs. Flint and the boy helped hold Conch's head up as he drank. Soon both bowls were empty.

"Is that enough?" Sy-wen asked as Conch searched the dregs left in each pot with a long tongue.

My blood is strong, Ragnar'k answered her.

His words proved true. In only a scatter of heartbeats, Conch was able to raise his neck fully from the beach. He even struggled to get his forelegs under him. His injured wings shook and spread, knocking the boy into the water.

"Look at its chest wound," Ewan exclaimed. "The edges pull together like a summer flower's petals at night."

"Is he going to live?" Sy-wen asked with her breath held.

My blood is strong, Ragnar'k repeated, an edge of scorn at her doubts.

Conch piped loudly, trumpeting his returning strength. His nostril flaps opened wide as he drew air deep into his chest. He slid back into the lake until he floated its surface like a dragon-prowed ship.

Flint stared out at him. "He'll live. He should be able to dive safely now and return to your people's leviathan."

"Then we can go?" Sy-wen asked, beginning to slide from her perch.

Flint held up a hand. "Conch can go." He turned his intense eyes upon her. "But, Sy-wen, you are bonded now, to Ragnar'k. It is time to let Conch return to his own bonded."

"My mother . . ."

"Yes, Ragnar'k has another path to take. You sense this, don't you?"

She lowered her head. How she wanted to deny the old man. But Kast's words echoed in her head: *My blood is yours to cast upon the seas.* She somehow knew they were not to be parted. She, Kast, and Ragnar'k were bound tighter than the strongest iron chain.

"Where do we go then?" she asked timidly.

Flint scratched the thin gray hair atop his head. "We need a place to rest and collect ourselves. I have a home on the Blisterberry Cliffs south of Port Rawl on the coast. It's not far from the Blasted Shoals. I chose it for its isolation. It should prove a good place to plan."

"Plan for what?"

Moris answered her. "For the Battle of A'loa Glen, the opening rally against the darkness that has overtaken Alasea. Prophecy said Ragnar'k would unite your two people—Dre'rendi and mer'ai—and forge a mighty army. It is this legion upon which the fate of both A'loa Glen and all of Alasea will rest."

Hungry, the dragon sent, interrupting them. Sy-wen felt an echoing gnaw in her own belly.

"We should be going," Flint said.

Sy-wen prepared to dismount, but again the old seaman held up a hand. "Perhaps it would be best if Kast stayed as Ragnar'k for now. The skiff is small and will fit only a few people. If you rode Ragnar'k . . ."

Hesitating, she chewed her lower lip.

Sea feeds dragon, Ragnar'k argued.

She was outnumbered and reluctantly nodded her agreement.

The dragon did not wait. Scuffling over the pebbled beach, his claws dug deep, and he slid smoothly into the water. She slipped her feet into the folds by his forelimbs. He was so much bigger than

Conch that she could barely reach them. But once she was in place, he tightened his folds snugly, holding her firm against his back.

He swam closer to Conch, who waited in the center of the lake. The two dragons eyed each other warily.

Little, very little dragon.

Sy-wen bristled a bit at Ragnar'k's insult of her friend. "He brought me to you. He almost died saving me."

I saved him with my blood. Now even.

Sy-wen frowned and let the subject drop. By now, the skiff was rowing toward them. Flint, Moris, and the boy shared the boat. Sy-wen glanced behind her and saw Ewan waving to them from shore.

Flint caught her look. "He wanted to stay. He hopes to help from the inside." Sy-wen saw the worried look in the old man's eyes. He waved her on.

Moris was at the oars. He had his robe pulled down to his waist to free his hugely muscled arms and shoulders. He had the skiff skimming behind the two dragons as Flint manned the rudder.

Flint called to her. "Sy-wen, can you let Conch know where we're going? Would he be able to tell your mother?"

"Yes, I can have him tell my mother the name of the place. But why?"

"For her to send an emissary there to meet with us. It is time for the mer'ai to return to the shores again."

Sy-wen nodded. She would do as he asked and so signaled Conch closer to her, but she doubted her mother would listen or respond. Her people had drifted so long in the Great Deep that lan'dwellers and the world of rock were no longer a concern to them.

She told Conch the message for her mother as they traveled the sea tunnel. Occasionally the rock walls around them would shake, and the sea would swell with tiny, agitated waves.

But the walls held long enough for them to reach the end of the channel and escape the tunnel.

Bright, Ragnar'k commented on the day's sun. Sy-wen stared out at the sunken city. A large, leaning sculpture of a woman in a flowing robe greeted her as she glided free of the bay. The statue seemed to be staring at her with sad eyes. It seemed as if days had passed since she had entered the sea tunnel with Kast and Flint.

In silence, they glided past the towers and half-submerged domes of A'loa Glen, winding themselves away from a city that now faced a greater menace than the creeping sea: a corruption that would swallow the island whole. No one dared speak lest the darkness reach out to them.

Once free of the city and into deeper water, Moris ran out the sail with the help of the boy and then led the way. Sy-wen only had a brief moment to say her good-byes to Conch; Ragnar'k would not let him even close enough to nuzzle her extended palm. With slightly wounded eyes, her mother's dragon swung from her and sank below the waves.

She had been right. By bonding, she had lost a part of her that would never return.

Hunt now. The dragon rolled a huge black eye at her.

Flint must have heard Ragnar'k, too.

"Let him eat!" he called out to her. "We've a long way to go!"

She waved her acknowledgment. Slipping the dragon's breathing siphon from between the blades of his shoulders, she slipped it to her lips. She patted Ragnar'k three times on the neck, indicating she was ready, then realized this was Conch's old signal. But Ragnar'k sensed the meaning behind the motion and dove.

Her inner lids blinked up as she leaned closer to his neck. She watched Ragnar'k stretch to his full length and marveled at his size. He had to be over three times as large as Conch. His black wings were rippling shadows to either side.

Ah, good water, good hunting . . .

She found herself drifting into the dragon's senses. Just as she had felt the jab of Ewan's glass lance when he drew Ragnar'k's blood, now she experienced the rush of water over scale, the varied scents mixed in the sea: squid ink, spoor of a school of yellowfin, even the tang of poison from a nest of sea snakes. She heard the echoes of distant whales in the water and, closer still, the noisy chatter of porpoises. She also sensed the strength in his body, his wings, to move with such grace and power. She gloried in the new sensations.

How blind she had been to the sea before!

Then a new scent was shared with her. It smelled like the finest rare perfume her mother wore. What was it?

Ragnar'k answered her: *Shark's blood.*

She cringed lower to the dragon's back. Suddenly Ragnar'k darted to the left. Sy-wen, sharing his mind, knew his move in advance and compensated by shifting her weight. He spun suddenly over a ribbed reef line and, snaking his neck down, jabbed his muzzle into the black shadows. He snapped his head back, a young male rockshark trapped in his fanged jaws.

In a flurry of razored teeth, the shark was shredded into pieces that could be swallowed. Ragnar'k skimmed the area, collecting every morsel. Sy-wen did not urge him otherwise. She savored the kill, the taste of blood in her throat, the satisfaction of a full belly. But mostly, she enjoyed how she and the dragon were united: one heart, one mind, one will.

She wanted to experience more.

The dragon sensed her wish. *I will show you more.* He, too, enjoyed the union. *Come see, come see . . .*

Suddenly he sped in a tight, dizzying circle, flaring out his wings, then shot away.

She saw where he intended to go!

Laughter echoed in her head, but she could not tell if it was her own or the dragon's.

Did it really matter anyway?

JOACH SAT IN THE PROW OF THE SKIFF. THE HUGE DRAGON AND THE GIRL had been gone a while now. Moris had kept the sails slack, waiting as the dragon fed. The sun beat warmly on his face. It seemed like forever since he had enjoyed the warmth of the sun.

Flint spoke behind him near the rudder. "What's keepin' the dang girl? We don't have all day waiting for the dragon to fill its belly. We've still a lot of sea to cross to reach port."

Moris just grunted, winding rope into perfect coils at his feet.

Joach did not care if they took the whole day. He stretched his body across the prow, the darkmage's staff across his knees, and worshiped the sun. He silently prayed that somewhere, across the many lands of Alasea, Elena was enjoying the same sun. He closed his eyes, dreaming his sister safe.

For now, the sun drained all his worries away.

Suddenly, an explosive eruption blew from the water near the boat. Joach jerked up, a cry of surprise on his lips. The boat rocked back as a huge swell caught the prow. He rolled toward the bow just as the dragon lunged from the water only a few spans from the boat.

It shot its entire length clear of the water, a tower of sinuous dragon displayed against the sun.

With an explosive beat of its huge wings, the black dragon swung in the air. It twisted and banked, revealing the girl on its back. With another beat, it sailed into the air. It winged high above the tiny skiff, a huge black shadow against the sun. From its glossy scales, sparks of brilliance outlined its flight. Its jaws were open, and a huge roar flowed from its throat.

It was not a cry of challenge, but of joy.

It headed west toward the coast.

From the stunned expressions of the two brothers, it seemed something else had been hidden from their prophetic visions.

Ragnar'k was more than just a dragon of the *sea*.

"I'm getting too old for all these surprises," Flint mumbled as they all stared at the receding dragon.

Book Five

SWAMP WIT'CH

25

At dawn, Elena stood at the edge of the towering cliff. She stared down at the fog-shrouded landscape far below. It was as if the world ended here at the Landslip. For as far as she could see, roiling mists spread to all the horizons, a dirty white blanket that hid the swamps and bogs of the Drowned Lands. Nearby, a hushed roar echoed in her ears from where the stream they had been following for three days cascaded over the rocky lip. Its waters fell in sprays and torrents to disappear into the blanket of mists.

Mycelle stepped beside her, Fardale at her heels. "Er'ril has the horses ready."

"Aunt My, you've not spoken much about what to expect below."

The older woman placed a hand on her shoulder. "It's difficult to describe. It truly must be seen to be understood. It is a harsh land, but not without its own dark beauty."

Elena turned her back on the sight and followed Mycelle to where the trio of horses stood saddled, their packs secured. They would not be riding the horses along the narrow trail that led down the cliff face. The grade was too steep and the switchbacks too sharp—a slip of hoof could kill both horse and rider. From here, they would walk the horses.

The trailhead was only a quarter league from the waterfall.

Er'ril finished stamping out their campfire and crossed to join them.

"How's your arm?" he asked Elena—as he had every morning for the past five days since they had left Shadowbrook.

She sighed in exasperation. "It's fine. The moss has not spread any farther."

Mycelle tried to deflect Er'ril's continuing worry. "Why do you keep asking? As I said before, as long as she doesn't use her magick, the vines will stay quiet."

Er'ril grumbled under his breath. "It harms no one to ask." He gave one final survey of the night's campsite, then waved them on. "Let's be off while the light is still early. It's a good day's trek down the cliff."

Mycelle nodded, apparently concurring with his assessment. With her crossed scabbards in place, she led the way with her golden-maned gelding. Elena had learned his name was Grisson, a fierce-hearted horse loyal to Mycelle's every word.

Elena followed behind with Mist. The small gray mare seemed a pony compared to the two larger mounts, especially Er'ril's dappled steppe stallion, who guarded their rear.

"C'mon, Horse," Er'ril urged. He had not bothered naming the beast. He simply called him "Horse." Still, this seemed to satisfy the stallion, and the mount responded well to his orders. The stallion followed the plainsman without even a tug on the lead.

Such was not the case with Mist. As long as no one was in Mist's saddle, the horse felt no compulsion to resist grazing. She kept grabbing at stalks and leaves from bushes at the forest's edge as they marched in file toward the trail head. Elena had to tug repeatedly on the mare's lead to keep her moving.

Soon they reached the beginning of the cliff trail.

Mycelle glanced back. "The path from here is steep, but there are generally few stones to trick a hoof or a heel. Move with care and keep an eye to the trail."

Elena nodded.

Fardale, surefooted and quick, took the lead. And so they began the day's journey down the face of the Landslip. It was a slow trek, but even the plodding pace wore on the nerves. The anxious horses nickered continuously at the drop by the trail's edge, seeming to sense the long fall that awaited a misstep. As Mycelle had stated, there were few loose stones on the path, but the rock was damp from the mists that rose from the swamps at night, and care had to be taken with each step. Occasionally alcoves in the cliff face offered spots to rest where the horses could back away from the cliff's edge and the party could sit and rub sore knees and calves.

At one of these small caves, Er'ril ran a hand along the stone wall of the alcove. "This has been dug out," he said. "Who built these way stations?"

"Swampers," Mycelle said. "A rangy and hardy lot that thrive at the edges of the Drowned Lands. They trade in wares collected from the swamps: medicinal herbs grown only in the bogs, the scaled skins of the swamp creatures, feathers from exotic birds, a variety of poisons."

"Poisons?" Elena asked.

"Yes, that's one of the reasons I initially traveled here: to study their art of poison. It was during my first journey here that I sensed the strong elemental force—a sly, fierce wit'ch—lurking deep in the swamps. Swampers tell tales of her: how strange, naked children would be seen moving through desolate areas of the bogs, but when approached, they would simply vanish. Occasionally one of these swamp children would even enter their raft camps, seeking information. Such a child was once caught and caged, but the next morning, only a mound of moss and vines was found in the trap."

Elena's face grew worried with the stories. She scratched at her left arm. Mycelle noticed the motion.

"And these caves?" Er'ril persisted.

"Built by the swampers. This is one of their trade routes to the upper lands."

Er'ril nodded, seemingly content with the explanation. For once, Elena was glad when Er'ril called them to move along. She had had enough talk for one day.

So the day wore on. By noon, the summer sun had dried the stone trail, making it easier to march, but the rays beat mercilessly upon them. Exposed on the barren cliff face, there was no relief, no shade, no cool streams to bathe a face. By late afternoon, they welcomed the swamp mists that eventually enveloped the lower trails. The sun's intense rays were finally quieted, and the heat's edge was dampened, but their relief was short-lived. As they worked farther down the trail, the moisture in the air became oppressive. Clothes clung; sweat ran in rivers down their faces. The deeper fog seemed to collect the summer's heat and trap it down here. Even breathing became oppressive, not only from the moist heat, but also from the rotting smell of the swamps.

"Swamp gas," Mycelle explained as she noticed Elena's curled nose. "You'll get used to it."

Elena scowled, doubting she ever would. She breathed through her mouth as she walked the last leg of the trail down the Landslip.

Even Fardale seemed bothered by the stink. He sent her an image of a skunk spraying a trail. She had to concur.

Soon they reached the bottom of the cliff, and the ground spread out before them. Finally being able to separate from one another was a relief. The mists had a certain suffocating feeling, and a bit of free space lessened the cloying sense.

Elena glanced around her. The late-afternoon light, blocked by the vapors, seemed more like a strange yellow twilight, giving all she saw a sickly cast. Ahead of her, the cliff's base was a tumble of rock and soil. A few scraggly bushes with huge thorns dotted the landscape. Farther ahead, hazed by the mists, was a shadowy wall of darkness, a huge slumbering beast hidden in the fog. Strange birds called from there, and unseen creatures croaked and splashed. Elena suddenly knew what lay ahead, recognizing the slumbering beast for what it was.

It was the swamp.

Over her shoulder, the towering cliffs of the Landslip disappeared into the mists. There was no retreat.

Suddenly Fardale began a low, throaty growl. At the wolf's warning, swords appeared in Mycelle's and Er'ril's fists.

A figure appeared out of the mists, seeming to detach from the greater darkness ahead. As the swamp vapors shifted, it was clear that the shadowy form was simply a man. Dressed in knee-high boots of a scaly gray leather and outfitted in a tight-fitted jacket made of some strange oily material, he approached their party. Elena cringed back. He was a youngish man with his head shaved to a coarse black stubble. Above a broken nose, his eyes were oddly slanted in a continual squint. But what startled and honestly frightened her was that the side of his face was a boiled mass of scars. One ear was gone, and the left edge of his upper lip was caught in the scars and drawn up in a perpetual sneer.

Mycelle's reaction was the opposite of Elena's. She sheathed her swords and dashed forward to scoop the man up in her arms. "Jaston! Sweet Mother, what are you doing here?" Before he could answer, she swung to face Elena and Er'ril, one arm still around the scarred man. "This is Jaston, the guide who led me into the swamp before."

Elena remembered the story. This was the man who had almost

given his life during Mycelle's first attempt to hunt the wit'ch. She stared at his ruined face. Such is the fate of those who venture too deep into the swamps, it seemed to warn.

Mycelle swung back to face the man. "What are you doing here, Jaston?" she repeated.

His attempt at a smile drew a shudder from Elena. His words did nothing to calm her misgivings. "The swamp wit'ch sent me."

By midnight, the blood hunter reached the deserted campsite beside the stream. The d'warf bent to sniff at the scattered ashes of the dead hearth. It stank of the wit'ch, a lingering scent no older than a half a day. Torwren straightened and stepped toward the cliff's edge ahead. He raised his nose to the breeze rising from the swamps. Poison, the winds cautioned, and decay. In the snatches of gusts, the swamp warned all away with threats of death.

Torwren crouched at the lip of the towering cliff. His red eyes tried to pierce the blanket of mists below. With the sun's setting, the swamp's shroud began to rise, reclaiming the sun-baked cliffs.

As he sat still, his stone skin began to harden. Over the past day, the stiffening grew worse with each idle moment. It was the curse of the Dark Lord: If he stopped for too long, the stone would stop flowing, and he would be trapped in an ebon'stone shell forever. To make matters worse, this sluggish effect was more pronounced if he did not feed. The stone was always hungry for human blood, and it had been two days since he had feasted on a fresh heart. But traveling through such isolated lands south of Shadowbrook had offered little chance to slake this ravenous thirst. As punishment, his skin grew sluggish whenever he paused, warning him against slowing his pursuit of the wit'ch and scolding him for not feeding.

Torwren straightened with difficulty from his crouch. He moved his limbs, bending his knees and working his arms. Slowly the stone gave way, and he found movement less of a struggle.

He sniffed at the air. The wit'ch's scent traveled east along the cliff's edge. He followed the trail, smelling the musky scent of horse, wolf, and the two others who traveled with the wit'ch. One reeked vaguely of poison, almost like the swamp. The other gave off a scent that seemed a mix of Standi loam and forged iron. His nose wrinkled at the scent: a most ancient iron.

He shook his head and continued on his hunt. In less than a league, the scent trail led to a path that headed down. He stopped. He had been sure she intended to follow the Landslip all the way to the coast. Why were they heading into the Drowned Lands? Why risk the fanged, slithering beasts of the endless bogs and fens? For a moment, a worry ran through his heart. Did they know they were being followed? Were they thinking to lose him among the thousand scents of the swamplands?

Impossible. They could not know he followed.

The black d'warf continued toward the trail, having to force his stubborn legs to obey after even such a brief stop. He must feed soon. Even this thought sped his legs down the narrow trail as night fully descended upon the Drowned Lands below.

The blood hunter did not need sunlight to guide his stone legs. The dire flames in his eyes lit his path. Nothing would stop his pursuit of the wit'ch.

Yet, somewhere deep inside the ebon'stone shell, wrapped tight around the white elemental flame that fed the black magicks of the blood hunter, laughter echoed up. A tiny sliver of the old Torwren, powerless and trapped from interfering, eavesdropped on the thoughts and actions of this creature forged by the Black Heart. The d'warf lord had sought to craft a cadre of ill'guard soldiers bent to his own will, ill'guard who could do what Torwren could not: who could free the Try'sil from its prison. He had failed and become an ill'guard himself instead. He laughed, not at the irony of this situation but at where the blood hunter was heading. How could he have anticipated such a twist of fate?

With this thought, he remembered his father's sage words: *Look no farther than your own nose for answers to your prayers.*

How blind he had been!

Deep inside the blood hunter, wild laughter accompanied the creature down the cliffs of the Landslip.

AMID GLOWPOTS THAT KEPT THE NIGHT'S INSECTS AT BAY, ELENA SAT cross-legged upon a woven reed mat and eyed the platter of odd fruit placed before her. Er'ril and Mycelle sat to either side of her, while Fardale hung a bit back. Elena did not know what to make of this offering. She had never seen such fruit and could not even fathom how to eat some of the weird-skinned fare. Did you peel that green bulbous gourd or just bite into it? And what of that fruit shaped like a star?

Elena glanced to their host. Jaston was pouring an equally strange brew into mugs before his guests. By the light of the lanterns, the scarring of their host's face appeared even worse. It was a storm on his skin, a roiling mix of wrinkled pink flesh streaked with white bands. Elena kept her eyes averted as Jaston left to retrieve the last of their meal. He must have sensed her discomfort and had raised a hood to shadow his face.

Er'ril, his brows dark, scrutinized the man as he left. The trip from the cliffs to Jaston's home had been a strained journey for Er'ril. Jaston had refused to explain further about his startling statement that the swamp wit'ch had sent him to meet them. "The story is long and best told over dinner," he had said, then turned to lead them away. Only Mycelle's insistence that Jaston could be trusted had finally convinced Er'ril to follow. Even so, the plainsman marched with one hand on the pommel of his silver sword.

Luckily, it was not a long walk to the trading town of Drywater perched at the swamp's edge, though *town* was an odd word to describe the ramshackle accumulation of rafts that supported the crude homes of Drywater. These raft homes were interconnected in a maze of floating piers and rope bridges. A few larger homes of brick and stone were built on the firmer ground above the waters, but most of Drywater grew from the rafts themselves, lopsided dwellings of scavenged wood and woven drapes. Some were even built in the towering limbs of the monstrous cypress trees that overhung the town, the lamps in their windows appearing like will-o'-the-wisps in the branches.

By the time the party had reached Drywater, true night had fallen. After leaving their horses in a stable at the edge of town, Jaston had led them over a network of floating piers that bobbed atop large, fibrous pods. "Bog weed," Jaston had explained, catching Elena's curious gaze at the pods. "Grows everywhere, but we plant it throughout Drywater to help keep us afloat. Won't do to sink in these waters."

With only these words, he had continued leading them through the maze of piers and bridges. As they traveled, Jaston would wave a hand to occasional fellow townsmen, a wary-eyed bunch with features worn hard by the swamp. But these rough men were not the only denizens of Drywater. A few children peered from behind drapes as the strangers passed. Somewhere a dog barked a warning, seeming to scent the wolf among their party.

Around them, as they had slipped through the outskirts of Drywater, the swamp awakened with nightfall, a cacophony of croaking, hissing, and the nesting calls of birds.

Even now, as they settled to a late meal on Jaston's home raft, the chorus of the swamps continued unabated. Occasionally something larger would grumble from deeper in the swamps, hushing the chorus for a short time. Elena knew from the quality of the sound that it echoed from far over the waters. Elena shivered. For the beast to make such a far-reaching cry, it must be huge. She noticed even their host's face would darken whenever this creature howled through the darkness.

As full night swallowed them up, the lights of Drywater began to dwindle around them, lamp by lamp, until only a scattering of lanterns dotted the maze of the town. Somewhere nearby a woman was singing softly to the night. She sang in a language Elena did not recognize. Some lullaby, Elena supposed from the mellow sweetness of the singer's voice, though the melody had a melancholy strain to it. The song touched upon the worries Elena had for her companions abandoned in Shadowbrook.

She spoke her concerns to Er'ril, keeping her voice low. "Do you think the others found Meric?"

"If the elv'in's still alive, they'll discover his whereabouts. Kral's an excellent tracker, and Tol'chuk has a keen nose."

Mycelle patted the girl's knee. She nibbled on a thick-skinned fruit with a purplish flesh. "In a moon, we will know. Once we're through the swamps, I'll go to Port Rawl and seek them out."

Elena lowered her face. She wished she knew now what had befallen their companions.

The wooden planks swayed slightly as Jaston returned to them, his arms laden with another platter. The smell of roasting meat momentarily drove away her worries. Jaston knelt upon his own mat and placed the tray next to the others.

Even Er'ril, who had remained sullen and cautious around Jaston, sat up a bit straighter. "What's that?" he asked with his usual manners.

Jaston smiled, his scars twisting the effect into a gruesome sight. "Filet of swamp python."

Fingers that had been reaching for the meat paused.

Jaston stared, baffled at their hesitation. "It's fresh," he assured them.

Mycelle reached for a slice of the steaming python first. "And if I remember, you know just the right way to prepare it. Not too spicy, but with just a touch of tarragon." From Jaston's blushing and sudden concentration on dishing out some boiled root, there was some hidden meaning behind this memory. Mycelle turned to them, the ghost of a smile on her own lips. "Try it. It's quite good. Tastes much like spring quail."

Er'ril used his knife to stab a slice of meat and flop it on his own plate. Hunger drove Elena to do the same. She watched Er'ril cautiously sample a bite first, and only after seeing his satisfied nod did she nibble at the tender offering. The seasonings and sweetness of the meat were quite a surprise. Elena needed no further encouragement to devour the remainder of her slice.

Mycelle passed a slice to Fardale, who swallowed the sample in one bite. In silence, they consumed their meal, hands reaching for more. Fardale nudged Elena's elbow with his nose, and she tossed him another slab.

Jaston, his eyes wary, stared as the wolf devoured the meat. Mycelle had already explained about Fardale, but the revelation of his shape-shifting nature had not lessened the man's concern.

Er'ril was on his fourth slice before he finally brought up the question that had been nagging him. "Jaston, your hospitality has been most generous." He wiped at his chin with the back of his hand. "But we need to know about this swamp wit'ch, and why you claimed that she told you to meet us by the cliffs."

Jaston lowered his mug. "It is no claim. Just this day, one of her swamp children, naked and filthy, appeared on one of the outlying rafts of Drywater. The child asked to speak to me." This last statement was said with baffled confusion. "When I came, the boy told that visitors would be arriving at the Landslip and that I was to meet them. Then when my back was turned, the child vanished. Not knowing what his message heralded, I decided to obey. I had no idea why I was chosen for this duty until I saw Mycelle standing by the cliffs. The two of us had searched for the wit'ch several winters back." His fingers wandered to his scarred face. "The wit'ch obviously knew of our connection."

"And this child told you nothing else?" Er'ril asked.

"He had one message from the wit'ch." Jaston glanced to the darkness beyond the lanterns and glowpots. "By dawn's light, you must enter the swamp. And I . . . I'm to guide you."

Mycelle spoke up. "We'd thought to rest a day before facing the swamp. We've journeyed hard and fast to reach here."

Jaston shrugged. "That was the message: by dawn's light."

The pleasant taste of python had soured in Elena's mouth. "How . . . how did she know we were coming?" she asked.

"I suspect," Mycelle answered, "that it has something to do with the vines on your arm. Its magick must be like a beacon to the wit'ch, marking our progress."

"Then there is no way to surprise the wit'ch in her lair," Er'ril said sullenly.

Jaston answered his concern. "If the wit'ch does not want to be found, you'll never find her among the swamps, let alone get a chance to surprise her."

Er'ril frowned at the truth in his words.

"It does not matter anyway," Mycelle declared forcefully. "I suspect the wit'ch will not hide from us nor harm us on the journey. She wants Elena for some reason, marking her with the vines to ensure she comes."

"And what about after we find her?" Er'ril asked. "What then?"

No one answered. Around them, the swamp croaked and growled. After a hushed few moments, Er'ril cleared his throat. "If we are to leave at sunrise, perhaps the women should get some sleep. Jaston and I will make preparations for our departure."

"No need," Jaston said. "After the message from the swamp child, I prepared for a trek, just in case. I have my pole boat already outfitted for the trip."

"Good," Er'ril said, standing, "then let's check out your supplies."

Mycelle still sat on her mat. "There is no need for that, Er'ril. Jaston is an experienced swamprat. He knows better than you what we'll need on this journey."

Er'ril's cheeks darkened with her words. "I'd still like to see for myself." He glanced at Jaston's scars. "Even an experienced swamp-rat can make mistakes."

Now it was Jaston's back that stiffened, but he kept himself civil. "If the plainsman wishes to see how I've stocked my boat," he said in a clipped tone, "he is more than welcome." Jaston led the way.

Mycelle persisted. "Jaston, there is no need to bow and scrape to this . . . this buffoon."

Jaston pulled his hood farther over his head. "It is only a short walk to the boat."

The two men left with Fardale trailing behind them while Mycelle scowled at their backs. "Men," she grumbled under her breath. Then, with a loud sigh, she turned to Elena. "We should get as much sleep as we can. Tomorrow will be a hard day."

Elena nodded. She wondered silently when a day wouldn't be hard.

Mycelle helped her spread their bedrolls on the deck near Jaston's one-room shack. The woman frowned at Jaston's home. Its walls leaned as if about to topple, and the drapes in the single window were tattered and threadbare. "Once he had a much finer house," she muttered sadly. "He's not done well for himself since I last saw him."

"Why's that?" Elena asked, rolling out her bedding.

Her response seemed to startle Mycelle, as if her aunt had not known she had been speaking aloud. She shook her head and joined Elena. "I'm afraid it's my fault. I should not have tried to reach the wit'ch before. But he was such a brave swamp tracker, full of pride and quick smiles that disarmed my trepidations. His scarring—" One hand waved to her own face. "—should have been mine. He saved me by sacrificing himself to the poison spit forth from the jaws of the king adder." She lowered her face. "I dragged him back to Drywater and helped heal him, but a part of him died out there."

Elena paused in opening her roll. "What do you mean?"

"I've seen him looking at the swamp. He used to love the swamp like a man loves a woman. He knew all her secret paths and faces. He showed me sights that took my breath away: ponds of glowing algae in a rainbow of colors, areas where the waters steamed and bubbled to soothe sore muscles, regions where moss grew so thick on water that one could walk on it. One time, on one of those beds, we even made . . ." Mycelle's soft smile dissolved as she realized to whom she was speaking. "But now it scares him, unmans him. I suspect the reason for his poor dwelling has something to do with this fear. A swamper will not fare well if his livelihood frightens him."

Elena remembered how his face had darkened with the grumbling of the large swamp beast, the spark of fear in his eyes. "Why doesn't he just leave?"

She shrugged. "I wager his scarring had something to do with that decision. He was once a handsome man." Mycelle must have seen the doubt in her eyes. "He truly was. I think his wounds reached deeper than just the skin. He hides here now, fearing to leave, fearing to stay."

Elena wondered at her words. "Will he be able to lead us to the wit'ch? Perhaps a less nervous guide would be better."

"No. He was chosen by the wit'ch just as surely as you were. He needs to take this journey." Still, Elena's question seemed to bother Mycelle. She turned away. "Let's rest," Mycelle said. "There'll be plenty of time to talk in the morning."

Elena did not argue. She slipped off her boots and got into her bedroll. She lay on her back beside Mycelle and pondered all she had learned that day. Overhead, the mists had lifted and thinned with nightfall. The moon and stars could be seen as vague ghosts in the skies above. To the north, the stars were cut off by the towering wall of the Landslip. In the distance, lit by moonlight, the cascade of a waterfall was a flow of silver across the black cliff face. Elena wondered if it was the same stream they had followed to the Landslip. As she watched, the foggy veil shifted. Suddenly a soft glowing arc of moonlight crested the mists of the falls.

Mycelle must have heard Elena's hushed gasp of wonder. "It's a moonbow," Mycelle explained somberly. "As I said earlier, there is much beauty hidden here, an inner magnificence that even the poisons of the swamp can't hide forever."

Elena remained silent. She knew her aunt's words did not refer just to the shining moonbow.

26

Er'ril was up before the sun's rays had even pinked the eastern skies. In truth, he had hardly slept. After returning from Jaston's boat, he had crawled into his bedroll, satisfied that their guide had outfitted them well. Still, slumber had escaped him. Instead, he had stared at the mists as the moon set, listening to the swamp's constant song.

Nagging worries kept him from rest. The journey ahead was a treacherous one, and Er'ril feared he had made the wrong choice. Why had he so readily accepted Mycelle's claim that only this swamp hag could cure Elena? He could have taken the child to A'loa Glen and let those brothers who practiced the art of healing attempt to free the bewit'ching from her. And now here was this scarred man sent to take them to the wit'ch. Er'ril had been around thousands of warriors about to go to battle. The eve of war soured many a soldier's will and heart, and Er'ril sensed that just such a weakness resided in Jaston. Er'ril had insisted on seeing the man's boat not just to recheck his supplies, but also to study the man further, away from Mycelle. He knew better than to voice such a concern to the swordswoman, since she and Jaston shared a history that seemed more than just seeker and guide, so he had pulled the man aside.

As Er'ril inspected the flat-bottomed boat, his concerns about Jaston were proven valid. Besides stocking the boat with more weapons than seemed necessary, the man was a sack full of jitters. Any sudden noise jolted him, and when Er'ril accidentally brushed against his side, the man jumped back as if stung. There was no doubt that Jaston bore a timid heart and would fare poorly as a guide on such a risky journey.

So, after returning from the boat, Er'ril lay awake in his bedroll and pondered his choices. He could either follow this frightened man into the swamps or leave with Elena in the morning and travel by horse along the Landslip to the coast. As he weighed his options, the moon set, and the stars to the east winked out. Finally, he fled his useless bedroll and faced the approaching morning, no closer to answering his nighttime questions.

He stepped carefully around his sleeping companions. Fardale, ever vigilant, raised his head, his eyes bright in the night, but Er'ril waved him back down and crossed to the darkened rear of the raft. As he relieved his bladder over the side, someone cleared his throat behind him—not in warning, but simply announcing his presence. Er'ril glanced over his shoulder to see a smoldering pipe glowing in the deeper shadows behind Jaston's dwelling.

"It's only me," the man said. Er'ril recognized the scarred man's voice. "Dawn's still a bit away, plainsman. You could have slept longer. I would've woken you with the sun's rising."

Er'ril finished and crossed to where Jaston sat in the shadows with his pipe. He leaned one hand against the wall; the wood groaned and tilted under his weight. "I couldn't sleep anyway," Er'ril said gruffly. From the other man's clothes and tired voice, he doubted Jaston had slept either.

"The swamp does that to you. It's a constant presence. Even when you shut your eyes, it still paints itself in your mind's eye with its noises." A small shudder passed through the man.

Er'ril slid down the wall to sit beside Jaston. The man offered a puff from his pipe. Er'ril accepted and drew a long, slow drag from its stem. The smoke settled like an old friend in his chest. It was good Standi tobacco, an expensive leaf—the best he had sampled in a long time. Considering the state of Jaston's living quarters, Er'ril suspected that tobacco of this quality was a rare treat for the swamp man. He passed the pipe back and reluctantly let the smoke loose from his lungs in a long, low sigh. "Mighty fine leaf," he said.

An awkward silence arose between them until Jaston finally spoke. "I know what you're thinking, plainsman. I saw your face earlier. Don't think I can't tell when a man has judged me worthless."

Er'ril stayed quiet. He would not lie or pretend otherwise. Elena's safety was too important for any false sentiment.

"Since I was scarred," the man continued, "I've had five winters of such looks. The other swampers smell my fear and treat me as if I lost both my legs. They wave and nod, but none will go swamping with me. These lands are not a place where you want a man whose hands tremble guarding your back."

Er'ril knew these words had festered in Jaston's chest for a long time and needed to be released before any healing could begin.

"When I was ten, my daddy was killed by an angry mother kroc'an. Tore his arm clean off the shoulder. He died before his punt could be poled back to Drywater." Jaston took a puff on his pipe, as if dredging up old memories. "Yet, even his death did not make me curse the swamp. I grew up among its sinking sands, quagmires, and bogs. They were my playground, my school, and eventually my livelihood. The swamplands became a part of me as surely as my hand or my foot. Don't get me wrong. I loved the swamp, but I never lost my respect for her poisonous side. Only a dead man ever does so. We have a saying among us swampers: 'You don't hunt the swamp, the swamp hunts you.' "

Jaston let his words sink in. The embers in his pipe glowed redder as he drew smoke deep into his chest.

"So what happened?" Er'ril finally asked.

"I've always known that life and death were a part of the swamp," he explained. "And I fully expected someday to die in its embrace. Every swamper knows she will eventually claim you." Jaston paused, pondering his pipe, then pointed to the scars on his face. "But death is easy to face. This was not."

His voice cracked as he continued speaking. "After the attack by the king adder, children shunned me, women would shudder as I passed, even men would only speak to me with their eyes cast down. I had known the swamp was a harsh mistress, but I had never suspected the true depth of her cruelty. To let me live . . . but only as this half man."

Er'ril nodded toward his own missing arm. "Not all men are whole." He began to push up from the planks. The eastern sky was beginning to blush with the approaching sun.

"Perhaps," he mumbled, "but you still have the face of a man."

Er'ril frowned and turned to leave.

Jaston grabbed at his leg. "I must go with you," he said, seeming to sense Er'ril's indecision about him. "I don't go to die . . . or to prove something to myself. I go to answer the wit'ch's call. She is said to be the heart of the swamp. Five winters ago, my life was stolen from me in a spray of poison. I will face this wit'ch and make her answer for this . . . even if it means my death."

Er'ril saw the determination in the man's eyes and heard the steel in his voice. Here was probably a glimpse of the man Jaston once had been. Still, brave words did not stoke a weak heart for long. If they were to risk the swamps, they would need some sign that this man would not become a hazard to their mission, some proof other than his mere word.

A small voice spoke from behind Er'ril, startling the plainsman. "Whatcha all doing?"

Er'ril turned around to find a small bare-assed boy standing at the raft's edge. He had a finger dug deep into one nostril. "We have to go," he said as he extracted his probing finger. "The sun's up, and a monster's coming to eat you all."

THE BLOOD HUNTER HAD REACHED THE BASE OF THE LANDSLIP JUST as the dawn's light brightened the eastern sky. Torwren paused to get a bearing on his prey's scent. The swamp filled his nostrils, trying to overwhelm his keen nose. Still, the wit'ch's magick was like a thread of silver in stone, bright and clear among the myriad odors of the Drowned Lands. Crouching, he sped along the scarp of broken rock and thorny growths at the cliff's base, his nose tracing the path.

She was close.

Though fearless, the black d'warf still moved cautiously; he did not want to spook his prey. With the sun's rising, the shadows would be few. Through the mists ahead, he saw the buildings of a ramshackle town. He followed the scent trail cautiously. It led first to a stone stable at the edge of town. Torwren smelled the horses he had been following for days. He smiled, his yellow teeth bright against his black lips. His prey were on foot now. Only the fleetness of their mounts' legs had kept the wit'ch from his grasp. Now that advantage was over.

Still, to be sure, he slipped around the edge of the building and crept toward the door. If he slew their mounts, there would be no chance of escape. He worked the door open and wormed into the stables. Instantly the horses erupted around him with whinnying cries and stamping feet. The first horse kicked savagely at its door, the crash like a thunderbolt in the narrow confines. He had to work quickly before an alarm was raised.

Torwren followed the scents to the second stall. Inside he spotted a small gray mare. A trace of the wit'ch's magick clung to it like the moss on a tree. The beast's eyes were rolled white with fear. It backed from him as he pulled open the stall's door.

He meant to step inside when a small voice rose from near his feet. "You're not supposed to be here."

Torwren glanced down to see a small human child standing in the crisp hay of the stall. He wore not a stitch of clothing. And worse yet, as filthy as the child was, he gave off no odor. The d'warf backed a step to study the boy. "Who are you?" he asked, curiosity staying his hand from snapping the child's neck. The boy's heart would make an excellent fuel for his chase.

The child removed a stem of hay from his mouth. He waved it at the hulking d'warf. "Go away. You don't belong here."

Torwren scowled. Already he had paused too long. His skin grew stiffer and his limbs sluggish from lack of blood. Curious or not, he needed to feed. He reached for the boy. But his hands ended up gripping only piles of damp moss. The boy was gone.

Shaking the slimy strands from his stone palms, he caught a whiff of magick hanging in the air. He sniffed at it, trying to capture its scent. But it faded too fast. He rubbed at his thick nose. Why did that brief whisper of magick seem familiar to him? It was like stepping into a room and suddenly getting an inkling that you had been there before.

Cursing, he backed from the stall, forcing his sluggish limbs to obey. By now, the horses were wild around him. Both the escalating noise and the strangeness of the boy drove him from the stables. The wit'ch was close. What did it matter if her horse lived? The wit'ch would never again see these stables.

Skirting the edge of town, Torwren crept toward the shadowy fringe of the swamps. Ahead, a thousand creatures woke to the morning. He meant to circle the town's border by traversing the swamp, staying cloaked by the night until he discovered where his prey hid among this maze of shacks and rafts.

But first . . .

An older woman stood near a section of trampled-down reeds at the bank of the swamp. She was busy pulling crab cages from the shallows. Her back was to him as he crept up on her. Only at the last instant did she suspect something and spin around. Her eyes widened with terror at the sight of his monstrous black form, but before her horror reached her lips, one of Torwren's fists clamped her throat. She dug at his flesh, tearing her nails on his hard skin. He did not have time to play with her. A sharp snap and the battle was over. He dragged her carcass over to the shade of a low-slung cypress.

Ripping open her chest, he fed quickly upon her. For a heart so old, it was especially tender, but perhaps his appreciation was exaggerated from supreme hunger. He feasted, then licked his fingers. Old or not, it warmed his core and loosened his limbs. The fire in him was stoked for the last leg of his long chase. He rolled the body into the water with a small splash. Let the denizens of the swamp share in his bounty.

He straightened from his crouch and wiped his hands on his belly. It felt good to feed.

Suddenly, from a branch overhead, a snake struck at his face, but its poisonous fangs broke upon the d'warf's stone skin. The bright-colored viper dropped dead onto the muddy bank of the swamp, having finally met something more lethal than its own fangs.

The d'warf ground the snake under his heel as he stepped into the swamp. Even among these treacherous lands, nothing was more poisonous than the blood hunter.

ON THE DOCK, ELENA SHIED AWAY FROM THE SWAMP CHILD. THE BOY stood shorter than Elena's waist and wore a blanket around his nakedness at Er'ril's insistence. Though he was not the same urchin who had accosted her in Shadowbrook, the boy bore a strange likeness to him. His hair was a different color, more blond than dark, and his nose was smaller, but something about his eyes marked this youngster as a sibling of the other. Like any other boy, his gaze was bright with curiosity, but behind his eyes, Elena sensed something much older staring out at her.

The boy caught her appraising study of him and stuck out his tongue.

She blinked at his insult. Before she could react further, Er'ril called to her. "Elena, join Mycelle in the boat. We need to shove off."

Backing with a final glance at the boy, she stepped toward the flat-bottomed boat. A punt, Jaston called it. To Elena, it seemed more like a small raft with short raised sides. The scarred man stood near the stern with a long pole in his hand. Bundles of supplies lay stacked at his feet.

A few onlookers hung around on neighboring docks, watching their departure and pointing to the odd boy. They all seemed to know this child was a minion of the swamp wit'ch, and they had come to see what was happening. One blunt voice echoed across the misty waters as Elena climbed aboard the punt.

"The swamp wit'ch has come to fetch Jaston," a bearded man said. "Finally she'll put the sorry bloke out of his misery."

Elena saw how these words tightened Jaston's grip on his pole. She stepped over a few swollen water flasks and crossed to join Mycelle on a seat near the bow of the boat. Her aunt, too, had stiffened with the man's words. She glared over at the bystanders as Elena sat beside her.

Fardale seemed to sense her aunt's tension and glanced back from where he stood at the prow of the punt, his front paws on the short raised rail. Mycelle patted his rump reassuringly, and he returned to monitoring the scents of the swamp ahead.

Er'ril untied the rope from a stanchion on the dock and hopped into the punt. He raised a hand to help the boy into the boat, but the child simply threw his blanket at Er'ril and stood naked on the dock.

"I don't like boats." With these words, the boy jumped into the swamp and disappeared under the green waters. Jaston began to pole away from the dock.

"Wait!" Er'ril said, his arm reaching over the side to fish for the boy. "He'll drown!"

A few chuckles arose from the neighboring raft at the plainsman's words and actions. Jaston's voice, though, was sober. "The boy is of the swamp. He cannot die."

Still Er'ril searched, his eyes determined to discover the boy's whereabouts.

"I wouldn't do that if you want to keep your last arm," Mycelle said to him. "One of the first rules Jaston taught me was to keep my limbs out of any water that wasn't clear."

Er'ril pulled away just as the back of something large and scaled humped out of the water where his arm had been. Missing its meal, the creature sank out of sight.

"Kroc'an," Jaston said. "A young one."

Eying the water with more respect, Er'ril slumped to the bench seat behind Elena. He slid out of his shirt and wrung the foul water from his soaked sleeve.

Elena watched his muscles work as he struggled one-handed with his shirt. Again, she was amazed at the smoothness of the scar that marked his shoulder. It must have been a sharp blade that cut his arm from his body. Never once during their long journey had he said how he'd lost that limb. As curious as she was about this, she found her eyes lingering on the thin layer of dark, curled hair that marked his chest and ran in a trail down his belly. Her cheeks blushed hotly when she found Er'ril's eyes on her own.

He held out his shirt. "Drape this over the bow to dry," he said.

Numbly, she took his wet garment and spread it out across the wood rail beside Fardale. The wolf sniffed at Er'ril's shirt. She was glad to find something to divert her attention.

The sharp noise of a slap, though, brought her gaze around once again. "Cursed bugs!" Er'ril slapped his palm again at his bare chest. Two spots of blood marked where he had squashed a pair of biting insects.

"Light one of the glowpots," Jaston said. "Or soon we'll be swamped with blood feeders. The heaviest swarms lurk just outside Drywater's pall of glowpot smoke."

Mycelle used a taper to snatch a flame from one of the lanterns, then lit the wick of a ceramic pot filled with perfumed wax. A curl of pungent smoke arose. Its scent reminded Elena of boiling razorleaf, used to soothe aches. She felt a sting on her neck and struck at it. Her fingers came back with a drop of blood. Another unseen insect bit her arm. Soon the boat erupted with sharp gasps and the sound of palms striking flesh. Even Fardale whined and pawed at his nose.

Only Jaston seemed unaffected as he poled them deeper into the swamps. "I've been living so long in Drywater that the smoke of its thousand glowpots has not only sunk into my skin but also into my blood," he explained. "The feeders don't much care to take a meal from a swamper, not when they have fresh targets." Elena thought she detected a hint of amusement in the man's eyes.

Grimacing, she swatted at another bite. She could not imagine traveling the entire swamp like this. Soon, though, the glowpot's smoke grew into a thin cloud about them, driving away all but the most determined insects.

Jaston continued to pole slowly through the green waters. "There's also a salve made from the herb that's in the glowpots," he said. "It's not as effective but it'll help. Once we reach one of the swifter currents, you'll need it, since we'll be moving quicker than the smoke can keep up with us."

Elena settled back to her seat, relieved that the plague of stinging bites had abated for now. She studied the swamp around her. Drywater had vanished behind a curtain of moss and cypress branches that brushed the oily waters. Again the mists had lowered with the sun's arrival. The light became a hazy, yellow-tinged glare off the water that soon made her eyes ache. Nearby, branches reached for their boat, but Jaston was a skilled poleman and kept them from the lowest of the overhanging limbs, where nests of coiled snakes hung like Winterfest decorations, bright yellows and vibrant reds, writhing slowly as the punt passed. Occasionally she would spot one of these fancifully colored snakes swimming in sluggish whips of its tail through the dark waters.

Jaston saw her attention on one of them. "Sweetheart adders," he named them. "Their bite hurts like a flaming brand on the skin but will only make you sick for a day or two."

"So why call them sweetheart then?"

"Because their bite doesn't kill you. Among the denizens of the swamp, their bite is nothing more than a kiss."

Elena settled deeper into the center of the punt. Mycelle put one arm around her. "Don't fret, Elena. The snakes are nothing to fear. As long as you don't disturb them, they'll leave you be."

"But there are other creatures that aren't so generous," Jaston added. "So, once we're deeper in the swamps, keep your eyes and ears alert."

As they poled around a slow curve in the channel, a sweet scent flowered the air. It drove back the smell of rotten eggs from their noses. Elena was startled at how accustomed she had become to the constant stink. The scents of daffodils and lilacs were a balm on her spirit, a reminder of home among these treacherous lands.

Jaston's voice grew grim. "Keep your heads down."

Mycelle glanced over her shoulder to him. "Is it a moonblossom?"

"Yes, and from the stink, I'd say it's a large one."

Mycelle hunkered down lower in the punt and pulled Elena off the bench seat to sit on the bottom of the boat. "Stay there, honey."

Fardale joined her, on guard.

"Strange to find it still hunting this late in the morning," Jaston mumbled.

They glided slowly around the bend. Ahead, the source of the sweet scent appeared: a monstrous purple blossom the size of a small calf overhung the channel. Its huge petals were curled back invitingly from its center. The boat would pass under those petals, but Jaston poled the punt as far away as possible. As they drew closer, Elena saw the reason for his concern. The stem of this huge flower, as thick around as her thigh and wrapped like a creeper around the branches of a huge cypress, was festooned with hundreds of thorny vines. Yet it was not the long, barbed spikes that drew her eyes, but the poor creatures that hung impaled in their grips. Wrapped in the thorny coils were a few white-plumed birds and a scatter of small furry animals with bushy tails. Nothing moved. As she watched, the vines slowly crept and uncurled, like snakes coming awake with the heat of the day. Elena suspected it was not the warmth of the sun but the smell of their blood that awakened this giant.

Frames of old skeletons dropped from its grip to splash in the water as it reached for fresh meat. Vines swung toward their boat, but even Elena could tell they were too short to reach them. She allowed herself to relax. Then, the flower's stalk suddenly convulsed. Its stem lurched farther along the cypress branch, dragging its blossom and vines closer to the punt. A small squeak of fear escaped Elena's lips.

"Get down," Mycelle warned, planting a hand atop her head and forcing her lower. Yet the sides of the punt were so low that Elena could still see the creeping flower reach for them. Hundreds of vines, some thicker than her arm, unfurled to probe at the passing boat.

Jaston used his pole to push aside these reaching fingers as the punt glided along. Where his pole touched, the vines snapped around the wood, but its smooth and polished surface offered no purchase for the thorns. Determined, a thick vine slid past his pole and tried to wrap itself around their guide's chest, but Er'ril was there, sword in hand. His silver weapon flashed, and the flower's limb splashed to the water, severed clean with the one strike of the blade. Jaston nodded his thanks to the plainsman. Once past the last of the vines, Jaston shook off the clinging remnants of the moonblossom from his pole and rinsed off its surface. "Sleep poison," he explained. "Wouldn't want to get it on a cut."

Elena stared behind her as the moonblossom vanished around the bend, its vines curling in frustration, its petals closing for the day. It would wait until nightfall to bloom again and lure the unsuspecting with its sweet scent. Elena shuddered. Was there nothing out here that didn't want to eat you?

Soon they reached a wider channel, where a small current caught their boat and drew it languidly toward the deeper bogs. Jaston now only used his pole to guide them, rather than propel them forward. With the easing of his burden, he became more talkative—though Elena suspected he talked more to keep himself distracted than for companionship. He told them which plants contained healing oils and which fruits could kill with a nibble. He spoke at length about the kroc'an, one of the larger swamp predators, an aggressive, scaled carnivore with razor-sharp teeth that hunted the waters but nested on mud banks. They were a prized kill. Their skin made an excellent leather, and their meat was rich with fat. He even explained their mating habits. "A pair bonds for life," he explained. "When you hunt them, you must kill both male and female, or the surviving mate will seek you out. They are vengeful beasts. But the worst is a nesting female. She will attack a boat merely for passing too near her eggs. Only a skilled swamper tackles a kroc'an hunt."

"Hopefully we won't encounter any," Elena said.

Jaston's eyebrows rose with this statement. "We've passed fifteen so far."

Elena's lips parted. She had not seen a single one.

"They hide in the muddy reeds." Jaston pointed his pole. "There's one now."

It took further clues to finally discover the pair of black eyes peering from between bunches of rushes. Its scaled snout barely poked above the water. It lay stone-still, the bulk of its body hidden in the water, but its thick armored tail lay draped on the bank behind it. It had to be as long as the boat.

"Just a young bull," Jaston said, appraising it. "I doubt it's even bonded yet. A full-grown adult can grow twice that length, and I've heard tales of kroc'an giants that can be even larger—beasts that could swallow this boat whole."

Elena leaned closer to Mycelle.

Er'ril tired of these nature talks. "Do you know where we're going?" he asked Jaston.

The scarred man nodded. "These are well-traveled byways. I plan to take us as far as the swampers have mapped. Beyond that, we'll have to trust Mycelle's seeking to guide us."

"How much farther until we reach these untracked lands?"

"We'll be there by nightfall. A swamper knows he risks his luck to spend more than one night out among the sloughs and bogs. 'One day out and one day back' is an old hunting rule."

"Why's that?" Er'ril asked.

"After a night, the swamp has your scent and begins to hunt you. Swampers that are gone for more than five days are mourned. Only a handful of men have survived longer than that in the swamp, and most have come back missing limbs or badly poisoned."

"How long were you and Mycelle out while searching for this wit'ch the last time?"

"Seven days," he said sullenly, glancing to his feet. "The longest anyone has risked the swamp."

"And how far do you think you penetrated?"

Mycelle answered. "We traveled for three days into the swamp before we were forced back. Even that hard-won distance, I believe, only touched the fringe of its dark heart. To reach the core will take easily twice that."

Er'ril pondered this news with dark brows.

"But this time the wit'ch wants us to come," Elena said, rolling back her sleeve to expose the vines of choker's nest that wrapped her arm. "She marked me with her calling. She won't be hiding from us."

Mycelle nodded as Elena shook her sleeve back over the vines. "Perhaps," she mumbled. "But who knows the mind of someone who could live so long in these poisonous lands?"

"Does anyone know how long she's been here?" Er'ril asked.

Jaston answered. "Tales of the wit'ch go back for generations. Hundreds of years. Some say since the Drowned Lands were first formed. Others say it was the wit'ch herself who sunk this region long ago."

Elena sat straighter in her seat. "What do you mean sunk? Hasn't this always been swamp?"

"No," Er'ril said, his voice a pained whisper as he stared at the poisonous lands. "It was once a part of the plains of Standi."

THE BLOOD HUNTER CROUCHED, HIDDEN AMONG THE TALL REEDS IN THE shallows near the edge of Drywater. He had circled the ramshackle pile of rafts to its southern point. His prey's scent left the town here and headed into the swamps. He stopped to ponder the path that the wit'ch chose to follow. Why was she risking the dangers of these treacherous lands? It made no sense, not when it was an easy trek to follow the Landslip to the coast.

Torwren slipped into the depths of the swamp, his head sinking below the green waters. His limbs moved easily as he plodded through the muck at the bottom of the channel. He marched steadily, the fresh blood heating his skin. He relished the new strength in his limbs as he pushed aside tangling roots that snagged at him. Large predators swam toward him, blacker shadows in the murk, bared teeth like beacons in the gloom. But as they neared, it only took a glance of his red eyes to twist them away. A flash of their thick, scaled tails, and they were gone. Swamp eels writhed around his ankles and up his legs, then were poisoned by his touch. Their carcasses floated up, leaving a foul trail in the wake of his passage.

As he followed the waterway, he rose to the surface occasionally—not to breathe, since his body had passed beyond that need and blood fueled him now—but to sniff at the wit'ch's trail, to make sure he did not stray from her path. With little resistance from the denizens of the swamp, he moved well. He would soon catch this wit'ch and taste her heart.

As the sun crested to midday, he reached a stronger current in the waters. He cursed under his breath. The swift waters would carry the wit'ch farther away from him, faster than he could march. Scowling, he increased his speed as the sun began its slide toward the western horizon. Still, where the current gave an advantage to the wit'ch, the night was a blood hunter's friend. His prey needed to sleep. He did not. He would use the midnight hours to close the gap. So, like a boulder rolling relentlessly down a mountainside, he continued, unstoppable, determination smoldering in the flames of his red eyes.

As he continued, Torwren again wondered why his prey had

chosen this route. Did she perhaps think to lose him among the bogs and fens?

He rose and sniffed at the trail. Her spoor was sharp and clear in the humid air. No, he would never lose her trail.

Never.

NIGHT HAD FALLEN BY THE TIME THE PUNT GLIDED UP TO A SMALL island. Rope in hand, Jaston hopped to the small dock protruding from its muddy bank. "We'll overnight here," he said, tying off the punt.

A stone shack stood atop a short rise. Elena stared longingly at the cottage. It seemed much more substantial than its watery surroundings. The stacked rocks that composed its walls must have been ferried here to build this stout structure; nowhere in the swamps was there such solid building material. Even the door appeared to be ironwood, a tree foreign to these lands.

Er'ril stepped out next to their guide. He had his sword in his fist as he studied the island for any threat. Satisfied, he waved Elena out next. Mycelle followed, her arms burdened with their packs. Fardale guarded their rear.

Jaston led the way, kicking aside a snake from the path. It slithered into the reeds. Still, Elena kept her eye on its last location as she was led to the cottage. Snakes were sneaky.

Their guide pushed open the thick door; there was no lock. But then again, Elena thought, who would be thieving way out here? Jaston raised the lantern and surveyed the interior before allowing anyone to enter. He shone the light into every corner and even up into the rafters. His search was quick, since there was not a stick of furniture. The room was an empty cell. Not even a window pierced the walls. "It's safe," he declared, and allowed the others to enter.

"What is this place?" Elena asked, creeping carefully inside.

Fardale loped past her thighs and did his own search, using his nose for a more thorough survey of the cottage's corners.

"It's a hunter's lodge," Jaston said. "A place to rest with stone protecting your back. A few other such lodges are built along the edges of the swamp, none farther than a day's journey from the Landslip."

" 'One day in, one day out,' " Er'ril mumbled.

Jaston nodded. "Beyond here are areas rarely traveled by any but the foolhardy."

With his dire words, the party set up camp inside the stone hut. Bedrolls were spread, and a cold dinner of dried fish and hard bread was served in silence. "We've an early start," Er'ril declared, dusting off the crumbs from his lap. "I'll take the first shift."

"The lodge is secure against predators," Jaston said. "There is no need to post guards."

Er'ril stared at their guide. "You'll take the second shift."

Elena crawled into her roll, glad to leave the others to watch for snakes and kroc'an. Though she had spent most of the day seated in the punt, exhaustion nagged at her. The constant tension of their journey wearied her even more than the hike down the Landslip had. As she recalled the previous day's events, an unanswered question arose in her mind. She rolled to her back and spotted Er'ril by the lantern.

He twisted the lantern's wick to a low glow.

"Er'ril," she said, drawing his eye, "you said earlier that the swamps were once a part of Standi. How is that possible?" she pressed.

Mycelle paused from climbing in her own roll to glance at Er'ril.

He sighed, apparently resigning himself to this tale. "Before the Gul'gotha came to Alasea, there was no Landslip. This region was as flat as the rest of Standi. Even the neighboring Archipelago once numbered twice as many islands before the region sank." His voice grew distant, his gaze wistful. "This was beautiful country here, scattered with wooded hills and countless brooks that flowed from the Teeth to the coast. When I was young, I used to hunt deer among these lands with my father . . . and once even . . . a long time ago . . ." His voice trailed off with some private memory.

"Then what happened?" Elena asked, pulling him back from his memories.

Er'ril's eyes focused back on her. He scowled. "We were naive, blind to any thought that Alasea could ever be conquered. But one day, tremors and quakes shook the lands, heralding the arrival of the Dark Lord to our coasts. It was as if the very land were repulsed by his foul touch. At first, we thought it only a natural phenomenon. Quakes were not uncommon in the coastal areas. To further this misconception, word reached A'loa Glen of a huge volcanic eruption far to the north. It was told that the sun disappeared under a blanket of soot for almost an entire moon, and whole forests were turned to stone by its ash and heat. When the smoke finally cleared, a monstrous cone lay where only flat land had once spread. Barren and burnt black, it was a smoldering blister along the coastline."

"What was it?"

"It was the birth of Blackhall."

Gasps met his revelation. Blackhall was the seat of the Dark Lord, a great mountain that had been carved and hollowed into a sprawling subterranean city.

Er'ril continued his story. "As the clouds of soot faded and the tremors calmed, we assumed the worst was over. Then after a time, rumors were heard of strange and vile creatures spreading forth from the mountains. Horribly deformed monsters and pale, winged creatures.

"Skal'tum," Elena said in a hushed voice.

Er'ril nodded. "Our leaders investigated, sending out scouts, but they never returned. By the time we realized that Alasea was under assault, it was too late. The Dark Lord was firmly entrenched in his volcanic fortress. It was at this time that his Gul'gothal armies arrived in massive fleets that stretched across the horizons. They attacked A'loa Glen first. For many moons, the oceans of the Archipelago ran red with blood, yet still we prevailed. The magick sustained us." The plainsman's eyes were bright with past glory.

Then slowly the fire in his gaze soured. "But Chi abandoned us. As we fought, mages lifted their hands for power but pulled back only stumps. Without our magick, the tide of battle slowly turned. D'warf armies and Gul'gothal dog soldiers reached the coasts and began their march to the Teeth, aided by the Dark Lord's beasts and black magicks. We could not withstand their forces. After ten winters of slaughter and bloodshed, only A'loa Glen still stood against their ravages, with enough pooled magick in her to sustain a long siege. From this last bastion, we struck at the Black Heart's dominion of our lands. As long as A'loa Glen stood, there was hope in the people."

Er'ril faced the floor. "Then one day a mighty quake tore into this region. During this upheaval, not only did the Archipelago sink until only the tallest mountaintops remained above the waves, but even this wedge of coastline tore and slumped from the higher plains. Rivers tumbled over the new cliffs and swamped this region. Ripped open by the cataclysm, hot vents heated these waters, and the creatures of the coastal marshes and bogs spread inland to claim this new territory. And so the Drowned Lands were born."

Silence met his tale. Finally, Mycelle asked, "But what happened to A'loa Glen?"

Er'ril grew somber. "During the assault, we thought the whole island would sink, but at the last moment, the quake ceased and the highest levels of the city still stood above water. Fearing further attacks, the mages sought to hide the island, to let the Dark Lord think the city sunk and defeated. The Brotherhood used almost all the remaining magick to build a cloaking wall against prying eyes, impenetrable without the magick of one of three wards. From this hidden post, the surviving mages thought to wage a war of stealth against the Gul'gotha. But it was a mistake. With the disappearance of A'loa Glen, the people of Alasea lost their heart." Er'ril's face hardened, his brows furrowed deep. "By hiding, we handed the final victory to the Dark Lord."

"But h-how did he sink these lands?" Elena asked.

Er'ril shrugged. "It was never discovered."

Jaston spoke up for the first time, his voice a worried murmur. "As I said before, some say it was the swamp wit'ch."

Er'ril rubbed his stubbled chin and straightened. "Whatever the cause, it grows late."

No one spoke against this statement. Each was left to his own thoughts as bedrolls were pulled up to necks. Elena's left arm itched with its vines, keeping her awake for a long time. As soft snores rose around her, Elena's thoughts were still plagued with all she had learned.

If the wit'ch was powerful enough to sink these lands, what did she want with Elena?

Nearby, Jaston moaned in his sleep and thrashed against invisible attackers.

And if the wit'ch had been hidden for so long, scarring and killing those that approached, why reveal herself now?

Outside, the swamp's nightly chorus of hunters and prey was a constant reminder of the dangers that lay ahead. Elena pulled the edge of the bedroll over her head to muffle the keening screeches and warbling croaks, and she tried to imagine she was home in her own room in the orchards. She failed. Still, after a time, exhaustion did finally claim her, and sleep swallowed away her fears.

She slept deeply, too tired even to dream, until someone grabbed her arm. Her eyes flew open, a gasp on her lips.

"Hush," Er'ril whispered, and pulled her from her bedroll.

Elena struggled free of her blanket and stood. She had no idea how long she had been sleeping but sensed it was well past midnight, yet still far from morning.

Er'ril shoved her behind him as he faced the ironwood door. Jaston and Mycelle were already out of their bedrolls. Her aunt had her two swords, and Jaston clutched a long skinning knife.

Beside them, Fardale stood with his hackles raised. The wolf's silence was unnerving as he stared intently at the door.

Glancing around her, Elena did not understand the danger until the quiet of the room penetrated her. Not a sound disturbed the night—not a single croak, whistle, or hiss.

Beyond the door, the swamp lay dead quiet.

PUSHING ASIDE A WALL OF DENSE REEDS, THE BLOOD HUNTER CREPT ONTO the island, ropes of soggy moss clinging to his shoulders. A flutter of frogs fled from his step, splashing into the shallows.

Ahead, the stone cabin lay at the top of a short hill. He approached its rear cautiously. The scent of the wit'ch led here. He stepped to the rock wall and sniffed at it. Even through the rock, he scented her spoor. His lips pulled back to grin at the night. He had finally caught up with his prey.

He circled the cabin, pleased by what he discovered. No windows opened in the walls, only a single door. There was no escape. His quarry was trapped within this stone prison. He crossed to the only entrance and crouched before the ironwood door. Here her lingering scent was strong. He straightened, glancing behind him to ensure that their boat was still tied to the dock. Through the mist, he saw the punt rocking gently in the night breeze.

Grinning, he faced the threshold, savoring his victory.

Raising his arm, he let fire dance in his stone palm. His polished black features reflected back the flames as they grew fierce. Once satisfied, he thrust his hand to the door. As his ebon'stone flesh met wood, the door exploded away from him, shredding into thousands of ironwood darts that blasted into the chamber ahead. Before the debris settled, Torwren stalked through the cloud of trailing smoke.

He found the cabin empty of all but a scattering of rumpled bedrolls. Dismayed, he marched into the room and searched its corners. No one was here. As flames ran in streams across his stone skin, he turned to the door, staring out at the night.

She may have slipped his snare this time, but now he knew his prey was wary. He took a step back into the swamps, determined to show her the skills of a true hunter.

Soon, he thought as he entered the dark waters. Soon I shall taste her heart.

27

In the distance, a muffled explosion echoed across the swamp. Elena did not need to turn around to know it came from the stone lodge they had just fled.

"The boy spoke the truth," Mycelle whispered. "Someone is stalking us."

Elena stayed ducked down as the strange boat sped along the swamp current. She stared at the small naked boy who stood at the bow of the vessel. Redheaded and freckled, he was clearly one of the wit'ch's swamp children. This time, she did not shy from the dirty child. If it had not been for the boy's timely arrival, all of them would have been trapped in the stone cabin.

The child had come knocking softly on the lodge's door shortly after Elena had been pulled from her bedroll. Er'ril had warily peeked out to discover the boy standing there. The fiery-headed youth had hissed at them to leave before they could even collect their supplies. "Leave it," he had scolded. "Dead men don't need bedrolls."

At first, no one had moved. Finally, Mycelle had sighed and sheathed her twin swords. "The wit'ch knows these lands. If she says run, we'd better heed her minion."

The boy had grabbed her aunt's arm, obviously relieved to find an ally, and practically yanked her toward the door. "The monster comes. Hurry!"

Er'ril was less convinced. He kept a hand gripped on Elena's shoulder. At the door, the boy had raised his gaze to the tall plainsman. "I do this to save your wit'ch. If you wish to die, then stay. But let the girl live."

Even Elena could tell it was not a mere boy that spoke. It was the swamp wit'ch.

Grumbling, Er'ril had finally relented and pushed Elena forward.

The boy quickly led them out the door and away from the dock. "This way!" he had insisted. He guided them to a crudely constructed craft nestled among the reeds. It was smaller than their own punt, but with no supplies, the boat was roomy enough. It seemed to be constructed of tightly woven strands of some thick vine and was encrusted with a layer of yellow moss.

While Fardale sniffed at it, Jaston had studied the craft doubtfully, then shrugged and stepped into it. The others followed as Jaston searched for the pole to work the boat. Before he could finish his search, the crude vessel had simply slipped away from the bank on its own and glided into the deeper waters.

Now, as the echoes of the explosion from the lodge died around them, the small boat picked up speed.

"It's traveling faster than the current," Jaston commented, wonder and fear equally mixed in his expression.

Without a lantern, the swamp was a black cave around them. Even the stars and moon were masked by the night's clouds and mists.

"Only a fool travels the bog at night," Jaston mumbled near the stern.

The boy glanced back at his words, his face twisted with exaggerated fear. "Then I'd better run home," he said, and toppled overboard.

Er'ril's arm reached out for the boy; then he caught himself with a dour shake of his head. "I hate when they do that," he said under his breath.

"I think the wit'ch tires," Mycelle said from beside Elena. "I wager it takes immense concentration and strength to create one of her moss children. If she's forced to move and guide the boat, she probably can't maintain the child any longer. There are limits to an elemental's ability."

"We should've used more caution," Er'ril said. "Who is to say the boy's talk of monsters was real?"

"I felt a stirring," Mycelle argued. "Something strangely muted, but corrupt. I couldn't tell for sure what it was, except that whatever pursues us has been touched by black magicks."

Her statement silenced the conversation. It felt uncomfortable to speak in the darkness anyway, as if their mere voices would bring some new foul creature into their midst.

Yet the swamp held no such qualms. The music of the night returned to claim the darkness. Strange, warbling cries echoed back and forth across the waters, and under it droned a constant croaking, chirping, and creaking.

Something huge suddenly splashed into the water only a stone's throw away—or at least it sounded that close to Elena. She huddled closer to Mycelle. Her aunt put an arm around her. "Why don't you try to sleep?" she whispered in Elena's ear.

Darkness hid Elena's incredulous expression. Sleep would never claim her this night.

As the boat glided through unknown dangers, her eyes slowly grew accustomed to the blackness. The darkness was not as complete as Elena had first suspected. In the distance, strange glows would shine forth in the mists for a few heartbeats, then fade away. Closer, swarms of sparking insects swept away in huge clouds from their passing boat. Occasional hanging ropes of moss glowed a soft green from branches overhead; some even pulsed languidly in the night breeze. At one point, the vessel swept through a dark pond, but in its wake, the disturbed algae blew bright with an azure hue, leaving a brilliant trail behind them.

The wondrous sights were not lost on the others. "There is much beauty here," Mycelle whispered.

"But beware its pretty face," Jaston answered her. "Among the bogs and fens, beauty is often used to lull the unwary to their death. Remember the pleasing scent of the moonblossom."

As if to support his claim, a viper swam past the bow of the boat, its body gleaming a radiant crimson as it twisted through the waters.

"Still, beauty is beauty," Mycelle said with a sigh.

So the night passed. No one slept. But as nothing directly threatened them as they traveled, they were able to relax and, in some small way, appreciate the wonders hidden among these lands. For brief moments, Elena could almost understand Jaston's ability to call the swamps home.

At long last, the skies to the east began to lighten with dawn. And while the sun was welcome, the calm of the night was shattered by what the new light revealed.

Around them, trees had grown so high that their crowns vanished into the foggy clouds above. Boles of these swamp giants were as big around as the stone lodge they had fled, and monstrous tangles of huge roots rose from the waters, creating twisted arches over the channel. Creatures of leathery wings and sharp claws hung upside down from these roots as they passed beneath them, wings wrapped like cloaks around their sleeping bodies. Walls of webs also lay draped across the snarls of heavy roots, with spiders the size of small dogs hunched in their center, fangs dripping a red oil as their boat passed.

Elena glanced away. The spiders reminded her too much of Vira'ni's poisonous demons that had plagued them last spring, like an ill omen warning them away. She turned to study the swamp channel.

Under them, the waters were no longer green but a deep black like a starless night sky. In the dark channel, beasts churned and swam. Schools of fish darted around the boat, and even from above, their sharp teeth could be clearly seen. Wide wakes marked the paths of unseen beasts, obviously curious and drawn by their boat. For a brief moment, a huge white fin rose from the waters ahead, then sank back down.

A gurgling splash drew Elena's eyes to the right of the boat. A striped python as thick around as an og're's chest was writhing from its perch in a fork of a tree and slipping into the black waterway. Before its full length slid into the depths, the boat had passed out of sight. But other snakes lay around them on all sides. Nests of pale vipers lay as thick as piled snow along the muddy banks, while their more colorful cousins hung in choked tangles from low-lying branches.

Everywhere Elena looked, the swamp squirmed and crawled with deadly menace. Yet nothing approached the boat directly or threatened immediate harm.

"They . . . they let us pass," Jaston mumbled.

"The wit'ch's magick," Mycelle said. "It must be keeping them back."

Er'ril spoke from behind Elena's shoulder. "And what if this wit'ch decides not to be so accommodating after we meet? How will we ever get out of here?"

No one had an answer.

As the boat shied around a slow bend in the channel, what Elena had thought was a small island buried in a bed of floating moss opened a huge black eye and stared at her. It then sank from view in a swirl of bubbles.

Elena hugged her arms around her body. Even the rising warmth could not dispel the chill that had settled around her heart. Her hand rubbed at the moss under her left sleeve. How were they ever to escape these swamps, especially without her magick?

Jaston stood near the stern of the boat and grabbed at fruit hanging from a vine overhead. He managed to collect half a dozen, dropping them at his feet, before the boat slid past the fruited canopy. "Fen apples," he named them, settling back to his seat. "Though I've never seen them so large."

He passed them around. Without their supplies, they did not even have water to share. While Fardale rolled one of the large red-skinned fruits across the bottom of the boat with his nose, sniffing at it, Elena needed both hands to grasp her own. Her eyes crinkled. This was like no apple she had ever seen. Following Jaston's example, she simply bit into it. As her teeth pierced the fruit's skin, sweet juices ran down her chin, and she found the flesh of the "apple" crisp and oddly cool. It wasn't until her mouth was full that she realized how hungry she was. She devoured the fruit in silence, as did the others. Too soon, she had gnawed it down to its core. But even then she did not stop. She chewed on the seeds inside and discovered they tasted a bit like hazelnuts.

Satisfied and full, she found the nervous chill in her chest strangely abated. Just the act of eating, this small achievement of survival in these poisonous lands, fortified her resolve. She leaned back, the tension fading from her shoulders. She would live today.

So the remainder of the day passed.

Elena even found herself dozing during the late afternoon as they glided, undisturbed, past horrors that would turn a brave man to stone. As she watched, now less concerned with something attacking her, she was able to appreciate the cycle of life in this strange place: the mother kroc'an with her tail wrapped around a nest of eggs, a pair of long-legged cranes with beaks like swords leading a line of fledglings and showing them how to hunt the shallows, the obvious courting ritual of a pair of rock turtles as big around as mountain boulders. Even here, poison could not keep life from continuing.

Eventually night again swallowed away the swamps, and Elena sought truly to sleep. Her belly was full from a late meal of something Jaston called a "potato weed," a fibrous tuber growing in chains that he had snatched from the waters. It was not all that tasty, but it was filling. Content, she drifted toward slumber, her head cradled on Fardale's side as the wolf lay curled at the prow of the boat.

At least this night, nestled among friends, Elena felt safe. Still, deep inside her, she suspected this peace would not last for long. So she would savor this moment. Tomorrow's worries could wait on the dawn.

She closed her eyes and let the poisonous lands lull her to sleep.

THE BLOOD HUNTER PUSHED THROUGH THE DEEPER SWAMPS. HERE THE waters ran with creatures far larger than himself, but still they shied away when he drew near. The foulness of his stone skin repelled the beasts' keen noses.

Torwren surfaced again to check the scent of the wit'ch. A trace of lightning burned in the air. Back at the island, he had soon enough caught his prey's scent. He had studied the trampled rushes and reeds. Another boat had awaited the wit'ch, one hidden in the shallows.

After tearing apart the muddy bank for further clues about her unknown support, he had discovered nothing. He was forced to pursue her on foot, slogging through muck and fighting the ever-thickening growth of roots and moss. He had trailed her throughout the remainder of the night and the following day. From the way her trail grew faint, she traveled faster and was leaving him far behind.

Still, as night descended again, he pursued her. As long as there was a trace of scent, she would not escape him. Eventually she would slow or stop, and again he would catch up. But this time, he would be better prepared.

With these thoughts clouding his attention, he failed to notice a huge predator that had swept closer than most dared. It was only when the beast was upon him that he finally grew conscious of the attack. Before he could move, its huge jaws clamped around his waist, dragging him from the muck. Teeth with serrated edges wore at his stone skin. Torwren's flaming eyes stared into the large black eyes of the scaled creature, monster studying monster. The swamp lizard used the weight of its tail to thrash and twist at the stone d'warf.

Torwren found himself tossed about like a child's doll in a dog's mouth. The creature weighed easily five times his own bulk. Any ordinary d'warf would have been long dead. But Torwren was no ordinary d'warf. He was at no risk of drowning, and his stone skin resisted the teeth of the creature. As its clawed front legs scrabbled at him, searching for a weak spot, he simply waited. Like most cold-blooded creatures, this beast was designed for a sudden attack and a quick kill. Prolonged fighting was not in its nature. It would soon tire.

The d'warf's assessment proved true. Soon the creature's thrashings subsided. Yet it was not exhaustion that weakened the monstrous lizard but the touch of poison in the blood hunter's skin. Now the creature's waning struggles were aimed at dislodging the foul prey from its mouth, seeming to sense the corruption it held as its blood lust faded. But Torwren would not be denied his kill. He hung on to the beast's snout, refusing to allow himself to be tossed off.

In only a few heartbeats, the beast lay still and floated to the surface with Torwren caught in its dead jaws. He pried himself free and pushed the lizard away. Near the bank, he spotted the lair of the scaled creature in the muddy reeds. Eggs like big speckled rocks filled the hollow of a shallow nest.

No wonder the beast had attacked when no other creature would dare. The mother's instinct to protect her offspring had doomed her. Torwren shoved the she-lizard's bulk out of his way.

Dumb beast.

He stalked back into the swamp. The wit'ch's trail had grown even fainter while he had battled the monster. Silently he cursed the creature and its maternal instinct. How awful it must be to be guided by forces beyond your control, to be a puppet to primitive instincts.

The blood hunter rose to the surface and sniffed at the air.

NEAR DAWN, THE BULL KROC'AN NOSED ITS DEAD MATE, THEN SEARCHED its nest. The eggs were still intact, but without his mate, the clutch would not survive. His nest was as dead as if it had been trampled.

He raised his nose to the sky and trumpeted his pain and rage. His thunderous call silenced the swamps for leagues around with its echoes.

Once done, he returned to his mate, nuzzled her, and wrapped his tail one last time around her. Massing three times her size, he held her tenderly, pulling her close to him. He lay in her embrace until the rage in his heart would not let him hold still.

He broke free with a thrash of his mighty tail, striking a tree near shore and snapping it in half.

He sniffed at her snout, confirming the scent of the one who had killed his bonded.

Then he sank beneath the waters.

His death hunt began.

THE SUN AWOKE ELENA JUST AFTER DAWN. SHE UNCURLED FROM Fardale's side and stretched to greet the morning. The wolf stirred at her motion but did not wake. Elena glanced at the rest of the party: Everyone slept. She was the only one awake. Even though it was obvious that Jaston had been left to guard the last watch of the night, he had not made it to morning. He sat near the stern of the boat, his chin resting on his chest. Gentle snores rose from his sleeping figure.

Elena worked a kink from her neck and glanced at the morning mists around the boat. Nothing but walls of swirling fog encircled their vessel. Her first thought was that the mists still hid the surrounding trees and banks. But as her eyes cleared of sleep fog, she realized the mists were not that dense. She sat straighter and, in a slight panic, glanced all around her.

Her sudden motion stirred Fardale enough that his head rose from his paws. He yawned so large that all his teeth shone bright in the dawn's light. He pushed slowly to his own feet as his eyes surveyed the waters around the boat. Then he stiffened. His gaze swung to Elena. A picture formed in her mind's eye: *A wolf flies off a high cliff and falls through empty air.*

She knew what he meant. She shook Mycelle's shoulder and woke her aunt with a start. Mycelle sat up, instantly alert. "What is it, hon?"

Elena waved her arm to encompass their surroundings. "The swamp is gone." Around the boat, the growing sunlight revealed the proof of her words. The mists were thin enough that their view stretched for at least a league in all directions—and nothing lay around them. Even the hue of the waters had lightened from a deep black to a clearer blue.

By now, the rest of their party had awakened.

"The channel must have emptied into some lake," Jaston said as he stared around him. His voice was low and embarrassed. He would not meet Er'ril's intense stare; he knew he had failed his watch.

Er'ril sighed loudly at the featureless surroundings. The swamp noises still carried to them across the waters, but the croaking and screeching were clearly some distance away. The boat had traveled deep into the lake.

Mycelle settled back down. "The wit'ch still draws the boat. Swamp or not, we are heading toward her."

"Or she might be chasing us off," Er'ril said harshly, "getting us lost when we weren't looking." He glanced meaningfully to the stern where Jaston sat.

The swamper did not acknowledge Er'ril's words. He just stared out at the waters, but Elena saw his cheeks redden.

Suddenly Fardale growled from the prow of the boat. All eyes swung in that direction. Through the mists ahead, a large dark mass appeared. The boat sped toward it. As the fogs parted, it soon became clearer. Sheer steep cliffs rose straight from the waters to reach for the skies.

"It's an island," Elena said. Her eyes strained to pierce the mists.

"No," Er'ril said, "it's not."

The mists lifted with the sun's warmth to reveal more of their destination. What had initially appeared to be cliffs were now revealed to be *walls*. Stone and mortar climbed from the lake's waves, their ancient surfaces draped in curtains of moss and lichen. Black holes of old windows stared down at them as the boat curved around the huge structure. From these windows, huge leather-winged creatures burst forth, disturbed by the boat's passage. Their cries raised the tiniest hairs on Elena's arms.

She craned her neck back. The structure rose high into the morning skies. Far above, Elena spotted battlements topping its crown. As the boat glided around its base, the walls curved so gently that it became clear the structure was a tower of immense girth.

"I know this place," Er'ril hissed.

"You do?" Mycelle said, her neck bent back.

"It's Castle Drakk," Er'ril said coldly. "Or what's left of it. This is the tip of its highest tower. The rest of the foul place must be drowned below us." He studied its mossy walls with his lips curled as if ready to snarl. "As much as I hated losing these Standi lands when the plains sank, it was a consolation to know Castle Drakk had been destroyed."

"Why?" Elena asked.

Er'ril shook his head. "It was the keep of the Assassins' Guild: a caste of poisoners and men who moved in shadows. Unwanted children of many lands—bastard children, babes born into hardship, deformed births—were sold like cattle to the lords of the castle."

"What became of them?"

"They were apprenticed as assassins, though some tales said a portion of the children sold were used for the training of the others, living targets for the black skills."

Elena's eyes grew round while Er'ril's brows darkened further. "But that was just one of the rumors surrounding Castle Drakk," he continued. "Some stories spoke of treasures buried deep in the castle's roots, stored blood money from the centuries of exorbitant fees collected by the caste's assassins. And other tales warned of weapons so sinister of nature that only the skilled hands of an assassin could wield them without harm to their bearer."

As Er'ril finished, the boat glided around to the far side of the tower, where a stone stair curved out of the water to wind up toward the distant battlements. The vessel glided to the narrow staircase and finally stopped its voyage.

The boat was silent as everyone stared up the mossy stairs. The day's heat had already begun to build, and a sheen of sweat glistened on their upturned faces.

"It seems that something survived in Castle Drakk," Mycelle said.

"The wit'ch," Jaston added needlessly.

No one made a move toward the stairs until Elena noticed water seeping into the bottom of the boat. "We're sinking!"

Er'ril and Jaston quickly hopped from the vessel and helped Elena and Mycelle out onto the narrow stairs. Just as the boat sank into the depths, Fardale leapt free. On the stairs, the wolf shook his legs to dry his paws.

The party stood clustered near the base of the staircase and watched their only means of escape drift down into the depths of the lake. Huge fins soon cut through the waters, curiosity drawing predators to the sinking craft. Er'ril herded the party farther up the steps as one of the beasts briefly surfaced. A large black eye rolled into view, its huge maw lined by hundreds of shredding teeth.

"It seems we've arrived where the wit'ch wants us," Mycelle said.

"And means to keep us," Elena mumbled, eying the circling fins.

Er'ril waved Mycelle forward. "Let's see what this wit'ch wants."

Her aunt led the way, with Fardale at her heels. The stairway was only wide enough to allow two persons to walk abreast, so Er'ril kept close beside Elena as they climbed the stairs. Jaston followed last, guarding their rear with his long skinning knife.

They climbed in silence until the waters of the lake were far below, and yet the tower staircase still continued into the mists. The steps had to be trod with care since moss slickened the heel and vines threatened to betray a toe. Due to their cautious pace, it was well past midday when they finally reached the top of the stairs. There, they found a large iron door blocking their way into the tower.

Elena glanced up. The battlements crowning the tower lay only a few stories farther up the structure. Above these fortifications, a large brass cauldron hung over their heads, stanchioned between two stout posts. The brass was green with age, and ropes of moss hung from its supports.

Mycelle noticed Elena's stare. "The cauldrons were used to pour flaming oil upon the tower's attackers. Any army that attempted to take the tower would find these stairs to be a trap. Did you notice the small holes along the walls as we climbed?"

Elena nodded. She had thought them just old mouse burrows.

Mycelle explained their real use. "Defenders would thrust sharp pikes through those holes at the enemy as they climbed the stairs, stabbing at them and shoving them from the staircase to topple to their deaths."

With her nose crinkled, Elena shied away from both the cauldron and the mouse holes as Er'ril tried the iron door. He found it latched tight.

"What now?" he asked, facing the others.

"Maybe we should knock," Elena offered.

Er'ril glanced at her as if she were daft, but Mycelle merely shrugged. "Why not?"

Shaking his head, Er'ril unsheathed his sword and used its silver pommel to strike the door solidly three times. This close, the clang of silver on iron stung the ear. Its call echoed over the still lake waters. Once the ringing sounds died down, Er'ril faced them. "Any other ideas that you'd—"

The sharp click of a latch's release from behind him halted any further comment. All eyes turned to the door. With the tortured screech of rusted hinges, it slowly pulled open.

They needed no orders to retreat down a few steps. Er'ril moved in front of Elena, his sword still raised, its tip pointing at the door. At his side, a tight growl flowed from Fardale's throat, while Mycelle stood beside Elena, both swords in hand.

From the doorway, a tall vision of slender legs and supple curves stepped forth. She wore a white silk gown finely embroidered with green leaves, yellow buds, and twisting curls of tender vines. Her hair, framing a heart-shaped face adorned with full red lips and large blue eyes, hung in a fall of auburn curls to her waist. Her smile was warm and inviting. Not a flicker of guile marred her features. "Welcome," she said, her voice soft and even. She did not even seem to see the swords or knife pointing in her direction, but simply stepped back and waved a sculpted china hand toward the tower's entrance. "Please feel welcome. My boys have prepared a warm meal for you weary travelers."

Even now the odors of baked bread and honey flowed out from the open doorway, and somewhere a roast was smoking above a hot fire.

As tempting as the smells were, no one moved. "Who are you?"

Her smiled faded to a bemused grin. "Why, *the wit'ch,* of course. Now please do not fear. I mean no harm."

Mycelle moved first, but suspicion ran thick in her words. "For someone who means us no harm, to bewit'ch an innocent child with a choker's nest makes us doubt the sincerity of your heart."

Her aunt's words seemed to wound the woman. Her smile faded to a serious expression. "I must apologize for the crudeness of my invitation. But to reach all the way to Shadowbrook tapped my resources to an extreme, and it was vital that the wit'ch come here before proceeding to A'loa Glen."

The mention of the sunken city, their secret destination, loosened Er'ril's tongue. "How do you know so much about us?"

"Come inside. I will explain all during dinner."

Still no one moved. "Free the child of your bewit'ching first," Mycelle said. "Then we can talk."

The wit'ch bowed her head and beckoned Elena forward. "Come to me, child. Let me see your hands."

Elena glanced to Mycelle, who nodded. Cautiously, Elena climbed the stairs to the door's landing, slipping off her gloves. Mycelle and Er'ril followed her. Her aunt sheathed one of her blades and gripped Elena's shoulder in one hand.

As Elena reached the landing, two swords guarded her: Er'ril's gleaming silver to her left, Mycelle's steel blade on her right. Still she had to force herself not to flinch as the wit'ch reached for her bare hands. But the woman's touch proved gentle and undemanding as she knelt before Elena and examined her fingers, palms, and wrists.

She first studied Elena's ruby hand. "Wit'chfire," she muttered, and glanced briefly at the sun. It was sinking toward the western horizon. Sighing, she picked at Elena's vine-encrusted fingers for a few moments. Finally, she clasped both of Elena's hands between her own and gazed into Elena's eyes. "You don't know half your true strength, child," she whispered so quietly that Elena doubted the others even heard the words. As the wit'ch pulled back, Elena caught a whiff of her perfume; the scent was oddly familiar.

Before Elena could recall where she had smelled the scent before, the wit'ch released her hands and straightened up to face the others. She took a step back. "I'm sorry. I will not be able to lift the spell until nightfall."

To either side of her, the two swords raised higher.

"I tell you the truth," she said with sincerity. "I have not expended such energy and brought you all this way just to kill you. I have a need of this child's magick. But to aid me, she must have access to her powers. The weed," she said with a nod toward Elena's left hand, "is not a means of stealing her magick. It was the only way I could ensure she would come and hear me out. Once free of the spell, the choice of whether or not to assist me will be hers and hers alone. Either way, you all will be free to go afterward. All I ask is that she first hear my plea."

The swords pulled back slightly.

Mycelle spoke first, her words directed at Er'ril. "She is the only one who can lift Elena's spell," she argued. "We can at least listen to her story until the sun sets."

Er'ril scowled, but even Elena knew the problem could not be solved on the point of a sword. He lowered his blade.

The gracious smile returned to the wit'ch's face. "Come then. Come inside and let us exchange stories over dinner." She led the way into the tower, moving with such grace that Elena felt like a plodding cow behind her.

Again Elena was struck by her tall lithe figure and cascade of curled tresses. Jaston's prior warning repeated in her head: *Among the bogs and fens, beauty is often used to lull the unwary to their death.*

As Elena followed Mycelle past the iron door and into the shadowed entry of Castle Drakk, it was more than just the stony coolness of the hall that shivered her flesh. In the enclosed space, Elena again caught a whiff of the woman's scent and finally recognized its pleasant fragrance. She recalled the deadly flower that had smelled so sweet and again pictured its vines embracing its prey in a thorny grip.

Silently, she named the source of this scent: *moonblossom*.

Er'ril studied the woman across the oaken table from him. As the others sampled the delicacies offered to them, he found no stomach for the assortment of dark breads and jams, or the slender pods of a swamp bean swimming in butter and lemon, or even the roasted steaks of a wild boar. Instead, he sipped at his mug of bitter ale and studied their hostess.

The wit'ch had tied back her auburn curls with a green braided ribbon as she oversaw the serving of their dinner. As they made their introductions, she had given her name as Cassa Dar but offered nothing more as she went about checking on the spitted boar or stirring a kettle. Once the meal was under way, she settled in a seat opposite the table from Er'ril, but her eyes were only on Elena. The girl sat next to him, nibbling at a slice of bread slathered in berry jam. From the girl's tense shoulders, Er'ril suspected the weight of the wit'ch's gaze unnerved the girl, but she need not have been so worried. Mycelle was seated to Elena's far side. The girl was safe between their two swords.

The rest of their party, Jaston and Fardale, shared the wit'ch's side of the table. The wolf crouched on the floor beside the wit'ch's chair, nosing his plate, while Jaston sat stiff beside the handsome woman and tried his best to keep his scarred features away from the light.

The only other occupants of the huge dining chamber were the wit'ch's servants, three of the swamp boys clothed in brown pants and white shirts. The trio now watched from beside the crackling hearth, eying the table like hungry hawks, awaiting a mug to refill or a dirty plate to replace with a clean one.

The woman's eyes finally met Er'ril's stare, a bemused smile on her lips. "You teem with so many questions, plainsman. Perhaps I try your patience and should now talk."

"You misjudge me," he replied. "All I wish is for Elena to be rid of your bewit'ching. I care nothing for your story or your words."

His harsh statement did nothing to remove the amusement from her eyes. "So you have no curiosity about a wit'ch living in Castle Drakk?"

He just stared.

"Well, if he doesn't, I do," Mycelle said. "Cassa, how did you come to live in these swamps?"

Her gaze moved to the swordswoman. "Come to the swamps? Why, I've always been here. It was the swamps that came to me."

Mycelle's eye twitched with this declaration. "Are you saying you've been here since the lands sunk?"

"Even longer, I'm afraid. I was apprenticed to the assassins' caste a decade prior to the great cataclysm."

All seated at the table wore shocked expressions, but it was Mycelle who spoke. "That would make you over five hundred years old—as old as Er'ril. But that's impossible . . . Or does some magick sustain you?"

Cassa Dar shrugged. "I am rich in elemental magicks. But you know this and know my power. Though vast, it cannot stop time's aging."

"Then how did you—?"

The wit'ch held up a hand. "You dwell on the trivial."

"Yes, she does," Er'ril said. He knew a way to test the veracity of this wit'ch's statements. "If you speak the truth, then prove your words. Show us your assassin's mark."

He had expected her to balk and seek some excuse, but instead she leaned over the table closer to one of the thick candles and tilted her head to the side. She fingered back the trail of curls from behind her right ear to reveal a small tattoo of a bloody dagger done in red and black dyes hidden there. She ran a long painted nail along the hilt of the tattooed blade, tracing a vine wrapped around the handle. A small flower bloomed just at the apex of the hilt. "Nightshade," she said, naming the deadly plant. "I was a poisoner."

The disgust could not be kept from Er'ril's face and was clearly noted by Cassa Dar. "Poison is just another weapon," she said. "Like your sword or Elena's magick. Why do you judge it so harshly? It takes as much skill to master the art of poisoning as it does to master your sword. How much nettleburr will kill a man versus incapacitating him? Which poisons kill quickly and painlessly, and which kill slowly and torturously? How do you lace a blade so the merest scratch will either fester a wound or kill instantly?" She nodded toward the spread of food. "And how do you prepare poisons that the tongue can't taste?"

She smiled at their glances of horror. "Fear not," she said. "I told you I meant you no harm, and my word is good. If I wanted you all dead, I could have done it in a thousand ways. So, Er'ril, if you are done testing me, perhaps we can move to more appropriate topics."

Er'ril was undaunted. "One more question. What happened to the other members of your foul caste?"

"Foul caste? You do seem a well of prejudices, plainsman. I would have you know that the master who ran this keep was as noble a soul as you. He cared for the rejected, cast-out children of both Alasea and lands beyond and paid good coin for the honor. He fed us, clothed us, treated our injuries, and taught us to survive. And at the last, he gave his life freeing the surviving members as the waters rose to claim the castle. So I will not have you disparaging his good work."

"Good work?" Er'ril said. "He created killers."

"And what do your schools of swordplay teach? Do they teach you how to use your swords to knit wool into sweaters? Death is death, and the art of stealing a life is no nobler at the point of a blade than from a powder mixed in a drink."

"But what of rumors that some of the weaker children were used as sport in training?"

"Just that, swordsman—*rumors*. In the libraries here, I have read the histories of the assassins' caste as far back as the foundation of

Castle Drakk. We served the land and its lords as justly and evenly as any knight. The assassins here were oath-bound to our elder members. The elder council judged the worth of any assignment before undertaking it. We did not kill on the whim of some errant lordling who needed an inconvenient person eliminated."

Er'ril snorted. "So you stabbed folks in the dead of night, but you did it nobly?"

"Some matters are better dealt with quietly. Sometimes a battalion of mounted swordsmen is not the best way to solve a problem. Sometimes it takes a well-placed knife or a hidden poison to make a problem go quietly away." Cassa Dar nodded toward Mycelle. "Sometimes poison in tiny jade vials solves many future dangers."

Mycelle's eyes widened. "So you know of my work?"

The swamp wit'ch waved one of her boys over to her and placed a hand on his shoulder. "These are my children, constructs of moss and illusions. They are my eyes and my ears in the swamp and around its edges. There is little I don't know that occurs in my lands, including the city of Shadowbrook. When the wit'ch arrived, I watched and listened . . . and suspected that in her magick lay a chance of salvation."

"Salvation for whom?" Mycelle asked.

She held up a hand. "In due time. What I *can* tell you now is that your other companions in Shadowbrook did escape the destruction of the Keep and are already on a barge toward the coast."

Elena sat up from where she slouched in her chair. "Did they find Meric?"

"The elv'in? Yes, he is injured but lives. I am afraid I can't give you much more detail than that. It taxes my strength to stretch my reach that far. But I can tell you this: When they broke the Keep, something escaped—something that has since been trailing your party."

"The thing that tried to attack us at the lodge?" Jaston asked.

She nodded. "I have been unable to get a clear look at it—something black and foul of form. Its dark magick obscures my vision. And after being thwarted at the lodge, it grew more wary and stays hidden in the waters. I lost it somewhere in the deep swamps. But little passes through that area without my help."

A grudging respect for this wit'ch grew in Er'ril with her tale. She had managed to hone her elemental gift over the centuries into a formidable tool. Yet could she be trusted? He wished he had Kral here to judge the truth of this woman's tongue. "So why did you help us?"

"To offer your wit'ch a bargain."

"And what is this offer?" Er'ril asked.

"I will free her of the bewit'ching no matter what she decides, but I can also offer her a tool that will prove invaluable in her war upon the Black Heart. All I ask in exchange is a small promise."

Er'ril's eyes narrowed. "What is this promise?"

"That when you are finished with this tool, you return it to its original lands and its rightful place."

"Where is that?" Elena asked meekly.

Cassa Dar stood up from the table. She glanced sadly at Elena. "Before we bargain, I must first put aside all illusions." Standing, the wit'ch reached up with her arms, and with a slight shake of her body, as if slipping from loose clothing, her illusions fell away from her. Trailing vines and mounds of moss fell away from her body until her true form was revealed.

Before them hunched a misshapen creature, squat of form and pale of skin. Her back was bent with age, and her pendulous breasts drooped like rotten melons. Her face, as she shied from the light, was more wrinkles than features. Only her ebony eyes still shone with the keenness and intelligence of the one named Cassa Dar.

Er'ril knew what he was looking at. He had fought such creatures on the battlefields with the coming of the Dark Lord. "You're a d'warf!"

ELENA WATCHED FARDALE AND JASTON DANCE BACK FROM THE REVEALED wit'ch. The wolf growled and retreated around the table. Soon their entire party clustered on the far side of the room. The stout oaken table stood between them and the d'warf.

"I *am* a d'warf," Cassa Dar admitted as she kept her face in shadows. Even her voice was a harsh gravel compared to its smooth tones from a moment before. "But as you disparaged the assassins a moment ago, you now misjudge my people."

"Misjudge?" Er'ril spat. He had his silver sword in hand. "It was your armies that ravaged our lands."

She lowered her head, as if its weight were too heavy. "I know. But before you lay blame, hear my story. I—"

"We have no time to hear your sick tale," Er'ril declared hotly. His cheeks had darkened to a deep red. Elena had never seen him so disturbed. "Between your people and the dog soldiers, we were slaughtered. I saw a cousin of mine torn to shreds by the beasts leashed to d'warf overlords. They laughed at his screams. And you ask me to hear your tale?" Er'ril's voice had risen to a sharp pitch. "May your people be forever cursed!"

Elena saw how his words wounded the wit'ch, how her back seemed to bend under his assault. Finally she raised her face toward him; tears ran in rivulets across her marred features. "If it gives you any relief from your sorrow, we were cursed, plainsman." The pain rang clear in her hoary voice. "We were cursed before we ever set foot upon your lands."

Before Er'ril could vent more bile, Elena placed a hand on his arm. He glanced down at her, his eyes aflame with rage. She had to tense her knees not to balk from his gaze. "I wish to hear her story," she said softly.

He started to argue.

She squeezed his arm. "No, I will hear her out."

Er'ril pulled back and could only nod, obviously fearful of even speaking lest he lose control.

Satisfied he would mind his tongue, Elena turned to the d'warf. "I will listen to what you have to say."

The creature nodded but remained quiet, collecting her thoughts and composing herself. When she finally spoke, her voice was hushed. "In the southern mountains of Gul'gotha, we lived in peace, trading our forged goods to the human settlements of northern Gul'gotha and sometimes even across the waters to neighboring lands. That is how I remember my people and our homeland. I still remember racing in the tunnels as my brothers and I played games of sneak-and-seek. I remember our scolding mothers and proud fathers. I remember the strike of hammers on anvils echoing through the valleys, and the flames of a hundred forges glowing like stars across the mountains."

She dwelt in her memories in silence for several heartbeats. When next she spoke, her voice had hardened. "But then it all changed. A troupe of deep miners discovered a vein of ore leagues under the mountain. They had never seen such a stone: blacker than the darkest tunnel and impervious to any tool. Undaunted and determined to mine this vein, they used the kingdom's strongest hammer to attack the stone. They employed the Try'sil, the Hammer of Thunder. Its magick-wrought iron was said to shatter any stone. And this claim proved true. The stone was mined and given the name ebon'stone by its discoverers. At first, it was greatly treasured; every d'warf lord lusted to work a piece, to prove his skill at fashioning the new ore. Bowls, cups, plates, swords, even statues were carved from the material.

"But then something happened. The stone began to warp and bind our people in ways we did not understand. The lands, too, began to sicken and poison. Volcanoes grew, and the ground constantly shook. Gasses and ash soured the skies. Poisonous beasts, the mul'gothra and skal'tum, began to appear from pits deep under the mountains. From somewhere, the Dark Lord arose among our people, almost as if out of the bowels of the land. Some said the Black Heart was a d'warf, one who had succumbed to the stone's black magick, while others said he came from the stone itself, released by our miners from an ebon'stone tomb. No one knew for sure, but all knew that the corruption of our people was under way. Some tried to fight it; some fled from it. My parents sold me to the assassins, not for the silver from the sale, but to get me from those lands. I was sent out here to Alasea before the stranglehold of the Black Heart was complete."

Cassa Dar turned her gaze to Er'ril. "I, too, saw the result of the Dark Lord's hold on my people. It was a d'warf army that came to Castle Drakk and slaughtered my teachers and friends here. They came with beasts and monsters and laid siege to our keep. I saw the deadness in their eyes and knew them thralls to the ebon'stone and its master. We tried to enlist the aid of surrounding hamlets, but our messengers were spat upon and reviled. So much for the nobility of your Standi clansmen!"

It was now the wit'ch's turn to grow angry. She glared at Er'ril. "But they paid for their pettiness. To our castle came a blackguard, the foulest of the ill'guard. Where the ill'guard are bound to their ebon'stone talismans, the blackguard were fused to the stone itself. Their very skin was impenetrable ebon'stone. We attacked this foul creature with every weapon and magick in the castle's arsenal, but all failed to pierce its stone skin. It was an unstoppable storm that swept over us, killing all in its path. While we fled up the tower, it marched to the roots of our school. Only I had an inkling of its true purpose. Only I understood the weapon held in its black fist. It had come to Castle Drakk with the Try'sil."

"Why?" Elena asked as the wit'ch paused her story. "Why did it come here?"

Cassa Dar wiped at the beads of sweat on her brow, as if she were experiencing it all again with its telling. "Do you have a map?"

Er'ril nodded, his brow wrinkling.

Cassa Dar waved a hand for her boys to clear a space on the table. Her servants, as ever, were quick. "Spread it out," she instructed Er'ril.

He did so, unfolding his map and flattening the parchment with a pass of his hand. His growing interest in her tale was clear in his eyes: It was the history of his own lands. Keen curiosity had damped his prior rage.

The wit'ch bent over the map. "Across the world, there are points where the land's core magicks rise close to the surface, locus points of its energies." She traced a crooked finger along Er'ril's map. "If you follow the southern and northern cliffs of the Landslip to where they meet in the west, do you see where the cliffs point?"

"Toward the Teeth?" Er'ril asked, obviously unsure of her meaning.

Cassa Dar sighed as if exasperated with a foolish child.

Elena, though, stared closer at the map. "It points to the Southern Fang," she said.

The d'warf woman's eyes swung to Elena. "Very good, child. So it does." She placed a yellow, cracked nail on the map. "The Southern Fang is one such locus of the land's deep magicks, as is the Northern Fang. Have you never wondered why the ancient mages placed their school in the shadow of the Northern Fang?"

Elena spoke up, remembering when she had received her amulet from her uncle in the hidden chamber under his cottage. "My Uncle Bol said that the mages may have chosen Winter's Eyrie because of the rich elemental energies in the area."

"And so the founders of Castle Drakk chose this site. From these two Fangs, potent magicks flow out like snowmelt from the other peaks to form channels and rivers of energy through our lands. Below the cellars of Castle Drakk lies just such a river. It fed this entire region all the way to the Archipelago."

"What does this have to do with the sinking of these lands?"

"I am coming to that. You see, at first, I also failed to understand what the blackguard was doing skulking through our cellars with our people's most treasured possession in its foul fist. So I followed the creature. It ignored me, believing me a member of its d'warf army. The creature delved deeper into caves under the cellar, places I don't even think the founders knew about. But the blackguard moved unerringly, as if it were on the scent of some prey. Finally, it came to rest in a huge cavern, as large as a ballroom. Along the floor lay a thick vein of pure silver."

She glanced up from the map. "But even I could tell it was more than precious metal that ran through this vein. The magick contained therein sang to the elemental powers in my blood. Though only crudely trained in my magicks, I knew that here lay a font of pure power. Before I could react, the blackguard stalked to this vein and smashed it with the Try'sil. The hammer tore the vein of silver, and the entire world shook. The cavern swelled with magick as the channel burst. It bathed me in the raw magicks, swelling me with potent energies. As the quake settled, I touched my magick. How could I not, since it was everywhere? Vines and moss bent to my will, sprouted from rock, and attacked the blackguard. I knew what the creature did was an abomination to the land and had to be stopped. So I thrashed at it, but its stone skin was impervious to my magick. Vines cannot choke stone. Undeterred, the blackguard raised the Try'sil again and hammered at the vein of silver. Even more violent quakes occurred. I swear I heard the land itself split with this second strike. I knew if the hammer struck again, the vein would be completely severed, and these lands would be forever lost. I renewed my attack. As I lashed out at the blackguard, my probing vines discovered tiny chinks in its stone skin where reverberations from the use of the Try'sil had cracked its ebon'stone armor. I sent my smallest vines and mosses through these chinks to attack the d'warf inside. I tore at him and shredded him from the inside. As he fell dying, the Try'sil tumbled from his raised fingers to strike his head. The hammer split the blackguard's stone helmet and revealed the d'warf inside. With death near, he was finally released from the Dark Lord's enslavement. He turned to me with eyes that recognized the horrors he had committed."

Cassa Dar closed her own eyes and was silent for a breath. "I knew this d'warf." She opened her eyes, and her gaze bore upon

Er'ril, daring him to doubt her. "It was my own brother, the one with whom I played sneak-and-seek in the tunnels of our childhood home. As the waters rose, it was his dying thanks, as he choked on my vines, that finally chased me from the chamber. Sick at heart, I did not think to grab the Try'sil but simply ran."

Exhausted by her story, Cassa Dar sat down on her chair. "The hammer still lies down there, under the roots of Castle Drakk, awaiting its next master."

"The Dark Lord has never tried to retrieve it?" Elena asked.

"No, he used the Try'sil, then cast it aside—just as he did my people." She glanced to Elena. "But I believe your magick can call the Try'sil forth from its watery grave. I will show you how, but only if you swear a promise to me."

"To return it to your lands," Elena said, recalling the wit'ch's previous request.

The wit'ch nodded. "Use its power to break the ebon'stone might of the Black Heart. Avenge my people, then return it to Gul'gotha. Legend has it that as long as the Try'sil is returned to our homeland that our people will survive. Return it, and I pray the legend will prove true."

Elena felt her pain. "But why don't you return it yourself?"

Cassa Dar lowered her face. "I wish I could. But when the vein of silver ruptured and I engaged my magick to attack the blackguard, the magicks mixed and a part of my spirit was drawn into the land itself. That is how I've lived so long." She turned a tired smile upon Elena. "I am no longer just a d'warf; I am also a part of this land, this swamp. I can never leave."

Elena's look of sorrow drew a small chuckle from her. "Don't pity me, child," she said. "I love these lands. When I called these moss constructs my children, I was not lying. This entire land grew from me, and I cherish all of it. Here is my home. Though I may be lonely sometimes, I am content."

Silence settled around them as her story ended. No one knew what to say. Finally Elena spoke. "I will try to do what you ask," she said. "If given a chance, I will return the Try'sil to your homelands. But—" She held up her moss-shrouded hand. "—I can't do it like this. Will you lift your spell?"

Cassa Dar pushed back from the table and stood again. "No," she said, to the shock of the others, "you'll do it yourself. The power to dispel the bewit'ching has always been yours."

Elena's eyes grew wide. "But if I engage my magicks, the vines worsen."

"Come," the swamp wit'ch said. "I will show you how."

Cassa Dar led them to a staircase and guided them up its twisting course to the castle's top. As Elena stepped out into the night air, she was surprised at how clear the sky was above the castle. Stars shone brightly, and a half-moon glowed crisply in the early evening. Around the castle lay a blanket of swamp mists, but the tower itself rose higher than the clouds, thrusting its battlements up to the clear night sky.

Elena breathed deeply. Free of the swamp's gasses, the air smelled almost sweet.

"It stinks up here," Jaston said with a crinkled nose.

"You've just never smelled normal air," Mycelle said, clapping her friend on the shoulder.

As the other members finished gazing at the wondrous sights, Cassa Dar approached Elena, waddling on her squat legs. "When you first arrived and I examined your hands," she said, "what did I say to you?"

Elena remembered the wit'ch's whispered words. "That I didn't know half my power."

The wit'ch nodded and knelt beside her. "So true." She picked up Elena's two hands. "Why do you only use your right hand for magick?"

Elena's brows furrowed. "What do you—?"

Er'ril interrupted. "Because a mage can only bear the gift of Chi with one hand."

Cassa Dar glanced in his direction. "It is not Chi we are dealing with here, is it? It is not a male mage that stands before me. After Elena's arrival in Shadowbrook, I searched ancient texts and scrolls in the castle library. Some scribes wrote of Sisa'kofa bearing two forms of magick—wit'chfire from the sun and coldfire from the moon."

"We know that," Er'ril said. "Elena has practiced both. If she renews in sunlight, she bears the power of fire. If she renews in moonlight, she bears the power of ice. This we already know."

"Yes, but did you know that Sisa'kofa bore both at the same time?" Cassa Dar seemed to enjoy their surprised expressions. "An old text spoke thusly," she continued. " 'Like two faces of a coin, so the wit'ch of spirit and stone bore her wild magicks, fire in her right fist, ice in her left.' "

"That's impossible," Er'ril said.

"But have you ever tried?" Cassa Dar asked, searching all their faces. "I didn't think so."

While the others debated, Elena studied her left hand and its twisted vines. Surely, as Er'ril had said, such a thing wasn't possible. Before anyone could say otherwise or before her own fears could dissuade her, Elena raised her left hand into the moonlight and wished for power.

She gasped as her left hand vanished. The vines fell free from her arm, dead as if the roots had been cut off.

"Elena?" Er'ril said, finally realizing what she was doing.

With her body trembling, she pulled her arm down. Her missing hand returned.

Horrified, she held both arms up to the sky. Her right and left hands now matched. In the moonlight, both now swirled with the ruby stain of blood magicks.

28

THE BLOOD HUNTER MADE BETTER PROGRESS ONCE HE REACHED THE LAKE in the heart of the Drowned Lands. In the open water, the tangle of roots and the centuries of moldering debris that had clogged the narrow channels cleared from underfoot. The lake's floor, a soft clay, was cluttered with only an occasional uprooted tree that had flushed into the lake from recent floods.

As in the swamps, huge creatures lurked here too: beasts with quick tails and arcing fins. A flurry of tentacles suddenly swept out of the dark waters to wrap around the hunter's face, a beaklike mouth gnawing at his stone ear. He did not even bother to reach for it. His skin's poison killed the attacker within two steps, and it fell away dead. Other lake creatures investigated but kept their distance. A school of blue phosphorescent fish swam close, then with a flash of bright light, darted away in unison like a startled flock of sparrows.

Yet his flaming red eyes saw none of this. He plodded through the muck, determined to reach his prey this night. Soon the lake grew so deep that even his magick-wrought vision had difficulty piercing the midnight waters. Nervous at his poor sight, he forced his way to the lake's surface and tested the air.

Lightning still scented the winds. She was close.

As he struggled to keep his stone form afloat, he peered ahead. In the distance, seen as a phantom through the moonlit mists, rose a huge structure. He squinted his eyelids. The black magick sharpened his vision enough to pierce the whorled layers of fog. A structure of stone and mortar, draped in vines and moss, rose from the waters and reached toward the moon.

He stopped paddling and sank back into the murk. She was there! The wit'ch's spoor marked the night breezes flowing from the ancient structure. As soon as his feet settled into the clay of the lake floor, he forged on into the depths of the lake. He now knew where he was going. This time he would stay hidden in the deep waters. She would not sense him and slip away again.

As he marched, something huge passed nearby, its form hidden by the black waters. Only a shifting of shadows and a flash of an eye revealed its presence. Then it was gone.

Fearing nothing, he pushed on.

Soon the waters grew so deep that even his stone skin felt the depth's pressure, and the inky darkness was complete. He did not see the submerged castle until it suddenly loomed up directly in front of him.

Out of the gloom appeared the lower levels of the castle whose tower protruded from the lake. Its first floors lay half submerged in silt and clay. Tumbled stones marked where ancient battering rams had toppled its outer walls. He climbed past the piled and crumbling rubble to the inner courtyard. Ahead, wide doors lay open to the lake, shattered by old axes and pikes. Broken windows still held shards of glass, appearing like the fanged mouths of aquatic predators.

Torwren pushed into the lower levels of the submerged castle. Furniture and human bones lay underfoot, both crumbling to a soft mire under his stone tread. Algae lay thick upon the wall sconces, and waving fronds of kelp grew from between the bricks of the floor. Overhead, an ornate chandelier in the grand entryway now drooped with curtains of a thick black moss, reaching like limp fingers toward him.

As he continued toward the staircase, crabs scuttled from underfoot and a freshwater lobster scooted behind a large porcelain vase. Schools of darting fish fled his intrusion into their home. Another of the tentacled creatures shot a soft green cloud of glowing dye at him and vanished in its wake.

Undeterred, Torwren paused at the base of the grand staircase, its marbled steps now slick with algae. He meant to mount the stairs and begin the climb, but deep inside him, something stirred, a sliver of spirit that called him *down* rather than up. For a moment, he pictured a treasure awaiting in caves below the castle.

Frowning, he shook his head at this odd thought and shoved aside this errant desire, ignoring the small scream deep inside him. His path lay *up*, not down.

The blood hunter took to the stairs and began the long climb toward the lake's surface. His savage grin chased away his momentary hesitation. Creatures fled from his approach, and ancient bones smashed underfoot.

Somewhere above awaited his true treasure—the tender heart of his prey.

ELENA LOWERED HER HANDS. AT HER FEET LAY THE REMAINS OF THE choker's nest vines that had plagued her. While she should have been happy to be rid of them, the cost was too high. She stared at her left hand. Whorls of dark ruby stain slowly swam across her skin.

She raised her gaze to find Er'ril's wide eyes fixed upon her left hand. The usually stoic plainsman wore an expression of horror. Elena remembered how he had always shied away from the touch of her right hand when its stain was exposed. Now, with both her hands cursed with dire magicks, she felt as if a barrier had been raised between her and the plainsman. As long as her left hand had been normal, she had been able to reconcile herself with her wit'ch heritage, claiming herself at least half a woman; with her left hand plain, she had been able to touch the world like any normal person.

Staring into Er'ril's stunned face, she knew a part of her had died with the choker's nest. As Cassa Dar had dropped her facade and revealed the d'warf inside, Elena was forced to shed her own illusions.

She was not an ordinary woman. She was a wit'ch.

Tears rose in her eyes, and she sank to her knees atop the tower.

Mycelle appeared at her side and swept her up in her arms, kneeling beside her. "Hush, child," she whispered. "You are strong enough to handle this. You have your mother's intelligence and your Aunt Fila's backbone."

"But . . . I . . . I'm so scared," she sobbed. She could not meet her aunt's eyes.

Mycelle pulled back and wiped the tears from Elena's cheeks. Then she raised Elena's hands, not showing any shyness about her ruby flesh. "These are not curses," she said. "These are your wings. Like a fledgling teetering at the edge of a nest and scared to fly, you will overcome your fears and learn to soar." She clasped Elena's hands between her own and leaned close to Elena's face, staring her in the eye. "A hawk without its wings is not a hawk. This is who you are, Elena. Do not fear what makes you soar above others."

"But . . . I don't want any of this."

Mycelle settled back to her heels before Elena. "You are no longer a child, Elena. Sometimes responsibilities are thrust upon you when you are least prepared. Growing up means bearing the burden of responsibility as best you can and doing what must be done."

Elena sniffed back tears as Fardale nudged her arm with his nose. She glanced to his amber eyes. Images entered: *Wolves standing together as a pack. Bitches fostering each other's litters while others hunted. Males teaming up to bring down a deer*. Elena understood. In this matter, she did not stand alone. She was part of a pack.

She placed her palm on the wolf's cheek, silently thanking him. Then, taking a deep breath, she pushed to her feet. Mycelle stood beside her, a hand still on Elena's shoulder. Elena stared squarely at Er'ril for a silent heartbeat. The plainsman's stoic demeanor had returned, but in his eyes, Elena noted a glimpse of genuine concern.

Cassa Dar shambled over to them. "I'm sorry. I didn't mean for all this to upset you."

"It's not your fault," Elena said. "I needed to learn this eventually."

Cassa Dar nodded but seemed suddenly distracted. She glanced out toward the mist-shrouded night and stared silently.

"Is something wrong?" Elena asked.

The d'warf woman did not move. "I'm not sure," she finally mumbled. "I thought I sensed something, but then it was gone."

Er'ril nudged Mycelle. "Are you sensing anything unusual?"

Mycelle's eyes narrowed. "There are too many whirling magicks about this castle for me to seek clearly."

They all turned to the d'warf woman. She remained frozen for a few moments more, then shook her head and turned to them. "I don't like this. Perhaps we'd better see about retrieving the Try'sil and getting you all on your way. Come," she said, glancing back one last time before leading them toward the tower stair. "We must go down to where the lake has claimed the castle."

She guided them back to the kitchens, where the remains of their meal had already been cleared by her servants. She continued past this chamber and deeper into the interior of the great tower. At the end of a curving hall, they reached a wide staircase winding down toward the heart of the castle. Fresh torches flickered in bronze sconces, marking the way down. "Come this way," Cassa Dar said. "It's a long climb, but it's all downhill."

Er'ril stayed by Elena's side as they took to the stairs. Ever wary, he kept his hand on the pommel of his sheathed sword. "You don't have to do this, Elena," he said. "Free of the wit'ch's curse, we can leave for the coast at dawn."

"No, this Try'sil may prove a potent weapon against the Dark Lord's black magick. It's foolish to pass by such a tool." She glanced up to Er'ril. "Besides, I gave my word."

He nodded, almost as if she had passed some test. She felt a momentary flash of ire at his attitude. The journey continued in silence.

Mycelle and Jaston were ahead of them, conversing with Cassa Dar in low tones. Fardale padded silently behind them, a dark shadow on the stair. Halfway down, they came upon one of the swamp boys waiting with fresh drinks and a platter of cheeses. They rested for a short time.

During this break, Mycelle stepped up to where Er'ril and Elena sat on the stair. "I've been talking with Cassa," she said, settling beside them.

"Has she had more of those strange feelings?" Elena asked, worry itching at her resolve.

Mycelle patted the girl's knee. "No. All seems quiet."

"Then what were you talking about?" Er'ril asked.

"I was curious about the fusing of her spirit with the land. I find it interesting. I've traveled through other marshlands and swamps along the coast but have never encountered such a poisonous land as this. Well versed in toxins myself, I can assure you that the variety of venoms in these swamps is astounding."

"What of it?" Er'ril asked, fingering a chunk of a peppered cheese.

Mycelle lowered her voice. "I have a theory. I think these lands are a reflection of her spirit. Somehow when the land took a part of her essence, I think it also took a bit of her knowledge of poisons taught to her by the assassins, utilizing her skills as a poisoner for its own protection."

"Is that possible?" Elena asked. "I thought that the land's elemental magick was just raw power. Do you think there is some form of intelligence in this magick? Something that could interpret the memories of the swamp wit'ch and put them to use?"

Mycelle shrugged. "I don't know, but I find it intriguing." She nodded farther down the stair, to where Jaston and Cassa Dar were still deep in some discussion. "But it seems I'm not the only one who finds the wit'ch's company interesting."

The d'warf woman laughed at something Jaston said. The swamper waved his hand in the telling of some story. He, too, wore a grin. His shyness with his features was absent as he talked with Cassa Dar. It seemed that compared to the wracked and wrinkled form of the d'warf, Jaston did not find his own scars so troublesome.

Elena glanced to her aunt. A slight frown shadowed Mycelle's lips as she stared at the two of them. "Perhaps we've rested long enough," Mycelle said. "I'd like to retrieve this d'warf hammer and be on our way with the first rising of the sun. We've still a long way to reach the coast."

Her aunt pushed to her feet, drawing them after her.

The last leg of the journey was made in silence, everyone lost in thought. The remainder of the descent passed slowly. Just as Elena was wondering if the steps would ever end, the staircase suddenly widened enough that a battalion of men could have marched the steps abreast, and the stairs soon emptied into a cavernous chamber. Decaying frescoes marked the high ceiling, and four huge chandeliers, long and dark, hung down, their burnished surfaces now stained with green-and-black scars.

The party perched at the last step, unable to proceed into the grand room since the chamber had no floor. Instead the placid surface of the lake reflected the dark chandeliers and faded frescoes in its black mirror. Here the lake claimed the rest of the castle.

Two torches marked where the staircase entered the waters. Their flaming light failed to reach the far side of the huge room. It was as if only the lake lay beyond this last step.

Elena stared out across the dark surface. "How do we proceed from here?" she asked. "What am I supposed to do?"

Cassa Dar waddled over to her. One of her boys, naked this time, trailed behind her. When she reached Elena's side, she pulled the child up in front of her. "I have tried to send my children after the Try'sil. I know where it's hidden. Using their small hands, it took me nearly a century to clear the debris and discover the route to the cavern where the Try'sil lay lost. But only living hands can grasp its handle and carry it forth."

"So are you saying someone has to go down there?" Er'ril asked.

The d'warf woman nodded. Her eyes settled on Elena.

"Me?" Elena asked, her voice high with shock.

"Yes," she answered, placing a hand on the swamp boy. "One of my children will guide you."

"But how am I to breathe? Or even see through this murk?"

"Let me show you. I've had hundreds of winters to practice." She waved her boy into the waters. Without hesitating, he simply walked down the steps into the lake. "Come closer," Cassa Dar urged. "Come see."

They all knelt by the water's edge. Deeper in the lake, the figure of the naked boy glowed in the depths. His flesh shone with a soft green phosphorescence, the same hue as some of the glowing mosses seen on their travels here.

"Now watch!" Cassa Dar said. "It took me many winters to crossbreed a type of coastal air bladder with some of the local molds. I then built one of my children from it." She waved her arm across the water.

As they watched, lit by the mold light, the boy's skin began to bubble. From his pores, air flowed out. After a few moments, the agitation of bubbles cleared, and the boy stood in a clear pocket of air.

Mycelle glanced to the swamp wit'ch. "Can you expand that bubble enough to allow someone to travel with the boy?"

"Not before now," Cassa Dar said and turned to Elena. "I did not have enough magick. But in Shadowbrook, I sensed your raw power and suspected you might have the magick to accomplish it."

"What am I supposed to do?" Elena asked. "I have the barest control of my magicks."

"Skill is not what I ask. I need only your raw energy to fuel my creation." She waved her hand over the water, and the boy climbed back out, dripping wet, unchilled by the dank waters.

"And how do I empower your creation?" Elena asked.

Cassa Dar nodded toward the boy. "He needs your blood."

"Now wait," Er'ril said. "I've heard just about enough of this nonsense. Even if what you say is true, I won't have Elena climbing into the depths of this lake for a hammer. And if you think—"

Elena ignored him. "How do I give the boy my blood?"

"Nick your palm and grasp his hand in your own. I'll do the rest."

Elena remembered sharing her blood with both Uncle Bol and Er'ril when they were injured. Cassa Dar was not asking her to manipulate her magick, simply share its power, as she had done with the injured men. She nodded at the d'warf woman's words and drew her wit'ch's dagger. Its silver blade shone bright in the torchlight.

Er'ril suddenly grasped her wrist. "I can't let you risk yourself like this."

Mycelle stood at Er'ril's shoulders. "Perhaps the plainsman is right. This sounds more dangerous than it's worth."

Elena stared both of them down and yanked her arm from Er'ril's grasp. "I will take that responsibility," she said, using Mycelle's earlier words. She placed the tip of her knife to her left palm and dragged a line across it. Blood welled blacker than her ruby skin.

She turned. The naked boy had come beside her and had his tiny hand raised up toward hers. Elena instinctively reached to accept the offered palm, but then she hesitated. She stared into the boy's face and realized this was the boy who had accosted her on the streets of Shadowbrook: same mud-colored hair; same small, slightly pugged nose. She recalled the last time she shook hands with the little urchin.

"I won't hurt you this time," he said, noticing her hesitation. "I promise."

Elena was suddenly unsure. Whom should she trust? Should she listen to Er'ril and Mycelle? Or should she trust this wit'ch who had taught her a new side of her magick? She stared into the boy's eyes for a heartbeat, then gripped his hand with her bloody one.

She would trust herself.

ER'RIL WATCHED AS ELENA SHIVERED IN THE KNEE-DEEP WATERS. SHE had stripped down to her undergarments and waited as Cassa Dar finished her preparations. As Er'ril studied the girl, he sensed it was more than the cold waters that rattled her teeth, but his further protests against this endeavor had only firmed Elena's resolve to attempt it, and now his words only fell on deaf ears.

"It'll be cold at first," the swamp wit'ch explained to her as she stood beside the girl in the waters, "but once you're submerged and the bubble envelops you, you'll warm up."

Elena nodded.

"As you walk the stair, keep close to the boy and keep a firm hand on his fingers." Cassa Dar reached and clasped her own hand around the joined fingers of the boy and the girl. "Never let go."

The d'warf woman studied Elena for a moment more, then slowly passed her hands over the boy's naked flesh. Where her wrinkled palms touched, the boy's skin burst with sharp light. She nodded at this result. "More than enough power," she mumbled. "And with only a few drops of your blood." She straightened and backed from the waters. "No wonder the Black Heart fears you."

"Sh-should I go now?" Elena asked as Cassa Dar stepped from the waters.

"Yes, child. Proceed slowly. Give the air bubble time to grow strong around you."

Elena's eyes met Er'ril's for a moment. He could see the fear in her gaze and knew her vulnerable. He sensed if he pushed hard right now she would fold to his wishes. He opened his mouth to do just that, but his heart would not let him. He stepped closer to the waters. "Be careful, Elena. I know you can do this."

She smiled weakly at him. A mixture of pride and determination firmed her stance. She straightened her shoulders and, with the boy guiding her, she moved down the stairs into the deeper waters.

Now it was Er'ril's turn to shiver as he watched the lake swallow her away. He had to hold himself back from diving in and pulling her back into the air and light. His hand had closed to a tight fist.

"She'll be fine," Mycelle said at his shoulder, but her voice quavered, betraying her worry.

From where he sat beside Er'ril, Fardale nosed Er'ril's fist. The wolf sought reassurance, too.

Er'ril let his hand relax and found his fingers working through Fardale's fur. "Elena can do this," he repeated.

He watched the boy's light flare brighter in the waters. From the depths, the silent tableau of boy and girl glowed like the lamplit stage of a mummer's act. Elena fought to keep beside the swamp child. The buoyancy of the water did not seem to affect the boy. He simply stood on the step as if no water eddied around him, whereas Elena, using the boy's arm as an anchor, struggled to keep her footing.

Suddenly the bubbles again burst forth from the boy and swallowed the scene away in a flurry of phosphorescent froth. Er'ril held his breath until the bubbling cleared and he saw Elena. A huge pocket of air encased the pair now, lit from within by the boy's glow. No longer buoyed by the waters, Elena stood on her own feet on the steps, hand in hand with the boy. Though she was soaking wet and obviously shaken, Er'ril could see the relief on her face. Cassa Dar's magick was working.

"It's hard and takes all my concentration," the d'warf said as she knelt at the water's edge. "But her power is rich and malleable. We will succeed."

Elena raised her face and stared up at them from the water's depths and waved. Er'ril and Mycelle returned her salute.

With their acknowledgment, Elena followed the boy down the steps and off into the waters. Soon their progress across the room was only evident as a fading glow on the surface of the waters.

Then that, too, was gone.

AS ELENA WALKED WITH THE BOY, THE WALL OF WATER AROUND them distorted the surroundings of the submerged castle. It was like staring at the world through a carnival mirror, she thought. As fish would dart up, their features would swell large in the curve of the bubble's walls. Huge eyes would stare back at her, then in a flick of tail, vanish.

Though a trace of fear still ran through her blood, a sense of wonder also thrilled in her. She was strolling through the bottom of a lake. Who else ever had a chance to do such a thing?

Her mouth gaped as she studied the ruins of the castle. With the stairs draped in algae and moss, she had to mind her footing, but her eyes were constantly drawn to the preserved remains of Castle Drakk. Tapestries still hung on the walls, billowing slightly at their passage. Ornate oil lamps hung from chains, home to tiny creatures that ducked into hiding as they passed. Carved pine tables marked landings, their wood preserved for centuries in the brackish waters. Some furniture fell apart as their pocket of air pushed back the waters, the old pieces unable to stand on their own any longer.

Just when her fears had faded to a vague sense of worry, she came upon her first skull. The flesh had long been nibbled away by the denizens of the lake, leaving the white bone bright against the green kelp draped on the stair. She gasped and raised a hand to her throat to stifle back a scream.

"You're hurting my hand," the boy said from beside Elena.

Thankful for the distraction, Elena tore her eyes from the horrible sight to look to the boy. "I'm sorry," she said, and loosened her hold from its terror-tight grip.

"There'll be more," the swamp child said. "The assassins put up a fierce fight to keep their castle." Suddenly the boy pointed to an eel as long as four men as it writhed past their bubble. "Look. It's pretty!"

His boyish exuberance startled Elena. Cassa Dar had explained to her that the children she created were more than just moss golems. Though they were forged to her will and could not disobey, they also had a rudimentary intelligence that flavored their behavior. The swamp wit'ch could direct them and communicate through them, but her actions were shaded by the creations' own personalities.

"Cassa, if you can hear me," Elena said, "how much farther?"

The boy turned his small face up to her. "She says it's a long ways yet." The boy picked at his nose as he spoke. "We have to switch to a different staircase soon. Then it's a straight climb to the cellars." He examined his finger to investigate the success of his mining, then leaned over to wash his finger in the waters beyond the bubble's wall.

Elena winced as his finger pierced the bubble. She feared that breaking the seal would somehow disrupt the spell, but nothing happened. The magick sustained the bubble.

He licked his finger dry. "We'll leave the tower stair farther down and cross the castle proper to reach the back stair to the basements." He began to hum a tune as he continued down the wet stairs.

Suddenly a huge dark form passed overhead. It trailed tentacles as thick around as her own thigh. She shied down away from it, but it shot past with a flurry of suckers and limbs.

"Owww! Don't be such a scaredy-puss," the boy scolded. "She won't let any of the boogies get us."

Elena swallowed hard and nodded. She had to fight to loosen her grip again.

"Over there," he said sourly, pointing to a doorway at the next landing. "We have to leave here, cross through the servants' hall, pass the kitchens to the main hall, then follow it to the main stair. And I'm getting hungry. Do you have any cake?"

"No, I'm afraid not." Elena said, feeling less and less sure of her guide. "Maybe when we're done."

"I like mine with dollops of cream," he confided to her as if this were of utmost secrecy.

With this revelation, he led her through the landing's doorway and into the main body of the castle. As they progressed, Elena was glad she had a guide. Castle Drakk was a stone maze of rooms, halls, and cubbyholes. Alone, she would have been lost among these many twists and turns.

While walking, Elena kept her eyes from the growing number of piled bones, both human and otherwise. It was not just ordinary beasts that had assaulted the ancient castle. She passed one especially large skull whose shape she recognized and gave it a wide berth. A shiver passed through her. She recalled her own battles with the winged dreadlords of the Black Heart. The name *skal'tum* still gave her nightmares.

She hurried past, glad this battle was long dead.

By the time they reached the huge main hall, the boy's constant humming began to grate on Elena. "Cassa, must the boy do this?" she asked the empty air.

The boy glanced up to her and stuck his tongue out at her. "You didn't have to tell on me." He sighed loudly and bunched his shoulders, sulking, but at least he was silent.

She followed him to the back staircase. The way from here descended into a deep darkness. The black waters seemed to suck greedily at the boy's moss light.

The boy turned to her. "Do we really have to go down there?"

She squeezed his hand and nodded. "Yes, we do."

THE BLOOD HUNTER HEARD A WHISPER OF ECHOED VOICES PASS THROUGH the waters. He paused and cocked his head, straining for its source. For some time now, Torwren had been lost in the tangle of halls and rooms of the castle, unsure of how to reach the tower stairs. Backtracking and pushing through debris had eaten up volumes of precious time.

Then he had heard the voices and begun to follow, hoping that these voices were echoing down from above and could be used to track his way through the castle. Still, the acoustics under the water played a thousand tricks on his stone ears. He could not be certain he was going in the right direction as he followed the voices, his only clue in this sunken maze.

Soon he spotted a narrow staircase ahead, and his heart thrilled. Here must be the tower steps. As if to confirm his suspicions, voices and snatches of words again reached him.

He grinned in the dark water, scaring away a large lake trout that had investigated too closely. Surely he had reached the tower! He forced his legs to move, again feeling the growing torpidity in his stone skin. He had not fed now in over two days, and the ebon'stone had again grown hungry and sluggish. Still, he did not let this disturb him. He would soon feast on the heart of the wit'ch and regain his strength back a hundredfold.

Grinning, he pushed through the portal that opened onto the stairs, but when he discovered where the steps led, the smile crashed from his face. The narrow staircase wound *down*, not up. This was not the tower stair. Consternation stopped his feet. This was the wrong direction.

Then again the voices reached him. He swung his head. There was no mistaking the source in such close quarters. The smattering of conversation arose from below. His eyes squinted at the dark descent. Was he picking up a trace of light flowing from far below? He took a step toward it, then stopped again.

He did not have time for curiosity. The wit'ch lay in the tower above. He did not have the luxury to investigate the oddities of this drowned castle. He took a step back, but deep inside him, something fought with renewed vigor.

Down . . . down . . . down, this strange compulsion urged. Again a picture of some vague treasure flashed across his vision. It seemed to be some weapon—no, some trophy. A flood of desire surged through him, urging him to seek this treasure.

He shook his head. The wit'ch was his goal, not some buried treasure. Yet, still, he could not retreat from the stair. It was not the stiffening stone that trapped him, but indecision. Maybe he didn't have to fight this strange compulsion. Maybe both goals could be met. Whoever was speaking from below might know the way to the tower. And if not, his skin was starved for blood, and it would be good to feed before confronting the wit'ch. Both curiosity and hunger could be slaked by what lay below.

His decision made, the blood hunter began his descent down the stair. Deep inside him, something howled with glee.

ELENA HAD TO MOVE WITH DELICATE CARE. SHE NO LONGER STARED through the bubble's wall but kept her eyes on the rubble that lay strewn across the cellar floor. Its algae-slick surface sought to betray her footing with every step. She could not risk a fall and lose her handhold on the boy. If the bubble should break, she sensed the weight of the deep water would crush her instantly.

So she and the boy carefully picked their way across the jumble of boulders and bricks. The source of the strewn rubble soon became clear. The far wall of the cellar chamber had been exploded by some ancient force. The stone and brick lay ripped open to reveal the black caverns beyond.

"Just a little ways," the boy directed. "Into the caves and down a level is the chamber where the Try'sil lies."

She nodded. The two of them helped each other through the burst wall. Just as they stepped into the caves, the boy suddenly glanced over his shoulder, back into the cellar. His next words drove Elena's heart to her throat. "Something comes," he said. "Hurry!"

The boy sped into the deeper caverns. Lest she lose her grip on the child, Elena had no choice but to follow. "Wait! What is it?" she hissed at him, fear keeping her voice low but urgent.

"She's not sure," the boy said, referring to Cassa Dar. "This deep, she can't sense that well. She's tiring and needs all her concentration to keep the magick working." He yanked on her arm to urge her faster. "For her to sniff it, whatever it is must be close to us."

Elena needed no further urging—she would have sped past the boy if she knew the way. They dodged past fingers of rock that thrust up from the floor, while more stone fingers pointed at them from the cavern roof as they ran.

"Over there! Over there!" the boy urged, panic in his voice. He dragged her down a stone chute that emptied into a wide cavern chamber.

Elena stared through the wall of water around her. The chamber here bore its own light. It came from a bright river that split the cavern's floor in half. It was the vein of silver that Cassa Dar had described. The elemental magick in the silver glowed brightly, but its luster was strongest where the river entered the chamber from the rear wall. The glow in the silver channel nearest them, though, was only a weak shimmer. This section of the river contained only a feeble trickle of magick.

Elena saw where the bright channel abruptly became this weak dribble. Midway along, a section of the silver had been torn away. The collapsed bulk of a d'warf lay near this damaged section.

The boy tugged her toward the rip in the silver. "Hurry!" he urged. "Get the Try'sil!"

Elena sensed the boy's words were no longer his own but that Cassa Dar was speaking directly through the boy. She followed him to the body on the floor. It was not scavenged bone, but a statue of black stone. Even sprawled on the cavern floor, Elena recognized the squat form and thick limb: It was a d'warf.

The statue's head, though, was marred, cracked into shards of black stone that lay around its shoulders. Only here did bright white bone jut forth from the statue, a thick-browed skull.

"My brother," the boy said. Even through the panic, Cassa Dar's sorrow rang clear. The swamp child pointed to an object that lay near the statue's damaged head. "The Try'sil."

Elena knelt and reached for the weapon. There was no mistaking the ancient talisman of the d'warves: the Hammer of Thunder. Its wooden haft, as long as Kral's ax handle, was decorated with scrollwork and runes and ended in a forged-iron hammerhead as big as a pair of og're's fists. Its iron shone red, as if blood had been used to forge its might.

Elena hesitated. She could not possibly lift this massive weapon with only one arm, and she dared not let loose of the boy's hand. Still the fingers of her right hand wrapped around the haft. Gritting her teeth, she pulled hard, determined to carry it. To her amazement, the hammer rose at her touch as if it were but a light broom.

She held it up, her eyes glowing in the silver light.

"Beware, child!" the boy suddenly screamed. "Behind you!"

Hammer in hand, Elena swung around to see a monster stalk into the chamber from the other caves. At first glance, she thought that the black d'warf statue had somehow come back to life. Lit by the silver light of the river, the black form pushed into the room. Elena's eyes grew wide at the horribly misshapen form. She remembered Cassa Dar's mention of something foul escaping the Keep at Shadowbrook and pursuing them. Somehow Elena knew that here approached that dark hunter.

"It's another blackguard," the boy moaned. "How?"

As it neared, even through the distortion of the water Elena recognized the familiar shape. It was a stone-encased d'warf like Cassa Dar's brother. Its grin of yellowed teeth shone bright against its black lips. It spoke as it stalked toward them, its voice sounding drowned but its words comprehensible. "Where is the wit'ch?" it said as it neared.

Elena and the boy retreated from it, but it stood between them and the only exit. As they stumbled back, the boy's hand began to tremble in her own. The bubble of air began to expand wider around them, reaching toward the creature.

"Wh-what are you doing?" she asked the boy.

The swamp child's skin shone with a deeper glow. Elena could almost see through his skin to the tangle of vines and moss in his core. Whatever magick was being employed, it taxed the boy's illusion. He gasped as he spoke, tears glistening on his cheeks. "I'm trying to clear a space so you have room to maneuver."

"Why?"

"You must fight the blackguard," he said. "Use the Try'sil."

Elena's breath froze in her chest. The creature had to weigh ten times her own weight, all stone, muscle, and bone. How could she battle it with only this hammer? If she could access her magick instead, maybe she'd have a chance. But she could not let go of the boy's hand and had no way to pierce the skin of her right hand and release her powers. Raising the hammer between her and the creature, she was glad for its solidity, but she held no hope in its d'warf magick. She continued to back as the bubble expanded.

The stone d'warf stepped into the pocket of air. It still wore its grin as it left the lake. Waters hissed and steamed from its stone skin as it entered their bubble. "Now where is—?" It stopped as if its stone skin had suddenly frozen. Its nose raised to sniff at the air in the bubble for a few heartbeats. Then its eyes, flaming pits in its black head, fixed on Elena. "You!" Its grin spread wider. "You're the wit'ch!"

Elena raised the hammer higher in a trembling fist.

The blackguard's fiery gaze narrowed at the threat, as if gauging its danger. Then its eyes grew wide with recognition, and the foul flames dimmed in their sockets. It stumbled forward a step, and a small voice arose like a vapor from its foul lips. "The Try'sil," it gasped. "At . . . at long last."

The boy pushed in front of Elena. He spoke with the voice of Cassa Dar. "Remember your heritage, lord of the d'warves, and fight the Black Heart's control! Let us pass!"

The small voice was like a hissing whisper. "Too s-s-strong." The flames in the demon's eyes began to grow fiercer.

"Fight!" the boy screamed. "For our homelands! For our people!"

The fire in the pits of the blackguard's eyes flickered. "I can't stop . . ." His gaze suddenly swung to meet Elena's. His voice became a strangled gurgle. "Beware," he moaned, his words etched with sorrow and guilt. "Beware the Legion!"

Then the flames blew savage. Twin pyres of black magick flared from the demon's sockets, and it roared at the cavern roof.

Both Elena and the boy stumbled back. She knew the small flicker of resistance in the demon had been vanquished.

"He's gone," the boy mumbled, and fled to Elena's side.

The blackguard's gaze descended upon the cowering pair. A wicked smile stretched its stone lips. Before Elena could react, the stone d'warf lunged at her.

Blindly, she swung the hammer but knew it was too late. Yet, for some reason, the d'warf's leap began sluggishly, almost as if a bit of resistance still held some weak grip over its stone skin. Whatever the reason, her swing of the hammer had time to complete its arc, managing a glancing blow to the blackguard's head as it bowled toward her.

The boy, with surprising strength, yanked Elena out of the demon's barreling path. Again, the creature's sluggish response kept a stone hand from grabbing at her as she and the boy rolled aside. Scrambling away, the pair barely kept their feet, their hands only connected by their fingertips now.

Elena quickly regained a secure grip on both the boy and the hammer and faced the beast.

The blackguard swung around and raised a hand to his head. A section of his stone skull fell off with this touch. The Try'sil had lived up to its legend. It still had the potency to shatter ebon'stone.

As it probed its injury, Elena bit at the thumb that held the hammer. The demon, wise now to her weapon's power, would be more wary in its next assault. She needed her magick. She bit deep and finally tasted blood and went to reach for her wit'chfire.

"No, child!" the boy suddenly warned. "Don't call forth your magick! Its power is too wild and may disrupt my spell—but you've given me an idea."

As the d'warf picked another piece of loose ebon'stone from the side of his head, he tossed it aside and hissed at them, "You'll pay for that!" With no further warning, he charged.

"Stand still," the boy yelled at her as Elena began to flee.

Suddenly the bubble of air crashed down around them. The force of collapsing water shook the very roots of the castle.

Elena screamed, but the falling waters stopped only a handspan away from her nose. She was not crushed or drowned.

Such was not the case with the blackguard. Caught by surprise, the sudden weight of water crushed the d'warf to the stone of the cavern. The boy yanked on Elena. "Run," he urged. "We must get away."

They fled around the creature's sprawled form, giving it a wide berth even as it began to push back to its knees, stunned but quickly recovering.

"I'll try to delay it," Cassa Dar said, speaking through the boy as they ran from the cavern. "I can use the damage of the Try'sil to my advantage."

Elena needed no further urging. They fled as fast as they could run. Climbing the endless stairs, Elena's breath soon became a flame in her chest. But she ignored the pain, terror driving her forward.

From deep below, a bellow of rage pursued them.

"WHAT'S HAPPENING?" ER'RIL SNAPPED AT CASSA DAR. THE SWAMP wit'ch still knelt at the water's edge. Her wrinkled skin ran with sweat. Her shoulders trembled with exertion.

Jaston knelt beside the wit'ch, a hand on her bowed back. "Quit yelling at her!" he spat at Er'ril. "Can't you see how much this strains her?"

Mycelle stood next to Er'ril. "Jaston, we need to know: Is Elena alive?"

Cassa Dar's voice was a croak. "She lives. She flees. I do what I can to sustain the magick around her and attack what pursues her." Tears ran down her cheek. "I'm so sorry," she cried. "I didn't mean to risk her life. But my people . . ." Her voice trailed into sobs.

Jaston rubbed his hand on her back. "You didn't know. Do not whip yourself." He glared at Er'ril. "If she is to help save your little wit'ch, she could use your support and not your accusations."

Er'ril bit back a retort, but he could not fault the swamper's words. Right now, Elena's safety lay in the hands of this d'warf woman, and as much as it frustrated him, he would have to accept it. He could not even imagine the battle raging under the calm black surface of the lake and sent his prayers into the waters, willing his strength to Elena.

As he waited, his lungs ached from curbing his screams of frustration. His hand began to shake. Over the long journey, Elena had become more to him than just a wit'ch, and in this moment of impotent rage, he had to admit that more than fatherly concern shaded his emotions. He swallowed hard, refusing to allow himself even to name this other feeling. He pushed such thoughts aside. He must be ready.

Cassa Dar moaned nearby. "I can't stop him," she mumbled to the lake. "I keep trying to slow him, but his stone skin is more poisonous than my own venoms. And when I try to attack him through the damaged patch on his skull, he keeps ripping my vines away before they can take root and spread."

"And Elena?" Er'ril asked, this time not yelling.

"She flees and draws near to us . . . but the blackguard has regained his bearings and is quickly closing the gap."

Er'ril ground his teeth and pulled forth his weapon. Mycelle already had her blades out. Fardale growled at the lake.

Er'ril raised his silver sword.

Hurry, Elena! Come to me!

29

Elena limped as she ran, half using the hammer as a crutch. She had twisted her ankle on a loose stone in the stair. Only a frantic grab at the wall had saved her from tumbling back down the steps and losing her grip on the boy's hand. Trying to ignore her protesting limb, she struggled on with the boy. Pain and terror warred in her. Her burning lungs, aching side, and throbbing ankle all slowed her pace, while her panicking heart and racing blood urged still more desperate speed.

"He comes," the boy said beside her. Cassa Dar no longer spoke directly through the child. The wit'ch's full attention was on keeping the black d'warf from their heels. The boy sucked his thumb as he ran, his eyes wide with fear. "I don't want to die," he mumbled around his thumb.

Elena had not expected a survival instinct in the moss children. "We're not going to die," Elena assured him and herself.

She increased her pace, now pulling the boy. After passing back through the castle proper and reaching the tower stair, she knew the way. She sped up the stairs toward the distant surface of the lake.

The boy stumbled to keep up, his small legs struggling to match her pace. "Don't leave me behind," he cried.

"I won't."

The boy suddenly moaned. "He's right behind us. He's already on the stair."

Elena did not bother to glance over her shoulder. She bent, and using her grip on the boy's hand, she threw him over her shoulder onto her back. "Hang on!" she yelled. He squealed with fear, but his other arm wrapped around her neck.

Using the hammer as a balance against the boy's weight, she ran. Luckily the boy was lighter than a real child and not much of a burden. Her ankle screamed, but fear's fire had hold of her blood. She leapt like a deer up the steps. Back in her family's orchards, she and Joach had raced each other down the rows of apple trees. Though her brother had a longer stride, Elena had often still beaten him. She put every mote of strength in her limbs into this last sprint.

Overhead the dark waters suddenly brightened. She allowed herself a moment of relief. It was the torches at the surface. She sped on.

The boy then screamed in her ear. "He's here!" The child tried to climb over her back.

Elena glanced behind her. The hulking black creature lumbered up the steps behind her. He was a distance away, but his stride ate up three steps with every one of hers. Clinging vines fought at him, but he shrugged them off, hardly seeming to slow. His flaming eyes spotted her, and his pace increased.

With her attention turned, Elena's foot slipped on some loose kelp, and both she and the boy stumbled to the steps. The boy was up first. "Go, child!" he screamed—Cassa Dar again. "Swim for the surface. The boy will slow him."

As the child said these words, tears flowed down his cheeks—he didn't want to stay. Elena hesitated a moment, her heart going out to the terrified child. Then the little fingers let go of hers. "Go," he mumbled in a tiny voice. The pocket of air shrank quickly around her.

The monster was bearing down on them. Not wasting the boy's sacrifice, Elena dove through the bubble and into the lake. The bouyant water shot her toward the surface as she pushed off the stone stair. Bellows of anger rose with her.

Before she knew it, Er'ril's arm was around her, hauling her up the last steps and onto the dry stairs. Mycelle helped hold her upright as her twisted ankle gave way. Dropping the hammer from her numb fingers, Elena turned to where Cassa Dar knelt, orchestrating the fight against the creature. "The boy?" she asked.

No answer came from Cassa Dar's trembling form.

At the wit'ch's side, Jaston just looked Elena in the eye and shook his head. "She's too weak."

"Don't fret," Mycelle said. "The boy's not real, Elena."

Elena's lips grew tight, and she turned to Mycelle. "Give me my dagger."

Mycelle obeyed, retrieving Elena's silver blade from her discarded clothes. "We need to retreat up the steps," her aunt urged. "Regroup when it pursues."

"No," Elena said. She sliced a deep cut in her left hand, the one that had held the boy's hand, the one that had been born in moonlight.

Suddenly, behind her, the waters erupted in the still lake. Elena swung around on her good ankle. The black d'warf rose up, the boy's throat clutched in one fist. From the child's body, a tangle of vines burst forth and thrashed at the black skin of the creature, seeking purchase. Yet the battle was doomed, for where the boy's vines touched stone, they curled and died.

Blood dripped from Elena's slashed palm as she raised her arm. Where the red drops touched the lake, ice spread out across the waters in spidery traces. Elena touched the magick inside her, *igniting* it. Ice raced from her heart out to her hand and burst forth in a blaze of blue fire. Power again sang within her, and she let it rage.

She cast out her magick into the lake. Coldfire met the struggling blackguard and stunned him with its sudden frigid touch. Elena continued to pour her magicks forth, letting the magick run wild. This was no subtle spell, but raw power.

A scream echoed up from her throat as she cast out her coldfire.

The lake froze around the blackguard, trapping the creature in its tight embrace. Only its head, upper torso, and one arm were still above the ice. Elena poured forth more of her magick until the lake was frozen from wall to wall. Only then did she close her fist and stanch her river of coldfire.

As her eyes cleared, she blinked her frosted lashes and checked her handiwork. In the iced arm of the blackguard, the stone beast still clutched the small boy. There was no movement from either.

Elena sank to her knees, her hot tears like fire on her cold cheeks.

"You did it," Er'ril said, kneeling beside her.

Cassa Dar also stirred from the water's edge. Her eyes were wide with wonder at the frosted ice. The swamp wit'ch pushed to her feet, swaying slightly with exhaustion. With Jaston assisting her, she crossed to the discarded Try'sil. Jaston lifted the hammer so she could examine it. "Elena, you've accomplished a miracle," she mumbled, fingering the carved haft of the Try'sil with reverence and awe.

Elena did not answer, her eyes still fixed on the child frozen in the grip of the blackguard monster.

But at what cost? she silently wondered, thinking of a boy who liked his cake with a dollop of cream.

FARDALE WAS THE FIRST TO NOTICE SOMETHING WAS WRONG. THE WOLF stared out at the lake, and a wary growl flowed from his throat.

As Mycelle hurried to get Elena into her dry clothes, Er'ril stepped beside Fardale and studied the lake. He didn't see anything strange; the black d'warf still lay frozen in the ice's grip. He rested his hand on Fardale's back and noticed the wolf's hackles were up. "Do you scent something?"

Fardale took a step back from the lake's edge just as a sharp *crack* burst from the ice.

Everyone jumped at the sudden noise. All were instantly on their feet. Er'ril at first thought the noise was the ice breaking up, but he quickly saw he was wrong.

It was not ice shattering—but *stone*!

The ebon'stone d'warf was cracking apart. Its thick skull fell from its shoulders and rattled across the ice, breaking into even smaller pieces. Its arms snapped from where it protruded from the lake to crash like an axed tree. As the limb struck the ice, it too shattered into hundreds of ebon'stone shards. Nothing lay within. It was as if the d'warf had been a hollow shell all along. Soon all that protruded from the frozen water was its upper torso, like a black egg imbedded in the ice.

Fardale continued to growl.

Er'ril was unsure if any danger still lay out in the lake, but he had had enough of Castle Drakk. "I don't like this," he said. "Let's get away from here."

Cassa Dar had finished wrapping the Try'sil in a cloak and passed it to Mycelle's care. "I think you should," she said, her eyes still fixed on the remains of the blackguard. "Something smells wrong here."

As if hearing her words, a thunderous clap exploded, shaking the tower with its boom. One of the chandeliers above the lake broke with a screech of bolts and fell with a clatter to the ice. Chunks of painted plaster rained down.

Er'ril shoved Elena behind him. The girl hopped to keep her weight off her injured ankle. "Out," he yelled. "Now!"

In the center of the frozen lake, the torso of the d'warf had split open. Like some dark chrysalis, the stone peeled back in curled sections. From the heart of this foul structure a bloody mist arose above the ice, followed by the squirming, writhing mass of something pale as a corpse. It squeezed forth, contorting and swelling as it escaped its ebon'stone womb. Its body, the size of a large draft horse, plopped to the ice. Steaming a red mist from its pores, it rolled sluggishly. Then, like a butterfly fresh from its cocoon, it shook free moist wings, and a long sinuous neck curled from where it lay coiled close to its body. It turned large white eyes in their direction, searching blindly. Then huge flaps opened to sniff at the air, drawing it toward the huddled group on the stair. It spread its wings and opened its wet maw and screamed at them, a keening wail.

Er'ril did not wait for the creature to gain its bearings. "Back up the stairs," he ordered. He waved the others onward.

"Take the double doors at the next landing," Cassa Dar yelled, struggling in Jaston's arms up the steps. "A shortcut."

"No time!" Mycelle yelled.

They had not even climbed a dozen steps when the creature screamed again, its wail more strident. Still too weak to fly, it rose on a tangle of snakelike appendages and used its wings to propel itself across the ice at them. Its large bulk moved slowly, but its tentacled appendages were faster, like striking asps. A flurry of albino limbs shot up the steps after them.

Er'ril knocked Elena to the wall as probing appendages snatched at his legs. He swiped with his sword, severing the thick fingers. Where they touched, his pant legs smoked. He kicked the squirming sections away from his boots. The creature was sick with burning poisons.

On the far side of the stair, Mycelle fought the tentacles with her twin swords. She guarded over Cassa Dar and Jaston as the pair slowly climbed. Her blades were a blur before her. Er'ril was impressed with the havoc she wreaked. Splashes of poison smoked on her skin, but she ignored them.

Er'ril borrowed the plan of the others and slowly crept up the steps, herding Elena behind him. Progress was slow. Snaking limbs were everywhere.

Suddenly Mycelle yelled, a piercing cry. Er'ril glanced across the sea of tentacles and saw that a thick limb had wrapped around the swordswoman's waist. One of her blades had been knocked away; the other was wrapped in the grip of smaller tentacles. Mycelle was pinned.

Er'ril spotted the woman's fallen blade. It had landed near Jaston's feet. "Grab the sword," he yelled to the swamp man. "Help free Mycelle."

The man stood frozen, his eyes wide with horror. He did not move.

Cursing the swamper's cowardice, Er'ril tried to push Elena faster, but the girl slipped past him and stumbled down a few steps. Blue flames danced along the fingers of her left hand.

"Elena!"

"I can slow it," she yelled back, already raising her hand. "Free Mycelle!" A wave of coldfire shot from her fingers to slam into the bulk of the beast as it reached the base of the stairs. The force stopped its charge toward the steps and slid its bulk back across the slick ice. The tentacles were dragged along with it, clearing a path for Er'ril to cross to Mycelle. He dashed over and hacked at the thick limb wrapped around her waist. Her face was contorted with agony. Her clothes smoked, and when Er'ril finally sliced away the limb, he saw it wasn't just her shirt that smoked: Her very flesh lay burned around her waist.

He glared at Jaston. "Help Mycelle up the stairs."

Jaston came out of his shock and took Mycelle under one of his arms as Cassa Dar led the way up the stairs.

Fardale, who had no weapon and had been hanging back from the fray, suddenly barked and raced down the stairs past Er'ril.

Er'ril swung around. Elena stood before a wall of lashing tentacles. She washed her coldfire over the snaking limbs, keeping them at bay—but the magick did little else. Where her blue flames struck the creature, its pale flesh grew red hot and resisted the ice with some inner fire of its own.

Elena was losing her battle—and one of the appendages was creeping along the roof, over Elena's head, out of her sight. The treacherous limb now reached toward her unprotected back. But Fardale raced to protect her. The wolf leapt off the steps and flew through the air. He snatched the creeping limb in his jaws, and his momentum tore the appendage away from Elena.

The wolf landed on his paws and gagged the limb from his mouth. The fur around his muzzle lay singed, and his tongue, lolling from his jaws, had been burned black.

Elena switched hands, obviously hoping *fire* would work where ice did not. She had already bloodied her right hand, and scarlet flames now danced in her palm. She sent a shaft of wit'chfire at the beast. Its flaming touch had once pierced even the formidable protection of a skal'tum, but the magick seemed to have little effect on the foul creature here. The beast mewled at the assault and was driven farther back onto the ice. But where the stream of magickal fire struck, its pale flesh grew black, like frostbit skin, and doused the scorch of the flames.

The beast remained unharmed.

Fardale loped up the steps while Er'ril hurried down. Burdened with his sword, he urged Elena back. "The Dark Lord has grown wise to your magicks," he warned. "We must flee while we can."

Elena ignored him. Her skin ran with sweat, and her face was pale. She raised her right hand again. Flames roiled to a sun's radiance in her fist as she built the magick to a fierce heat.

Er'ril did not know what she thought to accomplish. "Elena?"

The girl thrust her arm toward the beast and released her magicks in a mighty rush. The fire struck, not at the beast, but at the ice under its tangle of tentacles. Her fire ripped into the ice, and the lake exploded under the creature. Steam swelled through the chamber. In a single breath, what had been ice became water once again.

Through the steam, Er'ril caught glimpses of the beast's flailing appendages and beating wings. Caught off guard, it struggled at the sudden change of its footing and lost. The beast sank into the waters.

"Wise girl," Er'ril commended her.

But Elena was not done yet. She raised her left hand and sent forth her coldfire. Steam became icy mist, and the lake froze over where the beast had sunk. Once again the room was solid ice.

Elena lowered her arm and turned to Er'ril, her eyes still raging with her magick's use. "We can go now," she said. "I don't know how long the ice will hold it, but perhaps long enough for escape." She tried to mount the stairs on her own but swooned with exhaustion.

Er'ril had to drop his sword to catch her. Jaston appeared at her other side. The swamp man's and the plainsman's eyes met over the girl. Jaston's face shone with shame, but also with determination.

He held Elena until Er'ril could retrieve his sword and sheathe it. "I'll take her from here," Er'ril said coldly as he scooped the girl up in his one arm. He headed up the stairs. Jaston hung back a moment, then followed.

Up at the next landing, Cassa Dar, Mycelle, and the wolf awaited them.

"This way," the swamp wit'ch urged, leading the way through a set of doors off the stairway. "This hall will take you directly to the exterior stair."

Er'ril followed Fardale into the passage. The wolf padded forward, ears cocked tall, listening for any new dangers ahead. The footsteps of the other members of the party echoed on the stones behind Er'ril. He hurried with Elena cradled in his arm. She had one of her arms hooked around his neck, and she leaned into his chest.

"You did well," he whispered under his breath.

She raised her head. "Did . . . did you say something?"

"No, just hang on. We're almost out of this cursed castle."

Suddenly a massive quake shook the tower. The stone floor danced under his feet. Er'ril almost stumbled atop Elena. He caught himself just as the explosive crash reached his ears.

"It broke loose," Elena said as he regained his balance. "Let me down."

Er'ril ignored her. He wasn't about to let her out of his grip again—not until she was safely away.

AT THE END OF THE PASSAGE, CASSA DAR WORKED AT THE SECRET DOOR. "Just beyond here," the d'warf woman said, "is the stair that runs along the outside of the tower, the steps that you all climbed up earlier."

Elena pulled her arm free of Er'ril's neck. "I'll be safe here," she told the worried plainsman. "Go help Aunt My watch the hall."

Er'ril nodded, lowering her carefully to the floor. Then he leaned close to Elena, exacting a promise from her with his eyes. "Don't go outside until I return."

She nodded her agreement.

Satisfied, he slipped down the hall to where Mycelle and the wolf guarded their rear. Nearby, Jaston stood in the swamp wit'ch's shadow, his face lowered, his eyes somewhere far away.

Cassa Dar talked as she worked, clearly anxious. "This was an old camouflaged door used by the assassins to sneak up on the rear flank of any marauding force that attempted to climb the stair. In the past, there were nomadic robber bands that—" The catch finally released with a snap, and the door sprang open a bit. The swamp wit'ch wiped her hands and stood. "There we go!"

Jaston called to the others, his voice cracking slightly. "The door's unlatched!"

While the others hurried forward, Cassa Dar hauled the heavy door wide open. Beyond the threshold, the night breezes greeted them. It was still dark, and the moon had long since set. "Daybreak must be near," Cassa said. "The swamp mists are always thickest upon the lake just before morning."

Elena had to trust her judgment. To her it was the darkest night outside, and sunrise seemed no more than a fanciful dream.

Mycelle hurried them forward. "We'd best hurry. I heard something in the hall just as Jaston called."

As if to emphasize her point, a wail erupted from behind them. No one had to say what monster made such a noise. "It's close," Er'ril hissed. "Everybody outside so I can get this door shut."

They rushed out onto the stairs, boots flying down the steps. Er'ril stood by the door, attempting to drag it closed. Even in the dark, Elena saw the veins bulging at his temples, the muscles of his arm bunching thick. The door was stuck.

"Er'ril?"

"Stay back, Elena!"

Mycelle placed a firm grip on her shoulder, silently telling her to obey.

"I need time to build a boat," the wit'ch said from the water's edge. "He must get that door closed."

A second bellow of rage erupted from down the hall; then the monster's shrieking changed in pitch. It had spotted Er'ril.

The plainsman's attack on the door increased. A reddish mist flowed out into the night from the open threshold. Elena's fist was at her throat. It must be almost atop him.

Suddenly, a questing tentacle shot out and snatched at Er'ril's neck. The plainsman gasped as his neck burned. Unarmed, his hand scrabbled at the choking limb. Before anyone else could react, Jaston raced up the steps, his skinning dagger clutched in his hand.

Reaching Er'ril in a heartbeat, he slashed savagely at the appendage. Its acid blood etched his dagger and burned his hand and arm. He screamed, not in pain from the poison's burn, but in a rage pent up over many winters. He ravaged the limb with his knife until Er'ril fell free of its grip.

"Hurry," Er'ril choked, and threw off the limb. Together, both men forced the door and slammed it shut. Leaning against the door, Er'ril patted Jaston on the shoulder. "Thank you."

Just then something huge crashed into the door, the shock so intense that Er'ril was knocked outward by the concussion. The plainsman cartwheeled his arm at the edge of the stair, but one arm was not enough. Jaston reached for him and missed. Er'ril tumbled off the stair and crashed into the lake below.

"Er'ril!" Elena ran to the stair's edge. Even in the mist-shrouded starlight, Elena saw huge fins arise and cut toward the ripples in the lake. Er'ril's head bobbed up, and he swam with vigorous kicks toward the lowest stair. But again, one arm made a poor swimmer. The fins closed quickly upon him.

"Don't fret," the wit'ch said, appearing beside her. Cassa Dar waved a thick arm across the water, and the fins turned away in unison and sank from view. "I don't have time to build a boat," she muttered as Er'ril neared. "I'll have to improvise."

With these words, Cassa Dar threw herself off the stair to land flat on her belly atop the lake. Instead of sinking, her flesh blew out in a nest of vines and moss, some glowing brightly in the night. "I told you I was more than just d'warf." Then her form was swallowed away as a raft of vines and moss formed around her. Her voice, though, still rose from the tangle of vines. "Hurry. Climb on board."

Everyone hesitated a moment, uncomfortable with climbing atop the vessel that was built from an old woman's body. Then another concussion shook the tower steps as the beast slammmed into the door again.

Er'ril swam up to the edge of the boat and clambered up. "What are you all waiting for?"

No one needed further prodding. The party scrambled onto the living raft. As soon as all were on board, the raft took off across the waters, quickly gaining speed. Cassa Dar's voice arose from the floor. "I'll not be able to talk with you much longer."

Fardale sniffed at the raft, his ears cocked and his head tilted.

"Powering the raft," Cassa Dar continued, "taxes my elemental abilities, and the farther from the castle I travel, the weaker my skill will become."

Er'ril ripped off his soaking shirt, freeing his arm of its clinging grip. He checked his sheath. His silver sword was still in place. "Will you be able to get us across the lake?"

"Yes, but after that, I must return to Castle Drakk, to my nexus of power. From there, I can guide you all the way to the coast."

"But what about the beast in the castle?" Elena asked.

"I don't think it will remain there long. Hopefully just long enough for you all to get lost in the deep swamps. Then I can return to my castle."

But Cassa Dar's hopes were not to be realized. A thunderclap suddenly roared over the waters. All eyes turned to the castle. The dark tower still stood like a shadowed island behind them. Against its black stone, a white form could be seen, aglow in the starlight.

"It's burst through the door!" Mycelle said in horror.

From the prow, Elena stared back and watched the beast take to the air, its wings huge white sails to either side. They cut through the mists like a predator's fins slicing through the lake. But Elena knew that no wave of Cassa Dar's hand would save them now. She glanced to her own hands. Both her palms were still red—no longer with the dark ruby of before, but with a weak scarlet. Her powers were low.

She stared skyward as the beast turned on a wing and dove toward them. Tendrils of its snaking appendages hung all the way to the lake now, leaving small ripples in the still waters with their foul passage. Earlier, when Elena had been at full strength, the beast had resisted her magicks; what could she hope to accomplish now?

Still, she slipped free her wit'ch's dagger.

Er'ril stood near the stern of the boat, barechested with his sword in hand. Mycelle stood armed beside him, marking the progress of the beast against the speed of Cassa Dar. She could see that they would not escape the lake. Seeming to sense her gaze, Er'ril glanced over his shoulder at her, an apologetic look in his eyes. He knew they would not survive this. Still, he raised his sword. At least he would die fighting.

And so would she, Elena decided. She drew the tip of her silver blade across each palm, then sheathed her dagger. Cupping her hands on her knees, she stared as the blood welled into her palms and released the dam of her magicks. As she allowed the power to sing through her blood, each hand began to glow. The Rose of her right hand grew into a fierce crimson, while the Rose of her left hand burst forth with an icy azure luminescence.

Here were the two sides of her power, and both were now useless.

Elena stared at her glowing hands. Suddenly her eyes grew wide. What if—?

Elena shot to her feet, moving so suddenly the boat rocked. Ahead of her, Er'ril grunted, shaken off balance. He glared over his shoulder at her.

It was too late to explain. The beast had reached them.

As it swept over the fleeing boat, its appendages writhed and tangled under it, grabbing at the raft and its occupants. As the others fought the beast with their swords, Elena saw Fardale yanked into the air by a coiled limb of the monster.

Jaston leapt after the wolf, flying over the edge of the boat, his knife clamped in his teeth. The swamp man caught the vinelike appendage with both hands, then loosened one grip to snatch the dagger from his mouth. As his palms burned, he sawed at the limb, a scream frozen on his lips, until the appendage severed and both he and the wolf tumbled into the lake.

Elena knew this was just a test of their strength. She stared up into the night sky. The main bulk of the beast glided on its huge wings. Its pale eyes seemed to study the boat; then suddenly it focused directly on her. It was no dumb beast that hunted them. A malignant intelligence lay behind this creature's dead eyes.

She knew the Dark Lord watched and guided this beast.

It studied her for a heartbeat more; then a scream of triumph burst from its throat as it dove toward her, wings tucked for speed.

"Everyone down!" Elena screamed, not bothering to see if she was obeyed. From here, she knew the battle was hers alone.

She raised her arms. Not just her right or her left—*but both.* She brought her two red hands together and entwined her fingers. This time she did not unite wit'ch and woman—but coldfire and wit'chfire!

She thrust her joined fists at the diving monster and let her magick rage forth. The power blew out from her with such force that Elena was knocked backward. She had to anchor her legs to keep her feet.

From her fists, a rage of cracking lightning, searing flames, and shredding winds swept out. The lake screamed with her magicks. Thunder boomed across the waters.

Elena knew the name of this awesome power.

Stormfire!

This new magick ripped into the beast, haulting its dive. Like a fly in amber, it hung trapped as crackles of lightning danced across its flesh and savage winds tore its wings to shreds. Flame followed and laid waste to all it touched. The beast writhed within a ball of fierce energies, wailing and thrashing its appendages.

Elena poured every last dreg of her magick into the creature.

Finally its skin cracked, its tentacles curled and blackened, and its wings became bone and ash. It crashed into the lake with a final keening scream.

Waves and swells rocked the boat; everyone standing was knocked down. When the boat's rocking finally calmed enough, Er'ril sat up and glanced to Elena to make sure she was safe.

She leaned up on an elbow and gave him a nod. No words were needed.

A voice called out from the lake. Mycelle crossed to the vessel's edge and helped Jaston crawl into the boat. He dragged the sopping wolf behind him. Fardale's fur was burned in thick swatches, but the shape-shifter lived.

Er'ril crawled over to Elena as the remaining swells died down. He helped her sit up. "What was that magick?" he asked.

"Stormfire," Elena said breathlessly.

Er'ril stared at her, then took her hands one at a time and examined them. He had no qualms about touching her soft white skin, bare of magick. He glanced back to her face, wonder in his eyes. "How . . . ?"

"You told me mages in the past could only bear magick in one hand." She squeezed Er'ril's palm as emphasis.

Er'ril nodded and kept his hand in hers.

"But I can wield both," Elena said. "And since no one but Sisa'kofa could wield two magicks at once, I knew the Dark Lord could not be prepared for such a united attack . . . so I took advantage of his blindness." Elena smiled shyly up at Er'ril. "But even I didn't expect such a show."

Er'ril pulled her into his embrace and hugged her hard. "You continue to amaze me, Elena."

She leaned into him, relishing his warmth and scent. She hoped this moment would never end.

Then the lake erupted in a huge wave and jarred them apart. The boat almost flipped with the force of the sudden surge. From the waters to the side of the boat, a huge head burst forth, burnt and scarred, borne on a long sinuous neck.

Its maw swelled open, lined with thousands of shredding teeth. Its blackened eyes searched the boat, blind but still able to sense its prey by scent. It struck at Elena.

She screamed and raised her hands, but no power lay there. Er'ril threw his body atop hers, knocking her down and protecting her with his own life.

Suddenly a second surge rocked the boat, knocking the vessel back from the beast. Er'ril pushed up to see. Elena followed.

Up from the lake rose a monstrous, scaled head, huge jaws hinged wide open. Its teeth, shining in the light, were as long as Elena's forearm. With a whip of its huge tail and a clacking roar, it burst forth, snatched the Dark Lord's creature by its long neck, and shook it savagely. The pale beast squealed its death cry, thrashing in the jaws of the huge swamp creature.

With the beast already weakened, the lake monster finished what Elena had started. It twisted and tore at the pale creature until the head of the burnt beast fell limp in its jaws.

The swamp reptile, still holding its prey clamped in its huge jaws, rolled a huge black eye toward the raft, then sank below the waters.

Jaston spoke from the edge of the boat. "A bull kroc'an."

"Was it called up by Cassa Dar to save us?" Elena asked.

The swamp wit'ch's voice rose weakly from the floor, just a whisper. "No. It was no magick of mine."

Jaston stood at the boat's edge, staring out at the black waters. His wet clothes clung to him. He turned to the others, no longer hiding his scars. "I know these swamps, and I know the kroc'an. That roar before the bull attacked was a cry of revenge." Jaston turned back to stare at the lake. "These swamps are my home," he said, his voice a blend of warmth and pride. "Out here, creatures know how to survive."

Elena sensed he spoke of more than just the bull kroc'an, and from Mycelle's sad smile as she stared at Jaston's back, she knew her aunt must also suspect the extra meaning behind the swamp man's words. Though still scarred, something vital had finally healed in the man.

Sighing, Elena stared out across the calming waters and remembered Mycelle's words back at the Painted Pony in Shadowbrook: *Not all wars are won with swords and magick.*

Elena studied her white hands.

Somehow those words made her happy.

TWO DAYS LATER, IT WAS STILL DIFFICULT TO SAY GOOD-BYE. EVEN though the swamps had held such horrors, Elena would truly miss her new friends, allies forged in fire. But with their party's wounds treated and their plans finally laid, they were ready to strike for the coast.

So, as the sun rose on the day of their departure, the party stood on an island at the edge of the large swamp lake. Er'ril busied himself with packing the boat while Fardale nosed the plainsman's handiwork. Mycelle and Elena still faced Jaston and Cassa Dar, finishing their good-byes. From here, the wit'ch would guide them directly to the coast.

"You could still come with us," Mycelle said to Jaston.

He shook his head. "I have the horses to attend to," he said. Jaston was going to arrange to have their mounts, still stabled in Drywater, join a swamper's caravan to the coast. Elena had insisted that Mist not be abandoned. The mare would not thrive as a swamper's mule—loaded with gear, stopping every fifth step to chew razorgrass, and refusing to budge until her belly was full. No, Mist would not make a good workhorse.

Jaston stepped back from Mycelle. Their trials at Castle Drakk had revitalized the scarred man. He hardly seemed like the sullen man they had first met. He now held his back straight and spoke with good humor, unashamed of his scars. "Besides," he said, "my home is here in the swamps."

Elena saw how his words wounded her aunt, as did the brief glance Jaston gave the wit'ch as he mentioned his love of the swamps. Her face sad, Mycelle turned away and straightened her shoulders. Elena saw the resignation in her eyes. Some flames gone to ash could not be rekindled, even when a small spark was still left. "Then I guess we'd best be off," Mycelle said with false cheer. As she walked away, her aunt held a hand to her side, where the poisons of the tentacles had burned deep. But Elena suspected it was more than just the wound that pained her.

So Mycelle and Jaston parted—more than friends, less than lovers—leaving only Elena to say her good-byes. She hugged Jaston and turned to Cassa Dar. The wit'ch had redonned her magickal garb, standing again as an auburn-haired beauty. Her slender hands reached to Elena's gloved fingers. "You bear the heritage of Sisa'kofa. There is much power in your hands," she said, then raised a palm and rested it against Elena's chest. "But your true strength will always come from your heart. Remember that, child."

Elena's eyes misted up.

"And please . . . remember also your promise to me," she continued. "You're my people's only hope."

Elena nodded. "I will see to it that one day the Try'sil is returned to its rightful place."

Cassa Dar smiled, and they hugged. The illusion of the wit'ch was so strong that even with her arms wrapped around Cassa Dar, Elena could not discern the ancient d'warf hidden within the moss magick.

At last they parted company.

Elena's group climbed aboard the boat and settled in. With a soft bump, the vessel receded from the bank, moving on its own, borne away by Cassa Dar's swamp magick.

Elena, sitting at the stern, turned for one last view of Jaston and Cassa Dar. The pair still stood on the mossy bank, arms raised in farewell. Elena noted how the wit'ch slipped her hand into Jaston's as she waved them off. Elena smiled. So it seemed Mycelle was not the only one with an interest in Jaston.

This small display of affection by the wit'ch did not pass unnoticed by Mycelle either. Her aunt's cheeks reddened, and her wave of farewell was perfunctory. She quickly swung back around to discuss some detail with Er'ril, bowing her head away from the scene behind the boat.

Elena was glad her aunt had turned away and missed what transpired next. Just as their boat disappeared around a bend, Cassa Dar raised a hand to the swamp man's cheek. Where she touched, the man's scars vanished, swept away by moss magick. Jaston examined his face with tentative fingers, wonder in his eyes. But as he turned toward Cassa Dar, Elena caught a glimpse of something more in his eyes—something that suggested Cassa Dar's interest might not go unrequited.

Elena smiled to herself and twisted forward. Jaston had always said he loved the swamps. Now perhaps he'd have a chance to prove it.

From near the boat's bow, Er'ril suddenly cursed as he rubbed a balm the wit'ch had given them on his raw neck. His skin lay blistered and red from where the poison tentacle had touched him. He then wrapped the wound with a bandage and settled deeper in the boat. "I'll be glad to be rid of these poisoned lands," he muttered.

"As will I," Mycelle echoed, her voice a whisper as she glanced one last time behind them.

Elena placed a hand on her aunt's knee. There was no medicinal salve that could soothe this pain. All Elena could do was offer Mycelle her support.

Her aunt gripped Elena's hand and did not let go.

It would be a long trip to the coast.

30

Six days after leaving Castle Drakk, Elena stepped on the first solid ground in what seemed like ages. Her feet were slightly unsteady after the many days of traveling through marshy soils and bobbing on rafts through swamp channels. She adjusted her pack to balance herself and tested the ankle she had twisted on the flight up the castle's stairs. Only a dull twinge remained, like a distant memory of its former pain.

Beside her, Fardale stretched each of his legs, arching his back and relishing the release from the boat. The wolf clearly enjoyed the clean sunshine after the constant mists of the bogs. Elena studied the swaths of clipped fur on the wolf's torso; his burns were scarring well. The swamp wit'ch's salve was helping the others' injuries, too.

Er'ril stepped next to her, wincing slightly as his pack brushed his bandaged neck. Mycelle walked carefully behind him. She had sustained the worst injuries. The poison ring around her belly still pained her often.

Luckily, the hike from here wasn't far: half a day's journey at most. Er'ril knew someone who owned a remote cottage among the bluffs, a place were they could hide and rest while their wounds healed.

It was the promise of the cottage—of real beds and hearth-cooked meals—that kept the party moving.

Yet the luxuries of a clean bed were not the only motivation for their hard pace. In less than half a moon, Mycelle would need to journey to Port Rawl and search for the other members of their party. Elena looked forward to seeing Kral, Tol'chuk, Meric, and Mogweed again. She missed them dearly.

With their boots on real ground, Er'ril led them on the last leg of their long journey from Winter's Eyrie to the coast. As the sun climbed the sky, he guided them east toward the ocean, aiming slightly south.

The land rose gently higher as they left the marshlands and entered the rolling coastal hills. Birds called and rabbits bounded from their path as they left the poisons behind them. The air was scented with green meadowgrass and purple jonquils, while patches of honeysuckle swarmed with the buzz of bees. Summer claimed these hills, but the heavy milkweed pods that hung like the heads of drunken men warned of summer's end.

By noon, they crested a large hill. Not far ahead, the ocean appeared. Elena stared at it, gawking. It was as if the world ended beyond the bluffs. From horizon to horizon lay the blue waters of the great ocean. Nothing interrupted the smooth expanse except for an occasional misted green island.

"The edge of the Archipelago," Er'ril said, pointing toward the distant isles.

And, Elena thought wearily, their next destination. She sighed. But that was another day. For now, she would enjoy the sunshine and the scent of ocean breezes and forget for a time that she was a wit'ch. She refused even to glance at the two deerskin gloves that hid her ruby skin.

With the ocean in sight, Er'ril called for a meal break, passing out the last of their ration of dried meat and hard bread. It was a glum meal until Mycelle offered Elena a few berries that she had gathered from a small barbed bush nearby. Elena's eyes widened. She knew those ripe berries. They were her favorite—blisterberries! Accepting them greedily, she popped them in her mouth. They were tart and sweet at the same time. Her mother had grown such bushes in their family's garden, making the most excellent tarts from those few berries that Elena had not already picked and consumed by the time they were ripe.

Elena glanced around the hills. More of the small prickly bushes dotted the slopes. She grinned, her teeth stained purple. The journey from here didn't seem so bad.

Mycelle spoke to Er'ril as Elena finished the last of the berries. "So this friend of yours out here in the bluffs," she said. "Is he to be fully trusted?"

Er'ril nodded as he packed away their gear, then sat back on his heels to eye Mycelle. He rubbed absently at the stump of his arm. "He's a brother of the Order. I have full faith in his loyalty and would put my life in his hands without any misgivings."

Mycelle studied Er'ril a moment before speaking. "But it's more than just your own life this time."

Er'ril's gaze flickered toward Elena and back again. "I know my duties," he muttered, and returned Mycelle's stare. "If you don't trust this man, then trust my judgment."

Mycelle stood up slowly, protecting her injured belly. "I do, Er'ril."

The plainsman's eyes widened slightly at her declaration. He covered his surprise by snugging his pack closed. "Then let's be off while the daylight holds."

With their meal finished, they moved on through the hills. After a time, they reached a rutted path that hugged the coastline and made their pace easier. The bluffs were lonely country. From the fields, a few curious sheep and sleepy-eyed cows watched them pass, and they met only a single wagon on the road, the driver tipping his hat. Unfortunately, the rig was heading in the wrong direction to beg a ride.

So they continued on foot. The hike stretched endlessly, and the day had turned to twilight by the time a small cottage appeared ahead. It stood atop a tall bluff overlooking the seas. Its thatched roof and hewn stone walls seemed the finest palace to Elena's tired legs.

A dog barked and ran out to meet them as they approached. But when it scented Fardale, it grew less sure and backed away. A few goats also noted the passage of a wolf near their midst and bleated feebly and moved off. Only a gaggle of ducks actually waddled over to greet them, quacking for scraps of bread or seed.

Elena smiled at them.

Er'ril, though, shooed the fowl from underfoot as he led their party off the wagon path and across the yard toward the cottage. At the door, he rapped soundly.

At first, no one answered, and for a moment, Elena feared that maybe no one was home. But then the steps of someone sounded from within. Somewhere deeper in the cottage, a voice called out. "Git the door already!"

Er'ril smiled. "That would be Brother Flint," he whispered to her. "Always in a foul mood, but with a heart as big as the sea."

Whoever bore the brunt of this man's rough affection finally opened the door. He stood just a little smaller than Er'ril. The plainsman nodded, not recognizing the red-haired young man—and for just about two heartbeats, neither did Elena. Then her eyes grew huge, and she shoved Er'ril aside. She flew at the man in the doorway and wrapped her arms around the shocked fellow.

"Um . . ." he said awkwardly, stiffening in her embrace.

Elena pulled back and looked him in the face. He had grown a head taller over the past year, and even a bit of red beard now sprouted on his chin. She grinned up at him, and tears of joy ran down her cheek. "Joach, don't you even recognize your own sister?"

He blinked. "Elena?" he said, tentatively at first, then seemed finally to see past her dyed and shorn hair. "Elena!" He grabbed her up and hugged her so hard she thought her ribs would break, but she didn't protest or urge him to lighten his grip. She just held him. In Joach's arms, she rediscovered the strength of her father, and in his close warmth, the heart of her mother. United in tears, they were a family again.

"How . . . ?" She both laughed and sobbed into his chest, unable to form words, her vision blurring. She squeezed him tighter. He was not a figment of a cruel dream, a ghost to disappear on waking. Over the past moons, she had dreamt often of her brother, but this was real. He was flesh and bone. She could not stop crying. "How did you. . . ?"

He raised a palm and touched her cheek. "Hush."

By now, a grizzled, gray-bearded man strolled up behind her brother. He had a pipe clenched between his lips. "So it seems you two know each other," he said gruffly.

Joach loosened his hold on Elena at the approach of the old man but refused to let her go completely. He kept one arm around her shoulders as he introduced her to the man. "This," he said, grinning his boyish smile, "is my sister, Elena."

"Yes, the wit'ch. I figured as much." He nodded toward Elena and passed her a handkerchief for her tears. He surveyed the rest of the party, his eyes growing large at the sight of the huge treewolf. Then he beckoned them all inside as if they had just come from a neighboring farm. "About time you got here, Er'ril."

Joach had started to turn away when Mycelle stepped from behind Er'ril. Her brother's head snapped back around to face the swordswoman. "Aunt My?" he asked, his voice shocked. "What . . . what are you doing here?" Joach let go of Elena and reached to embrace his aunt.

Elena smiled, having momentarily forgotten there was another member of their lost family present.

As Joach reached for Mycelle, their aunt held up a hand. "Whoa there, Joach. I just saw how you hugged your sister. I've got wounds that can't withstand that kind of love." She leaned and gently hugged him, then let go. Her eyes filled with tears. "You've grown even more than your sister," she said, wiping at her eyes.

"Flint," Er'ril said, ever gruff, ever serious, "how did you ever come by the boy?"

"Moris found him in A'loa Glen," he said, waving off the question. "But the story's long, and I've got a pot of stew simmering. It'll burn if I don't get back to it."

Before they could enter, a deep roar cracked across the hills, freezing everyone in place.

Er'ril reached for his sword.

As they all turned, a winged shape suddenly swept up from below the bluff's edge behind them. It arched and swung toward the cottage.

"Skal'tum!" Elena cried.

Joach wrapped his sister up in his arms. "No, El, it's nothing to fear."

Er'ril drew his sword, as did Mycelle. Fardale growled.

Flint pushed through them all. "Jumpy sorts, aren't you all?" The old man ran his eyes up and down Mycelle's physique as he passed. He glanced at Er'ril, pursing his lips appreciatively. "C'mon," he said with a nod toward the bluffs. "My stew will have to wait. I sent a messenger out to rally some forces, but it looks like she's returning early. And I don't like what that implies."

Er'ril followed, his eyes narrow and suspicious. "What's going on, Flint?"

Elena, her eyes on the skies, did not hear the old man's response. In the last rays of the setting sun, Elena saw it wasn't a monster of the Dark Lord that glided the coastal winds, but a striking figure of iridescent black scale and silver claws. As the sun set behind them, the last rays sparked a brilliant radiance off its scales. It spun on the tip of one huge wing and swept back toward the bluff. Elena's mouth hung open as she followed on numb feet, her neck bent back to study the handsome beast's flight as it moved with power and grace across the darkening skies.

Elena trailed behind the plainsman, her brother's arm around her shoulders. Ahead, the huge black creature landed at the bluff's edge, digging gigantic claws into the rich soil. As it perched above the crashing surf, it swung its stately black head in their direction as they approached. Eyes of cobalt and ebony studied them.

"It's the dragon Ragnar'k," Joach explained.

Now closer, Elena spotted a small girl seated atop the dragon. Her green hair blew like a sweep of willow about her face. Joach raised his arm, greeting her. The girl returned the gesture. "That's Sy-wen," Joach explained to Elena. "A mer woman."

Elena's eyebrows rose high. The mer were supposed to be creatures of myth, but after all Elena had seen, she did not doubt her brother's claim.

As they crossed the meadow to join the dragon and its rider at the bluff's edge, Flint and Er'ril were deep in conversation. Elena drew close enough to hear their words. Er'ril's face had darkened with the fading light. "So A'loa Glen is lost," he said, dismayed. "And my brother . . ." His voice cracked, and the plainsman could not speak any further. His eyes stared far off. Elena had never seen him so distraught.

Flint chewed his pipe. "I'm afraid so. I've heard reports that flocks of skal'tum have been seen circling the towers of the city. Boats report other strange beasts seen in the waters around the island, and five times more the number of ships go missing at sea than before. I'm afraid the Dark Lord is digging in his heels. If we're ever going to get the Blood Diary, we need an army."

By now, their group had reached the bluff. They kept their distance from the dragon, though it had already lost interest in them and stared out at the ocean. Elena's and Sy-wen's eyes met briefly. The mer woman nodded at her. Elena suspected they were around the same age.

Flint spoke to Sy-wen. "How did it go? Were you able to convince your mother to help?"

"Conch had already reached my mother," Sy-wen said, "and passed on your request for aid." She waved an arm to encompass the seas below the bluffs. "And there is her response."

Beyond the crashing surf, the blue waters undulated in slow, regular swells. Nothing lay there but empty waves.

Elena noticed the old man's shoulders slump.

Then the small mer woman reached and touched her dragon's neck. At the quiet signal, Ragnar'k stretched out his long throat and bellowed across the waves, his call echoing along the cliffs.

Wincing at the noise, Elena leaned into Joach.

As the dragon's roar ended, the smooth sea beyond the frothing surf bloomed with hundreds of snaking heads as countless submerged creatures surfaced. "Seadragons," Elena whispered, awed. Like a scatter of jewels across the midnight blue waters, more and more dragons, in various hues and sizes, rose from the sea.

Each dragon bore a rider, an arm raised in salute.

"My mother sends her greeting to you," Sy-wen said with a ghost of a smile, "and pledges her aid."

Beyond them, huge behemoths of the deep sea rose like barnacled islands, spewing fonts of spray from holes along their backs. The spray caught the sun's glory, casting twilight rainbows to the horizon.

Flint whistled appreciatively. He fingered a small star-shaped stud in his ear. "You did it, Sy-wen," he muttered. "You've brought back the mer'ai from the Deep. The prophecies weave together this night. Can you feel it?" he asked Er'ril. "When the sun next rises, the war will be upon us."

His words—war and prophecy—chilled Elena.

Suddenly, the black dragon trumpeted again, a piping wail that startled Elena. His countless brethren below chorused back, a rising tune that somehow blended with the pound of the surf below them. It was a song that united sea and beast.

But deeper in the dragons' song, Elena heard more. She heard the drums of war, the beat of sword on shield, and the trumpet's charge.

Joach whispered in her ear as the light faded around them, his eyes wide upon the host below. "They're here for you, Elena."

His words brought her no joy. Tears rose in her eyes. From here, she knew nothing would be the same.

As if sensing her emotion, Fardale stepped to the edge of the bluff and added his voice to the chorus below, a long low cry that escalated into the ululating howl. The loneliness of his song spoke to Elena's heart.

Joach slipped his hand in hers and squeezed. She returned the silent affection. Whatever may come, Elena thought as she held tight to her brother and listened to Fardale's cry, at least she would no longer face it alone.

Hand in hand, brother and sister watched the seas turn dark as the day died. The warmth of family flowed between them, stronger than any ruby magick.

And so as Elena stares out at her dragon army, I must end this part of her tale. From this night forward, the oceans will run red with the blood of heroes, cowards will show their true colors, and brothers will raise swords against each other.

Yet is that not always the tides of war?

So for now, let's rest and pretend we don't hear the drums of battle in the pounding of the surf.

Tomorrow is soon enough for the lands of Alasea to bleed.

ABOUT THE AUTHOR

James Clemens was born in Chicago, Illinois, in 1961. With his three brothers and three sisters, he was raised in the Midwest and in rural Canada. There, he explored cornfields, tadpoles, and frozen ponds, dreaming of worlds and adventures beyond the next bend in the creek.

Eventually, pretending to grow up, he went to school at the University of Missouri, where he graduated with a doctorate in veterinary medicine in 1985.

During one especially icy midwestern winter, the lure of ocean, sun, and new horizons eventually drew him to the West Coast, where he established his veterinary practice in Sacramento, California. Presently, he shares his home with two Dalmatians, a stray Shepherd, and a lovesick parrot named Igor.